Rosemary Rogers was born in  school outside the capital city and history at the University of Ceylon, and got married in her third year. The marriage failed, and she fled with her three children to England. There she met and married an American airman who took her to the States. Their son was born in 1963, but that marriage ended the following year. Now a divorcee with four children to support, she typed and filed for the Solano County Parks Department in Fairfield, California. She spent her lunch hours at the library studying French and Mexican history. At night, while the phonograph played classical music, she wove her research into an exotic tale of romance set in the mid-1800's – SWEET SAVAGE LOVE.

Also in Troubadour paperback

Rosemary Rogers

Sweet Savage Love

Edited by Lesley Saxby

Futura Publications Limited
A Troubadour Book

A Troubadour Book

First published in Great Britain in 1977
by Futura Publications Limited

ISBN 0 8600 7466 8
Printed in Great Britain by
Hazell Watson & Viney Ltd
Aylesbury, Bucks

Futura Publications Limited
110 Warner Road
Camberwell, London SE5

"To C.E."

CONTENTS

PART ONE

❧

Prologue

Chapter One

Virginia Brandon was sixteen, that spring of 1862, and the thought of her first ball, now only two weeks away, was much more exciting than the letter that had arrived that morning from her father in America.

She had not seen her father, after all, since she was still a baby—perhaps three or four years old; and although he sent money for her care every month through his bankers in San Francisco, his letters were infrequent.

Why should it concern or upset her that her father had decided to remarry? As her Uncle Albert had pointed out when he read out her father's letter, William Brandon was still a young man—in the prime of his life. And his bride, a young widow, was eminently suitable—a Southern gentlewoman, owner of a large plantation near New Orleans.

Virginia remembered that Tante Celine's gentle eyes had looked troubled as the letter was being read to her. Tante was too sensitive; she was obviously thinking about Ginny's maman, who had been her own sister—the lovely Genevieve who had died so tragically and so young.

But I don't remember maman very well, Ginny thought rebelliously. And why should I care if Papa has married again? It is not likely that I will ever live with him and my stepmother; after all they are fighting a war in America—a civil war that might go on for years.

"Cousine Ginnie—if you will only stand still!"

Pierre's voice had a note of exasperation in it that would normally have kept her quiet and still as a mouse, but this spring morning Ginny's spirits were too high for her to be able to contain them.

"But I'm tired of standing still! And I'm excited at the thought of going to a ball, and the so-beautiful dress I will wear."

Green eyes, sparkling as brightly as emeralds, narrowed when Ginny smiled, and Pierre Dumont sighed again. How could he paint anyone as restless and volatile as his young cousin? And why had he imagined he'd the talent to try?

Ginny's face was a shifting canvas—his was far too still. Sixteen, he thought despairingly. How could one ever capture the moods of a sixteen-year-old?

He coaxed her, bribing her as he had done when she was much younger.

"Hold still for just a few moments longer—your head slightly tilted as I showed you—just a few more minutes, or I will contrive to take a terrible cold on the night of the ball and you will have no escort!"

Dark lashes veiled green eyes like storm clouds. The girl's soft, childlike lower lip pouted.

"You wouldn't—you could not be so—"

"Well, perhaps I could not be such a bear as to disappoint you, *petite cousine,* but you promised to pose for me this morning, and the light is just right. Come—just a few moments?"

"Oh, very well then! But pray remember that I'm to go riding in the park very soon, and I have to go upstairs and change first."

Repressing a smile at the bored sophistication in his young cousin's voice, Pierre turned back to his canvas.

In comparison with Ginny's sparkling beauty, her painted image seemed to have no life, no depth at all. Here, on his canvas, was merely the picture of a young girl in a green dress, standing beneath an old apple tree, her face turned slightly upward to catch the slanted light that filtered through the branches. He had portrayed her coloring well enough—the green eyes, slightly tipped at the corners, which were the first thing one noticed about her. And the hair, the palest shade of polished copper. Missing, however, was the liveliness and vivacity that could make Ginny's small face seem not merely vapidly pretty, but downright lovely at times. And the stubborn way she could tilt her chin—how could he duplicate that?

Brushing back a lock of blond hair that had fallen forward onto his forehead, Pierre Dumont sighed. It was a good thing, after all, that painting was merely his hobby, and a job in the diplomatic service awaited him later, through the influence of his father. No—he could do still life passably well, but portraits—pah!

Biting the end of his paintbrush, Pierre squinted at Ginny. He had half a mind to make a dramatic gesture and rip his canvas in two, but in spite of her grumbling over having to stand still, he knew that Ginny was excited at having her portrait painted. Well, he would just have to keep trying, that was all.

For a change, she was standing quite still, her face tilted obediently. Pierre had a suspicion that she was daydreaming as usual—thinking about the ball, perhaps. He studied her face, now in repose. His aunt Genevieve had been considered a beauty in her day, and Ginny had inherited her coloring and the shape of her face, but the mouth and chin were Ginny's own. Her chin was small, with the barest suggestion of a cleft, her nose straight. But the mouth—ah, yes, that mouth, it was the mouth of a courtesan, a demi-mondaine. Perfectly shaped, with a short upper lip and full, sensuous lower lip, it was a woman's mouth, promising untold delight for the man who kissed it. Combined with her hair and rather high cheekbones, it gave her face a smoldering, gypsyish look in repose. Only when she smiled, and her lips curved upward, flattening slightly, did Ginny look childlike.

Almost against his will, Pierre found his eyes travelling lower, to the rounded curve of her young breasts, the small waist, and the billowing folds of her skirt. A woman. He corrected himself. An almost woman. She was only sixteen, after all, and he had known her since childhood. She was growing up, this was evident, but he could not, must not, think of her as anything but a child—and his cousin.

"That's enough, you may relax," Pierre called sharply, more sharply than he had intended.

Ginny blinked her eyes. She had been lost in some childish daydream after all, then.

"Have you finished? May I see it?"

He covered his canvas hastily.

"Not yet—of course it isn't finished, I told you it would take time! I'm going to fill in some of the background now, while you go upstairs to change." He pulled at a strand of her hair teasingly as she came by, swinging her wide hat. "No peeking! You promised, remember!"

Annoyed, she turned her head away.

"Its not fair that I shouldn't be allowed to look."

She might have stayed to argue with him, but her aunt had sent Marie down into the walled garden to remind Ginny that she must change. With what she hoped was an airy shrug of her shoulders at her grinning cousin, Ginny flounced indoors.

Upstairs, Marie had laid her clothes across her bed in readiness, and while the woman helped her change, grumbling as she usually did that mademoiselle was always late, mademoiselle must remember she was no longer a child but a young lady; Ginny went back to her daydreams.

Against her will, she thought again about America. Strange, that she should have been actually born there, although it was France she loved, France that was her real home. People shrugged and said that America was scarcely civilized yet, but her mother had loved New Orleans, and her father was a man of wealth and education.

Why then, had her mother left him and come back to France? Tante Celine had never told her the whole story, Ginny was sure of that.

"Your maman was always delicate, even as a girl, you understand," Celine had said. "The climate in Louisiana did not agree with her, and in those days your father travelled much. She was alone too often, and my poor Genevieve hated to be alone. Your papa was busy making his fortune in the goldfields of California, but your maman wanted only to be near him—"

Why, then, had she taken her small daughter and left? Was there some secret about her papa that no one would tell her? Once she had ventured to ask Pierre this same question and he had laughed at her.

"You read too many romances, Ginny! Your mother became sick, and she wanted to come back home. Your papa could not refuse her. That is all there is to it."

"But why didn't he send for me? Did he not want me?"

"A man, living alone—travelling in rough and remote parts of the country, what would he do with a young child? No, your papa is a practical man, and I'm sure he knew it would be best for you if you were allowed to remain here, with us. Aren't you happy here, cousin?"

Of course she was. Certainly she would not want to live anywhere else, Ginny told herself. And yet—she shivered, involuntarily. Her father had spoken of sending for her when the war was over. Had he meant it? Above all, did she want to go?

"You must not worry about this," Uncle Albert had said. "The civil war in America, it might drag on for many years, who can tell. And the choice will be yours to make, Virginie."

"This is your home, child, and we love you," Tante Celine had added, tears in her soft brown eyes.

Ginny shrugged determinedly as she stood before the mirror, admiring herself. Why think about the possibility of leaving France when it might never happen? She had so much to look forward to here—the ball, two weeks away, and the puzzled, almost unhappy look in her cousin Pierre's eyes when he looked at her.

He has noticed at last that I am growing up, the girl thought triumphantly. He does not like to admit it, but he does think I am pretty.

It seemed to her that she had always been a little in love with her cousin, who had treated her only with a kind of affectionate comptempt, as if she had been his sister. But ever since the day his friend, the Viscomte De la Reve, had met them in the park, and had not been able to hide his surprise that she had grown up, nor his evident admiration for her, Pierre had been different.

Good, Ginny thought, as she went downstairs. It is high time he noticed. She hoped that all of his friends would be at the ball, and that they would notice her too. I will act very sophisticated, very bored, she planned. And when I am asked to dance, I will flirt.

She was filled with a sense of freedom, of standing on the very threshold of life itself. And when she thought, as she often did, what will the future bring, who will be the man I am waiting for? the thought brought only excitement. There was nothing she was afraid of. She was lucky, she had almost everything she wanted, she would have more.

Only her Aunt Celine worried. Standing beside her husband at the foot of the stairs she watched the way her niece almost danced down, her face flushed, her eyes sparkling. Suddenly, she was reminded of Genevieve, who had looked that way once—sparkling, beautiful Genevieve, always so full of life, so greedy for excitement, for love.

And what, in the end, had happened? When Genevieve returned to France she had been subdued, a shadow of what she had been when she had left. She had said nothing, admitted nothing, but Celine knew that something had hurt Genevieve; that somewhere the girl had lost her dreams and perhaps her illusions, and without them, she could not live.

Do not let it happen to Virginie, Celine prayed. The girl pirouetted, her wide skirts swirling round her for an instant.

"Hmm—you look like a gypsy dancer!" Albert teased her.

Last year they had visited Spain and watched the flamenco dancers—Celine could not help smiling when she remembered Ginny's excitement, the way she had declared that she too would like to dance like that.

Ginny lifted her chin and smiled at them both.

"I am glad, now, that I am not a gypsy. I would not like to dance because I had to, for money. No, I would much rather dance the waltz, I think."

"Well, you will have your wish, soon. And remember, young lady, I claim the first waltz!"

Gallantly, Albert Dumont offered his arms to his wife and niece, and they walked outside, still laughing.

She makes us all feel young again, Celine thought wistfully. Just like Genevieve. But perhaps Genevieve's daughter would not be so easily hurt. There was a kind of stubbornness in Ginny in spite of her dreamy ways and her romantic ideas; a kind of strength that Genevieve had lacked.

They returned early from the park, because the sudden gathering of clouds warned of a spring shower.

Disappointed, Ginny had returned to her room and changed back into her pale green dress. She leaned her elbows on the windowsill and looked out rather disconsolately at the small walled garden where Pierre had posed her for her portrait only hours earlier.

There were rain clouds scudding across the sky now and everything looked gray and lifeless. The branches of the apple tree bent and its brave spring blossoms seemed to droop and cower. Soon it would rain and the streets would become shiny. The water would drip off the eaves in long, thin streams. It was always boring to be cooped indoors when it rained. It was cold again, and soon Marie would be coming upstairs to light the fire—perhaps she could go downstairs to Uncle Albert's library and find a book to read. What else could one do on a rainy afternoon?

The raindrops had already begun to spatter down when Ginny remembered that the book she had been reading earlier—a collection of essays by Emerson, an American, was still outdoors where she had left it. With an exclamation of dismay she ran out of her room and down the narrow staircase, hoping that no one would see her.

In spite of her haste, Ginny was quite soaked through by the time she started back indoors. Her hair, clothes, everything except, fortunately, the book, which she had snatched up and concealed inside her bodice.

She paused for an instant in the doorway and let the rain beat down on her upturned face.

Chapter Two

There was nothing in common between the green-eyed girl in France and the young Union army captain in Louisiana except that they were both wet—and he had lived in Paris, a long time before.

His blue uniform was soaked through already, and he cursed the rain and his errand that day.

Promoted from the rank of lieutenant only recently, and transferred from a lonely outpost in the Territory of New Mexico to New Orleans because he spoke fluent French, Steve Morgan had thought he would enjoy his tour of duty here. But instead he had found himself instructed to perform guard duty—to "keep an eye on" the Beaudine plantation and its chatelaine, who just happened to be married to a U. S. Senator from California.

Now, caught in the slashing downpour, his ears almost deafened by thunder, Steve Morgan damned his luck and the lady he was looking for. What in hell was she doing riding out alone in a thunderstorm? And where was she? He hoped that at least she'd have had the sense to take shelter from the storm somewhere.

"Miss Sonya, she rode off someplace—" the sullen-faced housekeeper had told him when he'd come up to the house that afternoon with an invitation from General Butler. And that was another of the things that galled him—that he should be reduced to the position of either a messenger boy or polite escort; riding out on the general's errands, and for the rest of the time set to "guard" an icy cold Southern lady from possible molestation. Because Sonya Beaudine had been fortunate enough, or clever enough, to get herself remarried just before the war broke out, and to a Union Senator, at that, she was treated very differently from the rest of the women in this conquered city. Steve Morgan, with four or five troopers, was expected to be on hand whenever she wished to shop or visit friends. Five bluecoats, with their captain feeling foolish at their head, trotting beside Madame Brandon's carriage like lackeys—lounging around her garden when she was home—not good enough to be asked inside the house because they were, after all, only Yankees.

Even the Negroes, ex-slaves, all of them, treated the Yankee soldiers with a kind of veiled contempt; while the native Louisianans themselves were much worse—not even bothering to hide their contempt and disdain for their conquerors.

Sonya Brandon, in spite of her Northern connections, was a native Southerner and still accepted by her friends. She made no attempt to disguise her dislike for her escort—in fact, she seemed to take a delight in letting it show.

So it was with something like dismay that Steve had heard the lady had left the safety of her house to go riding that morning—alone, and with a thunderstorm brewing.

"Have you any idea where she might have gone?" Steve had asked her servant curtly, and the woman, shrugging, had mumbled something about the river—that her mistress sometimes liked to go to the high ground that overlooked the river, so she could watch the boats.

"Oh hell!" Steve had sworn out loud, forgetting to be cautious. He turned disgustedly to his corporal, a stolid-faced, rangy looking man. "I suppose I'd better go look for her—the general will have my hide if she's met with an accident."

The grinning corporal saluted smartly and offered half-heartedly to go along, but Steve had instructed him to stay close to the house with the rest of the men, in case she came back. "In which case," he said grimly, "you can come looking for me."

As he turned his horse around to leave, Steve heard the black woman mutter from behind him in French that her "maitresse" would no doubt prefer the perils of a thunderstorm or the snakes out in the woods to the company of a bluebelly. Forgetting himself, Steve told her in the same language that she could have saved her mistress from such a terrible fate by going with her, or having the sense to stop her. Leaving the woman gaping with surprise he kneed his horse into a gallop, making for the river and the wooded land that lay between it and the house. The first large drops of rain began to fall before he had quite reached the trees.

The rain dripping off the visor of his cap almost blinded him, and with a muffled oath Steve pulled it off his head and shoved it in the pocket of his uniform. Damn the woman, where was she hiding herself? He was close to the river now, following a path he had recognized by pure instinct. The thought struck him that she might not have followed this trail at all—she could very well have taken a short cut back and might be at the house by now, laughing at the idea of his half-drowning out here in the rain, looking for her. He gritted his teeth with rage. Well—he'd come this far already, so he might just as well go all the way up to the river now and look around before he headed back.

Coming out of the dense woods into an unexpected small clearing, Steve reined his horse in sharply. If he had gotten himself lost it would be the last straw! Then he saw the crumbling, abandoned warehouse at the other end of the clearing and her mare, its head tossing nervously, tethered by the door.

So she did have some sense after all—she must have decided to wait out the storm here, which wasn't, after all, such a bad idea. Grimly, he wondered if she'd be surprised to see him.

Sonya Brandon sat huddled up on an old wooden crate she'd found and turned on its side, her arms wrapped around her knees to keep herself warm. She was soaked to the skin, and vastly uncomfortable, but the thunder frightened her more than anything else, and each time she heard an angry explosion overhead she shivered and closed her eyes.

Her straight blond hair had escaped from its decorous chignon and hung in rat tails down her back, and the velvet of her new riding habit was utterly ruined. She knew she must look a fright, and she felt much worse. *Why* had she been so determined to ride today? She had known that a storm was coming, and she had always been afraid of thunder. If only Tante Victorine hadn't told her it wasn't proper for her to go riding alone—if only she hadn't hated the thought of seeing those Yankee soldiers hanging around her house again, playing cards and criticizing Southerners and the citizens of New Orleans in particular, in their loud, nasal voices! And their captain—she detested him most of all. He wasn't polite enough to hide the fact that he resented having to escort her wherever she pleased to go, and she'd noticed the bold and almost derisive way he'd assessed her body from head to toe—as if she'd been some quadroon slut on the city streets.

Oh God, why had she agreed so complacently to let William go to Washington so soon after their marriage? And why, why had she so naively agreed to stay and look after the plantation and their interests while he attempted to drum up support for the Southern cause in California? All his efforts had been in vain, after all—California had elected to join the Union and they were separated. In spite of her conviction that the South was right and their cause a sacred one, she had the depressing feeling that they might actually lose the war in the end. Look how easily the Yankees had taken New Orleans!

The Yankees! She hated their arrogance, their attitude towards the city they had conquered and its proud people; and in spite of her own unhappy beliefs, she hated their calm, sure assumption that they would win the war.

An extraordinarily loud burst of thunder, sounding almost directly overhead, caused Sonya to clap her hands over her ears and give a small scream of fear. And then, as the shaky wooden door burst open and a man stood outlined for a moment by a vivid flare of lightning, she screamed again, this time with pure terror. He looked like the devil himself filling the doorway for an instant, with his black hair plastered to his head, and his dark blue eyes seeming to gleam evilly in the half-light.

He walked inside, closing the door behind him, and she heard his voice, lazy, mocking.

"Why ma'am, you look like you've seen a ghost! And

here I thought you'd be relieved to see me come to your rescue."

Unreasonably frightened and angry, she sprang to her feet.

"You! What are you doing here? How dare you follow me?"

"Just performing my duty, ma'am."

He seemed quite unperturbed as he stood there, shaking the water from his hair and clothes like a wolf. And indeed, that was what he reminded her of at this moment—a dangerous, feral animal. There was something about the way he stood, with his legs slightly apart, the reckless slant of his lips, the thin, straight nose with nostrils that curled slightly as if he scented her . . . now, what had made her think that?

An unreasoning, blind panic took hold of her.

"Get out!" she whispered hoarsely, and then, more loudly, "get away from me!"

"But ma'am, I haven't come anywhere near you!"

His voice sounded coldly reasonable, but she'd seen the way his eyes had narrowed, the way his mouth twitched in a mocking, somehow knowing smile. She could almost sense it now, his sudden awareness of her—the velvet habit clinging snugly, rainwet, to every curve of her body; her wide, frightened eyes and lips that parted as she panted with fear and unexplainable, irrational panic.

And as they eyed each other warily, she, in her turn, became aware of him—as a man instead of a hated blue uniform. She saw a tall man, slim-hipped and hard-muscled, with wide shoulders and a lean, sun-browned face that formed a surprising contrast to his very blue eyes. His wet uniform, plastered closely to his body, left nothing to her imagination, not even the fact that he had begun to desire her.

Instinctively, shockingly, Sonya's eyes had dropped downward, and now she raised them quickly with a muffled, horrified cry, her pale cheeks flushing bright crimson.

"Do you expect me to apologize? There are some things a man cannot control, I'm afraid."

His voice was pleasant, but he smiled at her impudently.

Sonya took a backward step, her hands crossing instinctively over her full breasts.

"Don't—don't come near me! I'll scream if you take one step—"

"You think anyone will hear if you do? Over that noise?"

A sudden rattle of thunder seemed to shake the whole building and she jumped, gasping, frightened even more by his words. Perhaps he sensed something of her blind terror, for he shrugged, studying her face.

"You have no cause for worry, ma'am, believe me. I've no intention of raping you, if that is what you fear. In spite of evidence to the contrary—" he added wickedly, his eyes fastened derisively on her.

She stood still, feeling trapped, and with a kind of despair she saw that he had started to take off his jacket. With a small choked cry she backed off against the wall, and he spoke to her quietly and reassuringly, as if she was not quite bright.

"All I'm doing is taking off this wet jacket. I promise you I'll undress no further, if that thought alarms you." He flung the jacket from him and looked at her again, measuringly. "Would you mind if I sat down? No use our starting back until this storm's over." He let his glance flicker around the small space. "Maybe I can get a fire started."

His calm assumption that he was going to stay here with her made her heart pound.

"Oh please—" she whimpered suddenly, "please go! I—you make me so afraid!"

"For God's sake!" he said impatiently, "what do you take me for? A devil? A wild animal who'd take a female against her will? Or was it the sign of my damned male urges that frightened you so? Let me tell you, madam, that desire or not, I won't touch you unless you want me to. New Orleans is full of women who are not only beautiful and desirable but willing as well!"

He stood frowning angrily at her, a muscle twitching in his cheek, and had half-turned to stalk outside and leave her when there came a blinding flash and an explosion of thunder so loud that not only the building but the floor as well seemed to vibrate.

Sonya's mouth opened and she screamed hysterically as she heard a crackling, crashing noise outside and realized that the lightning had struck something nearby. Steve Morgan, his face both angry and alarmed, cleared the distance between them in two long strides and caught her by the shoulders. He shook her roughly.

"Damnation! Will you shut up? You're safe, I tell you—it was outside—stop screaming now, or I'll have to slap your hysterical face!"

His roughness and the cruelty of his words silenced her screams while provoking her, at the same time, into a blind fury that made her bring her fisted hands upward and pound them against his chest.

At one moment her hands flailed against him, and at the next—she could not recall, later, how it came about—her hands were clinging to him instead, as if she was drowning. She felt the linen of his shirt tear under her clutching fingers and she felt his muscles tense, and then her head fell helplessly back under the onslaught of his mouth on hers.

She felt her body bending backward, felt the length of his hard body against hers, and then somehow, they had almost fallen onto the rough, dirty stone floor together, still kissing. Their hands found and uncovered each other, and then, without preliminaries, he was over her, penetrating her roughly and deeply and, after her first cry of despair, completely satisfying.

It was only afterwards, when it was all over and they lay panting and exhausted together, that Sonya began to sob uncontrollably. Her suddenly awakened realization of what had taken place, coupled with a deeply cutting sense of humiliation and revulsion at herself, made her turn her head away and close her eyes, the tears trickling forlornly down her face. They had not even taken the time to undress completely—somehow, that seemed to make it much worse!

With a sudden change of mood that was all the more startling because of his earlier harshness and the rough, crude way he'd possessed her, Sonya felt the man pull her into his embrace and begin to stroke her hair and face tenderly. His surprising caresses soothed her as if she had been a child. Lying shivering and helpless in his arms, Sonya became gradually aware of all kinds of small things—the incessant dripping of the rain, the mutter of thunder, the fact that his shirt was made of fine linen and his voice had no nasal Yankee accent, but a deeper, almost lazy drawl. Whoever he was, he had at least been a gentleman at one time. He murmured soft, tender endearments to her, gentling her until her sobbing stopped; and gradually, as his hands continued to caress her she became aware of him, again, in the physical sense.

"Oh, God, I'm so ashamed!" she whispered brokenly, and felt him kiss her tear-wet cheek again, and then her mouth. Gradually, her body warmed and stirred under his roving hands, and she began to murmur incoherently and clutch at his shoulders; her head shaking in silent protest even while her body moved to accept his once more.

"I—I'm ashamed!" she wept again. "What will you think of me now? How can I live with myself?"

"Hush, sweet—you're a woman, remember. A live and passionate one, under that icy surface. It's nothing to be ashamed of ..."

She could hardly believe that he was ready for her again so soon; but she felt the proof of it and yielded to him, letting his hands do their work while his body rocked gently against hers—slowly, teasingly, while his hands moved like burning brands over her skin, making a complete wanton of her.

Afterwards Sonya felt as if she had come to rest after a long and tiring journey, and she said no more about feeling ashamed. That came later, when she was alone in her room, and the precepts of her rigidly conventional upbringing warred against the sudden discovery of her own passionate nature.

Oh, yes, later she despised herself and hated him but when she saw him again and he acted so formally polite, as if nothing had ever happened between them, then she wanted all of it all over again—his hands on her body, his lips stopping the moans that came from her mouth, and most of all, to have him inside her, taking her with him to the point of animal forgetfulness.

Steve Morgan had told her bluntly that any repetition of what had happened between them would have to be of her own will and wanting, and although she hated him all the more for saying it and meaning it, she found herself helpless to resist her own suddenly awakened desires.

They met again and again after she had finally broken down and forgotten her pride, asking him to escort her to the river bluff one morning. Sometimes they had their secret, stolen meetings in the abandoned warehouse where it had all begun, and sometimes she'd insist he come to her in her own bedroom, late at night. But he never spent a night with her—never stayed longer than an hour or two at most, and she learned to her anger and chagrin that he was not to be pinned down or questioned. His moods were unpredictable and changeable. Sometimes he was rough and brutal with her, quick to possess her and to leave her. But at other times he could be as gentle and tender as any ardent lover—kissing and petting her and taking endless time and pains to arouse and satiate her.

Just once, she asked him half-fearfully, "But—do you love me?" and he'd laughed shortly.

"I love making love to you—I want you. Isn't that enough for you, Sonya?"

And she wondered how many other women he had, and said the same thing to—whether even now, when he was her lover, he saw other women as well. She dared not ask—he refused to answer questions, and merely looked at her with a raised, mocking eyebrow, ignoring her sulks and tantrums.

She would tell herself, over and over, when she wasn't with Steve, that she had no right to question him. They weren't married—she was married to William, and she loved him, deeply and comfortably. Sometimes she'd think, oh, if only William would come, and take me away with him! And then, desperately, she'd find herself praying that he wouldn't, not yet!

This is only an episode, she would tell herself in her saner moments. I'm married to William, he'll come back here for me and it will have to end—that is what Steve says, that we are both lonely and so we console each other—and yet, and yet she was bitterly jealous and resentful of the time he spent away from her, and all those other, faceless women she knew he must meet and enjoy and perhaps possess in much the same way as he did her. Lightly, casually; sometimes with concentration and even affection, but always selfishly—never really giving too much of himself.

Sonya Brandon attended General Butler's ball, mainly because she hoped that Steve would be there. He was, but beyond a polite bow in her direction, he stayed away from her. The General himself took pains to entertain her, and introduced her to all his senior officers, but Sonya had a miserable evening.

The old Governor's mansion was crowded—the musicians played well and the food was excellent. But none of her friends were there, and she saw too many brown and café-au-lait faces—"they" were everywhere now, it seemed, and she could not understand how the white Yankee officers could so obviously and openly enjoy dancing with quadroon and octoroon women who would, just a few years ago, be forced to attend their own balls or stay hidden in their small, secret apartments.

She was dancing the waltz with a Major Hart, a rather portly man who paid her a lot of respectful attention, when she caught her first glimpse of Steve Morgan, dancing by with a girl who was young, breathtakingly beautiful, and obviously a quadroon. He was holding her very close, and smiling down into her face with the lazy, half-mocking smile that Sonya both hated and loved. And it was clear that the girl adored him—her eyes never left his face, and every now and then she'd laugh breathlessly and happily.

Sonya caught her partner staring at her with a puzzled expression and caught herself.

"I'm sorry—" she murmured apologetically. "But I find I—I cannot quite get used to that!"

"I know just how you feel, ma'am," the major said, squeezing her waist very slightly. "I'm originally from Tennessee myself, and we don't like it much either. But you know—this is why we're fighting the war!"

She was drinking a glass of punch with a Colonel Beamish when she had a first opportunity to talk to Steve Morgan. He walked by, rather abstractedly, and Sonya's light voice halted him.

"Why, it's that nice captain that General Butler sent to look after me! Are you enjoying yourself, Captain Morgan?"

He bowed to her politely, but she could see an almost appreciative glint of devilry in his eyes.

"Yes ma'am! It's good to see you here, ma'am."

How well he plays the country bumpkin, she thought viciously, even while her lips were curving upward in a smile.

"Are you going to escort me back tonight?" she asked sweetly, knowing that he was supposed to be off-duty.

"I believe Major Hart has already volunteered for that pleasant assignment, ma'am," he said, and this time the laughter in his eyes was apparent.

Colonel Beamish cleared his throat, and Sonya gave him her most brilliant smile.

"Are all of your young officers so shy, Colonel? I declare—here I see Captain Morgan almost every day, and he hasn't even asked me to dance."

She had him this time, there was no way in which he could escape his duty now. She saw him glance apologetically at the colonel, who growled impatiently, "For heavens sake, Morgan, we don't want Mrs. Brandon to think we're all mannerless savages, do we?"

The musicians were playing another waltz, and Steve Morgan bowed to her again.

"I would be honored, ma'am."

He danced well, although he did not hold her as closely as she had seen him hold the quadroon wench; and although she had half-expected him to be angry with her, he was only amused.

"You could have asked me to dance before!" she pouted, and he grinned at her teasingly.

"You're a Senator's wife, Sonya, sweet. Being a mere captain, I could not have presumed . . ."

"You presume a lot more!" she snapped at him, but he refused to be drawn into an argument with her.

"I didn't think you would actually come today," he said lightly. "Is it quite proper, with your husband away?"

"William knows, of course. I wrote to him, and he agreed that I should be—friendly. Especially since General Butler himself invited me. He's an acquaintance of William's."

"I'm glad your husband is so understanding."

She glanced at him sharply, but his face looked quite expressionless. And against her will, she found herself wondering if he was impatient to get back to his partner—if the girl had been his partner. Perhaps he was only being polite? She wanted to think so, but the way he had held that girl, the way she had laughed up into his face made her feel differently. How could he? How dared he? And yet, she knew him well enough by now to keep her thoughts on the subject to herself.

Steve Morgan did not ask her to dance again, and it was Major Hart who escorted Sonya back home that night. After he had left, she lay awake for hours, with sleep eluding her, even though she knew that he wouldn't come.

The war dragged on, the spring dragged on, straggling

into summer eventually; and their affair continued, some-what cursorily.

Sonya heard regularly from her husband—he was busy in California. Politics and his other business affairs kept him away, he explained reasonably enough. Travel was ex-tremely dangerous, she was safer where she was, although of course he missed her. Sometimes she hated William for staying away and longed for the safety and sanity that his return would bring her. What am I doing? she would won-der sometimes, despairingly. What is happening to me, what am I turning into? But she did not want to face the answers. She was Captain Morgan's mistress, his casual light-of-love—and although she sensed that was the real extent of their relationship she refused to admit it.

Because she needed to feel that their relationship was more than a purely physical one, Sonya occasionally ques-tioned Steve about himself, even though she had learned that he either avoided or brushed aside her curiosity as a rule. Sometimes, though he would let slip little pieces of information or trivia that intrigued her more.

He was younger than she, of course—only twenty-four, and had been sent to New Orleans because he spoke French. Had he travelled much? It was obvious he had, but he would give her no details, although just once he mentioned off-handedly that he had lived in France for two and a half years. It surprised her. How had he man-aged it? Did he have relatives in France? He merely grinned at her mockingly.

"My—my stepdaughter lives in Paris," Sonya offered. "William says he will send for her when the war is over."

"Oh?" he said without interest, and then he leaned for-ward to kiss her, and the subject was closed. It did not take Sonya long to realize that he knew exactly how to silence her when she was in a talkative mood.

Once, when Steve arrived late for one of their meetings in the woods, coming up softly behind her and scaring her half to death, she said petulantly,

"Why, you even walk like a—a cat, or a wild Indian!"

"But I am one," he teased her, kissing her between her breasts. "I lived with the Comanche for three years. If I'd seen you then I'd have taken all your lovely hair and worn it at my belt—" he pulled it loose as he spoke and Sonya shuddered, half-believing him.

"Well—you are like a savage, you know! There is some-

thing—something untamed and uncivilized about you. I
think that you are quite without scruples or conscience,
and it frightens me."

He only laughed, his lips moving down below her navel
as he unfastened the hooks that held her gown together,
one by one, and she forgot, after a while, to be afraid.

Sonya Brandon thought often about the danger of their
liaison and how it must eventually end—for the sake of
her marriage and her own peace of mind; but when it
happened she was completely unprepared for it, and the
circumstances that caused it.

They had fallen into the habit of going riding together,
quite openly, for after all, everyone knew that she had always enjoyed her daily rides, and his duty was to escort
her. But one morning she waited for him and he did not
come. Then, early in the afternoon a strange sergeant
came instead, touching his hat to her.

"Where is Captain Morgan?" She was in a rage by this
time, and her anger made her blunt. She wondered why
the man seemed embarrassed and reluctant to speak. Imperious and insistent in turn, she finally wormed the whole
sordid story from him.

There had been a duel the previous night. Over a
woman. And the captain had shot and seriously wounded
his superior officer of all people—a Major Hart.

"Dear God!" Sonya burst out, unable to hide her feelings. "What did they do to him? Where is he now?"

Shuffling his feet awkwardly the sergeant admitted that
Captain Morgan was under arrest, and a prisoner in the
stockade. And if the major died, which seemed likely, he
would in all probability be executed.

"Oh, God!" she said again; and then, "this woman—the
one they fought over, who was she?"

The man obviously did not want to tell her, but when
she threatened to go to the general himself and get the
story from him, it all came out.

The Captain had a woman—they said he had been
keeping her, although that of course was merely rumor.
True or not, he'd been walking with the woman on the
street last night, in civilian clothes, when the major had
come upon them. No one knew what exactly had happened—they said the major had made some disparaging
remark and angry words had followed. But the captain

had challenged him and the two men had fought with pistols at twenty paces in a deserted churchyard.

It was only later, from her friends in New Orleans, that Sonya heard the whole story of the scandal that had set the town gossips buzzing. The woman was a quadroon.

The long years of rigid training in etiquette and deportment that were her birthright as a Southern lady helped keep Sonya outwardly calm and unruffled. She told her friends, with a shrug of distaste that she had never liked or trusted the man—had always sensed there was something wicked about him.

"My dear—" one of the older women leaned forward, her face falsely commiserating. "I really think you should consider yourself fortunate. I mean—imagine a man like that appointed your escort! I mean, one never knows, with his kind . . ."

"No, one doesn't," Sonya agreed.

Outwardly placid and unchanged, she raged inwardly, and despised Steve Morgan completely. She hoped they would hang him. And she prayed that her husband would return to her soon, to take her away from the war and its attendant nastiness.

Chapter Three

As the second week of his incarceration limped slowly by, Steve Morgan also prayed in his own way that something would happen.

The major lingered, hovering on the edge of death, and Steve stayed in the small gray cell they'd put him in, with only one hour's exercise allowed him every day.

He hated it—this impersonal imprisonment. Even worse than the thought of the hanging or the firing squad that might await him. All his life he had enjoyed the outdoors and the sense of freedom that open spaces had given him. And now, because of his own burst of temper and his too-good aim, he found himself locked in here.

He spent his time either pacing restlessly around his cell or sitting morosely at the rickety wooden table with his chin in his hands, staring into space. Occasionally, he forced himself to read. Books he hadn't seen nor thought about since he had attended the university in Paris. He remembered a doctor from India whom he had met in London—a gentle, philosophic man who had spoken of an ancient religion he called yoga. They had travelled to Italy and to Germany together, and Gopal had tried to teach Steve about detachment and the power of the mind. But in those days, he hadn't been quite ready for philosophy or a way of life that withdrew from life itself. Now—he had time. Too much time—or not enough. It depended on how he looked at it. At any rate, he found himself thinking and remembering more and more about Gopal, and his yoga teachings. Strength, that was it. A man's strength comes from within himself and from the knowledge that he is part of everything that is.

"We do not look for outside help from some deity, you see," Gopal had said once. "To us, each man is God. There is a potential in all of us that needs to be understood to be tapped."

Trouble is, Steve thought ruefully, I've never been penned in before. Not for this long, anyhow. He wished, sometimes, that Major Hart would die and get it all over with.

The only visitors Steve Morgan had were his erstwhile corporal, who brought him daily bulletins on the major's condition and the general's mood, and Denise—the lovely quadroon girl over whom he'd fought the major. Denise, who had been the perfect mistress—uncomplicated, undemanding, and completely uninhibited. She came daily, in spite of the leering looks and ribald comments she received from the soldiers who guarded him; and she brought him books and fresh fruit and cried—every single time.

They spoke in French so that the soldiers who lounged outside his cell would not understand, and Denise blamed herself, while he reassured her impatiently and sometimes irritably. Occasionally, when he'd been angry with her, tired of her eternal tears and unnecessarily harsh, he would think that this time she wouldn't return. But she always did.

Sonya Brandon neither came nor sent any message— but he'd expected no such thing from her in any case. Only her icy unapproachability had attracted him to her in the first place—and later, for a time at least, the surprising passion and abandonment he'd discovered in her. But she was too full of guilt feelings, and she had begun to cling and pout and demand too much. Steve put her out of his mind easily without any pangs. As a matter of fact, there had only been one woman, apart from his mother, that he had not found too easy to forget, and she had been his Comanche wife. He had married her when he

was only fifteen, and she had died in an Apache raid, carrying his child. Since then, there had been many women,
but he had loved none of them. He made love to them,
and in a way he needed them, but he was ruthless and in-
nately selfish in his dealings with women. One would do as
well as another, and if he took the time and trouble to
arouse a woman physically it was only because he preferred taking a woman who was willing and passionate.
Sonya Brandon had begun to bore him, but for Denise he
felt an almost unwilling kind of affection, perhaps because
of her naturalness and spontaneity. At least Denise had
never demanded or tried to pretend.

On the evening of the fifteenth day of Steve's imprisonment, Major Hart finally died. Steve spent most of the
night writing a long and rather difficult letter to his grandfather, who was his closest living relative. He had already
been informed in no uncertain terms by General Butler
himself that if the major died, his own sentence would be
carried out without delay. Army officers in wartime did
not engage in duels with each other, no matter what the
provocation. And an example must be set, not only to the
Union soldiers, but to the citizens of occupied New Orleans as well.

Dispassionately, Steve Morgan understood the truth behind the general's reasoning. If he did not particularly
want to die, he was not afraid of death either. It was
something he had long ago learned to live with and accept
as inevitable. He had been close to death many times, and
the thought had ceased to frighten him. There was, in
fact, a streak of recklessness in Steve's nature that had
made him, on several occasions, almost tempt death. He
enjoyed taking chances and found a kind of excitement in
danger. His only regret now, when he allowed himself to
think about it, was that it had to be this way—locked up
like an animal to wait for death, instead of going out to
find it.

When they came for him the next morning, he was already dressed and waiting. Tossing the letter he had written onto the table, he asked one of the soldiers to give it
to Denise when she came. He had scrawled her a short
note, lightly worded, asking her to see that the letter to his
grandfather was safely despatched. And he had enclosed,
as well, all the money he had on his person.

Now that everything had been taken care of, Steve

Morgan left his cell with the soldiers, wondering only, with a detached kind of curiosity, why they hadn't bound his arms, or sent him a priest.

He expected to be taken out into the courtyard and summarily executed, but they escorted him, instead, to the general's private office.

General Butler came from behind his desk, looking angry and disapproving. A medium-built, rather nondescript-looking man in civilian clothes turned away from the window, where he'd been standing and glanced at Steve, studying him without seeming to, his gray eyes cool and non-committal.

"All right—you soldiers may wait outside," the general said brusquely. They saluted smartly and wheeled around, closing the door behind them; leaving Steve standing at attention before the general's desk.

A frown drawing his bushy eyebrows together, Butler turned abruptly to the civilian.

"There's your man Mr. Bishop," he said gruffly. "A foolhardy, undisciplined ruffian, if you ask *my* opinion, but I suppose he might meet *your* qualifications." His glance swept coldly over Steve. "Captain Morgan, you may consider yourself under orders to answer any questions Mr. Bishop may put to you. Mr. Bishop," he added dryly, "is with the Department of the Army in Washington—Special Services. It appears he's been studying your dossier for some time."

Turning his back, General Butler stamped off to the window, where he remained looking out, his stiff carriage showing his patent disapproval.

With a slight, mirthless smile, Bishop walked behind the desk and sat down calmly, leafing through some papers there.

He looked up at last, and met Steve Morgan's carefully guarded eyes with a level glance.

"Well, Captain Morgan, I think I have your complete file here, but there are a few questions I'd like to ask—a few gaps you might fill in for me, if you please."

Jim Bishop had, at first glance, impressed Steve as being colorless and ordinary. But by the end of a half-hour Steve had formed a grudging respect for the man, who was not only coldly intelligent, but surprisingly clever and knowledgeable as well. He seemed to know more about Steve Morgan than it was possible for anyone to know—

and what he did not know, his blunt questions had soon informed him of. Steve was frank with the man—after all, he had nothing left to lose, and it had soon become apparent to him that he might have something to gain—it was obvious that Bishop had something in mind; he would hardly make the journey here from Washington, or be so interested in Steve's past history if he did not have a purpose for doing so.

All the same, he listened almost unbelievingly when Bishop offhandedly offered him a job—of a sort; and then went on to outline its risks and possible disadvantages in his concise, rather pedantic manner.

"You understand, Captain Morgan, that technically, at least, you'll be branded a deserter. But since you are under sentence of death, it will not surprise anyone that you'd seize a chance to escape, if such an opportunity presented itself. In actuality, you will still be carried on the army payroll and will retain your present rank, although you will not be wearing a uniform. But your name will only be carried on our books." Bishop glanced down at the papers before him for a moment before he looked up again. "You have travelled a lot, and you know several languages; that alone will be an asset to us. You will still be required to travel. Perhaps in Europe, where we are having trouble with Confederate spies trying to drum up support for their cause—and perhaps in the Western states and territories of this country. You're a Western man, and for the most part, this area will be your base of operations. On occasion, you may be sent into Mexico.

You'll be contacted from time to time by—other members of our organization, and given various assignments. Needless to say, all these will carry a considerable amount of risk and danger. But you're used to that, of course."

Bishop's eyes were hooded, for a moment. "If you are ever apprehended, it must be understood that naturally, we'll disclaim all knowledge or responsibility for you or your actions."

He looked inquiringly at Steve, who said a trifle wryly, "Oh—naturally!"

Bishop gave one of his thin smiles.

"Good—we're beginning to understand each other, I think!" He continued, "After you leave here, I will see that you are contacted by—um—one of our more experienced men. He'll fill you in about the type of assignment you'll be handling, and what we'll expect. And—as a suggestion—you should build yourself a reputation as a gunfighter—a fast draw—a man who will hire his gun out for pay. But try, if possible, to stay *just* on the right side of the law. I think you know what I mean, and it would save needless complications. If you have to kill a man, try to make it happen in a fair fight—in front of witnesses. Do I make myself clear?"

"Quite clear, sir," Steve said politely.

"Well, then!" Bishop actually looked quite pleased. "I think you will find this assignment more—er—suited to your temperament than the one you are just about to vacate." His voice was bland, but Steve sensed an undercurrent of something close to humor in the man, which surprised him.

"Well—" Bishop said again, more briskly, "we'll arrange for your escape tonight. You'll leave New Orleans on a flatboat. We'll talk again of details after you've breakfasted, and I will meet you myself in Los Angeles, California, in two months' time."

Steve saluted, and had turned to leave when Bishop's voice halted him.

"Oh, by the way, Captain Morgan—in case I should forget to mention it later—the bullets they'll be shooting at you when you escape will be real ones. Do try to be careful."

PART TWO

Beginnings

Chapter Four

Four years certainly brought many changes. Pierre Dumont, dining with some of his friends at Maxim's in Paris, sounded rather melancholy as he lamented the fact.

"He's still pining for his little *cousine*," Jean-Jacques Arnaud commented, winking at the Viscomte De la Reve, who sat on his right.

"Well—but in spite of her obstinate ways I suppose I do miss her," Pierre confessed.

"Ha! Of course he misses her!" René du Carre laughed. " 'Face of a *demi-mondaine*, body of a woman—' you see, I remember what you told us four years ago."

"That was true enough *then!* And you'll remember, when my *chère maman* insisted that I escort Virginie to her first ball, I added that she had the mind of a child, excited by small pleasures. Yes, but alas, she grew too clever for me."

"And heartless, too," the Viscomte stated self-pityingly. He flashed a quick, apologetic look at his friend's reddening face. "No need to look so annoyed, my old one. You know very well that I offered for her in all honor, and she turned me down. Told me she had only been practicing on me, in order to learn how to be a flirt—because someone had told her she was becoming too much of a bluestocking to be appealing to a man."

"I plead guilty!" Pierre admitted. "I was afraid, you see, that her success at all the smart salons my esteemed papa dragged her to would spoil her. But—well—she turned me down too, although I knew, of course, that it would never do—for we are cousins."

"Quite so—but you fell in love with her, and she twisted you around her little finger!" René said slyly. "Remember that time she teased you into taking her to dine in one of those discreet little rooms upstairs, because she wanted to find out how it would feel to play at being a *demi-mondaine*?"

"*Dieu!*" Pierre said, clutching his head in mock-anguish, "why do you have to remind me? She embarrassed me with all the—very *searching* questions she asked—and when the waiter came in she sat on my knee with her arms about my neck, so that she would not embarrass me, she said. Thank God my parents never found out!"

"You never did tell me that story before," his friend the Viscomte said, frowning. "Damn—I wish she had not been your cousin, Pierre!"

"Well—it is of no consequence now, is it?" Jean-Jacques interposed lazily. "She's left France—she'll probably marry some rough, crude *Americaine* with lots of money in the end. Where did you say she was going to live, with her papa?"

"Oh, in some Godforsaken place they call California—they discovered much gold there some years ago, you remember. A very rough place, and crawling with wild Indians, I've heard."

"Ah, yes—also they fight duels with pistols in the very streets, and every man carries a pistol on his hip . . ."

They started on a lively discussion of life on the American frontier, while Pierre stared dourly into his wine. Why had they started to speak about Virginie? Damn, but De la Reve had spoken truly. If only she hadn't been his cousin, and he hadn't discovered her charms so late—he might have made the chit fall in love with him—why, at sixteen she had obviously adored him! How she'd blushed whenever he teased her or looked at her long enough.

He wondered where she was, and what she was doing. He even hoped kindly, for her sake, that there were parts of America that were civilized. Poor, lovely Virginie! Her beauty, her elegance and her wit would be quite wasted in America. Perhaps, at last she would begin to regret that she had left France, that she had left him.

Pierre would have been surprised, all the same, if he had known that his cousin was actually, and at that very moment, thinking of him with affection, and even a twinge of nostalgia.

Chapter Five

Ginny lay in a bed, a real bed, for the first time in weary weeks of travelling, and found that she could not fall asleep. She was overtired, overexcited, and the bed was even too soft, after what she had begun to get used to.

Ever since she had arrived in America, she had been travelling. The two weeks she had spent in New York now seemed almost dreamlike and unreal. Whenever she closed her eyes she imagined she could feel the swaying, bumpy motion of the coach which had brought them here, and that had been much worse than the rocking of the ship that had carried her to America, and those dirty, cinder-filled trains that had brought them from New York to Louisiana.

Closing her eyes, Virginia Brandon thought firmly about Paris—and then about her cousin Pierre. Poor Pierre, she thought now. He had looked so unhappy!

"But I'll write to you often," she had promised, and he'd shaken his head lugubriously.

"You won't. You—you're flighty, dear cousin. You'll find yourself a dozen new swains to dazzle before you're halfway to America!"

"But that's different—you're my cousin, and you know

me so well!" she'd reminded him laughingly. "Oh, Pierre—you know very well I never dazzled you. You only pretended, because—because it was the fashion, and your friends liked me. Why, you always considered me a nuisance before, and much too much of a bluestocking. Remember? You told me so yourself. Besides," she'd added coaxingly, "you've always been my confidante. Who else would I talk to?" But though she'd teased him, she remembered that she had been quite infatuated with him when she was younger. What a lot had happened since then!

Crossing her arms beneath her head, Ginny thought about it all. America—the country she had been prepared not to like at all, was young, and vital and exciting; and when she had met her father and her new stepmother, all her initial misgivings had disappeared.

Her father had seemed genuinely happy to see her and glad to have her with him after all the years they'd been separated. And Sonya, his wife, was surprisingly young—blond, petite and spontaneously affectionate. It was impossible not to love her.

"I think it will be quite all right if you call me Sonya," she had whispered after Ginny had called her 'madame' for the third time. And her father had smiled indulgently.

He liked her, and he had shown that he was proud of her and trusted her. Hadn't he taken her into his confidence right away, to show that he accepted her completely?

Ginny smiled in the darkness. It was really her father's plans and ambitions that had made everything so exciting.

At a party they had attended in Washington, Ginny had overheard a man refer to her father as an opportunist—a man with no scruples and too much ambition. But the sneering words had made her feel proud, instead of angry. She understood that a lot of people must be jealous of her father—envious of his wealth and his power and above all, his drive. He was the kind of man who obtained what he wanted, and she admired him tremendously, just as Sonya did. To think he had taken the trouble to explain it all to her!

"I mean to carve myself out an empire, Virginia, he had said. Other men have done it. The time is right, with people milling around uncertainly and aimlessly since the war's been over—and whole territories to be taken for the asking."

Well, she thought, why not? Why shouldn't her father do what other men had done and were doing? Maximilian had been crowned Emperor in Mexico, with the French armies supporting him—and she had been happy to learn that her father had connections with the French. Bordering Mexico, Texas and California were states, but between them stretched the vast territories of Arizona and New Mexico, and beyond that Baja California. Who could know what might not be achieved, with the support and alliance of the French, and Maximilian too, of course? A really strong man could do anything—look at the first Napoleon. She was not only excited but flattered that she was to play a small part in her father's plans.

Ginny Brandon was now in San Antonio, Texas. A very old city, her father had explained. It had been built by the Spaniards a long time ago and the Texans had fought for it and taken it in the time when Texas was still the Lone Star Republic.

It was a city of contrasts, with old brick and stone buildings and ancient squares lying cheek by jowl with recently constructed, false-fronted wooden structures. Fine hotels and private houses mingled with gaudy saloons and gambling halls. A kind of headquarters for cattle ranchers, all rushing to sell their herds to the meat-starved north and east—and, inevitably, for gamblers and Indians and renegade gunmen as well as cowboys who came to town for excitement. A rich town now—full of movement and excitement and danger. But not to her, of course, or to Sonya, for her father was here to protect them, and he had already hired several men, who would be working for him.

In a few days, when Senator Brandon's plans were completed, Ginny and Sonya would travel overland by wagon train to California, while he would have to return to Washington for a while. Her father had bought a small herd of a new breed of white-faced cattle in Galveston—ordered all the way from Europe by a rancher who was unable to pay for them when they arrived. They would be driven to his ranch in California, following the wagon train. But—most exciting of all, the wagon train would also carry something more. Gold bullion, concealed in the false bottom of the wagon that Ginny and Sonya would ride in. And surplus army rifles and ammunition as well, in another wagon. All to help the French armies in Mexico. Louis Napoleon of France was careless about paying his troops there, and Maximilian would be grateful for help. An empire, straddling both sides of the border, her father had said once, and Ginny believed, as Sonya did, that he would make his dream a reality.

A sudden burst of laughter from the room next to hers made Ginny come back to the present with a frown. Not for the first time, she regretted that her father's suite did not connect with her room, but lay at the other end of the passageway instead.

It was a hot, humid night, and she was forced to keep her window open. No doubt the occupants of the room next door had done the same thing, and the sound of their drunken revelry carried clearly into her room. Annoyed, Ginny sat up in bed, glancing across the room at the small cot where Tilly, Sonya's maid, slept deeply and soundly, with her mouth half-open. Poor Tilly, she had been working extra hard, and must be exhausted. I'll let her sleep, Ginny thought, and close the window myself. Even if I half-suffocate it will be better than having to endure that noise all night!

She heard women's voices in the next room, loud and raucous, and her lips tightened disapprovingly. What kind of women would sit up half the night, drinking and partying with men? The question answered itself in her mind. Only one sort! There were no intelligent and sophisticated *demi-mondaines* in this part of the world, in these still uncivilized, roaring, bawdy western states. Women were either "good" or "bad," with no half-world of elegant courtesans dwelling between the two categories.

Ginny had seen these "good" women, dowdily dressed in ugly, old-fashioned clothes, looking much older than they could possibly have been. And she'd caught glimpses of the gaudily dressed "bad" women in their enormous feathered hats and tawdry satin gowns. They all looked hard, and somehow shop-worn. Ginny herself had sometimes used rouge in Paris—a discreet trace of it on her lips and cheeks, but the women she'd seen who used it here looked as if they were painted—bright, ugly splotches of color standing out grotesquely against their too-pale skins. Yes, she'd seen women of that sort in New York and Washington and New Orleans and Galveston, and had recognized them for what they were without having to ask Sonya or her father.

One of the women in the adjoining room began singing, and Ginny climbed determinedly out of bed. This was too much to bear! Tomorrow she'd tell her father, and he'd have her room changed. A pity, in a way, because it was such a nice, large room, and had windows overlooking the street—even a narrow balcony outside the big windows, with a carved wooden railing around it—to be used in case of fire. But even if she had to occupy a room that was much smaller and did not have a view, it would be much better than having to put up with this kind of disturbance when she was trying to sleep.

With the thin silk of her nightgown swishing about her legs, Ginny walked to the window; and then, with her hands upraised to pull down the heavy shutter, she froze.

The voices of two men sounded as if they stood right next to her, and it was a few startled moments before she realized that they must be standing at the open window of the next room. The faint smell of cigar smoke drifted to her, and she wrinkled her nose with distaste.

One of the men spoke with an accent that she wasn't able to place at first.

"You are bored, *amigo*? But she likes you, the blonde one."

The other man's voice sounded faintly contemptuous.

"Oh, sure! She'd like anything wearing pants—with money. And since Bishop's won most of our cash—maybe she'll turn her attention to him. Think he'd like her?"

The first man laughed delightedly.

"Poor Jim! He looks as if he's afraid of her!"

"Well—" Ginny could almost feel the man's shrug, "this little card party and the girls, was his idea. Me, I'd prefer to get some sleep."

"Maybe you had better. That man Haines—he's looking for trouble. I think he remembers you from some place—he doesn't believe you're really a wagon scout, or that your name is Whittaker."

"Don't care what he believes. If he keeps pushin' he's going to get himself killed."

The cold, unemotional certainty in the drawling voice made Ginny shiver. She couldn't move—and she was unable to resist eavesdropping while the men continued their conversation.

"You could just wound him—"

"That would be a waste of time. He'd get himself all healed up and come looking for me another time, and maybe I wouldn't be ready for him then. No—if Haines still wants a fight tomorrow, I'm through backing off."

"Better be careful then. I've heard the Marshal here doesn't cotton to gunfights in the streets of his town. Particularly when we have distinguished guests."

"I've met up with tough marshals before. And we won't be sticking around town too long in any case."

"Steve—Steve, honey? What you doin' over there so far away? Thought you wanted to hear me sing!"

A woman's voice this time, petulant and rather shrill, from somewhere within the room, and Ginny heard one of the men chuckle softly.

"See what I mean, *amigo*? She likes you."

"God—not too much, I hope! She's not my type. Think I'll have Mimi send over that new French gal she was talking about—a redhead from Louisiana, she said."

"Tonight? Better not—this one will kill you!"

"Steve!" The woman's voice called again, shriller than the last time, and the man lowered his voice slightly, but Ginny could hear an undercurrent of amusement in it.

"Ah, hell, I guess not. Guess I'll just have to wait till tomorrow night."

The voices faded, and she heard more laughter and the sound of clinking glasses from inside the room.

Seething with anger and disgust Ginny banged down the shutter. Let them hear! Maybe that would quiet them down. Men could be quite loathsome, she thought—talking about killing and women of ill repute in almost the same breath. And whoever those two men were, she hoped that she would never meet either of them.

Chapter Six

Ginny woke late the next day. Even as she stretched and yawned lazily, she realized that it must be almost noon, or past, for it was hot, and the sun left a wide yellow stain on the floor by the window. The window! Her forehead wrinkled as she remembered last night—those men, and the horrible women with them. In spite of the tightly closed window that had made her room seem unbearably stuffy, the sounds in the next room had kept her awake for hours. And now—how much of the day had she lost already?

Stretching again, Ginny sat up in bed, noticing that Tilly had gone, leaving the window open, fortunately, and the blinds drawn.

Her eyes felt heavy-lidded and swollen, and she had half a mind to stay in bed, but there was too much she had wanted to do today—go exploring the town with Sonya, and sit in the old, tree-shaded plaza watching the people go by. Sonya, as soft-hearted as usual, must have told Tilly to let her sleep late.

Before her resolve weakened, Ginny got quickly out of bed. She longed for a bath, but there was no time to order one now, and she was hungry. Perhaps if she hurried there would be time to have lunch downstairs.

Most of her clothes were still carefully packed away, but Tilly had unpacked a few and left them to hang in the small closet that the room provided. Stripping off her pale silk nightgown, Ginny pinned her hair up and washed herself all over with water from the pitcher on the bureau. A sponge bath, after all, was better than none at all, and it refreshed her considerably.

Choosing a cool organdie dress that did not look too wrinkled, Ginny slipped into it and studied herself critically in the small mirror. Its pale cream color, sprigged with tiny green and red flowers, suited her rather pale complexion.

Of course, it was considered fashionable to be pale, but she wished in spite of it that she had more color in her cheeks. In France, she had sometimes used rouge, but Sonya had already warned her that people here were a little more old-fashioned. Peering at her reflection, Ginny pinched her cheeks lightly and frowned back at herself. If only her mouth was a little smaller, her forehead higher! Still, it wasn't too bad a face, and she had been told she was a beauty; which, though it was surely exaggeration, was still flattering. I suppose I'm passable, she told herself, arranging her hair high on her head, and brushing it into ringlets that fell around her face and down her neck. At least I have nice ears, she thought, and I like the new hairstyles. No more smooth, decorous chignons—following the Empress Eugenie's example women in Paris had begun to arrange their hair differently, and it was now quite proper for a lady to let her ears show. Ginny had had her ears pierced before she left for America, and now she wore her favorite earrings—tiny pieces of jade set in antique gold studs that had belonged to her mother.

Turning away from the mirror, Ginny walked impulsively to the window and pulled the drapes aside so that she could look down into the street. It had been getting dark when they had arrived here last night, and under the hot sun, everything looked different.

The heat, reflected off the small balcony just outside the window, seemed to assault her senses.

It must be just past noon, she thought, shading her eyes. The dusty street seemed to shimmer in the glare, and there was no breeze to cool her cheeks. She supposed that it was the intense heat that made everyone stay indoors, for there was hardly any activity to speak of. Horses, tethered to hitching posts that lined the avenue, hung their heads; a few loafers sat rolling dice or smoking on the porch of a saloon just opposite.

The street was wide, but at this time only an occasional buckboard or a lone rider travelled its length. She had been told that wagons sometimes rolled through the streets of San Antonio, that it was a busy, bustling town. But this afternoon it seemed lazy and half-asleep—almost too quiet.

Voices carried up to her, through the still, hot air. A good town for eavesdropping, Ginny thought wryly, but she could not help listening—perhaps because of the rather tense note in the voice that spoke first.

"He's in that saloon, Bart. Been drinkin' in there with that half-breed sidekick of his since mornin'. Want me to go hurry him up, some?"

"No." The second voice sounded nasal and flat. "If he's drinking, he's scared. I can wait. He'll come out some time."

Curiosity made Ginny lean out cautiously to look down. Three men stood on the sidewalk beneath her window, completely unaware of her presence. One of them was tall and rather thin, dressed like an Easterner in a black suit, his hat a fashionable derby. His two companions wore typical western clothes.

The man they had called Bart spoke again.

"You find out who he is?"

"Naw. Calls hisself Whittaker, an' he came in with that wagon train, all right. All the way from Louisiana."

"He sure don't wear his gun like no scout," the third man put in. "I asked around, Bart. No one recognizes him for sure, but I heard one man say he used to ride shotgun for Barlow & Sanderson. Kind of sidewinder that travels around a whole bunch."

Bart made a short, cold sound that could have been a chuckle.

"So do I, Ed. An' I recall seeing him before, even if the name he's using ain't familiar. The marshal's office didn't have a poster on him, but I'd swear he has a price on his head."

"You'll collect it, then, Bart. You're faster than any gunman I ever seen, and I guess he knew that. He sure stayed real quiet when you were needlin' him yesterday, didn't he?"

The black-garbed man's voice sounded suddenly sharp and dangerous.

"Mr. Casey didn't like the way he run them wagons through the river ahead of his herd. Lost him valuable time, he said. And me, I just don't like the way he sets. You sure you gave him my message, Tom?"

"Sure I did, Bart. You saw me go in there. Mebbe he slunk out the back door—mebbe he didn't cotton to the idea of meeting you."

"He's going to like it less if I come looking for him."

Above the men, Ginny stood motionless, her mouth suddenly dry, her heart beginning to beat faster.

The man they were waiting for was one of the men she had heard talking last night. What a coincidence! But—these men had implied he was afraid, and it hadn't seemed that way. She remembered the cold assurance in his voice when he'd said he'd kill Haines. That must be the man they called Bart.

What was going to happen now? Would there be a gun-fight? Ginny knew that she ought to close her window. Forget about everything she'd overheard, and run down-stairs to safety. But a certain sick curiosity and excitement held her helpless. She had never watched a duel being fought before, and her father had told her that in the west, gunfights were common. *I want to see what it's like*, she thought. *I'm safe up here—I want to find out. Will he come out of that saloon? Has he really run away?*

Some instinct told her that the three men who waited like predatory birds were killers. They would wait, and a man would walk out from that saloon into the sunlight, and be shot down.

I do not want to see this—she thought dazedly, staring down into the glare of the dusty street. And yet, some-thing held her there. She had to see it all begin—and end.

With a suddenness that startled her, Ginny saw the swinging door of the saloon across the street pushed open. Two men came outside, pausing in the shade of the porch.

"Kill him now, Bart, while his eyes ain't used to the sunlight yet—" one of the men below said urgently.

But the black-clad man laughed softly and sneeringly.

"No need for that. I want to see him draw against me—and I want it known I was faster."

A feeling of unreality seized hold of Ginny. She almost felt as if she might be watching a play, safely ensconced in her box at the theatre. She found her eyes fixed on the taller of the two men who had come out of the saloon. This must be the man they called Whittaker. He had walked to the edge of the porch now, while the other man who had come outside with him stepped to one side, slightly behind him. Actors, taking their places. She must cling to that illusion!

Whittaker wore a black, flat-crowned hat pulled down over his forehead so that it shaded his eyes. He wore a short black leather vest over a burgundy red shirt, and dark blue, closely fitting breeches tucked into black, high-topped boots. His gun belt, with its tied-down holster, rode low on his right hip. Surprisingly, he didn't seem to be afraid. He stood there on the edge of the porch, his stance almost negligent except for the hand that seemed almost to brush the butt of his revolver.

Although nothing had happened yet, a kind of stillness seemed to hang in the air. The loafers on the porch scuttled out of the way, and a small group of men farther up the street, who had been talking casually among themselves turned to watch.

The man called Bart took a forward step out into the street where Ginny could see him clearly, without needing to crane her neck downward. He was a tall, rather thin man, his shoulders hunched under his black jacket.

His slightly nasal voice sounded cold, thin-edged with contempt.

"Took your time comin' out here, Whittaker, if that's your name. I was beginning to think I'd have to come in after you."

The lithe, dark-featured man with Whittaker smiled as if he had heard something to amuse him, his teeth flashing whitely under his thin mustache. He leaned back against the saloon wall, and began to roll a cigarette.

"Hurry back, *amigo*. Don't forget you have a drink to finish."

One of the men who had been talking to Haines laughed nervously, but Whittaker himself merely shrugged and stepped off the porch. He began to walk slowly towards the man who stood waiting for him, his boot heels making small puffs of dust at each step. He wasted neither motion nor words, and Ginny could not help being aware of an almost catlike grace in the way he walked and carried his lean body. Surely, he would have to pause soon? Surely he would have something to say? There was something menacing about the way he kept coming, so indolently, and so silently, and the other man seemed to sense it and grow tense.

"Damn you! What do you think—"

"Haines, I'm walking. You said you had business with me. You make the move."

Whittaker's voice was soft and almost disinterested, as if he didn't care one way or another, but he neither paused nor hesitated, and the distance between the two men narrowed.

Where before Ginny had been positive that the man called Bart was the more dangerous of the two, now she felt differently. Whittaker reminded her of an animal stalking its prey. In spite of his casual, unconcerned manner she could sense something infinitely dangerous about this man, and it was obvious that Haines felt it too.

With a muffled, unintelligible oath, Haines made his move; stepping back and sideways as his hand seemed to blur downward for his gun.

Ginny supposed afterwards that Whittaker must have moved too. When horrified realization hit her, he had a gun in his hand and he was standing with his knees slightly bent, firing. There were three shots at least that seemed to merge into one rolling explosion. Haines' gun dropped before he could bring it up—the man seemed to have been picked up and flung backward by the murderous force of the bullets that pounded into his body.

Ginny leaned against the window frame, her nostrils stinging from the smell of burned powder, her eyes fixed with a sick, frightened fascination on the broken body that lay sprawled like an ungainly puppet in the dust, blood seeping from holes in the black coat.

She was hardly aware of the voices that floated upward, of the footsteps of men who came running.

"My God—Haines never even got a chance to shoot!"

"Never seen anyone draw so fast in my born days . . ."

"Somebody better get the Marshal, I guess. But Haines was asking for it."

"If the Marshal wants to talk to me, I'll be in the saloon, finishing my drink."

How could any man who had just killed another sound

so coolly unconcerned? Duels had always seemed so romantic, so dramatic, but there had been nothing so very dramatic or noble about this one—and even when she closed her eyes, Ginny could see the broken, bleeding body, just lying there.

Half-sick with revulsion, she stumbled away from the window and found herself sitting on her bed, fighting to control the waves of nausea.

Chapter Seven

Senator Brandon had reserved a private dining room that night so that his family and guests might eat in privacy. The hotel they were staying at boasted a French chef and the fine wines that accompanied their meal that night also came from France.

Tonight it was easy to imagine that they were dining in a fine Eastern restaurant. The large table was adorned with a snowy linen tablecloth, set with heavy china and silverware—the waiters were well-trained and unobtrusive.

It was amazing, Ginny thought, what could be achieved with enough money and influence—creating a civilized oasis in an uncivilized world was just one of the smaller things. I shouldn't think that way, she thought guiltily. Why, I've been told that San Francisco, for instance, can hold its own with any of the larger European cities. And yet, it was almost unbelievable to imagine that she was still in San Antonio, Texas, where outside on a street that was an unpaved expanse of red dust, a man had been shot dead in front of witnesses.

Ginny took a sip of her wine, willing herself to forget about the early afternoon and the scene she had watched. A man had died violently—she must get used to it. She was fully aware that she might watch worse things happen on the long journey by wagon to California.

"My dear child," her father had warned her, "I do not want you to imagine that this journey you have undertaken is without risk. There might be hostile Indians— some white men who are as bad or even worse, because they have turned renegade." His voice had been serious, she knew that he was worried and perhaps a little uneasy about the prospect of his wife and daughter travelling alone to California. And yet, he was a practical man too. He had admitted quite honestly that it would prove a tremendous political advantage to him—the fact that like so many other emigrants to the golden state, his wife and daughter had undertaken the long and arduous journey by wagon train. There was also another factor to be considered, and that was the safety of the gold, the importance of their mission. No one would suspect that William Brandon would send help to the French in Mexico, or that two women would be entrusted with a mission of such critical importance. If Brandon's motives were suspect in any circles (and he had also admitted that there were some who had these suspicions) they would never imagine that he would take his wife and daughter into his confidence. Westerners put "good" women on a pedestal—Sonya and Ginny would be much admired for their courage in undertaking such a long and hazardous journey without the Senator's immediate protection, and the gold and arms could be delivered into the right hands without suspicion being aroused in the wrong quarters.

My father is an intelligent man, Ginny thought proudly. She looked up and met his approving glance as it rested on her for just an instant.

Tonight, in honor of the Senator's guests, both Ginny and Sonya had worn evening gowns purchased in Paris, but it was apparent, soon after they had descended the staircase, that the latest styles had not come this far west as yet. There were five other women present—wives of the wealthy cattle ranchers who were Brandon's guests, and their hoop-skirted gowns in dark shades of brown or maroon were uncompromisingly highnecked in spite of the almost oppressive heat. Ginny could feel the disapproving glances of these older, dowdy women rest on her from time to time, and although she was stubbornly determined to show no embarrassment, it was hard to feel exactly comfortable! She was glad that she had been seated next to Carl Hoskins, her father's young foreman; and gladder still to learn that Mr. Hoskins would be accompanying them to California.

Carl Hoskins was an extremely handsome young man, with blond hair that gleamed in the candlelight, and a small, carefully trimmed mustache that enhanced his good looks. He was, Ginny learned, the younger son of a recently impoverished plantation owner, and had been a captain in the Confederate army. Now, he intended to make his fortune in California.

"I mean to learn all I can about the cattle business," he confided to Ginny, made slightly dizzy and reckless by the combination of her beauty and the wine that flowed so plentifully. "I'm not going to waste my time searching for gold—there are bigger and more stable fortunes to be made by ranching, so I've heard. Someday, when I've saved up enough money, I'll buy a ranch of my own; build up herds of Hereford cattle for beef and Jerseys or Guernseys for dairy products"—he broke off, embarrassed at the effect his own ill-timed enthusiasm might have on this dazzling, sophisticated young woman beside him.

"Go on," Ginny said softly, her emerald eyes seeming to glow. "I'm not at all bored, if that's what you are afraid of. I want to learn all I can about California, and the way people live there."

Her green velvet gown matched her eyes, and when she leaned towards him as she was doing now, Carl was almost uncomfortably aware of the slight, rounded curve of her breasts, revealed by the extremely low décolletage of her dress. Her shoulders were bare and gleamed like ivory—matching green rosettes held her gown together at the shoulders, and she wore long gloves that reached to her elbows. *I can tell these old biddies don't like her gown,* Carl thought bemusedly, trying to keep his attention on her conversation, *but I sure do. If that's the latest style—it suits her, and she's sure got the figure to carry it off!* Suddenly, he found himself looking forward to the long journey to California, even though, at first, he had not been exactly enthusiastic about the fact that they were to have two women along.

Born a Southern gentleman, Carl Hoskins possessed both charm and good manners, in spite of the fact that he had not thought it necessary to avail himself of more than a formal, cursory kind of education. Books and foreign languages had never interested him; he had had other things to occupy his time and his mind. And when he had returned home from the wars to find his father's acres seized by a carpetbagger government for non-payment of taxes, Carl had been philosophic enough and angry enough to be able to turn his back on it all and head west. It helped when his father wrote to William Brandon, who had been an early aquaintance of his. And Brandon trusted him—Brandon had plans that would include Carl in the adventure as well as the profit.

Not usually at a loss for words or compliments where women were concerned, Carl found himself shy and almost tongue-tied around Ginny Brandon. He had never met a woman exactly like her before—combining the graceful charm of a young girl and the intelligence and sophistication of a woman. And she was flirting with him—he didn't know quite how to react to it.

What Carl did not realize, because she hid it so well, was that Ginny was bored. And when she was bored, she talked more than usual, her conversation light and frivolous.

Did the men here have nothing to talk about but raising cattle and selling them? Had the women no other interests but their homes and their children? But then, in this vast and half-empty land, what else was there?

They were well into their third course now, and Ginny allowed her glass to be refilled, smiling when she caught Sonya's eye. She had already noticed that most of the other women did not drink any wine at all, or merely took small, polite sips. It was another thing that she felt they must disapprove of, and she didn't care. No doubt they would go home tonight and gossip among themselves that the Senator's daughter drank too much wine and was fast. The thought made her smile again, and Carl, who thought her smiles were all for him, felt his heart beat faster.

Her father was talking to Mr. Black, on his right, and because he was wearing a small frown on his face, which was unusual, Ginny found herself paying attention to his words.

"Do you know anything about a man who calls himself Whittaker? I was talking to your town marshal today, asking him if he could recommend a good scout for my wagon train, and he told me this man knows every trail between Texas and California. But it's strange I hadn't heard his name before."

Black, a portly, cheerful-looking man with a full beard, chuckled.

"Marshal Trevor always gets kinda nervous when he gets a famous gunfighter in his town. And this *hombre* you were just talkin' of shot Bart Haines just this afternoon— Bart was supposed to be one of the fastest, but the way I heard it, he hardly got to clear leather."

Involuntarily, Ginny's fingers tightened around the stem of her wineglass. She felt her whole body grow stiff. But the other gentlemen had joined in the conversation now, and her sudden tension went unnoticed.

"He's a *gunfighter?*"

Vance Porter, who sat on Ginny's right, leaned forward to answer her father.

"Sure. One of the fastest guns for hire. But I've heard he's ridden shotgun for Barlow, scouted for the army, and taken a few herds up to Abilene too."

"He comes from your own state, Senator," another man broke in. "And Whittaker isn't his real name either. It's Morgan—Steve Morgan."

Sonya, who was usually never clumsy, dropped her ivory fan with a clatter, and Ginny glanced across at her as one of the men picked it up gallantly and handed it back to her. Sonya's face, usually so placid and composed, looked flushed, and her eyelashes dropped to hide her embarrassment as she murmured her thanks.

It's too much, Ginny thought. First it is cattle and now it's gunfighters! She had half-opened her mouth to say that she had actually witnessed the gunfight these men had talked about, but catching sight of Sonya's face, unusually pale now that the color in it had receded, Ginny thought better of it. Perhaps the thought of killing upset Sonya, too.

Snatches of conversation came to her amid the subdued clinking noises the waiters made as they cleared away plates and empty glasses. Even Carl Hoskins seemed more interested in her father's plan for hiring a scout than he was in her. He was leaning forward, his fair head gleaming in the lamplight, and Ginny slanted a wicked glance at him. She remembered a story she had heard once, about a certain Parisienne lady who had deliberately loosened the

strap of her evening gown to cause a diversion when her
lover had appeared too interested in a rival. Unconsciously, Ginny's fingers touched the velvet rosette on
her right shoulder—it was loose, she suddenly remembered
that she had meant to have Tilly sew it on firmly before
she dressed for dinner. But no—it would never do! These
sharp-featured women with their disapproving looks—how
horrified they would be! And Carl Hoskins, even though
he was very handsome, wasn't worth it. All the same, the
mere idea made her want to giggle.

"Ginny my love—" Sonya's soft voice caught her attention. "I wonder if you would mind fetching our shawls
downstairs? I believe it is actually getting rather chilly."

Poor Sonya, her face had an unaccustomed pallor, and
Ginny thought she could see her shiver slightly.

Smiling consolingly at her stepmother, Ginny made her
murmured excuses, glad of a chance to escape for a while.

One of the waiters directed her to the back staircase—
she had no desire to use the one that led down into the
lobby and run the gamut of bold masculine stares that she
had encountered earlier in the evening when she and
Sonya had descended to dinner on her father's arm.

Lifting her long, trailing skirts, Ginny went quickly up
the narrow, rather winding staircase that would take her
up to the second floor. Its threadbare carpeting
proclaimed that this must be the servant's staircase, lying
at the end of the passageway that was furthest from her
room.

Pausing at the top of the stairs to catch her breath,
Ginny noticed for the first time how dimly lighted the narrow corridor seemed to be at night. It looked deserted,
and somehow its emptiness and the silence up here almost
frightened her.

It's nonsense, and I'm being silly, she told herself firmly.
I'll find my room first, and then Tilly can help me find
Sonya's shawl.

But the feeling of uneasiness persisted and she walked
swiftly, and as quietly as she could along the lonely corridor, with its shadowy walls. All the doors looked exactly
alike, and it was almost impossible to read the numbers
that had been painted on them. To make things worse,
when she reached the end of the passageway she found
that one of the lamps had been allowed to go out and it
was quite dark.

"Oh—oh, *darn*" she whispered to herself, annoyed because she could not even remember exactly where her room was located. "*Merde!*" she whispered again, daringly, the sound of her own voice making her feel braver. A thread of light showed under one of the doors, and she bent closer to read the faded numbers. She could make out a two and a five—257, hadn't that been the number of her room? Tilly usually kept the lamp lighted—perhaps she'd stayed awake.

Ginny hesitated for a moment and then tapped very lightly at the door, waiting impatiently for Tilly to open it. But what happened next took her completely by surprise.

The door opened very quickly from the inside, and before she could utter a sound she felt her hands grasped firmly as she was pulled, unceremoniously into the room.

She was only half-aware that the door had thudded shut behind her—too shocked and startled to do anything but gasp her dismay, Ginny found herself gazing into a pair of the darkest blue eyes she had ever encountered. They gleamed wickedly at her, half-shadowed by the longest eyelashes she had ever known a man to possess.

The darkness of his face, with its rather rakishly slanted eyebrows formed an almost startling contrast to those blue eyes, which narrowed as they studied her boldly and openly. She was petrified with fear and astonishment, her lips parted, but no words came from her dry, contracting throat.

The man smiled suddenly, and she thought, almost wickedly, showing a flash of white teeth; and she noticed, irrelevantly the grooves that deepened on either side of his mouth as he smiled.

"Well, by God!" he said slowly, his eyes travelling insolently over her body, "so you're Frenchy. Mimi really delivered the goods this time!"

His hands still held firmly onto hers, and before she could find the strength to utter a word, Ginny found herself jerked forward and gathered into the man's unwelcome embrace—and worse, felt his lips come down over hers, harshly, and somehow possessively.

She had been kissed before, but never like this! Nor had any man dared hold her so closely that she could feel the entire length of his body against hers. His mouth was hard and merciless, instead of merely touching her lips gently it seemed to sear into them like a flame, forcing them apart under the onslaught of his kiss.

He held her with one arm just above her waist and the other around her shoulders so that she felt crushed and completely breathless; and when she would have moved her head away to escape, she felt his hand slide upward, catching the curls at the back of her neck to hold her pinioned.

Ginny felt her head begin to spin—it fell back helplessly as waves of dizziness and heat washed over her. To her horror, she felt his tongue pillage her mouth, forcing little involuntary whimpers from her throat. Oh, God, God, she thought weakly, do men really kiss like this? What is he doing to me? What will he do next?

Quite suddenly, when she was on the verge of fainting, his hold loosened somewhat, and he raised his head slightly to look down into her face.

"I didn't think any woman could be this beautiful, Frenchy," he whispered. His eyes were narrow and hard with a kind of desire she could sense but could not fully understand. She fought to regain her breath, to exercise some control over her suddenly weak and trembling body, and he bent his head again—she felt his lips burn into the hollow at the base of her throat.

"No!" The one word was all she could manage and it came out as a despairing gasp. She felt his fingers pull teasingly at the loose rosette and gasped again with outrage. Almost unconsciously she spoke in French.

"*Monsieur—non*! Oh—what are you doing?"

The rosette came off and he laughed.

"Forget the stupid rose—I'll get you another." His lips muffled her cry of protest as he murmured against hers. "I'll buy you another gown too, sweetheart, for I've a mind to tear this one off your body. You know I want you, and I'm an impatient man."

His mouth seemed to attack hers again as his arm tightened around her waist, drawing her closer. Ginny felt her knees grow weak, so that she swayed against him involuntarily. She felt only half-awake—this is a bad dream, it cannot be real, her mind repeated dully, and she was aware of a strange, creeping sensation of languor, of a terrified kind of acceptance that had nothing to do with either her mind or her will. With a feeling of almost dreamlike detachment, Ginny felt his tongue explore her mouth, felt the gown slip off her shoulders as his hand caressed the curve of her breast. Her hands were trapped between their bodies, and could only press ineffectually against his chest, while her helpless struggles only seemed to excite him further, and drive him to taking even bolder liberties.

Helplessly, she felt his fingers find and press against the rapidly hardening point of a nipple, and the sensation was like a shock-wave running through her body, snatching her back to reality. Now she struggled in earnest against his encroaching hands and lips, horrifyingly aware that his shirt was open to the waist and her bared breasts, protected only by the thin silk of her chemise, were pressed against his bare, warm chest.

The pressure of his body, the animal heat of it, and the naked demand of his kisses were too much to bear. With her head swimming, Ginny forced herself to go limp in his arms. Surely, if he thought she had fainted, he would not continue this—this attack on her body and her senses?

He released her so suddenly that she stumbled backwards, to be brought up short by the alarming, unexpected pressure of the edge of a bed against the back of her thighs.

With a wail of pure terror, Ginny's hands came up to cross involuntarily over her breast as she saw him walk towards her with that stalking, catlike tread she remembered so well.

"Frenchy—will you stop acting so damned coy and take off that gown? *Now*, or I'll take it off you!"

She saw his arms reach out for her again, and like a cornered animal, Ginny brought one hand up with all the strength she could muster and felt her palm crack against the side of his face with satisfying force.

The look of stunned surprise on his face filled her with a savage pleasure, and instinctively, she brought her other hand up, longing to rake at him with her nails. But this time, he managed to forestall her; catching her wrist and squeezing it cruelly until she cried out with pain. They stood eye to eye for a split-second, his blazing with anger, and hers shining with tears of pain and frustration. She would have struck him again with her free hand, but he caught it too and held it in his harsh, merciless grip.

"Goddam it, you French bitch!" he said through his

teeth. "What kind of stupid game do you think you're playing?"

The cold fury in his voice and the dangerous look in his eyes would ordinarily have made her shrink back in terror if she had not been so angry herself.

"You—you rude, abominable m-monster!" Her voice shook with fury. "How dare you treat me this way? How dare you drag me into this room and—and then *attack* me as if I were a—a—" Her indignation at this point was so great that further words failed her and she stood panting, struggling to free her hands so that she could strike at him again.

From anger, the look in his eyes was turning into one of puzzlement, and then, slow-dawning dismay.

His black brows drew together in a frown as he took a backward step, holding her at arm's length now as he studied her. Sobbing with rage and humiliation, Ginny became suddenly aware of the state she was in—her gown slipped off her shoulders, her hair falling down her back in tangles.

"If you're not the girl Mimi was supposed to send over, then who—"

"Will you let go of me? I am *not* the—the *slut* you were obviously expecting—couldn't you wait even to *ask* before you fell on me like an animal?"

Breathlessly, blinking back tears, Ginny stormed at him fiercely, her anger making her brave, "You—you're worse than any savage, you murderer!"

She saw his eyes freeze into chips of ice for an instant, and then he quirked a slanted black brow.

"Never have murdered a beautiful woman, though," he said reflectively, and then, his tone suddenly becoming harsh, "*yet!*"

Still holding her wrists, he gave her a swift backward shove before he released her, and Ginny found herself floundering into a sitting position on the bed.

"Ohh!" she gasped, her eyes widening with shock and fear.

She saw a corner of his mouth twitch with amusement as he looked down at her.

"Suppose you just sit there for a minute and tell me—quickly, if you please, ma'am—who you are and why you came tapping at my door? After all," he added reasonably, "I was expecting a—female guest. How was I to know that you were not she?"

In spite of the softly reasonable tone of his voice there was an underlying steely quality to it that made Ginny answer him, a trifle sullenly.

"I—I mistook your room for mine; there was no light in the corridor and I couldn't read the numbers on the door. And then—" she flashed a hateful look at him, "you dragged me inside without giving me a chance to say a word, and you—you—"

"Attacked you?" he supplied helpfully and rage swept through her again when she saw that he was actually grinning at her. So he thought it all very amusing, did he?

She sprang to her feet angrily, forgetting once more to be afraid, and this time, he stepped back cautiously, although his eyes still mocked her.

"Now ma'am—don't you go attacking *me!*"

He heard her indrawn breath of fury and the dancing, mocking lights in his eyes seemed to intensify. A corner of his hard, reckless mouth lifted in a teasing smile, and Ginny, seeing it, gritted her teeth.

"You are the most objectionable, hateful—"

"It was really your fault, ma'am. It was your beauty that carried me away. Why, I couldn't believe my luck when I saw you—I had the irresistible impulse to kiss you, and I—"

"Will you stop trying to make a—a *joke* of what you did?" He was teasing her, he had the effrontery to think that she was some stupid ninny of a girl who would allow herself to be coaxed and cajoled and teased out of her well-founded rage!

"I cannot see how you could possibly mistake me for the—the type of female you were obviously expecting," Ginny went on coldly, trying to ignore the annoying smile on his face. "Although I must confess I feel sorry for your female visitors if you are used to greeting them in such a *forcefully* affectionate manner! Are you afraid they will refuse your advances unless they are not given the chance to do so?"

His glance flicked over her from head to toe, making her cringe instinctively. She had never encountered such obvious, crude insolence in any man's eyes before! It was as if he stripped her naked with a look.

"If you'll forgive me for saying so, ma'am," he drawled,

"I'm certainly not used to seeing *ladies* dressed the way you are—not in this little town, anyhow. Not that I'm complaining, mind," he added wickedly. "In fact, you look even more desirable just the way you are now . . ."

Ginny could feel the blush that spread all over her body as she became miserably, angrily aware all over again of how she must look at this moment. Her hands snatched for her gown, pulling it up over her half-naked bosom, and tears of rage and frustration filled her eyes.

"You are the rudest, most detestable man I have ever met!" she spat at him, her voice choked. "Will you stand aside and let me go? I'll not stay here another minute and be further insulted!"

He made no attempt to move, however, and she saw him frown.

"You'll either let me go or I'll scream!" Ginny's voice was high with a rising hysteria she tried to control. Surely, after what he'd done already, he didn't intend to—to—

"You can't walk out like *that*." His voice was flat, impatient. "And as for screaming—you didn't scream before, why should you now? I'm sure you're too intelligent to want to create a scandal."

He was actually threatening her, trying to blackmail her! Ginny stared at him with a mixture of fear and contempt, wondering what he would do if she did scream after all.

He seemed almost to read her mind, for he frowned again, shaking his head at her impatiently.

"Now look—I promise you I won't try to—er—attack you again! But please try to be reasonable. You cannot possibly—"

He broke off as a soft knocking at his door startled them both, and for just a second they were like fellow conspirators, exchanging looks of apprehension.

The knocking came again, this time louder and more insistent, and Ginny's hand flew to her mouth. Whoever it is, she thought despairingly, if they find me here like this with him, my reputation is ruined! No one would believe—they'll wonder why I didn't scream—oh, God, what will I do now?

A woman's voice with a heavy accent called softly from the other side of the door.

"Étienne? Steve Morgan? You can open the door, it is

me, Solange. Mimi told me you'd be expecting me—are you there?"

Ginny had to fight back the impulse to burst into hysterical laughter. And something must have shown on her face, for she felt Steve Morgan's fingers close meaningfully around her wrist, and flinched.

"That, I suppose is your Frenchy!" Ginny whispered, making her voice as cutting as possible. "Will you kindly let go of my wrist and tell me what you intend to do now?"

She noticed, with satisfaction, that for a moment he looked as much at a loss as she, and then as the woman's voice called his name again, louder and more petulantly this time, his manner became purposeful.

"I know one thing," he said shortly, "I can't leave her out there raising hell! She'll have everyone in the damn hotel in here, wondering what's going on."

He dropped her wrist, and then leaving her standing in the middle of the room he reached the door in two easy, purposeful strides and flung it open.

A woman of about twenty-five, well-formed, and wearing a red satin dress that clashed with her fiery red curls burst in, laughing.

"Ah—but you take so long! I thought you were not here, but now—yes now I'm glad that you are—you are ver' handsome, Mimi was right!"

Steve Morgan was locking the door, and as he turned back to her the woman flung her arms around his neck, pressing her voluptuous body closely against his.

Amazed, and fascinated in spite of her own embarrassing predicament, Ginny saw the young woman's bright, painted lips part and then glue themselves to the man's, in spite of his obvious stiffness and hesitancy.

In a moment, she had flung her head back to look up into his face.

"What is the matter lover? Don't you like me?"

And then, over his shoulder, her dark eyes met Ginny's cool green gaze, and her eyes widened.

Stiffening with outrage, Frenchy let her arms slip from around Morgan's neck as she stared at Ginny, her dark, angry eyes taking everything in.

"I think I am begin to understand," she said, her voice shrill with rage. "Who is she? An' what is she doing here?"

The woman's arm pointed dramatically, and she took a

step forward, but Steve Morgan had grabbed her quickly around the waist.

"Now wait just a minute—her being here is an accident . . ."

"Oh, an accident, hein? An' her gown all tore from her shoulders, that is accidental too?"

With a coolness she was far from feeling, Ginny shrugged.

"No, indeed it wasn't! It seems that Mr. Morgan mistook me for you, and without giving me a chance to explain or to defend myself he—but why don't you ask him to explain? I'm sure he'll do it much better than I could!"

"You're doing quite well," Steve Morgan said grimly. He dropped his hand from Frenchy's waist and looked at her quizzically. "I'm sorry, sweetheart, but she's right. She knocked at the door, and I thought it was you. Guess I got carried away!"

Expressions of anger, doubt, incredulity and finally amusement chased each other across the Frenchwoman's face as her eyes went from Morgan to Ginny and back again.

Finally, surprising them both, she began to laugh, throwing back her bright head.

"Oh—but this is the best joke I have hear! So—" her eyes flashed at Ginny, "he think you are me and he don't want to wait, hmm? Well—you are pretty, *cherie*," she admitted generously. "How can I blame him? Men are so impatient sometimes!"

"Impatient is hardly the word I'd use for Mr. Morgan's actions," Ginny snapped, giving him a malicious look.

Steve Morgan, his face unreadable now, walked over to the bureau that was set against one wall and poured himself a long drink from the half-empty bottle of bourbon he had left out.

"I think," he said politely, "we should all have a drink and discuss how we are to get miss—miss—" he raised an eyebrow at Ginny who stared back at him mutinously, her lips pressed tightly together, and then went on, shrugging, "this young lady back safely to wherever she came from, with her gown intact."

His words suddenly reminded Ginny of her errand upstairs—the fact that even now Sonya might have sent someone upstairs to search for her, and her eyes widened with dismay.

"Oh no!" she gasped, "if—if my father ever finds out where I am, or what happened, he'd—he'd kill you, and I'd be *ruined!* What on earth am I to do?"

"Yes, think of something," Solange chuckled teasingly, her small, dark eyes crinkled with amusement. "You do not wish for an angry papa to find his daughter here, do you, Steven *cher?*"

"That, believe me, is the last thing I wish!" he said grimly, and slammed the glass down on the bureau. Ginny felt his glance flick over her and blushed again, but he added, as if he hadn't noticed her discomfiture, "thank God you're not hysterical any longer, at least. Perhaps you could get back to your room and—er—sew the gown back together? I only ripped that stupid little rose off your shoulder—it ought to be around here somewhere—"

"*Only!* You took all kind of unforgiveable liberties, and now you try to pretend that—"

"But wait!" Solange cast a calculating look at Morgan and turned to Ginny. "He is right—it only needs just a little stitch at the shoulder here, you see? An' me, I always carry a needle and thread with me. So—I will fix it. An' you, *mal homme*, you will find that rosette for us, *oui?*"

Her head whirling with a mixture of rage, frustration and humiliation, Ginny forced herself to stand still while Frenchy wielded her needle with surprising efficiency, chattering away all the while in French. She had been delighted to discover that Ginny spoke her native tongue, and her eager questions about France and the new fashions were almost pathetically revealing of her homesickness. In spite of the fact that this Solange was, no doubt, a bad girl, Ginny could not help liking her—there was something so friendly, so honest and direct about her that it was impossible not to feel sorry for her, and of course, she had already confided that it was a man who had brought her to the profession she was now engaged in.

Men! Ginny thought, were the root of all women's troubles. Look at the trouble that the detestable Mr. Morgan had caused her!

She flashed a quick look at him from beneath her down-cast lashes and caught his gaze on her, but this time his startlingly blue eyes wore a somber, almost thoughtful expression. What was he thinking? And what kind of a man was he? She answered herself bluntly. A gunman. A man to whom human life meant nothing, obviously. And a man who would take what he wanted without any scruples, even if his victim was a defenseless woman! She had looked away from him nervously, but she could not help recalling the way in which he had held her imprisoned in his arms, the brutal kisses he had forced on her. She could not help shuddering, and Solange asked solicitously if she were cold.

"I will be finish in just a minute—and then you can get your shawl, yes, and go back to your papa. Perhaps you will say you felt unwell, yes?"

As much as she hated having to lie to her father and to Sonya, Ginny supposed that it might be the best excuse she could give—and she had, after all, drunk quite a lot of wine with her dinner.

Chapter Eight

The excuse that Frenchy had suggested served Ginny well enough after she had returned to the dining room downstairs, with her shawl and Sonya's over her arm.

"Ginny! Why, what took you so long? I was beginning to feel quite worried about you!"

And certainly, Sonya's face wore a white, distraught look that was unfamiliar, and caused Ginny a pang of guilt.

She bent over Sonya's chair as she handed her the shawl and whispered that she had run too fast up the stairs and had begun to feel quite dizzy . . .

"And then, of all things, I discovered that the rosette here, on my shoulder, was quite loose. So I stayed to sew it back on. I'm sorry, I really am!"

Sonya gave her a smile that seemed only a little forced, and squeezed her arm as if to make up for it.

"You don't need to apologize, my love! And the gentlemen have been so wrapped up in their conversation I'm sure you were hardly missed!"

Ginny heard her father chuckle as she slipped demurely back into her seat beside Carl Hoskins.

"Women and their dilly-dallying! Primping before a

mirror, weren't you daughter? Here, try some of the famous Texas coffee and tell me what you think of it."

Even though the meal had long since been cleared away, the men lingered over their cigars and coffee, and the women, obviously used to being left out of their husbands' discussions, talked softly among themselves. Ginny longed for the civilized customs of Europe and the east coast of America where the women would withdraw discreetly to leave the men to their boring talk.

Carl Hoskins was paying much more attention to her now, and his obvious admiration was like balm to her wounded sensibilities. What charming manners he had—he was a gentleman. How different he was from Steve Morgan! She found herself wondering what it would feel like to be kissed by Carl Hoskins. His kisses would be gentle and undemanding, she was sure of that. He would treat her with respect. And he did not look like a pirate, or a bandit! His blond hair contrasted well with his tanned face, and was carefully trimmed, as were his discreet sideburns. Steve Morgan's sideburns had swooped down the sides of his face, almost to the jawline, and his thick black hair had, she recalled with distaste, been allowed to grow too long, so that it curled at the nape of his neck. Yes, all he needed was a mustache or a beard and gold hoops in his ears and he'd make a villainous pirate.

I hate him, she thought. I despise and detest him! And I hope that I never have to set eyes on him again.

There were no sounds of revelry in the next room that night, although Ginny was careful to lock both her door and her window. All the same, she could not help wondering if Frenchy had stayed, and if he had been as eager to tear her clothes from her body as he had seemed to be earlier. A shudder went through her body when she thought of it. Last night it had been the woman who had sung so badly, and whose embraces he had wanted to avoid. Tonight—but no, she told herself firmly. A rake—a libertine like that—he is not worth thinking about. It is over, and I need never see him again.

It was only when she was lying in bed, trying to compose herself for sleep, that the horrible thought struck her that her father had actually spoken of hiring this same Steve Morgan as scout for their wagon train. Hadn't he explained earlier that he needed a man who knew how to use his guns?

It would be the duty of their scout to guide them through wild and rough country that was infested with savage Indians, and to see to their defense in case of attack. But how could anyone trust such an unscrupulous man?

"The Western gunfighter is a strange breed," William Brandon had said. "He's a professional killer, and he works for pay, but he is at least loyal to the man who pays him. It's a matter of pride, and of reputation. And very few outlaws will mess with one of these professional gunmen, because they are afraid of them. They're ruthless —and yet, you would be safest with such a man to guard you."

But if the man were Steve Morgan, *would* she be safe? For the second night in succession, sleep was long in coming.

Ginny would perhaps have slept earlier, and more soundly, if she'd known that Steve Morgan was not in his room next to hers.

He had spent quite a pleasant hour with Frenchy, who was young enough and attractive enough to please his somewhat fastidious tastes, and indeed, she had proved so adept, once they were in bed, that he'd quite looked forward to having her spend the whole night with him.

Unfortunately, Mr. Bishop had different ideas, and when Paco Davis had knocked at the door to tell Steve regretfully that he'd been invited to join in a late poker game, Steve had consoled Frenchy with thirty dollars and a promise to visit her room later, if the game did not go on until morning.

Bishop had engaged a private gaming room at the Cattleman's Rest, and when Steve arrived there by way of the back staircase the room was already stuffy and filled with cigar smoke. Empty glasses and bottles stood on the table, and as usual, Bishop, who played poker with ruthless concentration and a great deal of luck, had been winning.

"Got in a game with some drummers from back east," Paco said laconically. "They just left, or I'd have come looking for you earlier. But you would not have liked that very much, hey, *amigo*?"

Steve returned Paco's white grin.

"No—you're right. I sure wouldn't have appreciated being disturbed much earlier!"

Bishop had been playing solitaire while he waited for

Steve. Now he looked up expressionlessly, gesturing at the table before him.

"Cut for the deal. This is supposed to be a serious poker game, remember?"

"It's going to be serious for sure, if you keep winning all my money," Paco grumbled as he dropped into a chair.

Steve lit a cigar and sat opposite Bishop, waiting for the man to speak. The cards were dealt, and he studied his hand silently. It had to be urgent, or Bishop wouldn't have sent for him in the middle of the night. Perhaps Bishop had learned something new since this evening—he'd been expecting a man from up north somewhere; one of their couriers who spent his time travelling, and collecting information at various points. It was like doing a puzzle—everybody in the service had some of the different pieces, but it was up to the men like Bishop to put them all together and make them fit into some recognizable pattern.

"I talked to Yancey tonight—" Bishop said suddenly, glancing up from his cards. "He's already on his way to Sante Fe. But he had the information I needed. Brandon's got the money—in gold bullion."

Paco whistled softly.

"Gold? But why gold? It's heavy—clumsy to carry around in that much bulk too, and pretty damned dangerous as well, I'd say."

"He'll have thought of a clever way to send it wherever it's supposed to go. Don't underestimate the man. He's not only intelligent, he's dangerous as well, and he's got a lot of people working with him we don't even know about yet." Bishop's voice was sharp.

"Like that Eastern syndicate he's formed?" Paco's voice showed unwilling admiration. "Some of the richest men in the country, and they're still greedy for more—more land, more power."

"Texas, Arizona, New Mexico—not to mention all the territory just the other side of the border. A monumental land grab, with most of the dirty work being done by someone else." Steve shot a look at Bishop, and saw him frown.

"Senator Brandon is a man of ambition," Bishop said drily. "And he's certainly picked the worst time for us. The only real law in Texas is a handful of Rangers, and the territories of Arizona and New Mexico are even worse off. Also, you know as well as I do that the Indians have practically had things their own way during the war; and to cap it all off, with the French fighting the Juaristas in Mexico—"

"It's a great big powder keg!" Paco finished grimly.

"And we're supposed to stop it from blowing up?" Steve lifted an eyebrow at Bishop, wondering what the older man had in mind. Bishop always had a plan of some kind, and fortunately, they usually worked.

"Gentlemen, we've talked about this already. And luckily for us, at least we have some inkling of what's afoot. Let's take the facts we know, shall we? His eyes went from Steve to Paco, his voice was colorless. "For instance, we know that on this side of the border, the Indians are being provided with arms and ammunition, and certain chiefs are talking of forming treaties between all the tribes. We know that the Texans are unhappy, to put it mildly, with their reconstruction government, and their discontent is being fomented by the corrupt, power-crazy carpet-baggers who have been sent out here to run things. The individuals themselves are unimportant—they'll be easily gotten rid of when the time comes. It'll be the job of my men in Washington to find out who picked them.

"South of the border now—you two know better than I do how things are going. We've been giving Juarez what help we could during the war, and the French realize by now that their position in Mexico is a trifle shaky, to say the least."

"Bazaine's been paying his armies out of his own pocket," Steve said sharply. "But it hasn't been enough—so he's given them license to loot and kill. And Maximilian pretends to know nothing about it—"

"That gold Brandon is carrying is supposed to pay the French army," Bishop interrupted. He added softly, "But I don't think they'll see much of it. You see, Brandon has a contact—a friend you might call him—in the French army. A Colonel Devereaux." He sat back in his chair, the cards held loosely before him. "Devereaux got married recently—a rich *hacendado's* daughter. He doesn't want to leave Mexico. He's made friends with several of the richest landowners, and my information says he's got his own ideas about that money."

Paco Davis swore softly in Spanish.

"So—he helps Brandon build his empire, in return for a share of it."

"We think so." Bishop's voice was cool, emotionless.

"What's our part in all of this?"

A thin smile touched Bishop's lips. His eyes met Steve's briefly.

"You'll steal that gold. We've promised Juarez more help, more money. He gets the gold, and when he's back in power, we'll have a good friend in El Presidente."

"You make it sound so easy." Steve poured himself a drink out of one of the half-empty bottles on the table. He had been drowsy and irritable when Paco had routed him out of bed and Frenchy's arms, but now the old, keyed up feeling of excitement and anticipation sharpened his mind and swept him with exhilaration. He grinned at Bishop, who had been watching him silently.

"Where's the gold? Here in San Antone?"

"That's what I was coming to." Bishop's voice sounded dry and pedantic. "Senator Brandon is not going to accompany his wife and daughter to California. Not immediately, that is. He has to return to Washington very soon. He has the gold now, but naturally he will not carry it back there with him."

"The wagon train ... that's it! Why, the cunning, hungry bastard!" Paco's voice was soft, his eyes narrow. "He's going to use his wife and daughter to make it all look above board and natural, isn't he?"

"Sure—he sends his womenfolk to California with a wagon train and some cattle. And that gives him a perfectly reasonable excuse for hiring as many men to send along as he has."

"You're right—" Bishop nodded at Steve. "It's not only a good political move, but a clever one. Somewhere along the way one of the wagons gets—lost, shall we say? It's my guess this is meant to happen somewhere in New Mexico or Arizona. No one is any the wiser, but Devereaux will have the first shipment of gold and Brandon will be safe in Washington where no one can pin anything on him. I suspect he knows we keep tabs on him, but he doesn't know we've learned about his rich friends and his syndicate. In fact, if you do succeed in stealing the gold, I doubt if Brandon will dare make a fuss about it—no one is supposed to know . . ."

"A man who'd use his own family, set them up as

decoys, that is the warst kind," Paco said unctuously.

Steve shrugged carelessly. "Hell, the women are probably in it themselves! What woman can resist the thought of being a princess?" He looked at Bishop. "I take it we wait till we're close to the border before we snatch the gold?"

With the back of a fork, Bishop began to trace lines on the green baize that covered the card table, while Steve and Paco leaned forward intently.

As he drew his invisible maps, Bishop talked, giving them all the information he had—details and instructions to be memorized.

As usual, he forgot nothing, even his normal, cursory reminder to the men that once they had started on the job, they would be on their own.

"Needless to say," he mentioned dryly, "the United States Government has no knowledge and can take no responsibility for this—ah—operation."

Steve remembered the first time he had met Bishop and the warning he had been given then and chuckled. Bishop was not amused.

"If anything goes wrong, and you are fortunate enough to be taken to jail, we'll arrange an escape, if it's possible. But chances are that if Brandon's men capture either of you, you won't be allowed to live that long. You realize that, I'm sure." His formal warning given, his manner became more relaxed. He took a sip of his warm bourbon and refilled his glass.

"Gentlemen, let's play cards. As you know, I'm leaving on the stage tomorrow, but we still have time for another hour's play."

"You mean you still have time to clean us out completely," Paco grumbled, beginning to study his hand. "I'll have to keep some of that gold for myself if my luck stays as bad as it has."

They knew Bishop well enough to needle him now and then.

"If I were you, I wouldn't play poker with anyone who doesn't know you, Jim," Steve advised, keeping his face straight. "They might threaten to shoot you for cheating."

"Never cheated in my life," Bishop said blandly, "but I've always been lucky!"

Had Jim Bishop been asked seriously what his secret

was he would have replied that he was a student, not only of cards, which he could memorize at a glance, but of human nature. And it was really the latter which was the clue to the kind of game a man would play.

These two men sitting across from him were his best, and he had more or less trained them personally. They were, too, men that he trusted completely; and were intelligent and resourceful enough to use their own initiative if something went wrong with his carefully thought-out plans. He hoped they'd both come back in one piece—he couldn't really afford to lose them.

Outwardly concentrating on his cards and their play, his eyes hooded, Bishop went through the initial part of his current operation, as he chose to call it, in his mind.

There was no doubt that Brandon was in a hurry to get his wagon train started for California, and it seemed more than likely now that Steve Morgan and Paco Davis would be hired as his scouts. Bishop had arranged for their being here very carefully, just as he had seen to it that there were no other men who'd meet with Brandon's exacting specifications in San Antonio at this crucial time. The man Brandon had expected to hire had suddenly been offered a far more lucrative job taking a wagon train to Sante Fe, and had already left, and Marshal Trevor, who happened to be a friend of Bishop's had already suggested to Brandon that he might hire Steve Morgan. When Brandon arranged for a meeting, Steve would inform him that he always worked with Paco Davis. And the groundwork would be laid.

If nothing went wrong, Brandon's wagon train should be ready to leave within the next two or three days.

Bishop, his hand called, put down three aces and raked in the pot. Nothing would go wrong! He remembered that Morgan had warned him Sonya Brandon might not be too happy if he was hired—that unfortunate business in New Orleans! But Mrs. Brandon was hardly likely to confess an old affair to her husband—and Morgan had a way with women. A man of few scruples where his country's security was concerned, Bishop kept his face impassive while he allowed himself to wonder if Steve's past association with Sonya Brandon might not be of some use, after all. She was a beautiful woman, but weak. No—he did not think she'd say anything to her husband!

Looking up to meet Steve Morgan's eyes, Bishop said suddenly,

"I think you might just have a—hum—very pleasant journey after all." Steve would know what he meant!

Chapter Nine

In the days that followed, Ginny Brandon kept finding new and stronger reasons for the dislike she had already developed for Mr. Steve Morgan.

First, there was the small, private dinner party, where her father had announced that he had hired Morgan and his partner, Paco Davis, as scouts for their party. Ginny, who at first had not wanted to go downstairs for dinner, had finally let Sonya persuade her that it would only upset her papa if she did not dine with them.

She had expected—she did not know what she should expect! Confusion and embarrassment on Mr. Morgan's part, perhaps, when faced with cool disdain and hauteur on hers. She had been relieved to learn that Carl Hoskins would also be present, along with an older man called "Pop" Wilkins, who would be their wagon boss.

Ginny, once she had made up her mind to go downstairs to dinner, dressed with unusual care that evening, in one of her favorite gowns; this time in a soft shade of yellow that brought out the coppery brightness of her hair. She would put the uncivilized Mr. Morgan in his place once and for all! Rather to her surprise, she discovered that Sonya too had obviously paid careful attention to her dress—a deep crimson velvet, worn with rubies that made her blondness seemed almost ethereal.

"You both look very lovely indeed," Senator Brandon complimented them.

"It's probably the last opportunity we'll have for months to get all dressed up for an evening of dining," Sonya murmured deprecatingly. She would not—could not admit, even to herself, that there might be another reason for her careful toilette. After all, it had been over four years ago, and living during the war, under the shadow of the war, had made everything seem so different. If this Steve Morgan was the same man, perhaps he'd changed. Sonya Brandon was too wise, too mature to think that she could hide from something by trying to escape a confrontation. The sooner they met and faced each other, the better, and somehow, she did not think he would give her away.

Ginny, her cheeks flushed becomingly, spent the evening dazzling Carl Hoskins, who could not seem to take his eyes from her sparkling beauty. She ignored Steve Morgan, as she had decided to do, but it piqued her, in turn, that he seemed pleased enough to ignore her, and spent most of the evening talking to her father and Mr. Wilkins. Paco Davis, a lithe, rather dark-skinned man with a thin black mustache, seemed content to say little and leave the talking to his friend.

And, apart from his low-voiced conversation with her father, Steve Morgan's comments had to do with the inadvisability of taking women on such a long and difficult journey, and the danger from Indian attacks.

"He's a vile man, I detest his type! Did you notice how he raised his voice for our benefit every time he told some horrible tale of Indian atrocities?"

Ginny could not contain her repressed anger, once she and Sonya had excused themselves and tactfully withdrawn upstairs, leaving the men to their drinks and their discussions.

"But, love," Sonya remonstrated gently, "I did not think any of his stories so very horrible! In fact I'm sure he watered them down for our sakes. He was merely, I believe, warning us about the dangers of such a trip."

"How could you defend him? Why—he's not even a gentleman! I liked Mr. Davis better, at least he did not boast, or have too much to say."

Sonya changed the subject tactfully.

"Well, at least—you did make one obvious conquest this evening. That poor young man! I'm sure he's in love already."

"I should hope not, for men in love get far too sloppy," Ginny retorted. "And then, they become too, too boring."

"In that case, my love, I would not let his infatuation become too great. He's a nice young man, but hardly one your papa would think suitable."

Ginny glanced sharply at Sonya, and shrugged. Sometimes she could almost think of her stepmother as a contemporary, but there were times . . . she decided that they were both tired, and excused herself to go to her room.

Later, Ginny was to be only too thankful for the long and comfortable night of sleep she'd had. She learned from her father at breakfast the next morning that they were already to begin preparations for their journey, and that these preparations were to include wagon drill and practice in shooting and loading both guns and rifles. And before that first tiring day was over, Ginny was to wish fervently that she had never had set eyes on Steve Morgan or his friend Paco Davis.

The nine wagons they were to take on their journey were hitched to six-mule teams and taken to a flat, arid stretch of land about five miles out of San Antonio, and it was here that Morgan had decided to have them practice wagon drill. Ginny had been annoyed to hear that she, Sonya and Tillie would have to take it in turn to drive their own wagon. By the time her first day of wagon drill was over she was not only hot, tired and aching in every muscle, but almost speechless with anger as well. It seemed as if she could do nothing right.

Tillie found driving the wagon, bringing it into place in a quickly formed circle at a shouted command, to be an amusing kind of game. Sonya endured it stoically, and her determination to learn earned her the grudging admiration of both scouts as well as her husband's praise.

But Ginny—she thought rebelliously that Morgan chose her to deride in particular; using her as an example of the wrong way to go about things. Her wrists were delicate, her hands soft—even the gloves she wore did not protect them from the chafing bite of the reins she was supposed to hold. She hated the mules she was supposed to drive almost as much as she hated Steve Morgan!

On one occasion, when they had almost dragged her off

the high wagon seat and only Morgan's swift intervention had stopped the team from bolting, Ginny told him breathlessly and angrily what she thought of him.

He listened, politely, pushing his flat-crowned hat back on his head to study her flushed, furious face.

". . . And what is more," she ended up, made even more angry by his silence, "You seem to make a particular point of picking on me!"

At that point he ordered her coldly and flatly to start off again from the beginning, and to try and get her wagon in line with the others this time if she could, please, ma'am.

He rode away then, before she could frame an answer which was rude enough, and after that it was Paco Davis who put her through her paces. He was a little more patient and more polite than Steve Morgan, but just as exacting, and by the time the first day was over Ginny had no energy left to think about anything except a hot bath and her bed.

She had planned to protest to her father, but his very first words the next day made her bite back her words and lift her chin in stubborn determination.

"Ginny, my dear," he said doubtfully, "are you sure you are strong enough to survive such a journey? I keep forgetting that you were raised in Europe, and that the American west is very different from what you are used to."

"If Sonya can do it, so can I!" was all Ginny could bring herself to say.

They started out three days later, the same day that Senator Brandon left by the morning stage on the first part of his journey to Washington. The gold bullion had been concealed secretly in a carefully contrived space under the floorboards of the wagon that the three women were to occupy—the bars carefully arranged end to end and wrapped in heavy sacking. It meant that Ginny and Sonya would have to manage with the barest necessities in the way of clothing during the journey, so as not to attract notice to the lack of space in their wagon.

"You understand now, my dear," Brandon had said soothingly, "why it is so much better that you and Sonya and Tillie drive the wagon yourselves. A man, studying the inside of the wagon, or driving for you, might begin to wonder what makes it so heavy."

And even Ginny was forced to concede that he was right. Only Carl Hoskins, besides themselves, knew of the existence of the gold, and of the rifles and ammunition that were carried in the wagon that supposedly contained Sonya's household goods.

Ginny found that she missed Carl Hoskins' attendance and help the first day on the trail. He had already explained, apologetically, that he had to stay with the cattle until they had settled down for the journey.

"Don't know too much about this new white-faced breed, but longhorns are real spooky until they get trail-broke," he explained, and she tried to look knowledgeable. At least, she thought after he had ridden away, he tried to explain things to her. He treated her like a woman and a human being, instead of a necessary but unwanted piece of baggage!

She told herself as that first long day wore on that it would get better once she got used to it. Now that San Antonio lay several miles behind them, the country seemed to stretch endlessly in all directions, dry and arid, with the heat shimmering off the sandy dust.

After they had stopped to rest for what the men called the nooning, it was Ginny's turn to take the reins, and she sat uncomfortably on the high seat, glad for once of the unbecoming sunbonnet she wore.

Sweat trickled down Ginny's face and onto her bodice and down her neck. Her armpits were soaking wet, and she realized with a feeling of distaste that the wet patches were spreading down her sides. Sweat poured down her legs as well, and she wondered dully why she had ever thought this journey would be an exciting and exhilarating experience that she would not want to miss.

There was nothing exciting about driving a team of mules, and being jolted and jerked over ruts and stones while her arms grew sore from pulling on the reins and her shoulders burned from the onslaught of the sun. There was nothing in the least interesting about the nature of the landscape they were passing through. Vast, undulating plains, sometimes sparsely covered with bunchgrass, but for the most part dry and sandy with cactus and mesquite thrusting skyward. Used as she was to the carefully tended, checkered fields of France, the orderly towns and tree-shaded avenues, this empty vastness was too awesome and too lonely not to be rather frightening.

By the time it was Ginny's turn to crawl back thankfully into the wagon and let Tillie take the reins she was not only acutely uncomfortable but had a headache as well. Rebelliously, Ginny pulled off her thin cotton gown and stretched herself out on her narrow bunk. It was too hot and stifling inside the small, enclosed space to rest fully dressed in any case! She glanced at Sonya, who lay sleeping exhaustedly, and wondered how she could possibly fall asleep in this swaying, creaking vehicle. Her sunburned arms and shoulders throbbed, and she wondered dismally if this was what they would have to endure for the whole, long journey that lay ahead.

Closing her eyes determinedly against the slight feeling of nausea that was creeping up on her, Ginny tried to keep her mind on other things—memories of cool spring days in her beloved Paris; of balls and stolen kisses; and the long, exciting discussions in fashionable salons. A bluestocking, Pierre had teasingly called her, but she wasn't that at all, there was no reason why a woman could not be intelligent and feminine as well! Pierre had kissed her once, very lightly, very tenderly and apologetically, and before that—there had been a girl, a *comtesse* in the convent school, who had crawled into her bed one night and kissed her passionately on the mouth. Some girls did this, and some had wanted to touch her body. Locked up with each other, they had been curious and had talked of nothing else but men, and the way a man might make them feel. Ginny too had been curious, but she had always had a slight sense of unease, of drawing back. Even then, she had thought to herself, there has to be something more than this! And, "no" she would whisper fiercely to the girls who had wanted more than just kisses, so that after a while they learned to leave her alone.

With a feeling of humiliation and anger, she remembered the way that Steve Morgan had kissed her, ignoring her struggles until she had been incapable of resistance— was that how men really kissed, like—like an invasion? Men are all animals, her friend Lucille, who was married at seventeen, had told her. They want one thing, and all their courtship, their charming, tender manners, all lead up to that. But—the thought came snakelike, unbidden— what will it be like? How will it feel to lie with a man and to have him—Ginny could feel herself blush, and she pushed the thought away firmly. Perhaps if she could concentrate on keeping her mind a blank, she too would be like Sonya, lucky enough to fall asleep.

Two hours later, when Carl Hoskins rode by the wagon to tell the women that it would soon be time for them to make camp for the night, he saw only Tillie.

Carl looked tougher, older, in his trail clothes, with a gun at his hip, and the brown-skinned woman's eyes glanced appraisingly over him for an instant. Tillie, at least had no illusions about men, and she knew this was going to be a very long trip.

She met Carl's eyes when he spoke, asking where Miss Brandon was.

"Back there—sleepin', both of them. 'Specially Miss Ginny, she was sure tuckered out, poor young lady."

Tillie had a soft, educated voice, and Hoskins glanced at her strangely, really noticing her for the first time. She was amazingly pretty, too, for a mulatto wench, he thought, with straight black hair and strange, gold-colored eyes. Maybe sometime—reading his look, Tillie smiled, revealing white teeth.

"You got any message for the ladies, sir?"

He hesitated for just a moment, sawing back on the reins of his horse to stop its nervous prancing.

"Nothing important—just thought, since the sun's goin' down, one of them might feel like riding ..."

He looked idly over Tillie's shoulder, unwilling to meet her somehow too-knowing eyes, and a slanting ray of the sun, glancing into the wagon, reflected off Ginny Brandon's hair. Ginny, sleeping on her back only half-dressed, with the sweat-sheen still on her bare arms and shoulders, and her hair spilling down beyond the narrow confines of the bunk she lay on. Unable to help himself, Carl felt the involuntary tightening in his crotch. She looked so—so relaxed and unwary. As if she waited for a lover to find her that way—waited for him. He caught Tillie's eye, suddenly, and something knowing, slightly amused, set him to silently swearing.

He couldn't just stay here staring—he couldn't let the woman suspect what he was thinking.

"We'll be making camp for the night pretty soon," he said harshly, wheeling his horse around. "Better wake the ladies up."

Giving his horse its head, Carl rode quickly away to the west, where the herd that was his responsibility showed as a dark, dusty blur in the distance. Damn it all, he should have stayed back there, finding a good place to get the cattle bedded down for the night. But all he could think of right now was Ginny Brandon, and how much he'd like to get her bedded down.

Go slow, he warned himself. She's not like most of the other women you've met. And Brandon wouldn't like it— Brandon had already hinted he had big plans for his daughter. But this was a country where a man stood a chance to become anything he wanted to be, and his family was just as good as Brandon's—it's a long, long trip we have ahead of us Carl thought. A lot can happen!

Chapter Ten

The days and nights and the weary, bone-shaking hours on the arid, dusty trail fell into a relentless, unremitting pattern. Because of the cattle, they travelled slowly, hunting every river and waterhole, although these were few and far between and they had all been instructed to conserve their water.

Even the routine became familiar. Ginny had become used to waking very early in the morning when the sky showed only faint traces of pink; dressing hurriedly inside the wagon and going outside to join everyone else at breakfast—always preceded by a scalding hot cup of strong, black coffee. She had even forced herself to become used to the coffee that the cook produced. She sometimes wondered if old Lewt, the cook, ever slept. His fire seemed to go all night, just in case some tired cowboy wanted to snatch a cup of coffee to keep him awake.

"Ca-aa-tch up!" Pop Wilkins' raucous bellow would come after a while, and the teams would be hitched, the mules always cantankerous and balky at first. By the time Pop called his first "stree-tch out!" the whips would be popping, and slowly, protestingly, the wagons would begin to roll. This was the time Ginny loved best—the early morning, before it became too hot. Then the air had a fresh, pristine quality to it that seemed to soften even the jagged outline of distant hills they never seemed to reach.

They made camp just before sunset, circling the heavy wagons into an untidy kind of horseshoe shape, and always the chuckwagon would be ahead of them, the cook fires burning brightly. By the time the sun had set and the night seemed to rush in around them, the enclosed space with its glowing fires would seem warm and safe. It was hard to imagine that somewhere out there were Indians— that even worse dangers might lie ahead.

Now that the herd seemed to have settled down, Carl Hoskins often rode over, usually with a spare horse or two from the remuda, and both Ginny and Sonya enjoyed the long rides with him, ahead of the wagons and their dust. Most often, it was Ginny who rode with Carl, and his manner, though always respectful, grew more relaxed and informal.

Ginny enjoyed these rides, expecially since she had altered one of her riding habits to permit her to ride astride, instead of side-saddle. Her divided skirt, purchased in San Antonio, was of soft buckskin, with a tightly fitting basque that emphasized her slim figure, and unmistakeably, Carl Hoskins at least, was very much aware that she was a woman.

Even Sonya remarked how handsome Carl looked now, with his fair hair bleached by the sun and his skin already tanned to a golden brown that contrasted with his gray eyes. He looked broader, harder, and in consequence, more attractive to Ginny. It was fun to have a man to ride with and flirt with, although from the look she sometimes glimpsed in Carl's eyes Ginny knew that one of these days he'd try to kiss her. And what then? Should she let him? How would it feel? She had already learned that all men did not kiss a woman the same way—Steve Morgan had taught her that, and she hated him more each time she remembered the way he had treated her.

He's hardly a gentleman, she reminded herself, and he's obviously unused to associating with ladies! And yet, she could not help remembering that when he'd joined them for dinner at her father's invitation, his dark suit, worn with a deep blue silk waistcoat had been as impeccably tailored as her father's, and his company manners had shown that he should certainly have known better than to act the way he had the previous night.

I shouldn't think about him at all, Ginny thought crossly. He's the type of man I completely despise, and I'm glad he's stayed out of my way since the journey began.

Even Pop Wilkins, who always became garrulous over the campfire after their evening meal, admitted frankly that he didn't know what to make of Steve Morgan.

"He's a loner, I guess," Pop said. "Most fast guns are. Seems like they're a breed apart—allus keepin' to themselves. Morgan now, he knows what he's doing far as scoutin' goes, but he sure don't talk much, except to that compadre of hisn."

"What would a man like that have to talk about?" Ginny said scornfully, and Hoskins, who sat beside her, grinned.

"Nothing that would interest an educated young lady, I'm sure," he murmured in a low voice meant for her ears alone, and she flashed a smile at him.

They were camped for the night on the evening of their sixth day on the trail, and because the scouts had discovered a small creek, its banks shaded by willows and pecan trees, they had decided to make camp earlier than usual. The cattle had been watered already and were bedded down in a natural hollow in the plain some two miles to the west—the enormous casks in the water wagon had been laboriously filled to the brim.

"Probably our last good water for quite a ways," Pop had commented sourly, adding, "never been much of a water-drinkin' man myself, but there been times, trailin' across the desert when that's all I'd dream about."

"Why couldn't we have camped closer to the stream?" Ginny asked him. She gave Sonya an almost pleading look. "I'm longing for a bath—a real bath!"

"Too much cover over there for hostiles," Pop explained. He rose to his feet and stretched. "Orders are, everyone stays in camp. Injuns now, they know every water-hole and crik in this part of the country, and they're liable to act like they own it. Morgan's out scoutin' sign right now."

"I don't believe there are any Indians around here," Ginny said petulantly. "We've been travelling through such flat country, wouldn't you think we'd have seen signs of them? Besides, I don't think even an Indian would want to live around here, it's almost a desert!"

"Injuns are funny," Carl said pacifically. "Never have figured them out, or the way they think."

"Well, at least Mr. Davis seems to feel safe enough! And he does have a nice voice, doesn't he?"

From somewhere at the other end of the camp, where the cowboys usually ate around their own cookfire, Paco Davis sang softly, accompanied by his guitar—songs in Spanish that Ginny could not understand.

Carl Hoskins gave the women a look that mirrored a kind of distaste.

"Don't know about his singing—but he's a good scout, I guess," he admitted grudgingly. "It's just—" he hesitated and plunged on, "well, he's a 'breed. I hate 'breeds. Never met up with one I could trust, yet."

"Breed? You mean—because he's half Spanish?" Sonya knitted her brow, gazing inquiringly at Carl.

"Spanish? No ma'am, I mean he's half Mex—Mexican. They like to call themselves Spanish, I guess, but most of them are mixed with Indian."

"Mr. Morgan looks like one himself, except for his eyes ..." Ginny said sourly.

He'd ridden briefly into camp earlier, she remembered, only taking the time to swallow down a cup of coffee and eat a bowlful of beans, standing up. Strange how his manners seemed to have deserted him completely, for his only acknowledgement of their presence had been to touch his hat politely. She'd thought then, viciously, that he belonged out there in the country beyond the safe circle of their wagons, with the wolves and coyotes. Even the clothes he wore blended in with the brown, arid plains. Fringed leather pants that eliminated the need for chaps, and a buckskin shirt, open at the neck, with the usual kerchief knotted around his throat. And he'd taken to wearing two guns. She'd thought then that he looked like an Indian himself, especially with his face burned brown by the sun.

Carl Hoskins leaned forward now, slightly lowering his voice.

"Strange you should say that," he said to Ginny. "I've heard rumors myself that he's a breed. But of course no one dares say so to his face—he's shot men for less. A man as fast as he is with a gun is nothing more than a cold-blooded killer. Easy enough to provoke a man into a gunfight, and then cut him down." Heatedly, Carl added, "they ought to change the laws out here—do something about the way some professional killers can shoot down innocent men and get away clean, just because it was supposed to be a fair fight!"

"Well—I just resent the way he thinks he can give us all orders!" Ginny said crossly. She was tired, hot and sticky, and above all things she longed for a bath. She felt as if the trail dust had worked its way into her scalp and under her skin—no amount of rubbing ineffectually at her body with a damp washrag really helped. With a stream so close, why shouldn't she have a bath? She didn't believe there were Indians anywhere around—Morgan was merely trying to scare them all, to make them think he was earning his pay.

Abruptly, startling them all, Ginny got to her feet. The willow grove that hid the creek from view wasn't too far away, and there was still about an hour left until sunset. If she hurried—

"I think I'll go back to the wagon and find Tillie." Ginny said casually. But, almost as if she'd read her mind, Sonya followed her.

"Ginny—surely you don't mean to disobey orders? It could be quite dangerous, only think before you do anything precipitate, please!"

They paused by the wagon and Ginny swung around to face her stepmother, her determination showing in the stubborn tilt of her chin. Oh dear, Sonya thought despairingly, how very much like William she looks when she does that! She could not blame Ginny for wanting to bathe, but it was surely her duty to try to dissuade her. Personally, no matter how much she might have enjoyed being cool and clean again, Sonya had heard too many frightening stories about Indians to dare take any risks. And she couldn't let Ginny risk herself either.

"Ginny, I do beg you to change your mind," Sonya ventured again, her big blue eyes worried. "There may very well be Indians watching us at this very moment! I'm sure that if it was safe Mr. Morgan would have—"

Because she was tired and irritable, Ginny interrupted impatiently.

"Mr. Morgan! I'm tired of hearing what he has to say! He's always warning us about something—or criticizing. And I don't believe in his Indians either." About to climb into the wagon, she added scathingly, "I hardly think Mr. Morgan will dare to shoot me for disobeying his silly orders in any case!"

"Ginny, no! It's far too dangerous. I cannot let you—"

Seeing the hurt and anxiety in Sonya's eyes, Ginny bit back the retort she had been about to make. Instead, she bent down to touch Sonya's arm, and said firmly, "Sonya, I'm sorry! But I will have a bath. You heard what Mr. Wilkins had to say, it might be weeks before I get another chance. I'll take Tillie with me, she can wash our clothes, and I promise you I'll wear my thickest petticoat, and—and I'll take a rifle. But I'm going to feel clean tonight, for a change."

In spite of the fact that Sonya followed her inside the wagon and renewed her pleadings, Ginny remained adamant. And Sonya herself admitted that she was far too nervous to go along with them.

They had already been down to the small, clear stream earlier, to fill their water keg and canteens, and at last, with Tillie following her, Ginny made determinedly for the particular spot she had noticed before. It had been difficult, making Sonya realize that she insisted on having her way, and even Carl Hoskins had been doubtful. But when she had pointed out that Tillie would carry the rifle and was a better shot than she was, he agreed reluctantly to see that none of the men would disturb them.

"And I promise I'll be right back," Ginny had murmured coaxingly, putting her hand on his arm and smiling at him prettily. "Ten minutes—that's all I need. Oh, please, Carl, don't you start fussing at me too!"

Her use of his first name, and the pleading, yet slightly provocative look in her eyes confused him, and made him shrug helplessly.

"Don't forget—you see or hear anything, fire a shot and we'll come running," he told her finally, and when she turned back once, to look, he was still watching her.

In spite of her brave words moments earlier, Ginny found herself acting with excessive caution as she approached the small stand of trees that lined the creek on this side. But nothing stirred except a few birds who rose screeching and flapping annoyedly from the shrubbery at her approach.

"That shows it's all right, Miss Ginny," Tillie said with a relieved sigh. "Them birds wouldn't've been sitting there so peaceful like if there'd been anyone else around here but ourselves."

Ginny wondered fleetingly where Tillie could have learned something like that, but it made sense, and the sight of what she had already labelled as her spot made her forget everything else but the prospect of a bath at last.

Here, well-hidden by the trees, the creek curved gently inward to form a miniature bay. Grayish-white stones, rounded by the tumbling action of the waters, gleamed through the shallows, and would make an ideal spot for washing clothes. A little beyond, where the branches of a gnarled old willow tree slanted over the water, she would bathe, Ginny decided.

She studied the opposite bank carefully, noticing how it sloped gently upward. Trees outlined the top of the rise, but enormous boulders, scattered all over the bank, would render it inaccessible, she thought. There was no sign of life, except when the tree branches moved in the gentle breeze. She heard bird-calls, and that was all—that, and the soft, rushing sound of the water.

Pushing her sleeves back over her elbows, Tillie knelt on the bank, scrubbing efficiently at the clothes, and Ginny laid the clean dress she had brought along over a tree stump before she stripped down to her oldest petticoat, tossing the gown she had been wearing to Tillie.

Ginny waded into the stream cautiously, shivering when the icy-cold water first came in contact with her hot, sunburned skin. She ducked her head underneath and came up with her hair streaming wet, making her head feel heavier with its weight. *It feels so delicious, this is heaven*, she thought dreamily, running her fingers through her hair, rubbing her scalp to get all the accumulated dirt and dust loose. She had brought a cake of scented soap with her, and now she used it freely, rubbing perfumed lather through her hair, scrubbing at her skin until it tingled. Only Tillie's worried "please miss, we promised to hurry back," recalled her to reality. Again she immersed herself under the water, holding her breath for as long as she dared, and came up sputtering and laughing.

"Tillie, this is—oh, it's sheer heaven! You ought to join me!"

Tillie shook her head primly, and handed Ginny a large, fluffy towel as she emerged reluctantly from the stream, her petticoats clinging to her body.

"You don't know what you're missing," Ginny teased Tillie, who was still rinsing out their wet clothes.

She sat on a flat, warm rock and began drying her hair, rubbing at it vigorously with her head almost enveloped in the folds of the towel. A sudden, frightened gasp from Tillie made her look up, startled.

"What is it? Tillie, what—"

"A—a man, miss! I swear, I saw him one minute ago, right up against the sky there, among those trees, and the next, he was gone! Lord, miss, do you suppose it was a ha'nt?"

"If you saw someone, it certainly wasn't a ghost!" Ginny said bracingly, although her heart had begun to thump alarmingly. "Where did you put that gun, Tillie?"

She scrambled to her feet hurriedly, more than a little frightened by now, and felt her foot slip on the wet rock, tumbling her backwards into the water. It was a wonder, she thought afterwards, that she hadn't hit her head on one of the small boulders at the bottom of the natural pool, and been drowned!

Ginny came to the surface spluttering and gasping for breath, with her hair in her eyes, and felt her hand grasped and held as she was pulled roughly and unceremoniously to her feet.

Steve Morgan's voice, usually so indifferent and cold, said furiously,

"What in hell are you doing out here alone?"

Blinking water out of her eyes, Ginny found herself speechless as she gazed up into his dark, angry face.

He was astride his horse, having ridden it, apparently, right into the stream, and her first foolish thought was how did he get here? Where did he appear from? Before she had time to speak he leaned down further, and holding her wet, struggling body by the waist he hauled her (like a sack of potatoes, she said furiously to Sonya later) onto the bank.

Tillie sat back on her heels, round-eyed and silent, but at a word from Morgan she began to gather up the wet clothes hastily.

He came off his horse like a panther and caught Ginny's shoulders, shaking her until she thought her breath would never return.

"You little idiot! Didn't I give orders you were to stay

in camp? Don't you realize what kind of danger you've
been putting yourself in?"

She cried out then, with anger and pain and frustration,
and he released her as abruptly as he'd put his hands on
her, staring at her suddenly as if he'd never seen her before. Only then did she realize the sight she must
present—half-naked, or worse, considering the way her
petticoat clung to her body, revealing everything.

His eyes travelled very slowly over her, and the way
they did so made her flush with rage. Instinctively, she
crossed her arms over her breasts, half-sobbing with reaction.

"No use doing that—ain't no way to hide anything, the
way your petticoat's soaked through," he drawled wickedly,
and took a hasty backward step when she struck out at
him blindly.

Like a vengeful cornered animal she made a grab for
the rifle, lying just a few tempting feet away, but he put
his booted foot over the barrel and yanked her up to face
him by her hair, now as angry as she.

"Reckon I've told you before about guns—you leave
'em alone unless you're damn sure you can use one, and
must."

"Oh, you—you bully!" she hissed at him. She pushed
wet hair from her face and glared at him, panting with
rage. "How dare you come spying on me? How dare you
treat me like a—like—"

"You're damn lucky I happened to choose this way to
get back to camp," he said bluntly.

He didn't tell her he'd had the same thing in mind that
she'd had—taking a bath.

She was so mad she was shaking—mad enough to
spit—or to kill. And in spite of himself, Steve couldn't
keep his eyes off the curves and hollows of her body, outlined so revealingly under the outrageously thin petticoat
which was all she had on. Her nipples, hard and pointed,
seemed to strain against her bodice, and he could glimpse
the slightly darker triangle where her legs met—and she
had noticed what he was looking at, of course, and was
getting madder by the minute.

If she'd been a girl like Frenchy now, or even some
young Indian girl, taken unawares, he'd have thought
about tumbling her backwards onto the long grass under
the trees and making love to her. But she was Miss Vir-

ginia Brandon, and he'd better remember that; hadn't he stayed away from her deliberately these past few days? Ever since he'd kissed her that night and had felt the swell of her breasts under his fingers, he'd desired her, and now—

She had gone quiet, watching his eyes, and he knew quite suddenly, without any words being said, that she was thinking about the same thing. For an instant her eyes looked into his, a bright, hard emerald green, and then she'd veiled them with her lashes.

"Would you—will you please go away and allow me to get dressed, now that you've said what you had to say?"

He had to admire the way she'd controlled her temper, pulling a cloak of dignity around herself with an effort.

He was angry with himself now, for letting his guard slip.

"Better hand Miss Brandon her dress," he said harshly to the frightened mulatto girl who stood silently by, watching them both.

Bending, Steve scooped up the rifle and walked a little way off, turning his back on the women.

"I'll give you five minutes to get dressed, before I turn around. And then I'll see you back to camp. Damn it," he exploded violently, not able to help himself, "there was Indian sign about two miles upstream! If some young brave had come by here like I did, and saw you—" he bit off the words when he heard her startled, indrawn breath, and because he didn't quite trust himself, walked to where his horse stood, contentedly snorting into the water.

It took her less than five minutes.

He heard her voice, as brittle as breaking glass,

"You may turn around, Mr. Morgan. I hope I don't offend your sense of decency now."

Wheeling around, he saw that she was still damp-looking, but fully dressed—and braiding her hair, as cool as you please.

It was getting quite dark, and he followed Ginny and Tillie all the way to the camp, with all three of them quite silent; turning off only when they were close enough to see the wagons and the firelight.

Chapter Eleven

It did not in the least improve Ginny's temper to discover, the next morning, that there really had been Indians prowling around the previous night. A small band of them, accompanied by a few squaws and young children, overtook the wagons soon after they had broken camp, begging for coffee and sugar; and, as Ginny remarked scornfully to Sonya, they did not look dangerous at all.

"Perhaps that is only because they see we have so many armed men to protect our party," Sonya said gently, and Ginny was forced to concede that this might indeed be the case, for acting on Steve Morgan's instructions, several of the men had ridden up and sat their horses casually, holding loaded rifles across saddles.

It was Morgan himself who had ridden back with the Indians, and had suggested to Pop Wilkins that it might be best if they gave the Indians what they wanted and sent them on their way. When Pop would have protested he added quietly that there might be useful information to be gained from these same Indians, and, indeed, while the bargaining was going on, Steve sat his horse some distance away, with a scar-faced, rather disdainful-looking Indian who was obviously the chief of the small band. Pop said rather sourly that these were Wichitas, and that the gesturing that was going on was sign language.

Against her will, Ginny found her eyes straying towards Steve Morgan, who with his hard brown face and black hair could have passed for an Indian himself. What kind of man was he? Unlike Carl, or any of the other men she had met, he was not the type one could neatly label or categorize; to say, he is this, or that, type of man. She had not forgotten his almost brutal lovemaking the first evening they had met, nor the desire he had evidenced for her then. And yet, ever since, he had all but ignored her, except to criticize her. And then, last night, in spite of his anger and the biting, sardonic way he had spoken to her, she had seen the look of desire in his eyes again. He finds me desirable, Ginny thought, frowning unconsciously, merely because I am a woman. That is how men are, they have no wish to see what lies beneath a woman's face or figure—they would prefer it, no doubt, if women did not have minds at all!

Sonya and Tillie seemed fascinated by the Indian women, and especially by those who had tiny babies strapped to their backs, but Ginny, lost in her thoughts, now looked up again and directed a glance of resentment and dislike at Steve Morgan—a glance that he, turning away from his sign-conversation with the Indian chief at that moment, happened to intercept.

She had half-expected the usual sarcastic lift of an eyebrow with which he usually greeted her when their paths happened to cross, but this time, to her surprise he actually smiled, making her notice all over again the startling blue of his eyes.

Taken aback, and ashamed of her own sudden confusion, Ginny looked away quickly, but a few moments later, when Morgan cantered his horse over to their wagon, there was no way in which she could ignore him.

Fortunately, Sonya spoke first, her voice anxious.

"Are you sure that they will go—and leave us in peace?"

"Oh, they don't mean us any harm, ma'am. In fact, they're in a hurry to get back to their own camp. The chief was telling me he wants no brush with the snake people."

Before Sonya could question him, Steve Morgan glanced at Pop Wilkins, who stood by with a sour face. It was common knowledge that Pop hated Indians, ever since a marauding band had wiped out his family while he was away.

"He told me there's Comanches about—a small war party. Guess Paco and I will ride out ahead after a while; split up and see what sign we can find."

Sonya gave a small, smothered exclamation, and Morgan grinned at her, his teeth flashing white in the brown face.

"I don't think the Comanche will bother us, ma'am, not if they're only a small raiding party. But that's what Paco and I want to find out for sure." He gestured ahead of them, and glanced again at Pop. "Maybe we ought to make camp kind of early tonight. There's a place up ahead that would make an ideal spot for a defense, if it comes to that. You'll know the place I mean when you get up there—used to be an old creek bed. I'll ride over to the herd and warn Hoskins right now."

"The Indians we saw today didn't strike me as looking very dangerous," Ginny said scornfully, unable to help herself. She saw darting glints of laughter in Steve Morgan's eyes, but it was Pop Wilkins who answered her.

"Them Comanches ain't like most other Indians, miss —they're devils! But don't you worry none—" he gave her a reassuring look. "I'm gonna have some of the boys ride along with you from now on. They ain't too close by, or them Wichitas wouldn't have stopped like they did."

Ginny hardly heard what he said, she was too conscious of the way Steve Morgan's eyes stayed on her, warm and faintly amused. And why, she wondered annoyedly, did he have to stare so? Involuntarily, her hand crept upward to brush loose tendrils of hair off her face. She remembered that she had not taken the trouble to brush her hair before she had braided it hastily that morning—and no doubt, her bonnet was askew and he had noticed it. She remembered the way he had looked at her last night, the bold way his blue eyes had travelled over her body, making her feel as if she had nothing on. Even when he was acting half-way civilized, he gave the impression that there was something savage, something primitive and dangerous barely held in check under the surface he presented to them all.

Morgan had turned away to talk to Pop, and Ginny noticed that from time to time he rubbed the side of his face, where the black stubble of an incipient beard had begun to show. Bearded, he'd look more like a buccanneer than ever, she thought. He looked like an outlaw, with those two guns he wore on his hip, that dangerous rakehell face. He wore his usual buckskins, but the shirt was open almost to the waist, and the kerchief knotted around his throat was of rich, deep brown silk.

The black stallion moved impatiently under him, and she watched the way he controlled it easily, merely with the pressure of his knees. Unlike most of the other riders she had seen, he didn't wear spurs.

Perhaps Sonya had been noticing too. Ginny felt the touch of her cool hand as Sonya whispered,

"He rides a horse like an Indian, doesn't he? There is something strange and unreadable about him—he didn't upset you too much yesterday, did he?"

Ginny shrugged and picked up the reins.

"I don't think about him, because I don't like him! Do you want to get some rest now, Sonya? It's my turn to drive the wagon, you know."

Already, Pop Wilkins was yelling "stretch 'em out —stre-etch em out!" down the length of the strung-out wagons.

Steve Morgan's horse whirled around and came alongside.

"Either of you ladies care to come along for a ride as far as the herd?" he asked surprisingly. "Hoskins will be glad to escort you back, I'm sure. Paco and I will be getting us enough grub to last a couple of days, and then we'll be on our way."

"A couple of days? You are difficult to understand, Mr. Morgan!" Ginny burst out. He had looked directly at her when he had made his calm invitation, how dare he imagine that after his vile behavior she would be willing to go meekly along with him, for a ride, of all things—as if this was just an ordinary day like any other?

She caught Sonya's startled look, but went on, her dislike for him making her voice taut.

"You said these Indians are dangerous, and yet you'll go chasing after them alone? And are we supposed to sit around and wait until you decide to get back—if you get back?"

His eyes assessed her coolly, while a small, mocking smile twitched the corner of his mouth.

"Miss Brandon, your concern is really touching! But I assure you that I can take care of myself, and that you certainly won't have to sit around and wait for my return. You didn't seem very frightened last night, when I told you there were Indians around," he added wickedly, "but since the thought seems to make you nervous this morning, then perhaps Mrs. Brandon would care to ride with me?"

"Ooh!"

Ginny's face reddened, and her lips formed a gasp of pure rage. Narrowed, emerald green eyes like a cat's seemed to spit fire at him.

But he was ignoring her now, as if she didn't exist any longer, and his eyes rested on Sonya instead.

"I—why—yes, I would enjoy a ride I think, and I haven't seen the cattle close up yet. Thank you, Mr. Morgan!" Sonya's voice was soft with a mixture of confusion and pleasure, and Ginny was forced to pretend complete indifference while Steve unhitched Sonya's gray mare, which trotted behind the wagon. Ginny pulled back viciously on the lines—the mules slowed down to an amble, and with a murmured warning, Steve Morgan swung Sonya by the waist from the wagon seat onto the horse.

Ginny watched them go, a strange mixture of anger and frustration making her breath catch in her throat for an instant as she flapped the reins viciously and swore at the mules as she had heard some of the men do.

How dare Steve Morgan take her father's wife out riding? He had meant his invitation for her, and although of course she had turned him down with the scorn that he deserved, it was too bad of Sonya to accede so eagerly. For the first time, Ginny felt an unreasonable flash of what was almost dislike for her stepmother. She should not have gone with him, she thought angrily. She should have refused—and then, sneaking, unbidden—I should have been the one! It's just the right time for a ride, and I would have enjoyed it, even with him along. And now he probably thinks I'm afraid either of the Indians, or of him!

Ginny hardly noticed the country through which they were passing, although the distant, forbidding-looking mountains seemed closer today, their bare peaks covered only with stunted bushes and twisted trees. Armed men rode by the wagons, as Pop had promised, and after a while, Ginny made idle conversation with one of them, seemingly almost a boy. His name was Zack Merritt, and he was very shy and blushed easily.

Ginny told herself that her feeling of relief when she finally saw Sonya and Carl cantering towards them stemmed from the fact that trying to draw Zack out into talking about himself had proved a positive strain.

Sonya looked unusually pretty, with her blond hair escaping from its smooth chignon; her face was slightly flushed from the sun and fresh air, and she was laughing and more animated than usual. Ginny supposed she should be flattered, though, at the way Carl's eyes went straight to her and lingered—and a few moments later, when he suggested that she might enjoy a short ride she went willingly with him.

Carl was handsome, and attentive, and it was not difficult to draw him into talking about himself. He was too much of a gentleman to try to rush matters or take advantage of their being alone, but he let Ginny see quite clearly that he was more than a little interested in her.

"You're—you're really the prettiest girl I've ever met, you know," he said to her quite shyly, and her green eyes sparkled teasingly at him. Some spirit of devilry made her tear her unbecoming bonnet from her head, and the heavy braids of hair she had stuffed under it so carelessly that morning swung free, catching the sunlight.

She galloped her horse forward, leaning over its neck, and when Carl caught up with her he felt his heart begin to thud as she turned her head, laughing up at him. Without thinking, he caught at her mare's bridle, halting it, and he could not take his eyes from her lips, with the small white teeth gleaming invitingly between them. What a mouth she had! Perfectly formed, poutingly sensual in repose. Before he could stop himself, Carl leaned forward and kissed it. He heard her little "mm!" of surprise and then she was leaning quite pliantly against him until the nervous movements of their horses took them apart.

She was staring at him, with her eyes wide and fathomless—without a word to show whether she was angry or pleased.

"Ginny—Miss Brandon, I—I couldn't help myself," he stammered. "I'm sorry—"

"Are you, Carl?" Her mouth curved into a knowing,

teasing smile, and her lashes dropped, veiling her eyes for a moment.

Before he knew what to expect, she had turned her horse around, and was cantering back towards the wagons.

"Never tell a girl you're sorry after you've kissed her!" she called back over her shoulder, and he found himself wondering how many other men had kissed her, and if she'd responded in the same way.

They were silent for the rest of the way back to her wagon, and after he had left to go back to the herd, Carl did not see Ginny again until after they had made camp that evening.

They had built their cookfires in the shallow, natural depression formed by a long-ago stream, now dry, with the wagons on the higher ground around them. Tonight, Pop Wilkins had arranged for the men to take it in turns to watch for the approach of Indians or anyone else, and Ginny heard him admit almost grudgingly that this place was almost perfect for defense; situated as it was in the center of an almost flat plain, where anyone who approached would be in plain sight for miles. About two miles off to the west, where the cattle were bedded down, the small fires that the cowhands had built looked like tiny, sparkling fireflies. Overhead the stars looked larger than usual, and brighter—Ginny found it hard to believe that danger could lurk somewhere in those bleak-looking mountains that were now merely a blurred outline against the night sky.

"In about two days, mebbe three, we're gonna have to travel through a pass up there," Pop said, pointing towards the hills. "If there's Injuns about, that's where they'd plan to attack us—if Morgan don't find 'em first and cook up some plan to get us through."

"But isn't there another way around the mountains?" Ginny asked, and he shook his head dourly.

"Could be—but it would lose us a heap of days goin' around. With all the men we got with us though," he added hastily, "it ain't likely they'd try too hard to stop us. Injuns are smart enough sometimes to realize when they're outnumbered—though Comanches are worse than most."

One of the men who was standing guard outside the circle of wagons called out that there was someone coming, almost at the same moment that they heard Paco Davis' voice shouting "hola the camp—I'm coming in!"

They surrounded him anxiously when he came into the firelit encampment, tossing the reins of his horse to Zack.

Paco Davis looked dusty and tired. And he refused to answer any questions until he had had a cup of steaming hot coffee, spiked with some tequila he poured into his mug from a bottle he produced out of his saddlebag.

"Well?" Carl Hoskins demanded impatiently. He stood with his thumbs hooked in his belt, glaring down at the slim Mexican, who had accepted a bowl of beans from the cook, and was now sitting with his back against a wagon wheel.

"Why can't you tell us what happened? Did you see any Indians back there? And where's Morgan?"

Paco shrugged negligently.

"One question at a time, *amigo*." His black eyes rested almost guilelessly on Carl, but there was a touch of steel in his voice that made the other man pause, and clear his throat awkwardly.

"We cut Indian sign all right," Paco continued softly. "Two bands, it looked like at first. An' they split up, right near the foot of the hills back there. So Steve and I, we split up too. Caught up with my lot 'bout two hours later, and they was just a bunch of old men, squaws and kids, travelling real fast, like they were gettin' out of the way. Reckon, like Steve thought, the other bunch of 'em was that war party the Wichitas were tellin' us about."

"Suppose he don't get back to tell us about 'em, and they try jumpin us?" Pop Wilkins sounded upset, and Ginny remembered how much he hated Indians. Paco must have thought about that too, for his eyes seemed to sharpen, although his voice sounded deceptively calm and unconcerned.

"I know Steve. He'll get back. Could be he decided to parley with them—he knows Indians pretty well, and I know for sure he speaks Comanche."

"I don't trust any Injuns!" Pop exploded. "They're all nothing but a bunch of thievin', murderous critters."

"We've got the men and the rifles—" Carl Hoskins said harshly. "Why don't we just go after them and attack before they decide to? We could take them by surprise—and if the wagons kept moving they'd be through the pass before the Indians know it."

Paco came agilely to his feet and faced Hoskins across the fire, his mouth a thin, warning line under his black mustache.

"You keep forgetting, Hoskins, that with Steve gone, I'm in charge when it comes to the defense and safety of this party. Are you *loco*?" His voice was bitingly sarcastic. "Talkin' about leaving the camp and the women practically undefended to go chasin' after a band of Indians who'd know you were comin' a mile off? This ain't like any war you ever fought in or heard of, Hoskins, and these Indians are the most unpredictable bunch on earth. I've fought 'em and been friends with them, just like my partner has, and that's why the Senator hired us to do the scoutin'. That clear?"

Ginny thought for a frightening moment that Carl might go for his gun, but Pop Wilkins, by accident or design, interposed himself between the two men.

"All right, all right! Guess what you just said makes sense, Davis. So—what do you suggest we do now?"

"We'll follow the orders Steve gave me just before we separated. Break camp before five tomorrow mornin' and keep travelling as far as we can before sundown. It's gonna make longer, harder days, but we'll get close to the mountains. And the Indians know we're headed for that pass, so if they're planning to attack, that's where they'll be waiting. No point in their trying to attack us on these flat plains where we can see 'em comin for miles off! An' you can bet they know already how many of us there are!"

"What happens when we get to the mountains?" Carl said with a sneer. He had not forgiven Davis yet, nor forgotten that he'd had to back down.

"That's gonna take us some days, even travelling faster than usual. But we'll hear from Steve before then. First things first."

They had more questions, more arguments, but Paco wasn't in the mood for them. He walked calmly to his blanket roll, spread it out under one of the wagons, and lay down, closing his eyes. If they were to get a real early start, he needed some sleep.

The others were still arguing out there by the fire, and he heard Carl Hoskin's angry voice, demanding what in hell Morgan thought he was doing, staying out there—sending back orders. Surprisingly enough, it was Ginny Brandon's cool voice that quieted him down.

"For heaven's sake, Carl, is there any point in our standing out here and discussing it? I'm sure Mr. Morgan knows quite well what he's doing."

So she thought that, did she? From what he'd observed, she hadn't seemed to cotton to Steve at all, not one bit, and Steve had been unusually close-mouthed on the subject.

All the same—just like Hoskins, Paco could not help wondering what in hell Steve was up to.

Chapter Twelve

Steve Morgan was hunkered back on his heels before an Indian campfire. He was stripped to the waist, and the kerchief he'd worn that morning was bound tightly around his arm, stained with his own blood. He wore a blanket around his shoulders to keep off the night cold, and his face, like those of the Indians who sat around the fire, showed no emotion at all.

The pipe came around, and when it was his turn for the ceremonial smoke he handled it respectfully, in the approved manner; drawing in the acrid smoke and letting it escape slowly.

He passed the pipe to the tall brave on his right. This was Mountain Cat, his new blood brother—the same warrior Steve had fought earlier, to prove he was still one of the Snake People and had not gone back to the safe, soft ways of the white man.

It had been a good fight. The older man, wearing the ceremonial headdress of a warrior chief, began to speak now, describing the fight, expressing his pride in the fact that one who had been a Comanche warrior never forgot that fact, no matter what trails might have led him away.

Steve knew that once started, the traditional, ceremoni-

112

ous speeches would probably go on for most of the night. The muscles in his heels and calves had already begun to ache a little, for it had been a long time since he'd squatted in front of an Indian campfire. But his face, carefully trained, showed no sign of strain.

Listening to the speeches with only a part of his mind, Steve found himself hoping that Paco had gone back to the wagons, and would start them rolling early, as he'd told him to do. If all went well, he'd catch up with them before they reached the pass, and by then, the Apaches who usually roamed this part of the country and were their greatest danger, would be out of the way—for the moment, at least.

Lucky for him this particular band of Indians happened to be Comanches. They usually did not come this far south, but in this case they were after a renegade band of Apaches, led by Flaming Arrow, a chief's son. The war paint these Comanches were wearing was for the Apaches—who had raided their camp a week ago, making off with some of their younger, prettier squaws.

Following a hunch, Steve had trailed the Comanche war party for quite a way, and had ridden boldly and quite openly into their camp afterwards, greeting their chief, whom he had met once before—long ago, when he had been one of the People himself, his hair worn long and braided like the hair of the young warrior who sat beside him.

A good thing he hadn't forgotten how to use a long knife—he'd had reason to be thankful for that when this same young warrior had challenged him to prove he was still a Comanche, and hadn't grown soft from the white man's ways.

The fight had been bloody. Small nicks and cuts on the chest and arms of both men showed redly to prove it. And Mountain Cat had drawn the first real blood, when Steve, beads of sweat falling in his eyes to blind him for an instant, had lowered his guard slightly.

The gash in his arm might have been worse, if he hadn't moved quickly, turning his body out of the way. It had waked him up, made him vicious and less cautious. And, because of the blood he was losing, he knew he had to end the fight quickly.

Here the street-fighting days of the Louisiana docks,

and all the other river towns, had helped. He'd learned some fancy footwork, as well as some tricks with a knife the Indian wasn't familiar with. He'd pretended to trip, and then, moving fast on the balls of his feet, had thrown the knife from his right hand to his left. Mountain Cat, confused by this manoeuver and caught off-balance, had fallen, the knife spinning away in an arc.

Steve leaped for him like a cat, straddling his body, the knife now held against the Indian's throat. He'd seen the glittering, fearless eyes stare upward, and knew suddenly what he had to do.

Deliberately, he'd gashed the warrior's arm with his knife, just as his had been. This was the kind of cruelty, the kind of show that the Indians appreciated.

"Since I also am one of the people, I cannot kill my brother. But if you need more proof that I am one of the Comanche, I will help you kill Apache instead."

The calculated bravado of his words had won a grunt of approval from the other warriors; and for Mountain Cat, who had fought well, there was no loss of face. Later, his father the chief had performed the ceremony that made them blood brothers—formally making Steve, who had been the "son" of one of his old and respected friends, his son as well.

Tomorrow, before dawn, he would put on war paint and ride with them to find the thieving Apaches. For tonight, there were still the rest of the speeches to listen to, and perhaps one of his own.

Stoically, pushing away the thought of pain from his throbbing arm, Steve settled down to wait the night out. The arm he could take care of, with herbs, and it would heal eventually, but he hoped it wouldn't be too long before he was able to catch up with the wagons. He had a job to do—and he'd almost forgotten about it in the excitement of being back again in an environment which had once been his life.

The wagons, moving before the first early light painted the sky, trailed snakelike over the plains, with the cattle lumbering slowly and complainingly along, still keeping about two miles west.

Sonya was still asleep, but this morning Ginny sat on the high wagon seat beside Tillie, who was holding the reins. She had a thick wool shawl wrapped around her

shoulders, and her thick, pale copper hair hung in braids
down her back.

She could see Paco Davis riding a short distance ahead
with Pop, who was gesturing towards the mountains
ahead.

"Mister Morgan ain't back yet is he, Miss Ginny?"

Tillie's soft voice broke into Ginny's sleepy, half-dazed
thoughts, and the wide, sea-green eyes looked troubled.

"I suppose not. I wonder where he is? But then, he's
such an unreliable, unpredictable man!"

Ginny and Tillie had slipped into a kind of companionable familiarity when Sonya was not around—a familiarity
that Ginny, brought up in Paris where color was a matter
of small regard, had been the first to encourage. Sonya
was never rude, always invariably polite to her maid, but
there was a distance between them that they both took for
granted. With Ginny, on the other hand, Tillie found herself able to talk, almost as she would have to an equal.
When she thought about it, she knew it was rather
strange, but the Senator's young daughter was only a year
younger than Tillie herself, and she always acted natural
and friendly, as if she really liked her as a person.

Now Tillie glanced rather slyly at the young woman
who sat huddled beside her, still sleepy-eyed.

"You think he's found those Indians yet? Maybe they
found him first—although that Mr. Davis, now, he sure
don't seem worried."

"I'm not even sure there are any Indians out there,"
Ginny said sharply. "And if there are, I don't think Mr.
Morgan would be foolish enough to get too close to them.
In any case, I'm certainly not worried about him!"

By the time they prepared to make camp on the evening of the third day, however, it was certain that everyone
in the party was worried—for their own, different reasons.

Paco Davis was silent and grim-faced, and even Pop
Wilkins wasn't his usual garrulous self at mealtimes. Carl
Hoskins complained at the pace they were forced to
maintain, and warned that the cattle were losing too much
weight—they had already lost two calves.

They were almost at the foot of the mountains now,
and it was just as if a kind of sullen tiredness of mind and
body had seized them all. During the day, Sonya had been
unusually irritable, snapping at Tillie, who burst into

tears—this unusual reaction on her part causing Sonya to cry also. And Ginny, who had appeared to be in high spirits during the past two days, was abnormally silent, hardly allowing Carl Hoskins more than a half-hearted "oh, hello, Carl" when he rode into camp for supper and found her staring at her untouched plate.

The men began to argue, as they had been doing for the past two nights, and Sonya, her eyes still red-rimmed, said sullenly that if that was all they were going to do, she, for her part, was going back into her wagon.

"And, Ginny, you haven't even started to eat yet!" she said petulantly. "What in the world's got into you?"

"It's probably whatever's got into everyone else around here," Ginny retorted. "They can't seem to make up their minds!"

Paco, it appeared, was for going on—taking a few men to scout out the approach to the pass early in the morning, and then pushing through.

Carl announced that he was concerned about the fate of the herd—it wasn't likely that any Indians would molest a wagon train bristling with armed men, but would they pass up the chance to get themselves some cattle of a breed they hadn't seen before?

Pop Wilkins, it seemed, was for "setting tight" another day—maybe trying to find another trail around the mountains.

The argument was growing more heated when someone spotted a small dust cloud just clear of the shadow of the hills.

Paco grabbed for his field glasses and squinted through them.

"Lone rider—" he said laconically. "Don't do no firing. Could be an Indian or it could be Steve, comin' back— we'll wait and see."

He lowered the glasses and Pop made a grab for them.

"Here, let me take a look. Mebbe I got gray hair, but my eyes are still bettern' most young squirts!"

"If it's Morgan, he has his nerve, riding in here after three days without a word or a sign!" Carl Hoskins said furiously, not noticing the strange, almost considering look that Ginny Brandon gave him.

"Looks more like an Injun to me—but it could be Morgan, I guess," Pop said finally. "Hoss sure looks like his!"

As it finally turned out, they couldn't make out who their impatient visitor was for dust until he had ridden his horse right into camp with a wild Comanche war whoop that made the women cringe with apprehension, and the men grab for their rifles.

"You damned fool! Good way to get your head shot off, riding in hollering that way," Paco yelled in disgust as the man slid off his dust-covered black.

Ginny had come to her feet almost instinctively, and now she had to force herself to stand still, leaning against the wheel of her wagon as if his return hadn't mattered to her one bit. She bit her lip in annoyance at herself for not being able to stop the sudden wild thudding of her heart. It was that yell, she told herself—he'd had no right to scare them all that way!

She had privately given him up for dead already, and here he was, having ridden into camp screaming like an Indian, blue eyes alive with impudence and excitement.

As she took in the way he looked, her lips tightened with anger. It was disgraceful! Couldn't he have remembered there were women in camp? She certainly wasn't about to go and join the others who crowded around him, laughing and asking questions.

Steve Morgan was bare to the waist—his face and chest still showing traces of Indian war paint, and he still wore a fancy, beadworked headband around his forehead, Apache-fashion. His boots and shirt were tied to the horn of his saddle, and he wore moccasins on his feet. He was as brown as an Indian too—all over, Ginny could not help but notice.

She caught snatches of conversation as he hunkered unself-consciously down on his heels by a fire, pouring coffee while Paco fired questions at him.

"What took you so damn long, anyhow?"

"They were Comanches—I rode into their camp to talk; got myself persuaded into joining them in huntin' Apaches. Couldn't think of a better way to find out where the 'paches are hiding out, and how many of them are around."

"You bin out ridin' the warpath with Comanches?" Pop's voice sounded almost disbelieving, and Morgan grinned up at him.

"I used to live with the Comanches—long time ago. An'

they're about the only tribe them Apaches are really scared of. We went after some squaws the 'paches had the bad judgement to steal—got 'em back too."

"Do you mean to tell us you just met up with some of your old friends and took off with them—just like that? Leaving us here, not knowing what was going on?"

Carl sounded furious, and Ginny noticed that Pop Wilkins laid a warning hand on his arm.

"Now hold on Carl—"

"If there was any way of letting you know, I'd have done so—" Steve Morgan's voice was deceptively mild, but steel underlay it. "As it is—" his eyes swept the circle of faces and went back to Carl. "We won't be bothered by any type of Indians when we go through that pass. The Comanches are headin' back to their own stompin' grounds, and the Apaches will be lickin' their wounds. Weren't many of them left to make it back to their camp. They were Lipano, and a renegade band of 'em at that."

"You got some scalps on yore saddle—you take 'em yourself?"

"Yeah—as a matter of fact I did. Old Comanche custom. Guess they won't be in a hurry to mess with Comanche women again."

Ginny felt sick—against her will her eyes had gone almost fearfully to the black's saddle—but fortunately Zack had already led the horse away. How could he talk so casually about killing and then scalping men? He was worse than an Indian himself, and the matter-of-fact way he'd answered Pop's question showed it, if his appearance didn't!

"You got hurt—when did that happen?"

Paco asked the question, his voice sharp; making Ginny look quickly across the small distance that separated her from the group around the fire. Sure enough, the brown neckerchief he'd worn when he'd left camp was wrapped around his arm, still caked with dried blood.

"Knife," Steve Morgan said shortly.

"Here, you'd better let me have a look at it, *compañero*," Paco advised. "I know we got some medical supplies stashed away somewhere."

There was a sudden spate of talk, with Steve protesting he'd put some herbs on his arm and it didn't need anything else, Paco insisting the wound should be cleaned, and

Pop Wilkins yelling for one of the men to fetch him the medical kit.

"You'll probably end up with blood-poisoning—I don't suppose Indian knives are the cleanest in the world," Carl Hoskins said, swinging almost viciously on his heel as he walked away.

"We have emergency medical supplies in our own wagon. And since all you gentlemen seem so undecided and disorganized, perhaps you'll allow me to attend to Mr. Morgan's wound."

Without being told, Tillie had already brought the small box of supplies that the Senator had thoughtfully provided, and Ginny found herself walking coolly towards the fire. She saw the look of surprise replaced by something else—something unreadable and almost challenging in Steve Morgan's eyes as he came quickly and easily to his feet.

"It's only a scratch, ma'am. And I'm afraid I'm not exactly sanitary didn't have time to take a bath—"

Did his voice hold the slightest trace of mockery? If it did she ignored it, just as she ignored the looks she received from the others. Sonya's pale face showed amazement, and something like dismay, Pop Wilkins looked dumbfounded, and the glance that Paco Davis gave her was enigmatic.

"Mr. Morgan, none of us here is exactly clean after all that dust we've been riding through. If you'll come with me please, I'm sure we ought to fix that arm up right away."

The small medicine chest had everything in it that might be needed. Salves and bandages and raw spirits—even curved needles and catgut; and laudanum for pain. Everything the doctor in San Antonio had been able to think of.

Since Ginny had already turned to lead the way to her wagon, Steve followed her, shrugging.

When she gestured shortly he merely raised an eyebrow and sat obediently on the bare ground by the wagon, leaning his back up against the wheel. Without words, Paco handed him his shirt, helping him get one arm into the sleeve of the wrinkled buckskin garment.

"If you'll excuse me for just a minute, Miss Brandon," he said politely, taking the bottle Paco held in his other hand.

"Mr. Morgan!"

"Just a little whiskey, ma'am—to take the sting away."

His eyes smiled impudently up at her, and her lips tightened.

"Ginny," Sonya whispered from somewhere behind her, "are you sure that—I mean, have you ever tended a wound before? Sometimes it takes a strong stomach—"

"I can manage!" Ginny said tartly.

She took the small, sharp pair of scissors from its tray, and kneeling beside him, began to cut away the blood-soaked neckerchief. In spite of her care, bits of it adhered to the skin, and Ginny bit her lip.

"Needs to be washed off, ma'am," Paco offered, kneeling beside her. He grinned maliciously at Steve. "We're runnin' kind of low on water—try the rotgut. It'll sting some, but it's good for healing."

"Well—whatever you two decide, gimme another drink first!"

Steve scowled at Paco, then tilted his head back, letting the fiery liquor wash down his throat until Paco snatched the bottle away.

"You aren't serious?" Ginny stared at him questioningly, but Paco, after shaking the bottle, was already trickling whiskey over the bloody, open wound on his friend's arm.

Steve gritted his teeth against the searing, burning pain, but apart from a hissing intake of breath he made no sound, sitting there as stoic as an Indian while Ginny, face pale, used her tweezers to pick pieces of silk from the wound.

She had to wash the wound out again with spirits afterwards, wincing as she did so, and this time he went white under his tan.

"Jesus!" he gritted. "It didn't hurt this much getting that cut!"

"That'll be enough swearing, Mr. Morgan, if you please," Ginny said stiffly, although she was more than a little shaken herself. Surprising her, he apologized, turning his head to examine his arm as if it did not belong to him.

Drying the crimson, still-oozing knife cut with a piece of gauze, Ginny began carefully to apply some of the salve the doctor had recommended particularly for cuts, with Steve Morgan watching dubiously.

Ridiculous, she thought angrily to herself, that she

should choose this moment to notice how long and thick his eyelashes were. Who cared what kind of eyelashes a man possessed?

Her fingers faltered, and suddenly his eyes were looking right into hers, their strange blueness reflecting the leaping firelight.

"Hold still—it's difficult to see now that its so dark," she said unnecessarily. But why had she said that? And why did they suddenly seem to be alone?

She saw his lips curl in a slightly mocking smile and said quickly, surprising herself, "Why did you live with the Indians? Long ago, I mean. Were you kidnapped?"

"I was fifteen, ma'am—a mite old for them to want to kidnap!"

"You haven't answered my question. Is it because you don't want to?"

The smile left his face, and he seemed to look at her strangely.

"I lived with the Comanche because I chose to. But it's a long story, ma'am, and you'd get bored."

Exasperated, Ginny glared at him.

"Why couldn't you be honest enough to tell me you didn't want to talk about it? And by the way—I ought to remind you that you forget far too often to use bad grammar for your rough frontier scout act to be very convincing!"

He burst out laughing until she yanked on the ends of the bandage she had begun to wrap around his arm; and then he said "ouch!" and looked at her reproachfully.

"You're—"

A shadow fell across her shoulder, and Ginny looked up startled to see Carl Hoskins standing there with an ugly look on his face.

"Looks like our gunfighter went out to play Injun and got his gun hand crippled, doesn't it?"

Afterwards, Ginny could not remember seeing any movement, but Steve Morgan's gun, drawn from his left holster, suddenly lay against his thigh, pointing casually at Hoskins.

"Ain't nothing wrong with my other arm though—in case it worried you, Hoskins," he drawled. Ginny saw Carl's face go pale, and then, shrugging, Steve holstered the gun.

"Couldn't resist the chance to show off, could you?" Carl said bitterly. He glanced once at Ginny, and then, as if he controlled himself with an effort, turned and walked away towards the fire.

Ginny saw Sonya follow him quickly, putting her hand on his arm as she talked to him softly and urgently.

"What on earth is the matter with Carl?"

Morgan, his face unreadable again, had begun to slide his bandaged arm into the sleeve of his shirt.

"Could be he's jealous," he said shortly.

In some inexplicable way his curt observation annoyed Ginny all over again.

"That's ridiculous!" she said quickly. "I don't belong to Carl Hoskins, and besides, there's nothing to be jealous of."

"No?"

Her eyes widened slightly, and unconsciously, her tongue moistened her lips.

Streaks of bright pain stood out on his brown body, thrown into relief by the dancing firelight, and none of the angry, sarcastic words she wanted to use on him would emerge from her suddenly-dry throat.

"I don't understand," she said at last, the words sounding soft and hesitant.

"I think you do," he said abruptly, and the look in his eyes went through her like a jolt, making her heart pound dizzily.

Ginny was hardly aware that somehow, she was on her feet, his hands holding hers. He was thanking her, his voice polite and suddenly rather remote. Was he going to leave her? And why should the thought that any minute now he would turn around and walk away from her upset her so?

He had dropped her hands, and was frowning at her. She should say something, do something, but what? What is wrong with me, her mind cried out, and she felt mesmerized by his closeness, by the strange man-smell of him, the lean face with the whisker-stubble filling out all the hollows. She knew him and she didn't know him—and at this moment she neither knew nor understood herself. She had the almost irresistible impulse to sway against him, to feel his arms around her, touch the long, curling hair at the back of his neck.

"Better go back to your wagon, Miss Brandon," he said suddenly, harshly, breaking the spell that seemed to have seized them both for an instant. "Because if you don't I'm liable to grab a hold of you and kiss you—and they're all watching. Better go—before it's too late."

"Are you afraid of something Mr. Morgan? *You?*"

From a distance, Ginny heard her own voice, mocking, lightly teasing, and she knew instinctively that she'd said the right thing, for his eyes began to crinkle with appreciative laughter.

"And I was beginning to wonder if you'd lost your claws!"

"I sheathe them sometimes."

Deliberately, she let her eyes sparkle provocatively at him, and he laughed out loud.

From his place by the fire, Carl Hoskins glared angrily at them, his handsome face twisted with hate.

"Hadn't you ought to do something about that, Mrs. Brandon? Look at them—laughing together, flirting like none of us were here! I ought to—"

"You'll do nothing, Carl Hoskins," Sonya said sharply, although her face too looked troubled. "Please," she added more softly, "we mustn't have any trouble, not now! And you mustn't worry, Ginny's a sensible girl, she's only being friendly."

"It's him I don't trust! Morgan—a half-breed killer like him, he should keep his distance. His kind doesn't know how to act around decent women, doesn't she know how dangerous he is?"

"I've told you, there's nothing to worry about! Why, Ginny doesn't even like him, she's told me so."

"That's not the way it looks right now, though. Look at her, what's gotten into her?"

Dismayed, Sonya followed Carl's eyes and saw Ginny reach her hand up, running her fingers lightly over the paint streaks on Steve Morgan's bare chest.

"And what does that look like?"

Carl Hoskin's voice sounded muffled with rage and frustration, and Sonya herself could not repress a gasp of exasperation. Carl was right, what on earth was Ginny thinking of?

It was with a feeling of relief that Sonya saw Steve hold Ginny's wrist firmly, moving it away; saw his dark head bend towards her as he said something. Ginny was shrugging, but whatever it was he had said to her had some effect, for a few seconds later he walked away with a rather ironical bow, and Ginny, lifting her skirts without a backward glance, disappeared into the shadowy interior of the wagon.

Chapter Thirteen

Sonya had meant to talk seriously with Ginny, but with a cunning she would not have believed the girl capable of, her stepdaughter managed adroitly to avoid it.

Ginny was asleep, or pretending to be, when Sonya entered the wagon, after spending a good half hour pacifying Carl Hoskins, and Sonya, who was rather tired and depressed herself was almost glad to postpone their talk. The next morning, when they broke camp at about five o'clock, Ginny took the reins, advising Sonya cheerfully to get some more sleep while she had the chance.

But when Sonya woke up later on in the morning, still feeling unaccountably weary, only Tillie sat on the high seat, clucking at the mules. Ginny was gone.

Questioned, Tillie said rather sullenly that Miss Ginny had gone riding—she had said she wanted to see the cattle and the wagons travel through the pass.

"But—she surely didn't go by herself? Good heavens, there may still be Indians around!"

"No, ma'am, she didn't go by herself. Mr. Morgan, he came by, and she went along with him. Said they was going to ride up into the mountains a ways, an' catch up with us later."

"Oh, no!" Sonya's china blue eyes mirrored not only dismay but a kind of anger as well.

She bit her lip to keep back the words she wanted to blurt out—it would never do to let Tillie know how she really felt! But she was uncomfortably aware, as she climbed up beside Tillie, that the brown eyes studied her slyly. It didn't matter, of course, what Tillie thought, but it really was thoughtless and quite out of character for Ginny to act so—so sneakily!

Her own venom surprising her, Sonya thought viciously, "damn Steve Morgan!" Why did it have to be he William hired? And after all these years? And what was he doing with Ginny?

Steve Morgan was wondering the same thing, when they stopped for the second time to rest and water their horses on the long, steep slope that led down from the hills.

Why had he been crazy enough last night to promise he'd bring her up here? No one knew better than he that there might still be a few stray Apaches around, and with a woman along, especially one as inexperienced as Ginny Brandon—he told himself grimly that it must have been that rotgut Paco called whisky. But then, what had gotten into her?

The waterhole was really no more than a seep—a small underground spring he'd found under a huge, overhanging boulder. In spite of the fact that she'd sensed he was in a hurry to move on, Ginny had dismounted, and seated herself deliberately with her back against a smaller boulder, pretending that the long ride had tired her. She had pulled the hat from her head and was fanning herself with it, eyes closed; but she was well aware, all the same, that her companion was studying her, his face morose and unsmiling. She had asked herself all morning why she had come with him, and now, why she was here, but womanlike, she did not want to find the answer. She wanted—she didn't know what she wanted! She was here—let him make the first move.

So far, he had been polite—answering when she spoke to him, occasionally advising her to be careful when the trail they had followed grew narrow. Unlike Carl, he made no attempts to press his leg against hers when they happened to ride side by side. She had flirted with him last night, and he had responded, but this morning everything seemed changed. What was he thinking?

"We'd better get started. It's going to take all of two hours to catch up with the wagons as it is."

His voice came from somewhere above her, and Ginny pretended he had startled her.

"Oh! Is it really such a distance down this side of the mountain? It seemed to take much less time when we were climbing!"

An unwilling smile twitched the corner of his mouth.

"If you'll recall, ma'am, I think I told you that this trail we're following now kind of skirts around the hills. Takes longer that way."

He reached his hand out to her and she took it unwillingly, scrambling to her feet when he tugged.

"Ma'am! Why do you keep calling me that? You make me sound like an old married woman."

"Well, what would you rather I called you Miss Brandon?" he said drily, and something about the way his eyes looked her over, coolly and appraisingly, made her flush with embarrassment.

"You really are a very *exasperating* man!"

Ginny pulled her hand from his and walked over to her mare, turning her back on him.

"Ginny Brandon." His voice held an undertone of laughter now, as she felt him come up behind her. His hands touched her shoulders, turning her around gently to face him. "Why am I so very exasperating? What did you expect from me?"

She had to force herself to meet his eyes.

"I don't know. Honesty, perhaps. Most men are not honest with women, you know. They pretend and play-act and force us too into playing a role." Her voice faltered for an instant, and then gathered strength. "Perhaps, Mr. Morgan, you—intrigued me because you are different from the other men I have met. You give the impression that you say what you feel; do as you want. You are not afraid of what people may say or think, are you? I don't know if I should be frightened of you or—"

His fingers bit into her shoulders and she winced. The laughter had gone from his eyes and they looked hard and bleak.

"For God's sake! You find me intriguing because I mistook you for a whore the first time we met—and treated you like one? If you want the truth, you've intrigued me ever since—particularly since I could have sworn you kissed me back. But I learned a long time ago to run like hell from panting little virgins, full of curiosity and teasing little tricks."

"Ohh!" Her gasp was full of outrage, but he went on inexorably, his hands bruising her shoulders.

"No, don't try to pull away, I'm not through yet! You wanted honesty, remember? I want you, Ginny Brandon —I have from the beginning, and I'm sure you've known it. But I've tried to stay as far away from you as much as possible, because you're the worst kind of poison. A nice girl, a Senator's daughter, and by God, a virgin. I've not been respectable for most of my life—I've wanted women and taken them and never bothered too much with preliminaries. What I'm trying to tell you, I guess, is that this whole thing is crazy—I had no right to ask you to come up here with me, and you—damn your green eyes, you should have known better than to come!"

"Why not?" The same green eyes he'd damned flashed defiance at him. No, this time she would outface him, she would not back down. "You are right, you know, I *am* curious. And why should I not be, merely because I am what you call a 'nice girl?' I'm a woman, Steve Morgan, and you look at me as if I were a woman, and yet there are so many things I do not understand! You told me you want me, and I don't even know what that really means, or what I am supposed to feel! When Carl kissed me, I—"

His fingers bit into her shoulders and she gave a small cry of pain.

"So you're a virgin who plays at passion?" he said brutally, "and this, no doubt; is in the nature of an experiment? Very well, Miss Brandon, I'll try to oblige, just so you'll have a basis for comparison the next time you kiss Carl Hoskins."

Before Ginny could speak or move he had pulled her against him and his mouth came down over hers in a hard, angry kiss that took her breath away. There was no gentleness in him, no tenderness. His arms held her pinned against the length of his body, and he kissed her savagely and thoroughly, his tongue raping her mouth until she felt she would swoon, felt her legs become weak, felt a strange, feverish pounding in her temples that seemed to spread through her whole body and engulf her.

Without knowing why, or what she was doing, her arms

lifted, went around his neck and clung. She felt his hand move slowly and caressingly up her back, then tug impatiently at her hair, loosening it from its tidy, coiled braids. She felt her hair tumble down over her shoulders, and his mouth made a burning trail from her parted lips to her earlobe.

"Ginny—Ginny—" the words sounded like a groan, and a shiver of apprehension went through her as she felt his fingers start to unbutton the thin silk shirt she had worn with her riding skirt.

He mustn't—she mustn't let him—but his mouth found the hollow at the base of her throat and she made a little, helpless sound; feeling the shirt open under his hands, his fingers burn against her breast.

He held her close against him, one arm supporting her weak, trembling body, and when she would have protested against the liberties he was taking, his lips covered her open mouth, taking possession of it, stifling the words she tried to utter.

Ginny's head fell back and she began to whimper in the back of her throat. She felt drained of thought and will.

Suddenly, he had bent his head, he was kissing her breasts, his tongue tracing light, teasing patterns over their taut, sensitive peaks.

She struggled then, but only half-heartedly; both his arms imprisoned her again, she closed her eyes and let him have his way, feeling the desire to struggle or even to protest slipping away from her to be replaced by something else—something that grew like a tight, hard knot inside her belly, spreading a burning flush over her whole body.

He must have sensed her sudden, abject surrender. From somewhere far away she heard him laugh softly, and then, catching her roughly against him, he was kissing her again, his hands slipped under her shirt to caress the bare skin of her back.

This time Ginny arched up against him, half-sobbing, not yet understanding the strange new emotions that he had awakened in her body. She was all too conscious of the pressure of his long, hard-muscled legs against hers, of the feel of his shirt against her bare, tingling breasts, the crisp feel of his hair under her clutching fingers.

Somewhere in the recesses of her mind was the

thought: So this is how it feels—like a fever, like a coiled snake in the belly, growing, spreading heat like honey in her loins, rendering her incapable of everything but feeling, needing, and yet not wholly understanding what it was she needed from him.

It was only—as she was to realize later—only the sudden intrusion of a distant shout, from somewhere far below them, that stopped whatever was building up to a climax between them.

Ginny could feel the instant stiffening of his body against hers, the stilling of all motion, as if they hung suspended in space, and then she was free, standing on her own trembling feet as his hands fell away from her and he moved backwards.

"Oh Christ!" Steve said disgustedly as the same voice shouted again—

"Hola up there! Can you hear me, Steve?"

Ginny sank to her knees, her breath still catching in her throat, hands going up to touch her burning, flushed cheeks.

"It's only Paco," he said unnecessarily, and then, his voice tight with frustration, "tactful, isn't he?"

He cupped his hands over his mouth and yelled back.

"We're coming down, hold your horses!"

Already, Ginny was beginning to fumble with the buttons on her shirt. Sudden embarrassment kept her from looking at him. Oh, God, how could she ever face him again? How would she face the others?

He hunkered down beside her and brushing her shaking fingers aside began to fasten up her shirt, quickly and efficiently.

"It's just as well he called out when he did," Steve said quietly. "You know that, don't you? And I guess I should say I'm sorry, but I'm not." He put his hand under her chin and turned her unwilling face up to his.

"Don't mess with me any more, Ginny Brandon. I've no time for romance and gentle kisses! I'm not used to curious virgins."

Something drove her to flare up at him. "Is that why you were so—so rough? Did you mean to scare me off, Mr. Morgan? Have you never been tender or even kind to a woman?"

He was already pulling her back onto her feet, but he

shot her a look that was almost surprised before he masked it with coldness.

"To tell the truth, when I've been with women before we've known what was coming. There's been no need to waste time on silly games. Take my advice, Miss Brandon, and forget what happened just now. I'm sure you'll find Carl Hoskins much better behaved, and more to your taste as a lover."

"You make it very easy to hate you, but I'm sure you know that!"

Pulling the shreds of her pride and dignity about her, Ginny mounted her horse, ignoring the hand he stretched out to help her.

They rode down to meet Paco in stony silence, and Ginny did not know whether to feel relieved or guilty when she saw that Carl Hoskins was with him, his face hard with suspicion.

Only Sonya Brandon's pleading and her extraction of a reluctant promise from him made Carl control his anger.

Steve Morgan's face told him nothing, but Ginny—surely her cheeks wore an unusually high flush, and her hair, he noticed, had been clubbed together in an untidy braid that swung over one shoulder. He had opened his mouth to say something when he met her eyes, and the almost defiant look in them made him clench his jaws with helpless rage.

"Mrs. Brandon was—quite worried when she woke up and found you'd gone riding," he said stiffly when the girl had cantered up abreast of him.

"I'm sorry," she said sullenly. "But I didn't want to wake her, and I did tell Tillie—"

"If anyone's to blame, I guess I am," Steve Morgan said pleasantly. "I asked Miss Brandon if she'd care to go riding with me, and it took longer than I thought it might because we had to stop and rest the horses a few times."

"I would think you could have been more thoughtful, Morgan—after all it was you who warned us all about Indians!"

There was much more Carl might have said, but the suddenly cold, warning look in Morgan's eyes stopped him.

Paco Davis said quickly and pacifically:

"Well, now that Hoskins can escort Miss Brandon back

to her wagon, I think that you and I, *amigo*, should find out what happened to all those Apaches your friends run off."

"Miss Brandon—my pleasure, ma'am."

Forcing herself to meet Steve Morgan's eyes, Ginny nodded coolly.

So it was to be over, before it had started? He thought he could flirt with her and kiss her in that savage, almost animally passionate way, and put his hands on her body so intimately—and then pretend that nothing had happened?

You'll not get away with it quite so easily, Steve Morgan, Ginny vowed silently. He had already ridden off with Paco, their horses half-obscured by dust, and she didn't realize that she was staring after them until she felt Carl Hoskins' hand on her arm, his fingers hurting her.

"What happened up there? What is there between you? By God, if he touched you, I'll—"

"You'll what, Carl? Will you challenge him to a gun fight?" A cruelty she had not realized she possessed made Ginny's voice and words deliberately taunting, and she saw Carl's face redden.

"What has happened to you?" His voice sounded disbelieving, it shook with the frustration he was trying to control. "You've been with him twice, and suddenly you're not the same girl! What has he done to you?"

Tired of him, tired of his questions, Ginny pulled her arm from his grasp. Her green eyes looked hard, unsympathetic.

"Nothing! Nothing happened at all! Does that disappoint you? But I'm sick of being treated like a child, sick of your questions! And if Sonya is so worried about me, perhaps we'd best hurry back to her."

Without glancing at him again she wheeled her mare around, kicking the startled animal into a fast gallop. Not knowing what else to do, Carl followed her.

The hours that followed Ginny's defiant return to the wagon seemed interminable to them all. Ginny refused to be questioned, refused to speak to Carl. To Sonya she only said shortly that she had wanted to go riding, and had done so; and that she would ride with whomever she pleased when she felt like it.

Finally, Sonya decided to hide her agitation and leave the girl alone until she was in a better mood. She took the reins from Tillie, leaving Ginny lying on the small bunk with her eyes obdurately closed, and could not stop herself from wondering what had really happened. Steve Morgan was capable of anything, hadn't she sensed that at the very beginning? And she had been foolish not to warn William against hiring him, but what could she have said without giving herself away? She had thought that perhaps the years had changed him—he hadn't tried to touch her, nor to remind her about the past, not even when he had asked her to go riding, and she had been alone with him. Why hadn't he? Was it because he wanted Ginny?

I don't know, Sonya thought miserably, I'm not sure of anything any longer! All these years, she had felt so safe with William, so secure—almost, she had made herself forget what had happened that long ago spring in Louisiana. And then he'd come back—acting for all the world as if he had forgotten too, but had he? I should talk to him, she thought; ask him—no, *tell* him to leave Ginny alone. But he wouldn't listen, it might make him want her more. Or he might think—hastily, she shut the thought away, concentrating on familiar, safer things. Plans for the new house William had built in California, waiting to be furnished. Plans for an empire, waiting to be taken.

Sonya shuttered and screened her thoughts, filtering through only those things about which she wanted to think. Ginny, moving restlessly in the uncomfortably narrow bunk, wondered what might have happened if Paco Davis had not chosen that particular moment to call out. Her thoughts were a mixture of anger and humiliation and yes, she had to admit it, curiosity.

"A curious virgin" he had called her mockingly. He had sworn at her, been deliberately rude to her, but he hadn't been able to hide the fact that he wanted her, had wanted to kiss her. Would he have stopped? Could she have stopped him?

That strange, half-weak, half-feverish feeling that had taken possession of her, making her helpless, was that desire? She shivered, wondering if it was always like that. So frightening, to lose control of one's emotions, to actually *want* a man to do with her as he had done. His lips on her breasts, burning into them, his tongue exploring her mouth, the taste of his kisses—it hadn't been that way with Carl. No, Carl would never treat her that way.

The wagon creaked and rumbled beneath her, tossing

her, keeping her awake when she needed to sleep. She
found herself wondering if Steve Morgan would come into
camp tonight, whether he'd look at her differently. He
will, he will, she thought stubbornly and her heart
pounded, so hard she thought she would faint.

Chapter Fourteen

Pop Wilkins was more talkative than usual over the campfire that night. They had made camp late, in the deceptively transparent twilight of the plains, with the hills behind them still appearing to gnash at the sky with serrated teeth.

"Made it through the pass after all!" Pop said jubilantly. "By Golly, I never did think to feel this good about any damn Injuns being around. But them Comanches, they're fighters, that bunch—only Injuns the 'paches will run from."

"Don't be too sure the Apaches are goin' to keep their distance for too much longer, though—" Paco Davis warned in his soft, Spanish-accented voice. "They bin used to having things pretty much their own way during the war, and there still ain't enough cavalry in these parts to stop 'em if they get real proddy—not yet, anyhow."

Pop pulled nervously at his white mustache.

"You tryin' to say you think they'll jump us? Seen any sign up ahead?"

"This is 'pache country," Paco shrugged. "In fact, it's pretty certain they're watchin' us right now, trying to make up their minds, should they leave us go or not."

"We'll be ready for them, anyhow," Pop said stubbornly. "I'd like to kill me a few 'paches. I seen too often what them devils can do . . ," lowering his voice, he went on talking, and some of the other men joined in.

Occasionally, Paco glanced across the fire at Steve, but tonight, Steve was letting the others do all the talking, and Paco could not help wondering if his partner's silence had something to do with the Brandon girl. What had happened between them? He hadn't asked questions, but he knew Steve Morgan. Women liked him—perhaps because he so obviously didn't give a damn and they were intrigued by the reckless danger they sensed in him. Steve used women—took them when he felt like it and left them, and most of the time the women knew it would happen, he wasn't cruel enough to leave them with any illusions. But Ginny Brandon was different. She was too civilized, maybe too naive. She looked all woman and she had a mouth that was made for kissing, but she wasn't Steve's type at all, she was too damn vulnerable, that was it.

Tonight, she was doing a pretty fair job of pretending she enjoyed having Carl Hoskins sit so possessively beside her at the other, smaller campfire close to her wagon. She had been flirting openly with Carl ever since Steve had appeared—dusty, tired-looking and unsmiling, with hardly a word for any of them, not even for Paco himself.

Paco wished he knew her well enough to warn her. "Losin' your papa's gold ain't goin' to hurt you, Miss Brandon; not half as much as you'd hurt if you let yourself get tangled with my partner."

It would have surprised Ginny, and even Paco himself, if they had known what Steve Morgan's thoughts were, behind his taciturn and almost sullenly withdrawn appearance tonight.

He should have been thinking about those Apaches, who were somewhere out there in the night, waiting. But he kept hearing Ginny Brandon's soft, teasing laughter as she made up to Hoskins; found himself unwillingly remembering the feel and texture of her flesh under his mouth. Damn Brandon! Why in hell did he have to send his women along to do his dirty work for him? And damn the complications that Ginny could cause if he let her. She didn't belong out here in the West—she should have stayed in Paris, or in some sophisticated drawing room back east.

Ginny Brandon's hair shone coppery in the firelight, and she was leaning against Carl Hoskins' shoulder. Carl would be better for a girl like her anyhow; he'd probably want to marry her right off if he took her virginity, and that way, if he was smart enough, he'd be cutting himself in for a bigger share of the profits in Brandon's grandiose schemes ... one of which, at least, he and Paco were supposed to nip in the bud.

Abruptly, Steve came to his feet. He caught Paco's quizzical look and yawned ostentatiously.

"Guess I'll turn in. Figure to be gone before daylight, so you can head 'em out around six, if I'm not back before then."

He disappeared into the darkness, and Ginny, in spite of her outward preoccupation with Carl, was vividly aware of his going.

So he thought he could ignore her? The memory of the way she had all but thrown herself at him—her own surprising response to the almost brutal intimacy of his caresses that morning, stained her cheeks with blood, and she was glad of the warm orange glow of the fire; glad that no one would notice. From now on, she thought viciously, it would be she who ignored his presence—she would act as if he did not exist, as if the interlude that morning had been merely amusing to her, a scheme to make Carl jealous.

Ginny laughed softly at something Carl had said, aware that his eyes had hardly left her all evening. Carl was nice—he was handsome, and he was civilized, which was more than one could say for Steve Morgan.

When Sonya suggested that since they were all tired and would have to start out so early in the morning, perhaps it would be best to retire, Ginny smiled at her sweetly and insincerely and begged that she might be allowed to sit a little longer by the fire. She caught Sonya's small, hurt frown, but preferred to ignore it.

They sat by the fire, she and Carl, until it had burned down into embers, and she needed the shawl he had so thoughtfully brought out for her earlier. Except for the cook, who lay rolled in his blankets by the chuckwagon, they were alone.

Carl's arm was around her waist—she felt his warm

breath against her temples when he kissed her lightly.

If it had been Steve Morgan, he would not have been content with that, she thought angrily. Why didn't Carl turn her face up to his and kiss her? Everyone else was asleep, why didn't he do something? I keep forgetting that Carl is a gentleman, she thought, he is hardly the kind of man who would pull a female roughly into his arms and kiss her until she falls breathless; he would not . . .

As if he had sensed her thoughts he said tentatively,

"Ginny? Perhaps it is time I took you back to your wagon now, your stepmother might think . . ."

She wanted to retort, "do you care so much what everyone else might think? Don't you *want* to kiss me, Carl?" but she only gave him a half-drowsy murmur instead, and let him help her to her feet.

In the small, dark space between her wagon and the next, he surprised her by taking her uncertainly into his arms, his mouth finding hers almost by chance.

Her mouth was soft, half-open under his, and made bolder by the fact that she did not attempt to pull away from him, Carl kissed her hard and almost desperately, drawing her body closer to his, wanting to feel the soft swell of her breasts against him. She had only wanted to make him jealous by riding with Morgan this morning, Carl was sure of that now. Maybe her sudden and unexpected flirtation with the man had been merely her woman's way of telling Carl to move faster—maybe he'd been too respectful, too patient and gentle with her. He had begun to feel, this evening, that under her soft and ladylike exterior there was a streak of wildness in Ginny Brandon. Let her find out that he was a man, as well as a gentleman.

Carl could feel his own breathing come harder, almost ragged. Her body was molded against his now, and desire swelled in him. By God, he thought, By God, she was his—he could take her, and she would not stop him. He forgot who she was and who he was, feeling only the urgency of the male need in him, the softness of her woman's body. It had been a long time since he'd had a woman—too long. Almost involuntarily, his arms tightened around her, and he heard the soft expulsion of her breath. All this time, she had neither responded nor rejected, merely accepting his kiss, but now, suddenly, he felt her hands come up and push against his chest, her head twisting to escape his lips. What in hell kind of game was she playing? And then the thought—had he frightened her with the ardor of his lovemaking?

"No, Carl, no!" she was whispering, face turned away from his now, small clenched fists still pushing against him.

"Ginny—honey, you're so beautiful, so—"

"Carl—" her voice stronger now, more urgent, "that's enough, Carl—you mustn't—we mustn't—"

"Oh, God, Ginny! I'd never hurt you, I swear! But you're enough to set any man crazy, just being near you—"

He let his arms loosen around her, in spite of the blood pounding in his veins that urged him to take her, push her up against the wagon and make her cry out to him with a need as big as his. But she was a Senator's daughter, and a decent woman—not the kind a man could force or seduce in a night. She'd want to be courted, of course, he had to be careful—

"Carl—I—I really think I ought to go inside now, I—"

"I love you, Ginny" he said almost desperately, arms still holding her, "I wouldn't do anything to hurt or upset you, you know that. I want to marry you, if you'll have me—I'll speak to your father."

"No!" she said sharply. "Carl—no!" And then, as if she regretted her sharpness she added hesitatingly, "It's too soon—I don't really *know* you yet. And—and I don't really know myself!"

He could not help himself—the more he felt her withdraw from him, the more he wanted her. Hating himself for pleading, he could not prevent the words.

"One more kiss then, Ginny—please, honey, just one more. And I won't push you, I promise, I'll let you take as much time as you want deciding—Ginny, let me kiss you—"

Because she was trapped, and she had deliberately led him into this impossible situation, Ginny turned her lips up to Carl's again, closing her eyes against the abject, hungry look in his face. Carl's mouth attacked hers again, his kisses wet and searching, and she shuddered uncontrollably, a shudder he mistook for desire. Why couldn't she feel anything when Carl kissed her? Minutes ago she had wanted his kisses, had deliberately led him to this moment, but when he'd put his arms around her she had merely felt stifled; when he'd kissed her she'd found it faintly repulsive. And now, she felt she couldn't stand the feel of his mouth on hers another instant. Instinct made her push fiercely against him until he released her, and with a mumbled "I'm *sorry,* Carl!" she picked up her skirts and stumbled away from him, back to the safety of the embered fire and her own wagon. And only the strongest amount of self-control made her wait until she was inside the wagon before she snatched up a damp washrag and dragged it fiercely across her lips, rubbing away the damp feel of his kisses.

Sonya called softly from her bunk,

"Ginny? Is anything wrong, love?"

"Nothing—I'm sorry if I woke you—it's so hot, that's all!"

Ginny was ashamed of herself the next moment, for having sounded almost harsh. Poor Sonya! And poor Carl too, she thought as she stripped off her petticoats and lay down. What is the matter with me?

Ginny felt as if she had hardly fallen asleep when the camp was aroused the next morning by shouts and the pounding feet of excited men. It was Pop Wilkins who broke the news. One of the guards they had posted had been found dead, with an Apache arrow in him; his body still warm. And there had been an attempt to stampede the herd which had failed, Pop said fiercely, because these cattle weren't as easily stampeded as longhorns would have been.

"Good thing them cowpunchers was kinda prepared for trouble," he explained briefly as the mules were being hastily harnessed. "Shot a couple of 'paches, they said, but the devils took their dead away with 'em like they allus do."

Ginny had to bite back the question that almost leaped to her tongue. Where had the scouts been? She remembered, last night, that Steve Morgan had said he'd be leaving before dawn. Suppose—

Surprising her, Sonya asked the question.

"Mr. Wilkins, one minute, please! Our scouts, are they all right?"

"Morgan, he's the one found poor Blackie. He took off after the 'paches, an' sent Davis to warn the men lookin' after the herd. Guess he got there just in time—they said he had about six Apaches screamin' after him." Seeing the expression on the women's faces, Pop said quickly that they weren't to be alarmed, they would move ahead very slowly, with armed men riding alongside each wagon.

Ginny insisted on driving the wagon, Sonya beside her with a loaded rifle across her lap. Thank God Sonya knew how to use a gun. And thank God for the reassuring feel of the pistol she had concealed in the pocket of her own dress. It didn't quite seem real. They had come all these miles without seeing a hostile Indian, and now, the knowledge that somewhere out there were hard-faced brown men in whose breasts burned a hatred for all white men and the desire to kill—well, it did not seem possible!

They camped just before noon, when Steve Morgan rode back to confer with Pop Wilkins; the wagons circling with the ease of long practice. But this, Ginny was soon to discover, was to be no ordinary nooning. They were going to prepare to defend themselves—already the men were working with grim efficiency, driving the mules and horses into a hastily constructed remuda—"sheeting" the wagons with extra thick layers of canvas stretched from wheel to wheel; linking the wagons together with heavy chains.

There was no time now to ask questions. Biting her lip, Ginny had to be content with keeping busy, helping Sonya and Tillie pile boxes, anything heavy against the side of the wagon from which the attack would come, with spaces between for rifles. Later, there would be bullets to make, extra powder and lead to be distributed to the men. Sonya worked silently, with a film of perspiration beading her pale face. Tillie was frankly terrified, her usually nimble fingers all fumbles.

From overhearing the men talk, they knew there was a large band of Apaches concealed somewhere in the bluffs ahead of them. Men who called this vast and forbidding country their home and knew every inch of it. Ginny found it hard to analyze her feelings. She was afraid—and yet the feeling of unreality was still too strong. It didn't seem possible that she was in the middle of this strange and unfamiliar emptiness, instead of being safely home in her beloved France. California seemed eons away now—would she ever get there, would any of them? And even her father's great plan, the heavy gold concealed so snugly in the false bottom to their wagon, that too seemed part of a dream.

What would happen? When would they attack? If she closed her eyes for an instant, Ginny could see them in her imagination—a horde of painted warriors, brandishing their weapons, screaming their war cries. She suddenly remembered the way that Steve Morgan had ridden into camp on that evening, his blue eyes bright with devilry, yelling defiantly like a Comanche warrior. And then the forbidden, shameful thought, why do I have to think about him? Why couldn't it be Carl's kisses that make me feel weak and helpless?

She had seen Carl that morning and he had smiled at her a trifle shamefacedly, but since their nooning he had been busy with their preparations for defense. Suddenly, some two hours later, she looked up from loading one of their pistols and he was there, his face serious.

"I'm going now with some of the boys to see to the cattle, but I'll be back as soon as I can."

Mistaking her silence for concern he said reassuringly, "Don't worry, Ginny, it's not likely they'll attack just yet. I was talking to Paco Davis a while back and he says they're still mourning their dead of this morning. He says it takes them quite a while. But I have to see that the cattle are bedded down someplace safe."

"Be careful, Carl."

There was nothing else she could say. He leaned down from his horse and caught her hand, squeezing it a moment longer than necessary.

"I'll be careful. I've got reason to be. You'll stay in the wagon, won't you? Anyhow, stay within the clearing."

Silently, she watched him ride away, aware of Tillie's sudden presence at her side.

"Sure is a handsome gentleman, that one," Tillie commented, and Ginny wondered how much the girl really observed.

The cook had a fire going already, and with Zack's unwilling help was starting to prepare supper. Occasionally, one of the men wandered over and helped himself to a cup of hot coffee.

Sonya was resting, having declared that she knew she wouldn't sleep a wink all night, and Ginny, who privately agreed with her stepmother, told Tillie that she might as well get some rest too.

"But lord, Miss Ginny, how's a body to rest knowin' any moment them painted devils could come rushin' out at us?"

"I told you, Tillie, we've done everything we can. And

we have enough men and guns to hold off a small army. Papa made sure of that before we left San Antonio. They'll attempt to attack us and we will beat them off. And that will be the end of it."

Ginny's words sounded braver in her ears than she actually felt, but having said them, she felt better. The sun beat hotly down on her, its burning heat seeming to seep into her body, and she was young and alive and the possibility of dying was unthinkable.

And yet, she thought a little later, walking with Tillie to the water wagon to refill their water casks, and yet if I'm to die today or tomorrow I'll be sorry at that moment, because I haven't really lived yet; there is so much I've not experienced, or only half-felt—there's so much more I want to know before I die.

She was to remember this thought later, when it was night and a quarter moon hung in the sky and after interminable hours of waiting the Indians still had not attacked. They had all eaten early, with little appetite, and the only fire permitted was a very small one, hardly more than a bed of embers in a scooped out depression in the ground. Two large coffee pots stayed warm here, but there had not been the usual talk and laughter over coffee that night.

They had waited all afternoon, keyed up and tense, and nothing had happened. And Paco Davis had said, with a reassuring look at the women, that Apaches seldom attacked at night.

"Look out for the first light, though," he added in warning to Pop. "They figure that's the best time to catch a man off-guard, when he's been up without sleep all night an' it's just beginning to catch up with him."

"Ain't gonna catch *us* nappin' though!" Wilkins said fiercely. His white-bearded face looked bleak and craggy in the dim light. Ginny remembered the story she'd heard about how Pop had come back from town one day to find his cabin burned and his wife and children dead and horribly mutilated. It must be a terrible thought for a man to live with, she thought; eating into him. No wonder he hated Indians so much!

And then there was Steve Morgan, who with his soft, strangely graceful walk was like an Indian himself, and had even lived among them and fought with them. She remembered the Apache scalps at his saddle and shivered.

He was a violent man. He'd fight with the Indians and against them—and he'd kill a white man as easily as he would an Indian. For pay. He was no more than a mercenary, and she must keep reminding herself of that, especially when his eyes met hers, as they sometimes did accidentally.

Night was a strange half-light on the restless plains and ridges. The movement of the wind could be the movement of Apaches, creeping on their bellies like snakes, and just as soundless. Men stayed awake, taking turns, while others slept under the wagons.

The small clearing in the center of the circled wagons looked completely deserted when Ginny, the moon and the night-sounds making her restless, pulled aside the canvas flap to peer out. Tonight even cookie slept inside a wagon, concealed like the rest of the men from eyes that might watch.

Two wagons away, she knew that Steve Morgan slept under the heavily constructed wagon that held their spare guns and ammunition. When Paco, half-joking, had declared that he sure wasn't going to be the one blown up in smoke by a chance fire arrow. Steve had shrugged laughingly.

"Don't make any difference to me. I'll take that one."

She'd watched him take his blanket roll and spread it under the wagon, only half-aware of the pressure of Carl's hand on hers.

"Ginny," he had whispered, "take care. Try to get some sleep."

She'd promised she would, and yet now, while Tillie and even Sonya slept heavily, tired out by the waiting and the tension, it was she who could not close her eyes.

It was intolerably hot and stifling under the heavy canvas top of the wagon. No air here, and yet outside the wind stirred tall grass and coyotes howled. I'm afraid, she thought, and then quickly, no, I'm not afraid, I'm just—I don't know, just restless. It's the waiting, the stillness, the not knowing. And being alone.

She was half-tempted to make enough noise to wake Sonya, so that they could huddle together and whisper their shared fears.

Ginny opened the flap again, and the faint glow of ashed coals, the black outline of the coffee pot drew her. If she had a cup of hot coffee it might help, although this west-

ern coffee was like nothing she had ever tasted before—
only bearable when drunk very hot, so that the burning
would take away some of the bitterness.

She had undressed for sleeping, wearing only her lightest
shift, but now, hardly thinking, she pulled the sweat-damp
garment roughly over her head, and put on one of her
dark cotton dresses. Strange, and somehow almost sensuous, the feel of the soft material against her bare skin.
Why were women forced to wear so much under their
clothes?

Stepping very carefully over Tillie's sleeping form, picking her skirts up high, Ginny lifted the canvas flap and left
the wagon.

She could not remember afterwards if she had somehow
known or only sensed it would happen. She crouched by
the small warmth of the burned-out fire, reaching for the
coffee pot, and she felt his hands in her hair. She could not
move, did not turn, but she knew who it was, just as if she
had been waiting for him.

"You shouldn't be out here."

"I know. I couldn't sleep. Why couldn't you?"

She hadn't turned her head yet, but she heard him
chuckle softly.

"I'm a light sleeper. And then again—"

His hands moved slowly down the back of her neck,
lifting the heavy coil of hair, and she trembled at the light,
warmly caressing touch of his lips.

"Nights like this, when even the wind is hot and the
coyotes howl at the moon and I know we'll be in a
fight—I don't usually sleep much. I'd like to be riding, or
maybe just running, no place in particular, like the
Apaches do."

She turned around quickly, trying to read his shadowed
face.

"But you're a man. If not tonight, then there can be
other nights. You're free to ride where you please, when
you please. It's so frustrating to be a woman, to have to
wait until someone accompanies you. Sometimes I feel
that being a woman is worse than being a child—we have
the intelligence and the feelings of adults, but we aren't
permitted to show them."

"Was that why you couldn't sleep? Because you feel
frustrated and restless?"

They were both kneeling, staring into each other's faces.

Her fingers plucked nervously at her skirt until he put his
hand over hers, stilling its movement.

"I wish—it seems as though every time we meet we
are either quarrelling or—or—can't we talk?"

"This isn't the time or the place for talking, and I'm in
no mood to play the gentleman and flirt with you under
the stars, Ginny Brandon," he said roughly. Before she
could answer he had pulled her to her feet, holding both
her hands.

"If you know what is good for you," he continued, still
with the same note of suppressed violence in his voice,
"you'll pick up your skirts and go back to bed to dream
your safe little virgin dreams. Because if you stay out here
I'm going to take you under that wagon with me and
make love to you. You know that, don't you?"

He was too close to her, she thought feverishly. There
was no time for thinking, and how could she think clearly
when he was already taking her with him?

It was warm and dark under the wagon, like a cave,
isolating them both. Her body felt stiff and unyielding as
he lay down beside her; like a board, she thought—that
would splinter and break if he touched her—and then his
arms took her and held her close against him, and after a
while, because he did nothing else, she could feel herself
beginning to relax. He held her quietly, his breath warm
against her cheek, and as some of the tenseness left her
she began to tremble slightly. Bemused as she was, from
somewhere she found the strength to whisper,

"I—I don't even know what—what it is I'm supposed to
do—what—"

"Hush. There's nothing you're supposed to do. I'm going
to kiss you, that's all. Turn your face to me, Ginny."

Blindly, not daring to open her eyes yet, she moved her
face up to his, and he kept kissing her for a long time until some of the warmth of his body and his mouth had
penetrated to hers and she began to kiss him back. Gently,
gently, while they kissed, she felt him take the pins from
her hair, letting the heavy mass of it fall over her back
and shoulders.

His lips moved slowly and lingeringly from her mouth
to her earlobe and she could feel him, for a moment, bury
his face in her hair. She could feel the stirring in him and
in her, and she wanted to speak, to tell him that she was

afraid, and then his mouth covered hers again and it was too late.

His hands moved over her breasts and down the length of her body, exploring its curves and hollows through the thin cotton gown. When his fingers began to unfasten the hooks and buttons that held it together she shivered, but could no more move to resist him than he, at this moment, could have stopped himself.

With her mouth still clinging to his and her arms around his neck Ginny forced herself by an effort of will to lie acquiescent under his hands. She had wanted this— with one part of her mind she realized dimly that perhaps she had wanted to lie with him just this way from the very beginning, when he had first seized her and kissed her so brutally. But none of her imaginings had ever been like this reality—"the thing that men and women do together" that she and her friends had discussed in whispers at the convent as something terrible and frightening but inevitable, had surely nothing to do with what was happening now!

Gentle, still kissing her, he was easing her arms from around his neck, and again Ginny shivered as she felt her gown, her last defense, slip from her body. She had not thought that he'd want her completely naked, and it was only by closing her eyes tightly and gritting her teeth together that she could control her own instinctive shyness and the protests that welled up in her throat.

At least, thank God, he seemed to know exactly what to do, exactly how to still her unspoken fears. For all his previous roughness and harshness, he was now only gentle with her, his hands patient with her shrinking flesh.

His own fully clad body half covering hers now, his leg thrown over her to keep her still, his hands resumed their exploring—his fingers brushing like fire against her skin.

She felt his mouth on her breasts, lips and tongue teasing her nipples until she groaned, a muted, strangely incoherent sound, and at the same time, taking her by surprise, his hands moved lower.

"Don't, love—don't cross your legs against me. Your body is so beautiful you've no need to be ashamed of it . . ."

He kissed her hair and eyes and face and the pulse that beat in the hollow of her throat and then her breasts again until she was flushed and shaking with a recurrence of the same wild and thoughtless emotions that had swept over

her before when he had held her and kissed her the last
time, up in the hills.

Suddenly his hands were between her thighs, stroking
the soft inner skin very gently, moving upward—she gave
an instinctive, incoherent cry as his fingers found her and
he muffled it against his mouth.

"Be still, love—I'll be gentle—just be still now—"

He spoke to her as softly and coaxingly as if she were a
mare to be tamed and gentled for her first mounting, and
after a while she forgot who she was and who he was and
gave in, letting his fingers have their way, her body
writhing and straining upward against his, aching for
something she couldn't yet understand or recognize until
she found it at last; her arms going upward to hold him
closer, closer, her body straining against his until she came
floating, shuddering back to reality, her eyes flying open.

She was aware, without actually seeing them, of the
blueness of his eyes, the shape and texture of his lips
against hers as he kissed her tenderly, caressingly, his arms
now holding her cradled against him.

"Oh God," she started to whisper, "I didn't know . . ."

"You don't know—not yet, my sweet," he told her
softly. "There's more. You're going to undress me now."

"I—I can't!"

"Yes, you can. There's nothing to be afraid of, you
know that now, don't you? And you've come too far to
back off . . ."

But in the end, because her fingers were shaking and
clumsy, he had to help her. Ginny kept her eyes closed until he forced her to look at him.

"A man's body isn't half as mysterious as a woman's is,"
he teased her. "You have the advantage, love, of being
able to keep your feelings better hidden."

"Oh!" she said softly, half-afraid, when he put her hand
on him; and he laughed.

"Is that all you have to say? You were more vocal a
short while ago."

"Oh, don't! I—you make me feel—I am embarrassed, I
suppose. Is that so strange?"

"All right, honey—I won't rush you. Let's start from
the top. Touch me—or aren't you curious any longer?"

Shyly, hesitantly, she reached out with both hands and
put them against his chest, under the shirt he still wore,

running her fingers along muscles that ridged under them.
Her exploration stopped abruptly.

"You—there is a scar, right here—you've been
wounded?"

"Bullet wound. And if you keep on you'll find more
scars—mostly knives or bullets. You see what a reckless
life I lead?"

"You make me feel reckless too."

She whispered the words and he turned over onto his
side and began kissing her again, his fingers moving very
lightly over the skin of her back and thighs.

This time, when she had found her breath again, she
became bolder, she found herself wanting to touch him,
wanting to become as familiar with his hard man's body
as he was with hers. Her hands moved impatiently, pulling
the shirt away from him, finding more scars, muscles that
moved under her fingers, and then finally, more slowly,
over his flat, hard-muscled belly, feeling him stiffen and
catch his breath.

The knowledge that she, with her untaught hands, could
excite him as much as he'd excited her, made her brave.
Her hand slipped lower, hesitated, and then touched, held
him.

"Oh, Ginny!" he half-groaned, and then added more
lightly, "there—that wasn't too bad, was it? No—don't
take your hand away, not yet—not until I've taught you
what to do with it when you have it—"

His hand taught her the motion and he began kissing
her again; hard and almost brutally this time.

She felt him nudge her over onto her back and her
hands dropped away from him as his tongue started to
trace patterns over her flesh, making it tingle. This time,
she let him part her thighs without a murmur, and his
hands were gentle between them. But when his head
moved lower, Ginny felt her body arch with shock—her
fingers caught his hair and she could almost have
screamed.

"No! Oh, please, Steve, *don't*—I don't think—"

"For God's sake, Ginny, you're as beautiful down there
as—ah, hell—" he seemed to catch himself, and his body
slid, slowly and reluctantly upward over hers, his weight
pinning her down helplessly.

"I'm going too fast for you, I guess, but it's damned
hard not to—it's damned hard to remember you're—"

She felt the molding of his body against hers, the hardness and impatience of him, and she was suddenly as tired of the waiting as he was.

"I don't want to be a virgin any longer. I want to know, Steve—"

"All right honey, all right—let's put an end to your damned virginity then—"

His knees were between her thighs, holding them apart. His hands held hers, and she felt his body rest against hers for a moment before it was lifted, poised, and then, as he began to penetrate her, his mouth stopped her moans.

He was gentle at first, as he'd promised, and very slow—lulling her into an almost-security until that final, terrible thrust like a knife inside her, making her body heave upward in agony, her scream lost and muffled against his encroaching lips. He stayed inside her without moving, embedded in her, his body a part of hers, and then, in another minute he began to move again, inexorably and steadily, ignoring her struggles which gave way, gradually, as the pain lessened and finally disappeared, to a kind of stunned complaisance.

Why had he changed so fast, from gentleness to that final, fierce hurt? Ginny lay under him, panting, her eyes open and staring up into his face until he released her wrists and told her to put her arms around him.

"You—but you hurt me!" she whispered accusingly, even while she was already obeying him, her arms clinging to him.

"It'll never hurt again, love—it'll only get better . . ."

She felt his hand on her breasts—his movements quickened, and then suddenly her body was moving with his, matching his pace and his rhythms, and she was discovering that he was right—there was no more pain; only the urgent, driving motion of his body as he took her with him.

Lying there against him with his arms still around her, holding her closely, she thought, Nothing can ever be the same again—nothing, and then, listening to the sound of his quickened breathing, Now I *know* what it is, to have a man—this is what it's like. . . .

It felt strange to remember that only a few weeks ago he had been a cold, hard and rather frightening stranger—a man she had disliked and mistrusted; and tonight, he was her lover. Ginny found herself wondering about all the other women he must have had, might have made love to as tenderly as he had made love to her. Had it been this way with that woman, the one he'd called Frenchie? And then while he still held her cradled in his arms she felt him begin to move within her again, and she did not want to think of anything but the fact that he wanted her, and he had made it wonderful and not at all frightening, and he must love her, he must, or he would not hold her this way, kissing her softly, calling her "love."

Her hands slipped down his back and felt the tensing and untensing of his muscles—up again to touch the long hair at the back of his neck that curled against her fingers.

Very gradually, Ginny felt the cadence of his breathing and his thrusting into her increase, and by instinct, she matched her movements to his. She felt again the now familiar warmth and pulsing in her loins and her own body's arching twisting movements as he took her to forgetfulness and fulfillment and back.

And afterwards she was so weak, her limbs so lifeless that she had hardly the strength left to return his kisses or to protest when he took a clean neckerchief, wet it from his canteen and sponged her hot, perspiring body very gently—the cold wetness making her gasp as he drew the damp cloth across her breasts, over her belly, and even between her thighs.

He helped her dress, over her inarticulate murmurings that she did not want to move yet, she was too tired. . . .

"If you stayed here with me, I'd be tempted to make love to you all night," he said softly, half teasingly. And then, more soberly, "have you forgotten the Apaches out there? Better go to your wagon and try to get some sleep."

He took her as far as her wagon, kissing her lightly, and she had to be content with that—that, and the fact that he stood there watching until she had crawled back inside and pulled the flap down behind her.

Chapter Fifteen

The Apache attack came with the first streaks of light—seeming no more than a kind of vapor that turned the edges of dark blue night sky to a paler, more translucent blue. They were already under the wagon then—Ginny and Sonya and Tillie—still half-asleep, protesting at having been awakened so long before dawn. Heavy boxes and cases protected them, with only the merest slits between them for rifle barrels. It was safer under the wagon, Pop Wilkins had explained. And there would be men with them. They were prepared for the Indians—waiting for them.

And yet, when the attack came, its initial onslaught coming from all sides, it only seemed as if it was a herd of wild horses that galloped towards them. There was a slight, puzzled pause until someone, Steve? Paco? yelled:

"Start shooting, you damned fools! This is it!"

Peering through one of the slits, Ginny saw the brown, squat bodies of the Apache warriors who led the horses, running almost as fast as the animals until they swung their bodies onto horseback with derisive yells.

The fusillade of rifle fire that followed deafened her. She was aware of being pushed aside and told to stay out of the way, and after that, for a while there was fortunately no more time for thinking or being afraid, for she and Tillie were too busy reloading the hot, smoking guns and rifles that were tossed aside when their chambers were emptied.

It became automatic, after the first fumbling efforts. No time to feel hands blister and burn from touching hot metal, no time to wonder what might happen if somehow a bullet or an arrow found its way into the wagon.

Sonya too, was using a rifle; and after the first time that Steve Morgan had snapped, "Take your time—make sure every shot counts!" she seemed quite cool and calm, although her shoulder must have been sore and bruised from the recoil of the rifle each time she fired.

Ginny had no time to feel jealous over Sonya and Steve being so close—their shoulders were almost touching. At least he was here, with them—she had never been more relieved than when she had seen him come sliding under their wagon in a kind of a running leap from outside.

Once or twice she was aware of the thud of bullets striking the boxes that protected them—the firing seemed continuous, intermingled with wild shouts and yells from Indians and defenders alike.

There was a short lull in the firing after the first two or three waves of attackers had been beaten back, with several brown bodies lying quite close to the wagons. Ginny did not even dare think how many of themselves might be dead as well—some of the same men who had exchanged smiles with her or touched their hats when she passed—it was still not quite believable that this was happening.

"They've gone already?" she heard Sonya ask excitedly, and it had been on the tip of her tongue to ask the same question, but now she was aware that Steve Morgan was shaking his head grimly as he reloaded his revolver.

"They're not through yet. They'll be back—so don't take your eyes off that tall grass out there. No Indians will leave their dead behind if they can help it."

The Apaches had obviously not been prepared for the strength nor the preparedness of the wagon train's defenders, but caution did not in any way dim the fury of their next wave of attack. This time they used more guile. Some of the warriors dashed forward on horseback, but others, hidden by clumps of long grass, snaked forward

half crouched on foot, or on their bellies under cover of
the more obvious attackers.

This time, some of the brown-skinned warriors gained
the inner circle, crawling between the chained wagons
with screams of triumph. From somewhere Ginny heard a
man scream—then a rattling burst of shots and a cry,
"We got him!"

"Keep firing!" Steve Morgan said quite calmly to the
suddenly shaking Sonya. His eyes swept over Ginny.
Crouched almost frozen, her nerves still jangling from the
shouts of pain and anger that seemed to come from everywhere.

"You too—you can shoot at anything you see—let Tillie
reload."

Without waiting for her reply he had already swung
around to guard their soft underbelly—the "safe" side of
their small, improvised shelter.

It seemed unbelievable that she, who had been in Paris,
safe and happy, only a few months ago now sat crouched
under a wagon in the middle of nowhere with blistered
hands and powder smudges on her face—trying to fire a
gun at enemies she could not even see.

"Keep firin', keep 'em off!"

Was that really Pop Wilkin's voice, now hoarse and
almost unrecognizable in the heat of the battle?

There was a thud, like that made by a body, against
their wagon and Sonya screamed. Ginny felt the empty
gun drop from her hands, she had barely the strength to
take the freshly loaded rifle that Tillie handed her.

In spite of her orders, in spite of her own fear she
turned around, and Steve had disappeared. There was a
strange, almost liquid, rattling scream just outside, and
Ginny's face blanched with fear.

"Oh, Gawd, someone jes had his throat cut," Tillie
moaned, and above the sound of firing Sonya, no longer
either calm nor composed screamed at her, "Will you shut
up, you silly creature?" And then as Ginny, the loaded
rifle gripped in her hand, started to crawl outside, Sonya
called again, her voice high with fear, "Ginny—no!"

She kept crawling, driven by some instinct outside
herself that was stronger than fear, to freeze, still on her
knees just beyond the shelter of the wagon.

Not two yards from her lay the still, twisted body of an
Apache, the streaks of war paint garish, his eyes staring

sightlessly. He was an old man; there were streaks of gray in the hair held by a headband elaborately patterned with beads.

Just beyond, two men locked in a silent, gasping combat, rolled over and over on the dry, sandy ground. She saw the glint of knives—and noticed for the first time that one of the men was Steve Morgan, the other an Apache.

"Oh God!" Ginny whispered aloud. She lifted the gun in her hand, and it felt so heavy she wanted to let it drop. For she didn't dare use it . . . and then something made her look up, and she saw Carl Hoskins standing watching, from just a short distance away.

"Carl—do something!" she screamed, but he didn't move—there was a strange, almost gloating expression on his face.

"Morgan can take care of himself," he muttered,. and then in an almost dazed voice, "You all right, Ginny? I heard a scream."

She ignored him, her eyes again fixed on the silent struggling combatants. Steve's shirt was cut to ribbons—she could see the straining of his muscles as he and the other man grasped each other's wrists, each denying the other the chance to use his knife. What had he done with his revolver? There was blood everywhere—on him, on his antagonist, and they fought, the two of them, like wild animals, engaged in their own private war while another one went on all around them.

An arrow missed Ginny by inches, and she did not even scream, merely looked at it stupidly until Carl, diving across the space that separated them, knocked her backwards.

"Ginny, for God's sake, take cover!"

Pushing her ahead of him, he crawled into the small space where Sonya and Tillie lay huddled.

"Start firing! Here, give me that gun!"

Carl snatched a gun from Tillie and began to fire through the slitted opening, and Ginny stubbornly taking advantage of his preoccupation, peered outside again.

There was something primitive, elemental, about two men fighting with knives, although she could not have put it into words. Somehow, they had separated, were circling each other, bodies taut with the need to spring, fighting against caution that urged waiting. And somehow, she could sense these things, even if the guttural Apache tongue sounded strange to her ears. She knew that they taunted each other, promising each other death.

Again she lifted the gun, and the hammer made a clicking sound, and the warrior sprang for Steve, his knife reflecting the sunlight so that it blinded her for an instant and again, she could not bring herself to fire.

She heard a cry and a grunt, and the Apache fell backward, knife dropping from his hand. Half-dazed, Ginny saw Steve straddle his body, the knife flash upward and down even as she screamed to him, "Don't! Oh, don't!"

He turned to look at her at last, with the blood oozing and trickling from the cuts on his body, and his knife all bloody as well, and his eyes were cold.

"You wanted me to let him live with a knife wound in his belly? He was a warrior, and a warrior should die clean and quick."   :

Without a word, Ginny went back beneath the shelter of the wagon, staying there until again there was a cessation of the firing. While she reloaded for Carl, trying not to notice the reproachful look he gave her, her thoughts tumbled over each other. This was the second time she had seen him kill—and it was worse, much worse with a knife than it had been with a gun. And yet, those same hands had touched her so gently last night, that same body had lain over hers and become part of her—dear God, what kind of man is he? Am I insane to feel this way? And what, exactly, do I feel for Steve Morgan?

She had time to think about it later—after the Apaches had gone, taking their dead. And this too, strangely enough, was because Steve, arguing firmly with Carl and Pop Wilkins, had insisted.

"They'll keep coming unless we let them take back the bodies of their fallen warriors, even though they know by now we're too strong for them to take. One of you put a white cloth on your rifle barrel—they understand that— and I'll parley with them."

"We've got them now—why should we be the ones to show the white flag?" Carl had been furious, but in the face of the sudden savage light in Steve Morgan's blue eyes even he had given in sullenly in the end.

And so the Apaches had gone, as suddenly and as silently as they had first come in the early light of dawn. And a few hours later, after Paco and Steve had ridden out and returned to report that it was safe to continue their journey, the wagons had begun to roll ahead, just as if nothing had happened.

Two graves, piled with stones, had been left behind to mark their recent battle, and at least five other men who had been wounded rode in the wagons. As she rode in silence beside Sonya, Ginny remembered the short passages that Pop had read from the Bible, and tears stung her eyes again, as they had done earlier. Death and violence! They seemed so far from civilization, so far from all that was dear and familiar, and she realized now, more than ever, how wild and untamed this land still was, with its painted savages who belonged, surely, in another century; and its men who were equally as savage, killing casually and without conscience.

She thought about Steve Morgan, and reason told her that he had had to kill the Apache, that it was only the fact that she had seen it happen that had frightened and revolted her so. And yet, it only forced her to realize that he was a killer by profession and must have chosen his own way of life. Honesty forced her to admit that he had attracted her from the very first, and that in spite of all her efforts to hate him and stay away from him she had been helplessly drawn by some strange yearning in her own body and nerves that she had not understood before.

A grimace of distaste pulled at the corners of her mouth. Oh, God, she was no better than he, than any loose woman who had no control over her own baser emotions! How easily she had given herself to him— another conquest in a long line of them, no doubt. Well, he would not find her as easy again—not him, nor any other man.

Deliberately, pleading exhaustion and a splitting headache, Ginny stayed in her wagon that night, letting Tillie bring her a cup of light broth that was declicious.

"But—it almost tastes like chicken! How did you manage it, Tillie?"

The girl grinned at her.

"It's rabbit—or somethin' like that. Mist' Morgan, he shot it and gave it to me. Said to tell you he was sorry you're not feelin' so good."

How dare he pretend concern for her now? She had an impulse to fling the cup of steaming broth at Tillie, but instead she said in a voice that was carefully casual, "That was kind of him. Is Mr. Carl all right?" Let Tillie think her main concern was for Carl—the girl always acted as if she knew too much.

"Oh, Mr. Carl, he's real worried about you! Real upset he was, until Miz Brandon calmed him down." Tillie dropped her voice and leaned forward conspiratorially. "Heard him tell Miz Brandon how much he thought of you, miss! Ain't that somethin'? You got the two best lookin' gentlemen courtin' you already—almost got in a fight a while ago, they did, when Mr. Carl said somethin' about lettin' those Injuns get off so lightly today . . ."

Ginny sat up with a jerk, almost spilling the broth over herself.

"They almost got in a fight? Oh, God, Carl won't stand a chance against him if they do!"

"Thought you liked Mist' Morgan best."

The girl was sly—Ginny longed to give her a set down, but uncertainty as to whether Tillie had been awake last night and had seen her leave the wagon, made her bite back the angry words that sprang to her lips.

"Mr. Morgan is—an unusual man, but he is *not* a gentleman. I'll be glad when we finally reach El Paso."

But would she be?

In the days that followed, Ginny was often to ask herself that same question. There were no more Indian attacks, and everything went smoothly, even the crossing of the Pecos River. Carl Hoskins made constant excuses to ride beside their wagon, and in the evenings, when they made camp he courted Ginny in earnest, undaunted by her flimsy evasions as to why they should not wander off into the darkness alone, or talk of anything as serious as an engagement between them.

"But this is hardly a natural situation," she would tell him, "and we do not really know each other yet. Besides, Papa would be furious with us both if he thought—"

"Yes, yes, of course I understand! Ginny, I know you are right, and so logical, my stubborn little darling. But I have fallen quite hopelessly in love with you, and nothing will change my mind."

And she would think, if he only knew! How he would despise me—yes, he'd change his mind, all right. Perhaps he'd ask me to be his mistress then, but never his wife!

Back in Paris, how glibly she had declared to her closest, most intimate friends that of all things, she would like to become a famous courtesan.

"Marriage," she had declared vehemently, "is only another form of slavery. Why should I have to put up with his mistresses and be saddled with a child every year, not daring to take a lover of my own? I would like to be able to choose my own way of life, my own destiny, like any man can, merely because he is a man."

How facile it all sounded now, and how naive! She lived in a man's world, a world that put women on pedestals and worshipped them only as long as they conformed to accepted standards of behavior for women. Her virginity, that despised tiny piece of membrane that had sealed her away from any man but the right one, had been given away too lightly and too easily to the wrong man. And it galled her to think that he, Steve Morgan, had not even attempted to court her. He had made no declarations of love, no promises.

"I want you—" he had declared flatly and uncompromisingly—not, as she might have wished to hear, "I love you." No, and worse yet, he had not even shown her the respect due to her position or her inexperience. His kisses had been rough and demanding, he had treated her as if she were a cheap dance-hall girl, and she had let him, had been crazy enough to want more, to allow him, of all people, to be the one to satisfy her curiosity.

Ginny had been determined to ignore him and to avoid his presence as much as possible; but being feminine it irritated her unaccountably to find that far from seeking her out, or trying to coax her into a repetition of what she still thought of as "that night," he seemed to keep out of her way quite purposefully.

She was becoming used to Carl's kisses now, although they did not stir her in any way, and she would not let him take any further liberties beyond touching his lips to hers.

Still, there was a demon inside her that seemed to sit detached from the reasoning, logical part of her mind at times—nagging at her with the secret thought that she did not enjoy Carl's kisses at all, and had certainly responded to Steve Morgan's—that even now, on some nights, her body ached with the need for something, for the feel of lips and hands on her, for the sweet sense of dispossession she had felt when he had so craftily built her desires up until they were unbearable and then had slaked them with his body.

Like the others on the wagon train, Ginny counted the
days until they would reach El Paso, but for a different
reason. The wagon train would stop for two or three
whole days at El Paso, to rest the cattle and replenish
their supplies. And it was here, if everything went well,
that they would hear from an emissary of the Emperor
Maximilian. Her father would be arranging matters from
Washington even now—and if all materialized as he'd
hoped, she and Sonya might find themselves journeying to
Mexico City as guests of the emperor and empress.

"You, Ginny, with your important connections at the
French court," and here her father's eyes had twinkled at
her, "you shall be my little Ambassadress. Remember to
give your most special smiles to Marshal Bazaine, for he,
as commander of the French armies, is the real power behind the throne."

It had all seemed so exciting, listening to her father tell
of all his plans and his ambitions. Like something from a
novel by Monsieur Dumas. She had imagined herself as
the cloaked heroine, hurrying into danger on a vital errand—but the Indian attack had taught her, at least, the
unpleasant fact that danger was by no means pleasant;
that the thought of dying, even for a cause, was even
more terrifying.

Suppose they left the train at El Paso, using some
trumped-up, last-minute excuse (but no, she thought annoyedly, there would be no need for that, there would be
a message from her father waiting and he would have arranged everything, leaving nothing to chance, as was his
way) what would happen?

What would happen to the rest of them? Would Steve
Morgan miss her presence, or wonder why she had
changed her mind about California so abruptly?

To Sonya, when they discussed it, it all seemed unimportant.

"We do not even need to give them any explanations,
Ginny dear. After all, they were hired by your father to
take a wagon train and some cattle to California, not to
question us! We will simply announce that we intend to
stay on in El Paso because your father has changed his
plans and will join us there. Or—or—well, we will think
of something, I'm sure!"

How wonderful to have Sonya's sweet, unruffled
nature—to be so very certain that nothing could possibly

go wrong! But at least, she would tell herself firmly, she would not have to see Steve Morgan again; to be afraid of looking up and meeting his cold, sapphire blue eyes and feel herself jolted all the way down her spine by an unnameable, unthinkable yearning to feel his mouth against hers again, and hear his voice call her "love."

Chapter Sixteen

On the last night they would spend out in the lonely, rugged Texas plains before they reached El Paso, storm clouds began to gather overhead, adding to the strange feeling of gloominess and depression in Ginny's heart.

Lightning slashed at the darkening sky overhead, and the rattling of thunder made Pop Wilkins predict pessimistically that cattle were nearly always spooked during a bad storm.

"An' them Texas storms is the worst of all I've seen," he added. Carl, looking anxious, had hurried off with some of the men to see to their herd, and Sonya put Ginny's moodiness down to the fact that she missed his presence by the fire. Trying to console her sullen stepdaughter, Sonya squeezed her arm and whispered that she would soon forget her depression when they reached El Paso.

"And dearest, if you are thinking that Carl will forget you if we decide to travel to Mexico, then you must not—he's told me himself how much he cares about you. In fact," she added teasingly, "he's even asked me to speak to your papa and feel him out! But I'm afraid that it will be you who will soon forget him if we visit the emperor's court at Chapultepec. I hear it is magnificent, and there will be all the handsome officers from France and Belgium and Austria there—indeed, there'll be diplomats from all over the world! Just think how exciting it'll be, Ginny! All the balls and receptions we'd attend—and there's even the chance that your father might decide to join us there, you know."

Ginny did not have the heart to spoil Sonya's own excitement, but before she could frame some ambiguous answer she had felt his presence. Steve Morgan, who had avoided their campfire so assiduously on preceding nights had suddenly come up behind them, and now, without a word of apology he jackknifed his long legs to sit easily beside her.

He walks as softly as an Indian, Ginny thought angrily, noticing that tonight he wore knee-high Indian moccasins instead of boots. Ignoring the unwanted thudding of her heart, she found herself wondering how much of their conversation he had heard. And how dared he come up so stealthily? How dared he calmly assume that she would not mind his sitting beside her?

Biting her lip to hide her confusion, Ginny cast a warning glance at Sonya and faced him boldly.

"Why, Mr. Morgan, you're quite a stranger these days, aren't you?" She caught the look of amusement in his eyes, the lifted eyebrow and stumbled on quickly, hating the betraying color that sprang to her cheeks, "Mrs. Brandon and I were just discussing how strange it is that we are so very close to Mexico. It is only across the river from El Paso, is it not?"

"Yes, ma'am. Look across the Rio Grande and you'll see Mexico. Nice country when they're not fightin' wars over there. You ladies ought to visit it sometime."

He said the words so calmly that it was hard to read any hidden meaning into them. But what had he meant by his suggestion that they should visit Mexico? As if she sensed Ginny's slight hesitation Sonya stepped quickly into the breach.

"I was telling Ginny how exciting it would be to have the opportunity of visiting the Emperor Maximilian's court some day. I hear that Carlotta is an extremely beautiful and intelligent woman, and that they have done wonders for the poor, uneducated people there."

"Don't know about that, ma'am. But sometimes I wonder if those poor uneducated folk in Mexico really prefer a foreign emperor to the president they elected themselves." He caught the surprised glances of both women and shrugged. "Didn't mean to sound rude, of course, but I reckon we wouldn't like it too much if some other country sent their soldiers to keep order around here. In fact, we just got through fightin' a war of our own to keep the country in one piece, didn't we?"

"Mr. Morgan," Ginny said stiffly, her temper high, "I happen to know that the Mexicans themselves invited the French into their country to keep order. It was they who invited Maximilian and Carlotta to Mexico in the first place! Why, I have had the opportunity myself to talk with the very charming Señor Hidalgo in Paris, and he—"

"Miss Brandon, I sure didn't mean to make you mad!" The mocking lights in his eyes belied the smooth apology as he went on, every word enraging Ginny further, "An' I'm certainly not qualified to speak as an intimate of Napoleon's court in Paris. But I do know somethin' about Mexico and its people." He gave her a wicked look. "I'm sure you've heard it said that I'm a half-breed? Well, I guess that's partly true, dependin' on which way you look at it. My mother was Spanish, you see, and I was brought up in Mexico, ever since I was about five years old."

"And you feel that qualifies you to be a spokesman for the Mexican people?"

A trace of impatience came into his voice this time.

"I'm not a spokesman for anyone but myself, Miss Brandon. But I do know it's only the rich folk—the landowners who want to hang onto their big haciendas, and the Church, wantin' to hang onto its lands and powers, and the crooked politicians—those are the Mexicans who wanted Maximilian!" He gave Ginny an unexpectedly bitter look that dumbfounded her. "Those poor uneducated people, ma'am, are the ones doin' the fighting for their freedom and their country back from all the foreign powers that want to grab large chunks of it."

Unexpectedly, almost shocking Ginny, Sonya leaned forward to join in the argument. With her wide blue eyes fixed on Steve Morgan's face, she said sweetly, "Why, Mr. Morgan, you surprise me! You talk like a man with a cause! Next you'll be telling us you intend to go and fight for those—those *Juaristas*, or whatever they are called, who murder and mutilate French soldiers and innocent citizens and call it fighting for their freedom!"

Ginny watched, feeling stunned, as two pairs of blue eyes met and clashed. It must be the storm, what had gotten into Sonya? A strange, taut smile stretched her blond stepmother's lips, even though she shivered at a crash of thunder.

"I had no idea you felt as strongly as you do either," Steve Morgan said softly, and suddenly it was if a shutter had come down over his face, leaving it bleak and unreadable.

"I think this whole argument is pointless and stupid!" Ginny announced loudly, and felt as if she had broken some kind of spell that had held them all.

"You're right, of course!" Sonya said it quickly, with a little laugh. "My goodness, I can't think what got into me!"

"Maybe it's the storm. Most women tend to get kind of nervous when there's a storm coming up."

He said it casually, almost lightly, but Sonya's face grew flushed and she gave a sudden exclamation, her hands tightening on the folds of her gown so that the veins stood out on them.

"I hate storms! They—they terrify me, and remind me of—unpleasant things."

A particularly vivid flash of lightning made her wince and she sprang to her feet.

"I'm going back to the wagon—I'm sorry to be such a coward, but I really can't stay out here in this." She seemed to pull herself together with an effort. "Goodnight, Mr. Morgan. Your argument was—interesting."

He came easily to his feet, leaving Ginny to scramble up by herself.

"I'm sorry if I said anything to upset you, ma'am."

But he didn't sound sorry, Ginny thought angrily—he didn't sound sorry at all! And what had upset Sonya? Was it only the storm?

Sonya was saying stiffly that she wasn't upset by any means, and that it was not necessary for Ginny to come with her just because she was unreasonably afraid of loud noises.

"Carl will be back soon, I'm sure—he'd be sorry if he missed seeing you tonight," she said to Ginny, sounding her sweet, considerate self once more.

Reluctantly, Ginny watched her go, too much aware of Steve Morgan's closeness to her. But I'm not afraid of him, she told herself sternly. I will not let him think that I don't trust myself to be alone with him.

"Would you like to continue our discussion?" she asked him coolly enough. "I can assure you that I am not as easily upset as my stepmother, and storms do not distract me in the least."

She sat down by the fire again, and wondered if she had really noticed a slight hesitation in his manner before he joined her.

"The discussion was pointless—you said so yourself." The note of harshness in his voice made her glance at him in surprise.

"But you seemed to know so much about the Mexicans, why should you feel ashamed of expressing your views?"

He leaned forward without speaking to pour himself a cup of coffee, but Ginny could see a muscle in his jaw twitch as if he fought to hold back words he might regret. Or was it—the thought struck her, making her eyes widen—was it because he felt as disturbed by her presence as she did in his?

Sitting back at that moment he met her glance, and she noticed that he was frowning.

"My views, as you call them, happen to be shared by most of the Mexican people," he said abruptly, as if he had only just heard her question. "But I'm afraid they're not of much importance to many people in this country. For your own sake though, I hope you'll not think of visiting Mexico until it's all over, and there's no more danger for unwary foreign visitors."

"What do you mean—until it's all over? Until what is over?" A pulse pounded in her temples and she told herself it was anger—rage that he should dare presume to advise her. "Really, Mr. Morgan, I'd think you are hardly the person to warn me about danger—and a danger which, in this case, I'm sure does not exist. The French army is more than too much for a few peasants with few or no weapons, I'm sure! And," she continued, her voice rising in spite of herself, "if I do decide to visit Mexico some day you may be sure that I shall do so, without asking anybody's permission first!"

"Mexico, in case you did not know it, is in a state of war!" he said between clenched teeth. "Have you ever been in a war, ma'am? Or seen its effects? And I can assure you that if there's shooting, no one will stop first to make sure whether their targets are male or female! And furthermore—the Mexicans have had their bellyfull of foreigners—it's a matter of time before the *Juaristas* take over the government again, and I'd hate to think of anyone as pretty as you having to face a firing squad, which might well happen if you decide to do anything so stupid and foolhardy as visit Mexico at a time like this!"

"You overheard us then! You're contemptible! How dare you sneak up on other people's private conversations and then presume to butt in?"

His face had grown dark and forbidding with anger, and she thought his eyes almost shot sparks of blue flame at her.

"Goddam it! Do whatever you want, then. And since I don't want to be forced into a fight with your beau right now, I think I'll leave—before I do something I might regret later."

Carl Hoskins came up just as Steve Morgan stalked angrily away, and as they happened to pass each other, Carl had opened his mouth to make some scathing comment. One look at Morgan's face, the dangerous, almost challenging look in his eyes made Carl clamp his jaws together as he made his way towards Ginny. This was no time for a fight—not here, not now—but some day, as he'd already vowed, he'd take care of Steve Morgan!

One look at Ginny's flushed face, with tears of anger making her sea green eyes seem even larger, was almost enough to make Carl change his mind.

"Ginny! What's wrong? What has he said to you? By God, if he's done anything to upset you I'll—"

"Oh, for Heaven's sakes, Carl, there's no need to look so forbidding!" She had spoken more sharply than she had intended, and bit her lip in exasperation. How stupid, to let *him* push her into such a state! How he must be laughing now, as he thought how easily he could upset her.

A tendril of pale copper hair fell across Ginny's cheek and she brushed it away irritably, softening her tone with an effort.

"Oh, Carl, I'm sorry! I didn't mean to snap at you, but—it was only a silly argument, that's all. I'm afraid I let myself get baited into losing my temper."

Mollified, he dropped to the ground beside her, taking

both her hands in his own and stroking them lightly as if he wished to smooth out the tension he could feel in them.

"I hate to see you this way, Ginny . . . all tense and upset. I hate to think that he's done this to you! I'm going to tell him to stay away from you . . . a man like Morgan is worse than an animal, he's no fit company for a lady! Why does he make a point of annoying you this way?"

With an irritated exclamation, Ginny pulled her hands away from his.

"Are you implying that I encourage him to annoy me? Why, I—I've never known a man that I more cordially detest! And if you think . . ."

Carl's handsome face showed amazement at her outbreak; she saw frown lines come to his forehead as he interrupted her quickly and almost roughly.

"Ginny, Ginny! What's gotten into you? I made no such allegation, I know how much you hate that man, almost as much as I despise him and his kind myself! Please, sweetheart, don't let *us* have a quarrel!"

Ginny resorted to subterfuge.

"Forgive me, Carl! I—I swear I don't know what's the matter with me this evening. It—it must be the coming storm. There, I could vow I felt a drop of rain . . ."

Carl could not resist the appeal in her upturned face, those wonderful eyes that still sparkled with tears. He felt masculine and protective, all at once.

Helping her to her feet, Carl took Ginny back to her wagon, and he was surprised and elated by the way she responded to his good-night kiss. Instead of accepting it passively as she usually did she flung her arms around his neck and pressed her body against his. He noticed that she was trembling, and in spite of all his good intentions, he felt his desire for her rise. How tiny her waist felt under his hand, how firm her small breasts thrusting against his chest!

He raised his head to murmur hoarsely to her, but she said urgently,

"Kiss me again, Carl, kiss me!" and then in a small whisper, "I feel so frightened tonight, so lonely, I wish you could stay with me for a while and talk to me—"

With a groan of mingled passion and frustration, Carl bent his head again and kissed her wildly, feeling the aching throbbing in his loins. My God, he was thinking, she doesn't know what she is saying . . . it's only the storm

... but I want her, I've got to have her ... Does she understand what she is doing to me?

Had he known that over his shoulder Ginny had caught a glimpse of Steve Morgan, standing talking to Paco in the shadow of one of the wagons across the circle from them, he would have been even more frustrated.

As it was, half-demented by his own need and Ginny's unexpected surrender, he half-led, half-carried her into the wagon that stood next to hers, piled with boxes and bits of Sonya Brandon's furniture.

Whatever he had let himself hope, Carl found himself disappointed in the end. Inside the darkened interior of the wagon, Ginny's mood of barely suppressed abandonment and ardor seemed to vanish. She suffered him to lie next to her and to touch her breasts very lightly through the thin material of her gown at first, but pulled away from his arms almost immediately, protested in a choked voice that she was afraid, that she did not know what had gotten into her, that he must promise to behave. . . .

They stayed together only about ten minutes, during which time she babbled almost hysterically of how afraid the thunder made her—how exciting the prospect of a journey into Mexico seemed, and then, when he insisted upon knowing, admitted reluctantly that she would miss him very much.

"But you'll forget me, of course. By the time we return you'll have found yourself another sweetheart . . . I know that men are like that."

And in spite of his protests, his insistence that he loved her and wanted more than anything else to make her his wife, she would not commit herself to anything beyond "we'll wait and see; we both have to be very sure first, don't we?"

All in all, it had turned into a most frustrating evening, and by the time Carl had escorted Ginny back to the safety of her own wagon he was in a particularly bad mood.

The storm broke during the night, and did nothing to mend the ragged tempers and frayed nerves of almost every member of the party.

They seemed to turn upon each other, tempers flaring. Cookie complained that Zack did not yet know how to start a proper fire, and the boy overturned a pot of coffee and ran for his horse, declaring that he was a cowhand, and not a cook's helper.

Sonya and Ginny had words, starting when Ginny came back to the wagon at an hour that Sonya declared was ridiculously late, adding that if Ginny did not watch herself she would get the reputation of being cheap; whereupon Ginny retorted fiercely that she had been with Carl, and not Steve Morgan, following her statement by asking oversweetly whether poor Sonya was actually jealous of her?

With compressed lips and backs carefully turned they spent the rest of the night in silence, although neither of them could sleep after the rain started to beat down on the canvas overhead.

Hitching mules to the wagons the next morning, in a slashing downpour, with the ground already boottop-deep mud, was almost chaos. Some of the horses gathered into the roped-off remuda bolted, and Pop Wilkins blamed the wrangler, Dave Fierst, who promptly shouted back that he had a good mind to quit.

Carl Hoskins rode up just then, his black slicker spattered with mud, and demanded wrathfully to know why in hell the wagons weren't moving yet—the herd was restive and ready to stampede right through camp if they didn't hurry it up.

Pop had just opened his mouth to swear when Steve Morgan chose that same unfortunate moment to ride his big black into camp, looking like the devil himself, Pop was to say later, with his head bare and his black hair plastered closely to his skull.

"Goddamit! You're supposed to be holding those cattle. What the hell are you doing here?"

His angry, almost contemptuous tone flicked the raw wound of Carl's own injured vanity, and he lost his temper.

When Ginny, alarmed by Sonya's scream, clambered onto the high seat of their wagon, mindless of the rain that soon soaked her hair and gown, all she could see was two men, both completely covered with mud, slugging it out within a circle of shouting, almost obscenely excited onlookers.

They were both of a similar build and height, and at first it was difficult to make out who was who, particularly since the thick mud was smeared on their faces as well.

But it did not take Ginny long to recognize Steve Morgan—he fought with the raw, vicious fury of an animal. Carl, she knew, fancied himself as a fighter. He had once boasted to her that he had studied boxing, and even Cornish-style wrestling. But Ginny knew, after she had watched for only a few moments, that none of his skill would help him.

She could almost hear the sickening thud of fists against flesh, almost sense the hate that flared between them. They circled, came together, fell and rolled, fought free and struggled onto their feet again. She was reminded of gladiators in a Roman circus, of a fight to the death between two angry leopards.

"Stop them!" Sonya moaned, her hands pressed against her mouth, "for God's sake, why doesn't somebody stop them?"

"Because they're all enjoying it, can't you see that?"

Ginny had meant to be extra nice to Sonya today, to apologize for her temper last night, but her voice came out sharp and high.

She wanted to scream, but not with fear, as Sonya had done. Rather, with the surge of almost primitive excitement that had taken hold of her. Her pulses drummed, her heart beat so loudly and so fast she felt faint. She did not want to watch, but she could not help herself—it was like that day when she had watched Steve and the Apache fight—it was almost like the bullfight she had watched once, wondering then at all the women who leapt to their feet and screamed exultantly for blood. But today, today with the rain streaming down over her face, with the shouts of the men ringing in her ears and the thunder growling somewhere high overhead, she knew how they had felt. She was dimly aware of the heaving chests, the pounding blows, the primitive male encounter there in front of her; and acutely aware of her own body under the drenched, clinging gown she wore. It was as if a kind of insanity had seized her.

There was a cry, a groan, and one of the men stumbled backwards, falling headlong into the mud.

She heard Paco's warning shout, "Steve! That's enough!" And the man who had remained standing, half-crouched as if he was going to spring forward again, to finish it; hesitated, straightened, and walked away.

It was over then. She threw herself from the wagon

seat, ignoring Sonya's frantic cry, and ran forward. Her instincts were driving her, it was to Steve Morgan she ran, oblivious of the rain and the mud and the staring faces that followed her stumbling progress. And then he turned around, and she saw the cold anger in his dark blue eyes, turning them almost black—the hateful twist of his mouth under the black mustache.

"What do you want, Miss Brandon? Shouldn't you run to your lover instead?"

The words registered in her mind like a blow, stunning her. Without thinking she swung her hand outward and up, only realizing she had slapped him when she heard the crack of the blow and felt the tingling ache in her fingers.

Somebody gasped—she saw an expression of shock and fury spring into his eyes and thought for a moment that he was going to strike her back.

"You brute—you coward—that was for what you did to Carl—" She could barely force the words from between her stiff, cold lips, and she panted as if she had been running all morning.

He stood there without a word, his lips taut with fury, and suddenly she could not bear to look at him, nor to see the ugly red mark her hand had left on his face.

Swinging on her heel, Ginny ran towards Carl and fell to her knees beside him. The rain tasted salty—it was sometime before she realized that she was crying, the tears gushing from her eyes like the rain itself.

Chapter Seventeen

Captain Michel Remy, Comte d'Arlingen, had been waiting impatiently in the small Mexican village across the river from El Paso for the Brandon wagon train to arrive. Part of his impatience was due to the fact that he had been in this hell hole for two days already, and it was growing more and more dangerous for French soldiers to linger this close to the United States border. The *Juaristas* were everywhere these days—in spite of their lack of weapons and lack of organization they had proved themselves a stubborn bunch, striking in the most unexpected places. In fact, as Captain Remy gloomily contemplated his half-empty bottle of wine, he was thinking of the rumors he'd heard just before leaving Mexico City, that they would soon have to evacuate Chihuahua and drop back to Durango, leaving the *Juaristas* more or less in full possession of most of the north.

He frowned angrily. It was incredible! Here they were, the invincible armies of France, the Mexican Irregulars, troops from Austria and Belgium as well—and they still had not wrested a complete victory for Maximilian over the ragged forces of Juarez. As one of Marshal Bazaine's aides, he had of course heard that the United States was in sympathy with Juarez, and since their civil strife had ended they were supplying arms and ammunition to Juarez, and turning a blind eye to the gunrunner who operated on both sides of the border. It was too bad! If only people in America and the rest of Europe and yes, even in Paris itself, realized what a wretchedly poor country this Mexico really was! The peasants were starving, their living conditions worse than those in Europe during the Middle Ages, and still they stubbornly rejected all the reforms and the help that poor Maximilian wanted to give them. The only civilized Mexicans were, of course, the *gachupines*, who were proudly jealous of their European descent and took care that their bloodlines were not mixed with Indian or *mestizo*.

Not legally, that is, Captain Remy thought wryly to himself, remembering a certain Carmen in Cuernevaca, with pale amber skin and marvelous tawny eyes. Very little Indian in that one! She boasted of the fact that her *padre* was one of the richest *hacendados* in the area.

From Carmen, Michel's thoughts wandered, in natural order, to Ginette. Ginnie Brandon, whom he had always called Ginette, ever since the night he fell in love with her at the theatre, in Paris.

He had known Pierre, of course, from childhood. And remembered Ginnie as a thin-faced girl, with extraordinarily large green eyes. Pierre's *petite cousine*—he had not paid her any attention. Why should he? And then he had enlisted in Napoleon's army, had come home on leave one winter, and seen Ginette. But my God, what a change! She had grown beautiful, *ravissante!* And when he had visited her box to renew his acquaintance with Pierre, what self-possession! It was he who had stumbled over his words like a green schoolboy. She had been charming, teasing, so sure of herself!

If he had not been unexpectedly recalled to his regiment he might have persuaded her to marry him. Certainly, in spite of all her other admirers, she had seemed to prefer him. Even Pierre, who, for a mere cousin, seemed inordinately jealous of Ginnie's *beaux cavalieres*, had not seemed to mind too much.

"We'll write," she had promised him when he left. She had cried, but had firmly refused to elope with him the previous night. Not surprisingly, he reflected somewhat bitterly, the letters had dwindled to nothing in about six months. After all, he was a soldier, he was not much of a letter writer himself, and how could a man court a girl who was many thousands of miles away, in the midst of all the gaiety in Paris?

But now, soon, he'd see her again. His Ginette. He wondered if she had changed, hoped she had not. *Ma foi,* would this waiting never end?

If Michel Remy had but known it, his waiting ended that same night. While he was engaged in his melancholy reflections, the wagon train rolled into El Paso right in the middle of the thunderstorm that raged on both sides of the river.

He arrived at the only decent hotel the town boasted, masquerading as a civilian; fatalistically aware that he might, if he was unlucky enough, be arrested and shot as a spy. But at least, he thought with a surge of self-confidence, his English was almost perfect, and he was wearing a suit of clothes that was impeccably cut by the best tailor in Paris.

Most of his misgivings were dispelled when he was greeted by Madame Brandon, a tiny, exquisitely pretty blond woman with large china blue eyes and an enchanting laugh. A man named Hoskins, an American who seemed unusually taciturn and sported a bruised and battered face, escorted him across the river. Tactfully, Michel did not mention the bruises, but he wondered what had happened to the man. These Americans, always fighting! Even in Mexico City, they continued to fight their civil war that had just ended—sometimes with cutting words and sometimes with weapons. Secretly, he sided with the Southerners, who were gentlemen. Now if they had won the war, Maximilian's troubles would have been ended!

As they waited for Ginny, Captain Remy noted uneasily that the small hotel dining room seemed unusually crowded. Sonya Brandon, as if she had sensed his unrest, whispered to him that these were only men from their own wagon train, celebrating the end of part of their long journey.

"This is the first town we've been in since we left San Antonio!" she said, shuddering prettily. And she assured him that she had already mentioned him as a friend of her husband's from California, so he must not worry.

"Ginny does not know that it is you who are here," she confided. "I have told her only that the French officer who is to escort us has come. Have you known her very long, Monsieur Remy?"

They had agreed that she would use the less formal mode of address, and he was relieved that she had not forgotten. And then, his answer was lost in the sudden beating of his heart as Ginny Brandon seemed to float down the stairs.

How could he have imagined she would change? If anything, she was even more beautiful. She wore a green velvet gown cut in the latest fashion, one that he knew at once could have been tailored only by Worth. No crinolines for his Ginette—following the style set by the Empress Eugenie her gown's neckline plunged low in front to show the bold curve of her bosom, and clung all the way to the hip, to be swept into artful folds of drapery at the back. Her hair was piled at the back of her head, high up, and it shone under the lights with the pale, coppery sheen he remembered so well. A single curl fell down over her shoulder, and she wore emeralds in her ears that were outshone by her eyes.

Michel thought that every man in the room gave a sigh of sheer pleasure at her beauty. Certainly none of the fine ladies, some of them titled, that adorned the Emperor Maximilian's court at Chapultepec could outshine her! He rose to his feet, their eyes met, and he could see how hers widened in stunned disbelief.

Then she gave a little cry of greeting and sweeping her long skirts up carelessly with one hand, she ran down the few steps that remained. With an effort he remembered his manners and the gaping faces that surrounded them, and meant only to kiss her hand. But she came to him artlessly, and flung her arms around his neck, crying out his name.

"Michel! Is it really you? Oh, but I cannot believe it, you of all people!"

He bent his head almost without thinking, and felt her lips cling to his. It was only with an effort that he forced himself to draw away. Ginny chattered happily to him in French as they were seated, and he could not believe his luck. She called him her love, her dearest angel, and vowed he had broken her heart when he left Paris. Michel was overwhelmed.

They had champagne with dinner, and neither of them noticed what they ate. Ginny drank more than she ought, until she felt her head was swimming—from a distance, she seemed to hear her own laughter, sounding high and forced in her ears. But Michel Remy noticed nothing, except that Ginette was happy to see him. She seemed to glow with health and vitality, and he thought the warm, peach-colored tint of her skin suited her much better than the fashionable paleness of complexion that most ladies cultivated. Her face was a trifle thinner than he remembered it, of course, but this only served to emphasize the fine-boned look of her face, with its willful mouth and enormous green eyes. Michel could hardly take his eyes off her all evening, and he was not the only one.

Carl Hoskins sat glowering at the same table, and even Sonya's whispered explanation that Ginny had known the French captain from childhood did nothing to alleviate his growing anger and frustration. What was the matter with her this evening? She was acting like a—a trollop! And to add to his humiliation, she ignored him almost completely, under the eyes of half the men in the wagon train who knew that he had been her beau. Bad enough that Steve Morgan should have the audacity to be here as well, together with his friend Davis and two brightly dressed females of obviously easy virtue. It was much worse knowing that Ginny would be leaving for Mexico within the next few days, and that Captain Remy, and not he, would be the one to accompany her there.

As Ginny's spirits seemed to soar higher, along with the champagne she consumed, Carl's sank lower. It was with an effort that he forced himself to sit tight during the meal—soon after it was over, he excused himself, explaining tersely that they had to make an early start the next day. Ginny hardly noticed him go.

If she was hardly aware of Carl Hoskins any longer, Ginny was, in spite of her champagne haze, very much aware of Steve Morgan's presence in the same room. The memory of his cutting words had stayed with her, even after they had reached El Paso, flooding her with a sense of humiliation each time she thought about it. She was glad, glad that she had slapped his angry, sneering face—glad each time she recalled the barely suppressed fury in his eyes after she had done so.

It was with a sense of shock, therefore, that she looked up to find he had had the effrontery to approach their table; making his false, polite excuses to Sonya and ignoring her.

"Don't mean to disturb you, Mrs. Brandon, but I understand you won't be going on to California with the wagons, after all. So I thought it better that you should hear this first from me—Pa ɔ Davis will be leading them when they get started tomorrow. I'm quitting—I'll be leavin' for New Mexico tonight."

"But Mr. Morgan, I don't understand! My husband. . . ."

"The reason your husband hired me, ma'am, was because you and Miss Brandon here were going along. You don't need two scouts, nor a hired gun, to get the herd and the rest of the men through to California. Naturally, I won't expect to be pickin' up the rest of the money I was to have been paid when we got to California."

"Naturally!" Ginny heard her own voice, sounding sharp and almost shrewish. "I suppose it was too much for my father—for any of us to expect a man of Mr. Morgan's sort to be gentleman enough to fulfill the terms of an unwritten contract." If she had expected to wither him with the wealth of scorn in her voice, she was mistaken. He had at least deigned to notice her for the first time in the evening, but he met her vituperation with a carelessly raised eyebrow, waiting politely for her to continue.

"Ginny!" Sonya's voice was horror-stricken—she looked appealingly at Steve. "Mr. Morgan, my stepdaughter is not herself. The strain of the journey has been too much for her, and since our old friend Monsieur Remy is here we have decided that he will accompany us to San Francisco by stagecoach—he had been visiting relatives in De Hanis, you see, and . . ."

"I'm sure Mr. Morgan isn't in the least interested in our feelings or our plans, Sonya dear! But since you are here, Mr. Morgan, how very remiss of me not to present our friend Michael Remy, the Comte d'Arlingen—Mr. Steve Morgan, our *ex*-scout."

Sonya all but wrung her hands—Michel Remy, sensing the tension that almost hummed in the air, without understanding it, came swiftly and rather uncomfortably to his feet, extending his hand.

"I am happy to meet you, sir. But please—" he cast an unhappy look at Ginny, "I don't use my title in this country. It is not—very democratic is it?"

Steve Morgan shrugged, clasping the Frenchman's hand.

"Why not? Us simple folk here kinda go for titles, since we don't have any ourselves." He looked again at Sonya and bowed. "My apologies again, ma'am. But to tell the truth—it's better this way all around, especially since Hoskins and I can't get along. Goodbye, Mrs. Brandon— Miss Brandon. Mr. Remy."

Words struggled to Ginny's lips, but she dared not say them, and bit them back. She was very aware that Michel was watching her quizzically, that Sonya was flushed with embarrassment. Only Steve Morgan, his casual farewells made, retained his composure as he left them—going back to his table to join his companions.

Ginny was gayer than ever. Half-laughing, she whispered to Michel that indeed she apologized for being so naughty and so rude, but she had taken an un- conscionable dislike to this Mr. Morgan, who was the rudest, most insufferable man she had ever met in her life and needed a set down.

And thank goodness I never need lay eyes on him again!" She added. "Why, if Sonya would only stop frown- ing at me, even she would agree that she's relieved. Come, be honest, you did not like him either, did you?"

"That is no excuse for bad manners, Ginny!" Sonya said firmly, but she allowed herself to be coaxed into accepting another glass of champagne shortly afterwards, and the rest of the evening passed quite pleasantly and without further incident.

Captain Remy escorted both ladies to their room before going to his own, which was at the end of the same passageway. Before he fell asleep, he congratulated him- self again upon his incredible luck at having been present in the marshal's office, when the matter of an escort for Senator Brandon's wife and daughter had come up. He had volunteered immediately, of course, and when Bazaine had learned of his previous acquaintance with Ginette he had finally agreed. The gold, of course, was his main responsibility, he must try to remember that, but his thoughts stayed with Ginette, and the long weeks that they would spend together. This time, he told himself, he would have her. He would persuade her to marry him, to arrive in Mexico City as his fiancée, before any of the other of- ficers there had a chance to lay eyes on her. And because he was a man, with a man's virile appetites, Michel Remy

thought also of other things—of how it would feel to hold
Ginette's warm, softly accepting body against his, to initi-
ate her into the rites of love. . . . He was a gentleman, of
course, and he intended to marry her, but perhaps, who
knew? During the long weeks that they would be thrown
together there would be warm Mexican nights, the scent
of flowers in the night air, the moon, and the mariachi
players to serenade them. Perhaps they would have their
honeymoon first. Now that he had met her again, he was
impatient to possess her completely.

If Ginny had any idea that Michel had already planned
her future, and her seduction, she kept it to herself during
the days that followed, even in the face of Sonya's growing curiosity. Sonya, since she had learned that the handsome Captain Remy also happened to be a count, actually
encouraged Ginny's flirtation with him. He had a title, and
even though he had chosen to become a soldier, he was
rich—Ginny had already told her so. Even William could
have no possible objection to that kind of match for his
daughter! Sonya felt sorry for Carl, when she happened to
think about him, but she felt sure that Carl would soon
find a girl in California who was better suited to him. He
was a serious and ambitious young man, and she had liked
him, but Ginny was really too much of a butterfly—too
giddy and inconstant for Carl. And certainly—every time
Sonya thought about it she sighed with relief—it was a
good thing that Ginny had so quickly gotten over her
strange friendship with Steve Morgan. That relationship
would have led to nothing good, and no one knew it as
well as she did. It was just as well that Ginny had seen
him kill that Apache and wakened to seeing what kind of
savage, uncivilized ne'er-do-well he was.

Ginny herself went through the first two days of their
travel into Mexico in a kind of daze. She had drunk far
too much champagne the night before they left El Paso,
and had awaked with a terrible, splitting headache the
next morning.

And then, to make matters worse, she had had a most
unpleasant encounter with Carl Hoskins, who had forced
his way into her room after Sonya had dressed and gone
downstairs—demanding to know exactly how he stood
with her, and what Mr. Remy meant to her. She had actually felt ashamed of herself then, and sorry for herself too,
for Carl was really angry and upset. He had called her a

flirt and a tease and a little baggage, and then, when she
had burst into tears had grabbed her hands and kissed
them, apologizing—begging her not to forget him, to
remember that he loved her.

To be rid of him and the whole ugly situation he had
placed her in, she had ended up promising to do nothing
drastic about Michel—to give herself, and him time.

When Carl had finally gone, Ginny had watched the
wagon train rumble out of town in a thin drizzle, and had
found herself feeling curiously bereft. She hoped that they
would all reach California safely, that there would be no
more graves left somewhere in the arid, empty wastelands
of New Mexico and Arizona. Yes, she would actually miss
them all, even old Pop Wilkins, with his gossipy ways.

Together with Michel, they had left El Paso in their
own wagon under cover of an early, rain-swept night. The
French soldiers who were to be their escort were waiting
on the other side of the river, and the gold transferred
quickly without incident to the compartment under the
floorboards of the "diligencia" that they would travel in
for the next few weeks.

Adjusting to the swaying, jouncey motion of the coach
as it lumbered over the bad Mexican roads had not been
difficult for Ginny and Sonya; used as they were to their
wagon. But Ginny, who had ridden on horseback every
day, found it almost intolerable to be cooped up for hours
on end in the cramped, stuffy interior of the diligence.

It was true that Michel often dropped back from his
position with the rest of the small troop, to ride alongside
and keep them company; but even his droll stories of life
at the Emperor Maximilian's court in Chapultepec, his attempts to help Ginny with her rusty Castilian Spanish
(which he assured her was still spoken by the *gachupines*
and the better-class Mexicans) did nothing to dispel the
feeling she had of being stifled.

Michel kept assuring them that they were safe—they
had nothing to worry about, but his reassurances made
even Sonya feel more nervous than ever.

They were travelling through rough arid country that
reminded Ginny of Texas, but at the small *cantina* where
they had stopped to water the horses and stretch their legs
on the first day of their journey, Ginny had overheard the
proprietor talk to Michel about "*bandidos* and *Juaristas*."
Even her small knowledge of Spanish enabled her to un-

derstand that much! It was only a slight consolation to know that they carried American passports and letters that would serve to introduce them to the American representative in Mexico City as wives of Americans from the defeated southern states who had bought estates in Mexico. Perhaps the letters they carried (more evidence of careful planning on Senator Brandon's part) might serve to protect them from molestation from the supporters of Benito Juarez, who counted on the friendship of the United States, but if they should be attacked by bandits. . . !

Michel told them that the French were still in nominal control of this part of the country. He repeated the rumor he had heard that Juarez had in fact flown the country and was reputed to be hiding out somewhere in Texas. And as for the bandits—he told them airily that they preyed mostly on their own kind and would not dare attack a coach guarded by French soldiers for fear of reprisals by the French. His presence and his reassurances helped. After all, what was the use in being afraid? They had already embarked on their journey and on their mission—hadn't Ginny herself pooh-poohed the thought that she feared the dangers they might run into? When she wasn't thinking of Michel and how glad she was that they had met again, she found herself unwillingly remembering the night that Steve Morgan had warned her about journeying into Mexico.

"Mexico, in case you did not know it, is in a state of war!" he said, almost shouting the words at her. If the nature of their mission were discovered, would that make her a spy? The thought was almost laughable. Ginny knew that if she mentioned any of this to Sonya she would be told that she had read too many romances.

They had been travelling for two days, following roughly the contours of the Rio Grande, and stopping often to rest while Michel sent some of his men ahead to reconnoitre. But now, he warned, they would be travelling along a trail that skirted the lower foothills of the forbidding Sierra Madre and would lead them, if all went well, safely into Chihuahua.

"From then on, it will be much easier," Michel said, with a meaningful glance at Ginny's flushed, tired-looking face. "We will be away from this heat—wait until you feel the coolness of the mountains! And you will see—after we get to Chihuahua there will be no more fears of bandits or *Juaristas*."

"Does that mean that we have both those possibilities to contend with now?" Ginny asked with some asperity but he refused to take offense at her tone, leaning down from his horse to grasp her hand through the open window of the carriage.

"You have nothing at all to fear, *belle amie!* See, I am here. I am armed to the teeth, have you not noticed? And there are also ten French soldiers, carefully picked by the marshal himself!" With an apologetic glance at Sonya he said more softly, in French, "if you have anything to fear, little love, perhaps it is myself. It is getting harder and harder for me to be content with the chaste good-night kisses we are allowed, under the eyes of your pretty step-mama. Perhaps tonight I will spirit you away under the stars and hold you in my arms for as long as you will let me."

Ginny dropped her lashes under the ardent, hot gaze he turned on her, but she smiled, and he took heart.

"Perhaps I would like that—very much," she admitted in a low voice, speaking also in French.

Michel, touching his tall hat, rode on to join his men, and Sonya, who had begun to feel a trifle piqued by their *tête-à-tête*, decided to ignore their slight breach of manners. After all, they were both still young, and, if she was not mistaken, they were falling in love with each other— all over again, perhaps. Sonya thought again how romantic it all was.

To Ginny, however, there was nothing romantic about this journey. If not for the presence of Michel, and the way he looked at her, even when she was hot and bedraggled, it would have been quite intolerable. Thank God for dear Michel—he took her mind off other things. She longed to reach the end of their journey, to be cool again, to mingle with civilized people among surroundings that would be safe and familiar. Sometimes she could not believe she was the same girl who had arrived in America, longing for adventure and excitement. She had had dreams of romance, too, but how different reality had turned out to be!

They were travelling into higher country now, almost indiscernibly, but steadily; the river left behind, the mountains looming ahead. The trail they travelled had been used by heavy pack trains from Spanish times, Michel had told her—it was a *camino real*, but the Spanish name meant nothing to her. It was merely a dusty, rutted track that went up and down, and sometimes she felt as if her head would be jolted from her body.

As the trail sloped up into the foothills, the desert scrub of creosote bushes, cactus and mesquite gave way in part to stunted, twisted trees—oak juniper and piñon pine. Their canteens, filled the previous night, were already half-empty when they stopped to rest in the afternoon heat. Red dust covered the lathered mules that drew the diligencia and the horses of the French soldiers. As Ginny stepped down from the coach, Michel warned her to watch for snakes—they were everywhere, he said. Sonya gave a small scream and insisted that she would rather stay inside the shelter that the vehicle provided but Ginny, her legs cramped, let Michel help her outside.

Removing his hat to squint upwards at the sun he smiled at her cheerfully, his teeth gleaming against the sunburned skin of his face. His glossy chestnut hair hung in boyish ringlets across his forehead. Unlike most of his contemporaries, Michel Remy was clean-shaven except for the long, thick sideburns that seemed to emphasize the leanness of his face, with its high-bridged nose and chiselled mouth. A few years ago Ginny had thought him the handsomest man she had ever seen—not, she told herself again, that she wasn't lucky; lucky to have such a man, such a very eligible young man (she could barely repress a small smile, remembering Sonya's words) pay her so much attention.

They had stopped in a small canyon, or *barranca*, its almost sheer walls providing some shade. Ahead of them lay a tortuous, winding trail that seemed to cling to the hillside, but Michel had been quick to assure them that they would soon come out on a small plateau where they would spend the night at an Indian village boasting a single *cantina*.

"It's a small, shabby, and I'm afraid, rather a dirty place—hardly fit to take you into," Michel apologized. "But it's better than having to spend the night out here ..." he gestured at the arid emptiness of the hills around them and Ginny shuddered.

"With all these rattlesnakes and bandits you warned us about? I should think so!"

He had led her some distance away from the diligencia, and now with a sudden movement he captured both her hands in his.

"Ginette! You know how I feel about you—how I felt from the very beginning when I saw you looking like an angel in your white dress. If only I had the right to be near you tonight, to protect you from everything you are afraid of, just to hold you in my arms, as I have dreamed of doing for years."

"Michel ..." Ginny did not know, for a moment whether she would burst into tears or hysterical laughter. What did he expect her to do? She took refuge in subterfuge. "Your soldiers—they can see us, what will they think?"

"Petite amour—it does not matter what they think. They cannot help but know my feelings for you. If we were not at war, I would court you endlessly, my Ginette, but things are different here. God knows where I might be sent after we reach Mexico City. I must know how you feel—I must know if what your eyes tell me is true."

He did not give her a chance to answer, but swept her ruthlessly into his arms and began to kiss her. Surprisingly, Michel's kisses did not repel her as Carl's had done—she found them quite pleasant. His arms enfolded her firmly, masterfully, and it felt so comfortable to lean against him! Here was no whirling, half-faint feeling of helplessness, of being swept away in spite of herself—here was security; the feeling of being in the arms of a man she could trust, who would be kind to her, who would be gentle too. Ginny let the safety and the tender affection of Michel's embrace take her. Half sobbing, she lifted her arms and let them cling to his broad shoulders as she began to kiss him back, her lips warming under his.

The French soldiers who were sitting, leaning against the rocky walls on either side of the trail became busy with their canteens or rubbing down their horses as they pretended not to see.

So the *capitaine* was not wasting any time! Of course, from the very beginning they had noticed how his eyes were constantly on the pretty *mademoiselle*; how many excuses he made to ride back to speak with her. Who could blame him? Assuredly, she was quite beautiful, and she had the manners and accent of a lady. Corporal Valmy thought resignedly that no doubt they would travel much faster now than they had been for the past two days. The capitaine would be in a hurry to reach Chihuahua, where he would undoubtedly arrange circumstances so that they could be discreetly alone. And again, who could blame him? One could get tired of dark-haired, dark-eyed *señoritas* very easily.

The corporal, who had decided to busy himself cleaning his pistol, had no time for further musing, for at that moment there was a terrible screech from somewhere above them—a burst of rifle fire, and to his dazed, dilating eyes it seemed as if the hillside above them and to all sides of them swarmed with menacing figures.

"Those shots, little *soldados*, were merely to warn you. It is hoped you will be sensible."

Relaxed as they had all been, and completely off-guard, the Frenchmen were taken by surprise. Menaced by rifles and pistols, they remained frozen, only glancing towards their equally surprised captain for guidance.

Michel Remy was a soldier, and under ordinary circumstances far from being a coward. But in this case there were women to think about, and in particular there was Ginette, whom he still held in his arms. He put her gently from him, but she still clung to his arm, her green eyes large with fear.

He studied the men who surrounded them; some of them already beginning to slide or scramble down the steep slopes towards them. Fool that he was not to have taken more precautions! He was bitter with anger and frustration. He had volunteered for this errand, the women and the gold they carried were his responsibility, and now—he hoped grimly that these men were not *Juaristas*—even bandits were preferable to the former if you were a Frenchman in this Godforsaken country!

To Ginny it seemed part of some monstrous nightmare. To be torn from Michel's warm arms only to find this! She had heard Sonya scream from within the diligence, but now even she was silent—either fainted or having hysterics, no doubt! With horrified fascination, Ginny watched the Mexicans approach—they looked frighteningly dangerous with their huge *sombreros* shading their swarthy faces, and cartridge belts looped from shoulder to hip and around their waists as well. Some of them carried wicked-looking knives with wide blades; all of them wore pistols. She had no idea how many of them there were.

What did they want? And worse—what would they do? One of the bandits who had remained on the hilltop above them was obviously their leader, for it was he who had spoken earlier, and it was he who continued to give orders in the guttural bastard Spanish that was spoken by the *mestizos*.

The French soldiers were red-faced and tightlipped with anger as they were ordered to throw down their weapons and raise their hands. Corporal Valmy hesitated, and one of the bandits clubbed him with his rifle butt, laying open a bleeding cut on his cheekbone. The senseless cruelty of this action, coupled with his own intolerable sense of impotence made Michel Remy lose his temper.

Ginny had dropped his arm, although she still stood close to him as if for protection, and now he brought his pistol up from his belt, cocking it as he did so and firing, with an explosion that seemed to deafen him as he felt himself sprawling backwards; realizing only then that he had been hit by a bullet himself.

Blood gushed from a wound in his shoulder and he heard Ginny's scream of anguish as she bent over him.

"Oh God, Michel! My brave darling—poor angel—are you badly hurt?" Her fingers pressed against his wound, trying to staunch the flow of blood, and he bit back a groan of pain.

From the distance that seemed to widen enormously all around him, Michel Remy faintly heard more shots and tried to struggle upright, reaching for a gun he could not find. Where was it? Had he dropped it?

"Lie down! Michel, lie still or—"

Ginny's words trailed away as his eyes closed. She had turned her head to look over her shoulder when she heard more shots, and two French soldiers, who had bravely attempted to take advantage of the diversion their captain had provided, lay inertly on the dusty earth.

There were no more attempts at resistance, and only Ginny, whose mood of hysteria had made her forget even her fear dared ask any questions of the grinning men who seemed to move so silently and efficiently, picking up the discarded weapons of the soldiers. Sonya and Tillie had emerged from the carriage by now, Sonya half-fainting, her eyes dilated with terror.

"What do you want with us? You devils! We're

American citizens, and if you dare harm us you'll answer to the United States armies!"

One of the bandits was shaking his head in exaggerated admiration for Ginny's courage.

"Such a brave *señorita!* I salute your bravery!"

She was attempting to bind Michel's wound with strips of cloth torn from her own voluminous petticoats, but she looked up angrily at the sound of the man's taunting voice.

"Never mind me—I demand that you leave us alone— you'll have the French army after you too, you know! We have nothing that you need—no expensive jewelry—oh, look what you've done, you murderers!"

She did not know whether the man understood her or not, but obviously his leader did. She heard a laugh from above her, mocking, and somehow tauntingly familiar.

"Tell her, *Pedrito.* Such courage deserves an answer."

He spoke in Spanish, and now the man who had spoken to her earlier smiled, showing stained, irregular teeth.

"We look for money, *señorita*—much money." He spoke in halting English, but well enough for her to understand. "We follow your *diligencia* many miles—we ask ourselves, it is strange, no? That such a little carriage, carrying such dainty ladies, leaves such deep tracks. We are curious men, *señorita.*"

Ginny heard Sonya's choked exclamation, and flashed her a warning look.

"Oh, Ginny! How did they—"

"Sonya, don't! They're bandits, don't you see that? They think we're rich. Give them whatever jewels we have, and maybe they'll let us go—"

"Ah, the *señorita* is sensible, too!" The man came closer and Ginny shrank away. He smelled! Of dirty, unwashed clothes and hair of—of death! The nightmare was real, this time she was not going to wake up in the safety of her bed.

While some of the men tied up the French soldiers, Ginny's tormentor came closer, smiling still.

"*Señorita*—why would two American ladies travel with French *soldados*? Ah, *los Francescos*—pigs!" He spat elaborately. "No, I think we will find something interesting in your *diligencia*—perhaps much money, no? Enough so that poor *bandidos* like ourselves will be rich men?" He laughed then, and the rest of them laughed with him.

In an instant, he seemed to tire of his game. Ginny heard him snap orders, and three Mexicans ran to the wagon with their machetes—she heard the sound of more laughter and tearing wood as they proceeded to rip up the interior.

The gold—they knew about it! But how?

"*Señorita*—he will live, your so-foolish capitan. Now if you will join the other ladies—" She noticed then, that Sonya and Tillie were being tied to one of the wheels, their wrists behind them. Tillie's mouth stayed open as if she wanted to scream but didn't dare—Sonya looked as if she had fainted already, leaning back against the wheel with her face as white as a sheet.

For a moment, Ginny stayed motionless, her face a mask of defiance. Then she heard, in French, the broken whisper of Michel's voice.

"My pistol—dropped." And then, questioningly, "Ginette? Ginette, where . . ." again he struggled to sit up and she cried out sharply for him to lie still.

"Please, you will not kill him? Once you get what you want, you won't?" she forced herself to plead with the dirty bandit who stood leering at her, but she was conscious, at the same time of the weight of Michel's gun against her thigh, the coldness of the ivory grip. He had dropped it, and when she had flung herself upon him, her skirts had covered it. Almost without thinking, she'd slipped it into the pocket of her gown. Perhaps . . .

So far the bandits had not attempted to molest her, nor Sonya and Tillie either. Perhaps they meant only to take the money and flee. But in any case, if they tried to lay hands on her she'd shoot—what did it matter, anyhow?

Again the bandit leader on the hill above called out something in Spanish, his tone harsh. The Mexican who stood in front of her shrugged, but moved back.

"There will be no more killing, *señorita*, if we can help it. And now, if you please."

Ginny glanced again at Michel, who still seemed unconscious, but at least her bandage appeared to have stopped the bleeding. Unwillingly, she got to her feet, pretending to brush off the folds of her skirt. Thank God, the gun was still there—they hadn't noticed!

The bandits who had searched the coach were coming out, carrying the gold in its heavy sackfuls. There were whoops and chortles from the other men who crowded

around, helping. And even the bandit leader, handing his
rifle to the man who stood next to him, had decided to
grace them with his presence. They had forgotten her for a
moment, and Ginny shrank back against the wheel of the
coach, next to Sonya.

"Look—the money—jes' like we expect, no, *amigos*?
Such a nice present for poor men such as we are!"

He had turned back to her, was coming towards her. I
won't let them tie me up, Ginny thought wildly. I won't be
left tied here while they massacre those poor soldiers, take
the gold. Panic overrode reason as she began to tremble
with reaction. The pistol came free without any conscious
effort on her part and she was pointing it at the man,
holding it steady with both hands.

"You come any nearer and I'll shoot—and you'll call
off your men, too, or . . ."

He stood very still, an almost comical expression of incredulity creeping over his flat, Indian features. The
bandits had stopped their laughing too; they all seemed
frozen in ridiculous positions, some with the sacks of gold
still slung over their shoulders.

"She is crazy! *Señorita*, you are being very stupid, you
cannot think . . ."

"If you do not untie those soldiers immediately, then
you, *señor* bandit, will be a very dead man." Her voice
sounded almost too calm in her ears, but the hammer of
the revolver trembled under her thumb.

"We shall have to kill you, *señorita*, it is too bad. You
can take my life, *sí*, but I do not think . . ."

"Pedro, wait. The young lady is hysterical, I think. Let
me reason with her."

She had forgotten the bandit leader until he spoke,
switching to Castilian Spanish that even she could understand. His voice sounded muffled, but unhurriedly even.
"*Señorita*—I will drop my gun, see? And we will talk. You
are being very foolish, you know! Do you think a few
lives are important to us in comparison to the gold?"

His voice came closer as he walked towards her, but she
dared not take her eyes from Pedro, who had now stepped
cautiously backward, shrugging.

Biting her lip to keep back hysteria, Ginny pointed her
gun at the tall man who walked steadily forward, just as if
the gun she held unwaveringly was a silly toy. Unlike the
rest of them, he wore a handkerchief knotted at the back

of his head to hide his features, like the cowboys who rode drag when they'd guided her father's cattle through the dusty Texas plains. And even though he was garbed just like the other men, with a wide sombrero and serape covering the upper part of his body, there was something naggingly familiar about the way he walked, something—

"So you're their leader—a man who covers his face like a coward!" Her words poured scorn on him, although by now Ginny was more frightened than she had ever been in her life. "Perhaps if it is your life that is endangered they'll let us go."

"If you shoot me, it will mean the lives of all of your companions. Do you want that? I do not think you are stupid, *señorita*, just foolish, perhaps. Give me the gun, and I promise there'll be no lives taken. We will be magnanimous and spare even *los Francesos*. Come, hand it to me."

He was within a yard of her now and he held his hand out, keeping his head down so that he could watch the gun.

The sun poured down on her head, its heat intolerable. Beside her, she could hear Sonya's sobbing, her incoherent pleas for Ginny to be sensible, not to get them all killed.

As Ginny hesitated the man made a sudden, rattlesnake-fast grab for her gun, and she heard it explode, the recoil knocking her backward. She was close enough to see the bullet go through the folds of his serape, and then she was conscious of an aching, numbing pain in her wrist as his hand slammed downward, knocking the gun from her nerveless fingers.

And, as if she needed further horror piled upon all the horror of the last quarter hour to drive her across the thin line into hysteria she had it now. She knew him. Even before she heard him swear at her, forgetting to disguise his voice, even before she brought her hand up, clawing at his face like a wildcat, tearing away the black neckerchief, she knew him.

His dark blue eyes were as bright and as pitiless as the blue bowl of the sky above them, his fingers bruising her wrists cruelly as he caught them, pinioning her against the diligence.

"You!" she panted, and then, with rising hysteria, "You! Oh, God, I should have killed you!"

"You always were a bad shot, Ginny. And just as well.

You calmed down yet?" That he should dare smile at her
so tauntingly!

He released her, turning his head to say something to
the grinning Mexicans, and she flew at him like a cornered, half-demented animal. Her nails raked at his face,
she would have gouged his eyes out if he hadn't caught
her hand. With a quick movement that caught him unprepared she bit his hand and heard his hissed, indrawn
breath of pain before he slapped her backhanded, half
stunning her. She fell backwards against the coach and felt
his fingers bite into her shoulders as he caught her, spinning her around.

"You goddam hellcat! You're more trouble than any of
the others put together! Will you hold still!"

But she would not. She screamed and kicked and bit,
struggling against him until her strength ran out and she
felt him push her forward, twisting her arms behind her
until she fell onto her knees in the dust, sobbing with pain
and defiance.

Now that Ginny's actions had ended the need for con-
cealment, Steve Morgan took charge quite openly. It had
seemed like a nightmare in the beginning—but what was
to follow was, unbelievably, worse.

Crouching in the dust with her wrists tied painfully behind her, Ginny could hear the staccato orders he issued,
overlying the groans of the wounded Frenchmen and
Sonya's sobbing, pleading voice.

In English, Steve was saying quietly and conversationally
to Sonya that he regretted the inconvenience.

"Sorry it had to happen this way, ma'am, but if you'll
remember I warned you about traipsin' into Mexico. And
it's too bad your stepdaughter had to act up the way she
did. . . ."

"Oh, but please," Sonya wept, "you're not going to—
you *can't!* You've got the gold, what more do you want
from us?"

Her scared blue eyes fixed themselves pleadingly on his
frowning face, with the dark eyebrows drawn together so
menacingly. She could see no pity in it—read nothing at
all!

"I'm afraid, ma'am, that I'm left with only two
alternatives, both rather unpleasant. I can have you all
killed, so there'll be no witnesses, or . . ." he paused con-

sideringly, and Sonya released the breath she had been holding with a sob of pure terror.

"Please! Oh, please, not that! I swear—if you'll only go away and leave us alive I'll never tell anyone I recognized you! I'll make *them* promise too, I *know* I can! For God's sake!"

Her dilated, horror-stricken eyes saw the twitch of his lips, as though he had almost smiled. Still hesitating, he shrugged and looked down at Ginny, who had not said a word since they'd tied her wrists. Now, as though she had felt his gaze, the girl looked up at him through tear-swollen eyes, her face twisted with hatred.

"I'll make no promises, you—you *canaille,* you unmentionable filth! You had better kill me then, because I swear that if you don't I'll have you hunted down and destroyed like the thieving, traitorous dog that you are!"

The world seemed narrowed down to the two of them as their eyes clashed—Ginny felt a shiver go through her, although she forced herself not to look away. At this moment, she did not really care if he killed her. Let him! He had betrayed her and struck her. He'd caused the death and wounding of innocent men, and all for gold—for money! She tasted a bitterness that was almost too much to bear—if her mouth had not been so dry she would have spat at his feet.

"Perhaps there's another way. We'll take you with us, as insurance, you might say. Get to see a lot of country that way, an' that's why you came to Mexico, isn't it?"

Ginny's mouth opened in a silent, thunderstruck "O" and his glance seemed to flick over her with a contemptuous kind of amusement before he turned back to Sonya, who was already protesting.

"No! No you cannot mean it, you won't . . ."

"Mrs. Brandon!" His voice cut like a whiplash over her stumbling, incredulous words. "There is no other alternative, madam, unless you prefer to be a martyr for your gold. Your stepdaughter will go with us to insure there's no pursuit. Within a month or so I'll see that she is returned safely to Texas—or to Mexico City, if you prefer." He bowed ironically to Sonya, who began to weep hopelessly.

"I won't go! You can't make me—I'll fight you, I'll scream, I'll—" Ginny was almost incoherent in her extreme anger and agitation, especially since she had noticed that Michel's eyes were open—he was gazing at her with an expression of horror.

"Michel! Oh, thank God, you're alive, at least—Michel, don't let them."

Steve Morgan pulled her unceremoniously to her feet, holding her against him in the steel vise of his arm and laughing, like the rest of his men, at her attempts to kick him.

"*Olé!* Such a wildcat, that one! You will have a hard time taming her, *amigo!*"

Although Ginny did not understand the Indian dialect the men spoke, Michel did, and he groaned silently, as much from mental anguish as from his wounded shoulder, which certainly throbbed like the devil.

Because of his wound, perhaps, and his having been unconscious the bandits had left him untied, but now as he attempted to move, one of them raised his gun, to be stopped by a sharp word from the American he had recognized and now knew to be their leader.

"Leave him! We'll take their guns, and in this country, it's as well they have someone to untie them after we leave. *Señor soldado—*" still holding the struggling girl Michel now *knew* that he loved to distraction, the American switched to the easier Castilian that Michel understood better than the polyglot dialect the other men had spoken. "If you place any value on the—shall we say, continued good health of this young woman, you will see to it that we're not followed too closely. The gold, you may be sure, will be spent well—as for Miss Brandon, what happens to her will depend on you."

"Leave her! You can take me instead." Michel Remy struggled to sit up, but fell back weakly with a muffled gasp of pain.

"Very touching! As was the tender embrace we were forced to interrupt! But I'm afraid, *señor*, that we are wasting time. You will please remember that if you wish to see Miss Brandon as well as she appears now, you will do exactly as I've said." The harsh voice sneered at him, and Michel Remy had never wished more passionately to kill than he did now.

"The—the lady is my fiancée, and if you harm her you'll never be able to show your face in this country or in your own!"

The young captain heard Ginny scream as she was

dragged away, heard Sonya Brandon's wail of fear and pity. In spite of his growing weakness he forced his aching body into a sitting position, closing his eyes against the pain. But when he opened them, she was gone—all of them were gone. He heard the muttering of Madame Brandon's mulatto maid as he attempted to drag himself over to where his men lay bound, staring at him in silent commiseration, but the words made no sense to him in his present condition.

"I always *knowed* that man was no good," Tillie was saying. "Knew he was a devil, an' I tried to tell Miss Ginny so, but she wouldn't listen—"

"Shut up, will you shut up!" Sonya screamed. "He has her now—oh God, what will I tell William? What will happen to us all now?"

PART THREE

The Conflict

Chapter Eighteen

They had been riding forever! Aching in every bone of her body, half-dazed with weariness, Ginny was sure of it. Night had fallen a long time ago, and the horses still plodded on, though more slowly now than they had at the beginning. She had no idea where they were or where they were heading, and it had, for the moment, ceased to matter. It was cold, and her clothes, soaked through from stumbling waist or neck-deep through mountain streams, clung soddenly to her shivering body. They were somewhere in the mountains, she knew that much, and already a few of the men, each carrying their share of the gold, had ridden off in separate directions.

She had wondered, in the beginning, if they were really bandits, or followers of the deposed President Juarez. She had tried to count heads, to remember how many of them there were—she had even made an attempt to notice in what direction they were travelling. But now it didn't matter, and had ceased to matter a long time ago, when it had first begun getting dark, and the gnarled and twisted trees and bushes that grew here had begun to look like crouching animals in the half-light.

Dear God, when would they stop? The utter exhaustion

of mind and body that seized her now made Ginny feel that she might faint. She had struggled and kicked earlier, trying to throw herself off the horse until Steve Morgan, his face set and cold had slapped her twice across the face, his carefully calculated blows swinging her head back and forth, making it reel. He'd forced her to ride in the saddle before him, her wrists still tied behind her back—and when he'd reduced her to helpless, angry sobs he'd held his rifle across her body, under her breasts, tightening it against her whenever she attempted to struggle again so that she felt her breath cut off.

Now, she slumped wearily and dispiritedly against him, uncaring; even vaguely thankful that he'd thrown his serape over her shoulders for warmth.

Without knowing it, Ginny began to whimper softly, like a wounded animal. Why didn't they stop? Would they ever stop?

It seemed hours later when they finally made camp, in the shadow of an enormous misshapen boulder that seemed to loom over them like a prehistoric monster, forming a natural cave that gave partial shelter from the wind.

Steve Morgan had to carry her off the horse and prop her up against the rocky wall, for she was too stiff to move or to offer any resistance.

Working silently with their knives, the men cut branches that they tied swiftly together, interlacing other branches to form a makeshift shelter. They fed the horses from nosebags tied over their heads, speaking softly to them and rubbing their sweaty coats dry with bunches of grass. Obviously, there were to be no fires built tonight.

Ginny had begun to shiver uncontrollably, her teeth chattering from cold and exhaustion. Morgan brought a blanket from his saddlebag and put it around her, but she could not stop shaking. Squatting beside her, he cut her wrists free and began to chafe them roughly. Had she the strength, she would have pulled away from him, but as it was, she was forced to endure his careless ministration, and the agony as her circulation, almost cut off by the tight rawhide strips they'd bound her with, began to be restored.

The men, talking softly among themselves, had begun to drink from their canteens and chew on strips of dried beef. Some of them produced bottles of *pulque* or *tequila*

and drank thirstily. Somehow, even in her befuddled state,
Ginny was left with the impression that they were used to
this kind of travel—riding by night, building no fires to attract pursuers—what kind of men were they, and what
was Steve doing with them?

Morgan offered her some jerky, but she shook her head
sullenly.

"Better eat," he advised her flatly. "It's all you'll get."
He swallowed deeply from his flask of *tequila* and held it
out to her, but she turned her face away.

"You're shivering with a chill," he said impatiently, and
then with harshness creeping into his voice, "you'll be no
use as a hostage when you're dead of pneumonia!"

Brutally, he forced her head around with his fingers digging into the soft flesh of her face, and held the bottle
against her mouth. Because in a minute he would have
poured it forcibly down her throat, Ginny drank, choking
and gagging on the raw, burning liquor. But he'd been
right, in a few minutes, she felt almost revived, the *tequila*
seeming to form a warm, glowing spot in her belly. He offered her some jerky again, and this time she took it,
realizing suddenly that she was hungry.

The men were beginning to roll themselves up in
blankets to sleep, unmindful of the rough ground they lay
on.

Through dull eyes, Ginny saw Steve Morgan get up and
stretch elaborately.

"You'd better try to get some sleep too—we'll be riding
again in about two hours."

She was so tired that she scarcely understood what he
had said. Two hours? It wasn't possible—he must be
crazy, like them, like anyone who would choose to live in
this terrible, Godforsaken country!

Now he bent over her, tying her wrists again, but more
loosely this time, and in front of her. There was no point
in resisting, she had learned that already. She watched him
spread a blanket on the ground, and then, quite calmly, he
lay down beside her and pulled her down against him as
he lay on his side. She began to struggle then, although
her limbs felt weighted and strangely lifeless, but his arms
held her too tightly and too closely, and after a while she
stopped struggling and lay there stiffly. He chuckled softly.

"Body heat's the best thing for keepin' warm on a night
like this," he said tersely.

Ginny was silent, miserably aware of her own helplessness. He could do anything he wanted with her, anything, and she could not prevent it. The thought made her shiver with fear and a kind of terrified anticipation; but he did nothing—continuing to hold her until she felt warmth creep into her aching body at last and slept in spite of herself.

Slept only to be awakened in what felt like almost immediately. Jerked unceremoniously to her feet and deposited once more across his saddle. The deep night-blue of the sky lightened into the paler blue of dawn as they rode deeper into the mountains, sometimes along trails that seemed no more than narrow footpaths, clinging precariously to the edge of deep canyons into which Ginny dared not glance.

The sun came up to beat fiercely down on their heads, and one of the men, with a sidelong, grinning glance, produced a battered straw hat which Ginny accepted apathetically.

She lost track of direction and time, and even, she thought, of days. When they stopped it was only to water their horses and fill canteens from tiny mountain streams. They ate jerky, and she became used to the fiery taste of *pulque* and *tequila*. At least, because they seemed to accept her as Steve's prisoner, there were no attempts to molest her—indeed the hardbitten Mexicans seemed even to have gained some admiration for her stoicism; not realizing that it was caused simply by her own utter exhaustion of mind and body that made her feel drained of all emotion, even fear. She heard them refer to her as *"la niña,"* the little one, and when her gown had begun to fall in rags about her, one of them, a slim youth who could have been no more than eighteen or nineteen, produced from his saddlebags a rather dirty pair of *colzones,* the loose trousers worn by Mexican peasants, and an equally loose *camisa,* or shirt. He gave them to Steve, with an apologetic shrug and a torrent of words in his own dialect, glaring at some of the other men who laughed and made ribald comments.

It was late afternoon, and since they had climbed higher into the mountains, growing chilly as well. The land was almost frighteningly wild and magnificent in its bleak loneliness. The day before, one of the men had shot a puma, using only a bow and arrow. They had grinned at

Ginny's expression of mingled fear and disgust, but had been surprised when later, she had refused to eat its meat.

Now, they had paused in their relentless, headlong flight to wherever they were going—this time on a small plateau thickly covered by pine and juniper trees.

Ginny had grown used to taking orders, but she hung back rebelliously in this instance when Steve began to lead her deeper into the grove of trees, amid the good-natured gibes and laughter of the others.

"I won't—I won't wear those—those disgusting garments!"

Angrily she bit back the rest of the words she had been about to utter, but he gave a short laugh that sounded more taunting than amused.

"Would you prefer to ride naked? Bare-breasted, like an Amazon warrior? I'm not saying that it would not be interesting for me, but my friends back there might find the temptation too great." His voice changed, becoming curt, almost harsh. "Ginny, don't waste time arguing with me. Or—do you want me to tear your clothes from you? As I recall, you did not make it too difficult for me to undress you, once."

"Oh!" The color drained from her face and she took a backward step when she saw the look in his eyes. "Is nothing too low for you? Do you dare to remind me that—that you—"

"Don't provoke me, Ginny!" His voice held a warning note that made her grow cold with fear. "And don't pretend any sudden modesty. You've taken off your clothes for a man before. For me, and for Carl Hoskins, and no doubt for your French captain who called you his fiancée. Why do you continue to play your silly games with me?"

He had untied her wrists so that she could eat, and now Ginny found her fingers curling into her palms, aching with the desire to claw at his dark, mocking face. She had clawed at him before and he still bore the faint scars—now she wished she had taken his eyes out.

"Games?" she hissed at him in a fury, "do you think I could possibly feel anything but hate and loathing for you? I hate you, hate you, hate you, Steve Morgan! You sicken me. The thought of your touching me makes me ill! Yes, I'd rather be Carl's mistress, or Michel's, or the mistress of any other man whom I chose myself, rather than have you touch me again, you—you dirty half-breed dog!"

His face remained as impassive as an Indian's, but she could see from the sudden opacity of his eyes and the white lines about his mouth that she had finally succeeded in penetrating the cold control he normally kept over himself.

"You almost tempt me to find out how much you really hate me," he said at last, and came towards her, making her recoil instinctively, her hands coming up as if to ward off a blow. But he only flung the clothes at her, laughing contemptuously when she gave an involuntary gasp.

He put his hands on his hips and gazed at her coolly, a Mexican brigand with blue eyes, the crossed bandoliers over his chest making him look even more menacing.

"Hurry up and change, Ginny. Or I'll be forced to think your coy hesitation means something else."

Flushing with humiliation and pent-up fury, Ginny turned her back on him and did as she was told, miserably conscious of his eyes on her, even though she could not see the expression on his face.

They rode on again, with Ginny riding astride like a boy. But since their confrontation in the trees, the subtle shading of her relationship with Steve Morgan had changed again. Where before she had been silent and sullen, almost, at times, apathetic; now she could feel the hate and despair inside her grow and grow until she thought at times that she would burst with frustration. God, how she despised him, how she hated him! The hate seared into her, becoming as much a part of her as eating and breathing. There was not a moment when she was not aware of him—of the warmth of his body as he forced her to lean against him—the hardness of his hands when he tied or untied her—the mocking blue brilliance of his eyes against his sunburned skin.

She cursed him and resisted him at every opportunity so that he was compelled to force her onto his saddle and off; to eat, to drink, or even to lie down beside him to sleep.

"I hate you!" she would whisper to him at every turn. "Thief—half-breed!" And when he grew tired of hearing the constant invectives she hurled at him, he would tighten the rifle he held against her breast until she felt her breath cut off by its pressure and collapsed, sobbing her rage, against him.

They started to descend from the mountains, in what

direction, Ginny did not know. But again, almost imperceptibly, some of the men started to drift away. They would wake up from a sleep to find someone gone—or sometimes after a whispered discussion one or two men would take a different trail. Ginny was sure there was some hidden purpose to their seemingly senseless movements. Perhaps they had all arranged to meet again, and this was merely a ruse to throw off pursuit. When the men talked among themselves, however they used an Indian dialect that she was totally unfamiliar with.

And as they came down from the mountains into an arid, desertlike country that reminded Ginny vividly of parts of Texas, she began to be afraid again. What would happen to her? Where was he taking her? She was even more apprehensive because she knew that Steve wanted her.

It was as if by her scorn and rejection of him she had brought herself back to his attention as a woman; not merely a pawn in some game he was playing—a hostage for his own safety.

When they slept together under his blanket she could feel the rising of his desire for her, although he made no overt moves to do anything about it. And sometimes, as they rode he would let his hand brush against her breast or shoulder, or insist upon braiding her hair, as matted and tangled as it had become. She thought at such moments that he did it deliberately, to hurt her—sometimes the tears started to her eyes at his careless tugging, although she would not let him see. At times, he'd rest his hand on her hip or belly, caressing her against her will while she squirmed and struggled furiously against him, pouring out her hatred for him, her disgust at his touch. But since that first day when he'd flung the clothes at her, he would not let her taunt him into losing his temper, nor his control.

She wondered, fearfully, what he had in mind, but when she'd ask him when he would let her go, he only shrugged.

"When I've no more use for you, baby," he told her once, and the note of cold finality in his voice made her shudder.

Only Pedro and the boy Juan, who had given her his clothes remained with them on the night they rode into the small Indian village.

Juan had left his horse and slipped ahead an hour be-

fore to make sure that all was safe, but when he came
back wearing an exuberant, face-splitting grin, they rode
into the small clearing where thatched huts, some built of
crumbling adobe, seemed to huddle together for protection.

"*Mi casa*—" Juan said, speaking Spanish for Ginny's
benefit, and by now she was so tired that she welcomed
any kind of shelter, even that of a mud hut.

Juan's parents—if that was who they were—seemed
very old. From the excited greetings, the *abrazos,* it was
clear that Pedro, too, was some kind of relative. They had
been warned of Ginny's presence, for there was no more
than a mild curiosity in the wrinkled face of the woman
who greeted her, leading her to the small fire that filled
the room with smoke and the odors of cooking.

After the jerky she had become used to, the corn
tortillas she was offered seemed delicious, and Ginny
wolfed them down like a hungry animal, unaware that
Steve was watching her until she looked up once and
caught his brooding gaze on her face. What was he thinking? She looked away immediately, but he crossed the
small room to her with a stone mug that was half-full with
some kind of sweet liquor that burned her throat as it
went down.

The men talked, low-voiced. Juan's younger brother,
Pablo, who had run outside to attend to their horses came
back and sat by them, his large, dark eyes shining like
black stones in the firelight. Beside Ginny, the woman sat
silently, her occasional shy sidewise glances at *la gringa*
her only betrayal of curiosity. Close-up, the woman was
not as old as she had seemed at first. Clearly, she was
much younger than her husband. But her figure was shape-
less under the dark-colored *reboza* huddled over the shoulders, and there were wrinkles in her face, under the straggly
dark hair. Ginny felt a sudden rush of pity for her.
What an existence! To have to live all her life in a
place like this, condemned to nothing but hard work and
childbearing—to know nothing of the world outside!

She found herself growing almost overpoweringly
drowsy ... and then, because she was so tired, she slept,
leaning her head and shoulders back against the wall.

A hand shook her roughly awake. Her eyes flew open,
startled, and she found herself looking into Steve Morgan's
face.

"It's warm enough in here——" she hissed at him, suddenly conscious of the fact that they were the only ones
left awake—the others lay huddled by the fire wrapped in
the inevitable blankets. "You don't need my body to keep
you warm tonight."

"I can think of other uses for that body you try so hard
to hide," he said softly, and she went cold inside, all the
way to the pit of her stomach.

"No!" she whispered fiercely, glaring her hate into his
implacable face. "No—I won't let you touch me!"

"You were willing enough before, remember?" he said
cruelly.

He wrenched her to her feet, pulling her along with
him.

"There's a place back there we can use. Juan had an
older brother who was studying for the priesthood, before
the soldiers killed him. They fixed it up for him, so he
could have some privacy, and tonight . . ."

He didn't have to finish what he had started to say—his
meaning was clear enough. Ginny strove to pull back, but
his grip was too strong, too painful.

There was only a makeshift curtain of some rough,
coarsely woven material separating them from the others.
He had made preparations already, for a small oil lamp
had been lighted and placed in an alcove in the rough
adobe wall, and he'd spread his blankets on the floor.

He released her, standing between her and the doorway
and began to take off his cartridge belts, and then his
guns, placing them carefully in a corner. When he turned
around, Ginny still stood there as if she had been mesmerized, staring at him with eyes that looked like bits of
green glass. And something in the way she looked at him,
like a terrified animal held at bay, almost made Steve
Morgan hesitate. With her hair dirty and uncombed, lying
in tangled ringlets down to her waist she looked like a
wild gypsy. He could see the heaving of her breasts, even
through the loose *camisa* she wore, and the thought of
them, and the ease with which she had given herself, first
to him, and then to Hoskins and, no doubt, to her French
lover, hardened his purpose.

"Since it's so warm in here, might as well take off your
clothes before you lie down," he said, motioning with his
head at the blankets. And at that, the sense of being held

mesmerized left Ginny and she gave a small cry of outrage.

"I will not! I'll kill you first!"

She flung herself desperately for his guns, and he
knocked her backwards with a sweep of his arm. She fell,
hitting her head with a stunning force that left her dazed
for some minutes.

"Stop fighting me, Ginny. You ought to know by now
it's no use." She felt him bend over her, undressing her in
spite of her struggles.

The lamp still burned steadily in its alcove, and somehow, being forced to see the way he looked her over made
it even more intolerable. Ginny reached desperately for
the blankets as she attempted to cover herself, sobbing
with rage and fear.

"You animal! Dirty half-breed! Oh, can't you see I'd
rather die than have you touch me? I hate you, hate you!"

Calmly, he finished undressing and came to her. She
opened her mouth to scream, and with a quick movement
he pressed his hand over it, bruising her lips.

"Please—try to restrain your cries of ecstasy. We don't
want to wake our friends back there, do we?" Grim
amusement twitched the corner of his mouth in a tight
smile that did not reach his eyes.

She tried to cry out, to protest hysterically against his
violation of her, and felt the weight of his body come
down over hers. He held her immobile, taking his hand
from her mouth only to kiss her savagely while his hands
fondled her breasts. And now he took his time, playing
with her, leaning the weight of his body on hers while she
expended all her strength in her desperate, futile struggles.

Finally, when she was breathless and exhausted, her
head still throbbing painfully, he rolled half onto his side,
one hand over her mouth to keep her quiet, his leg over
hers to hold her still.

"That's better," he whispered in her ear, and his hand
moved slowly over her body as if they had still been
lovers—caressing, teasing, by turns; exciting it subtly.

There was nothing she could do but submit—and this
was much worse than she had expected. She had forced
herself to be prepared for a quick, brutal rape, but
instead, against her will and the silent, screaming protest
of her mind, her body, vital and young, was beginning to
respond to his caresses.

"No—no, please, no!" she whispered, but he laughed softly and kissed her on the ear, and then more gently on the mouth; and all the time his hands moved on her body, his fingers teased and aroused it until she was twisting and turning under him, desiring release, craving it; whimpering against his mouth while he whispered Spanish love words, sex words, and everything grew mixed up until she felt him spread her thighs with his knees and arched her hips to receive him—his hardness and maleness as he drove into her endlessly, demandingly, until she heard the crashing in her ears like sea-breakers and her body became one; gathering rising, and falling gently, gently, back from fulfillment to reality.

Only afterwards did the feelings of shame and revulsion engulf her, so that she lay sobbing uncontrollably in his arms. She felt them tighten around her, and then as she stiffened, heard his voice sounding as cold and rejecting as her own thoughts.

"For God's sake—*now* what is the matter?"

"You promised!" she sobbed. "When you took me away you promised you'd release me as soon as you were safely away. You promised you wouldn't—that you would not."

He leaned over her, all gentleness gone.

"I made them a threat, Ginny—not a promise. And damned if I don't find myself reluctant to do what I threatened! But I'm not releasing you as long as having you with me might prove useful. As soon as they stop following us, maybe I'll let you go—*maybe*," his voice grew harder, "unless they get too close."

"Follow? Threaten? I don't know what you're talking about! We're not being followed, how could we be? You're lying to me, you're lying because—"

"Keep your voice down, damn you!" his voice grated harshly in her ear and she shivered at the anger in it. Her mind whirled with unspoken thoughts.

He said more quietly, "We've been followed for the last week. And whoever they are, they're mighty persistent, and mighty smart too. Got an Indian tracker with them, I think. And it's you they are after, Miss Brandon. They're Americans, about five of them. Your father works fast and he's efficient, I'll say that for him."

She stared at him unbelievingly.

"But it's not possible! How long have we been travelling? My father would hardly have time to . . ."

He chuckled mirthlessly. "Baby, I've my own means of getting information, even out here. Your stepmother went back to El Paso. They have a telegraph office there. Who knows? Maybe she wired your father. All I know is we're being trailed. Why do you think we started separating? No one's going to get that gold back, and maybe they're smart enough to realize it, but they obviously want you. And probably me as well. I'll bet your father has some real nice plans in mind for me—if he ever catches up with me."

"It's just not possible," she whispered again. And then, more slowly, as the meaning of what he'd just told her began to seep into her consciousness, "So that's why . . . oh, but you can't mean it! You think to use me as bait, to lead them away from the gold, is that it? And this—the way you have treated me, is that your revenge on them for following you?"

"Revenge? Is that what you'd call this?" He kissed her again suddenly and savagely, tasting her tears, and she felt his body roll on top of hers and cried out against his mouth as he took her again; this time brutally and violently, without preliminaries.

Chapter Nineteen

They left the Indian village early the next morning, with only the faintest blush of pink in the sky to herald dawn.

A mixture of weariness, humiliation and anger kept Ginny silent. Her thighs were sore, even her legs ached; and the bitterest thought of all was the fact that last night her own body had betrayed her, had actually responded to his hateful caresses—and he had known it!

Now they rode on alone, she and Steve Morgan, and he seemed as preoccupied with his thoughts as she was. Ginny supposed he was thinking of their pursuers—if he hadn't been lying to her about it, to justify the brutal way in which he'd used her body last night. She shivered slightly, remembering the intimacy of his caresses, her own involuntary, unwanted response, and felt his arm tighten around her. She thought, miserably, Oh God, and what will happen now? What is he going to do next? He was completely unpredictable, of course—it seemed as if she was always asking herself that question. It was intolerable to find herself completely at his mercy, and even more so now that they were alone. Would he insist, every night they stopped, that—she shivered again, unable to

complete the thought, and he asked her sardonically if she
could actually be cold with the sun beating down on them.

She wouldn't answer him. She was determined that she
would never speak to him again, if she could help it, but
before nightfall, with the red desert sand gritty on her
face and even in her throat she was demanding to know
where he was taking her, when he would let her go.

The heat was unbearable, and the country they were
riding through seemed endless and changeless. Ginny had
the impression that they had been riding all day in
pointless circles. Did he actually think someone was
following them? It seemed impossible, for even a dust-
cloud should be visible for miles. They rode through dusty
red plains, with mountains, flat-topped and rocky, ahead
of them; seeming to rise like huge stone images against the
sky.

This, Ginny thought anxiously, was the kind of desert
where no man or animal could survive—and yet, surprisingly, they managed to do so. Water was scarce here,
and yet Steve seemed to know every waterhole and every
seep, and because he seemed tireless and unworried, she
found some of her earlier fears of being lost in the desert,
left to die without water for the buzzards to pick clean,
diminishing.

They kept moving, keeping mostly to the shelter of
huge buttes that towered over them. And now, they slept
only in snatches, mostly in the daytime when it was hottest—travelling fastest at night. Since the night they had
spent in the Indian village, Steve had not touched her
again, except to put an arm around her when they slept.
In spite of her tiredness, and her moments of apathy when
nothing seemed to matter, Ginny thought constantly of escape. To be free! To be free of him, free of this endless
running, of being dirty and hot and dusty all the time—
knowing that she was becoming almost as deeply tanned
as he was. She saw her own reflection once, in a waterhole, and did not recognize herself.

"I look like an Indian!" she accused him. "I look even
worse than that! Where are we going? When will we
stop?"

It was then he announced, quite casually, that he was
taking her back to El Paso.

For a stunned moment, Ginny stared at him incredulously.

"You have gone insane! El Paso? But where are we now? We were in Mexico."

"We were in the province of Sonora, my sweet." He had taken to calling her that, teasingly, enjoying the way she flushed with anger when he did. "But we happen to be in New Mexico right now. In Apache country," he added hastily, seeing the way her mouth opened, "so I wouldn't scream, if I were you."

She could not have screamed in any case, with her throat as dry as it was. But even while her eyes threw a look of hatred at him, her mind had leapt excitedly to the possibility that he had decided to set her free.

It almost seemed as if he knew what she was thinking, for she saw his lips curl in a derisive smile.

"Don't get your hopes up, Ginny! We're going to El Paso for several reasons of my own, and one of them is that it's the least likely place. Think I've lost that posse, but I've got to make sure, first."

Nothing she could do or say would induce him to tell her more, or to make her any promises. She went to sleep sullenly that night, thankful that at least he seemed to have lost his desire for her.

They reached the outskirts of what Ginny thankfully thought of as "civilization" before it dawned on her that she herself hardly looked civilized, or even human.

We are just like hunted animals, she thought furiously, hiding out in the daytime, riding at night. She turned against him suddenly, making the horse rear, hearing him curse.

"What the hell's the matter with you now? You trying to break your fool neck?"

"I won't be taken anywhere looking like this! I won't be paraded down the streets as if I was some—some—"

His anger gone, he laughed.

"You look just like a little Mexican *puta*, a whore who got caught in a dust storm. Is that what you were thinking of, *niña*?"

"Damn you! Oh, damn your soul to hell! You dirty greaser pig—you look worse than a savage yourself!"

She felt his arm tighten around her breasts, making her choke with pain and rage.

"Remind me to teach you some real swearing, Ginny," he said. "The only words you seem to know are beginning to wear mighty thin!"

He thought that she would probably swear some more
if she knew where he was taking her. In a way, he even
had some qualms, but he'd dismissed these earlier on. Lilas
was about the only person in El Paso he could really trust,
and he'd known her for years—used her place as a hide-
out before. She ran the fanciest place in El Paso, and kept
it expensive and exclusive. It was a big house, off of one
of the smaller side streets, with a saloon downstairs and a
brothel up above. And it was the whorehouse he knew
best. Lilas boasted that her girls were the best in the
business, and the prettiest—he wondered how she'd react
to the first sight of Ginny. Well, tonight he'd find out. And
Ginny would be in for a shock. She was silent now, her
body stiff with outrage, and he looked down at her,
wondering what she'd look like when she was clean again,
with her hair brushed out and shining. And laughing
inside, he wondered how it would feel to make love to her
in a bed for a change.

Ginny was half-asleep, dazed with fatigue and hunger,
when they rode into the outskirts of El Paso, late that
night. She leaned against Steve with her eyes closed,
hardly noticing the dark shape of the building that suddenly seemed to loom up in front. There were few lights
in this part of town, and none at all at Lilas' back door.
The unobtrusive, unlighted back door was especially for
the use of some of Lilas' customers who did not want
their comings and goings known. She catered to many
married men—rich ranchers and businessmen—and even
an occasional outlaw who wanted a woman before he rode
on to wherever he was going, and could afford Lilas' fancy
prices.

In order to "protect the innocent" as Lilas drily put it,
there was always a man on guard there—sitting at a
small, open window with a shotgun to see that no one attempted to molest the madame's customers. A policy that
had paid off in added bonuses for the woman many times.

Now Steve Morgan rode boldly and directly to the door
he'd used so often in the past, and hitched the black to the
rail there alongside two other horses. Later, Lilas would
see that his horse was taken to her own small livery stable
to be fed, rubbed down and settled for the night. He
studied the other horses carefully, noting the brands they
wore, but recognized none of them.

He felt Ginny stir against him and kept a tight hold of her arm as he helped her down.

"Try making a fuss or screaming and I'll break your pretty nose," he warned her softly, and hearing the hard note in his voice she believed him and stayed silent.

The door opened inward on well-oiled hinges, even before he had time to knock.

"Hola, Manuelito," Steve said as casually as if he'd been there only a week before. It had actually been almost a year, but the fat man who stood there with the shotgun under his arm recognized him and stepped back, his face wreathed in smiles.

"Señor Esteban! It has been a long time! Will you wait a moment? I must tell madame at once, or she will be very angry with me. Wait . . ."

When the man had disappeared through another door, concealed by velvet drapes, Ginny turned furiously on Steve.

"Where are we? What is this place? I don't want . . ."

"Shut up!" he snapped at her, suddenly tired of her questions and her nagging. His fingers tightened cruelly over her arm, forcing her to grit her teeth in order not to cry out with pain.

"Does it make you feel better to hurt me? Do you need to prove how much stronger than I am you are?"

Half-ashamed of himself, he let his grip on her loosen, and at that moment, Lilas came to them with her skirts swishing, her arms outstretched in greeting—all rich satins and bleached hair, her perfume almost overpowering in the small space.

"Steve! Steve Morgan! Well—I must say I'm surprised to see you back here of all places. I've been hearing things about you, you wicked, wicked man!"

Feeling slightly sick, Ginny watched them embrace. The woman was obviously old enough to be his mother, and yet Steve kissed her full on the lips, hugging her, with every evidence of enjoyment.

When at last he held her away from him, he shook his head almost imperceptibly when Lilas opened her mouth to say more.

"Lilas, my love, I have a guest for you, if you've a room to spare. And don't be misled by her appearance, it is a girl, and she's even passably pretty when she's clean."

Burning with humiliation, Ginny felt the other woman's small eyes flicker over her, taking in everything.

"Oho—so it's like *that!* Well—better come upstairs with me quickly—most of the girls are busy in the parlor right now, and if I guess right, the fewer people who see her the better, eh?"

Still talking, Lilas turned to lead the way. Ginny felt herself picked up in Steve's arms and carried along in the plump woman's wake, in spite of her feeble struggles. Her head whirled with shock and anger and yes, with embarrassment too! How dare he talk about her that way, as if she weren't there, and couldn't understand? And what kind of a place was this, what kind of woman was Lilas?

She was being carried upstairs in Lilas' billowing, perfumed wake—Steve's arms holding her closely and easily in spite of her struggles. Ginny had a vague impression of thickly carpeted opulence—a long corridor that reminded her of a hotel, with doors opening off it. And Lilas, in her lowcut blue satin gown, reminded her of something—someone. . . .

She was being taken into a room that was dominated by an enormous bed—an elaborate dresser, covered with bottles and combs and brushes had three mirrors, and Ginny turned her face away from her own bedraggled reflection. Lilas wore rouge and bright lip salve. She flirted archly with Steve as she said she'd be sending a maid upstairs soon to fill the hip bath that stood behind a small, carved screen.

"No need to stir yourself, little one—the bath's right in front of the fire, and that's been lit—I don't stint on anything up here. And I'll have one of my young ladies bring you some clothes later."

Her eyes went critically over Ginny, who could not help shrinking under their amused, inquisitive regard.

"And as for you, Steve—I know someone who will be just dying to scrub your back for you, you handsome devil! Just knock at the door at the end of the hall—you know which one—whenever you can tear yourself away."

If only she could hide! Ginny tried to ignore the arch way in which Lilas looked at Steve, the way he smiled down at her. Huddled in a chair, she could find nothing to say. And in spite of her growing dislike for Lilas, she disliked even worse the prospect of being left here alone with Steve Morgan.

She told herself later that her instincts had been right. No sooner had the door closed behind Lilas than he was raising his eyebrows at her, ordering her to take her clothes off—ripping them off her body when she refused. And to make matters worse, she'd been forced to stand naked and blushing under the eyes of the shy, giggling Indian maid who brought in pails of steaming hot water and a large cake of heavily scented soap.

Having a bath, which had been something she'd longed for and looked forward to for weeks, became a miserable ordeal when Steve had insisted on washing her himself, even her hair—heartlessly pushing her head under the soapy water when she balked.

"I want to make sure you're clean all over, my sweet," he said laconically. And then, when she cursed at him wildly, he held her face steady and rubbed soap in her mouth until she gagged and choked.

"Been meaning to do that for a long time," he grinned. "Somebody ought to have told you that all that swearing and name-calling is hardly ladylike!"

Afterwards, he held her pinioned between his thighs while he dried her quivering body, taking his time over it—lingering over her breasts and belly and inner thighs.

"Oh, stop it!" she moaned, "haven't you abused and punished me enough? Let me go!"

He tossed the towel carelessly away and continued to hold her captive.

"Stop struggling, Ginny! You know it isn't any use, don't you? Why don't you give in and try to enjoy our enforced companionship?"

She knew her struggles were useless, she had reason to know he'd take whatever he wanted from her in any case, but his words goaded her to further squirmings, especially when he began to move his hands teasingly and very slowly over her body . . . she felt his lips follow his hands and cried out wildly that he must stop, and then, to her utter relief she heard the maid's soft tap on the door.

She brought Ginny a filmy, diaphanous silk wrapper that concealed nothing—and then, at last, the food that she had been longing for.

Thinly sliced roast beef with a delicious gravy—baby peas and enormous baked potatoes swimming with melted butter. There was even a tall bottle of red wine and two glasses.

Unable to help herself, Ginny ate hungrily. It would have eased her pride to refuse dinner, but the smell and the sight of the food were too much—she felt starved, it was impossible not to stuff herself.

Steve himself ate sparingly, and when she looked up occasionally she would catch his eyes on her, the amusement in them making her almost choke on her dinner. And she did notice that he drank considerably more than he ate—sending the maid for another bottle of wine when she came back to clear away. Ginny herself drank two glassfuls when he insisted, and she had to admit that it was palatable and made her feel warmer inside. But the coldness and misery came back when she saw him rise, stretching, and go towards the door.

"You promised I should have some clothes! Where are you going?"

"Is it possible that you don't want me to leave you?" He took her chin in his fingers and laughed shortly when she flinched away.

"I didn't really think two glasses of wine would change your mind that fast, stubborn one. I'm going to have my bath now, and talk to a few old friends. But I'll be back. You'll wait for me, won't you?"

Her cheeks flaming, Ginny heard the lock click behind him, but in spite of it she tried the door several times, then pounded on it, hoping that someone might hear and let her out.

Finally, after spending several minutes pacing around the room, Ginny decided against trying to hang herself with the sheets from the bed, and determined to get herself drunk instead. From what she had witnessed, getting intoxicated must be quite a pleasant, if not euphoric, sensation.

With a stab of homesickness that went through her like a dagger she remembered how Uncle Albert and his friends had always seemed more jovial after they had been at the port for a while. And once, when Pierre had come home very late and had thrown pebbles at her window so that she would wake and let him in, he had hardly been able to stand for laughing.

Sullenly, Ginny sat in the chair, which she pulled up in front of the fire, and began to drink. She got tired of using the glass and refilling it so many times, and drank from the bottle instead, as the bandits had done with their *tequila.* But did she really feel any different? She looked into the fire and wondered why it suddenly appeared so much brighter, and so hot. The bottle, surprisingly, was empty, and she got clumsily to her feet to tug at the bellpull which would summon the maid, and found herself unusually clumsy. Why did her feet stumble so on the rug? And why didn't she feel happy? The room seemed to sway around her and she put one hand up to cover her eyes, wondering dazedly if the wine had been drugged. Oh, but she wouldn't put that past him—he was capable of anything, anything at all!

Amazing herself, Ginny began to cry. She felt very sad, and very sleepy. She tore the wrapper from around her body and threw it at the door that stayed closed. It was too hot for clothes—and what did it matter, he would take if off her quickly, if he pleased. Still sobbing, she fell across the bed and was asleep almost immediately.

Steve Morgan came in later—so much later in fact, that the fire had burned down to embers, leaving the room in darkness except for the single lamp that burned on the dresser.

He undressed quietly, looking down at Ginny's sleeping profile that still showed traces of tears. So she'd been crying? Certainly not for his absence, he was sure of that much. The empty wine bottle, lying on its side by the chair caught his eye and he began to grin. Damn the little witch anyhow! She was drunk.

He leaned over her, smelling the fumes of wine, and the sweet curving of her uncovered, unconscious body made him feel something like regret. Perhaps he should have stayed with her tonight. But he'd had to talk to Lilas, make arrangements; and then Susie, a pert brunette whose charms he'd tasted before, had given him a bath, joining him in the large tub that was Lilas' own. Susie had the cleverest hands and the sweetest little body—her mouth could do things for a man that could make him stay crazy-wild for her, hour after hour. They had drunk champagne, and one thing had led to another.

It was good, having a woman who neither cursed nor struggled nor pretended she hated every moment, every touch, until the very last . . . and tonight, he hadn't been in the mood for war, he'd needed to relax. Susie was good at providing just that.

Steve got in bed beside Ginny, a smile touching the corner of his mouth. In her sleep, she moved instinctively closer, snuggling her body against his with a sigh. Shrugging, he pulled the covers up over them and put his arm around her. Habit was a funny thing. He'd grown kind of used to having her body up against his this way at nights. Her hair smelled sweet and clean, and although she lacked Susie's opulent curves she was soft against him, her flesh warm and yielding for once. He realized to his own amazement that he wanted her—but not like this. Something that was almost pity made him tighten his arm around her. There was always the morning. . . .

Ginny woke first in the morning, her head aching, a horrible taste in her mouth. Without daring to open her eyes just yet she tried to move, and found her hair caught under the shoulder of the man who lay beside her with his arm and one leg thrown possessively over her body.

Her eyes flew open and she stared at a ceiling ornamented with paintings that would have made her blush at any other time. But there, for a moment she had been dreaming that she was home, lying in her own room above Tante Celine's, with fat Marie coming in to wake her with a cup of hot chocolate.

But now, too soon, the moment of being caught between dreams and waking had passed, and reality came flooding bitterly back. Ginny could not repress a small cry of mingled pain and disappointment and the sound, coupled with her involuntary movement, woke Steve up.

He opened one red-rimmed eye and gazed critically at her stiff, unyielding body.

"Must you be so restless and noisy this early in the morning, my love? Or is this your way of telling me you're impatient for the pleasure you were cheated of last night?"

This time her gasp was filled with rage.

"Ohh—you dirty lecher!"

"I see that a good night's sleep in a bed has done nothing to improve your temper," he interrupted unfeelingly, opening both eyes and gazing into her flushed, angry face.

With her hair all tousled and her green eyes heavy-lidded from sleep he thought she looked uncommonly desirable this morning. Reading his look, Ginny tried again, unsuccessfully, to move as far away from him as possible; and then she cried out with fury when he pulled away the sheet that covered her warm, naked flesh.

"Beast!" she panted. "Oh, *why* won't you just let me be?"

"But you'd be disappointed if I did not notice how very alluring you look this morning—now wouldn't you?"

Leaning up on his elbow, Steve let his eyes roam slowly over her cringing body. And, as Ginny realized bitterly, there was nothing she could do to stop him, nothing at all. She felt hot, shamed blushes covering her face and neck as he studied her intently.

"Open your legs, Ginny," he said softly, and she thought for a stunned moment that she could not possibly have heard right. His hand moved teasingly over her belly, fingers pulling at red-gold curls.

"I'm beginning to find out you have lots to learn, my sweet. Come on now, stop fighting me, for a start. Open your legs for me." His voice was soft and wheedling, and she felt him press tiny, tender kisses along the side of her neck, but she was hardly conscious of it, for the rage that drummed in her head.

"No! No, I won't! I won't give in to you, Steve Morgan. Whatever you want from me you'll have to take by force, for I'll never submit willingly, never!"

"Don't make promises you might not keep, sweetheart," he taunted her.

He tangled one hand in her hair and began to kiss her on the mouth, his lips bruising hers. She felt his tongue in her mouth, seeking, and felt his hand on her belly, sliding downward—his fingers on the soft inner flesh of her thighs. She struggled, pounding against his encroaching body with her fists. Tears streamed down Ginny's face and she was choked by sobs of terror and frustration.

"You brute—you wild animal!" she wailed, feeling his hands riot over her body, touching, invading, probing until she squirmed against him, pleading abjectly with him to stop.

Oh, God, what was he doing with her? She felt him drag her thighs apart and lift her legs over his shoulders and gave a muffled scream of outrage. He held her with his hands on her breasts, fingers torturing her nipples, and then his mouth found her. She heard her own wild sobbing, her moans of shame that were mixed, humiliatingly, with desire as his tongue drove deeply into her softness.

Her body writhed; unthinkingly her fingers caught his head, holding him, pulling him closer to her.

"Ohh—" she cried, her head rolling helplessly from side to side. "Oh—damn you, damn you!"

His mouth seemed to sear into her like a hot iron, branding her his possession as all restraint left her and she cried out wildly for release.

When it came, leaving her shaking, completely helpless and half-fainting with reaction, he slid his body upward and over hers. This time, when he entered her, she made no protest at all, except to shudder weakly when he whispered in her ear, "And some day, sweet, you'll do that for me, too."

What was the use in protesting? No matter how much she hated him, he had only to begin caressing her and she was lost—powerless to prevent him from doing as he pleased. And now, in spite of her own revulsion, he was proving it all over again—moving slowly, so slowly and steadily against her that her treacherous body was awakening again, arching up greedily to meet his.

"Put your arms around me, Ginny," he commanded and her arms complied, raising slowly to twine themselves around his neck.

"I hate you, I hate you!" she whispered, but even in her own ears the words sounded like a caress, and he only smiled down into her face, increasing the rhythm of his movements until she forgot everything else.

Chapter Twenty

She had grown to hate this room that held her prisoner. It had been a week already, and Ginny felt like a caged captive in some Sultan's harem. Even this room—her velvet cell, with its entwined figures on the ceiling, its conveniently mirrored dresser and rich plush—everything here reminded her of what she was and where she was.

He was gone all day, and sometimes for half the night as well, and she had almost lost track of the division between day and night. The whorehouse blossomed at night—during the day most of the girls slept. She knew now, of course, to what kind of place he had brought her, and she tormented herself with questions and with her own feeling of abject humiliation.

Whore—I'm his whore—his plaything, she thought. And that's all I ever was at the beginning—a new experience, a stupid, foolish, too-willing virgin! Oh God, I flung myself at him, in a way I asked for this. So now he keeps me in a bordello for his personal pleasure. But afterwards—this was the thought that would make her shudder and grow cold with fear, afterwards, when he's tired of me, what will he do with me? I know too much ... he daren't let me go after this, and when he's finished with whatever

business he has out here that keeps him gone so long—
what then?

She had wept a lot in the beginning, planning continually how to escape. But as the days passed she became
almost resigned. The room was locked—the windows were
not only barred but heavily shuttered as well. Her meals
were brought in by the Indian maid, but always behind
her the man Manuel lounged, with his shotgun ready. Her
hysterical outbursts were met with cold, blank faces, and
once Lilas herself had come and had told her, in an incongruously husky, friendly voice, exactly how she treated her
recalcitrant girls.

"You must understand of course, my dear, how—shall
we say—fortunate you are? To have just one lover? But I
can't have trouble—it's bad for discipline and the girls are
complaining . . . so you see, if you can't behave . . ."

Terror-struck, feeling physically sick, Ginny had
managed to control her outbursts after that—confining her
weeping to moments when she was alone; muffling her sobs
in the pillow.

She received no sympathy at all from Steve, who for
the most part seemed tense and abstracted when he forgot
her presence.

To pass the time, and because she found herself almost
unbearably lonely and starved for any kind of companionship, Ginny began, at first shyly, to chat desultorily with
some of Lilas' "girls," when they came in curiously on the
pretext of bringing her meals.

One of them, a vivacious French-Canadian who called
herself Lorena, was more friendly than the others, and
kinder, once Ginny had become used to Lorena's frank
manner and blunt speech.

As the days passed, Lorena came quite often to visit
and talk in her bright satin wrapper, sitting yawning on
Ginny's bed, her black eyes bright with friendly amusement at the new girl's obvious naiveté.

Like the other girls, Lorena talked mostly of men—
their likes and dislikes in bed, and their peculiarities. They
thought Ginny lucky to have a lover who wanted to keep
her for himself—luckier that her lover happened to be
Steve Morgan.

Lorena told Ginny bluntly that she was a fool to think
constantly of escape.

"Where would you go, *ma petite*? Back to your papa?

No—after this, I tell you it is too late! That is the trouble with being a "good" woman, once a man has had you then you are bad, hein? Now me—I am a whore because I have to survive and the work is easy. Hard work—being someone's maid, perhaps—scrubbing floors—that is not for me!" Lorena shuddered delicately. "After my man was killed in a fight with knives I learn fast that all men, they are alike. They want to be made to feel good—want something different, you comprehend? Something their good wives won't give them."

It did not take Lorena long to discover that Ginny did not comprehend. Laughing, she promised to teach her about men.

"For," she said shyly, rolling her liquid black eyes, "it is possible that if a woman is very good, very clever in the bed, she can make a man wild for her, so wild that *he* is *her* slave, in fact—and me, I know this!"

Bored, with nothing else to do, Ginny found herself listening in spite of herself—learning about things she'd never dreamed of. Lorena, or one of the other girls perhaps, would stroll into her room to share a meal, and regale her with details of their lovers of the night before. Occasionally, if a man had been too rough, a girl might sport a bruise or two. Lorena admitted that once she had gone with a man who wanted to beat her, and had offered her a hundred dollar tip for herself if she would let him.

"I do it for the money, that time—but never, no, never again!" Lorena cried, shivering with the memory of pain.

"Oh God! Why are men such beasts?" Ginny burst out, horrified, and Lorena patted her hand consolingly.

"Well—maybe not all of them, yes?" Her eyes twinkled and she looked sideways, teasingly, at Ginny. "You promise you will not be jealous? Your Steve—he is *magnifique* in the bed, I know! Once—but very long ago, *cherie*, don't hate me for it—we spend one whole night together, and not once did I 'ave to pretend. He is a stallion, that one! You're lucky, *p'tite*."

"Lucky!" Ginny echoed bitterly, her mouth drooping. "How can you say that when you *know* I'm not here of my own choosing? I hate him—and I'm so afraid—Lorena, what will he do with me?"

Lorena shrugged. "Life is uncertain. Who can tell what any man will do? But I think he likes you more than he will admit, and perhaps more than you suspect too, little innocent! Why else would he run off with you? Perhaps he will even marry with you some day, who knows? You say he was the first man for you—that makes a difference to a man."

After Lorena had gone, Ginny's thoughts were more bitter than usual. Marry her indeed! And Lorena did not know that Steve thought there had been others after him—Carl Hoskins, and even her dear, dear Michel. She would never tell him different of course—let him think the worst, let him think that she'd taken other men and preferred them to him! And as for marriage—she knew well enough what his thoughts were on that subject.

"Women make marriage a trap for men," he said once. "I intend to stay clear of it, and of love—another female excuse to cling, to put chains on a man and keep him in one place. Me, I'm footloose, baby—never could take staying in any one place for too long."

She wouldn't marry him if he begged her on his knees—not even if he was the last man on earth, Ginny vowed to herself. She'd escape from him somehow, before he tired of her and planned to discard her. Some way, she'd go back to her father's love and protection and he'd find a way to make things right. Perhaps he would let her go back to France, and even if she never married, at least there she would have the freedom to take lovers of her own choosing. Like the famous Ninon, perhaps she too might become a courtesan. I'll be rich, yes, and independent—a *demi-mondaine*, a courtesan, but never a common whore, she thought rebelliously—never that! I won't let him turn me into one!

Over and over she'd tell herself this, steeling herself for the time he'd return to the room, dirty and travel-stained, refusing to tell her where he had been or what he was doing.

A week passed, and another day—Ginny felt she could no longer bear it, and the unseasonable heat put her nerves on edge so that she felt like screaming, clawing at the walls that enclosed her with her nails, beating at the door until her fists were reduced to pulp.

She was not expecting Steve's sudden return just before noon, and surprised him by the frenzied way she flung herself at him.

"Why won't you let me go *out*? Can't you see I'm dying here by slow degrees, that I'm stifling to death? For God's sake, Steve, I feel I'll go mad—is that what you want me to do?"

He held her away from him, looking down at her tear-contorted face with a forbidding frown.

"Control yourself, Ginny! I've got to leave again in a minute. Maybe I'll take you riding tonight, if I get back in time."

"But you've taken me with you before—where do you go? What are you doing? Why can't I come with you now?"

He smiled at her mirthlessly.

"I suppose I should be flattered at your eagerness for my company. But not today, Ginny. There's a posse hunting me, and they're too damned close right now. I'm laying a false trail for them, leading them away from here so we can leave."

Her eyes widened. "You mean—you actually mean there's help this close? Why won't you let me go?"

He had turned away from her but she ran after him, pulling at his arm.

"Please! Oh, please—if you'll only let me go I'll see my father pays you—any ransom you name! And I'll make him stop them from coming after you—don't you see? Then you'll be free too!"

He jerked his arm from her clinging grasp and caught her by the shoulders, his fingers digging cruelly into her flesh.

"I'm going to keep you with me for as long as I have to, as long as I need to. I'm sorry, Ginny, but you're my ace in the hole, you might say. There's a U.S. marshal leading that posse, and not even your father is going to stop them—only the fact that I have you keeps them from getting too close. They got wind of a lot of gold being exchanged for guns, you see, and so—" he laughed, suddenly, "so I've been running across the border, letting them get a glimpse of me now and then—leavin' a trail they can't resist following. It's been like a game, baby—a pity you can't join in."

"You dirty, rotten bastard!" She was learning how to swear, and the word came easily to her lips.

"I'm getting tired of hearing you swear," he said, and she shivered in spite of herself under the flat coldness of his regard. "The fact is—I'm also goddam tired of your nagging and your bitching and your hatred hitting me in

the face the minute I walk in this door. I'll be leaving you
alone tonight, Ginny—so enjoy it!"

She spun her body around, staring at him fearfully. He
meant it! He'd jammed his hat back on his head, was
hefting one of his saddlebags to throw over his shoulder,
and was already at the door.

"But you said—where are you going?" She almost
screamed the words at him, and saw the lines at the corner of his mouth tauten.

"If you must know, sweet, I'm going to another room.
I'm going to have a bath and change clothes and then I'm
going downstairs, where I will play cards and get slightly
drunk and find me a woman who's willing and warm.
Good day." He bowed to her politely and sarcastically before he left, leaving her staring at the door.

Ginny found herself strangely restless and keyed up
after Steve had gone. Ginny paced the room, her thoughts
giving her no rest. Dear God—suppose he didn't come
back? Suppose he decided to keep riding, without her? Did
he hate her so much in turn that he'd decide it would be a
big joke to leave her here, to become one of Lilas'
whores?

Clad only in her thinnest wrapper because of the heat,
Ginny alternated between pacing the floor and flinging
herself on the bed to cry her rage and fear into the pillow.
There was a heavy gilt clock on the nightstand by the bed
and she watched it balefully as the hands moved forward
pitilessly and inexorably.

She fell into a light, troubled sleep and woke up feeling
herself in a kind of stupor. Mechanically, she forced
herself to walk about the room, lighting the lamps. Dear
God—seven o'clock already! Where was he? "Come back,
damn you!" she raged into the crumpled bedcovers, "I
won't be left here, I won't stay—you can't do this to me!"
But couldn't he? Cold—ruthless—calculating—he was all
of those things. Perhaps he had decided she was a millstone around his neck—too dangerous and too full of fight
to carry around with him any longer.

Footsteps, heavy and deliberate, came down the hall-
way—paused at her door, hesitating, and then moved on.
Ginny realized only after the man had gone that she'd
held her breath with fearful anticipation. She'd heard
them before—Lilas' clients, her girls' customers, passing
her door.

The thought that she was trapped here, forced to lie here and wait for whatever fate he planned for her, was too much to bear. But what other choice had she? Ginny's eyes went hopelessly to the window. But she had tried that before and found that the bars were thick and heavy, embedded into adobe and stone. And beyond the bars were the shutters that closed her in and were never opened to let in the light or fresh air.

Ginny began to pace again, more nervously this time, her hands clasping and unclasping before her. He had to come back, he *had* to!

Every time that footsteps passed the door Ginny froze, the color draining from her face and then returning as the footsteps went on. He's making me into a whore, she thought furiously, feverishly. Yes, for I'm becoming just like one of them—waiting, listening for the footsteps of the man who—who will own me tonight. God, I can't let him do this to me, I must be calm!

Walking over to the dresser, Ginny snatched up her hairbrush and began to pull it through her hair, tugging viciously until her scalp ached and tingled. And in some odd way, the pain helped—enabling her to think more clearly.

She saw herself in the wide, elegantly decorated mirrors that tripled her reflection—patches of color standing out on her cheekbones as if she'd used rouge—her green eyes seeming larger than ever. Footsteps passed the door again, then returned. A voice came from the other side of the door—drunken-sounding, from its thick speech.

"Hey—hey you in there? You number seven? You the li'l ole redheaded gal she promised me?"

Speechless, frozen with fear, Ginny heard the doorknob rattle.

"Hey! You gonna let me in or not? Durn you, I already paid Lilas plenty, but I'm aimin' to pay you more if you're as purty an' nice as she tol' me . . ."

She hadn't even heard his footsteps, and yet, there he was! And the redhead he was looking for—surely, surely it wasn't possible! He was rattling at the door again, swearing. All she had to do was stay quiet, and someone would come and remove him. Of course they would!

But if—if—hardly pausing to let her thoughts go further, Ginny ran to the door, clinging to the knob.

"Mister? Mister, I'm locked in, you'll have to open the

door from your side if you—if you really want to, that is." Belatedly, she'd paused and tried to make her voice sound softer, and more appealing.

Could he have been sent up to her on purpose? But in that case—wouldn't they have told him that the door was locked on the outside? Wouldn't they have told him to walk right in and surprise her?

But if he hadn't been sent, and he was drunk and had made a mistake when he looked at the room number, then—"Oh God! she prayed silently, "Let him be very drunk—so drunk I can handle him easily."

She heard a drunken chuckle, more fumbling at the door, and wondered, almost crying with suspense, if the lock needed a key to open it. No—she couldn't remember that Steve had ever paused to use a key, surely she would have heard one rattle in the lock. She prayed again, "Don't let anyone come right now—not yet!"

She heard the click of the lock at last and moved back as the door swung open and a man stumbled in. Before he could utter a word she bent swiftly forward, and grabbing her hairbrush, jammed the narrowest part of its handle between the door and the jamb—just enough so that it could not lock itself again.

"If—if you let it go back all the way then you'd be locked in here too," she explained breathlessly.

"Can't see that it would be a bad idea, now that I seen you, little filly!"

Ginny straightened cautiously, still moving backward and away from him, hoping her actions would not prove too noticeable. Seeing the man's loose, blubbery lips spread as he chuckled with amusement at his own sally, and catching the look he gave her, now licking his lips, she realized suddenly what a picture she must present to him.

All she wore was the thin wrapper that hid nothing from his lecherous gaze—her hair hung loosely around her shoulders and down her back. And now, suddenly, she had misgivings, and her heart began to beat heavily.

"By God, Lilas sure wan't lyin' to me this time! Plumb beautiful—a real little jewel you are! Come on, li'l baby-doll, no reason to put on that innocent act for ole George. Come give me a big smack, huh?"

Leering, the man lurched towards her and Ginny backed away from him fearfully, not daring to take her eyes off his face.

"Please, mister—oh please, wait a minute! You have to listen to me, you *must*, please!"

His eyes had a glazed, animal look in them, and she was aware that he had big, beefy red hands that stretched out towards her. Dear God, had he no shame? He was older even than her own father—a gray-haired, balding man with a paunch that hung over his belt, and watery blue eyes. He was smiling, cunningly, his eyes squinting under a low, bulging forehead.

"C'mon, babydoll—George likes his young fillies wild and eager—no need to pretend, I tol' you—gimme a kiss, a kiss first, huh?"

He laughed, and Ginny went almost sick with terror as she realized that she could back away no farther, the edge of the bed caught her against the thighs and she almost screamed.

"Mister! Will you listen to me a minute?" She licked her lips nervously, willing her voice to sound soft, wheedling. "What's the hurry, sw—sweetheart? See, here I am, all yours, but you have to let me talk to you a little first—you have to be *patient* with me, you understand? Oh, please ... !" He didn't understand, she flung her hands out towards him in despair and tried again. "I—it's my first time, *please*—don't you understand that? That's why she keeps me locked up here—so I won't run away, but you—you look so kind, and you're—you're handsome—distinguished, you know?" He had stopped, swaying on his feet, to peer uncertainly at her, and Ginny felt a surge of hope. At least he was listening to her now! She put all the pleading she could muster into her voice, uncomfortably aware of the bed behind her.

"You—I could tell right away you're a gentleman—you'll help me, won't you? They—they keep me here by *force*, but you're going to rescue me, you will, won't you?" Her voice broke in spite of herself, and she saw his small eyes peering at her with a kind of doubt.

"Now—now looky here! Lilas tol' me you was a purty redheaded piece an' would give me a ride fer my money—said you was a lot of fun. Don't go gettin' all teary-eyed on me now, I don't wanna hear no problems, just came to git me some fucking ..."

She saw his eyes take her in—the way his tongue snaked out to moisten his thick lips, and felt her heart sink. Oh God, he *had* to listen to her!

"Why don' you shut up with that claptrap—come on
here an' gimme a kiss like I bin tellin' yuh."

Ginny forced herself to smile at him and toss her head
coquettishly.

"You're so big and so strong, why your arms would
crush poor little me in a minute! Why don't you . . ."

Grinning, he started to fumble with his belt and she said
quickly, leaning forward, "You—you have to go real slow
now, promise? I—really I'm new to all this and I don't
know—"

"Look, babydoll, I paid Lilas already. Don't you try to
pull no wool over George's eyes. I know about you li'l
whores, and the more innercent you look, the badder you
are. No, don't go givin' me any more lies, now!"

"But I'm *not* a whore! I don't want to be! Listen—you
look like a smart man, one who wouldn't be fooled by
outward appearances. Wouldn't you like to earn yourself a
reward? A whole lot of money? Maybe as much as ten
thousand dollars, mister, you'll be able to name your price
if you take me back to my father."

Something in the frantic urgency of her voice, the
fingers she kept twisting together got through to the man,
as lecherous and fuddled as he was and he paused to stare
at her.

"You *loco*?" To her despair, she saw that his little piggy
eyes had gone hard, and he was staring at her with anger
starting to show on his face. "Now look, I didn't come up
here to play no games! I know the kind of gal Lilas keeps
up here, and ain't none of you tramps in this 'gainst your
will."

"My name is Virginia Brandon. *Brandon!* For God's
sake, won't you just listen? My father is a Senator from
California, and he'll have rewards posted for my return, I
know it! If you'll just take me with you, please!"

"Uh—huh!" he was shaking his head, still leering at her,
a cunning smile on his mouth. "Looky here, babydoll, you
gimme some *first*, and then we'll see, after that!"

Wild with fear she saw him loosen his belt and sus-
penders, still grinning at her. "Come on now, you be real
nice to me an' I'll see whut I kin do, hear?"

He reached for her with his pants still around his
ankles, and his hands brushed at her breasts.

With a cry of mingled fear and desperation, Ginny

rolled sideways and backwards, across the bed, and he came after her, his hands already tearing at the wrapper.

"No—no! Take your dirty hands off me!"

"You're the kind wants to fight, huh? Want a man to give it to you rough? Ol' George is goin' to get what he paid for."

She tried to roll off the bed on the other side, but his hands, clawing for her, caught her leg and she heard him chortle. His other hand grabbed for her crotch, fingers splayed, and now, at last, she cried out. Her hands went out, and she touched the night stand—the clock!

Hardly capable of thought by now, Ginny curled her fingers around it and brought it down on the man's head, as hard as she could.

He gave a sound that was like a croaking grunt, and she thought his heavy body jerked horribly before he lay still—fingers still clutching at her.

Sobbing, shaking with terror still, Ginny looked down at him. The dirty, greasy old bastard! He deserved it. Even if she had killed him, he deserved it. He stank of sweat and unwashed clothes, and it struck her suddenly that all this time—even while he was undressing in anticipation of having her, he had not bothered to take off his boots nor his filthy underwear.

She scrambled from the bed, tearing what remained of her wrapper off her body, and ran for the armoire. Thank God that at least she had some clothes—Lorena, taking pity on her, had brought her two dresses just two days ago. All that Steve had thought to get her so far was a cotton shirt and a riding skirt!

No time to search—Ginny took the first gown that came to hand, a green flouncy garment of lace and satin, cut very low at the neck, and dragged it over her head. Her fingers trembled as she forced herself to take the time to fasten the tiny buttons that held its bodice together. Panic—a dry fear that left her shaking like a leaf, drove her on now.

Pushing her feet into high-heeled, unsuitable slippers, Ginny rushed to the mirror and pinned her hair up carelessly, swirling some of it on the top of her head and letting the rest hang down her back. A touch of lip salve—if anyone saw her she must not look different from any of the "girls"—and then she was away from the mirror, stumbling towards the door, pausing for the merest instant to make sure the man was still unconscious. He was stirring—God, he moved! And groaned. Not wanting to see more, Ginny ran from the room, only stopping to make sure that the door was locked behind her.

She had escaped from her room, at least, but in the narrow, silent passageway outside it Ginny gave a small, despairing sob as she wondered how she would ever contrive to escape from the building itself. The back door was out of the question with Manuel stationed there, but the staircase she was facing now led downstairs—no doubt to the saloon itself.

Her ears straining, Ginny heard a door open and close somewhere downstairs—the tinkling of a piano—a woman's voice, singing, and the sound of male laughter. Down there, there were people—bright lights and talking. Surely, among all the men who must frequent Lilas' saloon there might be one or two with enough decency to help her? And surely, downstairs and in public, they would not try to make a prisoner of her again?.

Quickly, before she could think about all the risks she was about to take, Ginny walked hurriedly past the closed doors and to the head of the stairs, thankful for the dim, rose-shaded lamps that Lilas kept up here.

The staircase curved slightly, and as she came downstairs as quietly as possible, her hands clinging to the railing, Ginny could see a small foyer, with swinging doors at one end that obviously led into the saloon. Her breathing quickened as she almost ran down the last few stair-treads. There had to be another door here, there just had to! But on reaching the bottom of the stairs she could have cried with disappointment, for there was only a full length mirror on one wall, reflecting her own scared-looking face back at her, and against the other wall a carved wooden stand with a bowl of wilted looking flowers on it.

She stood hesitating, and as she did the door swung open and a man and a woman, both laughing, came through it. The man was a Mexican or Spaniard, tall and slender, with dark hair and mustachios, and the girl was Lorena. He had his arm around Lorena's waist, and they were still laughing together at some joke until Lorena saw Ginny, who stood rooted to the floor, and her mouth fell open.

"Ginny! Oh, *cherie,* how could you. . . ."

"So—another pretty new one? But where does madame Lilas find you all?"

The man smiled, showing white, even teeth. "Perhaps, Lorena, this one would join us too? You know I have the money, I'll make it all right with Madame."

Before Lorena could say anything else, or the grinning man elaborate on his suggestion, Ginny brushed past them and ran swiftly into the saloon, driven by blind panic and desperation she was beyond controlling.

Her frightened, seeking eyes moved quickly to the right and left and noticed that there were not many people in the large room. A bartender wiped glasses behind the long, curving bar, and of the "girls," Susie, sat on the piano with her legs defiantly crossed to show her mesh-stockinged calves and ankles as she sang some saucy new ballad.

The saloon was not as wide as it was long, and as soon as she had seen the location of the front door, Ginny picked up her skirts and fled towards it, running faster than she had ever run before.

She heard Lorena call out behind her, "Ginny, stop! You must not . . ." and then she had burst through the big double doors and was running blindly, hardly knowing or caring where she was fleeing—aware only that she had to run and keep on running now, to escape from whatever Steve might do to her if he'd seen her.

Ginny heard the clattering of her own heels sounding monstrously loud on the uneven boardwalk, and then as other footsteps sounded behind her she turned and ran like a hunted animal out into the street, noticing only vaguely, the sound of her panting echoing in her ears, that it was narrow and dusty.

Her hair came loose and fell down over her face and shoulders, blinding her, and still she ran. She could feel the sweat pouring down her body, her breath rasped in her throat and she knew with a kind of utter despair that she was tiring, her steps starting to drag already.

Oh, God! Had she really hoped to escape? Where could she run to? One of her shoes came off and she stumbled; trying to save herself she spread out her arms and fell, sprawling ignominiously in the dust and dirt of the street.

She lay there sobbing hopelessly, feeling that all strength had left her and she could not move. What further degradation was there left?

Opening her eyes, she saw his boots, standing astraddle before her face. It would have to be *him*—who else would have come after her? His voice drawled mockingly from somewhere above her.

"Really, my love! You might have told me you wanted a stroll in the fresh air. Or could it be that you were pining for my company?"

Without giving her a chance to answer his gibes, he bent down, grasping her arms, and pulled her roughly to her feet.

She was still sobbing breathlessly, despairingly, and with a muffled, angry exclamation he tugged the neckerchief from around his throat and began wiping her face with it while his fingers, still holding her arm in a painful vice, held her motionless.

"You had better look a little more presentable than you do now when I take you back inside," he said coldly.

Ginny looked around wildly and saw that in spite of her feeling that she had run for miles they were only a short distance from the lighted doorway of Lilas' saloon. A liquid, hazy-looking half-moon hung low in the sky and by its diffused light she could see how angry he looked—the black brows meeting in a frown, lips thinned and compressed with annoyance.

"Come along now," he said, shaking her. "You wanted an outing—some amusement, and you shall have it. But first bend down and pick up your slipper—put it on—it won't do for you to walk in barefoot like some common Indian peasant girl, would it?"

"Please—" she murmured incoherently, but even as she began to plead with him she fell silent again, biting her lip, knowing that it was no use.

Anger, panic, hope—everything evaporated, leaving her cold with utter despair. Silently she walked beside him, hardly feeling the painful grip of his fingers on her arm, just above the elbow.

Chapter Twenty-one

Ginny had no remembrance, afterwards, of how many hours she was forced to endure in the brightly lighted, smoke-filled saloon. It seemed to her that an almost forced gaiety had seized everyone there after Steve had brought her back inside, seating her too politely at one of the small tables that were scattered throughout the room.

Lorena and her partner joined them, and she whispered to Ginny that Lilas had gone upstairs to soothe the man she had "entertained" shortly before. His aching head attended to he had been sent on his way to red-headed Patti, the girl he had been supposed to visit, with Lilas' reassurance that it was "on the house" this time.

"He thinks you are crazy, *cherie*—and of course it's just as well, hein? It was a crazy thing you tried to do . . ."

No one understood—not even Lorena!

Her color high, her eyes bright with unshed tears, Ginny sat stiffly at the table, sipping the drink that Steve had ordered for her. And he, on his part, proceeded to ignore her, except to remind her sharply to finish her drink—there was already another one set before her.

"Enjoy yourself, baby," he said sarcastically; "it's what

237

you wanted, isn't it? And be sure and act normally—flirt, if you like—you're good at that, as I remember!"

The piano player had been joined by one of the guests who fancied himself a fiddler, and some of the girls who were still downstairs had begun to dance, laughing shrilly as they were whirled around by their partners.

A young cowboy, his hair slicked down unnaturally, his clothes obviously new, asked Ginny to dance. She would have refused, but when Steve nodded grimly towards the space they had cleared for dancing, she was forced to rise from her chair like a puppet on strings—to dance with the young man who held her too closely and listen dumbly to his clumsy compliments. She could not help noticing that Susie had slipped into the chair she had just vacated and was now leaning against Steve, whispering to him, her hand clutching possessively at his arm.

The young cowboy told her his name was Dan and said she was the prettiest girl he had ever seen at Lilas' place. The sickly sweet smell of his hair oil made Ginny want to retch.

"I guess that lucky hombre back there has already booked you up for the night? Maybe next time I'm in town I'll be just as lucky." He paused and looked down at her. "Hey, you don't say much, do you? You new at this?"

"Yes—" she murmured, "very new."

Dare she tell him anything more? Would he help her, or would he be like the man George? It wouldn't be any use—she knew that! And Steve would only think of some worse way in which to punish her.

Steve and Susie were kissing when Dan took her back to the table after buying her a drink she didn't want. She drank it fast, trying not to notice the way that Steve was playing with the narrow bands of lace that were all that held Susie's dress up. Why should she care? She was relieved when he got up to dance with Susie, who obviously had designs on him, judging from the way she molded her body against his as they danced. Maybe he'd take Susie upstairs tonight ... but then, what would become of her?

Lorena, taking pity on Ginny's white-faced misery, came to sit beside her.

"Poor Rafael—he is always so quick—lot of talk, but then, just like a rabbit, phhtt!"

She glanced at Ginny and her voice softened.

"*Cherie—cherie* you must not look like that! He is angry now, but later, he will forget it. And that Susie—he only acts so with her to make you jealous. Smile, *petite*! Pretend that you do not care."

"But I don't care! Oh, God, Lorena, I wish he would keep *her* instead of me! Why couldn't he let me go?"

Ginny felt hysteria bubbling up inside her, but Lorena, leaning forward, put her hands up and pinched Ginny's cheeks hard, startling her into silence.

"There! I did not mean to hurt you, *cherie*, but you must not make him more angry, not now. And you need some color in your cheeks. Afterwards, you will see, it will be all right."

Lorena was wrong, but it was only much later, in the privacy of the room upstairs, that Ginny learned the full extent of Steve Morgan's anger.

By this time she was so tired, and half-drunk, into the bargain, that she could barely walk straight. Evading Susie, who had started drinking much earlier in the evening and now lay draped in a semi-stupor across the piano, Steve carried Ginny up the last flight of stairs; but there was no tenderness or consideration in the way he held her in his arms.

He slung her onto the bed as if she had been a sack of potatoes, and stood looking down at her with his thumbs hooked into his belt.

Ginny lay there sobbing, hearing his voice coming at her from what seemed like a great distance away.

"Don't ever try it again, Ginny! I don't intend to let you get away from me until I'm good and ready!"

"I didn't—I didn't do anything!" she heard herself sobbing. "I only wanted to *escape*, that's all . . ."

Ginny raised herself on her elbows and looked over her shoulder at him, her eyes still blurred with tears, and he was still standing there, looking down at her with a strange, withdrawn expression on his face.

"I'm sorry, Ginny. How in hell can I blame you for trying to escape when I'd have done the same thing myself?" His voice sounded flat, and oddly bitter, and since she had never heard him make any kind of apology to her before she could hardly credit her hearing.

"You'd better get dressed—as quickly as you can. No point staying around here now that there's a chance your friend George might start thinking about everything you told him. Once he's sober, he could start talking."

"But you're still going to take me with you? Is that what you are saying?"

"Ginny—I'm not going to argue! Put your riding clothes on, we're leaving in about half an hour."

How quickly his moods could change! From black rage to what had almost been contrition, and now back to impatient harshness.

Wearily, Ginny dragged herself from the bed. How could he expect her to ride feeling like this? Wasn't he capable of pity? Of anything besides anger and ruthlessness?

She began to understand him better in the weary, endless-seeming weeks of riding, and hiding, that followed; and even began to build up her own reserves and strength and stubbornness like a shield against his unpredictability.

Supporter of Juarez or not, he was an outlaw, she knew that by now. And he was used to running, to being hunted. Sometimes, she'd taunt him with that—ask him if that was all life had to offer him and if that was enough. And perhaps in his own way he had begun to understand her better too, for now he hardly ever lost his temper with her, in spite of the gibes and insults she occasionally flung at him still—only laughed or shrugged and told her she was a shrew and he'd be glad to get rid of her some day.

Some day! But when would that be? Would he ever let her go?

Sometimes it was difficult for Ginny to imagine any other kind of existence—she rode now as if she was a part of her horse, and she had learned to light a fire that was virtually smokeless—even to skin and eat the occasional small animal that Steve shot.

"You make me feel like a squaw!" she told him once, sulkily. They were deep into Mexico again, somewhere in the foothills of the Sierra Madre, and he would not, as usual, tell her where they were.

"Squaws have other uses besides cooking and skinning game and carrying all of the heaviest loads—," he answered her obliquely, pulling loose her braided hair. "And besides, you're not tame enough yet—your tongue's too vicious. Any self-respecting Comanche brave would have taken two other wives by now, and traded you for a horse."

She ignored his teasing, but it was impossible to ignore the demands of his lips and his hands on her bare, sweat-slippery body. There was no denying by now, even to herself, the strange, almost unnatural physical desire she had for him. She despised him, but she could not resist the power that his love-making had over her, even when she hated him most bitterly. And as for escaping, she had put that thought aside for the time being—ever since the morning she had awakened first, and seeing that he slept heavily and deeply, had taken his gun.

After that, the gun safely beside her, she'd made coffee, lighting the small fire very carefully as he'd taught her to do. She watched him, and when he opened his eyes she could see them narrow when he found himself looking into the unwavering muzzle of his own gun.

He was careful not to move—perhaps he had read the grim resolve in her own eyes. And finally he said, "Do I get any coffee first, or are you going to shoot that thing right off before you lose your nerve?"

"I'm thinking about it," she said calmly, and then, with barely suppressed fury, "I could kill you right now! Or I could shoot you where it would hurt a lot, and leave you here to die very slowly. It's what you deserve!"

She looked for any sign of fear in his eyes, but saw none. They measured her carefully, almost contemplatively.

"Guess that's quite a decision you have to make, isn't it? But if I were you, I'd think about a few other things too—like how you're going to survive out here by yourself."

"I'm quite capable of looking after myself!" she said sharply. "You've taught me well, Steve. I can shoot this gun without missing, and I can read signs. We can't be too far from a town or a village, and the French soldiers . . ."

"We're in Juarista country, my sweet," he broke in. "Think I'd risk getting too close to the French? There's nothing to prevent your killing me, of course, but have you thought about what could happen to you when they get you? They'll hear a shot, and they'll come to investigate. It isn't pretty, the things those guerillos can do to a woman—after they've all used her, of course."

Deliberately, he stretched and crossed his hands under his head, ignoring the movement she made with the gun.

"Make up your mind, love. I'm getting real hungry."

She felt like crying with frustration. Why hadn't he been afraid? Was he so sure she'd never have the courage to shoot him? And worst of all—had he spoken the truth about the *Juaristas*?

"Oh—damn you, damn you! Why'd you sleep so hard then?" Half weeping with rage by now, Ginny threw the gun at him, barely missing him. Biting her lip she turned her back on him and began to pour the coffee.

Surprisingly, he chose to act as if nothing had happened. Having buckled his gunbelts around his waist and replaced his gun in its holster, he came to her, hunkering down on his heels beside her, and took the cup of coffee she held out to him silently.

But before they saddled up to ride on again, he surprised her once more by producing another handgun from his saddlebags and handing it to her. She took the small gun, a serviceable-looking, two-shot derringer, and stared at it unbelievingly.

"You can keep it in the pocket of your riding skirt," he told her shortly. "Just remember, for God's sake, that it's loaded. Never can tell, in this neck of the woods, when you might need a gun. Even my friends the *Juaristas* could shoot first, if they caught sight of strangers, and not stop to ask questions later."

Not knowing what to think, Ginny dropped the gun into the pocket of her skirt. I'll be damned before I thank him for it, she thought stormily, but he had already turned away from her.

As they travelled deeper into central Mexico Ginny could see that Steve became more careful. The country to their left appeared flatter, hotter, and more like desert than the foothills. But he told her it was the best cattle-grazing land in all of Mexico.

"But where are the cattle, then? And the people? I'm beginning to think Mexico is a land of ghosts and bandits—or that this is a nightmare I'm having!"

"With all the fighting that's going on, I guess the people who aren't directly involved try to hide themselves," he reminded her. "And as for the cattle, I guess the *hacendados* in these parts are smart enough to see that they're grazed close to home. Everybody's hungry these days—even the French!"

Ginny remembered her comments about Mexico when

they were surrounded, a few days later, by a small armed band of incredibly villainous-looking men.

She sat her horse frozen, terrified, while Steve engaged in a long and heated argument with their leader, and tried not to notice the leering, lecherous glances of the others. Finally, when Steve produced a small, folded and creased piece of paper from his boot top, the leader of the *Juaristas* began to grin widely, and the conversation became obviously more friendly, while the men who had been pressing closer to Ginny moved back reluctantly.

Some of her fear left her and she began to listen more closely to the conversation, understanding only a little of it. They were discussing the French, and troop movements in the area. The French were retreating, they had evacuated Chihuahua already—General Escobedo was too clever for them—Ginny did not believe any of it!

Nor did she believe what Steve told her later—that on Bazaine's urging the Emperor Maximilian had signed an infamous decree which ordered the death of all suspected *Juaristas* without trial. She had heard of torture and mutilation practiced by the *Juaristas*—to imply that the French would stoop to that and worse was an obvious lie! She told him so, and he shrugged carelessly, but only a few hours later he forced her to ride with him to a hilltop, from where they could see a small village.

"Just visited by your friends, the French soldiers," Steve said grimly. "Take a good look, my love!" He handed her his field glasses, and what Ginny saw made her retch weakly, unable to stop herself. The tiny, doll-like figures scattered grotesquely in broken heaps in front of the thatched adobe huts resolved themselves into the bodies of men, women, and even children. She saw a tiny baby with no head—another with a pulpy mass where its head had been. Buzzards hopped clumsily over the carnage, their beaks ripping into flesh.

"Did you see how they had the women staked out?" His inexorable voice went on while her shoulders heaved. "Can you guess what agony they went through before they were killed? And you know why? Because those damned Frenchmen thought, only thought, mind you, that they'd given shelter to *Juaristas*."

The terrible scene he had forced her to look upon stayed with her that night and all of the next day, follow-

ing her even when late the next night they rode cautiously
into a small town.

Since it was dark, Ginny could not make out much of
the town, such as it was. What amazed her most was the
utter darkness and the stillness. There were no street
lights—under their horses' hooves the winding street
appeared to be dusty and deeply rutted. What buildings
there were seemed to crouch squatly against the velvet
dark night sky, and there did not seem to be any planning
in their placement—just a scattered collection of buildings
with gap-tooth spaces between them.

Ginny was tired, but she had learned better than to
complain. She dismounted when Steve signalled her to do
so and followed him, leading her horse, as he stepped into
the squalid darkness of an alley between two buildings. An
odor of rotten garbage and decaying vegetation made her
clap her hand over her nostrils. A good thing it was so
dark—she daren't look down to see what she was standing
on. If only he'd hurry!

Steve had found the door he had been looking for and
was tapping on it lightly, his fingers moving in a strange,
off-beat rhythm which was obviously a signal of some
kind. But the fat woman who opened the door was
cautious. She lit no lamp or candle, and as the door swung
rustily inward Ginny could barely see the faint gleam of
metal.

"No need for a gun, Mama Vera—it is Esteban."

"Esteban? Esteban Alvarado?" The woman's voice
sounded incredulous at first and then she broke into a soft
chuckle. "Still a rascal—still full of surprises, eh? But who
is this with you? You bring a friend?"

"You'll see when we get inside," Steve said briefly.
Lamplight suddenly flared in the gloom behind the
woman, and a small boy, grinning widely, ran past her.

"I see to the horses, yes, *señor?*"

"You take care of them, or I see to you!" Vera shouted
after him.

Her feet dragging with weariness, Ginny followed Steve
inside. Mama Vera's *cantina* doubled as a saloon, a
hotel, and a whorehouse. The rooms she rented upstairs
were tiny, with no pretensions of elegance. The one small
window that overlooked the street had wooden shutters,
and the room itself contained only a bed and a rickety
table that barely held a pitcher and a small basin. Even

so, the narrow bed was like heaven compared to the rough ground, and the warped, clumsily made shutters let in the fresh night air.

Stripping off her dusty, travel stained clothes, Ginny only took the time to wash her face and arms before she collapsed onto the bed. She slept deeply and dreamlessly, not knowing when Steve came back upstairs.

Chapter Twenty-two

Dusty streamers of sun, touching her face, forced Ginny awake. For a moment, when she first opened her eyes, she had a feeling of panic, not knowing where she was. As memory came back, she turned instinctively in bed, looking for Steve, but he wasn't there. Flinging aside the roughly-woven cotton blanket, Ginny ran across the room to try the door, and was surprised to find it unlocked. She stood looking at it for a moment, frowning thoughtfully. So he had decided to trust her, had he? Or was it only because he was very sure she would not have a chance to make good an escape?

It was stiflingly hot in the room, and Ginny still felt drugged from her long sleep. Even thinking seemed too much effort at the moment. Shrugging, she turned away to the small washstand and began to scrub the trail dust away from her body, using one of Steve's neckerchiefs as a washrag. She was unembarrassed by her own nudity now, and it seemed quite normal to stand there unconcernedly naked, washing herself. She had grown thinner. Except for her breasts, which had never been overly big anyhow, and the curve of her hips, she told herself that she could easily pass for a boy. There were hollows at the base of her throat, and when she surveyed her face in the small cracked mirror that hung above the washstand, it too seemed thinner; its gypsyish contours more pronounced.

A sudden commotion on the street outside made her forget herself and rush to the window, tugging at the heavy wooden shutters until they swung open. No sooner had she put her head outside than Ginny found herself looking into the barrels of at least five rifles, held by French soldiers who looked just as surprised as she.

Their smart red and blue uniforms made her feel homesick, and when a tall soldier wearing sergeant's chevrons called out to her in broken Spanish, begging her pardon a thousand times for having thought that the sound of her window opening might have meant an ambush, some spirit of mischief made her answer him in French.

The soldiers, horses rearing and prancing in the dust of the street, cheered delightedly, pulling off their kepis to wave at her. But it was only when a young man, wearing the insignia of a lieutenant, came galloping down the street to find out what was keeping his men, that Ginny realized the precariousness of her position. She had forgotten her own nakedness, the hair tumbling loosely over her shoulders, until his eyes made her conscious of it.

Her cheeks burning, Ginny drew back hastily, trying to ignore the laughing, admiring comments being made by the Frenchmen. She banged the shutters closed and hoped that they would go away. And then she thought, contradictorily, that it could not possibly have been these same laughing men who had destroyed the Indian village. She had only Steve Morgan's word for it, after all—it might have been the *Juaristas* themselves who had done it. And now—the thought struck her, driving away her embarrassment and mood of lassitude, that she was safe at last. Those Frenchmen would rescue her, she was sure of it! She could go to Mexico City with them, and let Steve try to stop her if he dared! Most likely, when she told them he was a *Juarista* himself, he would be shot. . . .

Rummaging quickly in her saddlebag, Ginny had barely pulled a thin chemise over her body when the door opened and Steve came in. Whirling around, she faced him defiantly, her chin lifted.

He banged the door shut behind him and leaned against

it, his face like a thundercloud. He had grown a beard
during the weeks they had spent travelling, and she
thought it made him look more like a pirate than ever.

"Your soldier friends are all downstairs," he said sarcastically, his voice a cold drawl. "They're calling for
Madame Vera's new French whore. Shall I send them upstairs to you, Ginny?"

Her face paled a trifle, for she hadn't thought of that—
that they would naturally jump to the conclusion she was
one of Vera's girls. But after all, and the thought was as
bitter as gall, what else *could* they think?

"Ginny, you little fool! For all that they're Frenchmen,
don't you realize that they've probably been without even
seeing a white woman for months? Don't you realize what
they want from you?"

"What difference does it make? It's the same thing *you*
want me for, isn't it?" Ginny snatched a yellow silk dress
out of the saddlebags and held it up against herself protec-
tively. "Don't look at me like that! There's not a thing you
can do about it now, Steve Morgan! Besides, when I talk
to their lieutenant, when I explain, he'll protect me. I'm
sure of it. And as for you . . ."

"Oh, for God's sake!" He crossed his arms negligently
as he stared searchingly at her with a disgusted look
spreading over his face. "Is that what you really think?
Are you still naive enough for that? It's entertainment
those men want right now—not some hard-luck story that
might take months to prove—are you willing to provide
their entertainment?"

"You always try to twist things around!" she screamed
at him. "And if you think to frighten me, you're mistaken.
I'd rather go down and brave those French soldiers than
continue to be your captive whore!"

To her surprise, he shrugged, hands dropping to his
sides.

"Very well, Ginny. If that's how you want it. But if I
may, I'd advise you to dress first. There might be some
misunderstanding if you went downstairs so scantily at-
tired!"

It was hard to believe that he'd give in so easily, and
Ginny stared at him suspiciously until a shout from
downstairs made her jump.

"I think your friends are getting impatient," Steve said
softly. "You'd better hurry, before they come up here to

look for you. Seeing you like this—the bed so conveniently in the background—they might not want to wait for explanations from you."

"You bastard!"

He raised his eyebrows.

"You know what I've told you about swearing, Ginny. What's more, they wouldn't understand it either. Especially if you intend to tell them you're a lady in distress."

"Damn you, get out!"

Her fingers shaking with rage, Ginny slipped the dress over her head—shrank away as he approached her.

"I wouldn't dare attack you, *niña*. Not with all those French soldiers downstairs, ready to come to your rescue! No, I merely meant to offer my help, your fingers seem very clumsy this afternoon."

Before she could protest, he turned her around impatiently, and she was forced to hold still, feeling his warm fingers brushing her skin as he hooked up her dress at the back.

"Your hair—I really think you ought to do something with it. Would you like me to brush it for you?"

Without waiting for her reply, he had seized her brush off the small washstand, and holding her in front of him, pinned uncomfortably between his lean, hard body and the table, he began to brush her hair in long downward strokes, ignoring her pained, angry cries as he tugged the brush through tangled curls.

"What—what do you think to gain by this?" she panted furiously. "You've admitted you cannot stop me from going downstairs, and you certainly cannot talk me out of telling that nice young lieutenant everything I know. If you are half as smart as you pretend to be you'd have made your escape by now!"

He dropped the brush and swung her around to face him, his hands suddenly rough on her shoulders.

"It's too late for me to run, Ginny. And besides, I never have enjoyed running away from danger. As a matter of fact, *querida*, I intend to escort you downstairs—it might prove kind of exciting, at that."

"You're crazy!" The words came out as a whisper. "They'd kill you!"

"But I'd take several of them along with me. And it's better than a firing squad, or torture, although I'm sure you'd be sorry to miss that."

"I'm not going to let you blackmail me into silence, Steve Morgan! I've too many scores to settle with you!"

"Then settle them with me, damn it! Tell them I kidnapped you, that you're here against your will—but you say anything about my being tied up with the *Juaristas* and there'll be a half-dozen or more innocent people slaughtered, as an example to the rest of the town. You saw that village? You want the same thing to happen here? I'll tell you how they do it, Ginny—they order everyone outside and start counting, and usually every fifth person gets it. But sometimes, they go berserk, your gallant Frenchmen—they find they can't stop shooting. And when it's done—you'll be here to entertain them, won't you? There's a whole troop of them—seven Frenchmen and about fifteen Mexican Irregulars. They should keep you busy until nightfall, at least."

"No, no, no! I don't believe you! You're lying—you've lied to me right along! They wouldn't."

A soft, nervous tapping at the door made Ginny fall silent, biting her lip to hold her anger in check.

"Esteban! For the Blessed Virgin's sake! Those French *soldados* are getting too rowdy! They threaten to come upstairs and tear the place apart if the *señorita* does not come downstairs."

"You can tell them she'll be down directly. She's just fixing her hair so it will look extra pretty, aren't you love? Don't worry, *mamacita*—just tell them what I told you to say—remember, you are not happy at having us here!"

Ginny heard the fat woman's footsteps recede, and found herself staring at Steve. He was dresed somberly, all in black except for his blue brocaded vest. The broadcloth jacket he wore was long enough to cover the holstered gun that rode low on his hip.

"You look as if you are dressed for a funeral!" She blurted out unthinkingly, and flushed with anger when he laughed.

"For my own, perhaps! And now, sweetheart, why don't you hurry up and do something with your hair? Our would-be conquerors obviously don't like to be kept waiting."

He took her arm when they walked downstairs, and Ginny, better attuned to his moods by now, could feel the tension—that high-strung, devil-may-care quality in his mood that usually went with danger. He was gambling on her, of course, but she was beginning to believe that he actually enjoyed the excitement of taking risks. She thought viciously that she intended to enjoy the afternoon too. She'd play a cat and mouse game with him; make him wait, wondering when the moment would come—and then she'd accuse him when he least expected it; just when he was beginning to feel sure of her. . . .

The *cantina* was noisy with loud voices calling in French and in Spanish for more liquor and louder music, more women. Uniforms were everywhere—there were no civilians to be seen. In a corner a small mariachi band played furiously, as if their lives depended on it.

The Frenchmen had drunk enough to become boisterous. Their Mexican counterparts were more occupied with Vera's selection of pretty *putas*.

"Hey, you fat old whore!" One of the soldiers called out in French as Ginny and Steve paused at the foot of the stairs. "Where's the woman?" There was a raucous laugh from one of his companions.

"The old one has a good head for business, I'll say that for her! Providing a little French *poule* especially for us . . ."

His voice trailed off as he looked up to see that the same little pigeon he'd been talking about had come downstairs at last, clinging tightly to the arm of a tall, bearded North American, who was staring coldly at him.

In the sudden hush that followed, Ginny could not, indeed, stop herself from clutching at Steve's arm. She had heard the comments they were making about her, and now, she saw naked desire that they did not bother to hide in the face of every man in the room.

In a drawling, somehow affected voice that suddenly sounded very southern, Ginny heard Steve drawl, "I'm afraid there seems to be some mistake. This lady, gentlemen," and he put the slightest sarcastic inflection on the word "gentlemen," "happens to be my wife."

Ginny sucked in her breath, anger blinding her for a moment so that she swayed. It was perhaps fortunate that Madame Vera chose the same moment to come bustling up, her arms akimbo, huge breasts quivering with every step under the bright red satin of her gown.

"There! What did I tell you? I did not want you here—I told you this was no place for a man with his wife. But *gringos*—" she turned to the table occupied by the slightly

built French lieutenant and threw out her arms in
despair—*"ay di mi*! What can one say to a *gringo*, tell me
that? He forced his way inside—he said they were too
tired to look further for accommodations—what could I
do?"

"Hold on here!" Steve's voice sounded annoyed. "I paid
you in advance, didn't I? Good ol' American dollars, too.
This goddam country! Rent a room for a night in some
fleabag place and my sweet li'l wife gets insulted! Well,
sirs, let me tell you—"

"Monsieur! If you please—a moment—"

The lieutenant had risen hastily and was making his way
towards them, bowing to Ginny as he came closer. *He* was
the one, of course, who had first made her conscious of
her nakedness by the way he had looked at her, and now,
against her will, Ginny found herself blushing when she
encountered his long, assessing look that took her in from
head to foot.

"Monsieur, you must excuse my men—we have been
travelling hard and long, you see—a natural mistake,
when we saw madame at the window—well—" he spread
his hands out, palms up, in an apologetic gesture, although
the shooting sidewise glance he gave Ginny was insolent in
its implications.

"I beg you, *monsieur*, to accept my apologies. We intended no disrespect, you'll understand how it is, I'm sure!
Perhaps you'll join me at my table for a while? Some
champagne?"

"Well, now, sir—that sounds like a mighty kind offer,
but I don't know if my wife—"

The stumbling hesitancy of the big American's speech
made the lieutenant dismiss him almost immediately as a
stupid oaf. A typical *Americaine*, of course! But the
wife—ah, she was too pretty to be a wife. His mistress,
more likely, and judging by how quickly the man's bluster
had died away in the face of his tact—who knew? Perhaps
some arrangements could be made . . .

While he was thinking swiftly, the Frenchman brought
his heels together and bowed gracefully to Ginny.

"If madame will permit me? I have been away from
France for two years now, and I crave the soft, pretty
speech of a countrywoman—the champagne is good, I
assure you—" he spoke in quick, idiomatic French and

Ginny hesitated looking up at Steve. He was glancing down at her, a strange, half-smile pulling at his mouth.

"I can't understand the half of what the feller's saying, of course, but if you wanna drink champagne, my love, then I see no harm in joining the lieutenant."

What was he up to now? What was he planning? Whatever it was, she would take care that it did not succeed! What an actor he was—she'd like to teach him a lesson; show him that she could act just as well!

Ginny smiled archly at the young soldier, and then bit her lip in mock-confusion.

"Well—well as long as you're sure you understand, and your men too, that I'm not—not—"

"Ah, *Bon Dieu, madame!* Do not think it! Again, I beg your pardon a million times . . ."

"Are we gonna have a drink or aren't we?"

Rather annoyed at having his speech cut short the Frenchman bowed curtly.

"But of course, *monsieur!* And permit me to introduce myself—Lieutenant François d'Argent—at your service, *monsieur et madame!*"

"Name's Gray. John Gray. And this little lady here is my wife Virginia."

Again, Ginny sucked in her breath, rage almost choking her. He was going too far! But she permitted the Lieutenant to lead them to his table, set slightly apart from the others, and smiled her acknowledgement of true French gallantry as his men all rose to their feet, bowing as she passed.

Before a half hour had passed, the bottle of champagne had become several bottles, and the rest of the Frenchmen had also crowded around, annoying their lieutenant. A stocky, rather sour-faced sergeant kept refilling the American's glass, and he, dolt that he was, seemed happy enough to drink all he pleased and smoke his cigar, smiling indulgently as the swift, laughing conversation in French flowed around him.

D'Argent noticed that the woman's face was flushed with pleasure and excitement, although no doubt the champagne had something to do with it as well. He took care to keep her glass full as well.

But they were certainly a strange and ill-matched pair, these two! He had already found out, by clever, off-hand questioning, that the big American was from Texas. He was a cattle buyer, and actually admitted that he was poor, since the war. He was in Mexico trying to buy cattle with what money he had left—planning to have them driven all the way to some outlandishly named town in Kansas where he thought to make an enormous profit.

"Gotta keep my babydoll here in silks and pretty gew-gaws," he'd chuckled in his crude way, and catching the glance that the woman threw at him, Francois could have sworn he read dislike in it.

Ah, he thought to himself with satisfaction, so all is not well here! Madame—if she is Madame Gray—is bored. Who can blame her? And her husband as much as ad-mitted, later on, that his wife had insisted on accompany-ing him on this foolish journey.

"My little Ginny is kinda jealous, I guess," he said with a foolish laugh. "Thought I'd be out chasin' pretty *señoritas* an' not attendin' to business unless she came along."

The pretty little Ginnette had choked on her champagne at that moment, and her rough idiot of a husband had made matters worse by thumping her unfeelingly on the back.

"Now, babydoll—you always do drink that stuff too fast. An' come to think of it, you do look kinda flushed. Mebbe we should find someplace to eat—I'm feeling plumb starved myself!"

Thinking quickly, d'Argent had managed to avert a domestic crisis by suggesting they should do him the honor of dining with him—no, but he insisted! Sergeant Pichon was an excellent cook—he would go ahead immediately and begin to prepare the meal. Madame Gray had begun to smile at once, saying sweetly that she would just love it—he was the kindest man; and when d'Argent, who had contrived to sit next to her, pressed her foot meaningfully under the table, she had continued to smile.

Ginny felt heady with the champagne and the excite-ment of the game she was playing. She hoped Steve was sweating it out. Let him! It was his turn now, and at any time she pleased she could turn the tables on him by telling these people who he was and what he was. And in the meantime she was enjoying being able to speak French again, to ask questions about her beloved Paris, and above all to be flattered and treated as a beautiful woman should be treated.

It was perhaps because of the champagne that Ginny did not realize that Lieutenant d'Argent was growing more and more puzzled as their conversation continued.

So Madame Gray had lived in Paris for many years and was, in fact half-French. From his carefully thrown-out questions he had already learned that she knew almost nothing about the more popular bistros, such as he and his friends had frequented. She talked of an uncle and aunt— named a quiet residential street whose houses were owned by the very rich and very influential—it could not be possible that she had actually lived in one of these houses, unless, of course, she had been a maid or a governess! And if she'd been the latter it would account for her ladylike manner of speaking. It had to be that, of course. A rich young woman of gentle birth would certainly not be careering around a country at war with an obviously boorish American. Nor would she sleep in a shabby *cantina* run by a madame of rather dubious repute.

As the wine continued to flow the Mexican Irregulars began to get more and more boisterous. Some of them had already retired upstairs with the *señoritas* of their choice. d'Argent noticed, with contempt curling his lip, that the American seemed to be falling asleep. It was clear he wasn't used to champagne, and indeed, that the good wine was wasted on him. But madame was a different matter—madame was growing quite gay, and prettier by the moment. Even the cheap and rather garish dress she wore did nothing to detract from her beauty. A lovely discontented woman—a husband who was too stupid to notice what was going on beneath his nose—what could be more perfect? And he, François, had not had a woman for over a month, if you did not count the few he had taken by force—dirty Mexican sluts who had screamed insults and struggled. This woman would not fight against him, he was more sure of it with every minute that passed!

Smiling, leaning closer to her under the cover of the conversation tactfully engaged in by his men, Lieutenant d'Argent let his compliments become more ardent, his innuendos more daring. Once or twice Madame Gray, or Ginette, as he had already begun to think of her in his mind, actually blushed. He became bolder, positive now that her uncivilized brute of a husband knew no French, and her beautiful green eyes dropped under his—he noticed that she glanced doubtfully at her husband, and smiled.

"He's falling asleep—your husband," he said softly in French. "Although me, I cannot understand how he could do so, with such loveliness beside him. Ah, if I could only show you how much I appreciate your presence here. . . !" Again, his foot pressed against hers under the table.

"You become too bold, *monsieur!*" she said sharply, adding in an undertone, "and if I were you I would not underestimate him. It could be dangerous."

Did she mean that her husband was jealous? Certainly it did not seem so. But perhaps she was only playing coy.

"Madame," d'Argent said earnestly, "I cannot blame any man for being jealous of such a precious possession! But if you'll permit me, as an admirer of your beauty and elegance, to ask an intimate question—what do you really do here, with such an unappreciative man? This is no place for a woman, this crazy country, and particularly not for one as lovely as you. In Mexico City, now—"

As he let his voice trail away suggestively Ginny thought confusedly that perhaps this was her chance to explain. The young lieutenant would surely be only too eager to help her, although she did not particularly care for his overly bold manner. But when he understood—

"*Monsieur,*" she began haltingly, trying to choose her words, "perhaps I should explain . . ."

"My love, it's getting late. Perhaps the good lieutenant's cook wasn't able to find anything to fix for supper. In any case I think we oughta leave these gentlemen to their warlike duties and find ourselves some place to eat. You know how sleepy I always get when I drink on an empty stomach!"

The lieutenant's face had darkened at the unfortunate interruption. And something in the tone of the big American's voice set his teeth on edge, although it was nothing to put one's finger on. But the man was a dolt, of course. One could not mistake it. D'Argent contemptuously dismissed the gun that the man wore. All American cowboys wore guns—to them, it was a part of dressing up. And besides, what could one gun do against a troop of French soldiers? He forced himself to smile and speak soothingly.

"*Monsieur*—no need to worry, I assure you! Pichon will be here in a few minutes, or better still, let us go now to my quarters—I have an excellent brand of champagne myself that I would love to have you try. And I am sure the meal will be to your liking, and madame's."

His glance at Ginny was languishing, and she flushed, although she was still puzzled and angry that Steve had interrupted when he did. She caught him looking at her with that infuriatingly mocking smile, one eyebrow tilted slightly as if to say he left the decision up to her. And even Lieutenant d'Argent was watching her expectantly.

"I haven't had a decent meal in months, as you very well know!" she said rather sullenly to Steve. And then, with a sudden smile she put her hand flirtatiously on his arm and looked up at him, fluttering her eyelashes in a deliberate parody. "Please—you cannot refuse me!"

He caught her meaning, of course, as she had meant him to do. Only she noticed the slight tautening of his lips, and she gloated inwardly. Let him walk the tightrope for a while longer! She could betray him at any moment she pleased, and he knew it. The thought gave her an intoxicating sense of power.

"My love—how well you know that I can refuse you nothing! And our thanks again, Lieutenant."

Steve stood up, pushing his chair over clumsily as he did. He saw Ginny wince, and smiled amusedly at her. The little bitch, she was enjoying herself! But he had to hand it to her—it was her turn to be on top, and she was taking it.

D'Argent was explaining hurriedly to his men that he was going back to his quarters and the Americans would be his guests. Some of the men gave him sly, congratulatory smiles that he pretended not to notice.

Outside the sun blazed down hotly, and Ginny shuddered, shrinking from it. With a perfunctorily apologetic glance at Steve, the lieutenant offered her his arm. Lagging slightly behind, pretending to look around curiously, Steve noticed the wrinkled Mexican peasant sitting dolefully on the edge of the cracked wooden sidewalk, huddled in his serape. The man, a refugee or a beggar by all appearances, appeared to be dozing, and yet Steve caught the white gleam of an eyeball as the man's look slipped sideways and away.

"Hey, that pore old guy looks like he ain't had a square meal in years! Take this, *amigo*, buy yourself some supper—"

The man scrambled in the dust after the carelessly tossed coin, his thanks a gabble in some obscure Indian dialect.

D'Argent and Ginny had stopped, and the lieutenant sounded annoyed.

"Really, *monsieur*! You should not encourage his kind of scum! Give them a peso and they expect it—and they'd turn around and put a knife in your back the next moment."

"Ah shucks—can't see a man looking as skinny and starved as he does," Steve said mildly. "We've seen too much of that since we been here, haven't we my dearest?"

"I prefer not to discuss unpleasant things," Ginny said sharply, refusing to play his game, whatever it was. Although she was unpleasantly aware of his presence at her elbow as they continued to walk up the street, she pretended to ignore him, saving her smiles for the Frenchman instead.

The French had set up their makeshift headquarters in the only sturdy-looking adobe structure, which happened to be the local jail. But, as d'Argent explained quickly, he was occupying the *jefe's* quarters next door, and he had seen to it that they were clean and comfortable.

"Jails always did give me a funny kinda feeling," Steve commented conversationally. "Got yourself any prisoners locked up in there?"

"Only one," d'Argent said, a trifle impatiently. "In fact, we think the man we have may be a *Juarista* spy—he did not seem to have any particular business here. Tomorrow we shall question him and find out."

"Oh?" The American actually seemed interested. "Think you'll get anything out of him? From the talk I've heard, these—whatever you call 'em—they're tough customers."

"We have our ways, *monsieur*. Believe me, if the man we have in jail is one of those filthy *Juaristas*, he'll be happy to confess when my men are through with him."

"I guess your laws out here are different from the law back home. Suppose he ain't a spy after all?"

D'Argent shrugged, his eyes bright. "We all make mistakes, *monsieur*. And this is war. The man's explanations did not satisfy us, and after a while, one has an instinct. . . ." he ended his sentence with an expressive shrug, but all the same, he felt almost relieved when the cigar-puffing American did not persist with his questions. He had been in Mexico two years, and yet the torturing of a man was not something he enjoyed. He had seen French soldiers, often mutilated before they were killed, and had no compunctions about carrying out Marshal Bazaine's orders to execute any suspected *Juaristas* without the formality of a trial. This was war, after all! But although the firing squad was one thing, torture, even though it was sometimes necessary, was hard on the stomach. He could order it, if he had to, but preferred not to watch it.

Fortunately, he had two American mercenaries standing guard over the prisoner right now—hardbitten gunmen from across the border who would rather earn big money for fighting the *Juaristas* than take their chances with the law in their own country. One of them, a tall, pale-eyed Texan who called himself Tom Beal would do the "questioning" of the prisoner. The lieutenant had seen Beal work before, and Beal enjoyed this kind of thing. He and the other man, who was known only as Blue, worked well together. They were both fast with their guns and completely ruthless; and they had already proved their worth as scouts, tracking down roving bands of Juarist "guerillos" who came and went like shadows, preferring to strike at the French soldiers from ambush rather than face them in battle.

The faithful Sergeant Pichon had done his best with the rather shabby quarters formerly belonging to the *jefe*. The floor had been polished, and the addition of a few handwoven rugs of local manufacture added color. As for the meal, there was no need for apologies here. Pichon had excelled himself—adding his own special touch to what had been available. Proudly, d'Argent served a dry white wine with the chicken, and was flattered when Madame Gray agreed with him that the vintage was one of the finest for that particular wine.

The American, her husband, ate stolidly and concentratedly, drinking down the wine as if it had been nothing but water. A waste, on such an undiscriminating pig, d'Argent thought to himself with a grimace.

But Madame Gray—Ginette—she was different! Such beauty and elegance was all too obviously wasted on her husband, and François d'Argent found himself growing more and more intrigued as the meal progressed. He made a perfunctory apology to the American for speaking in French, but the big man had merely waved his cigar ex-

pansively and told him to "go right ahead." What kind of
a man was he? The kind, no doubt, who would stoop to
using his wife to further his business ambitions, using her
as bait. And just as obviously, all was not well between
them.

Once for a short while, the conversation turned to
politics, and it appeared that madame, like d'Argent himself, had hoped that the southern states would win the recent civil war in America. Her husband, on the other
hand, had merely raised an eyebrow and advised her that
politics was not a woman's province.

"Oh—but you're insufferable!" she had burst out angrily, and her husband had grinned condescendingly, looking across at the lieutenant as if for support, with a shrug
of his broad shoulders.

Hastily turning the conversation to more personal matters, d'Argent discovered, by dint of careful questioning,
that the young woman was well-read, to add to her other
accomplishments. Her French mother had died when she
was young, but her father, also an American, was still living.

"You're from Louisiana then, surely?"

"Alas no, *monsieur*! I'd hoped to stay there longer, especially in New Orleans, but Papa was in such a hurry to
reach Texas ..." here she paused rather thoughtfully, as if
unwilling to continue.

"Oh, and that is no doubt where you met your husband?" d'Argent said encouragingly.

"I—yes, I did meet *monsieur* in Texas," she said
shortly. She might have said more, having drunk enough
to make her bold, but at that moment her fool of a husband stood up abruptly, his chair falling over with a clatter. D'Argent noticed that he swayed slightly on his feet.

"You gotta—gotta excuse me for a while. Damn good
food that! But I think I need—need some fresh air—they
got outhouses around here?"

Ginny blushed vividly, her face a mask of embarrassment and disgust and d'Argent, anxious to be rid of her
husband, even if it was only for a little while, intervened
tactfully.

"Ah, *monsieur*, my apologies! Let me show you."

"No—no—wouldn't dream of bothering you. Just you
tell me where an' I'll find it—bet it's out back, huh? Jes'
like home ..."

Smiling vaguely, stumbling as he walked, the bearded American fumbled his way to the back door which opened onto a small courtyard where the house formed an ell with the back of the jail itself.

The dolt! Let him find a convenient spot to relieve himself. Perhaps, with luck, he'd pass out. But at least he'd provided a golden opportunity for François himself, and he intended to make the most of it.

"I apologize, madame, for allowing your husband to drink too much," d'Argent said softly. "But I must confess that I have longed to be alone with you from the first moment I saw you! You cannot imagine how your loveliness has captivated me—I could gaze for hours into your green eyes—admire the softness of your lips—"

The young woman seemed a trifle confused, but d'Argent caught her hand, pressing it urgently.

"I'm infatuated with you! I say this to you so suddenly, so soon, because we are at war, madame! I might never see another woman as lovely as you again—you've swept me off my feet."

He was pulling her towards him when the shot rang out. D'Argent jumped hastily, guiltily almost, to his feet, while the young woman made a frightened smothered sound.

"Mon Dieu! The *Juaristas!"*

At that moment, the big American appeared in the doorway, a foolish, embarrassed grin spread over his face.

"Sorry. Sorry if I startled you, didn't mean it to go off, y'know. All I was doin' was checkin' the loads, see, an' the damn gun went off! Can't unnerstand it."

Before d'Argent could find words, Ginny said coldly, "And why, pray, did you find it necessary, suddenly, to see if your gun was loaded?"

"Huh?" The American's glance went from d'Argent to his wife and back again. He looked puzzled. "But honey, you know darn well I always start to checkin' my gun when I see the way guys look at you." He glanced at the dumbfounded lieutenant, still smiling. "Real jealous son-of-a-gun I am—just ask Ginny! Men are always lookin' at her, and I jes' keep getting mad. Even though I know my little babydoll here wouldn't give any of 'em the time of day. She hates makin' me mad. Don't you angel?"

D'Argent had begun to look a trifle alarmed, his face reddening. Surely the man had not overheard? If he'd been a Mexican, he'd have had him taken out and shot, but he dared not meddle with an American citizen, especially one with such a pretty and well-born wife—if she were well-born, and not just a little governess who had married for security.

The woman was speechless with fury, her eyes flashing, but d'Argent managed to find his voice, and was ashamed that it sounded so placating.

"B—but *monsieur*!" he said, stammering slightly, "you surely do not think that I—"

"Ah heck, of course not! No, you bin real nice to us both, hasn't he, love? An' you ain't Ginny's type at all. But I sure didn't like the way some of your men back there acted—I tend to brood on things, and I got to thinking— an' it made me mad, I guess!"

"*Monsieur*—" d'Argent said a trifle wildly, "I have already apologized for my men! But if you wish it . . ."

An urgent knocking at the door, and Sergeant Pichon's alarmed voice gave him the opportunity to break off and he straightened himself with some relief. "I'm afraid, *monsieur*, that your accidental shot has caused some alarm among my men. If you'll excuse me for a moment, I will explain to them." With a curt bow for the American and a languishing look at his wife, d'Argent opened the door quickly and went into the front room where Ginny could hear him complain in French that the stupid *Americaine*, the clumsy imbecile, was playing with his gun and—the closing of the door cut off the rest of his words, and Ginny, coming to her feet, turned angrily on Steve.

"Steve Morgan, I've had enough of this—this miserable imposture! I mean to . . ."

He took a swift step forward and gripped her wrist hard enough to bring an exclamation of pain to her lips; all the foolishness and drunkenness falling away.

"John Gray's the name, and you'd better remember it! And as for what you mean to do, Ginny, then you'd best think carefully first. They've got Paco Davis in that jail. I know it's him for sure now. He came to the window when I fired that shot, and I mean to get him out."

She saw the old reckless light dance in his eyes and gasped.

"But that's crazy! The town's full of soldiers, as you know well enough. You'll get yourself—"

He laughed suddenly. "Killed? But that should please you, love. Shouldn't it? All I'm asking is that you don't try to stop me from trying. If they do end up getting me, I'm sure it'll prove very convenient for you."

"I've no desire to be left at the mercy of a troop of soldiers who haven't seen a white woman in months—especially if the man they think is my husband has just been executed as a traitor!" she retorted.

"Try to look on the bright side of things. Perhaps the handsome young lieutenant will keep you for himself," he said softly. His eyes smiled down into hers, and for an instant she imagined that he intended to kiss her. But the moment passed, with the distant slamming of the front door. He released her and dropped into a chair, long legs stretched negligently before him as he reached for his glass.

D'Argent, apologizing for his delay in returning, poured more wine. He had noticed that Madame Gray looked flushed and rather sullen when he entered the room, and that she rubbed at her wrist almost absent-mindedly. So! Had her clumsy ox of a husband dared hurt her? Perhaps the man really was jealous, in which case, would more wine only make his jealousy uglier, or would it put him to sleep?

The lieutenant made a point of trying to draw the man out, but he seemed to have no conversation, unless it was about cattle, and he found himself answered mostly in monosyllables. Certainly, the American looked sleepy. He had drunk an enormous amount of wine, and his eyelids seemed to droop, while he had not even the manners to smother his yawns. Even the young woman had become silent and rather thoughtful—perhaps she was afraid of her husband, although that had not seemed to be the case earlier.

"Gettin' awful late—fall asleep right here if I don't get to bed," the American announced suddenly, his voice slurred.

"But, *monsieur*, another drink! See, the bottle is only half-empty, and I would hate to have to throw away good wine. Why, *monsieur*, I thought you Americans prided yourselves on being hard drinkers!"

D'Argent felt his cunningness at throwing out a challenge rewarded when he saw the scowl on the big man's face.

"Whaddya mean, you thought—sure, we can hold our liquor better than anyone else, I bet!"

Triumphantly, d'Argent watched the American reach forward for the bottle, tilt it over his glass. He could not forbear stealing a glance at the woman, and was flattered when he found her eyes on him. The corner of her lips tilted upward very slightly in the beginning of a smile before she dropped her eyes demurely. So—she knew what he was up to, and she approved! He began to feel more hopeful.

When the sharp rapping came at the door, therefore, d'Argent was understandably annoyed; he was even more disturbed when the door opened abruptly, before he'd had time to answer. Americans! They had no idea of tact, of protocol!

The man who came in, closing the door carelessly behind him, was Tom Beal, one of the men who was supposed to be guarding the prisoner. How dared he intrude?

"Beal! What are you doing here? I thought I had told you—"

"You told me to let you know the minute our prisoner wanted to start confessin'. Well, it appears he's in the mood to do just that. But he wants you to hear it."

Beal was very tall and thin, with a high-cheekboned, rather cadaverous face. His hair was straw-colored and plastered down against his bony skull with sweat and hair oil. His eyes were pale blue and expressionless, and Ginny could not help wanting to shudder when they touched her briefly.

Of them all, only Steve, his glass held to his lips, seemed completely unconcerned.

As a matter of habit, Tom Beal studied the room first, although he had been in here before. He was a killer by profession, and watchfulness was an instinct with him. He wore one gun, its holster tied low on his hip, and he set down the rifle he usually carried with him by the door, after he was sure how many people were in the room. It was the sort of pointless courtesy, he'd learned, that French officers insisted upon. And as long as it was safe, why not? They paid good money for his services, after all.

Beal had noticed the woman first—the minute he entered the room he had sensed her presence; knew right away that she was American, young and quite beautiful.

Like to get me some of that—the thought flashed through his mind. It had been a long time, too long, since he'd had an American woman, especially one like this, with the bloom not yet worn off.

Because he was in the French lieutenant's quarters, and because of the woman's presence, Beal made a mistake he would not normally have made. He let his guard relax, studying the woman openly while he spoke to the Frenchman. And because of it, he barely noticed her husband, who in any case was leaning tilted back in his chair sipping greedily at a glass of wine. He'd heard the French soldiers talk and had already dismissed the man contemptuously as a weak drunk. It was the woman—the woman that mattered.

D'Argent had not missed the way Beal's eyes seemed to grow even paler as he let his lust show openly, and the fact annoyed him. The man had no right to walk in as he had, and he had even less right to stare.

"You interrupted me, Beal. You were speaking of the prisoner?"

With some difficulty, Beal brought his eyes back to d'Argent's frowning, rather pompous face.

"Oh—yeah. Well, seems like he suddenly decided to confess, like I said—particularly when I started tellin' him all the methods I planned to use to get him to talk." Beal smiled wolfishly. "Says he knows where they hide out in the hills by here, but he'll only spill it to you, personal. Guess he thinks you might give him a pardon."

"I give no pardons to confessed *Juaristas*," the lieutenant began sternly. "But of course, the man need not know that until after he has confessed, I suppose! Yes, I think. . . ."

Bored by the lieutenant's self-important speech Beal let his eyes wander again.

They went past the woman, who was suddenly whitefaced and still, her head bent; and beyond to the bearded man who lounged so silently in his chair, the glass of wine still in his hand, as if he could not bear to let go of it.

Beal started to move his eyes away indifferently when something, some half-remembered spark of familiarity tugged at his brain, drawing his gaze back to the other American. Like most professional gunmen, Beal relied largely on his instinct, and the reason he'd stayed alive this long was that he believed in playing his hunches—messages sent like faint tremors from his subconscious mind. Instinct, more than memory, told him now that he'd seen this man before, and under different circumstances. And there was also the way the man was looking at him now, watching him steadily and coldly through very dark blue eyes that contrasted strangely with the black beard and hair.

That was it—those eyes! He'd seen them watching him before, over the barrel of a gun. Just once, and very long ago; but Tom Beal never forgot a man who'd managed to get the drop on him.

He cut sharply and rudely across the Frenchman's speech, taking a step forward, with his hand dropping to the butt of his gun.

"You—I've seen you before someplace, mister. We've tangled somewhere, sometime."

"Now Beal ..." the Frenchman began as the big American looked up in surprise, as if he'd been startled out of his drink-sodden stupor.

"Did you say Beal?" The man's voice was filled with sudden, drunken rage. But he didn't reach for his gun, as Beal had sensed he might. The unexpectedness of his shout startled Beal just as much as it had startled the others, losing him the split second he needed to pull his gun. That, and the quick movement of the man's hand as he flung the glass of wine at Beal's face.

Steve Morgan's body followed the movement of his hand as he lunged across the table, falling onto Beal as the table caught the surprised gunman across the belly, splintering like matchwood. Off balance, Beal had fallen backward, and now, before he could move, a fist crashed into his jaw—hands caught him by the hair, pounding his head mercilessly against the hard adobe floor.

"Beal, is it? You goddam son of a gun—think I wouldn't recognize any dirty bastard that tried to run off with my wife? Only reason I didn't kill you then was she made me promise I wouldn't, but by God, you're still after her, and I'll kill you for sure this time!"

It was the last thing Beal remembered before the blackness closed over him—a blackness laced with crimson streaks and agonizing pain.

When the table crashed over, Ginny screamed with real fear and sprang to her feet. D'Argent, completely astounded, stood with his mouth open, unable, for a moment, to comprehend what was happening.

"*M'sieur—m'sieur*, stop! Have you gone mad? For God's sake stop—you will kill him!"

He stooped, attempting to drag the infuriated American off the unconscious mercenary. The imbecile—he was obviously insane—what was the matter with him? Had he really recognized Beal, or was it the raving of a drunken maniac?

With a bellow of rage, the American swung his arm backward as D'Argent tugged at it, sending the Frenchman staggering. Before he could recover himself, the American had sprung to his feet and now caught his wife, who had been about to scream, by the shoulders. He shook her roughly as he swore at her.

"You cheating tramp! You led him on—flirting with him, smiling those sly smiles at him when you think I'm not looking, like you do with every man you meet. Like you were doin' this evening with the lieutenant here, and don't think I didn't see what was goin on, you bitch!"

The woman was gasping with shock and terror, fighting for breath. The pins flew from her hair, clattering to the floor and her hair spilled down over her shoulders.

"No—don't!" she managed to whimper, "please—don't!"

D'Argent's French gallantry was outraged. The drunken idiot! He had gone berserk. Mad with jealousy, he didn't know what he was doing!

"Stop it! I insist that you stop it! *M'sieur!*" He noticed with relief that the faithful Sergeant Pichon had come running from his quarters and now stood staring in astonishment.

"Oaf!" d'Argent yelled in French, "the imbecile American is out of his head—he will kill madame! Can't you do anything but stand there gaping? Come and help me!"

Together, they finally managed to catch the American's arms and pull him away from his sobbing wife. With a little shocked moan the girl dropped into a chair, hands up to her throat. D'Argent had expected to have difficulty in holding the big man still, as blind with rage as he seemed to be, but the moment they had him held fast he seemed to slump against them, swaying unsteadily on his feet.

"Not—not my fault—" he mumbled sullenly. "She always drives me to it—drink—only thing that helps—always men—"

"It's not true! Don't believe him, don't believe anything

he says!" the girl stormed, her eyes like green fire. "He's a
wicked, evil man. He hurt me!"

"Madame—madame I beg you not to upset yourself!
Your husband is drunk, he is not capable of rational behavior. I am afraid I will have to put him in jail—for
your own sake, of course, as well as for the sake of all the
innocent people of the town—my men—"

Just in case the American decided to lose his temper
again, d'Argent snatched the Smith & Wesson .44 from the
man's holster and stuck it through his own belt. He smiled
reassuringly at the dishevelled woman, who now stared at
him in a startled fashion.

"Jail!" she repeated, her voice strange, and the lieutenant hastened to soothe her.

"Do not worry yourself, I implore you! We will only
keep him there overnight, until he is sober. It will teach
him a lesson, madame, one he richly deserves, you must
admit." He turned to look warningly at the American.
"And you, *monsieur*, if you'll give me your word that
you'll give me no more trouble, I'll allow you to walk to
the jail with me like a gentleman, with no manacles on
your wrists. It is for madame's sake, you understand? But
I must also warn you that I will have your own gun pointing at you all the way there, so we'll have no more violence, if you please!"

"Jail—" the girl said again. She sounded stunned.
"You'll really put him in jail?"

"Believe me, madame, I must! For reasons of discipline,
you understand? But—" his voice dropped slightly and he
spoke now in French, the message in his eyes clear—
"after I have the matter taken care of I will return here,
to escort you *personally* to your hotel. You need not
worry, I will look after everything."

She blushed, biting her lip and he congratulated himself
again for having found her. What a beauty! And especially
now, with her hair all loose—he'd make her mad for him
with his caresses—he'd be very careful, very tender—

Her words brought him back to reality, she was asking
something of him.

"If you don't mind, I would like to go with you, to
make sure he's safely locked up. He's dangerous, I'd like
to see him behind bars!"

D'Argent smiled to himself. So! Now she had decided
she hated her husband. This was even better. Perhaps he

could persuade her to come with him to Mexico City—it would be nice to have a mistress again, particularly a woman as lovely as this one. Getting rid of her husband would be easy—let Beal have him, when Beal had recovered consciousness!

Monsieur Gray seemed to understand that he was in trouble. He was very quiet now, and shamefaced; his head hung abjectly. As he stood swaying on his feet, the man was almost pathetic.

"No—no more trouble—promise you—," he muttered, the words slurred. "Just wanna sleep, tha's all—sleepy—"

"I promise you, *monsieur*, you will sleep well in my jail tonight! You will have a *Juarista* for company, and I'm afraid they all smell bad, but it will not matter—we will execute him very early in the morning, so you may sleep as late as you wish!"

D'Argent smiled conspiratorially at the woman, but she continued to look rather sullen. Anger had left color flaring along her cheekbones that only rendered her even more attractive.

"I must see him safely in jail," she persisted.

"Come along then, madame," d'Argent said. "And you, *m'sieur*, it is only a short way. Walk slightly ahead of me, if you please, like so."

He turned his head to look with disgust at the broken table and crystal—his best linen stained with wine. Beal lay on his back like a dead man, only his shallow, ragged breathing showing that he still lived. This drunken American would no doubt be very sorry that he had attacked Tom Beal. Ah, well—he deserved whatever Beal and his partner decided to do to him!

"Pichon—you will stay and clean up this mess," the lieutenant instructed. "And do it swiftly, for I will be back as soon as I hear what this *Juarista* has to confess. And—you might as well see to Beal as well. Perhaps a cold compress for his head . . ."

"*Oui, M'sieur le Capitaine*. At once!"

Pichon came belatedly to attention as the lieutenant glared at him—how dare Pichon presume to promote him? When his superior officer left Pichon could not help sighing as he gazed around the room he had tidied earlier.

Lucky Lieutenant d'Argent! He had the foolish husband at pistol point, walking ahead—and an arm about the waist of the pretty wife. A true Frenchman, that d'Argent!

Chapter Twenty-three

The entrance to the jail, as d'Argent had stated earlier, was no more than fifty feet from the door of the *jefe's* house that the lieutenant had commandeered for himself. Nevertheless, walking very slowly behind the shambling, hang-dog American, d'Argent managed to whisper a stream of bold compliments in his companion's ear. She did not reply, but she *had* permitted him to put his arm about her waist, and he did not think she would balk too much at allowing him further liberties later on.

"You are much too beautiful to be wasted on this clod of a man, dear madame! You need someone to appreciate your charms, your so-lovely lips and body. Believe me, you should be dressed as you deserve, in the finest gowns, with jewels in your ears and around your neck. I'm not the kind of man who believes in beating a woman—I'd rather storm your citadel, Ginette, with kisses. I'll show you—I'll make you happy tonight, I swear it!"

"Monsieur!" Her whisper sounded almost pleading, and d'Argent laughed, squeezing her waist, sure of his victory.

"There's no need to pretend with me, little one. I've wanted you ever since I saw you at the window, your hair falling over your breasts, just as it is now. I knew then

270

how it would be with us." Carried away, d'Argent waxed poetic. "You'll have no complaints of me as a lover, *cherie*. I'll be gentle I swear it! And if you'll stay with me, I'll be generous."

The big American coughed suddenly and seemed to stumble, and d'Argent jabbed the pistol viciously into his back, hoping it would hurt. He realized that the woman had drawn away from his arm and was staring at him with tears of emotion shining in her eyes.

"You actually believe all the terrible things this—this *canaille* said about me! You really think I'm a cheap woman, don't you?"

He tried to calm her. Why were women so sensitive?

"But no, my sweet! You misunderstood me. Of course you are a lady, and I'll treat you as one. But believe me, I don't blame you for preferring any other man to this one."

Again the pistol jabbed harshly into his captive's back, driving him up the three shallow steps that led up to the door of the jail. He hoped the girl would not prove difficult at this stage—after all, she had encouraged him quite obviously, what did she expect?

"Come come, my little one, you must not think I don't respect you," he said soothingly. "Tonight I'll show you just how much respect and yes, admiration I have for you—for that beautiful body you are hiding under a gown that does not do you justice."

He replaced his arm around her waist rather roughly and pulled her along, knowing that some women preferred to be dominated and used thus by a man. And the next moment he had decided smugly that his judgement had been right, for she stopped protesting and came with him quite meekly.

The man known as Blue opened the door with his gun at the ready, a look of relief replacing the surprised one he'd worn when he saw the staggering, drunken prisoner the lieutenant had brought along.

The jail consisted of only two rooms—a makeshift office, and a large cell. The walls were of thick adobe, with the thick iron bars of the cell door and tiny window embedded into them. Behind the barred door, on a makeshift wooden bunk, a man sat hunched over; a dirty serape wrapped around his shoulders.

As the Frenchman and his captive walked inside the

man in the cell jumped up and came to the bars, shaking them furiously.

"*Americano—gringo* dog! I won't share a cell with a dirty *gringo!*" he began yelling.

"Shut up, you filth!" Blue shouted angrily, his fist raised threateningly.

What happened next was a blur—just like a nightmare and just as unreal, when the Frenchman looked back on it.

The big American—falling drunkenly against the bars as d'Argent pushed him forward. Falling, and throwing Blue off-balance as he did. One moment, Blue had been standing on his feet, head turned to shout at the *Juarista* prisoner. And the very next instant he lay writhing helplessly on the hard-packed earthen floor, clutching his groin and moaning like a sick animal. It was the bearded American who had done it, his drunkenness disappearing as his knee slashed wickedly upward, maiming the other man.

And now, his eyes cold and hard, his vacuous mask dropped, he held Blue's gun in his hand as he faced d'Argent with his back to the cell.

"Better drop that gun you're holding. Hesitate and I'll gut-shoot you." Still stunned by what had happened, d'Argent dropped his gun. The clipped, businesslike voice went on giving orders.

"Ginny—you get those keys and unlock the door. And try to hurry it, baby, we're sitting on a powder keg."

Silently, moving like a puppet, the girl walked forward, kneeling gingerly by the gasping, retching man on the floor to take the keys from his belt. Without being told again she unlocked the cell door and the prisoner walked out grinning; casually bent to pick up the gun d'Argent had dropped.

"Remind me to kiss you when we get far enough from town, Ginny," he said softly as he passed the girl. She stared at him blankly—d'Argent thought afterwards that she had looked as if she was in a trance.

A few minutes later, leaving d'Argent and Blue bound and gagged; locked in the cell; three people walked casually and slowly down the steps of the jail. One was a woman. They mounted horses, and they rode openly out of town. Since the American and his wife had been guests of the lieutenant, none of the men under his command did anything to stop them.

Once they had left the outskirts of the town, they rode very fast. Neither Steve nor Paco spoke, although it was apparent, after a while, that they knew in which direction they would travel.

Ginny still felt dazed. Her tawdry yellow dress was unsuitable for riding astride, but the saddle on her horse would permit no other alternative. Her bare legs felt cold, and after a few hours her whole body felt stiff and numb. Still, she did not complain, or beg that they stop to rest. And after all, if the French came in pursuit, they would be looking for her too. It seemed unreal!

They were riding into the foothills again, into pitch-dark, forbidding-looking terrain. Sometime during the night they stopped to rest the horses in the shadow of an overhanging cliff, and Ginny had barely strength left to stumble over to a boulder, which she leaned her back against, her eyes closed. Steve had lifted her off the horse—he'd given her his black jacket to wear against the night chill, and a canteen to drink from. But now he and Paco, merely darker shadows that merged with other shadows, talked softly together.

She was too tired to listen, too tired to want to. The jacket smelled of cigar smoke, and the smell made her headache worse. She felt as if her skull would split open if she moved her head.

Why hadn't she done what she should have done? D'Argent's manner towards her would have soon changed if she had told him who she was, and that she was a prisoner. Or would he have preferred not to believe her, for his own reasons? And why had she meekly followed Steve's curt orders and made herself a wanted fugitive too? She tried to tell herself it was only because she did not want Paco to be tortured and executed. Paco—but what was *he* doing here? Of course he had to have known Steve's plans from the beginning, he was a thief and an outlaw too, in spite of—in spite of—she was suddenly aware that Paco was standing over her, that he was thanking her; telling her he was leaving now, going in a different direction.

"Perhaps we'll meet again soon," he said. "Who knows? And you were wonderful," he added. "I'm grateful."

She murmured something—she could not remember what she had said. But suddenly he was gone, and Steve was bending over her, his hands surprisingly gentle as he helped her to her feet.

"We'd better get moving, *bébé*," he said quietly. She glanced at him strangely. He'd called her *"bébé,"*—a French word? But then, it was only a word, and a man could pick up a word or two of any language easily enough. He helped her up into the saddle and she said tonelessly, "How far this time?"

She saw him shrug in the darkness as they put their horses into a canter.

"Depends on how fast we can travel. We're going to come out into some flat country now, and I want to put as many miles between us and our friends back there as possible first."

"I have a terrible headache!" she said suddenly, with the first sign of emotion she had shown since they'd left the town. He laughed unfeelingly.

"It's probably a hangover, Ginny. You drank too much champagne."

She wanted to scream at him, hurl insults and abuse at him, but it would take too much effort. She relapsed into a sullen silence, closing her eyes against the pain that lanced through her temples with each movement of the horse.

Their travelling during the next forty-eight hours followed the old pattern that Ginny had been forced to become used to. Riding at night, hiding out somewhere to sleep during the hottest part of the day. The only other humans they encountered were an occasional peasant—a *vaquero* guarding a small herd of incredibly scrawny looking cattle.

Once they had left the foothills behind them the country seemed to undulate, to stretch endlessly before them. And all this land, Steve explained briefly, belonged to the big landowners—the *hacendados*. His voice had sounded almost bitter, making her glance at him sharply. At times like this, she would remember that he had a Mexican mother, and wonder—was that why he was mixed up with the *Juaristas*? Had he felt deprived and cheated in some way?

She asked him questions about Mexico, and about Juarez and for once he seemed to take her seriously, and gave her considered, honest answers. It was the big landowners, wanting to keep their miniature kingdoms, who had supported Maximilian. He told her of the system of peonage which rendered men slaves to their patron, working all their lives on land that could never belong to them. Juarez had wanted things to be different—he had broken the power of the church, insisted on schooling for even the children of poor Indians. He represented a threat to the way of life of the wealthy landowners, "*criollas*" most of them.

"And you," Ginny persisted, "what about you? Surely you don't consider yourself a Mexican? Why would you want to take sides?"

To this question, at least, he would not give her a straight answer. "Maybe I wanted to know how it felt to fight for a cause," he said once, lightly; and the next time she asked, "You're surely not forgetting I'm a half-breed?"

He continued to puzzle her. She was almost as familiar with the shape and texture of his body as she was with her own, and yet she knew nothing about him—who he was or what he was. He was no ordinary half-breed gunman, she knew that much. Sometimes he spoke like an educated man, and sometimes worse than any illiterate. He knew Indians, on both sides of the border, and he seemed to know the country they were travelling through, so he was as familiar with Mexico as he was in the United States. It seemed unusual, to say the least, that any man should have travelled so much in his lifetime—although, of course, she would tell herself with a little stab of contempt, he had probably spent most of his life running from the law.

"Where are you taking me this time? Dear God, I'm so tired of riding, of running!"

The plains, their emptiness slashed through by *barrancas,* or small canyons, seemed to shimmer under the heat, and Ginny felt unutterably dirty and weary.

Surprisingly, he stopped to draw her a rough map in the sandy soil.

"We are in the Meseta Central—here are the mountain ridges, the Sierra Madres, on either side—" he drew jagged lines—"and we're here, somewhere in the center, in the province of Zacatecas. Ahead of us there are more mountains—Mexico City. But that's quite a way farther, and don't look at me so hopefully, sweetheart, I'm not taking you there, not yet."

"But why? Why not? I'm of no use to you now, you can let me go, and travel more quickly without me, why do you need me now?"

She saw the way he looked at her and flushed, hearing him laugh softly.

"Blushes become you, do you know that? Even under the tan you've acquired."

"Oh, damn you, Steve Morgan!"

She whirled away from him and ran for her horse, mounted it with her ragged skirts flying, not bothering to turn her head to see if he followed. She dug her heels into the animal's side and felt it spring forward. A sudden, unreasoning fear, mixed with depression, seized her. What am I doing here? What will become of me? Why won't he set me free? She leaned low over the horse's neck and felt the hot breeze whip against her face. The hat he had given her to wear flew from her head, hanging from her neck by its cord.

She rode with a kind of desperate, mindless fury, feeling the fluid motion of the horse under her. It was only when the animal began to tire and slacken its speed that she became aware that all along, he'd been riding abreast of her. She lifted her head to scream her hate and fear at him and saw his arm come out, catching her around the waist and sweeping her from her saddle to his.

"I've missed riding with you and holding your body close this way," he said softly in her ear. "Ginny, you fool, did you really think I'd let you run away? What were you running to?"

"Away—anywhere, it doesn't matter—just away from you, from what you've turned me into." She half-screamed the words at him, gasping for breath. "Haven't you done enough? Do I have to be exhibited in cheap saloons and bawdy houses as your whore? Must I be dragged along wherever you go like a—a trophy of war? What are you trying to do to me?"

"Don't forget, *niña*, that I only took what you kept offering me in the first place! And then there were the others—Carl Hoskins, your French lover, the debonair Captain Remy—do you think he'll be waiting for you in Mexico City? Is that why you're so anxious to get there?"

She had goaded him into anger at last, she thought, and didn't care. Let him be angry with her, what could he do to her now that he had not done already?

"Whatever I am, it's what you've turned me into! And if being some man's mistress is all that's left to me now, then I'd rather be a demimondaine and choose my own lovers than be your cheap camp follower!"

"In that case, Ginny, if it's your ambition to be a *puta*, you'd best learn how one is treated! And remember, no fighting, no struggling, a man expects something in return for his money!"

Before she could say a word, he reined the horse up sharply and slid off its back, carrying her with him.

She would not yield, not this time. She would not let his arms and his kisses melt her. Perhaps, if she refused to fight, refused to *feel*, he'd tire of her and let her go.

He held her hurtfully by the arm, but at least he thought to throw his blanket-roll down among the clumps of sagebrush that littered the hard ground. Well, it wouldn't be the first time he'd taken her out in the open, lying on the hard, unyielding earth. She felt him push her backwards and lay stiffly and rigidly where he'd left her, noting almost with triumph the way the temper showed hotly in his eyes when she ignored his rude demand that she undress, and quickly.

"If that's how you want it," his muttered words were a threat—almost unbelievingly, Ginny saw him pull the knife he always carried in a sheath strapped to his leg. He used it on her clothes, then, while she forced herself to lie still—cutting them swiftly and savagely away from her shrinking flesh. When it was done, he flung the knife carelessly aside and stood over her, his hands unbuckling his belt.

"Spread your legs for me, *puta*," he said almost casually. "Let's see how much you are worth."

The words, the way in which he said them, his assumption of being able to take her so cheaply, so easily, brought sudden life back to her body and she felt as if a tide of furious rage bubbled in her veins, rendering her almost insane with anger and hate.

As he bent over her, she flung her arms outward in a paroxysm of sheer frustration, and her fingers touched the knife he had flung so carelessly away. Hardly thinking, all reaction now, Ginny snatched up the knife, driving the point upward at his body. She felt it slice through flesh— with a shock that jarred her whole body she knew the blade had glanced off bone. Blindly, in a frenzy of fear and fury, she would have struck again, but this time he was prepared for her. His hand caught her wrist and twisted it savagely. When she looked up at him, she saw that the whole side of his shirt was soaked with blood—he sat back on his haunches, Indian fashion, and stared at her as if he hadn't seen her before.

Ginny's wrist throbbed horribly but suddenly, as she gazed back at him, she was only barely conscious of the pain. Something stirred in her as she lay there naked under the hot sun, with the sky like a deep blue bowl overhead—something strange and unfamiliar and primitive. Her eyes locked with his, finding them unfathomable.

"You should have been a Comanche squaw after all," he said suddenly. "But if you had been, I'd be dead by now."

She said nothing, watching his eyes. There was pain there, she could see that now; and a kind of puzzled wonder too, but no anger.

The blood dripped down his side, down his pants leg, but he did nothing to staunch its flow.

"I still want to make love to you," he said quietly.

"You'll bleed to death first!"

But the words were a whisper, and even as she said them he leaned over her again and her body moved to accept his. She felt the warm, sticky wetness of his blood on her breasts, and when she opened her eyes again she could see the buzzards wheeling above them—tiny black specks against blinding blue.

He moved inside her and her body arched to meet his. Her voice sounded drugged, half-dazed.

"I might have killed you—they know—the buzzards. I can see them."

"And I prefer another kind of death—the little death that comes each time I fuck you, Ginny."

He spoke to her in fluent French and she gasped with shock and a return of anger, raking her nails down his back like a wildcat until he swore at her in Spanish and then in French, jamming his mouth down against hers in a kiss so violent that she forgot her anger, the words she wanted to scream at him, and became blind to everything but his body, and hers, and the savage hunger in both of them that had to be satisfied.

Chapter Twenty-four

The knife wound, when Ginny looked at it later, appalled her. A deep, wicked gash in his side, under the arm—but Steve told her calmly as she washed it clean that he had survived worse wounds than this one.

"Lucky my rib deflected the blade, or you might have found yourself all alone out here," he mocked her gently.

"You're not angry?" she said with surprise as she pulled strips of cloth tight across his chest. He shrugged, wincing as he did so.

"Guess I had it coming. And it'll teach me not to be careless with that knife in future." He gave her a strangely thoughtful, measuring look. "Nor with you either. I underestimated you, Ginny. And that streak of stubbornness in you."

She moved away from him sullenly, and stood with her back to him. She was aware how ridiculous she must look, wearing nothing but his shirt and a clumsy skirt improvised from a blanket.

"I suppose I underestimated you too," she said waspishly. "You speak French after all, and all this time, all these months you let me think . . ." She bit her lip in vexation, remembering some of the things the French lieu-

279

tenant had said to her. Why had Steve pretended? And how was it that he spoke such good French?

"Suppose we don't underestimate each other any more, then." He'd come up behind her, she was uncomfortably, tinglingly aware of his presence at her shoulder, but refused to turn.

"Ginny—" his voice was almost a sigh, surprising her. "Look—if you'll just be patient for a while, maybe things will work out. I was going to tell you back there, when you took off like a wild thing, that by evening tomorrow you'll be someplace safe. No," he added hastily, when she swung around to confront him, "not a room over a saloon, or a place like Lilas'. A house. Belongs to a friend of mine, but you'll have it to yourself. There'll be a woman to take care of you too."

"And you? You're going to leave me somewhere alone while you . . ."

"I would have thought you'd be relieved to be rid of me for a while!" His voice had turned flat and emotionless again, she could not tell what he was thinking. She was silent, waiting for him to continue.

"I have to go to Mexico City, Ginny. There are a few arrangements I have to make. And I can't take you with me, for obvious reasons. But when I get back—"

"*If* you get back!" she flung at him. "*If!!* You're a hunted man, Steve Morgan, and well I know it. Do you really think you'll be able to ride boldly into Mexico City, of all places, and come back out alive?"

"I'll come back. But even if I don't—my Cousin Renaldo will see to it that you're delivered safely back to your father."

He would tell her nothing more, even though she alternately pleaded and stormed at him. Nothing that she really wanted to know. He would send her back to her father as soon as he returned, he promised her that much at least. Wasn't it what she wanted? And if he didn't come back, Renaldo would see to it. Renaldo was not really his cousin, he admitted. More nearly a kind of uncle, although they were almost the same age. "But in Mexico we call all our relatives cousin or uncle," he said carelessly.

Well, at least he had promised to set her free, Ginny thought, leaning against him in the old way, sitting up straight again when she felt his almost imperceptible wince of pain. But along with the thought of freedom came a kind of fear, almost a kind of reluctance she was not ready to consider yet. When she did go back, what then? How would they all react—her father, Sonya, everyone who knew what had happened to her? *I'll go back to France,* she thought at last, and tried to force herself not to think after that.

The foothills behind them were turning purple with evening when Ginny saw the cattle. A sizeable herd of them, this time, grazing peaceably in the long twilight shadows. And where there were cattle. . . .

She shrank against Steve when she heard the sound of drumming hoofs. The two *vaqueros*, gaudily-colored neck-keerchiefs knotted around their brown throats under wide-brimmed sombreros, reined up alongside them. They wore guns, both of them, and one of the men had his rifle at the ready, so they were obviously mistrustful, but before she could do more than draw in her breath sharply, they had pulled off their hats, waving them crazily, with their faces breaking into broad grins of recognition.

"Don Esteban!" one of them shouted, "We did not know you were coming!"

"*Sí*, but I told Diego, I said no one else rides that way—and Don Esteban would not miss the birthday fiesta of *el patrón*. It has been a long time, no?"

Their eyes touched Ginny, slid away politely. For once she was relieved that Steve did not stop to talk at length. He grinned back at the men and made a joking comment about the fiesta and his thirst for *aguardiente*.

"But I cannot meet my grandfather or my friends looking like a ruffian—I will look for you tomorrow, my old friends, and share some *pulque* with you. Until tomorrow."

"*Hasta mañana*." The words were the essence of Mexico, Ginny thought rather wryly. Everything waited on tomorrow. And what would hers be?

To cover the embarrassment she had felt when the vaqueros rode up she asked Steve quickly, "Who were they? Did you know them well?"

"Very well. I used to ride with them, and get drunk with them sometimes. They're my friends."

"But they called you Don Esteban," she persisted.

"Oh," she could feel his shrug. "Don's a courtesy title. Like calling someone mister in the States. Did you expect

me to be something more than a poor *vaquero*? Does it
disappoint you?"

"Since I've learned to expect the worst from you you
could hardly disappoint me," she retorted; but curiosity
and the desire not to think about the place to which he
was taking her made her persist in her questioning.

"Still," she went on thoughtfully, "I would hardly expect
an ordinary cowboy to have as much education as you
seem to have. Or to speak fluent French either."

"Ah, Ginny!" There was a faint tremor of laughter underlying his voice, "I'm afraid I am a disappointment. I
never had any formal schooling, you see. I picked up what
I could from books and hearing how people talked. And
as for the French—I learned it from a French whore in
New Orleans. Does that satisfy you?"

She did not believe him—she longed to ask him
questions about his American father, but his last statement
silenced her. A man like him! Frequenting whores—it was
obvious he'd had no dealings with decent women in his
past. Her back had stiffened involuntarily, and she felt his
arm tighten around her waist.

"No need to be jealous, love—that was long before I
met you. And perhaps you can teach me something too."

His meaning was unmistakeable but she refused to rise
to the bait and sat in sullen silence until she saw the grove
of trees.

They were tall, and looked very old, even in the deep
blue light of late evening. Somewhere, she heard a dog
barking, and lights showed between the trees as they rode
closer. A strange feeling of desolation, almost of *deja vu*
swept over Ginny, and she heard herself sigh. A grove of
trees, welcoming lights, somewhere ahead a house. Perhaps it had been home to Steve once, but she was a
stranger. In spite of the odd feeling of familiarity, this
place was not familiar to her. And this cousin, what kind
of a man was he? How would he react to her presence?

There was no more time in which to ponder. They were
through the grove of trees now, following a curved driveway that led to the house. Ginny had the vague impression
of tall shrubs lining the driveway; the heavy scent of some
nightblooming flower hung in her nostrils.

A shallow flight of steps lit by twin lanterns, led up to
a narrow porch that extended all the way around the two
storied building. Expecting something smaller, Ginny was

surprised first by the size of the house, and then by the sudden, unexpected presence of two armed *vaqueros* who seemed to materialize out of the shadows. Two dogs, barking wildly, ran ahead.

"I suppose I smell different," Steve said dryly. Raising his voice slightly he called "Sit, damn you, you hell-hounds!" The barks turned to whimpers as the dogs obeyed, their tails swishing now.

"It's Don Esteban!" one of the men said. "We were half expecting you, *señor*, but it's so late, and the fiesta began yesterday . . ."

"Where the hell is my cousin? Renaldo! Isn't he here?"

Steve slid off the horse, tossing the reins to one of the grinning men, and Ginny felt herself lifted off and held close to his chest.

"Oh, for God's sake!" she found herself whispering, "you'll not take me in there to meet your cousin like *this?*"

The door opened, and light streamed out, silhouetting the tall and rather stooped man who stood there for an instant, and then ran lightly down to them, his arms outstretched in greeting.

"Esteban! I had a rather garbled message a day ago, but I couldn't make sense of it. I was half afraid you'd be in Mexico City by now. But it's so good to see you."

"I cannot return your *abrazo*, Renaldo. You see, I have a guest for the little house. It's unoccupied?"

By this time the man stood before them, but neither his manner nor his tone of voice betrayed any surprise or dismay.

"It's unoccupied, of course. I hoped you'd come, so I made sure of it. By now, Rosa is waiting there, and you'll find I had everything kept ready."

"In that case, I'll take my friend there directly. She's tired, and rather embarrassed at meeting you when she's not at her best, I think. You'll be introduced later."

Ginny's blush burned her face and neck. If she had not been so mortified she would have burst into angry tears. How dare he expose her this way? How dare he refer to her so lightly as his "friend?" A Frenchman would refer to his mistress as his "*petite amie*"—no doubt the phrase had its equivalent in Spanish! And so that was to be her role!

"You'll join me for a drink later, then? I'll expect you."

She could not help sensing the rather embarrassed look
that Renaldo threw in her direction. No doubt the poor
man was wondering whether he should address himself to
her or not. But Steve gave him no chance to do so, for he
was already walking with his long, easy strides along the
side of the house, carrying her lightly in his arms as if he
had not been wounded at all.

La Caseta, the little house. Later, by daylight, Ginny
was to think how aptly it was named.

It stood some distance away from the larger *estancia*,
nestled in a tiny clearing in the trees where one would not
expect any house to be. A crazy-paved walkway connected
the two dwellings, and in spite of the darkness, Steve was
as surefooted as a cat.

The door stood open, with warm lamplight spilling out,
and a fat, black-haired *mestizo* woman stood aside,
smiling shyly as Steve carried Ginny inside, walking
through the tiny, miniature living room, turning to the
left, and bending his head under a low-arched doorway as
they entered the bedroom.

The bed was enormous—probably, she thought, the
biggest and most comfortable-looking bed she had ever
seen. A brightly colored, handwoven spread had been
turned back to show white linen sheets. Patterned curtains
that matched the bedspread had been drawn to cover the
window that seemed to run almost the length of one wall.

This room, of course, was the focal point of the whole
house. It was much larger than the living room, the floor
was entirely covered by a kind of soft matting that sub-
stituted for a carpet, and instead of doors the arched
doorways were covered by heavy draperies.

Steve bent over to deposit her on the bed and suddenly,
surprisingly, Ginny felt nervous. She actually did not want
him to leave her yet!

"Wait," she said when he turned to go, and there was a
puzzled, almost startled look in his dark blue eyes as he
turned back to her.

"Aren't you anxious to be rid of me?" He started to
smile, his eyes becoming lazy as they narrowed very
slightly. "Ginny, can it be—"

"Stop playing games with me!" she snapped, and then,
irrelevantly, "you're bleeding again—you had better get
that gash taken care of."

Almost indifferently he put his hand up, grimacing as he

touched the warm stickiness of blood where it seeped through the makeshift bandages.

"Oh, yes, I guess I am. Well, Renaldo will see to it. Was there anything you needed, love?"

"I'm hungry, and I'd like to wash, and I need some clothes." She said it flatly, angry with herself now, and angrier with him.

"Rosa will get you anything you need. There's a bathroom back there," he nodded his head towards a curtained archway she had thought to be merely an alcove. "Tomorrow, you'll be able to see the patio, and the rest of the house, if you're interested."

He hesitated, and then bowed to her politely, and ridiculously formally.

"Sleep well, Ginny."

Rosa, when she bustled in, fussed over Ginny like a mother, her shy smiles hiding her normal curiosity. In spite of her rather unprepossessing appearance, and her inability to speak anything but Spanish, she also proved an excellent lady's maid, and for the first time in months Ginny felt spoiled.

The bathroom had a sunken Roman bath that made Ginny open her eyes wide in surprise.

"It's big enough for two—" Rosa said, and Ginny felt herself blush again. She had thought the same thing, and the unwanted thought embarrassed her. Rosa helped her bathe, rubbing her body with scented soap, washing out her hair and exclaiming at its coppery length and beauty. Afterwards, in the bedroom, Rosa massaged her aching, tired body very gently with cologne, and Ginny felt some of the weariness and stiffness leave her.

Her light supper, which she ate while wrapped like a Polynesian in a soft cotton blanket, was excellent—and accompanied by a light white wine which she found dry and delicious. For dessert there was fresh fruit, packed in ice, and Rosa hovered nearby, urging Ginny to eat more, clucking that she was too thin.

Afterwards, in the bedroom, Rosa brushed Ginny's still-damp hair in front of the full length mirror that hung there, exclaiming admiringly as she did.

"The *señorita* is very beautiful—such hair, such pretty soft skin. Tomorrow I will bring some pretty clothes—the *señor* will be pleased."

The reference to Steve reminded Ginny vividly that

after all, she was nothing but his prisoner and plaything. She could not help wondering where he was and what he was doing. Had he gone to see the mysterious grandfather to whom those *vaqueros* had alluded? And why was he so mysterious about all his relatives? She thought bitterly that they were probably all *Juaristas*—it was surprising that the French were so blind when it came to landowners. Perhaps Rosa would tell her more—all she wanted to know, in fact. But she'd have to be careful, letting the woman suspect nothing. She was far too tired tonight, though. Perhaps tomorrow morning. She did not even remember the exact moment she fell asleep—only half-recalled Rosa's voice coming to her from a distance, asking if that would be all.

PART FOUR

Interlude

Chapter Twenty-five

In the morning Ginny woke in an empty bed, blinking in the sudden sunlight that filled the room as Rosa pulled the draperies apart. She had hot chocolate and crisp rolls, sitting up in bed, and after she had washed the woman brought her an assortment of gowns, skirts and low-necked camisas to choose from.

"The *señor* sent them," the woman said in reply to Ginny's unspoken question. She added quickly, "The *señor* is on his way here now."

"And where," Ginny wanted to ask acidly, "did the *señor* spend the night?" But she said nothing, and when Rosa had left she chose a simple white muslin gown to wear, wondering as she did so, with an indefinable feeling of distaste, where he had obtained clothes for her so quickly.

Ginny was pinning her hair up when Steve walked unceremoniously into the room to stand looking at her with his brows quirked.

"You look like a lamb led to the slaughter," he commented dryly.

"Perhaps that is because you very often make me feel

like one!" she retorted, and his eyes crinkled with amusement.

She turned to study him, her eyes widening in surprise. He looked very Spanish today, in a tight-fitting *charro* suit, with a short jacket, and he had trimmed his beard more closely than usual.

Catching her look, he grimaced.

"My grandfather is old-fashioned, and a stickler for convention. I'm dressed like a dandy to please him."

"It surprises me that you'd put yourself out to please anyone," Ginny stated coldly. She turned back to the dresser and began fiddling with her hair. "And how did you find your grandfather?"

In the mirror, she saw him shrug.

"My grandfather is, as usual, very angry with me. I had forgotten his birthday fiesta. But in the meantime . . ."

"Yes." She swung around to face him again. "And in the meantime—what? What do you intend to do with me? I'm still a prisoner, I suppose."

"By no means, love. This is your house for as long as you wish to stay here. As we say in Mexico, *mi casa esta su casa*. My house is yours. Will you let me show you the patio now? It's cool there at this time of the day, you'll enjoy it."

"Don't try to put me off with clever words, Steve Morgan. Or should I follow the custom of the country and call you Don Esteban?" Anger flared in Ginny's eyes, making them look almost dark in the dimness of the room. Her hands clenched into fists at her side.

"I thought this was your cousin's house," she continued furiously. "How can you be so generous with it? And will you tell me what I'm supposed to do with myself while you are in Mexico City, or wherever you intend to go next? Will you leave me to become your cousin's plaything next, like—like the women who must have worn these clothes before me?"

"Goddammit Ginny!" His mouth had thinned into an angry line, and she saw a muscle twitch in his jaw. "You have an unfortunate knack for making me forget all my good resolutions. Come with me into the patio, now, and listen to what I have to say for a change."

He had seized her wrist, and willy nilly she went with him—through another arched doorway into a tiny, shaded patio with a small fountain at one end. There was a profusion of flowers everywhere; warm stones under her feet, bowers and jasmine and another, starlike blossom she did not recognize.

Two cane chairs and a rough wooden table stood here, and Steve pushed her into one of them, throwing himself into the other impatiently.

Ginny rubbed at her wrist and glared at him.

"Why are you always so rough with me? You push me here and you drag me there, and just because I'm not a man, and you're physically stronger than I am . . ."

He cut her off abruptly, squinting his eyes against the sun as he leaned back in the chair.

"Oh, for God's sake! When will you learn not to act so shrewishly? I didn't come here to quarrel with you Ginny. In fact, I'd hoped to surprise you still in bed, and in a better mood than you were yesterday, when you stuck a knife in me."

"I'm only sorry I didn't kill you! Oh, if you only knew how much I . . ."

"Were you going to tell me again how much you hate me? Don't bother, my sweet, I've heard you say it often enough to believe it. But"—he opened his eyes lazily at her and she shrank at the sudden flare of passion she recognized in them for just an instant—"I suppose that if you were always meek and eager for my embraces I'd soon be bored with you. As it is . . ." his eyes became opaque again and he changed the subject abruptly, as if he'd tired of it.

"I thought I'd introduce you to my cousin Renaldo. I think you'll like him, he's not at all like me. And perhaps I should mention that you need not fear that Renaldo will expect you to become his light of love when I'm not here. Women don't seem to interest him, except as friends. He was trained for the priesthood, in fact. I'm surprised he didn't become one in the end."

"Perhaps the way you turned out disillusioned him," Ginny countered.

"Perhaps so! But you'd find him a good friend, I think. Rosa's bringing us some orange juice. Will you come with me to meet him after that?"

The fact that he'd asked her instead of ordering her surprised her into nodding, if a trifle sullenly.

It was peaceful out here, after all. And what was the

point in quarrelling with Steve? He'd do just as he pleased, eventually, as always.

In the end, Ginny was to be glad of her friendship with Renaldo Ortega. She could sense, from the time of their very first meeting, a kind of quietness and inner strength about him. And above all, as she was to find, his manners were impeccable. Renaldo Ortega was a gentleman, in the old-fashioned sense, his courtesy and kindness towards her unfailing.

The first time they met—he was in the *sala* of his house, and he rose to his feet when Steve brought her in, waving aside the servant who would have announced them first in his usual careless way.

Renaldo Ortega was a tall man, only a hair shorter than Steve but slim hipped and just as wide shouldered. His dark hair was not overly long, and he wore it parted on the side, which gave him the look of an intellectual. Ginny thought, amazed, that with his light skin and amber-colored eyes he could easily have been a Frenchman or an Italian. Certainly he did not look like any Mexican she had seen before. Perhaps, then, he was a pure-blooded Spaniard, one of the *criollas* that Steve had mentioned so contemptuously.

She had been stiff, and more than a little apprehensive when Steve had brought her here, but now, meeting Renaldo's eyes and seeing the warmth and understanding in them, she felt the rigidity leave her.

He bowed over her hand correctly, touching her fingers to his lips.

She heard again the same words that Steve had used so casually to her earlier, "*mi casa esta su casa,*" but in spite of their formality she had the impression that Renaldo Ortega meant them. And after that first greeting, he conversed with her in English, with only the barest trace of an accent.

Tactfully, he ignored the strangeness of her position here, treating her with the same respect he would have treated any lady who was an honored guest. Renaldo's old-fashioned manners covered a warm heart and an intelligence that most people tended to underestimate. He was considered something of a hermit, preferring the books in his library to the usual sports of his young Spanish contemporaries.

Women had never interested him too deeply because he

felt they were too shallow, too foolish—at least, all of the women his granduncle used to insist he meet, trying to find a suitable wife for him. It was not the fault of the women, of course—Renaldo was aware that from infancy they were brought up to think of themselves as being somehow inferior to men; taught to look forward only to marry, bear children, and handle the affairs of a household. Education was wasted on women, and a woman who thought for herself and questioned her destiny was not to be thought of as a bride. It was a system that Renaldo deplored, but tried to ignore by burying himself in literature and his writing. He was a paper revolutionary. He despised himself for it—but the thought of bloodshed revolted him even more. While he had always been a thinker, his cousin Esteban, now, had always been a doer, seeming to crave the danger of action, of adventure. Perhaps it was because by nature they were such opposites, that they had become close friends.

Renaldo was the only member of Steve's family who knew what kind of profession his cousin really followed. He had envied his freedom in a way; although it was not the kind of freedom that he, Renaldo, would have chosen. Esteban was wild by nature, a reckless adventurer. He had always been wild, ever since Renaldo's cousin Luisa, Steve's mother, had brought him here as a child. From then on there had been constant battles, with Renaldo protecting his cousin as often as he could from his grandfather's rigid, inflexible disciplining. His grandfather! When he thought about Don Francisco, Renaldo could not help sighing. What would he think of his grandson's latest indiscretion? He had been angry enough when Steve had arrived late for the fiesta celebrations—thank God he had no idea that Steve's being here at all was only accidental! But when he found out, as was almost inevitable, about the young lady . . .

For the first time in years, Renaldo was really angry with Steve, although, in Ginny's presence, he did not show it.

They had had their argument last night, when Steve had come back to the house looking unwontedly pale under his tan, blood dripping from a knife wound in his side. Renaldo, who had studied as much as he could about medicine from his books, had attended to the wound himself.

"So—you're in some trouble again."

Deftly, his fingers had cleaned the wound as he talked, and he saw his cousin's lips tighten against the sudden pain.

"Tangled with a wildcat. She's all claws, especially when I least expect it."

"Oh?" Renaldo's brows shot upward. "It's unusual, isn't it, for you to have a mistress who's unwilling? And come to think of it, it's not like you to bring a woman here. You know that your grandfather . . ."

"I'm aware of the way he'd feel about the matter, if he knew. But I had no choice. You know I have to be in Mexico City soon, and I can't take Ginny with me. Damn it, if I had only thought of the consequences! But I lost my temper."

"That's unlike you. But couldn't you have left her wherever you took her from? Or have made some arrangements?"

But when Steve had grudgingly told him the whole story, Renaldo found himself at first astonished and then filled with anger.

"My God, Esteban!" he burst out, "this time, surely, you've gone too far. Even for you, this is too much! To kidnap a young woman of good birth and breeding and to treat her like a *puta*. What were you thinking of?"

They had argued until late into the night, but Renaldo found his cousin implacable. He swore the kidnapping had been unplanned, he agreed that his subsequent actions had been completely dishonorable and offered no excuses. But the fact remained that the girl was here. He wanted Renaldo's assurance that she should remain here, under his protection, until he returned from Mexico City.

"And what then?" Renaldo questioned grimly. He paced the room, his face white with fury. "Don't you realize the consequences to her? Don't you care? How will she face the world, her parents, after this?"

"Damn it, I'll think of something! She wants to go back to France—no one there need know what's happened, and I'll wager Senator Brandon won't be in too much of a hurry to talk about it either. I'll settle some money on her, make sure she has sufficient to keep her independent. That's what she wants, anyhow! She hates my guts, she tells me she despises men, and would like to pick her own lovers."

"And damn *you*, Esteban! What did you expect her to say? Thank you for ruining her life? I tell you, if you were not wounded I'd be tempted to call you out, even if you are a better shot than I! For God's sake, why did you do it? How could you do it?"

"I'll let you meet her tomorrow, perhaps you'll understand better," Steve said obliquely. And then, meeting Ginny Brandon the next day, Renaldo wondered if he did indeed understand.

She was beautiful. Beautiful, spirited, and a lady. How could Esteban, or any man, take this woman lightly? Or having taken her, how could any man bear to let her go? Renaldo was surprised at himself. It was very seldom a woman affected him. He had always respected women, found them pretty and ornamental. But this one was more—he could sense a kind fo resilience in her, combined with pride and indomitable courage. If ever a woman were a match for Esteban, it was this one. Esteban, because of his handsome face and his casual, arrogant manners had always found women easy conquests. But here was a woman he'd obviously been unable to tame. Renaldo found himself wondering what the outcome would be, just as he knew, inside himself, that having met her he would accede to what Esteban had asked of him, but for her sake, and not his.

During the short time that Steve stayed, having performed the necessary introductions in his usual negligent manner, Renaldo found himself observing them both. His cousin's dark face was unreadable, his manner towards the girl light, and almost teasingly affectionate. But there was something there, beneath the surface. Steve never showed anything that he did not want to show, except for occasional flashes of anger.

Ginny Brandon was more transparent. She had been horribly embarrassed at first, although she had bravely tried not to show it—later, Renaldo could see her begin to relax; once or twice she even smiled at him gratefully and he could feel his anger at Steve begin to rise again.

In the days that followed Ginny and Renaldo found themselves thrown together more and more. Steve was staying officially with his grandfather, although he sometimes contrived to "visit Renaldo" and spend a night with Ginny. Occasionally, he took her riding, always insisting that Renaldo accompany them too. They fenced, he noticed, almost like strangers who disliked each other. And yet—he was only too much aware of those nights that his cousin spent in the little house. There were no screams, Esteban bore no more scars, and Ginny always seemed quieter the following day, her eyelids heavy, a warm glow underlying her apricot-tinted skin. So she accepted the situation. ... but what, he'd ask himself fiercely, was her alternative? His unpredictable cousin had taken her as a virgin, had taught her body sensuality, no doubt. Steve had a way with women. And now, even though her mind might hate it, he was sure that Ginny's passionate female body could not deny its own urgings. What a situation! He wondered if, in spite of the brave and sometimes shrewish front she showed she was actually in love with Steve. Poor girl! He hoped she was not. At the moment, because she was like a wild thing not yet quite tame, Steve desired her. But later? What would become of her?

Ginny had almost stopped wondering that herself, except when she would catch Renaldo's sorrowful, sympathetic dark eyes on her and sensed his concern for her. She threw herself into the lazy, unhurried pattern of her days in the little house, not daring to think of the future.

Her days were no longer ruled by haste—she had all the leisure in the world. Renaldo seemed always to be there when she needed companionship; at other times, there were the books in his library, discussions that touched on almost every subject possible, games of chess. It seemed an unspoken agreement between them that they not discuss her relationship with Steve, although from time to time Renaldo would relate incidents from their boyhood. She wondered rather bitterly at times if Renaldo hoped to teach her to understand Steve better. If he only knew how pointless that would be, how impossible!

Steve had told her he must go to Mexico City soon, but he stayed for over a week—almost ten days, in fact. It was because of this mysterious grandfather of his, of course—he seemed to be the only person in the world that Steve respected enough to be considerate of. And yet, she could hardly reconcile it with what Renaldo had told her of the Senor Alvarado's sternness and insistence upon discipline—the way Steve had kept running away as a boy. Why, now that he was a man, did he come back? She was curious about Steve's grandfather, but dared not ask too many questions, even of Renaldo, who was growing more and more into a friend. She imagined the old man as being stern-faced and rather frightening, and wondered how he had allowed his only daughter to marry an Americano.

And as for Steve Morgan himself—she could not help noticing that in some subtle, almost indefinable way, he had altered. He came very seldom in the daytime, and when he did come at night she was usually asleep already—would wake to find him beside her, his hands caressing her, his lips on her temples or her breasts. She'd be too sleepy to protest, and he knew it. Her guard down, her body responded to his without reserve—almost by instinct. And when she'd open her eyes in the morning, ready to quarrel with him, he'd be gone.

When they were together, he was polite to her, but almost absent-mindedly so. She supposed that she ought to be relieved he left her to her own devices so much, and had forced no added humiliations upon her, but as the long, languid days passed Ginny found herself wondering what he did with himself all day, and where he went.

"Where is your grandfather's house?" she asked him carelessly one day when they were out riding together, and he pointed behind them.

"Several miles away. It takes me quite a while to get back down here."

"I suppose I should be honored?" she queried sharply.

She saw the grooves in his lean face deepen as he smiled.

"You don't know my grandfather. It takes a lot of evasion and quite a bit of lying to get away from him. In fact he's been hinting that I should decide to stay and help with—some of the chores around the place."

"You're quite good at lies and evasion. No doubt you must keep in practice."

He laughed outright this time.

"Touché!" With a touch of his knees he brought his horse closer to the mare he'd borrowed for her from Renaldo. "But I'm going to miss you when I leave tomorrow, and that's the truth."

"Tomorrow!" For an instant her voice was unguarded, betraying something like dismay.

"I'll be back in two weeks—if all goes well. Try to miss me a little, Ginny."

He put his hand on the back of her neck and turned her head, kissing her half-open mouth.

Afterwards, when she knew that he had really gone, she remembered that his kiss had been tender, and his words, although teasingly uttered, had sounded almost regretful. But what had he been regretting?

Chapter Twenty-six

With Steve gone on some mysterious errand to Mexico City, Ginny had almost too much time in which to think and torture herself with questions and doubts. She hated him! She had told him so, crying with vexation, when he had stopped by the little house very early in the morning, dressed quite incongruously as a Mexican peasant.

Why did he always have to be so mysterious? And if his business concerned her, why couldn't he tell her about it? What did he intend to do about her? She stormed him with questions, none of which he would answer. He told her to be patient, and finally, driven into a rage, he had told her coldly that she was turning into a shrew and he would be glad to be rid of her.

"Unfortunately," he said between clenched jaws, "my cousin Renaldo has reminded me that I am, in part, responsible for you. He agrees with you that I'm a dishonorable wretch for having kidnapped you in the first place. Well, believe me, I've had time to regret that precipitate action of mine! I'm afraid I've lived away from civilization too long, I'm used to taking what I want." His hands had bruised her shoulders. "As soon as I return,

Ginny, I'll see about taking you back. You'll finally be free—and by God, so will I!"

Even Renaldo's quiet presence was no consolation to Ginny that day. She hated Steve—she hoped that he would never return—she hated herself for her own body's sensuality and weakness. He hated her too, of course! Obviously, it was only physical desire that formed the strange, unmentionable bond between them. It had been that, and nothing else that had attracted her to him in the first place. But how dared he deposit her here so casually and then ride away? Why decide to set her free only when he had already brought her into the very heart of Mexico? For what secret purpose had he planned to use his captivity of her?

By the afternoon of the second day, the tumult in Ginny's mind had subsided into a sullen resignation. There was nothing to do now, but to wait. How she hated it, having to endure everything he forced upon her. She was reminded of the endless-seeming days she had spent in El Paso, locked in the small room above Lilas' fancy saloon. Here, at least, she had freedom of a sort, and Renaldo's companionship, but how, and when would it all end?

Ginny had taken a book out into the patio, but it was impossible to concentrate on reading, and besides, she had read this book, a novel by Alexandre Dumas, before. She needed movement, the blowing of fresh air against her face. If only she could persuade old Manuel to saddle up the mare! Ginny frowned, then, thinking with a feeling of annoyance that he would probably stammer and hang his head—make some excuse. He'd probably tell her again that it was dangerous—she did not know the country, and besides the *señor* had expressly forbidden that she go riding alone.

She'd been told this before, but when she'd protested sharply to Renaldo, he had, for once, agreed with Steve.

"It's not proper for a young lady to go anywhere alone. This is a country of *duennas*, I'm afraid!"

Only consideration for Renaldo's feelings had prevented Ginny from retorting bitterly that she would hardly be considered a lady if her real position here were known.

Now, she wished that Renaldo were home. But this morning he had explained rather apologetically that he would be busy all day going over accounts. She had seen him leave, and had wondered rather curiously whose books he was going over. But then, Renaldo was kind-hearted, helping everyone. Look how much he had done for her, and for her drooping morale!

I suppose, if I put my mind to it, there are any number of things I could find to occupy myself with, Ginny mused. Soon afterwards she thought impatiently that she was really far too lazy, and it was too hot. I'm going to end up fat and lethargic, insisting on my siesta each day, if this goes on much longer!" she scolded herself. She had laid her book on the wooden table beside her chair, and now, determinedly, she picked it up and began to read. But in a short while her mind had begun to wander again.

Renaldo had many books written in French in his library. She remembered that he had told her he'd visited France some years ago. "I had to take the grand tour," Renaldo had said deprecatingly. "My father was alive then, and he insisted upon it." Ginny wondered if it had been Renaldo who had taught Steve French. In some ways, Steve reminded her of the character D'Artagnan— but then he was by no means as polished a gentleman, nor gallant. He was not a gentleman at all; his manners were like a very thin veneer, cracking easily and often to reveal the savagery underneath.

The sound of horse's hooves, pounding at a furious gallop and obviously coming closer, startled Ginny into dropping her book again. Her eyes widened curiously as a horse dashed into the small clearing and its rider began to give a demonstration of fine horsemanship as she controlled the animal with her gloved hands, finally bringing it to a rearing halt only a few feet away from Ginny, who had instinctively risen to her feet.

The rider, a girl, smiled down at her rather mockingly.

"Were you afraid that Ilario would crush you with his hooves?" she demanded in heavily accented English. A look of barely controlled disappointment flashed in her dark eyes when Ginny shrugged and shook her head coolly, studying her unexpected visitor with some curiosity.

"Was I supposed to be frightened? You appeared to be an excellent rider, and perfectly able to control your animal."

"Yes, I do ride well. Everyone says so!"

Laughing a little in a pleased fashion, the girl dismounted gracefully, and stood facing Ginny, her eyes openly appraising.

Something about her bold, almost rude stare made Ginny uncomfortably aware of her own rather dishevelled appearance. Because of the heat she had dressed casually this morning, finding the loose camisa and colorful skirt of Mexico far more suited to its climate than the voluminous skirts and long sleeves of her other clothes. On her feet, she wore *huaraches*; again, the coolest and most comfortable footgear she could find.

Her visitor, on the other hand, seemed almost overdressed in her dark purple riding habit that was exquisitely cut to show off a figure of almost voluptuous maturity. And yet, close-up, the girl was much younger than she had appeared even at first. She appeared to be about fifteen or sixteen and had dark, wide-set eyes and straight, dark brown hair that was tied back with a wide velvet ribbon that exactly matched her riding habit. Privately, Ginny considered the color far too old for a girl so young . . . almost in self-defense she was studying her as openly as her visitor studied her own appearance.

"I am Dona Ana," the girl said abruptly. She gave an unexpected, short laugh, and looked more like a child for a moment. "I've run away from my *duenna*—on purpose, so that I could see you!"

Without ceremony she perched herself on the edge of a chair, not bothering to hide the look of open curiosity on her face.

"You are not in the least as I expected you to be," she went on, pulling the small, flat velvet hat from her head and tossing it carelessly on the table. "In fact, I might as well tell you that you are very different from the way I'd pictured you!"

Ginny forced herself to sit down, and answer the girl calmly, feigning a composure she hardly felt.

"Oh, indeed? And may I ask what you expected to find?"

The girl put her head on one side and seemed to consider.

"Well, for one thing, you are a little younger than I'd expected. And you don't paint your face. But I suppose Renaldo would not like that. He is such a stuffy and conventional type of man!" She burst out giggling. "At least, that is what everyone thought up until now, of course. Who would have thought it of Renaldo!"

Ginny's fingers curled in her lap from the sudden desire she felt to slap this girl's impudent, smiling face. But she forced herself to speak calmly.

"You seem to know a lot about me. Suppose you tell me who you are? All I can assume, of course, is that you're very young indeed, and that you must have come here for some reason besides idle curiosity. Surely you don't intend to keep me in suspense?"

A trifle disconcerted by Ginny's unexpected attack, and the coolly controlled tone of her voice, Ana had begun to flush rather angrily, and to look disconcerted.

"I've already told you my name, and why I came. Hasn't Renaldo told you anything at all about his family? I must say, he's surprised and shocked everybody! Who would have thought that Renaldo would suddenly decide to keep a mistress, and particularly a *gringa!*"

For a moment, Ginny was too angry and too dumbfounded to speak. Her green eyes narrowed dangerously, and her hands clenched into fists. This girl was not only rude and mannerless, but her contemptuous insinuations were too much to bear! To think that she thought Ginny was poor Renaldo's light of love! And how like Steve, to arrange things so cleverly that everyone would think thus!

Ana seemed pleased at Ginny's sudden and unexpected silence. Clearly, she thought she'd thrown her into a state of confusion by her bluntness. Now she leaned forward, her voice condescending.

"You need not fear that I'll tell *el patrón.* I can be discreet, sometimes! And besides," she said carelessly, "I'm sure he would not approve of my being here, and nor would my *duenna.*"

"And *who,*" Ginny's voice was only barely controlled, she felt that her whole face had gone stiff with anger so that she could hardly produce the words, "is *el patrón?*"

She saw Ana's stare of surprise.

"You ask me that? Why, everybody knows Don Francisco! You're living on his land, after all, and lucky for you that he . . . oh!" Childlike, her attention was easily distracted, and she had snatched up Ginny's book and was staring at it, frowning.

"You were reading a book written in *French?*" Her voice sounded incredulous; looking up she caught Ginny's flashing eyes and her own became rather spiteful. "Oh, perhaps at one time—before—you were a governess? Is that how Renaldo met you?"

"Perhaps if you had had a governess she might have improved your manners," Ginny said forcibly. She jumped to her feet, too angry to stay seated. "You really are a most provoking child," she went on, not caring that Ana's eyes had slitted, almost like a cat's. "But then, I suppose you were deliberately trying to be so. Why? Don't they teach children their manners here?"

"How dare you speak to me like that!" Like an angry feline, Ana, too, sprang to her feet. She faced Ginny with her eyes spitting fury. "Don't you know who I am? I'm no child, I'm betrothed already, to the heir of *el patron*. Why, I'll be the richest, most envied woman in the whole province when we marry—which is more than you can ever hope for, a woman of your type."

"You insufferable, spoiled brat! It takes a woman to recognize what type another woman is, and as for being married, believe me I feel nothing but pity for the poor man who's forced to marry you!"

Ginny felt her cheeks burn with rage, and she wasn't in the least bit afraid when she saw Ana's gloved hands tighten over the handle of her braided leather riding quirt.

The girl's voice shook with uncontrollable rage.

"Why you—you *puta*! Yes, that is what you are, I heard *tia* say so! A fallen woman, she said—a *gringa puta*—to think I had actually begun to feel sorry for you!"

"Well, don't waste your pity, little girl," Ginny snapped. She drew in a deep breath and tried to calm herself. "I really am surprised that an apparently well-brought-up child should use such language, and especially to a guest," she went on more coolly than she felt. "Why don't you make sure of the facts before you start flinging your ridiculous, insolent accusations around? I might as well call *you* a little trollop because you're here unchaperoned, and show an obvious lack of breeding and manners as well!"

"Oh, oh! How dare you?" Ana's voice was shrill with rage, she looked like an angry tigress. "When I tell Don Francisco, he'll have you whipped! Yes, and your precious Renaldo will be in trouble too, for bringing you here and flaunting you in the faces of everyone as his mistress."

The girl's rage gave Ginny the advantage and she

pressed it home with a small, sarcastic smile tugging at the corners of her mouth. "Since I don't know who this mysterious Don Francisco is, I see no reason to be afraid of him," she said reasonably. "But since you appear terrified at the thought of his rage, perhaps you'd better leave before someone catches you here and gives you the spanking you deserve."

"You—slut! Don't talk to me that way!" Almost sobbing with fury, Ana had actually raised her riding crop, but Ginny snatched it from her, and saw fear spring into the girl's tear-filled eyes.

"I'm both taller and stronger than you are," Ginny said grimly. "And I'm in no mood to endure any more of your rudeness."

Ana gave a small shriek as Ginny put her hand out and pushed her back into a chair; standing over her with the quirt held in both hands.

"You wouldn't dare strike me!" she whimpered. "Don Francisco would—oh, and I'd tell my *novio* too, he is very fierce, and always wears a gun—he'd kill you without blinking an eyelid, he can be *muy diabolico!*"

"Well, I'm not afraid of either Don Francisco or your silly, diabolical fiancé," Ginny retorted. "And you'll just sit quietly for a few minutes and listen to what I have to say without interruptions, or I will use this whip on you! I can be just as fierce as any man."

"I won't listen, there's nothing you can say to me that I want to hear," the girl muttered sullenly. "You'd better let me go—even Renaldo will not be happy when he hears of this!"

"Then tell me, why are you here? Is it because you are fond of listening to servants' gossip and wanted to have something to add to it? Or were you sent here by someone?"

"I wasn't sent—I wasn't! And I don't listen to servants' gossip either! But Renaldo—no one could believe it of Renaldo! I had to see for myself. Especially," the girl added sulkily with a sidelong glance filled with hate, "since my own *novio* has been seen here too—I was told he's often gone riding with you—I wanted to see what kind of a woman you were."

A terrible suspicion had started to build up in Ginny's mind; she felt as if she was beginning to have a nightmare. All the same it would not do to let this silly chit of a girl see her shock and growing dismay—she forced her voice to remain even with an effort.

"You've seen what kind of woman I am—I'm not to be trifled with, and I am not Renaldo's mistress, whatever your gossips may say. And as for your *novio*, whoever he might be, let me tell you that the only other man I've been out riding with happens to be the same despicable outlaw who abducted me and brought me here by force! And I cannot possibly believe that a little girl like you would be allowed by her family to become engaged to a man like Steve Morgan. A professional gunfighter—a murderer and a thief and even worse! Oh, no, it's just not possible! He's worse than a wild beast, he'd swallow you up in one mouthful!"

"Be silent! Be silent at once! I will not listen to any more of your lies!"

Springing to her feet, Ana actually stamped her foot in rage.

"How dare you speak so about Esteban? How dare you say such terrible things about him? It's only because he isn't here to defend himself that you talk this way—he would never bring a woman of your kind here—why, ever since I was a child it's been understood that we were to be married some day, only the other day Don Francisco was speaking to my father about it—he said . . . he said . . . oh, you're a horrible, horrible woman, a lying slut, and I don't want to look at your face any longer!"

"Then leave at once, before I lose my temper. Remember, I didn't invite you here." Ginny flung the riding crop at the girl, who promptly gave a small scream of fear and anger.

Grabbing it, she turned and ran for her horse, sobbing with frustration.

"You'll be sorry—you'll see!" she shrieked over her shoulder.

But Ginny had already whirled about and was running for the house, hardly able to breathe for the rage that boiled up inside her.

Even when she had reached the haven of her bedroom, and had flung herself across the bed, she found it impossible to control her feelings. Anger, humiliation, and above all, a searing hatred for Steve Morgan, who had brought her here, placing her in this impossible situation without a thought for the consequences. She pounded her fists against the pillows, longing to scream out loud. How sordid it all was! He was actually engaged to be married—Steve, who had stated so many times that he had no desire to be tied down to any one woman. And he had had the colossal nerve to bring her here, with his fiancé living close by. What had he hoped to achieve? Why had he done it?

She was working herself up into a fine state, and she knew it, but didn't care. To think he's told me so many lies! He had no qualms about taking *my* virginity, but I'm sure he hasn't even touched that spoiled little girl. No doubt her parents are very rich—he'd be the kind of man who'd look out for a big dowry. But why did he bring me here, except to humiliate me even more? And to make matters worse, he's gone off somewhere, leaving me here to face everything alone . . . oh God, what will I do now? Where's Renaldo? Why doesn't he come?

Ginny had not cried for a long time, but now the tears gushed from her eyes uncontrollably and her body was shaken by sobs. Rosa came rushing in, full of questions, trying to console her, but it was impossible. Her face worried, the woman sat by Ginny until her sobs trailed away and she lay in a kind of stupor of exhaustion. Gentle, then, Rosa undressed her. She brought towels, and a small copper bowl filled with cold water, and began to sponge the girl's tear-swollen face and perspiring body.

It was such a pity, such a shame! In spite of her loyalty to the Alvarados, Rosa found herself muttering under her breath. Don Esteban should have known better! It was clear to see that this one was a lady—and so beautiful too! How could he treat her so? She knew, of course, of Dona Ana's visit. A nasty little spitfire she was. And spoiled by her parents. By *el patrón* too, because he had been the one to arrange for a marriage between the girl and his grandson. Rosa could not help shuddering when she wondered what *el patrón* would do when he found out. Because of course Dona Ana would go straight to him. What would he do?

Chapter Twenty-seven

After Ana had left his study, still crying hysterically, Don Francisco Alvarado still stood frowning thoughtfully at the door, his riding whip held tightly in his still-strong hands. A handsome, distinguished looking man he was, in spite of his seventy-six years. Don Francisco's hair was completely white, but he had the erect carriage of a man much younger, and there was no trace of senility in any of his actions. However, he was a man given to command— as proud as his *conquistador* ancestors and just as arrogant, and it was obvious that what he had just heard had not pleased him. His mouth was a thin line under his full white mustachios, and his eyes, as blue as his grandson's looked fiercely out from over a high-bridged, aquiline nose.

"Jaime!"

He did not need to raise his voice. Jaime would be just outside the door as usual, waiting. He wondered casually how much the man knew. Almost everything, of course! The servants, the *vaqueros*, they would all know— although they'd not dare speak of it to him. Still, this was not a matter to be discussed in front of servants.

"*Patrón?*" The man moved silently and unobtrusively,

as always. Don Francisco had hardly realized that he had entered the room already.

"You will inform the *señor* Renaldo that I wish to speak with him. At once, if he pleases."

"*Sí, patrón.*"

When Renaldo entered the room, Don Francisco was sitting at his desk, a glass of wine at his elbow. He glanced up at his nephew and gave an almost imperceptible nod of greeting.

"You did not keep me waiting. One might almost feel there's still some hope for the younger generation!"

"You wished to see me on a matter of some urgency?" Renaldo's voice sounded guarded. In the shadowed room, his face seemed to wear an expression that was at once preoccupied and rather adamant.

"You may sit down. A glass of wine?"

Renaldo shook his head.

"No thank you, sir. In fact I was just about to leave when Jaime found me—there are a few things I have to take care of at my house."

"It seems as if you've had much more than usual to take care of during the past week or so!" Don Francisco was holding the glass of wine up to the light contemplatively, he seemed merely to be making idle talk. "In fact, I've hardly seen you of late. Whenever Esteban decides to honor us with his presence I find that unusual things begin to happen." Don Francisco looked up suddenly and caught his nephew's almost indiscernible frown. "I do hope my grandson has not involved you in any of his wild escapades?"

"It's my understanding that Esteban is in Mexico City, or headed that way," Renaldo said stiffly. "At any rate, I didn't see much of him during his visit here."

"Well—I suppose we should hope that whatever business he had to take care of there proves profitable." Don Francisco took a sip of his wine and glanced casually at his nephew as he continued speaking in the same inconsequential tone of voice. "I am rather surprised, however, that he could bring himself to leave the woman he brought here with him. Ana tells me she is quite attractive, in a bold sort of way."

Renaldo could not control the angry flush that came up in his face. So he knew! Somehow, Don Francisco contrived to learn everything that happened. He was uncom-

fortably aware of the piercing scrutiny of those blue eyes
that caught every detail of his confusion.

"Sir! I—I—" Renaldo was annoyed at himself for stut-
tering and stumbling over his words just as he had when
he was a boy. And even then it had usually been because
he was trying to protect his cousin Esteban from the consequences of some irresponsible action.

"For shame, my nephew! A learned scholar such as you
are at loss for words? I was hoping you would be able to
tell me more about Esteban's latest plaything—I understand that she upset my poor little Ana a great deal. I'm
surprised you allowed him to be so indiscreet. How could
you permit a woman of that type to occupy your
guesthouse and have so much of your company as well? Is
she so fascinating?"

"You do not understand! I don't know how Ana
managed to meet Ginny—Miss Brandon, that is—but I
assure you, sir, that she's not at all what you imply. She's
a lady, sir—and of good family. Esteban had no right to
place her in such a compromising position! In fact, I told
him . . ."

"And since when has my grandson listened to what anyone tells him?" There was a touch of irony in Don
Francisco's voice at last, his hooded eyes had narrowed
slightly. "So—you say this woman is a lady. In that case,
what is she doing here as my grandson's mistress? As I understand it, she is not exactly a prisoner, although she told
Ana some wild story of kidnap. Damn it, sir!" Don
Francisco suddenly pounded on the arm of his chair with
the handle of his riding whip, causing Renaldo to jump,
"Why am I not informed of what goes on in my own estates? Why do I have to summon you here and go to such
lengths to pry the truth from you? No"—his voice had
turned sarcastic—"don't wear that stiff look and tighten
your lips with such noble resignation. I suppose you were
preparing to tell me that some ridiculous idea of loyalty to
Esteban must seal your lips. I won't have it, do you hear
me? Remember that your first loyalty is to me! I'll hear
the whole story from you now, *señor*, with no evasions, if
you please!"

Renaldo Ortega was later to remember that interview
with Don Francisco as being one of the most unpleasant
occasions in his life. His uncle had been right, of course;
he did have a feeling of hare-brained loyalty towards Este-

ban, but at the same time he felt more than that towards Ginny—he couldn't quite understand his feelings; he felt pity for her, yes, mixed with a tremendous admiration for her fortitude and her indomitable courage, but was there something else as well? As his uncle pried the whole sordid story from him, he kept picturing her—that honey-colored skin, those wide, sea green eyes set like a gypsy's in her unwittingly sensuous face, her quick woman's mind, and her laugh ... how dare Esteban have treated her like some cheap woman he'd picked up off the streets, leaving her here to be vilified and insulted by a little chit like Ana? No, it was to her that he owed loyalty, and more than that, his protection.

But he was stunned when Don Francisco abruptly terminated their talk, announcing formidably that he intended to see for himself—he would visit the little guesthouse himself and talk to Miss Brandon. When his uncle made up his mind to take a certain course of action, nothing could stop him, he should have known that by now, but still Renaldo protested.

"But, sir, I beg you—"

"Finish doing your accounts, Renaldo." Don Francisco's voice was measured and dry, but Renaldo caught its veiled menace and winced. "I'm still capable of handling the affairs of my own estate, and my family, and I shall do what needs to be done. Jaime—see that my horse is brought to the front of the estancia, if you please. And prepare to ride with me."

When Don Francisco became el patón and dismissed one, there was nothing else to do but retire. Barely able to suppress his frustration, Renaldo made a slight bow and withdrew. But while he tried to labor over his uncle's books in a small room overlooking the patio, Renaldo found himself seeing Ginny's face. An unspoken prayer throbbed in his mind— Don't let him hurt her!

He need not have worried. The emotional storm that Ginny had been through since her meeting with Dona Ana had left her drained of all feeling, even fear. Like an automaton she had allowed Rosa to bathe her, after a while, and to dress her in the prettiest of the gowns that had been provided for her. Rosa even tied a green ribbon in her hair, and let it hang down her back. She drank a glass of juice and ate some fresh fruit—ice-cold papaya, with lime juice sprinkled over it.

"But why?" she had protested, "what are we preparing for?" Ginny had sensed that Rosa was on her side—but against whom or what? She expected Renaldo to turn up at any moment; dear, kind Renaldo would tell her what to do, he would help her. She only knew that she must leave, she refused to be here, waiting meekly, when Steve got back. She never wanted to set eyes on him again; he was a lying, treacherous monster!

Rosa kept muttering to herself all the time she was helping Ginny, forcing her to eat. She did not speak Castilian Spanish, of course, and Ginny often found it difficult to understand her, especially when she was upset and spoke fast, or under her breath.

"Dona Genia," (this was what Rosa insisted upon calling her) "you must look your best. Whatever might happen, it's good to be prepared."

"But what could possibly happen? I'm not afraid of a little girl's threats. No—even if this—this person she kept calling *el patrón* were to decide upon murdering me, I wouldn't care! In some ways, I'd prefer it."

"*Ay di mi!*" Rosa crossed herself quickly, "do not talk like that! It brings bad luck. But *el patrón*, though a fierce man, is also fair. Yes, he'd see justice done, although—I don't know—it's said Dona Ana is a favorite with him. It was *el Patrón*, of course, who arranged it all."

"Who arranged what? Are you seriously trying to tell me that—that *Señor* Esteban allowed this *el patrón* to arrange a marriage for him?

"But *Dona Genia!*" Rosa looked at her as if she had lost her senses, "It is the custom of the country. Among the large *hacendados* all such marriages are arranged between the respective families—I've heard that when Dona Ana was no more than a baby her father spoke to Don Francisco, and of course . . ."

"Wait—wait!" Ginny pressed her palms against cheeks that were suddenly burning. "Rosa, you have me all confused. Who is Don Francisco? Is he Esteban's grandfather? But then, why do you all keep calling him *el patrón?*"

"Because he *is el patrón.*" Rosa was round-eyed with surprise at Ginny's ignorance, but a note of pride had crept into her voice. "Ah, Dona Genia, I thought you knew—everyone knows Don Francisco Alvarado! Why, it is said he's one of the richest men in Mexico; certainly his hacienda is the largest. Not even the *Juaristas* dare attack these lands—even the French, those murderers, they are full of respect—once the emperor and empress visited here, and Don Francisco has stayed in the palace at Chapultepec."

Ginny had been standing, studying her reflection somewhat pensively in the mirror, but now she sat down suddenly.

She remembered Ana's shrill voice saying so proudly, "I'm to be married to Don Francisco's heir!" Steve Morgan, the man she had so contemptuously called a half-breed—the man she'd believed to be nothing more than a professional gunfighter and a thief—he was the grandson of a Spanish grandee, the heir to millions? No, it was unbelievable!

"So he's rich!" she whispered aloud. "He could have been a gentleman, he could have stayed here and married as his grandfather obviously wants him to do, but instead ..." She became aware that Rosa was staring at her worriedly, and her lips tightened. She was filled with a surge of fresh hatred, coupled with a burning sense of outrage. "He can't be allowed to get away with it! To bring me here, parade me as his mistress, treat me as abominably as he's done, when all the time—yes, all the time there's been no valid reason for any of his actions! Why did he have to steal my father's money? Why become an outlaw? Why take me and treat me worse than a whore when he's betrothed to this girl Ana, who's no doubt just as rich, and with a fat dowry to give him as well? What's the point?"

She was suddenly so angry that she sprang to her feet, brushing past the astounded Rosa as she sped into the living room. She did not know what she intended to do, perhaps find Renaldo, face him with her new-found knowledge and her bitter accusations. But she wouldn't stay here any longer, she would go, she would do—something! Anything to end this farce, to retrieve her own pride.

"Dona Genia, Dona Genia!" Rosa wailed behind her.

And at that moment, when Ginny had almost reached the door in her headlong flight, it was opened unexpectedly from the outside, and a man stepped into the room.

"What is wrong here? Why was there no one to answer our knocking?"

They stared at each other, the tall old man and the panting, distraught young woman. Don Francisco's cold blue eyes took in every inch of her appearance before they became hooded and unreadable—his lined, craggy face looked stern and implacable in spite of the faint, rather sarcastic smile that thinned his lips.

"*El patrón!*" Before Rosa could utter the words in a trembling, awestruck voice, Ginny had known who he was. Steve's grandfather. There was some resemblance; perhaps in the way his eyes had raked over her without seeming to.

Unconsciously, Ginny had straightened her shoulders, her chin lifted in an almost childish gesture of stubbornness and pride.

"I am sorry, Don Francisco, that there was no one outside to welcome you. Rosa was busy, attending to my toilette, and I'd hardly expected visitors."

"I'm sorry I had no time to give you formal warning of my visit, Miss Brandon. Unfortunately I had no idea, earlier, that I would be paying this call. Will you not sit down? I think we ought to talk privately." His eagle eyes flicked to Rosa. "You can go, woman. I've no intention of harming your mistress."

Politely, Don Francisco handed Ginny to a chair, his manners as courtly as Renaldo's. She was dumbstruck, feeling more than ever like a puppet, or a pawn in a chess game. What did he want of her? What was he going to say? Surprisingly, she was not afraid—she had come too far for that. But she was determined not to speak a single word until he spoke first.

There was always a decanter of wine left on the low table here, and Don Francisco walked over to it, pouring out two glasses of wine as casually as if he had been in his own house.

"You'll drink a glass of wine with an old man, *mademoiselle*?" Again Ginny was amazed that he knew so much about her, even the fact that she had been brought up as a Frenchwoman.

"Thank you," she said quietly, watching his face as he handed a glass to her, and then raised his own to sniff the bouquet.

"An excellent wine. My grandson has good taste in a few things at least, I'm glad to find. A pity that in so many other ways he is little better than a savage."

Ginny could not prevent herself from reddening. She took a sip of wine, to cover her sudden sense of embarrassment under his long, open scrutiny. Did he expect her to make some response to his gently barbed comment? No, he had come here on purpose to see her, let him instigate the conversation.

Don Francisco twirled the stem of the glass between his fingers, taking his time while he considered what he would say. She was a surprise, this Miss Ginny Brandon. A pleasant one, fortunately. Well, he could usually depend on Renaldo to speak the truth, but he preferred to form his own impressions, trusting no one.

In this case, however, his intuition had already told him that Renaldo was right. From the first moment he had set eyes on her, had seen her deep green eyes widen with shock, noticed the way in which she had so valiantly composed herself soon after, he had known this was no ordinary woman that his wild young grandson had seen fit to bring here. So it had been kidnap, had it? By God, Don Francisco thought with sudden rage, the young whelp has reverted to the dark ages! So he'd abducted a lady and treated her like a whore. But why? Could he, of all men, always so casual about his conquests, have actually fallen in love with this young woman?

She was, of course, fully aware of his long, brooding gaze. Cleverly, she had apparently decided to remain silent, allowing him to take the initiative. To his own surprise, Don Francisco found himself rather looking forward to the battle of wits which must follow. For this woman was no whimpering ninny, he had seen that already. And according to his besotted nephew, she was possessed of an unusual degree of intelligence and charm as well.

Don Francisco permitted himself to smile slightly at the green-eyed *mademoiselle*. Her long-lashed eyes gazed steadily back at him, but he'd noticed how tightly her hands were clasped together on her lap. He liked women with spirit. Clearly, Esteban had not been able to tame her yet—he could almost chuckle inwardly, now he had met her, when he recalled what Renaldo had told him of the knife-wound she had given his rash cousin.

"Well, *mademoiselle*," he said aloud, his voice softly persuasive, "don't you think it's time I learned your whole story from your own lips? You will have to excuse my directness—I'm an old man, and past the age when I en-

joyed preliminary sparrings. I should tell you that I've
heard a long and rather incoherent tale from Ana, and
I've talked to my nephew Renaldo, who seems to think a
great deal of you. Will you tell me if it's true?"

"But which story are you referring to, Don Francisco?
I'm quite positive that Ana took a violent dislike to me,
and I'm ashamed to say I lost my temper—but Renaldo, I
think, is my friend. I didn't know that Steve had—poor
Renaldo, he must feel terribly guilty!"

"*Mademoiselle*—I hope you'll not disappoint me by
playing with words." The sudden sharpness in Don
Francisco's voice made Ginny's eyes flash. Her look held
defiance.

"Words, sir? You must forgive me. If I hesitate and
beat around the bush it's merely because I'm rather confused, and embarrassed as well. After all, the reason for
my being here is so—so sordid, and yet so simple! Your
grandson, the man I knew as Steve Morgan, brought me
here. I'm his—his . . ." she had been going to say quite
straightforwardly that she was his mistress, and see what
conclusions the old man drew, but somehow the words
stuck in her throat, she bit her lip, and her eyes dropped
in spite of herself.

Ginny sensed rather than saw Don Francisco's hand
move impatiently.

"Miss Brandon! Again, I apologize. Naturally, this
whole subject is distasteful to you. But I can assure you
that if you choose to trust me with your confidence you'll
find that all the men of my family are not completely
devoid of honor!"

There was a repressed note of anger in his voice that
made her lift her head and stare at him wonderingly.

"But what can you do? It's too late, even I can see that
now. Steve kidnapped me—oh, at first he said that I was
to be a hostage—just to insure that his friends got away
safely with the money they stole—but afterwards—oh, no,
I don't think I can bear to talk about it! Please—think
anything you want to, I don't care! All I want is to get
away, to go far away where he can never find me, where
I'll be able to forget everything, everything!"

When Don Francisco frowned, his bushy white brows
came together, and he looked like a thundercloud. But in
this instance his frowns were not directed at Ginny—
rather, at his own thoughts.

"What! You say my grandson stole as well? And that he's treated you badly? Miss Brandon, come, live up to my first expectations of you, when I saw you standing there, your eyes flashing at me so dangerously. I must know everything, and not from any motive of ghoulish curiosity, as you'll learn when you come to know me better. I am the head of my family, mademoiselle, and honor, to me, is not an empty word. It is a way of life, it *is* my life! What touches any member of my family affects me—perhaps I'm old-fashioned—but there are some things I will not tolerate! You must tell me everything, I insist upon it!"

His fingers closed compellingly over her wrist; looking down Ginny saw the veined hand of an old man, but the fingers were as strong as steel—as imperious as Steve's had ever been. Suddenly, Ginny was beginning to realize the strength in this man, the power in his eyes that now fixed on hers so unwaveringly. She understood now why everyone she had spoken to here held him in such awe—no, not just that, but were actually afraid of him!

She felt mesmerized. In a toneless voice, stumbling over her words, she began to speak at last, sparing nothing, not even herself, and that part of the blame which attached to her for her own weakness, her first blind, virginal passion for the man she had begun to hate and despise so completely.

It was over at last—she had told him everything, her throat was so dry that she felt she could not utter one more word. She drooped in her chair, keeping her eyes turned away from Don Francisco's, and gulped thirstily at the fresh glass of wine he proffered her as if it had been nothing but water.

Now what would he do? Perhaps he'd have her killed, or gotten out of the way by some other method, to hide the stain on his family's honor! She could put nothing past him, he was Steve's grandfather, after all, and his harsh demands for her to talk, to go on speaking even when her voice trembled and her eyes had filled with tears, had been just as inexorable in their way as Steve's had been. Don Francisco was like a king here, among his people, the law could not touch him, no one could! And after all, who else knew that she was here? What could she possibly matter to him in comparison to his daughter's own child, his heir?

Why doesn't he say something? Ginny wondered wildly, why doesn't he do something to end this strain once and for all? After all, it doesn't matter to me any longer, one way or the other, I'm so tired, so mentally exhausted I just don't care!

"So—it's worse, even, than I had thought. He's gone too far this time, and I cannot permit his folly and reck- lessness to go further." Don Francisco spoke quietly enough, almost as if he spoke to himself, but some steely quality had been added to his voice that made Ginny tremble. What did he mean? Before she could ask him, he continued, still in the same low, rather harsh voice—the voice of a man who had brooked no opposition all his life, and was used to getting his own way. "I don't know what kind of stupid, irresponsible schemes Esteban has become mixed up in, but I'll find out when he gets back. You see, Miss Brandon, I hardly know my grandson! Ever since my daughter Luisa brought him back here as a child, I've tried to make a gentleman of him—even as a child he resisted me! I disciplined him, I've whipped his back until I drew blood, and yet, over and over again, he defied me. Then, when he was older, he began to run away. He'd be found, and brought back, but then he'd run away again. Finally I decided that like the wild falcons he needed room in which to try his wings—he needed life to teach him the lessons that I could not. And now I see what's happened. He has learned nothing, except to please him- self—to take whatever he wants without a thought to the consequences. Well, by God—this time he shall have some consequences to face! He'll fulfill his obligations as a gen- tleman and my grandson, or I will kill him myself, before the law of your country, or your father does so!"

Don Francisco's voice had become stronger, he slammed the riding whip he carried against the side of the chair, and Ginny put her hand against her mouth to stop herself from gasping out loud as his meaning suddenly forced itself into her muddled brain.

He turned towards her suddenly, his eyes sweeping over her keenly before he caught her cold hands in his dry, warm clasp.

"You're very beautiful, my dear child. And you're strong and spirited—I like that. Well, I cannot undo what has already been done, nor can I offer you sufficient repara- tion for the wrongs you have suffered, but I can offer you a solution that would spare you any further anguish or humiliation. My grandson will marry you, as soon as he returns."

For a long, stunned moment Ginny stared at him like a wild creature, unable to believe that she had heard right. Then, with a cry, she tried to withdraw her hands from his grasp, but he held them fast.

"No! You don't know what you are saying! Steve would not—he would never—oh, but you don't know him! He'd never submit to a forced marriage, this is the nineteenth century after all, and besides—besides I hate him!" she ended on a curiously childish note.

"Listen to me, Virginia!" The stern note in Don Francisco's voice made Ginny stare at him with her lips parted, still ready to burst forth with fresh denials. "You must set aside your quite natural reaction and try to realize that the solution I've offered you is the only possible one, for your own sake. It is to save your reputation that I suggest it. Too many people know that Esteban ran off with you, but if you were to return to your family later, as his wife, don't you see how different their reactions would be? An elopement—there'd be some whispering, no doubt, but you and your family could still hold your heads up. Soon, people will be saying how romantic it all was. You see, my child, I know human nature. You'd be a respectable married woman—and a rich one, I might add. I will make a marriage settlement upon you that will be more than considerable, and if you chose to return to America later, or even to France, you would be independent. Do you understand?"

"No," she said weakly again. "No, it's quite impossible! You must see that! Even if I agreed, Steve would never do so—he's not the kind of man who can be forced into doing anything he does not want to do. And he'd make me suffer."

"Esteban will do whatever I tell him to do in this instance! You're forgetting, my dear, that this is Mexico, and not the United States. He understands our customs, even though he's always rebelled against them. He'll do it—because I'll allow him no other alternative. And I'll see to it that he treats you with the respect and consideration that is your due as his wife. No—this time Esteban will not escape his responsibilities as easily as he's done in the past."

Ginny continued to stare at this strange, almost frighteningly domineering man; still feeling as if she were dreaming.

"But if he refuses?"

"If he refuses, he is no longer my grandson, and will take the consequences. Do you realize, young woman, that I've had men on my *hacienda* shot for much less? I think Esteban understands this much about me—when I explain matters to him he'll have no difficulty in comprehending that the only other alternative I'll give him is a felon's death!"

The inexorable note in Don Francisco's voice struck through Ginny's mounting feeling of unreality, and she felt the blood drain from her face. He meant it then, he meant every word that he'd been saying!

"I've dreamed of being revenged, of making him suffer. Yes, I've even longed for his death, and I've almost brought it about. But this—no, this is too much! I've seen enough violence, I won't be the cause of more."

"Then you'll marry him. Leave Esteban to me, he'll not hurt you again, for I'll see to it. He'll give me his word, and for all his irresponsible ways, I've never known him to break it, once given. If you've wanted revenge, child, this is your chance. You'll be his wife, and no matter what happens later, you'll bear his name, legally. He owes you that much, and more!"

"I don't know what to say!"

"You have agreed, have you not? Well, then—you must come with me now. I'll give you your own suite of rooms at the *hacienda*, and a *duenna*. No need to worry about gossip here—once I make the announcement that you are to be my granddaughter-in-law, you'll soon see that there'll be no more unpleasant talk. No arguments—you look exhausted. Rosa will pack for you."

Arrogant, not even listening to her feeble protests, Don Francisco swept all before him, and by nightfall, Ginny found herself installed at the grande *hacienda*—an especially honored guest of *el patrón* himself.

Chapter Twenty-eight

The full extent of Don Francisco Alvarado's wealth and power was revealed to Ginny during the days that followed her surprising and unexpected removal from the little house to what was known as the *casa grande*. From her first glimpse of the high stone walls surrounding parklike grounds; the tree-shaded avenue that seemed to stretch forever until one burst suddenly upon a scene that would have rivalled a storybook illustration of a medieval mansion; Ginny felt herself under a kind of spell.

One moment she had been living in seclusion, feeling herself under a cloud, and the next, she was the future granddaughter-in-law of *el patrón*—nothing was too good for her. Feeling herself taken in hand, and during those first few days, feeling more than a little bewildered at the speed with which things were taking place, Ginny felt herself swept along helplessly with the tide of events.

She was given the large apartments that had once belonged to *Dona Luisa*, Steve's mother. They were completely self-contained, but opened onto the same patio as the big house. Ginny found herself wandering through the rooms in a daze that first night—admiring the beautiful Spanish furniture and the expensive rugs. She had already

been introduced to *Señora Armijo*, known to the family
as *Tia Alfonsa*. *Señora Armijo* was to act as her unofficial *duenna*—the thought made Ginny feel like laughing
hysterically. She was also to have two personal maids of
her own—giggling brown-skinned girls who were obviously
more than a little in awe of her. "I'm going to wake up
tomorrow and find I've been dreaming all this," Ginny
kept telling herself. But the next day only brought more
surprises.

Her measurements were taken, and she was led by
Señora Armijo through a massive storeroom where bolts
of cloth and materials of all colors and varieties were
kept. Fashion journals—some of them from as far away
as London and Paris—were brought out and pored over,
with even the rather austere Don Francisco himself giving
his opinion as to the new clothes Ginny would be needing.

"We may be rather remote from what is considered
civilization here," he said dryly, "but the women of my
family have always dressed in the height of fashion. And,
my dear Genia, you'll find that you'll have innumerable
parties and *fiestas* to attend."

Everyone called her Genia, the name sounding quite
Spanish the way they pronounced it. The little maids
giggled when they discussed her forthcoming wedding and
the beautiful clothes that were being made for her. Even
Tia Alfonsa unbent far enough to comment favorably on
how well the emeralds Don Francisco had given her suited
her hair and complexion. Yes, there were the jewels too.
Ginny had protested, at first, to find her objections
brushed away imperiously. The jewels, she was informed,
were hers. All these years they had waited, locked up in
the safe, to be worn by Don Esteban's bride.

She was to have everything she wanted—anything. If
she wanted to ride, she had only to mention it, and a
spirited Arabian mare was brought around by the groom
assigned to her.

Sometimes Ginny felt that she had been produced out
of a hat, like a magician's rabbit. All these people—the
relatives who lived in the big *estancia*, and Don
Francisco's numerous friends and business acquaintances—had no doubt expected that Ana Valdez would
some day marry his heir. And then, out of the blue he had
introduced a strange female—an American, at that—as
his grandson's bride. And she was accepted without ques-

tion; more than that, with genuine kindness and consideration.

It was not hard for Ginny to let herself slip into the easy, pleasantly luxurious way of life she had been offered.

All she had to do was to let herself float through the days, being gently guided in this direction or that by people who had only her best interests at heart, and desired nothing more than to please her. And she would try, for her own peace of mind, not to think where all this was taking her—to the day when Steve Morgan would return, no doubt expecting her to be waiting in the little house he had brought her to, only to find that preparations were being made for a wedding.

Don Francisco's assurance that his grandson would do as he was told did not seem strange to her at all by the time she had lived in his house for a week. She had learned already that he wielded literally the power of life or death over the people who worked for him. Things Steve had told her about the great *haciendas* and the *hacendados* who owned them came back to her—long conversations with Renaldo and with Don Francisco himself helped complete the picture of a still-feudal society. But with this background, how had Steve broken away? And why had he wanted to do so? She felt that she despised him even more for what he had become. He was an outlaw and an adventurer not because he'd had to fight for survival, but because he was reckless enough and wicked enough to desire the type of life he lived. To make matters worse, he was a hypocrite—how dared he criticize the landowners, and the French who were there on invitation, when he himself was one of them? He'd talked as if he were a peasant himself—he supported, stole and killed for the cause of Juarez, who would take all he could from these same landowners and divide it among the peasants; the peons and bandits who were his supporters. She could never understand it!

Ginny did not want to think about Steve, but she could not help herself. Every now and then one of the women who now surrounded her would make some laughing comment, their sidelong gazes watching for her reaction.

"Oh, Dona Genia—these silk and ribbon nightshifts are enough to drive any husband out of his senses," one of the seamstresses cried, holding up a flimsy garment which had been made from a bolt of thin, pure silk brought all the way from China.

The maids, chattering to each other as they made up the bed every morning would make sly, bold comments about the day when the Señora Armijo would no longer share the apartments with Dona Genia.

Carmencita, who was the more forward of the two, would roll her eyes.

"That Don Esteban—*muy macho hombre*! We always said that when *he* marries it will be to an American— Dona Ana, now, she's not as beautiful as you are, Dona Genia, and she has a sharp tongue."

Privately, although they would not have dared talk about it aloud, the young women of the household thought it all very romantic, like something out of a novel, that their Don Esteban had run off with the young lady he'd chosen to be his wife. From under the nose of her tyrannical father too!

Even Renaldo, normally so tactful, made occasional references to her wedding. Invitations had started to go out already—he was helping Don Francisco send them out. Did she have any friends she wanted to invite? Against her will, Ginny found herself blushing; stammering like a schoolgirl over her words. No, she told him. No, there would be no time. She had already confided privately to Don Francisco that she would not write to her father until afterwards—he did not have to know when she had been married, just the fact that a marriage had taken place would no doubt help matters. Later, when she saw her father and Sonya again, she could explain.

There were times, however, when no matter how hard she tried, Ginny could not push the unwelcome thoughts from her mind. When he came back, when he found out, how would he react? Remembering how brutal he could be when he got into a rage, she could not help shivering. She was under Don Francisco's protection now, but what would happen later? The marriage settlement he had promised her would make her free to travel, to come and go as she wished, but what if Steve wished differently? She could not forget that marriage made a woman slave to her own husband, if he chose to exercise all his rights over her. And what had he said to her once, soon after she'd plunged a knife into him:

"Let's not underestimate each other any more." She

didn't dare underestimate Steve—she didn't really know him!

I'm afraid of him, Ginny thought, lying awake one extra-hot night. He's completely unpredictable, and capable of anything. I'm afraid of what revenge he might try to take. And yet, she reminded herself angrily, none of this was her fault at all. Her being here, the impossible position he'd left her in, all of it was his doing. Let him take the consequences, find out what it was like to lose the precious freedom he talked so much about. I hate him she thought again, fiercely. He'll find out just how much—I'll never give in to him again, never let myself be intimidated by him.

And yet there were nights when the heavy perfume of jasmine and gardenias drifted through her open window, and she'd tear the covers off her body, feeling herself on fire, unable to sleep. Over and over she'd tell herself that it was only the heat—the slumbering, languorous sensuality of a climate she was unused to. It was her body that was the traitor to her mind; aching for the caresses he'd forced on her, waking her from virginity to the knowledge of her own passion—the realization of desire and its fulfillment. No matter how much she hated him with her mind and shuddered at the memory of her forced subjugation to his demands, there were still nights when she was tortured by the need of her flesh for his—for the feel of his hands on her body, his lips crushing her half-hearted protests into silence, and the now-familiar weight of his body over hers that could make her forget everything else but the need for fulfillment.

Sometimes, on such nights Ginny would spring up, unable to stand the direction her own thoughts were taking. She'd fill the bath herself, with cold water, and lie in it until her teeth chattered. What is wrong with me? she'd question herself afterwards, am I a creature as contemptible as he is, ruled by passion—by my body, instead of my will? She would berate herself for her own weakness, for, she thought, I really do hate him, there's no doubt about it, and yet when he kisses me or touches me in a certain way I react like an animal—my senses rule me then, and he knows it—he knows he can do what he wishes with me! It's so unfair, being a woman!

There was no one she could talk to about these secret feelings—certainly not the old priest who now heard her dutiful confessions—not even Renaldo, as dear and understanding a friend as he was. She read books on philosophy and the science of reason until even Don Francisco teased her about spending most of her day in the cool gloom of his library. No, ironically, the only person in the world who might understand her dilemma was Steve himself—she gritted her teeth when she imagined the cynical smile he sometimes wore when he made some scathing comment about the female sex, or about herself in particular. The last words he had said to her before he left for Mexico City had been that he'd be glad to be rid of her. What would he think when he came back? The one thought that nagged at her ceaselessly during the long days and longer nights was that of all the men she had known only he, the man she hated and yet was to marry, had in a way really understood her. He had seen her as a woman, not a paragon of virtue or another pretty face, and he had used her as such.

Ten days had passed since Don Francisco had brought her so unexpectedly to his house, and in spite of the lazy, lethargic routine she had succumbed to, Ginny would, at times, feel her nerves stretched like bowstrings when she thought about the future.

She was reading in Don Francisco's library when she heard a great commotion outside and for a moment she felt herself freeze with fearful anticipation. He had arrived! He had finally decided to come back! She continued to hide herself in the library, pretending she had heard nothing, the letters in the book she was holding dancing before her eyes. She could hear Don Francisco's footsteps now, he was leading someone with him. His voice, as dry as usual, was saying, "She's in here, I'm sure. She spends all her time reading." But when the door opened and she was forced to look up it was not Steve who came into the room ahead of the old man but a woman instead—a plump, richly dressed woman who wore too much jewelry.

Don Francisco introduced the woman as *Señora* Maria Ortega; Renaldo's mother and the don's only surviving sister.

"My sister lives in Mexico City, with her oldest son and his family—she's here to attend your wedding, Genia," Don Francisco said with his old-world courtesy. He added, somewhat wryly, "She's anxious to make your acquaintance—I'll leave you together for a while."

"Yes, yes—we were all so curious about the woman who managed to capture that elusive grandnephew of mine!" Ginny found herself drawn into a moist, perfumed embrace, while the woman's small dark eyes travelled swiftly over her, taking in every detail. Before Ginny could utter a word she found her hands seized, and she was being dragged out of the room by Dona Maria, who did not stop chattering for a moment.

"Francisco—we'll sit in the patio, I'm sure it's cooler out there. And don't forget my orange juice, will you? I'm sure dear Genia will join me. "Goodness child," she went on, with a quick smile, "don't look so afraid of me! I won't bite—you'll soon find out that I'm just an old woman who loves to talk—bear with me, there are so many questions I must ask!"

Soon they were comfortably seated in the patio, the don's soft-footed servants hurrying outside with a tall, frosty pitcher of fresh orange juice for the Dona Maria. Her endless stream of talk never stopped, except when she paused to draw breath or take a sip of juice, and Ginny, feeling half-dazed, was relieved to find she did not have to contribute very much to the conversation, except for an occasional "yes" or "no."

The *Señora* Ortega, while being the most unlikely person Ginny would have imagined as Renaldo's mother, was also outspoken. She was quite frank regarding her opinion of most *Norte Americano's*—they were all uncivilized, she stated complacently, except for a very few of them she had met who were exiles from the South. But she forgave Ginny for being a *gringa*, because her mother had been French.

"And they're close enough to Spain to be tolerable," Dona Maria said kindly. She patted Ginny's hand. "You really are a pretty little thing, I must admit I'm pleasantly surprised. That wild devil Esteban has always shown a propensity for the wrong kind of woman, you know, it's worried us all tremendously! But when Renaldo wrote us to say that you were the daughter of a Senator, and such a quiet, well-educated young lady, I felt quite relieved! That's what I told my dear Sarita, my daughter-in-law. I said, 'My dear, Francisco would never have countenanced a woman he did not approve of,' and you know, my dear, my brother, for all that he seems to have turned hermit of late, is a man of refined taste and very decided opinions.

And he is fond of you—I could tell that right away. So is my youngest son, for that matter—I'm really amazed, Renaldo always seemed so wary of females before, but he thinks the world of you!"

Her companion's sudden switch in subjects made Ginny's head reel; she could only murmur feebly, "Renaldo? Fond of me?"

"Well of course, girl, who else would I mean? It's a shame he didn't meet you before that rascal Esteban did—you can't know what a disappointment Renaldo has been to me. He, the quietest of my sons, the one I did not expect to have any trouble with! First it was the priesthood—two years in a seminary and suddenly he changes his mind! It's all this reading he does, giving him radical ideas. I was in tears when he told me, I said, 'But son, you always said it was your ambition to help people, especially the poor peasants!' But no—he told me he could help much more by being a school-teacher, can you imagine my son a schoolteacher? And then, of course, I tried to get him married—you can't imagine how many eligible young ladies I introduced him to, but no, he'd have none of them! And now—it's too bad!"

"But—but, madame, I don't think I understand," Ginny stammered. "What is so bad about Renaldo's wanting to be a . . ."

"Pah, child! Of course you understand! Renaldo's as easy to read as one of his books. He's in love with you, of course—I could tell with half an eye, and even before I'd met you. Not that I blame you for preferring Esteban—he's quite dashing, I suppose—those good looks of his, and that insolent swagger—I suppose that it's not really surprising he turns the heads of so many females. And of course he's rich, or will be some day, when he's ready to settle down."

Ginny, her face reddening, found herself protesting vigorously.

"Really, madame, you embarrass me! I'm sure I . . ."

Señora Ortega merely waved her hand airily, her rings flashing in the sunlight.

"No need for that, dear child! I know you're not an adventuress after my brother's fortune—in fact, I'm sure you have quite a little fortune of your own, eh? And besides, Esteban aways did have a way with women—such a worry he has been to my poor brother, and to my dearest

Luisa too, before she passed away. I'm just glad he's finally ready to settle down, and with such a sweet, pretty girl too—but there's one thing I'll have to speak to him sternly about, if my brother doesn't do so first—why isn't he here? Surely, with the banns already being read for his own marriage that young scamp should have the good manners to stay in one place for a while? He's always off jaunting around somewhere—you'll have to put a stop to that, my dear, take a word of warning from an old woman—men will try to get away with *anything* if you'll let them! When do you expect your *novio* back?"

Ginny could easily have ground her teeth together with exasperation but she forced a smile instead and answered quickly that Steve had told her he'd be back within two weeks.

"He had some urgent business to take care of, but I'm sure he'll return in time for the Sandoval's fiesta," she said lightly, inwardly despising herself for making excuses for Steve's unpredictable behavior. Then, to forestall any further questions on the part of Dona Maria she added hastily, "you'll be going with us too, will you not, madame?"

"Please, my dear, call me Tia Maria, you mustn't stand on ceremony now you're to be one of our family! Of course I'm going—dear Don José, he's a very old friend, and the parties he gives are always exceptional—much more style and elegance, my child, than any I've attended in Mexico City, or even at the palace at Chapultepec." Dona Maria had produced an ivory fan, and was using it vigorously as she spoke. "Now *there* is a place you must visit sometime. You must be presented to the emperor and empress—their palace is quite a gay place—the empress likes to be surrounded by young people, you know, and it is always crowded—handsome young officers from all over the old world, the prettiest of our young ladies, like butterflies—I went with my son and his wife to quite a grand ball at the palace the night before I started out here, and you should have seen the crowds! In fact it was then I could have sworn I saw Esteban, of all people, with that bold, pretty French countess they are all talking about—I remember it gave me quite a start for a moment and then when I looked for them again they'd disappeared into the gardens! It was only because of the wedding invitation, of course—my son Alberto explained it all to me, and he has such a *rational* mind—I knew, of course that it would not possibly be Esteban, it was some *Norteamericano* adventurer, the court is full of them, and they say the Countess Danielle, when her husband is off fighting the *Juaristas*, prefers Americans as her lovers. Dear me—" Dona Maria broke off to stare at Ginny, "I surely haven't upset you with my silly garrulousness, have I? Of course it wasn't Esteban, it couldn't possibly have been! You do look strange, Genia, is the sun too hot for you?"

"Oh—oh, yes, I'm not quite used to it yet, you see! But I'm not worried, not in the least—why should I be?"

"Of course you shouldn't be! You're going to be married soon. it's something every woman looks forward to, is it not? But perhaps you're suffering from nerves—it's normal, my dear, we all have qualms, just before! Why, I remember . . ."

Dona Maria's voice droned on and on while Ginny sat upright beside her with her features carefully composed into an attentive, smiling mask. Hidden by the folds of her gown, her fingers clasped and unclasped in her lap; inwardly she seethed with an anger she could hardly manage to hide.

It had been he, of course! It could have been no other. 'The Countess Danielle, the bold, pretty French countess they are all talking about . . . He'd had an assignation with the woman—that was why he was in such a hurry to go to Mexico City, and why he'd insisted she could not accompany him!

'He's nothing but a *Juarista* spy—if only they knew! He's a vile traitor—how could he have the gall to attend a ball at the emperor's palace when all the time he's working against the poor man? Oh, but I should denounce him—I must be mad to think of marrying him, to think of tying myself to a man like that!'

Ginny's thoughts scurried this way and that, and by dinnertime she had developed a really splitting nervous headache that provided her with an excuse to stay in her rooms.

She closed her eyes, while Dona Alfonsa bent over her worriedly, applying wet cloths to her forehead. Teasingly, annoyingly, she kept seeing Steve's face against the curtain of her closed lids, his mouth curved in the all-too-familiar smile that was both mocking and hateful.

She no longer feared his anger now—she almost looked forward with a vicious kind of pleasure to his return.

Just you wait, Steve Morgan, she cried silently to her mind's image of him, I'll make you sorry you ever met me—I'll repay you for everything, everything!

She finally fell asleep with that satisfying thought to console her.

Chapter Twenty-nine

Steve Morgan did not arrive at his grandfather's *hacienda* until the very day of Don José Sandoval's name day fiesta, and by that time Dona Maria had transformed Don Francisco's normally quiet and orderly household into a state of perpetual hubbub.

She had taken over the running of the house immediately, and there were servants constantly scurrying here and there carrying out her orders. Every room must be cleaned from top to bottom—the floors freshly waxed, the furniture moved around. And she insisted on taking Ginny in hand, as she termed it. Every one of her new gowns had to be critically examined for even the slightest flaws, she must spend less time reading, and more time learning how to run a large household. She must wear more jewelry, she must have her hair arranged more elaborately.

Don Francisco took to locking himself in his study with his accounts—even Renaldo, quite unnerved by his mother's presence and her constant carping, came less often to the big house.

Ginny felt completely helpless, but in some strange way almost relieved to have the responsibility for planning her days taken from her. Dona Maria gave her hardly any time to be alone with her thoughts, although by the time Steve finally decided to turn up Ginny felt she had heard his name so often, mentioned always in a disapproving tone of voice, that she would go mad if she heard it again.

She felt nothing but a coldness inside her—a coldness born of a combination of anger and despair—when one of her maids burst into her bedroom, panting, with her eyes big with excitement.

"He's back! Don Esteban has returned at last!" Remembering her manners the girl dropped a kind of abrupt curtsey. "Dona Genia—he'll be here to see you soon, I'm sure! He's with *el patrón*, in his study now. May I help you to change your dress?"

Ginny found herself retorting more sharply than she'd meant to.

"Heavens no! What's wrong with the gown I have on? I've changed so often today I'm tired already."

When the girl had left, Ginny started to pace nervously around her room immediately. She caught a glimpse of herself in the mirror—the new gown Tia Maria had insisted she wear this morning was quite becoming, and in the very latest style, caught up in an intriguing bustle at the back. Not that it mattered, she caught herself thinking viciously, for he never noticed what she was wearing—his one aim in the past had seemed to be tearing the clothes off her back!

It did not in the least help Ginny's nerves when her *duenna*, the self-effacing *Señora* Armijo, came bustling in, all of a dither. It was she, in the end, who had to calm the excited *señora*, assuring her several times that indeed, she was positive that she was by no means nervous—she was quite calm, why shouldn't she be? It relieved her greatly, however, to be informed that Dona Maria was visiting her son this morning and would not be back until sometime later in the afternoon.

"Such a shame! She will be sorry to miss Esteban's arrival," Tia Alfonsa kept repeating, "she'll be very put out, I know it!"

Ginny had seated herself with some embroidery, more in order to calm her *duenna* than because she needed something to do. She kept telling herself sternly that she was not in the least afraid, not at all upset, but when she heard those familiar footsteps just outside her door she sprang quickly to her feet, feeling the blood drain from her face.

"You need not go," she whispered almost imploringly, "after all, it's not as if we're romantic children, or strangers to each other!"

"But he's your *novio*! Don Francisco said it was permissible for you to see each other alone," the woman said with some surprise. As soon as Steve appeared in the doorway, she made her excuses and hurried away tactfully.

There was no escape for her now, she had to face him, and hope that her face would not betray her inward quailing.

"I hear we are to be married," were the first words he said, and although his voice sounded surprisingly mild, Ginny was not deceived—she had seen the mocking, almost evil look in his narrowed eyes as he took in each detail of her appearance, before he veiled them again with his ridiculously long lashes.

He lounged against the doorway, apparently quite at ease, but she had seen immediately that his lips were drawn taut and white with suppressed anger, and he could not hide the frowning look that the drawing together of his black brows gave him.

He was carrying a package of some sort, which he now tossed carelessly onto a chair.

"I brought you a present—a new gown. Although I can see it was hardly necessary. But you might wear it tonight, if it pleases you."

How politely he spoke, and how calmly, but all the time he was raging inside, his anger just barely controlled—she had seen him like this before, and she knew too well what it meant when his eyes seemed to gleam like hard blue stones, and his nostrils flared just so . . . oh, he was furious! But just as obviously he was trying hard to control his rage, and the idea that she was safe from it, that he dared not raise his hand to her made Ginny's chin tilt slightly upward as she faced him boldly, her eyes staring contemptuously into his.

"Thank you! You must forgive my surprise—I'm not used to such considerate gestures from you."

"That's what my grandfather seems to think too—that I've treated you in an inhuman fashion. Shall I try to make amends? Perhaps I should court you with all kinds of sweet words and loverlike phrases—maybe that's the way to a woman's heart!" His eyes narrowed at her hatefully and he showed his teeth in a positively wicked smile. "You seem tongue-tied suddenly, Ginny. That isn't like you. Are you disappointed that I haven't greeted you properly yet?"

Before she was fully aware of what he was about Steve had crossed the room to her with his long strides and grasped her in his arms.

He brought his face closer to hers and Ginny closed her eyes instinctively against the blazing anger she could discern in his. Or was it merely in anticipation of his kiss? She did not know, she was merely conscious of her own weakness, of the almost hypnotic power his embraces still seemed to wield over her. He had not kissed her yet, but she could almost feel, like a physical thing, the burning gaze of his eyes on her face, her lips, her shoulders and breasts. What was he waiting for? How dared he hold her pinioned this way while he studied her, feature by feature, as if he had never seen her before? Ginny summoned up the strength to whisper fiercely, "No, don't! Let me go!" Her hands pressed against his chest, trying to push him away.

But his arms only tightened even more, holding her so closely that she felt her breath cut off.

"Hadn't you better get used to my embraces, my love? Is this the way to greet your prospective husband? I've been told how anxiously you were awaiting my return, why don't you prove it?"

Her eyes flew open at last and glared into his.

"Stop it! I hate you!"

He gave a sudden, sarcastic laugh that startled her into silence.

"Ah, yes, of course," he drawled mockingly, "how could I have forgotten that? And here I thought you'd changed your mind, and were marrying me for love! Are you sure you're not nurturing a secret passion for me, Ginny? Try kissing me back, I shall expect more willingness from you after we're married, you know!"

She began to struggle against him, but he had bent his head and was kissing her, long and hard and almost hurtfully, with his fingers tangled in her hair to keep her from turning her head away; pulling its carefully arranged coils loose and sending pins scattering all over the floor. She had tried to forget the way he kissed her; the way his mouth almost seemed to take possession of hers, bruising her lips, forcing them apart while his tongue ravaged her mouth; demanding, almost compelling her own response.

His arm was clamped around her waist, and as her head fell back under the fury of his kiss she was suddenly, painfully aware of the hard, muscular promise of his body against hers. Why did it always have to be this way? It was humiliating, degrading, to be forced thus into the full realization of her own weakness and the almost sordid sensuality that his touch could arouse in her.

Ginny was almost past reason when the kiss ended and she found herself freed as abruptly as she had been swept into his arms. She was still breathless, as if she'd run a long distance, and in order to stand erect she had to hold on to the back of a chair with both hands. It took her a moment to realize that Steve, on the other hand, seemed quite unmoved—he had stepped back, and his narrowed eyes surveyed her critically. Anger flared up in her, replacing the sensuous languor of a moment before.

Her hair fell loosely to her waist, her cheeks wore a feverish flush, and her eyes, which a moment ago had appeared a soft, cloudy green seemed to darken like the surface of the sea when a storm is at hand. Even her voice sounded stormy, and choked with emotion.

"What did you think to prove by *that*? That you are still physicallly stronger than I am? You disgust me!"

He had hooked his thumbs in his belt, a gesture she had always hated. And now he sneered at her, his voice a sarcastic drawl.

"I didn't always disgust you, as I recall very well. In fact, you seemed only too anxious to discover what it was you'd been missing all the time you were still a frightened little virgin! What I cannot understand is why you want to marry me. Do you crave respectability that much? Think of all the new experiences you'll be missing, Ginny—no more exciting new lovers—no more adventures. Won't you become bored? You're a very passionate woman, even if you are still too much of a puritan to admit it; it's so easy to arouse you, my love! Don't you remember how quickly you turned to Carl Hoskins after me, and then to your handsome French captain? Come, I know you could have done better than to choose me for a husband, I've no intentions of settling down, and I'm an outlaw, a miserable half-breed wretch, remember? How is it you've changed your mind?"

He might as well have slapped her—his sneering, contemptuous words drove Ginny almost out of her mind with rage. And still he stood there with that jeering half-smile twisting his lips, waiting calmly for her reaction.

"You dare say those things to me?" Her voice rose, and she had to use all her strength of will to control it. "You dare accuse *me* of—oh God! What kind of hypocrite are you? Do you think I don't know what you were up to on your mysterious, urgent trip to Mexico City? Or that her name is Danielle? Oh, yes," she went on furiously, pleased to see that her barb had struck home and the smile had vanished from his lips, "I'm not quite as foolish and ignorant as you seem to think! I knew exactly what I was doing when I told your grandfather I'd marry you—didn't I always swear to you that some day I'd be revenged, I'd make you sorry you ever decided to kidnap me in that high-handed fashion? Did you imagine I'd ever forgive you for the brutal, vicious way you've treated me? No, Steve *dear,* for once you're going to find out how it feels to be forced into something you don't want—you'll marry me and set *me* free; don't imagine I want to live with you and be your prisoner any longer! I mean to travel—wherever I want and whenever I want, and if I desire lovers I shall have them too—won't that be quite a change for *you* to be the one to wear horns? I'll keep you informed, of course, but there won't be anything you can do about it— take as many mistresses as you like, I don't care, but I'll be your wife, and *I'll* bear your name!"

She was breathless when she had finished, her narrowed, hate-filled eyes gleamed at him like a cat's.

"What a bitch you've turned out to be!" His voice sounded quiet and almost conversational, but Ginny was not deceived, she knew very well the extent of his anger. His face looked as if a mask had been dropped over it with every muscle in it strained and tense.

"But I've had such a good teacher, in *you,* Steve!" Deliberately, and almost flirtatiously she widened her eyes at him and was rewarded when she saw his jaws clamp together. For an instant she thought she had gone too far, and that he would spring forward like a wolf and crush her throat between his hands.

But he took a deep breath, and was suddenly smiling at her.

"Some day, my love, you must tell me what you and my grandfather have planned for me. But in the meantime, perhaps we should try to enjoy what time we'll have together. You're really magnificent when you're angry, do you know that?"

How infuriating he was! One moment she had almost expected him to be breathing fire, but the next he seemed to be maddeningly, completely self-possessed, his voice sounding cool and even slightly amused. How could he regain control of his emotions so quickly?

"Please don't bother to pay me compliments at this point," Ginny said haughtily. "I think we both know how we stand!"

"Well, I'm not too sure about that," he said thoughtfully. "You're a little bitch all right, but I think you can be brought to heel. Perhaps I've just used the wrong techniques! At any rate, I've been given my orders. I'm to treat you with nothing but respect—I'm to whisper sweet nothings in your pretty ears—my grandfather tells me it's high time I started acting like a prospective bridegroom. If we're to be married, I suppose we might as well make the best of it, don't you think?"

He reached his hand out and touched her face lightly, laughing when she flinched.

"You're as flushed as if you have a fever, my sweet! Are you sure you feel well enough to attend the festivities this evening? Which reminds me, I'll call for you promptly at seven o'clock, so do try to be ready then, my grandfather hates to be kept waiting, and we'll have a long drive ahead of us."

"You're really insufferable!" she said in a freezing voice.

"You're really quite like a gypsy, when your hair's down like that, and your eyes turn as dark as a sunless forest," he mocked her, his voice teasing. "You see, you can inspire even a hardened sinner like myself into becoming poetic! Actually, you're most desirable when you're all fiery and dishevelled like this, it's a pity we aren't married yet!"

"Ohh!" Ginny gasped angrily, "I can't take any more of this! Will you get out? I won't hear any more!"

She turned her back on him and ran like a coward for the seclusion of her bedroom, angrily aware of the sound of Steve's cynical laughter behind her. Ginny slammed the door shut as loudly as she could, hoping to close herself in with silence, but all the same she was obliged to put her hands over her ears to still the pounding of her heart.

It was only some time later, when her *duenna* re-entered her room carrying a package in her arms, her face reproachfully inquiring, that Ginny remembered what Steve had brought her. She did not want to open it. She would have preferred to rip the gown that reposed inside the carefully wrapped parcel to shreds! But under Señora Armijo's watchful eyes she had to force some excuse from between lips that still felt painfully bruised, and fumble with string.

However, once the wrappings were thrown aside and the gown lifted out, its folds and flounces shaken loose, Ginny could not repress a spontaneous exclamation of delight. It was a ball gown, the most beautiful she had ever seen—really exquisite! It appeared to be green until the light caught the material it was made from, and then other colors magically appeared in its folds—flashing, irridescent, constantly changing and seeming to merge into each other. She had never seen anything like this before, how was it possible that one piece of cloth should contain so many different, subtle shadings?

Even Señora Armijo's normally impassive face seemed transformed with admiration as she gazed at the gown—the beautiful, shimmering dress that was now laid carefully across Ginny's bed so that they could study and admire it further. It's cut so low in front! Ginny found herself thinking, most of me will be exposed! And yet, wearing it, I'd feel like a fairy princess!

Tia Alfonsa's voice cut across her thoughts at that moment.

"Oh! But I've never seen anything so lovely! You'll be the envy of every woman, Genia! It is a good thing you are safely betrothed, or I should never be able to keep all the young *caballeros* away. What excellent taste—how much dear Esteban must think of you!"

The mention of Steve's name brought Ginny back to earth with an unpleasant jolt, although at the same time her fingers could not help touching the soft, almost flimsy material caressingly.

Steve—why did he have to be the one to give her this particular gown? And where on earth could he have found such a treasure? No doubt, she thought resentfully, he had stolen it. Perhaps it had belonged to the Countess Danielle—oh God! Perhaps he'd gone so far as to steal it from the Empress Carlotta herself! He's capable of any act, no matter how low and despicable, she thought angrily. And yet, in spite of all her misgivings, Ginny knew that she would not be able to resist wearing the gown that very night.

It's green—and yet it reminds me in some way of an opal—a fire opal. Yes, that was it, she decided. She'd wear this gown tonight, and with it the magnificent fire opals that Don Francisco had presented her with. They were the only jewels that she could possibly wear with this dress.

"I'll wear it tonight," Ginny said aloud, and watched Señora Armijo take up the dress almost reverently.

"I'll press it myself," the older woman said. "I wouldn't trust either of those stupid girls with such a task. I'll bring it back soon, and hang it up for you—you ought to try and get some rest before tonight Genia, the dancing is likely to go on until dawn!"

"Oh, yes, the dancing," Ginny thought listlessly after her *duenna* had left once more. She felt strangely restless— and curious too.

What kind of role was Steve playing this time? And what methods had Don Francisco used to bend his grandson's stubborn will to his own? It really would be most interesting to find out just why Steve had given in so easily, it just wasn't like him, especially as he had made it clear he hated the idea of being married to her.

Thinking about him always had the effect of making her furious! With a muffled exclamation of disgust Ginny threw herself on her bed and closed her eyes, determined to conform to custom for once and take a siesta.

She would have been more than a little surprised if she knew that at this very moment, Steve Morgan was thinking about her—his thoughts almost as angry and full of bitterness as hers were.

He had returned to his room, and was preparing to take a bath, but for some reason he found he needed a drink more urgently. Wine! That was all his grandfather kept outside on the big sideboard in the main dining *sala*. He needed Scotch or bourbon, but the wine would have to do for now.

Morosely, Steve looked at his own stubbled reflection in the mirror and rubbed his jaw reflectively. He needed a shave badly—for two pins he'd stay the way he was and announce flatly to his grandfather that he intended to grow a beard again but the thought of another unpleasant interview following on the heels of the one they'd just had filled him with an unusual reluctance to force any minor issues. Damn it, he thought savagely, so I'll be cleanshaven tonight. Maybe it'll please her better too.

The thought of Ginny did nothing to improve his temper. Damn her for the sly little schemer she was! She'd been offered her chance to get even with him and had seized it eagerly—he had no doubt that she'd meant every threat she'd flung at him. He'd relieved her of her virginity and taught her that sex was enjoyable—and she'd promptly turned around and sought further enjoyment in numbers—until he'd been damn-fool enough to abduct her.

Dispensing with the glass he'd been using, Steve tilted the bottle of wine and drank half of it in about three long swallows.

Ever since he'd met Ginny Brandon things had started to go wrong. Although he had to admit reluctantly, that it hadn't been all her fault. He should have kept to his resolution to stay away from her in the first place. And in the second place, he should never have kept her with him all this time. It hadn't been hard to shake off his pursuers—he could have done it alone, without her to slow him up. So why in hell had he dragged her along, especially when he knew he was coming home? He might have known his grandfather would find out, and that being the kind of man he was he'd not be content until he'd met and spoken with the female his unconforming grandson had dared to bring home with him. He should have known what would inevitably happen—he should have taken precautions. Most of all, he should never have permitted himself to have anything to do with Ginny Brandon!

Steve swore to himself, and the Indian maid who was carrying in more hot water for his bath jumped as though he had bitten her. He smiled at her absent-mindedly and gestured rather vaguely for her to continue with whatever she had to do. She gave him a pert, rather shy smile in return, bobbing her head, and left to bring more water.

Steve stared broodingly at the door the girl had closed so carefully behind her. What a mess! He had returned from Mexico City as quickly as he could, with all of the information that Bishop had needed. In fact, Bishop him-

self, in the guise of a rich American cattle buyer, would
be at the Sandoval *hacienda* this evening, on the invitation
of Diego Sandoval, Don José's son, and Steve's friend
from childhood. Diego, an ardent, if secret supporter of
Porfirio Díaz, was also a part of the Juarist movement.
He had arranged for this meeting, having recently
returned from a trip to San Francisco—and he had, in
fact, told Steve before he left that Bishop had another important mission for him when he returned. What could he
tell Bishop now? "My grandfather treats me like a little
child—he's posted guards on me, he's even arranged a
wedding for me"—the thought made his face turn dark
with anger. There would be no quarreling with him over
his methods—in their branch of the service, men like
Steve would use any means they had to in order to attain
their ends. But in this case what it all amounted to was
that he had made a mistake—a stupid, costly mistake!
Thank God that at least he had the information they'd
needed so urgently. Even without him, they'd still be able
to act, carefully coordinating their planning on both sides
of the border.

In spite of his rage and self-disgust, Steve could not
help grinning when he suddenly imagined the lovely
Danielle's fury when she found he'd disappeared. She
would be even more furious when she found her new
gown, sewn for her in Paris by Worth himself from
material shipped all the way from India, had also disappeared. It had been a gift to her from a high-ranking
English admirer—a duke, no less. Yes, Dani would be
having screaming hysterics right now, he'd no doubt. What
a vixen she was, especially in bed! She'd been insatiable;
alternately pouting, pleading, clawing or screaming encouragement in gutter words she'd picked up in every
language conceivable. Still, he'd found himself growing
bored with her demands and her tantrums after a while—
it was more or less in revenge for her having begun to
make herself tedious to him that he'd appropriated her
new ball gown. Maybe she'd be more cautious in her
choice of lovers from now on—her husband really ought
to thank him for it!

But the thought of Dani's husband, away fighting Maximilian's war while she appeared publicly with her lovers,
made Steve start frowning again. Juana had returned
again, this time with the last can of hot water, and she

was standing expectantly by, ready to help him have his bath. An old custom in the bachelor wing of Don Francisco's house. At least, Steve thought bitterly, he had to give the old martinet credit for having that much consideration for the normal physical needs of hot-blooded young men.

But as for the rest of it—no, his grandfather still lived in a closed-in, autocratic world that should have vanished a long time ago. Grown man or not, his grandson was still his grandson, and *el patrón's* word was law. It was impossible! His grandfather must be made to understand that he couldn't keep him prisoner, like any one of his peons who had committed some misdemeanor!

His black brows drawn together in an unconsciously fierce frown that scared the pert Juana into silence, Steve began to undress, tossing his travel-stained clothes carelessly at the girl who blushed and began to giggle as she caught each one adroitly.

Thinking almost absent-mindedly about escape, Steve glanced once at the door and then shrugged. He supposed that Perez still stood guard outside his room. Big, taciturn Jaime Perez who was his grandfather's bodyguard, and had patiently taught him to shoot a rifle. The fact that Jaime watched him was proof enough that his grandfather did not trust him, and in fact Don Francisco had told Steve so quite bluntly.

"Any blood relative of mine who would forget his honor and do what you have done is not to be trusted," the old man had said icily. The mixture of anger and contempt in his grandfather's voice had made Steve feel, for a moment, like a stupid, callow youth again, and he'd been unable to prevent the slow, embarrassing flush that rose in his face.

The interview had gone badly from the start, and without raising his voice Don Francisco had not minced any words, nor tried to hide his scorn and contempt and cold, deadly anger. He had made Steve fully aware of the consequences he might have faced if Ginny had not agreed to a wedding—the same consequences he'd face if he didn't immediately give his word that he would marry her—and even more—treat her with unfailing consideration and respect.

"She deserves much better, I'm sorry to say," Don Francisco had said with disdain, "but since you've ruined her, it's up to you to make amends. I trust that you have some vestige of the sense of family honor and obligation I've tried to instill in you still left!"

Stiffly, cautiously Steve had given his word, thinking the matter would end there. He'd marry her, if his name would magically restore her respectability! What did it really matter, after all—he didn't intend to stay with her for the rest of their days.

But his grandfather, just as if he'd read his mind, had other demands to make, and they were phrased as outright commands.

Steve listened almost unbelievingly as he was ordered to hand over his guns. He glanced up casually, and Jaime lounged in the doorway, his rifle pointing floorward, although Steve was well aware how quickly the man could bring it up if it proved necessary.

He had, for one split-second of pure, unthinking fury, considered whirling around and going for his gun, but sanity returned just in time and he was forced into the realization of two things—that Jaime would not hesitate to shoot, even if it was to maim rather than kill—and that his grandfather would certainly do so, not caring whether he killed or not!

And as far as that went, he was fond of Jaime—the man had been kind and patient with him when he was a boy—almost as close as a father, in fact. Could he really have pulled a gun on Jaime Perez?

Silently, seething with a rage he could barely control, Steve had unbuckled his gunbelts and handed them to his grandfather.

"Good. And now—your word that you will not seek to obtain any other weapon, nor wear one again, until I give you my permission to do so."

His eyes blazing blue fire with an anger that defied his grandfather's, Steve refused.

"I've given you my promise that I'll wed the girl, and that I'll deal with her honorably from now on. But this time you go too far, sir! I'll not be treated like a green boy who can't be trusted to wear a gun."

"And I tell you, Esteban, that you have acted like one! The wearing of guns around your waist like any bandit from the mountains and the use to which you have put them is what has sent you to the depths of villainy in the company of other low-life thieves and murderers who carry weapons only for the purpose of killing! You've had every opportunity in life that I could offer you, but it wasn't enough. You were too stubborn to learn anything, even to live like a gentleman. And you've dragged the honor of my family in the dust by your heartless treatment of a young woman who was trusted to your care— an inexperienced girl whom you seduced; and as if that was not enough, abducted her from the care of her family and paraded her in the worst, most infamous places as your paramour! How would you have me treat you, you young whelp?"

His grandfather's lashing contempt had made Steve go pale and tense with anger, but he stood there silently until the old man had finished his diatribe. A stubborn sense of pride kept him from making any attempt to defend himself or offer any explanations—and in any case, what could he say without betraying himself or his "employers?" There were things that his grandfather could never understand!

"Your word, if you please," Don Francisco repeated when Steve said nothing.

"I'm sorry, sir. I cannot give it."

Steve noticed the way his grandfather's hands clenched themselves around the stock of the riding whip he invariably carried, and remembered suddenly his many "disciplinings" of the past, always inflexibly meted out—his eyes went to the silent, watchful figure of Jaime, still standing before the door.

Deliberately, Steve controlled the anger that might have shown in his voice, softening it to a tone of almost exaggerated patience.

"I would not, however contemptible you think me, lift my hand against you, my *abielo,* nor my old friend here, nor any of your men. I think you know that. But I must tell you—" his voice hardened slightly in spite of all his resolutions—"that at the first possible opportunity I intend to obtain another gun, and to wear it, if I feel like doing so."

Don Francisco's hooded eyes looked like chips of ice.

"I find you impudent, as well as irresponsible. You leave me with no choice but to make sure that you conform with my dictates, whether you will or not!"

Steve gave a short, bitter laugh.

"What will you do with me, grandfather? Turn me over

to the law? Load me down with chains? Or will you shoot me instead? It will be difficult for me to play the part of bridegroom under such conditions, won't it?"

"Guard your tongue, you reprobate!" Don Francisco struck angrily at the arm of his chair with the whip he held. His cold, angry eyes bored into Steve's as he spoke again, very slowly this time.

"There is another alternative, if you insist upon being stubborn. I could arrange matters so that you would meet with a slight accident. To your right hand. It will not cripple you, but you would never again draw a gun quickly enough to kill a man . . ." he halted in mid-sentence, seeing that no further words were needed, for Steve had sucked in his breath, his face whitening beneath his tan. So his grandfather would actually go that far? Still, he himself was too angry and too stubborn to back down.

"You do that, and you might as well kill me." Steve's voice was even, toneless. "You'd have to, before I'd let you even try."

His eyes locked with those of his grandfather in a battle of wills, and Jaime Perez, standing just inside the doorway, thought how much alike they were in some ways, these two. He found himself hoping that this time at least the *patrón* would not do as he had threatened—it was really too bad that Don Esteban had turned out to be so reckless and so willful.

Jaime could not know it, of course, but for an instant, as he looked into his grandson's eyes, Don Francisco saw his daughter Luisa, with the same long-lashed blue eyes challenging him after he had just declared passionately that he would have her Yankee lover killed. This had been after he and his most trusted *vaqueros*, after pursuing them for miles, had finally caught up with the eloping couple. Like her son did now, Luisa had faced him defiantly and without fear.

"You kill Daniel and you might as well kill me too," she had said softly. "He is my husband, and my life. Take his life, and I swear that mine is ended too."

Looking into her eyes he had known bitterly that she was no longer his—and that she meant what she said. He had let her go—Luisa and her husband, and when she had finally come back to him later, with her child, he had seen, with a terrible sadness, that she had spoken truly—her life was finished.

Now Don Francisco found himself thinking that perhaps he was getting too old—or too soft. This was his only grandson, just as Luisa had been the only one of his children to survive. And Esteban had always been too strong-willed and defiant for taming. Not even the many whippings he had received so stoically as a boy had changed his willful, headstrong nature. As a man, he was still just as stubborn, just as headstrong. Yes, Esteban's stiff-necked pride matched his own, the old man thought grimly. He would back down no further, even if it meant death.

To hide his unwonted emotion, Don Francisco banged the stock of his riding whip on the floor between his feet—so hard it sounded like an explosion. He continued to frown.

"If you will not give me your word, then I'm sorry to say that you will, from now on, consider yourself a prisoner here," he said forcibly. "You will be watched at all times, to make certain you do *not* obtain a gun, and you will not be allowed to leave here until I feel that you have earned the right to be turned loose on the unsuspecting world outside."

"I see! And am I to be watched on my honeymoon as well, to make sure I perform satisfactorily as a husband? Or am I not to be permitted to hold my blushing bride in my arms in case I might do the poor, unsuspecting girl some injury?"

In spite of his age, Don Francisco could rise from his chair as quickly as a man much younger, with no stiffness or creaking of bones. He stood up now, his craggy face white with anger.

"You will, for one thing, learn to curb your insolence in my presence, and in the presence of others as well. Perhaps this will serve to remind you that I am still the head of this family."

Don Francisco's arm lifted, and the quirt, wielded so easily and expertly by him, lashed down twice with vicious force—back and forth across his grandson's chest, drawing blood through the thin cotton of his checkered shirt.

Steve had half-expected what might happen, but pride forbade his trying to avoid his grandfather's blows, or cringing from them. His lips went taut, and he winced almost imperceptibly, but that was all. His arms stayed

down at his side, hands clenched into fists, and his eyes
never left his grandfather's face.

Don Francisco gave him a cold smile.

"A reminder that your manners need mending, my
grandson. And while we are on the subject—let me remind you that you are to treat your betrothed at all times,
with the utmost respect and consideration, both in public
and in private. You will not be watched in your marriage
bed, but I trust that even you would not force her to submit to your rough and uncouth passions unless she herself
is willing! A man who calls himself a man would surely
not rape his own wife—or is it impossible for you to persuade a woman to give herself to you of her own accord?"

Don Francisco's words cut deeper than his whip and
Steve remained silent under their sting. He felt every
muscle in his body tense with the strain of holding his
temper in check. How much more would he be expected
to endure? But clearly, his grandfather was not through
with him yet. Now his voice dripped with sarcasm.

"I take it, since you've seen fit to give me your word on
this at least, that there will be no foolhardy attempts at
running away until after the wedding at least?"

In spite of his anger and bitter frustration Steve began
to discover a kind of macabre humor in the situation that
made him smile rather wryly, surprising his grandfather. It
was really ridiculous that he, a grown man who cherished
his own independence and freedom above all things should
stand here so meekly and let an old man heap insults on
him—yes, and order his life and behavior as well!

"Why should I want to run away from my beautiful
bride?" he said, shrugging slightly. "Do you think she's so
lacking in charm that I'd desire to escape the prospect of
bedding her again?"

Don Francisco's eyes flashed for an instant, but he
responded coolly enough.

"I'm really surprised that in this instance, at least,
you've displayed some good taste. Meeting Ginny was not
only a pleasant surprise but a pleasure."

Although he did not relax his vigilance, Jaime Perez
found himself able to relax slightly at last.

Ah, these two! It was always like this. First the heated
words and the tension, and then a sudden quieting as they
remeasured each other's worth as adversaries.

"You had better go and make yourself a little more

presentable before you visit your *novia*," Don Francisco was saying now, as he poured himself a glass of wine.

Bowing formally, Steve turned to leave, but his grandfather halted him at the door with one last question.

"I find myself curiously puzzled that you should have brought the girl here. You are usually more discreet—or should the word be cautious?—about your pecadilloes. Have you considered that for once you might have fallen in love?"

Steve's eyes narrowed just a fraction at the unexpectedness of the question, but his face stayed expressionless.

"I had not given it much thought, sir. Perhaps, since we're to be married it might be more convenient if I were to feel some—affection, instead of dislike for her."

"It might be even more convenient if Ginny felt the same way, would it not?" Don Francisco said, and the conversation was ended.

Stripped, with his body immersed in water up to the waist, Steve Morgan was hardly in the mood to enjoy either his bath, or the attentions of the pretty Juana. The knowledge that Jaime stood on guard outside his door was frustrating enough—the thought that he was actually to be treated as a prisoner, with no freedom of movement, was intolerable. To make matters worse, there had been the meeting with Ginny. What was there about her that constantly had him losing his temper? This afternoon he would have dearly enjoyed striking her—slapping her into silence, and then flinging her backward onto the bed with all her brand-new petticoats thrown over her head while he exacted an unwilling, but inevitable response from her squirming body. That's what he should have done, and would have done if his grandfather had not forced him into a ridiculous position. How amusing Ginny must think it all! He gritted his teeth when he thought of the way she'd stormed at him.

Juana's soft, commiserating voice interrupted his black thoughts as she exclaimed with shock and pity over the weals that criss-crossed his bare torso.

She bent over him with her large black eyes soft with concern, and her full, unbound breasts were fully revealed under the thin cotton *camisa* she wore. Clearly, Juana did not wear more than the barest minimum of clothing, and just as clearly, she did not care if he knew this.

Her fingers trailed across the marks on Steve's chest.

"Ah, *señor*! They must hurt, no? I can get some salve, it will not take a minute . . ."

It was almost habit that made Steve take her hand and move it to his lips, tickling her palm with his tongue.

"It's not salve that I need," he whispered against her fingers, feeling them tremble uncertainly before she pulled her hand away with a nervous giggle.

"*Señor*! And you to be married so soon!"

He cursed inwardly. So it was to be soon, was it? It seemed as if everyone here knew more about his own wedding than he did. He felt trapped, and very angry—there had to be a way—some way out!

Aloud, Steve said insinuatingly,

" 'Soon' is a long time away from today and now, pretty thing. And you have beautiful black eyes—a man could easily lose his honor in their depths."

She giggled again, more from nerves than anything else, and almost imperceptibly, she leaned over him.

Steve smiled at her with his lips, but his thoughts were bitter. Honor! Why had that particular phrase sprung to his lips? "No honor" his grandfather had said, and he was right, of course. Honor was nothing but an empty word, used by old men to cover weakness. A man did what he had to do or wanted to do, as long as he was prepared to take the consequences of his actions.

It was possible, that this little Juana might be persuaded to find him a weapon. It would be easy for her to smuggle one in to him. And in any case, she was an attractive wench—her breasts were quite beautiful . . . Almost without thinking his fingers were pushing the loose blouse she wore down off her shoulders, freeing her really magnificent breasts. He heard her gasp softly as he bent his head and pressed his mouth against the hollow between the mounded flesh. Her skin was warm, and a small vein pulsed under his lips.

"Why don't you take those uncomfortable garments off and join me in the bath? There's room in here for both of us . . ."

His tongue found her nipple and her fingers tangled themselves in his hair.

"Ohh—*señor*!"

Neither of them noticed, after a while, that the water had become cold, and the floor was wet from their splashings.

Chapter Thirty

Don Francisco's carriage was large and comfortable, but the journey to the Sandoval *hacienda* took almost two hours, and seemed long and wearisome.

For most of the trip, Steve Morgan maintained an inscrutable silence, leaning back with his head against the cushioned backrest, his arms folded across his chest. He answered politely enough whenever either his grandfather or the Señora Ortega addressed some question to him, but for the most part he kept his eyes closed, as if he were unutterably weary—or bored. He had already explained shortly that he had been riding all day and was rather tired.

"It's the same with all you young men these days!" Tia Maria exclaimed, sparing him any further explanations. "Too weak—leading soft lives! In my day a *caballero* thought nothing of travelling over a hundred miles merely to claim one dance with his sweetheart. And chaperones were stricter in those days too, the only chance a girl had to converse with a young man was during the dancing. But we all made the most of it, I can assure you! We'd dance till dawn, without feeling the least tired!"

Tia Maria's voice droned on and on, carrying almost

the entire conversation, with the Señora Armijo adding an occasional comment of her own.

Don Francisco, seated next to Steve, frowned out of the window to hide his growing anger from the ladies, and Ginny, looking ravishing in her new gown, said hardly a word.

Under the cover of her own garrulity, Dona Maria wondered more than once what was wrong between the two young people. They certainly acted most peculiarly for a young engaged couple. She had even had to insist that Genia add a touch of coral rouge to her cheeks to give them some color, and as for her grandnephew, he seemed hardly his usual gay, devil-may-care self. She wondered if Esteban was sulking because he had not been permitted to have his *novia* sit next to him . . . and certainly, it was strange that her brother had not suggested it but had seated himself firmly next to his grandson. There was something strange going on here, something she could not put her finger on. For instance, why were two of Francisco's *vaqueros*, armed to the teeth, escorting them tonight? Was some trouble expected? Still, she was too tactful to ask, so she continued to chatter.

Steve, although he pretended to nap, was only too conscious of their armed escort. His escort. Jaime Perez and Enrico, another of his grandfather's *vaqueros*, had dogged his footsteps constantly since he'd set foot in the house. The taste of rage was as bitter as gall in his throat when he was forced to realize that even at the fiesta they would still be there, following wherever he went, watching him like hawks. How was he going to explain being in such a stupid, inconceivable situation? And above all—he had to talk to Bishop privately; how could he arrange it now? The only bright spot in his day had been Juana. Sweet, passionate, helpful Juana. The knife she had given him was her own, carried for her protection.

"The men here—they are always trying to grab me!" she had told him fiercely. "Pah! I despise them—pigs! Now they know that I will kill them if they try, and they leave me alone—me, I give myself only when I please!"

The knife she had given him was concealed in the lining of his high-topped, silver ornamented boot—he could feel it against his right calf. So much for his not being allowed a weapon of any kind!

With a mental shrug and a return of his old self-confidence, Steve decided that he would take care of each problem as it arose. He had, after all, escaped from jails before, and even, once or twice, from a lynching mob. When he was ready, he'd escape his watchdogs too. But right now, his other problem was Ginny.

Without her being aware of it, Steve opened his eyes a fraction and studied her from beneath the cover of his lashes.

He had to admit it—she was exceptionally desirable tonight. The stolen gown suited her far better than it would have the lovely Danielle. And he had recognized his mother's opals—blazing like pale fire on her ears and around her throat. She was really a beautiful woman—a pity she had turned into such a nagging shrew. But could he blame her for it? He had to admit in all honesty that most of the fault was his. The same thought that had irritated him with its repetition all day came back to nettle him now. Why had he brought her with him so far? Why did she, of all women have the power to annoy him so intensely that he lost his normal self-control and felt, at times, that he could easily strangle her with his bare hands? And why, goddam it, did he keep desiring her in spite of it all? She brought out the worst in him, and obviously the same was true the other way around. She could be charming, flirtatious, even spontaneously affectionate with other men. He had watched her fuss over Carl Hoskins—throw her arms around Michel Remy and offer her mouth for his kiss. It would have been the same thing, over again, with Lieutenant d'Argent, if he had not intervened.

Unconsciously, Steve had begun to frown. Damn Ginny! Damn her female guile and duplicity! One moment she was soft and kittenish and yielding, and the next a wildcat. He'd had to watch her every minute, and as soon as his back was turned she had wormed her way into his grandfather's good graces, agreeing quite meekly, no doubt, to marry him, just so that she could have her revenge. And then she'd dared threaten him with the scandalous life she'd lead once she was his wife. Well, they would see about that, he thought grimly. He'd marry her because he had promised to do so, and leave her at the altar. The abandoned bride. Let her face that scandal. His biggest mistake had been to keep her around long enough for her to become a habit—but habits could be broken and the world was full of beautiful women—women who didn't scream at a man that they hated him, loathed him, before they gave in and enjoyed what was inevitable.

Ginny was being unusually quiet tonight, when she should have been excited and triumphant instead. Again, Steve flicked a sharp, shadowed glance over her. Like Don Francisco, she appeared to be studying the countryside that rolled past the windows of the carriage. Her face looked quite calm and composed, and the slight color in her cheeks and on her lips was becoming. But he remembered suddenly how cold her hand had been when she'd held it out to him so unwillingly earlier that evening. Even when he had kissed it formally, complimenting her extravagantly on her appearance in an effort to needle her into showing her temper, she had refused to rise to the bait and had swept past him with a murmured "thank you, Steve—you're too kind."

A sudden, extremely unpleasant thought suddenly made him catch his breath and sit up straight, prompting Don Francisco to remark testily that he supposed they should be honored that his grandson had finally deigned to honor them with his attention.

"But anything you say always has my attention, sir," Steve responded mechanically, and was rewarded by a glowering look from under the old man's bushy white eyebrows.

Tia Maria glanced from one to the other of them sharply and began to talk volubly again, addressing herself to Ginny this time, so that the girl was forced to turn her head and give the older woman her polite attention.

Glad of the respite, Steve relapsed into his brooding reverie again, but the ugly suspicion that had popped into his mind quite suddenly a moment ago kept nagging at his mind.

Good God! Could it be she was pregnant? Was that the reason why she had let herself fall in so eagerly with his grandfather's plans to marry them off? And was that the reason for her changing moods, the alternation from abandoned, passionate mistress to hate-filled antagonist?

He looked at Ginny then, opening his eyes lazily, giving her a long, searching look that she could not fail to notice. No, her waist seemed as slim as ever, her breasts no fuller. He was imagining things—he almost laughed out loud—a guilty conscience? Perhaps, if he'd ever possessed a conscience.

The carriage had slowed down, and there were lights ahead—myriads of tiny, dancing flames that looked like fireflies; suspended against the inky blue night sky.

It took Ginny a few seconds to realize that the fireflies were tiny paraffin lights that lined the top of the tall walls they were approaching. Two strong lanterns swung from a carved iron archway, and the gaudily dressed, smiling *vaqueros* who stood there called out greetings as the carriage rumbled through.

Ginny could hardly believe her eyes—the magnificent grounds were ablaze with lights from Japanese lanterns, making them a veritable fairyland. More lights streamed welcomingly from every door and window of the enormous house they were now approaching. There were throngs of people everywhere, standing in groups or strolling around. As the carriage rolled to a stop and they alighted, Ginny could hear music. Small bands of mariachi players wove their way between the guests, and from somewhere came the high, plaintive sound of a flamenco singer.

Far to their left, lights that were brighter and larger than the lanterns showed through the trees, and Ginny could barely make out what appeared to be the outline of a huge arena. Noticing her stare of surprise Dona Armijo whispered that it was a bullring—later perhaps some of the younger men would want to try their prowess with the bulls.

"Yes, and sometimes they put on exhibitions of their riding skills to impress the ladies," Tia Maria said with a sniff. She added in a disapproving tone, "there have even been duels fought there. Our young men are very hot blooded."

"Hotheads would be more correct," Don Francisco snorted. They were at the foot of the wide stone steps leading up to the main entrance to the house, and he offered his arm politely to Ginny. But before she could take it she heard Steve say teasingly,

"Surely, sir, you would not deny me the opportunity to escort my *novia* inside? Perhaps the knowledge that she's mine will keep some of those young hotheads at bay."

Under the teasing there were undercurrents—instinctively Ginny would have held back, but Steve had already taken her arm firmly and was leading her up the steps. Don Francisco had taken his sister's arm, his face wooden with anger, and Dona Armijo trailed behind.

They were in the main hall now, and Ginny felt herself caught up in the rush of introductions, of embraces from the ladies, bows and handkissing from the men. She seemed to be borne, like a tiny cork, through a sea of faces, all smiling; some enviously. Voices beat against her ears, congratulating her, congratulating Steve at having chosen so well.

Here were the wealthiest people in the province—the oldest families. Outside, in the carnival atmosphere created by the lights and music, the patios were also crowded, but with younger people—guests from as far away as Mexico City. Once, as she passed an open French window, Ginny even caught a glimpse of uniforms—French, Austrian, and Belgian. She felt her heart falter, and then beat faster. Suppose—just suppose Michel was here? Or the horrible, pompous little Lieutenant d'Argent? Unconsciously she had stiffened, raising her head proudly. After all, why should she be afraid? It was Steve who had everything to fear, not herself.

She was relieved that as they moved through the crowd, Don Francisco and his sister stayed close. When Señora Armijo suggested that Ginny should give her her shawls and she would take them upstairs for her, Dona Maria left her brother's side and tugged at Ginny's arm.

"Come along, love—you can tear yourself away from Esteban for a few moments. Let me introduce you to some of the ladies who are among my oldest friends, they are all so anxious to meet you!"

All this time, she had felt as if she and Steve had moved and smiled and spoken like actors on a stage. He had said all the right things, his voice holding nothing but tender regard and pride. There were even times when she had imagined his hold on her arm tightened possessively; especially when some of the younger men, his friends, paid her elaborate compliments. But that was ridiculous! Steve was just a good actor, he enjoyed masquerades.

Dona Maria was leading Ginny with her now, her voice alternately explaining and scolding. Glancing back over her shoulder once, Ginny had seen Don Francisco put his hand on Steve's arm—was she imagining that they were engaged in some kind of argument? But she had no time for more imaginings. Señora Ortega was explaining that the older people, the more staid and conventional families, preferred to stay indoors. Instead of dining al fresco style outdoors, Don José's most honored guests and his closest friends would dine in the enormous main dining room of the house. They would dance later in the big *sala* to a more sedate band than the one playing outside in the patio.

"If Esteban has any sense at all he'll steal outside with you," Tia Maria commented. "I really don't know what's wrong with that young man this evening, his behavior goes from bad to worse I'm afraid! Perhaps you can change it—I'm sure you'll be an excellent influence, dear."

"Oh, yes, I hope so," Ginny murmured dutifully. She hardly knew what she was saying. Even while she was being introduced to a bevy of dark-costumed older women who held court in one of the smaller drawing rooms, Ginny could feel her mind whirling, full of questions that had no answers.

That afternoon she had thrown herself on her bed, hoping to sleep, but rest was impossible. Then Carmencita, the more talkative of her two maids had come sidling in with a cool drink for her, and had stayed to gossip, her eyes shining with excitement. She had seen Dona Genia's ball gown, it was so lovely, all the servants were talking about its magnificence. She had commented that Don Esteban was in a bad mood—there had been an interview with *el patrón* behind closed doors . . . and she herself had heard from Juana that *el patrón* had been so angry he had struck his grandson with the whip he always carried . . . did Dona Genia know that her *novio* was not permitted to wear his guns any longer? And Jaime and Enrico followed him everywhere, now.

"He's a wild one, that Don Esteban! We've heard that he's killed many men with his guns. *El patrón* would not like that!"

Seeing Ginny's expression Carmencita added pacifically that she was sure Dona Genia knew of all this already, she must forgive her for gossiping.

"Don't stop, now you've started!" Ginny retorted, sitting bolt upright in bed. "Who is Juana, and how does she know so much?" She was too angry at the moment to care if she did sound jealous.

Carmencita's eyes had widened, but they gleamed with a kind of mischief too.

"She works in the house, Dona Genia. You've seen her. The men think she is pretty, but she's wilder than a gypsy—her father is nothing but a *bandido*, but he used to be one of Don Francisco's *vaqueros*, until he killed a man and had to run off into the hills. It was her mother who brought her here and begged *el patrón* to take her in . . . trust Juana to know everything that that goes on!"

In the end, Ginny had managed to worm out of the girl the fact that Juana was not only pretty but ambitious. She considered herself too good for the common *vaqueros* and peons and enjoyed her work in the bachelor wing—she had many beautiful presents given to her by various young *caballeros* who had occupied those quarters—Juana thought Don Esteban was the handsomest man she had ever seen, also "*muy macho*." Had Carmencita been trying to make her jealous, or only to warn her, Ginny wondered afterwards.

She was angrier than ever with Steve. How like him this was, no doubt he'd taken advantage of the opportunity to try Juana's tempestuous charms—obviously he did not think her charming any longer now that she had shown him she was no longer his puppet, to be used and moved around as he wished!

Afterwards, when some of her rage had diminished, she had begun to wonder about the reasons for Steve's violent quarrel with his grandfather—the reason for the constant presence of the two *vaqueros* who had even followed them unobtrusively into Don Jose's *estancia* itself. And it was true that he was not wearing his guns. How well Ginny remembered those guns! When they travelled he had always worn two. . . . When he woke in the morning the first thing he did, almost, was buckle on his gunbelts. He was a man of violence, a man who lived by the gun—it had been almost a shock to see him unarmed.

Was it really possible that he was being forced to marry her? Was the thought of marriage to her so repulsive to him that his grandfather had had to disarm him and have him watched in case he ran away? She should have been happy at the thought that for once Steve Morgan was being compelled (as he had compelled her so often) to do something against his will. But instead it irked her strangely. He should have realized he could not get away with what he had done—he should have been prepared to take the consequences as gracefully as the circumstances allowed. After all, this wouldn't be a real marriage— merely one of convenience; she would certainly neither expect nor want him to stay at her side. But suppose Don Francisco had other ideas?

Ginny was filled with a sense of foreboding, almost of fear. When Dona Maria led her back at last into the *sala* she had no recollection of the names of any of the ladies she had met, nor what they had said to her, or she to them.

The scene here had more animation and color. Dancing had begun already and couples drifted across the floor to the dreamy strains of a waltz. Without knowing how or why her eyes had somehow caught sight of Steve, who was at the far end of the room where a long table had been set up like a bar, for the serving of drinks. He was standing with a glass in his hand, talking to a dark-featured, slightly built young man whom she vaguely remembered being introduced to as Don Diego Sandoval. She saw Renaldo, looking exceptionally handsome tonight in his dark formal attire, join them. For a moment their conversation seemed to become quite animated, and then, as Dona Maria gently propelled Ginny farther inside the spacious, lofty-ceilinged room, Steve looked away from his friends and saw her. For a moment it seemed as if the dark, gleaming blue of his eyes cut a path through the crowded room, stilling sound and motion as they met hers.

He said something to Renaldo, who smiled at her, and placing his half-empty glass on the table, made his way towards her. The next minute he was smiling teasingly at his grandaunt, telling her that she'd taken up enough of his *novia's* time already.

Dona Maria smiled and nodded approvingly as he put his arm around Ginny's stiffly unyielding waist and almost forced her into the swirling, dipping motion of the waltz.

"Remember we're supposed to be a happily engaged pair. You might at least try one of your beguiling smiles on me, my sweet!"

Inexorably, his arm brought her body closer to his, and with the dance hardly begun Ginny felt herself growing slightly breathless.

"Must you hold me so closely?" But she smiled as she said it, and saw his eyes crinkle with appreciation.

"What a good little actress you've turned out to be, Ginny! I can hardly wait to find out what other surprises you have in store for me." Almost without pausing his voice continued smoothly, "You're the loveliest woman here tonight. Where have you been? Flirting with some young *caballero* to make me jealous?"

Don Francisco danced rather slowly and sedately by with a stout woman dressed in crimson brocade, and his cold eyes moved over them. In his old-fashioned way, he inclined his head to Ginny as they passed.

Steve bent his head and brushed his lips against her temple and Ginny almost cried out with outrage.

"Stop that! You don't have to waste your flowery compliments and your kisses on me." She could not help adding waspishly, "You should save them for the pretty servant girls, like Juana!"

He threw back his head and laughed.

"Jealous, my love? You shouldn't be. After all, a man has to amuse himself sometimes, as you well know. And why grudge me an occasional mistress when you plan to take your own lovers?"

If she could have done so without creating a scandal she would have pulled herself from his arms and fled from him, and his mocking laughter.

"I don't care what you do," she whispered cuttingly. "But at least you could spare me servants' gossip!"

"Spoken as if you were a wife already! But, Ginny-love, why should I want to spare you anything? Since you've listened to backstairs gossip I'm sure you've heard everything." His voice became deliberately exaggerated. "Not only am I a prisoner of your beauty and your— other charms, sweetheart, but my grandfather's decided I need restraint as well. We're companions in misfortune, you see."

She could see quite clearly that the evening was going to be a disaster. They did nothing but quarrel, they were beginning to hate each other more, and still they would be forced to carry on with a sham—play the part of lovers. Why didn't the music end? She was out of breath and felt as if they had been dancing for hours.

It would be best, Ginny decided, if she didn't answer his barbs. She tried to ignore the fact that he held her far too closely, and that from time to time he bent his head and kissed her lightly—on the forehead, on the temple—she knew that people were watching them and were probably shocked. Of course, that was why he was doing it—to shock everyone else and to force her into an angry scene. He wouldn't have that satisfaction at least!

The dance ended at last, but Steve surprised her again by staying at her side, his manner falsely solicitous.

"You're looking quite flushed, my love. Wouldn't you like to stroll outside for a while? The atmosphere there is much less stifling, and Don José has even ordered a moon. Shall we see if we can escape from your *duenna's* eagle eye? I can see poor Tia Alfonsa now, she's looking for you; and quite frankly, I'd like to avoid my grandfather as well—he looks quite fierce, don't you think?"

She could not pull away from his grip on her arm without making herself conspicuous. But Ginny could not help wondering suspiciously why he was so anxious for her company suddenly. What did he have in mind? It made her feel safer to notice the two men who detached themselves unobtrusively from the crowd of watching servants and were now following them without appearing to. She recognized one of them as Don Francisco's bodyguard, Jaime Perez. How many others had noticed? But if Steve was seething with rage inside, he did not let her see it. His manner was easy, almost companionable, and they paused occasionally so that he could introduce her to late arrivals and friends of his who hadn't met her earlier. One of them was an American, a cattle buyer from Texas; hardly the kind of man one would notice in a crowd, or remember afterwards. . . .

Steve had felt his gloomy mood improve slightly since he had talked to Diego, and to Bishop himself, for a few minutes. Diego had been vastly amused, and Bishop sourly reproving, but the information that Steve had brought them had even produced a rare smile from Bishop.

"It took a lot of string-pulling to persuade Mr. Seward to come out so strongly in favor of President Juarez as promptly as he did," Bishop admitted privately to Steve. "However! We have our ways. It's even better to learn that some of the French troops are actually being withdrawn." He had added, in a lower voice, "You're sure about Lopez?" Steve's answer seemed to satisfy him, for he smiled again.

"Well then—perhaps it's my turn to give you some information you might not have picked up. It appears your

future father-in-law has put it about that his daughter is
visiting friends in Mexico. He'll be coming up for re-elec-
tion soon, I suppose he feels he cannot afford a scandal in
the family. Not a word about that gold, either. But I
should warn you, Morgan, you're on the list of just about
every bounty hunter on both sides of the border. The price
on your head, alive, is twenty-five thousand dollars."

Steve whistled, and Bishop, his face inscrutable, added
dryly, "This might be a good time for you to lie low for a
while. Perhaps you might even use the opportunity to have
a honeymoon."

Used by now to Bishop's brand of humor Steve had
merely shrugged.

"I've already told you what's behind this marriage. And
besides, we've already had the honeymoon."

Bishop had raised his eyebrows.

"Does that mean you'll still be working for us? Marriage
has a way of making a man overly cautious . . . you
saw how it was with Dave Madden."

Steve grimaced.

"Yeah—I saw! Dave was good, and I was glad to have
him alongside me in several scrapes we got into. Since he
met Renata he's been trying to flush cattle out of that
mesquite brush, scraping out a living—if you can call it
that. It's not for me—"

He thought that again as he tightened his hold on
Ginny's bare arm, feeling the softness of her flesh. He
needed adventure, the taking of risks, the new experiences
that his travels always brought him. And if he was afraid
of anything, it was of bonds—being tied down to the constant frustration of mediocrity. The prospect of having to
spend his life with one woman appalled him—he had had
too many to be satisfied with one.

They had emerged into the cool, covered verandah that
led into the main patio now, and from habit, Steve's eyes
scanned the crowd quickly, fastening on the small group
of French officers at the far end. Three Americans, probably mercenaries, stood slightly apart from the Frenchmen,
talking among themselves, and one of them—Steve cursed
inwardly. No mistaking that hook-nosed, predatory profile.
What the hell was Tom Beal doing this far inland? And
what was he doing here of all places?

"Steve! You're hurting me!"

"I'm sorry," he muttered automatically. Almost without

pausing he released her arm and grabbed both of her hands in his, whirling her around. Before she could protest Ginny found herself pulled into the shadow, her back to a massive, creeper-covered column—one of those holding up the galeria above.

"What's the matter with you? Why have you . . ."

Unexpectedly, overwhelmingly, he was kissing her; not giving her time to think, or to stiffen with resistance.

Over her shoulder, Steve saw that Beal and his companions were strolling towards one of the tables that had been set up outside for the serving of food and drinks. They wore guns, all three of them. He had already noticed the bulges of concealed revolvers under the dark jackets the men had elected to wear as a sop to convention. And tonight of all nights, he did not have one, thanks to his grandfather!

But he'd be damned if he'd run from Beal and hide himself for the rest of the evening. He'd think of something.

Caught off-guard, Ginny's lips were soft under his, parted. He held her closer, felt the swell of her breasts against his chest, and, for the moment, forgot about Beal.

Her eyes were wide, as deep and mysterious as forest pools when he released her at last.

"Why did you . . ."

"If you don't keep silent for a while, I'll kiss you again," he threatened, and the softness left her eyes as her lips tightened mutinously. He sighed.

"Ginny—we have to talk. How about a truce? Look," he went on impatiently, in the face of her stubborn silence, "you know as well as I do this whole damn situation is ridiculous! We can't go on fighting like cat and dog if we're going to be married in a few days, it isn't going to get either of us anywhere. And there's something I have to tell you."

"I wondered when you were going to get around to that," she said in a small, hard voice. "I saw him too. That horrible man who looked at me as if he were taking my clothes off—the one you nearly killed with your ridiculous play-acting!"

She had seen Beale almost at the same time Steve did, her eyes drawn nostalgically to the French uniforms. She had felt herself grow weak and almost dizzy with fear when Steve had grabbed her hands and dragged her off here. Was that why he kissed her so fervently? To keep her quiet, to keep her from being seen and recognized?

He looked down at her, half-smiling, but there was an almost baffled expression in his eyes.

"Oh, Ginny-love! What a little termagant you are! You're the stubbornnest and most unreasonable female I've ever encountered. What am I to do with you?"

"It's not me you have to worry about, Steve Morgan, it's that man over there! What are you going to do about him?"

He shrugged carelessly.

"But I haven't decided yet. He hasn't seen either of us, so at least the element of surprise is on my side. In any case," his arms went on either side of her, trapping her against the collonade, "right now, all I find myself thinking of is how much I want to make love to you. You have the most exciting, sensuous mouth of any woman I've seen. Even when your eyes are flashing fire, as they are now, your mouth gives you away."

Before she could retort, he was kissing her again, his arms going round her, gathering her closely against him. She thought faintly that he was quite unscrupulous, impossible to withstand, and completely mad! But as usual, when he kissed her with such ruthless concentration her body seemed to develop a will of its own—she became completely incapable of resistance as her lips took fire under his.

"Do you realize," she whispered when he had raised his head at last, "that there are other people here? And those two men—they're watching us! What will they think?" A stirring of anger came back and she said more strongly, "You're such a hypocrite! Why do you have to play games with me?"

"You're the hypocrite, my sweet. Why won't you accept the fact that no matter what we've said to each other and how we've fought each other, there's still this to be contended with?" His lips brushed hers again and she shivered in spite of herself.

"I don't understand you!"

"And I don't understand you, sweetheart. But you can see for yourself, can't you, that we can't go on battling each other forever. That's why I want to call a truce. For heaven's sake, Ginny!" his voice had become impatient, urgent, "even if this marriage of ours seems to be the only practical way out of the rather dubious position I've forced you into—yes, all right, I accept the blame for that!—don't you see there are still things we must discuss? And it would be better if we could talk reasonably, and without useless recriminations. Well?"

Ginny could scarcely bring herself to believe that he meant it—that he genuinely wanted to enter into a kind of truce with her, and there were no ulterior motives hidden behind his sudden change of manner. Still, what did she have to lose by merely listening to what he had to say? She wondered, during that instant when she hesitated, looking into his eyes, whether he intended to offer excuses, or to try and talk her out of marrying him.

She nodded her head rather sullenly, hoping that at least he'd release her. Why did he have to make such a public show of ardor?

The words trembled hotly on the tip of her tongue and she bit them back. But she had the feeling that he had somehow read her mind, because he smiled down at her teasingly.

"Ginny! Do I really frighten you that much? You look as if you were about to become a living sacrifice!"

Ginny couldn't remember afterwards what she said in reply, or even if she said anything at all.

Tia Maria's voice, sounding tart and rather breathless, broke in.

"There you are! I've been looking everywhere, and poor Señora Armijo was wringing her hands when I last saw her! Hiding in romantic corners is all very well, I suppose, but you two will have lots of time for that later! Ginny, here's a gentleman who's been most anxious to meet you ever since I mentioned your name—no need to look at me so sourly, Esteban, Colonel Devereaux was recently married himself. He tells me he's acquainted with Genia's father—a coincidence, don't you think?"

Ginny could feel herself going paper white, and then her cheeks began to burn. Steve's fingers seemed to bite warningly into her shoulder before he dropped his hand and made a somewhat ironical bow.

"My dear aunt! What very sharp eyes you have. I thought no one would discover us here. Sir, it's a pleasure."

Ginny barely realized that introductions were being performed. She held out her hand mechanically with a fixed smile on her lips and felt the colonel's mustache brush the back of her hand as he kissed it.

As he straightened she found herself facing a rather portly man of medium height, with dark brown hair that was only slightly brushed with gray. It was his eyes that held her—they were hazel, intelligent—and he was looking at her piercingly, his eyes holding a question; rather puzzled at the same time.

"Miss Brandon—I have the pleasure of meeting you at last. Your father did mention that you were planning a visit to Mexico when I talked to him last, as I recall. But it's rather a surprise to meet you here." Did he emphasize that last word, or had she imagined it? He continued, his voice a pleasant drawl, "I have the pleasure of a slight acquaintance with your uncle, too—a charming man, and one whose opinion the emperor greatly respects. I wonder if—" he turned to Steve with a deprecating smile, "with your permission, monsieur, er . . ."

"Esteban is the grandson of my brother, Don Francisco Alvarado. You have met him, I'm sure!" Tia Maria sounded pleased with herself; Ginny did not dare turn her head to watch Steve's expression.

"Ah, yes, of course! Monsieur Alvarado—I wonder if you'll allow me a dance with your charming fiancée? If she does not object, of course!"

"Nonsense, of course Esteban does not object! And I'm sure dear Genia will enjoy talking of mutual friends. You two will have the whole evening together, you mustn't be selfish, you know!"

"My aunt has removed all objections, as you see, Colonel!" Steve's voice held an undercurrent of teasing laughter, nothing else. "Go ahead and enjoy yourself, my love. Tia—" he bowed to his aunt, "you haven't given me the pleasure of a dance with you all evening. May I have the honor?"

Feeling herself struck dumb, unable to think coherently, Ginny found her hand taken by Colonel Devereaux—he was leading her down the steps to the dance floor that had been erected on the patio. All she could pray for now was that the man Beal would not recognize her, that he and his friends had decided to stroll elsewhere. Certainly, she didn't dare glance in the direction where she had seen him last.

She found herself hoping that Steve had been sensible

enough and cautious enough to take his aunt indoors to dance. In spite of her exasperation with him, a surprising thought had wormed itself into her mind—she did not want Beal to see him—she did not want to see him shot and perhaps killed without a chance to defend himself!

Chapter Thirty-one

Colonel Raoul Devereaux was an excellent dancer, and his mask of polite affability never dropped for an instant, but to Ginny it was one of the most uncomfortable experiences of her life.

"My dear *mademoiselle*," were the colonel's first words, delivered in a playfully scolding tone, "you don't know how glad it makes me to find you here, safe and happy." He placed a gentle emphasis on the last word that was umistakeable this time, and continued before Ginny could find an answer, "you know, your father has been quite frantic with worry! And since Captain Remy returned to Mexico City, he has been almost beside himself with anxiety. In fact he even wrote to your uncle—did you know that we now have a telegraph line to Paris?—I received an urgent message from him only a few days ago, we were to try and find you at all costs. It's fortunate my wife's family has a *hacienda* not very far from here—we received an invitation to your wedding, and when I was invited here this evening I hoped I'd find you here too."

Ginny felt herself going quite pale; she knew her hands had begun to tremble, for Colonel Devereaux grasped her a little more firmly.

"Sir, I didn't know—that is, everything happened so suddenly I—"

"There, there, *mademoiselle*!" he said soothingly, "I did not mean to upset you in any way! Let me assure you that everything has been done to suppress even a breath of scandal—no one knows what happened, your father has put it about that you are visiting friends in Mexico, and only Marshal Bazaine, Captain Remy and I, myself are aware of—forgive me for mentioning such a delicate matter—your abduction by the rebels, led by that American spy."

"Spy?" Ginny found herself repeating stupidly. To avoid the embarrassment his urbanely delivered statements had caused her she seized on the word as an excuse to clear her muddled mind.

"Did you say *spy, monsieur*? I thought they were bandits—after the gold—they divided it up among themselves and disappeared into the hills soon enough. But I—I was—"

"I understand, *mademoiselle*! And it is certainly not my intention to upset you. But I am naturally concerned, you comprehend? It is my suspicion that the men you naturally took for bandits were none other than some of Juarez' rag-tag supporters—and the man who led them—the man you so bravely unmasked, incurring his wrath—I know of him, of course. A mercenary—a travelling gunman. Yes, he'd do a thing like that, for money. But I understand he was supposed to escort the wagon train that brought you to El Paso—he left it suddenly, when you did. And then he turns up, at the head of a band of bandits, to steal the gold. Strange! Yes, he could very well be a spy—your government doesn't approve of our being here, I'm afraid. Your Mr. Secretary Seward recently made that very clear. A pity. But I would not put it past certain elements to arrange such a thing. And you, *mademoiselle*, what do you think?"

His long and rather thoughtful-sounding speech had given Ginny a chance to collect her wits. She was determined that he should not make her stutter like an embarrassed schoolgirl again, and yet, his sudden question took her by surprise.

"What do *I* think? Surely, *monsieur*, that can't be important! I don't know anything about politics—I've been through a terrible experience, being carried across the country as a hostage by a man worse than an animal, and just as dangerous—quite frankly I cannot yet quite believe I'm safe! Thank God I was rescued—I've been spending the past weeks trying to forget what I went through!"

Seeing her eyes, wet with the surface shine of tears, look so imploringly at him, even Colonel Devereaux' stern heart was moved.

Sacre bleu, but she was a little beauty, this Ginny Brandon! He hadn't realized, until he'd seen her, how attractive she was. It explained a lot of things, he supposed, but not everything—not enough! What was she doing here? How had she met Alvarado's grandson? Everyone had heard of Don Francisco, of course, who could help it? They said he was the richest man in Mexico. But his grandson, now, was a bit of a mystery, they said he came and went—that he owned a ranch in California. Where had they met? How had the Brandon girl turned up here so suddenly?

"*Mademoiselle*—how can I resist the pleading look in your eyes? Even a happily married man like myself cannot help being turned as weak as water! Still—"

Ginny said hastily, "I realize you must do your duty, Colonel. But please, try to understand! It's far too painful for me to talk about yet. I've been so ashamed, so unhappy! And then, Don Francisco has been so kind to me! I don't want to spoil this whole evening by being forced to remember the unpleasant past. Please, can't we talk later?"

Trapped! He could not tell whether she had done it purposefully or not, but Colonel Devereaux found himself trapped by a pair of sea green eyes, gazing so tragically into his. To persist with his questioning would make him a cad or a boor—or both! Gracefully, he resigned himself to the inevitable—for the moment at least. But he could make inquiries. There were too many puzzling things here, they did not fit together well.

"Very well, *mademoiselle*! How can I spoil your evening? But later—you promise you will talk to me? It's important—we want to see this man brought to justice, you see; and we cannot let the *Juaristas* get away with anything, they must find out that they cannot win, they cannot continue this stupid resistance!"

"I don't know anything about politics, especially not in this country, Colonel Devereaux! But certainly, I'll be glad to talk with you later—I suppose I have to face what happened some time!"

"Quite so, but come, do give me a smile, Miss Brandon—your fiancé will think I've bored you to tears!" Colonel Devereaux himself gave Ginny a benign, rather beguiling smile, and she began to understand how he had managed to obtain such a young bride for himself—the man had undeniable charm, when he wasn't trying to worm answers out of a person!

She gave him the smile he had asked for, and the Colonel's hazel eyes began to twinkle.

"That's better, much better! Tell me, Miss Brandon, what does your father think about your impending marriage? I'm sure he's pleased, as well as relieved. Such an excellent match, after all—the Alvarados are *gachupínes*, you know—of pure Spanish descent—although your fiancé speaks excellent English, of course! I suppose the Senator will be here for the wedding? I am looking forward to meeting with him again. If only all your American Senators were as sympathetic to our cause here we'd have no difficulty crushing this pointless revolution, you know!"

Again, Ginny felt herself grow cold with apprehension. What a clever, insidiously cunning man this was! She must never forget that . . . she did not stop to wonder why she was actually protecting Steve, for that was what she was doing—her evasions were instinctual, she somehow resented the way the colonel kept setting traps for her. How much did he know? What, exactly, did he suspect?

She murmured something noncommittal about having written to her father—"I'm not certain if he'll arrive here in time, though, I've been told the mails are very slow. In any case, I'll be going back to the United States soon—I find myself growing quite homesick!"

"Oh? But that's understandable of course. I'm sure your fiancé understands. But if I can be of any help—perhaps in telegraphing your father, you must let me know! Write out your message, *mademoiselle*, and I'll pull a few strings for you—it's unthinkable that your father shouldn't be here to give his only child away!"

Ginny was beginning to believe that this man was something of a Machiavelli. Under his gentle, urbane exterior he was actually suspicious of her story, and was determined to trip her up in some way! The thought annoyed her, and enabled her to flash him her most brilliant smile.

"But how clever of you to think of it, Colonel Devereaux, and how thoughtful! Why didn't I think of telegraphing Papa! I don't have a pen and paper here, of course, but I'm sure I'll be able to borrow some at the house, after I've eaten—you see, I was so excited about the fiesta I couldn't eat a bite all day, and now I'm absolutely starved! Isn't that a terrible confession to make?"

She slanted her eyes at him and saw that he was slightly disconcerted, for a change.

"Forgive me, *mademoiselle*! I've been thoughtless. But if you would only tell me . . ."

A hand clapped the Frenchman on the shoulder and Ginny found herself looking up into the laughing eyes and dazzlingly white smile of Diego Sandoval.

"Excuse me, Colonel! But I claim the privilege! Dona Genia, I've been looking everywhere for you, how could you have forgotten that you promised me this dance? I am desolated!"

Deftly, before the colonel could protest he had swept Ginny into his arms, with a murmured apology to the older man.

Taken by surprise, Ginny could say nothing, but she was uncomfortably aware that Colonel Devereaux was looking after them thoughtfully. She was certain that he would make an opportunity to talk to her again—to question her. And what would she tell him?

"Please don't look so worried! Devereaux is an infernally cunning man, but Esteban was sure you'd fend him off admirably. Did I rescue you in the nick of time? Please say so, it's always been my ambition to fly to the rescue of a very beautiful woman. Esteban doesn't deserve such luck!"

Diego Sandoval, who had six sisters, had adopted a lightly teasing, almost cajoling tone which Ginny found impossible to resist. Despite herself she began smiling and saw his appealing, boyish grin flash at her again.

"Good! I have made you smile, and that's a beginning at least. Tell me, Dona Genia, would you trust me? Please do say "yes," for I have a favor to ask of you."

He continued to smile at her, but his tone had grown more serious, and Ginny herself gathered a trifle more closely in his arms as they danced, so that he was speaking with his head bent down to hers.

"If you will follow me—I will dance you to the edge of this platform, there to the left of the musician's stand—and we'll slip away into the shadows when no one is watching us. It's really a shame that you haven't yet seen my father's famous ornamental gardens; if anyone asks you can say I've been showing them to you—with Esteban's permission, of course!"

For a moment, Ginny thought she must be dreaming. What was he saying to her? What did he mean?

She threw her head back in order to look up at him, her emerald eyes flashing dangerously.

"Really, Don Diego! I'm sure I mistake your meaning! Why are you asking me to trust you? And where am I supposed to go with you? I can't believe . . ."

"Please, Genia!" In his urgency he dropped the formality with which he had previously addressed her, and his hand tightened over hers. "Esteban told me you would argue, but I'd hoped my powers of persuasion would be sufficient! I'm taking you to meet him—I think he's had sufficient time in which to escape from the watchdogs who have been dogging him so closely. But there's a man out here, an American, who has scarcely taken his eyes off you since you began dancing with the good colonel. Wouldn't you like me to rescue you from *him*?"

Ginny could not help giving a small gasp of apprehension, although she retained enough self-control not to turn her head in order to look for the man. She knew who it was, of course, but while she had been busy stalling her previous partner, she'd completely forgotten about Beal!

"Very well then," she said between clenched teeth, feeling annoyance at Steve's high-handed ways boil up in her again, "I'll come with you. But I must say I'm surprised at your choice of friends! Does Steve imagine he's playing some kind of silly children's game of hide and seek? First poor Jaime and Enrico, and now this dangerous man Beal—not to mention Colonel Devereaux, whom you yourself admitted is infernally clever! Will you please tell me what on earth you are all up to?"

"Oh, Genia!" Diego's voice was exaggeratedly reproachful, but his eyes had begun to sparkle with mischief again. "Here I was rejoicing at the chance of dancing with you, of being allowed to sneak away romantically with the most beautiful woman here—and you scold me just like one of my sisters. I am crushed!"

"I'm beginning to think that all of Steve's friends are as bad as he is!" Ginny snapped. Diego made such a woeful face at that that she could not help laughing at him and he brightened immediately.

She resigned herself, merely closing her eyes when he began to twirl her around energetically, all the while carefully threading his way through the crowd of dancers until they were close to the edge of the platform.

"Now!" Diego whispered to her urgently, grabbing her hand. Holding her voluminous skirts up as best she could, Ginny let him drag her along with him.

She felt completely lost and rather nervous in the darkness of the garden, which seemed twice as dark once they had left the lights behind them and were in the shadows of some enormous trees. The moonlight, far above, only filtered through the leaves sufficiently to provide a sinister, streaky kind of luminiscence to the path they were following. Ginny gave a cry of dismay when her skirts caught on a branch and she had to pull them free, but Diego seemed quite unconcerned as he begged her to try and keep up with him. "Why is he in such a hurry?" she thought mutinously, and with a slight pang of apprehension wondered again where he was taking her. Was she being abducted again? Had Steve enlisted the aid of his friends to get rid of her?

Soon, she had no more opportunity to think. They had left the path and were threading their way through what appeared to be a dense shrubbery. Panting with exertion, Ginny found herself wishing that Diego would stop and let her rest—she couldn't run any farther.

Suddenly they came out into a small clearing—the dark outline of a small building loomed up before them. Still without the slightest pause or hesitation Diego gripped her hand more firmly when she would have hung back, and led her straight inside.

There was an indefinable scent of mustiness in here that terrified her, for no reason—and overlaying it, the faintest smell of incense. No lights showed anywhere, but almost as soon as Diego closed the heavy door behind them she felt an arm go around her waist. Only the sound of Steve's voice prevented her from screaming.

"No shrieks of fear, please, my love. By now I'm sure they're all looking for us."

She almost fell against him, her relief mixed with growing anger.

Diego was saying, in a hurried whisper, that he would be back soon, "with the others." "I'll prove my tactfulness and give you two a few minutes together," he said with an undercurrent of laughter in his voice that made Ginny burn with an unexplained fury.

She heard the door open and close again, and then Steve was pulling her down despite her involuntary struggles—she found herself sitting on an exceptionally hard wooden bench with a high backrest, his arm still clamped around her waist despite her resistance.

"Ginny—for God's sake! I've never known any female to blow hot and cold as inexplicably as you do. What did you think I planned to do with you? Rape you?"

"Steve Morgan, there's nothing, *nothing* I would put past you!" she declared in a voice shaking with anger. "What did you mean by having your friend bring me here? What kind of dirty work are you planning now?"

"Keep your voice down, vixen! And stop struggling—I only want to talk to you in private. I asked you earlier if we could declare a truce, remember?"

"Yes, I remember! But . . ."

"Ginny!" A suddenly harsh note in his voice stopped her in mid-sentence and she fell silent, biting her lip rebelliously. "If I had time I'd play the ardent lover again, and kiss you into silence, or cajole you into some semblance of reasonableness. But I don't have time—do you understand? You had better listen to me before they come back, I have a lot of explaining to do."

"You're right! You certainly do have a lot of explaining to do, Steve Morgan! Do you realize the position you're in? That Colonel Devereaux, for instance—all he wanted to do was ask me questions, I'm sure he knows *everything*, I had the feeling he was playing with me! And that other man . . ."

"Can it be you're concerned for my safety, sweetheart? I must say, the sudden concern you show touches me. At any other time, perhaps I . . ." he broke off suddenly and she felt him take her hands in both of his. "I'm sorry, Ginny. When I asked Diego to bring you here I was full of good resolutions. Somehow, you have a way of making

me forget them all. Will you please listen to what I have
to say before you burst into further recriminations?"

His sudden change in manner took her completely by
surprise and kept her silent. A sudden shaft of moonlight
came palely through a dusty window, as if the moon had
come out from behind a cloud, and Ginny started, her
eyes widening with shock.

"We're in the family chapel. It seemed a suitably
private place, and I don't think they'll think of looking here
just yet. What's the matter, does the thought of being here
upset you?"

"It's silly of course," Ginny murmured, "but it almost
seems sacrilegious." She turned her head, searching the
darkness for some expression on his face. "Steve—what
are you doing here? What has happened?"

"As you must have noticed already, my love, I seem to
have walked into a hornet's nest!" His voice was abrupt,
off-hand, but the pressure of his fingers tightened on hers.
"Beal knows I'm here—Devereaux knows who I am—and
my watchdogs keep trailing me to see I don't put on a gun
or try to run away! So you see, it's all liable to burst
about my ears very shortly." Almost unconsciously, his
voice had taken on a slightly bitter note that stirred her
strangely. She was not used to hearing an admission of
defeat from this man—not even that time when he had
been surrounded by French troops, and she had held his
life in her hands. Why didn't he escape now? She almost
began to say so.

"But you've eluded them already. You can . . ."

"Yes, I can run away. But you see, I gave my grandfather my word that I would not attempt to escape until
I'd fulfilled my obligations, at least—and I've had time
enough to realize that he's right. If you'll agree, Ginny, we
can be married tonight. Diego's gone off to fetch Renaldo
and the priest; they should return shortly."

Again, Ginny was seized by the feeling that she was
dreaming. She felt incapable of speech, as if he'd dealt her
a sudden, stunning blow. With a jerk she pulled her hands
from his grasp, and would have jumped to her feet and
run from him if he hadn't seized her arm and pulled her
down beside him again with an impatient exclamation.

"Will you stop jumping to conclusions so fast! Hold still,
you little wildcat, and let me finish!"

"I don't want to hear more!" she gasped, almost sobbing

with angry humiliation. "I've changed my mind—nothing on earth would make me marry you now! You're free to go, Steve Morgan—go on, run away! I'm no longer an obligation you have to take care of!"

"Ginny, shut up! You sounded so fierce and so practical this afternoon, what's the matter with you now?" His voice hardened and he gripped her wrists. "Stop acting so hysterical, as if I'd offered you the worst possible insult—I'm only thinking of your future, damn it!" Still holding her wrists, he pulled her closer. The mask of civility, of controlled patience had dropped away, and she had the impression that he was himself again—savage, ruthless, determined to take what he wanted. "Be silent now, and listen. I've no intention of running away—at least, not until I'm sure how much they know—Beal, and your friend Colonel Devereaux. But in case—just in case something happens, by marrying you, I can be sure you'll be taken care of. Maybe I don't have much of a conscience, and no sense of honor, but you didn't deserve what I did to you. In fact, my love, it was too bad for us both that we ever set eyes on each other, I'm sure you'll agree! But that's beside the point—you had better stop acting like a spoiled child and accept things the way they are—just as you accepted matters when you and my grandfather first hatched this plot between yourselves. Pull yourself together. God-dammit—what are you crying about?"

The note of exasperated disgust in his voice forced her head up defiantly.

"I'm crying with—with *rage!* What do you think? I'm sure no other woman can boast of such a—a vastly romantic proposal! You're suddenly very anxious to marry me, just so that you can make me a widow!"

"Well, once you've gotten used to the prospect, I'm sure you'll find it quite alluring!" he said drily. "However, I should warn you that I don't intend to commit suicide either. I've been in worse scrapes than this, but then . . ."

"But you didn't have a wife to worry about, did you?" Ginny put as much scorn as she could muster into her voice. "Well, you needn't worry about me—even if I must marry you to hold my head up in society, I certainly don't intend to concern myself about you—you can be very sure of that! What a choice you offer me—either I'm to be the widow of a criminal, or the wife of a hunted outlaw! But don't expect me to bury myself away to hide my shame," she continued furiously, "I mean every word I told you earlier—I shall go back to France, and I shall . . ."

The chapel door opened silently and she gasped, but Steve was already drawing her to her feet.

"Since you've agreed to marry me, sweet, let's get it over with first, shall we? No doubt, after it's over, we shall be rid of each other—in one way or another! Come on—lets not keep Padre Benito waiting."

Chapter Thirty-two

They were married—the brief ceremony, conducted in hushed tones was over at last. When Steve bent over her his lips merely grazed Ginny's in a cold and dutiful kiss—she felt as cold as ice, as if she were still in a trance.

How unreal it had all been, after all; she could hardly believe, so soon after, that it had happened at all! She was married, surrounded by strangers—even the man who had given her away, a seemingly colorless American friend of Diego's, was a complete stranger. Ginny had found herself wondering vaguely whether he could possibly be mixed up with the Juarists too—even Father Benito was a revolutionary. An emaciated, stooped old man in a shabby cassock, he had been hiding out in Renaldo's house for over a month because he had once led a small village in revolt against the Mexican Irregulars.

Against the light of the two flickering candles on the altar Father Benito's thin, stooped figure had appeared mysterious and in some way frightening. In contrast with his appearance, his voice, though low, was sonorous—his Latin pure and unaccented. Ginny remembered afterwards that at some points in the ceremony Steve's hand had held hers—how warm his fingers had been, how cold the feel

of the ring he had slipped over her finger. She had not
even asked him from where he had obtained it; certainly it
was too small to be his . . .

In any case, she was married. She bore a name that was
no longer her own but belonged to a man she still disliked
and mistrusted. It was almost with relief that she lifted her
face to accept the kisses of the other men. Diego, as irrepressible as ever, kissed her the longest, announcing that
it was his privilege as the one who had rescued her.
Renaldo's kiss was somehow searching, almost sad. Afterwards he gripped her hands tightly and told her he would
always be her friend—she could turn to him for anything,
at any time.

When Renaldo had disappeared into the darkness with
the priest, Ginny felt somehow forlorn. She followed him
with her eyes, feeling that he was her only real friend in
all the world, until Steve slipped an arm round her waist.

"I'm beginning to think you are in love with Renaldo!"
he whispered to her a trifle sarcastically. "Just think, you
might have married him instead. As it is," he added, his
tone still mocking, "you'll have to settle for pot luck, I'm
afraid. But don't look so tragic my sweet—I'm not going
to make any more impossible demands of you. I'm sure
you'll prefer being a wife to being my mistress."

They began to walk back towards the house, with Diego
and his American friend talking in low voices behind
them. For once, Ginny did not feel inclined to embark on
another battle of words with Steve—she felt so strange, so
empty inside! She no longer even cared what would
happen when they got back to the others, or what Steve
planned to do.

In the moonlight, Steve's face looked as if it was carved
out of granite. His features wore the cold, implacable look
that she had learned to recognize so well, but for once it
did not frighten her. She wondered only how he was going
to explain all this to Don Francisco—and how she could
explain her willingness to go along with such a sudden, unplanned marriage. Why had she done it? Why had she let
herself be manipulated? The thought suddenly struck her
that as Steve's wife, she could no longer give evidence
against him. No doubt, that was why he had rushed things.
How disappointing for poor Colonel Devereaux! And now
she need not even telegraph her father, unless it was to
announce that she was married.

"You're very silent." The words sounded harsh and grating, as if they had been forced out of him. Indeed, the sight of Ginny's white, strained face in the ghostly light had given him a hateful, unfamiliar pang.

Really! One would think that she'd forgotten all her firm resolutions to marry him in order to punish him and make his life miserable. One would think it was the other way around, and that she was the one who was being tormented. He remembered that even when he'd attempted to make her lose her temper again, soon after the wedding, she'd refused to say a word. Now she looked like a tragedy queen! What was the matter with her?

Now she looked up and said, in a calm, oddly-withdrawn voice, "What is there to talk about? In any case, I've nothing to say."

He had the angry, crazy impulse to stop dead in the middle of the path and shake her—to bruise her shoulders and send her hair spilling loose, flying around her face—to shatter her calm and hear her cry out with rage. How dare she act this way? After all, he was the one who had been forced into this peculiar arrangement in the beginning, and now she was playing the martyr. What an unreasonable, impossible woman she was!

It was only the memory of Bishop's unemotional voice, murmuring that he might need to take an enforced vacation—that women had a way of clouding a man's judgment, occupying his mind when he most needed to think clearly, that prevented him from snatching her into his arms—wiping that cold and tragic expression from her face.

Controlling himself with difficulty, Steve dropped his arm from around Ginny's waist and began to stride on ahead of her, his face dark with anger.

"If you have any regrets now, you'd best try to hide them," he said, speaking over his shoulder. "It's too late for qualms now, my pet, and you had better get used to the idea before we come face to face with my grandfather. I have the feeling he's probably in one of his worse moods right now."

Feeling suddenly deserted Ginny had almost to run a few steps forward to catch up with his long, pantherlike strides. She clutched at his arm, slowing him down.

"What on earth is the matter with you?" she demanded, panting, "What got into you suddenly? One moment you're asking questions as if you were really concerned about my silence, and the next you become sarcastic and—and horrible! Don't you want my protection when you face Don Francisco?' she went on, enraged by the look he gave her, just as if she was suddenly beneath contempt; "After all, he seems to be the only person you're afraid of! And now, of course, you've made certain that I won't be able to say anything about you—so you're safe from Devereaux, at least. That ought to please you!"

She was amazed when he gave a sudden shout of laughter.

"So you're back to normal again, aren't you? It didn't take you long!"

He caught her hand and swung it between them playfully, and she saw that the closed look had left his face, he was smiling down at her teasingly. Her surprise at the sudden change in his mood was too great for her to find an adequately cutting reply yet, and he forestalled it by remarking that he did indeed need to be protected from his grandfather's wrath.

"But of course I'll put all the blame on you—I shall tell him that you didn't want any of the fuss connected with a big wedding—that you couldn't wait to crawl into bed with me with the full blessing of the church—"

Ginny's cheeks flushed scarlet when she heard a smothered laugh behind her, which Diego promptly turned into a cough.

"Steve Morgan," she began in a furious whisper, "you are . . ." she broke off suddenly as they emerged from the shelter of the trees into a lighted area at the side of the sprawling house. Here too there was a wide, shaded verandah, with shallow steps leading down to a smaller, more private patio. There were chairs and a few tables scattered around here too, and in the shade of one of the big oak trees three mariachi players provided the music for a girl with swirling red skirts and an ivory comb in her hair. The small circle of men and women who surrounded her clapped their hands rhythmically in counterpoint to the incessant clicking of her castanets. She was beautiful, the red rose she wore over one ear emphasizing her jet black hair, and she danced with graceful, unstudied concentration. A man suddenly leaped into the circle to join her, his short black jacket open to reveal a dazzlingly white shirt—the silver ornamentation lining sleeves and lapels catching the flickering torchlight.

Ginny's breath caught in her throat and she forgot what she had been going to say. Something about the primitive, earthy quality of this dance captured her whole attention. Here was passion without words, the age-old man-woman relationship; the barnyard sex and the romantic flirtation; retold in dance form.

"Her name is Concepción—she's a gypsy. Dancing comes naturally to them—those are her brothers who play the guitar—it's probably her lover who dances with her. The fierce-looking man over there, with the large mustachios is her father—he's their leader. It's said they're *Comancheros*."

Diego and his friend had come up behind them, and his usually expressive voice sounded almost dreamy as he explained softly to Ginny. She had the feeling, without even turning, that his eyes were fixed hypnotically on the gypsy girl.

Since they were here, it would not be good manners to leave now—they must at least wait until the dance was over, Diego went on. With Steve fallen silent for a change, but still holding Ginny's hand, they edged up to the outskirts of the circle of fascinated, admiring *aficionados* and stood watching.

After a while, Ginny felt Steve's arm go around her shoulders, but he did it absent-mindedly. When she glanced at him, he was gazing fixedly at the dancers, with a strange half-smile tugging at the corner of his mouth.

Oh, to be able to dance like that! The woman portrayed all women—alternately she teased and taunted, displayed passion and coldness; came so close to her partner that her breasts brushed his shirtfront, and then turned her back on him. She played with him, alternately leading him on and repulsing him. Sometimes she smiled, her teeth sparkling like pearls, and sometimes she assumed a haughty, touch-me-not air.

The dance leaped to a climax with a crescendo of chords, the guitars thrumming dissonantly. The woman leaned towards her lover, face upturned, her arms like white stalks twining around his neck. But only for an instant—in the next she had whirled away, repudiating him. He stepped backwards, melting into the circle of watchers and the girl danced alone again, her smile this time for every other man in the audience. The music became slower, more plaintive; she seemed to offer herself to every man there. The castanets were silent now and her body moved like a willow in the wind, this way and that. Her hands went up to her hair, held up in a shining mass by the comb, and suddenly it tumbled down her back, long and straight and gleaming—then whipped around her face as her head moved back and forth. She held the rose between her teeth, and as the dance ended abruptly, she plucked it out and threw it, straight and violently, at Steve's face.

This is ridiculous, Ginny was thinking a few minutes later. How many women are there in his past? And how many more will there be in the future? her treacherous mind answered her. She didn't know what to think, whether she was more amazed or angry.

After the gypsy girl had flung the rose she'd followed it herself, her stride as purposeful as any man's, her hair swinging about her shoulders like a mane. There was a sudden silence and the crowd parted for her—for a moment Ginny had actually wondered if this crazy female was going to do something violent, and she had instinctively shrunk backwards. She had felt Steve's arm drop from around her shoulders—somehow, he had caught the rose, and he was actually grinning. How well she knew that teasing, mocking note in his voice—she was inexplicably resentful that this time it was there for someone else.

"You dance as well as ever, Concepción. And you're still a beauty. But where's your husband?"

The girl's eyes slitted like an angry cat's, and she looked ready to claw as she stood before Steve with her bare feet.

"Hah! And you, my fine *caballero*! Since when have you let a little thing like a husband stop you from visiting old friends? Husband!" She put a wealth of contempt into the words, "you know very well I only marry him because I am so mad at you—you . . ." the girl broke into a string of obvious epithets in dialect that made Ginny's ears burn, and caused Diego to burst out laughing. But surprisingly enough, even as she continued to berate him Concepción flung herself against Steve, her arms going upward, hands pulling his head greedily down to meet her mouth. And he kissed her back, very thoroughly too.

Seething with a fury she was barely able to contain, Ginny found her hands clenching into fists at her sides, she must have made some motion, or emitted some sound that warned Diego, for suddenly he was holding her by the elbow, whispering to her that she must understand that Esteban had known Concepción since childhood . . . they were merely old friends . . .

"Oh, yes," she insisted, "I can see what kind of friends they are—he has been kissing her for over two minutes now, what kind of a stupid ninny do you take me for?" She turned on the hapless Diego with her green eyes slashing him like daggers. "And you, *señor*—will you kindly stop defending that despicable man you call your friend? Let him defend himself for a change! Look at him, far from being embarrassed he's enjoying it. Ooh!" She stopped to draw breath, and happened to notice the small, silent knot of men who were converging on Steve and the girl like a band of avenging angels. One of them, she saw with satisfaction, was the girl's father—he of the large mustachios.

"Your friend is uh—rather irresponsible, is he not?" the quiet American murmured behind them. Ginny, in spite of her rage, was glad to note that his thin face looked disapproving. "Do they mean trouble?"

Diego had his hands full, holding firmly onto Ginny's arm and trying to soothe her injured feelings at the same time.

He mumbled something that she couldn't catch, his quick wits seeming to desert him for a moment.

"Oh—I'd like to see him defend himself from them!" Ginny muttered triumphantly. "They look villainous enough to take on an army alone!"

Her triumph was short-lived, lasting only long enough for the oldest of the men to bellow threateningly, "Concepción!"

Sullenly, his daughter disengaged herself from Steve's arms, and Ginny could not prevent herself from putting a hand up before her mouth to stifle a cry as the men moved forward menacingly. What was the matter with Steve? Didn't he have any senses left, or had that girl befuddled them completely? Why wasn't he making an attempt to save himself?

No, instead he was smiling as he extended his arms.

"Sanchez, my old friend! I didn't expect to see you here."

"So I could see!" the man growled dangerously. And

then suddenly his face broke out in a wide smile as he laughed uproariously.

"You young rascal! Still up to your old tricks, eh? Come here and greet an old friend properly—I'll disown you if you've adopted too many *Americano* ways!"

Disbelievingly, Ginny watched the two men exchange *abrazos*—and then the others had crowded round, Concepción's guitar-playing brothers grinning from ear to ear as they in turn embraced Steve in bear hugs. Only the man who had been dancing with Concepción hung back rather sullenly, and then he too forced a smile and came forward.

As if he'd only just remembered her presence, Steve reached out suddenly, pulling Ginny into the group.

"I'm forgetting my manners. This is Ginny, my wife."

How easily he said it, still smiling—just as if they'd been married for years and the marriage was already boring. And only a few minutes ago he had kissed the gypsy girl back with every evidence of enthusiasm, just as if he'd still been single; as if they, she and he, had not been married within the last hour! Well, even if that was his intention he would not succeed in humiliating her, as he'd find out!

A smile curving her lips, Ginny accepted their somewhat boisterous congratulations. Sanchez kissed her heartily on both cheeks, his mustachios tickling her. She had not missed the widening of Concepción's eyes, the look of shock on the girl's face that was almost immediately wiped away by a wide, slightly mocking smile.

"So wicked one, it's happened to you too, has it? I would not have expected it—but you're lucky, she is beautiful." For an instant the girl's cheek, warm, and slightly damp from the exertion of her dancing was pressed against Ginny's. "Don't mind the kiss," Concepción whispered, "we have known each other since we were children, Esteban and I." Her apparent composure was marred only by a wicked glint in her eye as she shot a glance at Steve.

There were questions on every side. When had they been married? How long? But surely the invitations had said a week from now? When Steve admitted laughingly that they had actually been married this very evening, Sanchez gave a great shout.

"So—then we have a wedding celebration, before you rejoin your fine friends inside, *sí*?"

Diego Sandoval gave a shrug and announced that he would see to it that there were drinks sent out here. He looked ardently at the lovely Concepción and begged her to save a dance for him. Laughing, she agreed. She seemed completely in command of herself now, only giving a smile and a slight shrug when Tomas, the man who had been dancing with her, kissed Ginny full on the lips by way of congratulation.

Ginny herself was at first taken by surprise, and then determined to let Steve see that she too could play at any game he could. The man kissed her fiercely and somehow despairingly—for the short moment that he held her in his arms she could feel the heat of his body and its slight trembling which he tried to hide by the unexpected fervor of his kiss. So we are both taking our revenge, Ginny thought. She hated Steve all over again—hated his easy assurance, the way he was smiling at Concepción, bending his head to whisper something to her even while his wife was being kissed by another man only a few feet away!

"You bastard!" Concepción was saying, her voice low, her eyes spitting fury. "Why did you do it? You're not the marrying kind, any more than I am. What's the matter with you?"

His raised eyebrow infuriated her, as he had known it would.

"*Chica*, bitchiness doesn't suit you. And don't pretend you're jealous, you married first, remember?"

"Pah!" Concepción stamped her foot, skirts flying. She was the type who didn't care who saw her, or what she did. "You know as well as I do that I married that pig to make you mad—I got rid of him a long time ago—now I do just as I please. But *you*—"

"Don't swear at me again. Such bad language, coming from such a lovely mouth—why it is that women always resort to swearing when they don't have anything reasonable or logical to say? As for my wife . . ." Steve frowned almost imperceptibly when he saw that Ginny was being kissed by another man, a perfect stranger who had obviously seized the opportunity to kiss a pretty woman. So she was determined to get her own back, it seemed. With what abandon she threw herself into the kiss, her eyes

closed, head back . . . he had the sudden and quit inexplicable urge to tear her away from the man and slap her
face, hard.

"Are you jealous already, reasonable one?" Concepción's
biting tone did nothing to relieve his flare of temper. But
Steve managed to smile at her amusedly.

"As I was saying, about my wife," he continued
smoothly, "it's a marriage of convenience for us both. My
grandfather's idea, really, but it's going to have certain ad-
vantages—the main one being that I can't be trapped into
marriage again!"

"Go and dance with her!" Concepción said abruptly,
starting to move away from him. "After that is over, you
can ask me to dance, and we'll talk—I'd rather sink my
claws into your flesh, you dog, but maybe I'll save that for
another time!"

The music had started up again, and just as Jaime
Perez, his face glowering, walked down the steps from the
house, Steve grabbed Ginny's hands and pulled her into
the circle that had been cleared for dancing.

The music was wild and pulsing, and after a while, as
other couples joined them, she found that she did not have
too much difficulty in following the steps. Perhaps her
anger helped her throw herself into the primitive rhythm,
the abandonment of the body to the music. Perhaps it was
the wine that was being passed around, even to the
dancers. In any case, Ginny found it easier to lose herself
in the dancing than to talk.

"You should have been a gypsy yourself," Steve murmured to her when the dance brought them together. She
smiled at him a trifle dreamily, but there was a wicked,
almost dangerous look in her narrowed green eyes. He
reflected rather grimly that this promised to turn out to be
quite an evening.

'I'll show him—yes, I'll show him!' Ginny kept thinking.
Her body seemed to move by itself, her feet kept time to
the wild, fast beat of the music, the deeply thrumming
guitars. She had not eaten, and the wine they kept passing
to her had gone to her head, she knew it and she didn't
care. She danced with a glass of wine in her hand, drained
it and flung it over her shoulder, like the others were doing. 'I'll show him that I can do anything he does—I can
turn men's heads as easily as that woman can. She's
nothing more than an obvious flirt, of course, but men

seem to lap that kind of thing up. I'm his wife now—no one feels anything more than pity for a betrayed woman, but a man who's deceived by his wife is laughed at—we'll see how he likes that!'

There were more and more people out here dancing now—perhaps the sensuous throbbing of the guitars, the cries and the clapping of dancers and bystanders alike drew more guests away from the more sedate melodies of the waltz. Ginny's feet had found the rhythm of the *corrido* and wouldn't lose it. She saw Concepción's look of surprise as she danced past.

Ginny was dancing with Tomas. She had watched Concepción without the girl being aware of it, and now she moved her arms too, curling them upward, over her head, her body swaying teasingly, green eyes half-closed.

"*Dios mio!* You dance like an angel!" Tomas muttered. His eyes had grown hotter, and darker, they moved slowly over her body and she laughed softly.

"I don't dance as well as Concepción, of course," she murmured.

"You were born to dance—are you sure you don't have gypsy blood? *Caramba*, why is it you are married already?"

He had forgotten that she was a lady, one of the guests, while he was merely one of the entertainers. With her full, sensually smiling lips and the artlessly sexual movements of her body she had made him forget everything but the fact that she was a woman and he was a man. She was not like Concepción, whose tongue cut like a knife, taking a man's manhood away from him, playing with him. . . .

She danced in the very center of the crowd, and her hair and eyes would have made her stand out by themselves, if the attention of every man in the crowd, dancers and watchers alike, had not been drawn irresistibly by something else. Her body, the gleaming whiteness of her shoulders as they moved sinuously, her unconscious but complete abandonment to the dance; and above all the look on her face—eyes half closed, lips smiling, it was the face of a woman being possessed by a man—dreaming, languorous, at one moment, and then teasing, daring. There was not a man here who didn't want her—who didn't crave her body, naked and writhing, beneath his.

"You didn't marry a lady!" Concepción snapped. She

was dancing with Steve, but even she had not been able to keep her eyes off Ginny. "She—why she's as much of a bitch as I am!" Her voice held a note of grudging admiration. "Are you going to put up with the way she's behaving?"

Sanchez himself had shouldered Tomas aside and was whirling Ginny around, making her skirts fly. They were both laughing.

"Even my own father—the old goat, look at him! You ought to stop it, drag her away. What are all your fine friends going to think?"

"That I married quite a woman. And you're right, *chica*, she is as much of a bitch as you are—I don't think she's forgiven us for that kiss."

"So she's trying to make you jealous? What a switch!" Concepción laughed angrily.

"Oh—Ginny's full of tricks," he responded a trifle drily. "Most of them nasty. At the moment, we are in a state of war."

"Then you must fight back, no?"

"Perhaps! But I've the feeling that right now I'm outnumbered." His glance went meaningly to the glowering Jaime Perez who stood watching. Just behind him, the Señora Ortega and Dona Armijo had just emerged from the house and their faces were scandalized.

Following Steve's glance, Concepción's eyes widened.

"I think I understand. There is more trouble with your *abielo*, eh? Well—if you need an ally, there is always me to turn to—" she moved close to him, fingers snapping, face teasing. "Perhaps you will need consolation, sometime, if your red-headed tigress of a wife is too much for you to handle!"

"Bitch!" he commented softly, but his eyes were amused, and the word sounded like a caress. They were really much alike, he and Concepción—they understood each other.

Concepción smiled.

"You had better rescue her soon, I think," she said softly. "She's dancing with Tomas again, and he is a very passionate man, I know! I think she is only playing a game, playing at being like me, but she can't handle a man—for if she could, *hombre*, you would not be looking at me in that way!"

Señora Armijo was clasping her hands tightly together

to stop herself from wringing them. Her voice was a soft moan.

"Oh—if I had not seen this with my own eyes I would not have—what on earth has gotten into Genia? Such a quiet young woman, so much of a lady—and look, look at the way she is dancing! With those common *vaqueros*—and the way they are looking at her—"

Dona Maria's face was red with annoyance, but she had crossed her hands over her plump bosom in a dignified manner, her eyes snapping.

"There's no use wringing your hands and whining now. We cannot very well march down there and drag her away! And besides," she added unexpectedly, "I think she is only trying to make Esteban jealous. I've noticed, if you haven't, the way he's been dancing with that *Comanchero* wench—isn't that the same one he used to run away to visit when he was still a boy?"

The thin *duenna* remained distracted.

"He's gone over to her now—if only he'd bring her away, it's really too bad of him to allow this to happen! And I tremble when I think of what Don Francisco will say . . ."

The poor woman almost fainted dead away when she heard Don Francisco's voice behind her. Even his sister jumped, and then exclaimed with annoyance.

"It seems that no one around here bothers to tell Don Francisco anything! I have to rely on my faithful Jaime—and I am, at this moment, extremely annoyed with him as well!"

"Really, Francisco, you might give people some warning of your approach! And you have been in a bad mood all evening—Señora Armijo and I had merely hoped to spare you further annoyance . . ."

"I see!" Don Francisco's voice was dry. "How considerate of you, my dear Maria." He added, almost to himself, his tone hardening, "That young pup! He's incorrigible! He's done everything in his power to anger me this evening, by showing his defiance. First he disappears, right under the foolish noses of my most trusted *vaqueros*, and then he has the impudence to show himself again—here, of all places!"

"Francisco!" Dona Maria sounded alarmed, "surely you wouldn't . . ."

"I don't intend to cause a scandal, you need have no

fears of that, my dear sister. But I have several matters to
discuss with that grandson of mine, whenever he can tear
himself away from these rather primitive festivities!" His
voice was grim, and his look became even more dour
when Señora Armijo gave a startled wail.

"I don't know what's happening to Genia! Look at her
now, she's unpinning her hair—and it took so much time
to arrange this evening!"

She was, indeed, doing just that, under Steve's angry
eyes and to the accompaniment of delighted clapping from
the onlookers. They were dancing face to face, and a mis-
chievous, somehow taunting smile curved Ginny's lips as
she slowly removed the pins from her elaborately curled
hairstyle, tossing them aside carelessly, one by one. She
had the dreamy, concentrated look of a woman undressing
for her lover—only the smile gave her away, and anger
fought with amusement in Steve's face.

"What in hell do you think you're doing? You're making
an exhibition of yourself!" He spoke in an undertone,
through clenched teeth.

"Why darling, you're making noises like a jealous husband! But I'm doing it for you—I thought you preferred
my hair down."

Concepción, with Tomas now, had planted herself next
to Ginny, and she gave a smothered burst of laughter
which was quelled by a glare in her direction from hard
blue eyes.

The last pin fell, and Ginny shook her head as her hair
came loose—a rippling, shining cloud that fell to her
waist; and there was not a man there who did not want to
bury his face in it.

"It's like a pale fire," Tomas whispered, his voice awed,
and under the cover of the shouted "*olés*" that followed,
Concepción brought her bare foot down as hard as she
could over his instep.

"Bastard—*hijo de puta!* You're dancing with me,
remember?"

Laughing, Ginny whirled around. "I feel like kicking my
shoes off too—" she murmured.

"Not yet—you damned little hellcat! That's enough
damage you've done to the hearts and nerves of all the
men here for now. I ought to beat hell out of you!"

Ginny pouted deliberately, her eyes sparkling with spite.

"Oh! Is that all you can think of? You disappoint me, Steve."

The movements of the dance brought her close to him and she moved her body deliberately so that it almost brushed his. Her arms went upward in a slow and sinuous movement as she lifted the mass of her hair away from her neck, and then let it drop again.

"That does it!" His voice was threatening with anger. "If you want to seduce me, madam, I'd prefer you to choose a more private place for it. As it is, you've gone far enough."

Before she could avoid it, he had grabbed her wrist, holding it so tightly and so painfully that she had to bite her lips to hold back a cry of protest.

Leaving her no choice in the matter Steve led her through the crowd of dancers, smiling occasionally to acknowledge comments and compliments thrown at them both. To her he said in a whisper, through his teeth, "You were putting on such a good act a few minutes ago—I wish you'd continue with it for the benefit of all our friends here."

"I don't—" she began hotly, but he cut her short.

"In this part of the world my love, wives are expected to be obedient, above all things. A quality in which you're sadly lacking. In any case, it's high time we mixed with the other guests here."

By this time they were at the foot of the steps, and Ginny met Don Francisco's rather quizzical look with a blush. She did not dare, as yet, look in the direction of her *duenna*, or Tia Maria, either, for that matter.

It was almost with relief that she heard Steve take charge, his voice smooth, veneered with a clever blend of amusement and apology.

"I'm afraid it was all my fault if we've worried you. I persuaded Ginny to slip away from me so that we could be alone in the moonlight for a few moments." He gave a slight bow in the direction of his stupefied looking grandaunt. "Tia Maria, if you and the Señora Armijo would be so good as to escort Ginny upstairs so that she can pin up her hair again, I'll join you in the patio later."

Ginny felt her wrist released with a final, warning squeeze that made her want to strike out at him in rage. But he had already turned to his grandfather, with an engaging smile.

"Sir, I wonder if I may have a word with you in private? Diego has already told me we may use his father's study."

Ginny thought she heard Don Francisco mutter under his breath, a softly explosive sentence that began with "You insolent young pup. . . !" but she was already being hustled away by two outraged ladies, both scolding and questioning her alternately.

Deciding that to remain silent might be wiser, she rubbed at her aching wrist surreptitiously as she went upstairs. A hasty glance over her shoulder as they reached the landing showed her that neither Steve nor his grandfather were anywhere in sight. She could not help wondering, how would Don Francisco take the news?

Chapter Thirty-three

As it turned out, once she had been safely escorted to a room upstairs, Ginny had no longer any time to worry about Don Francisco's reactions. She sat silent and rather sullen while Dona Armijo combed her hair out and tried to find some means of pinning it up once more; all the while shaking her head dolefully or nodding it in agreement with something Señora Ortega said. And the good Señora had much to say on the subject of Ginny's behavior.

Unable to bear it any longer after a while, Ginny protested that it had all been Steve's fault. He had been the one who had encouraged her to escape from the crowds for a time; and afterwards it had been he who had led her to join the gypsy dancers.

"He kissed that gypsy girl right before my eyes, with absolutely no compunctions at all," she murmured, narrowing her eyes in a fashion that made the Dona Armijo think she looked like a gypsy herself. "Why should I not have showed him that I too could be just as popular if I danced in the same abandoned fashion? I'm sorry, Tia, if I fall short of the standards set for Spanish young ladies, but I am not one—I could not bear to allow myself to be

treated in such a casual and offhand fashion! Why all the
men I've met here are flirts—and most of them are married too!"

She stopped to draw breath and the Señora Ortega,
who had been looking quite sour during Ginny's im-
passioned discourse shook her head in dismay.

"My dear Genia! You've seen our lives only as they
appear on the surface, I'm afraid. Do you really believe
that women here have such a bad time of it? Of course
not—they are quite happy with things as they are, I assure
you. They are petted and pampered and spoiled—nothing
is denied them. There is no reason for a young lady, especially one who is formally betrothed, as you are, to feel
she has to—well, putting it bluntly—to compete with some
gypsy wench. Your place, my dear, is up on a pedestal.
Men will take their fun where they find it, it's true, but
even in France you must be aware that this is customary.
No, dear Genia, there are some things you must learn to
accept—even to turn a blind eye to. After all you will be
Esteban's wife, and even if the dear boy has been rather
wild, I'm sure he'll soon settle down and recognize his
responsibilities—my brother will see to it!"

"But Tia, I don't want . . ."

The Señora Ortega merely waved her hand imperiously, curbing Ginny's instinctive outburst. "You've so
much to learn, my child! It's not what you want, but what
you must accept. It's a woman's lot, I'm afraid. But men
can be managed—there's the example of my own dear
daughter-in-law—such a quiet, unassuming little thing she
seems, and she's always turning to Alberto for advice, begging him to make all her decisions for her; and he adores
her! There's nothing he wouldn't do for her, and it always
ends up, somehow, that Sarita gets her way, although Alberto thinks that he has made the decision!"

"But Steve is different! Please, Tia, forgive me for
speaking out—I suppose that's not ladylike either! However I can't see myself pretending all the time to be
something I'm not. I'm a woman, but I'm also an individ-
ual—yes, I have a mind, I can think; I could never, never
act like a stupid little ninny just so that I'd make some
man puff up with self-importance and protectiveness. And
anyhow . . ." Ginny paused and bit her lip irresolutely,
wondering if she had gone too far, "anyhow Steve's not
that kind of man either. He's arrogant and overbearing,

and if I didn't stand up to him he'd walk all over me! In fact, he's even had the audacity to announce to me that the only reason he hasn't become bored with me before now is because I do have a will of my own!"

Dona Armijo, obviously horrified at the turn the conversation had taken now gave the last disapproving pat to Ginny's freshly coifed hair and stood back as the young woman sprang restlessly to her feet, her cheeks burning with a high color that was really quite becoming.

"I must say that I really cannot understand what has got into you tonight, Genia," Tia Maria sniffed. "But I can tell there's no use talking to you when you're in such a highly strung mood. Let's go downstairs again, then, and I can only beg of you to be—a little more *discreet,* my dear. It would not do for people to begin gossiping about you, especially just before the wedding."

It was on the tip of Ginny's tongue to blurt out that there would be no need for a big, formal wedding now. She was already married . . . but the fresh storm that such an announcement would inevitably bring about her shoulders made her bite back the words. Let Steve break the news, and let him cope with all the angry reactions that would no doubt follow.

She clung to the curving stair-rail as they descended slowly, seized with a strange, inexplicable reluctance all of a sudden. You are being quite ridiculous, she scolded herself. What is there to be afraid of? Don Francisco will not be too angry, I'm sure of it . . . and then, when Ginny had almost reached the foot of the stairs she saw Colonel Devereaux waiting for her; an unusually stern look on his face, his light hazel eyes reflecting the light so that they seemed piercing, almost frightening.

For once, Ginny was relieved that the Señora Ortega was with her. She had remembered suddenly, like a lightning flash, Steve's careless words of a few hours ago— "Beal knows I'm here, and Devereaux knows who I am." How could she have forgotten? In spite of the sudden, fearful plunging of her heart, she was filled with an unreasonable anger against him. How could he take it all so lightly? He had married her—his duty done he could have escaped, she knew very well his friends would have helped him. But instead he had deliberately chosen to stay and court danger; he had danced, he had kissed and flirted with his gypsy girlfriend, and then he had gone off quite calmly to speak with his grandfather, having packed her off upstairs. Where was he now?

Ginny found her worst misgivings realized—Colonel Devereaux had been waiting for her; he wished to speak with her, he said in a grave voice, on a matter of the gravest importance.

What followed next was dreamlike—so far removed from reality that Ginny had the greatest difficulty making herself believe it was all really happening. She had felt this way earlier at her wedding; that strange, cold little ceremony that had transformed her within seconds from mistress to wife. Now she wondered rather wildly if that too had been a mirage—something conjured up by her own imagination.

She sat in a comfortable chair in Don José Sandoval's study, her hands folded in her lap, face as pale as a lily, her large green eyes shining with an unusual brilliance. And she would only shake her head and whisper, "I don't know—I don't know," to all the questions that Colonel Devereaux put to her.

Suddenly, the portly French colonel, that dapper, debonair man of the world, seemed to have been transformed into a cold hard man of business—a soldier with an unpleasant duty to perform.

"You must understand, *mademoiselle,* that we are at war! I have my sworn obligations to fulfill, and I cannot let anything—not friendship, nor my own sympathetic feelings, nor even pity, stand in the way. Consider, if you please, the seriousness of your position! By your refusal to speak, you are placing yourself in the position of an accomplice. Are you not aware that as a soldier I am empowered to try summarily and even execute any person suspected of giving help to the rebels?"

Don Francisco had, to Ginny's initial relief, insisted upon being present at this "interview" the colonel had requested. But so far, while the colonel paced up and down, pausing every now and then to fire a question, Don Francisco had said very little. He stood by the mantelpiece as if he wished for the warmth of the fire that burned just beneath, and his craggy face was expressionless as if it were carved out of wood. In spite of her own predicament, Ginny found herself glancing toward him, wondering how he must feel at hearing his grandson accused of being a revolutionary, or even worse, an American spy or paid mercenary. To a man as proud as Don Francisco, this whole interview must not only be humiliating but degrading as well. He had always supported the Liberal movement, had supported the Emperor Maximilian and his government, and now—Ginny wondered how much Don Francisco really knew of Steve's activities. Had Steve finally been honest with his grandfather, and was that why he had been allowed to "escape" so mysteriously? When the French colonel had asked him diffidently if Don Francisco could inform them of his grandson's whereabouts the old Don had drawn himself up stiffly, his mouth thinning under his white mustachios.

"My grandson has always come and gone when and as he pleases, I am afraid. He has never seen fit to confide in me regarding the kind of life he's been leading on the other side of the border."

"I understand sir—please believe that I bring this matter up only with the greatest reluctance. It is by no means my intention to impugn your loyalty to the government, Don Francisco, and I regret very much that I had to be the person to inform you of your grandson's unfortunate connections with the Juaristas."

Don Francisco had made no comment—Ginny had had the impression he was holding himself in check with difficulty; that he was much more upset and angry than he would show on the surface.

Now, as the colonel ended his latest harangue with a veiled threat, Don Francisco interrupted at last, clearing his throat before he spoke, his voice dry and brittle.

"Colonel Devereaux—one moment! I won't have my granddaughter-in-law bullied. Whatever Esteban's shady activities, I'm sure she knows nothing of them. He is hardly the type of man to tell his business to anyone, not even to his wife."

"His *wife*, you say? Really sir, I do not wish to sound stubborn, but I recall receiving an invitation to a wedding—I was introduced to *mademoiselle* as the fiancée of your grandson—how can this be?"

Colonel Devereaux had gone as red as a turkey cock—his eyebrows seemed to bristle with frustration.

"You ask how this can be? Well—in a word, my grandson informed me only recently of his secret marriage to this young lady. Still, knowing how tongues will wag, I insisted on a second, formal ceremony to satisfy everyone.

Do you wish the marriage certificate produced, *Monsieur le Colonel*? Do you still have any doubts?" There was the faintest sarcastic undercurrent to Don Francisco's words which made the colonel clench his hands together behind his back, controlling himself with difficulty.

"That will not be necessary, I'm sure. The word of Don Francisco Alvarado is sufficient, even for a mere French interloper." Was there a note of bitterness here, too? Ginny felt as if she were attending a play—it would have all seemed so harmless, merely a storm in a teacup, if not for the presence of an armed French soldier at the door—a crop-haired Legionnaire who wore a captain's insignia proudly, and stood with his eyes fixed into space, as if he were deaf.

"In that case—" Don Francisco stood straight and tall, a commanding figure still, in spite of whatever inner turmoil he must be hiding. "There is surely no further point in your questioning Ginny? She has already told you that she knows nothing."

Colonel Devereaux seemed to collect himself. He had stopped his pacing, and his eyes suddenly seemed to have taken on a steely glitter that sent a tremor of apprehension through Ginny's body.

"I am afraid, sir, that it is not as easy as that." The colonel turned his head towards Ginny, and a note almost of triumph seemed to have crept into his voice. "Madame's marriage to your grandson makes her a citizen of Mexico. She is subject to our laws, now, and cannot claim immunity as an American. And though I can well understand your feelings on this matter, Don Francisco, I regret that my duty as a French officer must take precedence over my own inclinations. If you please—" he held up a hand as if to stave off any interruptions and continued sternly, "I must and will have more information from madame. You have already heard me speak of an American counterguerrilla who works for us—a man named Thomas Beal. He recognizes the lovely Madame Ginny without any doubt, as the same woman who helped an American gunman named Steve Morgan break a man out of jail—a confessed *Juarista* rebel! And we know now, also, that this same man is none other than your grandson, who calls himself Esteban Alvarado while he is in Mexico. *Voila*—madame has been travelling far and wide with her—husband. Madame helps rebels escape. Am I therefore such a fool that I must believe that madame did not know what she was doing? That here is a woman so blindly obedient to her husband that she risks her life without question, merely because he tells her to? No, no! Excuse me, but I must ask more questions, and this time I will have answers. Madame, you comprehend?"

"You go too far, Colonel! Don Francisco's voice was like thunder. "I had no idea that our *allies*, the French, are in such straits that now they resort to intimidating ladies in the name of our laws. You may arrest me if you think we're concealing any knowledge of my grandson's whereabouts. And you may be sure, sir, that I will be in touch with Marshal Bazaine himself regarding your rather shoddy tactics."

"I am acting on the marshal's instructions. In fact, I am his representative in this province. And if I may remind you, sir, it was the emperor himself who signed certain decrees a few months ago, giving us the authority to question all suspected revolutionaries—to interrogate them to the fullest degree possible, sir; do you understand what that means? And we can execute them too—without trial, if I feel it to be necessary as an example! Believe me, my questions tonight were designed only to spare this lady a great deal of unpleasantness. Do you think we're so nice in our questioning of peasant women?" He turned on Ginny so suddenly that she jumped, staring at him with wide eyes, her chin now tilting stubbornly. "Madame, I beg you to think, to be reasonable, for your own sake. If you keep silent through any mistaken sense of loyalty, let me remind you that you are half-French—France was your home for most of your life, was it not? And do you realize how many Frenchmen are dying each day for the emperor's cause? Do you realize that every gun smuggled across the border to the *Juaristas* is used against us? And it's men like Steve Morgan who are worse than the others—he is a mercenary—a spy, he has not even the excuse of feeling any particular patriotism, has he? And you, madame, must I tell you of the cowardly ambushes these rebels set? Of the tortures and mutilations? Or must I threaten you with arrest and execution before you will speak?"

"Colonel Devereaux." There was a sparkle of rage in Ginny's slanted green eyes, and her voice was coldly defiant. "You are threatening me, and I never have liked threats. And you may execute me, but you'd never get away with it. We have too many acquaintances in common, have we not, Colonel? There's my papa, the Senator—you know yourself how glad Washington would be of an excuse to intervene here. Our Secretary Seward does not like your presence here, does he? And there's my uncle Albert—he has your emperor's ear, as you well know. I'm sorry, but you will not find it as easy to bully or get rid of me as you would some peasant girl."

"Threats, threats! My dear madame, did you really think I'd execute a lady as lovely and as intelligent as you are? Or that I'd torture you, perhaps? Ah, no. You will find, when you know me better, that I am not nearly so crude in my—um, methods. But, madame—" the man's face had taken on its former almost benevolent look and he almost beamed down at her; "What shall I do with you? You are really being very stubborn, you know—I had no idea you were so much in love with your husband. In fact, from the tone of the quite frantic letter I received from your father, you were forcibly abducted—at gunpoint, and following on a dastardly attack upon some of my own men. There was a certain young captain who was badly injured, and in fact almost died, trying to defend you. Have you forgotten already? Is all your love and loyalty for France evaporated completely? Do you consider us all monsters now? Eh?"

His sudden *volte-face* confused Ginny, as the colonel had meant it to do. He shrugged now, casting an almost appealing glance at Don Francisco who stood with a rather amused smile twisting a corner of his mouth.

"Don Francisco—will you not help me make madame see reason? I know she knows more about your grandson's movements than she is prepared to say. I have executed others for less. You must see that I cannot let her get away with this foolish defiance—my career would be ruined in any case if the story got out that I had been made to back down by a slip of a girl; that I did not do my duty. You're a man of honor, sir, you understand how it is, do you not? If your grandson had nothing to fear, would he have run away, leaving his bride? I'm begging you to put your patriotism and your loyalty to the emperor before your own feelings—I know it's hard—"

"Enough, Colonel! You make your point admirably. So

you'd play upon my honor now, would you? What would you have me do—order Ginny to betray her husband?"

"What is this? What am I supposed to do? You know, Colonel Devereaux, that a wife cannot give evidence against her husband . . ." visibly agitated now, Ginny found it impossible to sit still. She stood up quickly, fingers nervously smoothing out the folds of her gown.

"Ah—so you admit that there is some evidence you are withholding? In wartime, Madame, one does not bother about minor technicalities, surely you must realize that!"

How quickly he had pounced upon her words! It was as if he was determined to trip her up, to frighten her and confuse her with the sudden changes of tactics he had shown already.

"I admit nothing! If my husband is what you say he is—he's told me nothing."

"But you've drawn your own conclusions, surely? Come, madame, you've already shown me you possess quickness of wit. Don't disappoint me now! You're a woman of spirit and breeding, a lady—why should you feel any misgivings about telling us what we want to know about a man who not only abducted you and forced you into doing his bidding, but deserted you when he found himself recognized, leaving you to face the consequences? Where's your pride, young lady?"

"I am very much afraid, Ginny, that he is right." Don Francisco's voice sounded heavy and old, suddenly; as if every word he spoke was an effort. Ginny could not hide her surprise, she turned to him with her lips parted, her eyes like green flames, imploring him not to desert her now. But he went on adamantly, leaning his elbow against the mantelpiece as if standing was too much for him. She realized with a pang of pitying understanding how much it was costing him to say what he was saying now, especially in the face of Colonel Devereaux' triumphant expression.

"You must think of yourself now, Ginny, as Esteban has done. He is my grandson, and I love him, but that does not make me blind to his faults—to his wild, irresponsible nature. If he is, indeed, a traitor or a spy, then—" the old man's lips twisted, as if in pain, but he went on inexorably, "then he must be prepared to take the consequences of his actions. You'll remember, we've talked of this before."

His eyes looked somberly into hers and their haggard

expression, so unfamiliar to her, made Ginny bite her lip in anguish.

"But Don Francisco, Steve is—oh!" she cried through her gritted teeth, looking imploringly at the implacable Frenchman. "He may be an outlaw, yes, even a mercenary, but he isn't a traitor! A traitor to what? You tell me, colonel, that you think he's an American spy—I deny it! And if he is, then my loyalty is to America! And no matter what you say about Juarez and his supporters, he is the elected representative of the people of Mexico. Just as President Lincoln was—and he had to use force to insure that the United States stayed united!"

"You see. He has converted her—she talks revolution, she supports Juarez!"

"I support no one, why must you twist my words?" Ginny's hands were icy cold, and she clasped them together, desperately seeking warmth, and courage. "I love France, I've always been proud to be half-French, but I'm not proud of our role here in Mexico as—as conquerors and oppressors."

"Ginny!" Don Francisco's voice rang out warningly. "You're overwrought—be careful what you say!"

"She has already said what she really thinks," Colonel Devereaux said grimly. "It's clear enough, unfortunately that she believes in this untidy revolution. A pity that her husband dragged her into it and then saw fit to abandon her! And you, madame—" his voice had become steely, "do you now comprehend that you have, in effect, convicted yourself? And before witnesses?" He took a short step towards her and paused, obviously trying to control his anger. "It grieves me, madame, that I am faced with the very unpleasant duty of placing you under arrest."

The unreality of the whole scene seemed to deepen. The firelight flickered over Don Francisco's ravaged, suddenly aging features, and turning her eyes from him to the Frenchman Ginny saw his lips move as he pompously recited chapter and verse from the emperor's edicts giving him authority to arrest, interrogate, and if necessary, execute suspected rebels. She began to giggle, seeing the humor in it all, and they all looked at her as if she had suddenly gone raving mad.

"For God's sake, Colonel Devereaux! Can't you see she's hysterical? She did not know what she was saying. I cannot let you do this! Whatever my grandson has led her into, I take the full responsibility. I insist that you arrest me. There's no need to make war on women."

"Don Francisco, your sense of honor does you credit, but I'm afraid it is not you, but your grandson's wife we must arrest. She can give us information, I'm sure, that could lead to the arrest of some of these rebels, if not her husband himself. And as soon as she does—she'll be released. You see, I do not willingly war on women, I can sometimes bend the law—one last chance, madame. I beg you, do not make me do this!"

Her head was suddenly clear; the coldness had spread from Ginny's hands to her whole body, stiffening it, so that she felt as if she was carved out of marble, even her lips.

She looked back at the portly colonel, and he saw the pearly glint of her teeth as they caught in her bottom lip—her eyes seemed to shine with an unusual brilliance, and he could see the quick rise and fall of her breathing as her breasts swelled over the low décolletage of her gown.

What a woman! he could not help but think admiringly. Such courage, such spirit, and when she's angry, as she was a moment ago, *ma foi!* What magnificent, savage beauty! It's really a pity.

He waited, giving her time to think, his eyes trying to read the thoughts that must even now be scurrying through her mind. Doesn't she realize the terrible position she's in? Is she really willing to undergo arrest and even possible death for her husband? He found himself wondering fleetingly, what had really happened between them— this young, beautiful girl that young Capitaine Remy had raved about and the man who had abducted her and taken her all over the country with him. There were even rumors that he'd kept her in a whorehouse—and then, to end up married to him! It was unbelievable—he felt foolish when he thought that earlier in the evening he'd fallen for her story hook line and sinker; wondering only how on earth Don Francisco Alvarado's grandson had managed to find her and rescue her. And then Beal had seen her, and described her "husband" and the whole sordid story had come to light. Such a pity!

"I must think . . ." Ginny said slowly, surprised that her words had emerged from between her cold, stiff, lips so clearly. She saw the colonel incline his head formally.

"I will give you three minutes, madame. No longer. You have already wasted too much of my time."

"Ginny—my dearest child—you must tell all that you know. Never think it betrayal. Think of yourself, of your own future. If I had only known, when Esteban left, what he was leaving you to face I would have stopped him myself. I would have turned him in."

She hardly recognized the hoarse, old voice as Don Francisco's. She was almost beyond the point of hearing anything but her own thoughts. She walked slowly over to the small window that overlooked the patio and stood looking out.

Faintly, the sound of music came to her, and laughter. Which was real, all that gaiety of which she'd been a part such a short time ago, or this? This small, hot little room, and the fat, pompous colonel whom she'd dismissed so lightly earlier; the same man who now threatened her with arrest? She wanted to laugh again. Why am I doing this? she wondered. I don't know very much, it's true, but what I do know is damning. All I have to say is that he admitted to me he's a *Juarista*, and it would be over—after all, he's gone, they'll never catch him now. A sudden spark of anger burned in her as she thought of the careless, cavalier way in which he'd treated her from the beginning. And then, this evening, he'd married her quickly and secretively merely to satisfy a promise made to his grandfather . . . he'd left without so much as a goodbye, leaving her to cope with all this unpleasantness. I must be crazy, she thought, why am I trying to protect him? All he has ever done is use me; he never cared two pins for me, and I suppose that now he's only too glad to be rid of me. What difference would it make to him if I ended up in jail, after all?

"Madame!"

So her time was up. The Colonel wanted an answer, what could she tell him? I'll never let him force me into betraying anyone else, she thought fiercely in the same instant.

Ginny turned slowly and the colonel, standing impatiently in the center of the room, thought he saw the faintest smile trembling at the corners of her lips, giving her a strangely sensuous, alluring air. Her arms and shoulders seemed to reflect the firelight, like her opalescent gown—

her skin looked tawny, her eyes like emeralds. He knew a fleeting sense of regret that he had not met her first. He had married his very young wife purely as a matter of convenience and because her family had wealth. Had circumstances been different he might have tried to make this woman his mistress. Yes, she was that type. She had the look of a born courtesan; an unconsciously natural air of seduction. She was born to be a mistress and not a wife . . .

"Well, madame?" Colonel Devereaux repeated impatiently, brushing his own thoughts away with some annoyance.

She seemed to bend her neck slightly as if under a weight. But even if she had made a gesture of defeat, her voice was as clear and as proud as ever.

"Well, Colonel? I vow, you've quite frightened me with all your nasty threats. Tell me, what would you have me say?"

He was conscious of a twinge of irritation. Was she implying that he meant to put words in her mouth and force a "confession" that was no real confession at all?

"Why don't we start at the beginning? When did your husband first admit to you that he was working with the *Juaristas*? Did he ever give you any indications that there might be some other agency behind him?"

"What a lot of questions. Am I supposed to answer them in order? Well, then—" She had remained by the window, leaning her elbow on the padded sill so that part of her profile was shadowed. The colonel found himself absurdly annoyed because he could not guess at the play of expressions on her face. Her voice continued, lightly mocking, it seemed to him. "Steve never did come right out and tell me he was working with the *Juaristas*. He did sympathize with their cause, I'm sure of that. But as for any other agencies, I really think you are barking up the wrong tree, Colonel. He seemed to know what he was doing, but he certainly never gave me the impression that he worked for anyone but himself."

"Madame, you are playing with words! And as I've told you before I do not have the time for any more evasions. I don't want your impressions, if you please, I want facts! Names—places. The names of villages where you hid out. The names of people who sheltered you both—persons this man considered as close friends—in fact, madame, anything that would help us round up as many revolutionaries and Juarist sympathizers as possible."

He managed to drive under her mask of reserve at last—her head came up and her eyes sparked angrily at him.

"You are asking me, in other words to act as executioner, and merely on suspicion! No, Colonel, I remember nothing. The names of villages mean nothing to me, I'm afraid I can't even remember faces. But indeed, I'm beginning to realize more and more why the people of this country resent your presence here as oppressors!"

She would tell him nothing else. Her defiant stubbornness drove the colonel into an equally implacable determination to crush her pride and force her into bending.

He changed his tactics only at the last moment, after he had informed her that she was under arrest, and that he must insist, regretfully of course, that she accompany him to his headquarters at Zacatecas. Even the threats and anger of Don Francisco could not alter Colonel Devereaux' decision, although he put on an air of paternal concern and promised that there would be no overt scandal. With Don Francisco's compliance, they would leave quietly, in Colonel Devereaux' own carriage. He could make her excuses to the Sandovals—the young lady had developed a splitting headache and was so sick that she had been sent home. And in the meantime . . .

"You may be assured that I'm not exactly a heartless monster. She won't be lodged in a jail cell, of course—I'll see that she occupies my own quarters, which are comfortable enough, I assure you!" The colonel's benign look had returned, his eyes twinkled as he lowered his voice. "Perhaps a little fright—the knowledge that I'm not bluffing—will help overcome her stubbornness. And of course—if her husband should decide to give himself up it will save us all a lot of trouble, won't it? I'll see to it personally that the young lady is released at once, in that case. You understand my position, Don Francisco?"

"There is no mistaking it," the old man responded harshly. He said nothing else to the colonel and embraced the silent, cold-faced girl with real affection.

"You must not worry. The matter is not ended here,

and I promise to move heaven and earth if need be to
secure your immediate release."

"You mustn't be upset. I'm not afraid, you know," she
said quietly, and almost wonderingly. Because she was not.
Not then.

PART FIVE

"La Soldadera"

Chapter Thirty-four

Steve Morgan had merely changed clothes in Diego Sandoval's room, with Diego's connivance—concealing a new pair of revolvers under his serape. He had then strolled down the back staircase to join the gypsies, and mingling unobtrusively with them, he left the hacienda at the same time they did.

The interview with his grandfather had not gone very well, of course, but Steve had not expected that it would. He had informed his grandfather that he had married Ginny, quite legally, and in Don Francisco's angry presence Steve seated himself at the writing desk and scribbled a short will which left everything he possessed to his wife.

"That should take care of it," he said in a casual tone of voice which only served to infuriate Don Francisco further.

"You seem to forget our earlier conversation!" the old man shouted. "I told you then that you were going to settle down to your responsibilities. What kind of low-life mischief are you up to now?"

"If I don't get away tonight, then you'll probably see an end to all the problems I've brought you when they haul me in front of a firing squad," Steve said calmly, looking his grandfather straight in the eye. In the same calm voice he went on to explain that he had in fact been mixed up with some revolutionary activities and there was a man here, unfortunately, who had recognized him as his alter ego. "Ginny knows, of course," he added; moving Don Francisco to comment in a voice edged with acid that perhaps he should have married the poor girl to Renaldo instead—certainly she seemed to be getting something less than a bargain in his grandson.

The old man had shouted and blustered, causing Jaime Perez to wince several times when he felt that the command to shoot the Señor Esteban was imminent. It was the unexpected entrance of Diego Sandoval that had saved the situation. Above all, *el patrón* had a strong sense of family pride and honor—no matter how he might personally abuse and castigate a member of his family, he would not want to admit any kind of a rift to an outsider.

In a half-amused whisper Steve had informed his grandfather that in case of any emergency Diego would know where to get in touch with him—at least for the next day or two. He then flung an arm around his friend's shoulder and they sauntered out of the room together.

When he left the Sandoval hacienda, sitting quite openly beside the flamboyantly beautiful Concepción, his features effectively hidden by the huge sombrero he wore, Steve began to feel at last the familiar quickening of blood in his veins. He reflected with some amusement that he was growing to like the elegant life less and less and becoming more of a ruffian at heart. The weight of the twin guns, sagging against his hips was familiar and welcome, and beside him, her shoulder brushing promisingly against his with every jolt of the small wagon, Concepción alternated between a string of vituperations and half-sighed demands to know how much time he'd spend with her this time.

When they had passed through the gates and were well beyond them, the wagons changed direction, no longer keeping to the well-worn roadway marked by many horses and carriages.

Concepción became silent and sultry, leaning against Steve, insisting that he take the reins. He put one arm around her and felt her hands all over him. They had known each other a long time, after all, and Concepción was not shy. But although his body provided, almost automatically, the response that the girl desired, Steve found his mind curiously and annoyingly distracted. What in hell was the matter with him? He was free again, as he had not felt himself to be for the past few months, having been obliged to cart Ginny around with him all over the country, and cope with her changing moods, her unexpected moments of sharp rebellion as well. She had even stirred his conscience, of all things, in addition to annoying him almost intolerably. Well, he'd made amends, hadn't he? In the darkness, his mouth curled sardonically. Honorable amends, to quote his grandfather. He had given her the respectability of his name, made his will in her favor, and left her free to do as she pleased. She ought to be relieved. He remembered her threat about taking lovers of her own choosing, and wondered why it didn't amuse him any longer. Well, he'd married her and hadn't touched her afterwards—there was no reason why either of them could not get an annulment later, if they wanted to, although he certainly did not plan on any more marriages! To be forced into it once was bad enough; God, but women became so boring when they started to cling and to beg for attention.

His own mind startled him with the sudden vehemence of the thought that sprang into it. Damned if I was ever bored by her. The little green-eyed hellcat—she always contrived to make me angry, somehow, and to forget all my self-control. And even when she wasn't conscious of it, she was a seductress—teasing, tempting, and drawing back sullenly the next minute—fighting, screaming her hate and contempt, and then turning into a hungry tigress. A witch, leaving her brand on a man.

He thought about the night he had seen her disappear into the wagon with Carl Hoskins, reappearing quite a while later, looking shamelessly dishevelled. He had hated her then, and despised himself for not taking her sooner than he had, and with less careful tenderness. Even if she had been a virgin, she was one of those women who were born passionate—once a man had aroused such a one, she was unable to help herself or control her strong desires. And yet, he contradicted himself, I was never able to completely tame her. Just when I thought I'd succeeded she'd turn on me. What a vixen, I suppose I should really pity her next lover!

But even when the wagons had stopped for the night, in a protected *barranca*, and he lay with Concepción in his arms, both of them exhausted momentarily from their lovemaking; Steve found himself thinking again, reluctantly, about Ginny. She should have expected his sudden departure, of course. She had even encouraged it, earlier. But had it been quite fair to abandon her so publicly, with the wedding announcements already sent out? There were a few vicious tongues who might enjoy making capital out of a secret marriage and his sudden disappearance. And since when had he had any qualms about what was fair and what wasn't?

Incredible! The truth pierced him like a shaft and made him curse himself savagely. Fool! Since he still desired her he should have brought her with him. She was his, even if he decided to have nothing more to do with her once his desire was slaked; and he'd kill any man she decided to take on as a lover!

When he reached that point in his thoughts Steve discovered that he was scowling balefully into the darkness. This was ridiculous, of course, and from a practical angle it was just as well he had left her behind. She had become a habit, that was all! And of all the countless women he'd known and used and forgotten, she alone remained a challenge. Well—it was over. He had recognized the trap he was falling into, and would take care to avoid it. The thought that he, of all people should be lying awake at night mooning about a woman like a lovesick calf was really insufferable.

Steve sat up and Concepción stirred sleepily, trying to trap him in her arms again.

"*Querido*—where are you going? I'm cold . . ."

"I'm just thirsty, for God's sake! All that wine and tequila I was drinking last night, I guess."

"Well, hurry up! I'm wide awake again. Isn't that a pity? Are you going to give me something that will make me sleep?"

"You're the greediest bitch I've known. Don't you ever get enough?"

But he was grinning when he came back to her. Before he could lie down again Concepción came up on her knees with a lithe, pantherish movement of her body, her arms clasping him around the waist. Her long hair tickled his thighs, and his reaction to her ministrations was inevitable.

"Hmm . . ." Concepción whispered after a while, a gurgle of teasing laughter underlying her whisper, *"que grande! Hombre*, you are as greedy as I, *sí?"*

He found his breath coming faster—as a lover, Concepción was like no other he had known. She was a woman who made no pretense at coyness. She's the kind of woman I should stick to, Steve found himself thinking, in a way she's like me—she knows what she wants and takes it.

After a while he twisted his fingers in her hair, pulling her head backward. In the faint, diffused light of the Mexican night he could see her eyes gleaming with a steely kind of sheen. She put her tongue out at him, and he began to laugh, pushing her backwards, feeling the immediate response of her wild, warm body. No complications here. She was as natural as an animal with its mate, and gradually, as their half-savage, half-playful lovemaking continued, Steve found his mind letting go as his body took over.

It was near dawn, and Steve felt as if he had only just fallen asleep, when he heard the pounding of hooves. He had rolled away from Concepción, for both of them had become overheated and were covered with sweat—he fell asleep lying face-down, knowing that Concepción was quite capable of waking up in a few minutes and wanting a repeat performance. Habit kept his ear against the ground, and he heard the horse, and knew that only one rider approached, so that he was dressed already when Jaime Perez, one of the best trackers in the province, rode down the *barranca.*

Steve listened to the man's urgent, panted-out story almost incredulously. His first thought was that his grandfather was playing some kind of trick on him, determined to get him back in the fold by any means, fair or foul. Impossible! Even that wily, clever bastard Devereaux wouldn't dare. But as Jaime continued to talk, Steve felt the beginnings of a cold, frustrated rage that almost blinded him. By God, it did make sense. Devereaux was cleverer, after all, than any of them had given him credit for. His logic was really beautiful—and inescapable. Ginny would be released if he gave himself up. It became, in essence, a matter of honor—what else, in this crazy half-

Spanish country? And if he didn't, Colonel Raoul
Devereaux would make sure that everyone soon learned
that Esteban Alvarado was content to hide behind his
wife's skirts and let her suffer for his crimes. And in any
case, could he really bear the thought of her locked up as
a prisoner, at the mercy of men like Tom Beal?
Devereaux chose to show a surface veneer of benevolence
and sophisticated gallantry, but Steve had learned enough
of the man's methods since he'd been appointed military
governor of Zacatecas province to know that he was completely unscrupulous.

He became aware that he had buckled on his gun belts
while Jaime was talking—that the man was looking at him
with a strange expression on his face. What did Jaime
really think?

"*Señor*—" there was a slight hesitation in Jaime's
voice, and his face suddenly contorted. "I did not want to
bring you this message." Again he hesitated and then his
words came out in a sudden rush. "Do not go, *señor*!
They will not dare to harm the *señora*—it is all a bluff!
But if they take you . . ."

From somewhere behind Jaime, Concepción flung herself against him, arms clutching, and Steve could feel
the trembling of her body, although her eyes were stormy
as they glared into his.

"It will be the firing squad—that is what they do with
those suspected of being revolutionaries! You fool! *Idiota*!
Are you really so tired of life? You know this man is
right—they will not dare harm a *señora*, a lady. Are you
so crazy about her then that you must rush to her at the
risk of your own life? I won't let you go." She looked
around frantically at the silent men who now ringed them.
"Well? You're his friends, no? Won't you stop him?"

"Concepción!" To silence her raging Steve kissed her
half-open mouth and was surprised to taste the saltiness of
the tears that trickled down her face. "Behave yourself,"
he said after a moment, deliberately hardening his voice.

"I won't! Damn you! If none of these,"—her scornful
glance swept the silent faces around them—"will do anything to stop you then I will!"

"Stop having hysterics, you know it doesn't work with
me." Steve pulled her arms from around his neck and
stepped back cautiously. She looked so furious, and at the
same time so desolate that he smiled at her tenderly.

"*Querida*, they haven't executed me yet. I'll see you again."

"Let him go!" Sanchez' voice roared out roughly. He grabbed his daughter's arm and held her firmly in spite of her struggles.

"Stop him, stop him!" she screamed.

Steve was already saddling his horse, and even Jaime had fallen silent now, although the grief in his normally impassive face was plain to see.

"And how would you stop him, stupid *niña*?" Sanchez said with heavy sarcasm. "Would you shoot him yourself before the French *soldados* do so, eh?" He continued roughly, "it's a matter of honor, *muchacha*. You wouldn't understand."

Steve heard Concepción's screaming invective in his ears long after he had ridden out of the *barranca*.

"Honor, shit! I spit on this honor! He goes for her, that green-eyed woman who is more of a bitch and a whore than I am! *Sí*, I know it, I felt it from the first time I saw her! You fool, you fool, she isn't worth it, you'll find out, just wait and see."

He got back on the road again, that beaten-down ribbon of dirt that masqueraded as a highway to Zacatecas. From there it continued south-east to Salinas and San Luis Potosí, which was where he had been heading when he started out. The sudden thought struck him that he probably wouldn't get any place beyond Zacatecas, after all, and a slightly bitter smile twisted his mouth for an instant. Well—*c'est la guerre*. And a firing squad was better than hanging at that.

Steve gave the horse its head, letting it take him at its own pace. Why not enjoy the ride while he could?

"He goes for her, that green-eyed woman." Ginny—Ginny—she had become an obsession with him, why not admit it? Ginny in all her moods, like the ocean he might never see again—worse than a tropical storm sometimes, and at others as calm, as deep and dreamy, as unfathomable as the ocean at its best. My God, he thought suddenly, I was in danger of falling in love with the woman, and I didn't even know it. What a trap!

Steve Morgan, who had always prided himself on his cold detachment from emotional entanglements now found, as he galloped towards Zacatecas, that the prospect of seeing Ginny again was almost worth facing a firing squad for. If they were going to execute him in any case, they would probably allow him a few minutes alone with her. He could take her in his arms and taste the wonderful texture of her lips again, and feel her small, perfectly shaped breasts pressing against his chest. He'd tell her— yes, what did it matter now? Before they killed him, he'd tell her he loved her.

Chapter Thirty-five

Ginny had not been able to sleep at all in spite of the fact that the colonel's quarters boasted a surprising degree of luxury, and his bed was wide and soft. Colonel Devereaux had, in fact, been surprisingly kind and considerate once they had left the lights of the Sandoval hacienda behind them.

She must not worry too much, he told her, patting her hand in an unexceptionably paternal manner. "We all lost our tempers, but these matters have a way of working themselves out. Don't think I blame you, my dear young lady—your loyalty to that no-good ruffian is really admirable." He had added more softly, "but does he deserve it, eh? Does he appreciate what a brave wife he has?" Almost to himself the colonel added under his breath, "we shall see—yes, we shall see."

He had maintained an amiable flow of talk, only occasionally interspersed with admonitions that she really must be sensible, she must see her loyalty was misplaced—she must understand that she had placed him in a very embarrassing position by her stubborn refusal to speak. "In front of that young *capitaine* of the Legionnaires too—it was really too bad of you, madame, you left me with no alternative, surely you can see that?"

For the rest of the time he asked her only questions that good manners forced her to answer—questions about her father and stepmother, and about the people she had met in New York and Washington. Once, he shot her a sharp look as he mentioned that Michel Remy, his wounds healed, had obtained Marshal Bazaine's grudging permission to join a fighting regiment; leaving the comparative safety and luxury of Mexico City in order to battle the armies of Diaz and Escobedo.

Ginny stirred restlessly, throwing the covers off her suddenly overheated body. She felt her head throb pitilessly.

What time was it? How long had she lain here with her thoughts torturing her? All night long—or what had remained of the night when they reached Zacatecas. By the time they had arrived at the French headquarters the feeling of trancelike unreality that had kept her isolated from these distastefully unpleasant circumstances had begun to wear off. It had been all she could do to keep her lips from trembling, to maintain an air of haughty disregard. She had even had the almost overwhelming temptation to burst into tears.

But in the end Ginny had maintained her self-control by sheer effort of will, pushed on by her pride. She had even managed to thank Colonel Devereaux for the use of his quarters and the loan of a nightshift and robe belonging to his young wife.

"Sometimes she surprises me by riding down here to spend a night or two with me," he had confessed, his eyes twinkling. "A very passionate young woman for her age, my little Dona Alicia . . ."

Ginny had not felt in the mood to make any comment.

Now, the thought that she lay in the colonel's bed, that very same bed he had shared so many times with his wife, gave her an indefinable feeling of disgust.

What's going to happen? What does he really intend to do? White-hot bars of sunlight slanted through the closed shutters, and imagining the heat outside made Ginny feel slightly sick. The reflected glare of the sun made her headache worse, and hearing the French bugles a few hours ago, as the soldiers drilled in the courtyard below, had done nothing to help her impression of being somehow marooned, here in this hot little room.

Ginny sat up with an effort and reached thankfully for the small water carafe that a sullen-looking Mexican woman had left by the bed. The water was tepid and tasted horrible, but it helped the intolerable dryness of her throat.

How absurdly theatrical this all is! Ginny thought suddenly. Any minute now, I'll wake up and find I've been dreaming, and I'll laugh and tell myself what an absurd dream it was. She was reminded forcibly of the Opera in Paris—some of those melodramatic plots that had never failed to make her giggle at their sheer improbability. But here she was, actually involved in a plot that rivalled that of any play she had watched!

Only last night she had been married, abandoned by her husband, and arrested as a revolutionary! It was really too comical! The thought that Steve might even consider giving himself up to save her she brushed aside as being absurd. Steve wasn't the nobly unselfish type at all. He was cold, hard, ruthless and completely calculating. By now, he was probably several miles away, congratulating himself on having arranged matters so cleverly. He'd married her and gotten rid of her—and if he happened to hear what had taken place afterwards he'd probably laugh. Yes, no doubt he'd be vastly amused to think of how the tables had been turned on her. That she would have to be the one to pay for his crimes.

Ginny found herself wondering again what would become of her. Was this room to be her prison? Would they question her again? Was it possible that Colonel Devereaux would really go so far as to execute her as an example? No—no, of course he would not dare! Don Francisco would undoubtedly get in touch with all his most powerful friends—with her father as well. She'd be saved—but did the urbane colonel intend to give her that much time?

She had a sudden, unwanted vision of Steve's dark, unsmiling face—the way his hard blue eyes could suddenly soften when he was in a tender mood, or become piercing and darker when he was angry. He had been angry last night and she had been delighted to think that she might actually have made him jealous. Such a ridiculous thought. She meant nothing to him, except as a convenient plaything—an object for the slaking of his masculine desires, no more.

There was a rattling at the door, and Ginny swung her legs over the side of the bed, reaching hastily for the robe she had tossed on the chair beside it.

"Señora—con su permiso . . ."

The Mexican woman came hurriedly into the room, telling Ginny that she must come with her at once, el colonel desired her company downstairs.

"But—but I'm not dressed yet! My gown, where is it?"

The gown had been taken to be pressed, and the colonel must not be kept waiting. The robe would do, and the *señora* must come at once.

Ginny was reminded, forcibly and unpleasantly, that she was, after all, a prisoner. She looked at the woman's hard face and noticed for the first time that she looked like a female warden. That stocky, strong body, the muscular arms . . . no doubt she'd be dragged downstairs like a common criminal if she hesitated. Better to cling to what shreds of dignity and pride still remained.

Although her face was flushed with humiliation and pent-up anger, Ginny stood up silently and tied the sash of the robe tightly around her waist. There was no time to do more than drag her fingers through the tangled mass of her hair before the woman grasped her arm with strong, bony fingers and led her outside.

Two French soldiers who had been standing just outside the door snapped to attention as she passed them, carefully averting their eyes from her obvious deshabille. Ginny could hear their heavy boots clattering down the narrow stairs behind her, through the sudden pounding in her ears.

The woman opened a door, pushing Ginny ahead of her, and she found herself in a small, surprisingly bright and cheerful-looking little room, with sunshine pouring in through the windows. How incongruous it all seemed! Here was the colonel himself, informally dressed in a Chinese brocade dressing gown embroidered with fierce dragons. He beamed at her over a table laden with a typically French breakfast that made Ginny's mouth water in spite of herself. Brioche, fresh yellow butter, steaming, fragrant coffee—an enormous omelette that looked as if it had only just been brought to the table. She couldn't believe it!

"Ah, come in, madame, do sit down! I trust you slept well?"

Ginny moved forward on leaden feet, hearing the door close gently behind her. What did this all mean? What was the urgency for her being dragged here so summarily?

"It occurred to me that you might be hungry, my dear

young lady—I wondered, later, if you had had the time to sit down to supper last night, after all. Come, don't look so upset! Please do sit down, and we'll have a nice, informal talk after we've eaten, eh?"

He came around the table to pull out a chair for her; as gallantly as if they had been at some formal dinner party. Keeping her eyes fixed on him disbelievingly, Ginny sat down, her hands moving automatically to pull the robe more closely across her breasts.

Colonel Devereaux' eyes glittered with amusement.

"My dear madame! Why hide such treasures? I assure you, that if I were not such a happily married man I'd do more than just gaze on your beauty, but as it is, I thought we could become friends."

"Colonel Devereaux!" Ginny tried to put all the scorn she could muster into her voice. "I am surprised, sir, that you would think so."

"But I've jumped to no conclusions, madame, let me assure you! You are a Frenchwoman, yes, there's no mistaking it this morning—you're exceptionally charming with your hair loose, if I may say so. Come, *cher madame*, let us have no more evasions between us, hein? There's no need to pretend any longer that you're nothing but a naive little American—we French are a much more intelligent and sophisticated race, are we not? We could help each other. Believe me, you'll find the emperor's court at Chapultepec a much more exciting place than the hacienda of Don Francisco, where you'd be followed around by a *duenna*. . . ."

Ginny's eyes had begun to sparkle with tears of sheer rage, and she half rose—only the fact that somehow the hem of her robe had become trapped under the foot of the chair prevented her from sweeping from the room.

"I find these—these suggestions of yours impossible to credit, *monsieur!* Even coming from you! If you'll excuse me, I'm not hungry."

"Sit down, madame!" He stood, his voice suddenly steely. "Must I remind you that you are my prisoner? Would you prefer to have a meal of tortillas and water with the rest of them, instead? Pah—that *canaille* would tear you to pieces—a lovely morsel like you! Sit down and be reasonable. Do not disappoint me with this sudden affectation of innocence, I beg you. I will not rape you—no, no, I am a Frenchman, and no true Frenchman needs to

take a woman by force. Will you sit, madame? Or must I
have you tied to your chair?"

His threats frightened her more than she would admit.
Biting her lip to keep back her mounting fury, Ginny sat
back, averting her eyes.

"That's better. You'll see, soon enough, that we have a
lot in common. Believe me, you can trust me! You'll find
that out, too. Now eat—come on, don't be stubborn, *ma
chère*, it doesn't suit the kind of woman you are."

Oh God, he was torturing her! Ginny found suddenly
that she could not remember when she had last eaten, and
the smell and sight of all this food made her feel positively
faint from hunger. The practical part of her mind came to
her rescue by whispering, What difference will it make if I
eat? It's all one—he can do whatever he wants with me in
any case, and if I've eaten it'll make me stronger. Yes, it
can't really hurt, I must be sensible. To let pride prevent
me from having a meal that I badly need would be stupid!

"Don't frown so thoughtfully! Go on, eat! It's almost
noon, and I'm sure you must be starved. Do you think I
always breakfast so largely? No, I had all this ordered especially for you. You see, I'm not so bad and wicked after
all, am I now? Eat, and we won't talk of anything you
find unpleasant until after our meal, eh?"

Ginny felt her stomach begin to cramp and knot and
she became quite alarmingly pale, so that the colonel
leaned over solicitously and poured her a cup of coffee,
dosing it liberally with cream.

"My dear, this won't do! Eat up, where are those bright
eyes that shot such flaming sparks at me last night? You
will never have the strength to resist my blandishments if
you don't have some nourishment, you know!"

It was all that Ginny could do not to begin to stuff
herself immediately. How easy it would be to break her,
she thought miserably. All they'd have to do was starve
her and she'd capitulate—it was too mortifying! But even
as she thought in this strain she was reaching for a still-
hot brioche, and the colonel, smiling benevolently, had
placed a large slice of the omelette on her plate. With a
sigh, Ginny resigned herself. She ate, and true to his
promise the colonel said not a word that might upset
her—merely helping her silently to more food as her plate
showed signs of becoming empty.

When she protested that she couldn't eat another bite,

and was sipping her second cup of delicious coffee, the colonel decided to entertain her with some of the latest jokes from Paris. In spite of Ginny's mistrust of the man, she had to admit, reluctantly, that he was a born raconteur. He was so droll—he made everything sound so funny! He gave her a third cup of coffee and continued to tell jokes until Ginny found herself laughing helplessly.

What's the matter with me? she thought with a vague pang of alarm, I must be going completely mad! This man has not only insulted and threatened me but he's made all kinds of improper suggestions, and here I sit like a ninny, laughing at his rather improper jokes!

A sudden suspicion struck her and she frowned across the table at her droll companion.

"I'm not usually so silly! Are you sure you didn't put something in this coffee? I wouldn't put it past you!"

"Ah, Ginny, Ginny! I am desolate to think that you would have such suspicions of me! Did you think I'd stoop to putting some—some aphrodisiac in your café? No, no—it's only Kahlua, a delicious little liqueur they make here in Mexico—I always add it to my coffee. In fact, it is made from coffee. What do you think of it?"

In spite of herself Ginny giggled again.

"I think you're just full of tricks! But you're funny, too. Aren't you going to tell me any more jokes?" She blinked her eyes at him archly, with one part of her mind standing aside quite appalled. "Or are you going to try again to seduce me? I warn you, Colonel, it's quite impossible!"

"Oho! So it's impossible, eh? You didn't say so last night, *ma petite*, when you snuggled so close to me in bed. What a little tease you are!"

He reached quickly across the table and caught her wrist, some subtle change in his voice warning her before her befuddled mind could make sense of his words.

It happened like a nightmare. Her robe falling open in front as she leaned forward across the table, taken by surprise, still giggling in a sort of stupid reflex action. Then the embarrassed cough at the door, making her twist her head around—the French corporal apologizing for not having knocked loudly enough—Tom Beal's wicked, leering laugh, and—she could not believe her eyes—Steve? What was he doing here? Why was he looking at her in that coldly murderous fashion?

Ginny felt the blood rush from her head, making her so dizzy that she stumbled backwards into a chair, still staring at him, unable to speak one word.

The colonel was saying something in a quietly triumphant voice—she did not catch what he said at once because she was noticing that Steve's wrists were manacled behind him, and there was a bruise along the line of his jaw, and his eyes—dear God, she'd never in her worst nightmares imagined she'd see such disgust, such hate in those same blue eyes that could smile so lazily, so mockingly into hers.

"And I must say you are to be congratulated, my dear madame. Our plan—*your* suggestion, I should say—it worked very well, did it not? But on the other hand, why wouldn't any man come to the aid of such ravishing loveliness? Take him away. You know what to do."

Ginny's clasped hands flew upward to cover her mouth —she was literally petrified, what was the matter with her? Through glazed eyes she saw Steve incline his head sardonically, a cold, twisted smile on his lips.

"*Adios*, my lovely wife. I'm certainly glad you've suffered no ill-effects from your incarceration."

"Steve!" she screamed frantically; "Oh God—no! Steve, please!"

But her voice came back too late, the door had closed minutes ago, and as Ginny stumbled blindly to her feet, Colonel Devereaux' arms went comfortingly around her shoulders.

"I'm sorry, *ma chère*—it had to be done. Perhaps, if we can make him very angry he will talk, yes? And that will be so much better for us all—" he patted at her hair, pulling her closer and she was so shaken by sobs that she literally could not move, could hardly breathe for the tears that choked her. "We will talk, soon—there, there, have your cry, you need it; and then you will be ready to listen, yes?"

As she began to cough and retch from the fury of her uncontrollable sobs, Ginny found herself wondering dully if she would ever stop crying—if she could ever learn to bear the complete, utter desolation she now felt.

Chapter Thirty-six

Quite a welcome, Steve Morgan was thinking sardonically as they marched him across the sun-baked courtyard. It was almost as if they had been sure he'd come. "Fool! *Idiota!*" Concepción had screamed at him, and of course she was right. Riding into Zacatecas like a goddam hero—a medieval knight out to rescue his lady-love. He had always been a cynic about women; why couldn't he have guessed that Ginny would know instinctively how to take care of herself? And why did the thought that she had spent the night comfortably curled up against the fat colonel in his bed still have the power to make him almost blind with rage?

Hell, Steve thought now, feeling the rifle barrels jab into his back when he stumbled once, there was really a wry kind of humor in the whole situation! He'd made a fool of himself, and little Ginny got her revenge, in spades. Fancy coming to her "rescue" only to find that she hardly desired rescuing! No doubt she and the colonel had cooked up the whole scheme while they'd been dancing. And by marrying her so suddenly, he'd only played into their hands further. She deserved admiration for the way she'd waited until just the right time, the right moment. And what single-

minded hate she must feel for him—no doubt it would
give her real pleasure to see him punished for the way
he'd messed up her life. "I'd like to watch you die, very
slowly," she'd flung at him once. It was too bad he'd underestimated her again; and this time, no doubt, fatally,
for him.

They had almost reached the far end of the courtyard
now, its earth hard-packed from the marching of the
Legionnaires who held Zacatecas. No point in resistance . . .
But as he looked up and suddenly realized what they intended to do with him, Steve Morgan could not help a
momentary hesitation, nor the crawling of his flesh.

"What's the matter, Morgan? Just the sight of it make
you nervous? Colonel told me I was to tell you you could
save yourself a whole lotta pain if you decide to answer
his questions. Me," Beal's voice dropped to a soft, gloating
jeer, "I hope you stay stubborn. Think I'm gonna enjoy
working you over."

The two hard-faced Legionnaires who were part of his
escort had moved up on either side of Steve, seizing his
arms as Beal unlocked the manacles. He had the wild impulse to break free and run for it and fought it back,
knowing how Beal would love that. No, there was no
point in resistance, not now. The firing squad would have
been better, Steve thought grimly as his arms were hauled
upward and lashed firmly with wet rawhide to the wooden
crossbar. A wide, beltlike leather strap buckled just above
the waist pulled his torso flat against the thick-bodied
wooden post. The soldiers worked fast, while Beal stood
aside grinning his thin-lipped wolfish grin.

"Ain't too comfortable now, are you? But don't you
worry none—pretty soon you'll get to screamin' and beggin' so loud you'll forget everything else. I ain't worked on
a prisoner yet I haven't broke. Why, you bastard, you're
just going to be praying for that firing squad to put an end
to your misery!"

They left him alone then—"to think about it" Beal said.
The heat of the early afternoon sun was like a blow, and
it seemed to reflect upward from the sun-seared soil as
well. Steve felt the sweat break out all over his body,
pouring down his face so that he had to blink it out of his
eyes. He cursed his own inanity all over again. He could
have been somewhere in the coolness of the mountains by
now; circling around to make contact with the ragged

Juarist armies under Escobedo, who were even now moving slowly and inexorably towards Zacatecas. And in Mexico City he had heard that Bazaine was calling his armies in; pulling them closer to the capital. "Not a retreat, of course, but a concentration," his informant had said rather pompously. Why hadn't Devereaux gotten his orders yet? A matter of time . . . and he could have waited. If he'd had any sense he'd have thought with his brain, instead of with his gut.

'But not me—Christ, what a complete idiot!' Steve swore savagely to himself. All he had been able to think about was Ginny—Ginny in prison; Ginny in the hands of men like Devereaux and Tom Beal—hungry and thirsty and frightened. He remembered, unwillingly, the little scene he'd witnessed. The breakfast table with its half-empty dishes; Devereaux still in his dressing gown, and she—she in that robe which did little to conceal the soft curves of her figure. She had been laughing the teasing giggle of a woman sated by a long night of love. But at least she'd had the decency to look white-faced and guilty when she saw him. If he hadn't known better he'd have imagined there was an appeal in her slowly widening green eyes. The bitch! Why did the thought of her still have the power to cloud his mind and his judgement? Why, even now, did he still want her? And hate her so violently for having succumbed so quickly and easily to another man? Even if it was only to save herself; that's still no excuse! Does she have to give herself to every man who wants her? Is that what she meant when she threatened to choose her own lovers?

The sun must be getting to him, Steve thought angrily. He was losing his detachment, all the rationality he had ever possessed. Yes, what he really found hardest to face was the knowledge that slowly, without his realizing it, she had become necessary to him. He, who had prided himself on being a cynic, on never trusting anyone, particularly a woman, he had allowed her to become his only weakness, and it was that thought he found intolerable!

But at least she needn't have the satisfaction of knowing that, he told himself grimly. Not even the thought of the pain and torture that now faced him had the same power to affect his mind that she had. Even while one part of his mind mocked himself for childish bravado, he was determined that no matter what they did he wouldn't cry

out—that would be too much, the last straw! She would
be watching, she and the colonel; waiting for him to
break; but even if he died under their torture he wouldn't
speak.

The French soldiers flung open the gates that separated
their parade grounds from the main square of the village.
There was no love lost between the Frenchmen and Mexican Irregulars who strutted through the town as if they
owned it, and the townspeople themselves—going about
their daily business with sullen-faced resignation. When the
French were gone, these same people who pretended loyalty to the emperor and cheered dutifully at the regularly
held parades would no doubt run screaming their welcome
to the *Juaristas*.

The French sergeant who headed the small detail that
now marched from house to house, banging at doors, had
long ago given up trying to understand the seeming apathy
of the people of this land. He had fought in Algiers under
the burning desert sun—had fought Arabs, who were the
worst and most dangerous enemies in all the world. But of
all the places he had been he hated this Mexico the most.
You could not trust anyone here—they'd smile into your
face, bow their heads politely, and knife you in the back if
they ever got the chance. He had marched into villages
where he and his men had been greeted with fiestas, like
heroes, on the previous night; only to be met with rifle-
fire. You could not even trust the little children here. A
small boy, carrying a stick of dynamite, had blown up
almost a whole platoon of Irregulars, once. What a dirty
country—a land of hypocrites. He cursed his luck at having been posted here, instead of to Queretaro, or Mexico
City, where at least you could walk the streets and find
your amusements without being cursed at from dark alleys
and fearing a bullet in your back at every moment. But a
man had his duty to perform. . . .

Sergeant Malaval's duty, at this moment, was to fetch
as many citizens as he could find during this time of siesta
to the parade ground—to witness the questioning of a
Juarista spy. A public flogging—it was supposed to act as
a deterrent to *Juarista* sympathizers, but hell, he was sure,
privately, that more than half the townspeople believed in
their El Presidente, anyhow. They would watch, as they
had watched executions and other floggings before, and it
would make no damn difference. This was a savage land,

and life was cheap. Moreover, when they decided to hate, these people hated hard.

Sergeant Malaval thought only vaguely of the prisoner, left to bake in the sun while he "considered" what lay in store for him. There was no question but that the man would break, in spite of the fact that he had looked and acted different from the usual run-of-the-mill *Juarista* dogs they captured. He had blue eyes, he'd carried a gun on his hip when they'd captured him—or was it really true that he had given himself up as a substitute for the pretty green-eyed woman the colonel had brought back with him? It did not really matter, after all. Beal, the American counter-guerilla was an expert with what he called a "bull-whip." Personally, for this kind of punishment, the sergeant preferred the use of the "cat." It was traditional, at least, and tradition and habit were what kept armies on the move.

Herding their quota of silent, resentful townspeople ahead of them, the soldiers returned to the courtyard. Time for the colonel's usual little speech, Malaval supposed, and then the main event. He cursed his luck again, having to stand at attention all afternoon in the sun, listening to the unfortunate prisoner's screams ringing in his ears. He hoped Beal would not take too long to break the man—he could use a nice, long drink.

The colonel had broken precedent by coming down himself to talk to the prisoner. The fact that he had done so only half-surprised Steve. Colonel Devereaux was a wily man, as well as being a dangerous enemy. No doubt he had some axe of his own to grind—and of course there was the fact that he had made Ginny his mistress. What man could resist the temptation to boast of a conquest like that, especially since she happened, unfortunately, to be Steve's wife. He had had time to adopt an almost fatalistic attitude by now. What would happen would happen. There was no way he could escape it, so why not face the inevitable with as much fortitude as he could muster? At least, he felt he could maintain an attitude of indifference to the colonel's inevitable needling. Or could he? The rawhide they'd used to tie him up with had already shrunk in the searing heat of the sun, had stretched his arms upward almost intolerably. Already he could feel the blood trickling down his arms where the strips of hide had cut into his wrists. It was like being stretched on a rack, and soon, to this present discomfort, would be added much more.

"Well, señor? Have you reconsidered? I would hate to have to go through with this, all things considered, but you understand, you have hardly left me with a choice!"

"Are you offering me a choice, then, *mon Colonel*? What can I possibly give you that you haven't already taken?"

Blue eyes clashed with yellow-brown, and Steve's fluent French mocked the colonel's rather pedantic Spanish.

"Ah. So you speak French as well. It explains a lot." The colonel's voice was thoughtful, rather than angry. He sighed. "I have a feeling you intend to go on being stubborn. For your sake, as well as your wife's, I had hoped not."

"My wife is hardly my concern any longer, *monsieur,* since you seem to have made her yours. And like your own marriage, ours was a matter of mutual convenience, after all. If all you need from me is my blessing for your little liaison, sir, you certainly have it! I'm an understanding husband—hasn't she told you?"

"Enough! I didn't come here to discuss your wife. It is your other activities I'm interested in—your spying, señor. Who sent you to Mexico? Who is paying you? It could not be Benito Juarez, for he doesn't have enough money. Why is your government so anxious to topple ours?"

Steve laughed, and saw the gleam of anger in Colonel Devereaux' eyes.

"But you have all the answers already, Colonel. Why ask me?"

"You have given us a great deal of trouble with your meddling in our affairs here, *monsieur*! You were becoming quite a hero to a few ignorant peasants. But in a few minutes, that heroic image will, I'm afraid, be dispelled when you squeal under the lash and beg to be allowed to tell all you know! Damn it—I'll have names from you— you'll betray all your accomplices—the places where I can find them!"

Colonel Devereaux had begun to pace around, his hands behind his back in the manner of Napoleon, whom he had always admired tremendously. And in spite of the unpleasant position he was in, it was all Steve could do not to laugh at the man again, and drive him into a towering rage. Devereaux looked up again, and it seemed as if he deliberately softened the tone of his voice, so that it was almost pleasant.

"Come now, Morgan—you're a reasonable man I'm sure. And so am I. What good does it do to lose tempers? You see, I have you. There's no escape. Still, if you'll have the good sense to tell me what I must know, you'll find me a fair and just man. You like danger and action, do you not? You enjoy these things? You enjoy life? You can still have them all, on our side. Yes, we could use a man like you, and once you've turned against your *Juarista* friends, well, then we can be sure you won't go back to them, won't we?" The colonel's eyes had begun to twinkle. "I believe that's what your Americans would call 'insurance,' hein? You'd be well paid, too, if money matters. Believe me, it would be so much better for you if you turned your talents to the right side. I have great respect for your grandfather, you know—think how pleased it would make him to know that at last you'd come around to what he believes in! What do you say?"

Steve drew in a deep breath, half-tempted to say too many things he shouldn't say. There was no point in uselessly flinging words of defiance, nor in continued fencing. Still, he realized with a feeling of distaste that he actually disliked this pompous, vain-glorious little man who had bedded his wife a few hours ago and now took it for granted he'd jump at the chance to turn traitor in order to keep his hide.

"Colonel—if I betrayed my friends I'd die anyway." Steve kept his voice flat and even. "You've lost the war already, and you know it. It's a matter of time now, that's all. And you stand to lose a lot more, personally. You're finished, as far as the big *hacendados* go. You were a guest of the Sandoval's and you arrested a woman. I must admit, she's very charming when she wants to be, my little wife—perhaps you managed to persuade her you could offer her more than I could—but what will happen when your wife's family finds out? And whatever happens to me—remember you've made an enemy for life in my grandfather. We have our disagreements, he and I, but he'll never take such an insult to a member of his family. He has enough money, and enough influential friends both here and in France, to have you broken. Your only chance to save your own skin is to apologize for the inconvenience and let me go."

"*Mon Dieu*, but your insolence knows no bounds! You dare to threaten me? I made a mistake, I see, in offering you a gentlemen's agreement, but you are not one—you're a dirty *Juarista* dog, a spy—and in case you'd forgotten it, my prisoner! We will see who will break!"

His face crimson with rage the colonel turned on his heel and marched away. Steve shrugged mentally. Well, he'd given it a try. He'd almost hoped that Devereaux' practical streak might outweigh his stiff-necked military pride. Too bad he wouldn't be around to see what happened to the Colonel himself in the end.

Too bad he had to stand out here in the sun with his muscles strained uncomfortably and painfully, waiting . . . his only hope now that he would be able to endure their torture without giving way under it. But how did a man know how much pain he could stand until the moment when he was actually required to suffer it? The sunlight felt like a burning brand against his skin. The whip would be worse. Steve licked lips that were already cracked and dry and leaned his forehead against the wooden post, deliberately concentrating on nothingness. It was possible, Gopal had told him in that long-ago time when they had been friends, to isolate the mind and free the body of all sensation. It was necessary, by concentration, to enter a trancelike state.

Steve had tried it, on occasion. Once, when he'd been shot in the shoulder, the bullet lodged against the bone, and no doctor within miles, he thought he'd succeeded. It had been in a bar, and while the bartender had probed clumsily with a knife under the gun of Steve's friend, he had sat, immobilizing himself, eyes fixed on a crack in the dirty ceiling. And had hardly felt the pain. Not until hours later, when his shoulder had begun to ache and throb agonizingly and he'd had to remain in what was practically a drunken stupor for days.

He became aware of the shuffling of feet, of muffled whispers, nervous movements, the rustling noise made by the skirts of women. A child began to cry and was hushed almost immediately. He didn't have to open his eyes to know there were people surrounding him now. The damned French! Always having to make an example out of something. In this case, he was it. His screams were supposed to have a demoralizing effect on any of the poor devils here who might think about going over to the *Juaristas*. Let them all witness how the French treated their prisoners, and beware! God, what a farce this was turning into.

The soldiers, with their passion for orderliness were marshalling the unwilling spectators into rows. Feeling something like the prize exhibit at a zoo, Steve let his eyes rove casually over them—those that he could see, anyway, Anything to keep his mind off what was coming . . .

His eyes moved, stopped and came back to a particular pair of dark eyes. Without knowing he did so, he frowned. That woman with a black rebozo wrapped around her head, in the second row . . . he could have sworn—their eyes met, hers wide and dark and wet with the sheen of tears; his flashing a warning as he recognized her. Steve groaned inwardly. Concepción! Now who was the *idiota?* She had no business coming here, and for her own sake she'd better not have some wild scheme in mind. There wasn't a chance in hell that he could escape now, under the guns of a whole platoon of French Legionnaires. He hoped she wouldn't do anything stupid—these French would take pleasure in torturing her, too.

Booted feet marched up behind him. Stopped. Rough hands took hold of his shirt at the neck, ripping it away to bare his back. This was it, then. Now. No more waiting. Only a few seconds left of ghastly anticipation, and then the pain, wiping out everything else.

Steve felt his heart begin to pound, and the sweat that popped out on his body suddenly seemed cold. He was afraid. He was suddenly sick to the pit of his stomach with primitive, animal fear.

Tom Beal's sneering voice, filled with a barely held-in gloating, sounded from behind him.

"You ready, Morgan?" Steve sucked in a deep breath, and was not able to prevent the involuntary shudder that ran through his body. Was a man ever ready for something like this, when it was inescapable and inevitable? He had seen what a bullwhip could do to a man and he suddenly knew he would not be able to stand it. In spite of all his resolutions, he wasn't strong enough to stop this crazy, cringing fear that came from nowhere, urging him to cry out, to tell them to shoot him instead . . .

He heard Beal laugh and knew the man had sensed

what was in him now. Beal knew, and Beal enjoyed the
feeling of power it gave him.

"You still got time to change your mind, if you ain't
feelin' as brave now as you pretended to be a while ago.
See where the colonel is? Up on that balcony, with your
wife. Guess she didn't want to miss the show either.
Watch his arm, Morgan. He's gonna give a little speech to
your sympathetic friends here, an' then when he raises his
arm, I go to work. Reckon it won't take me more than a
few minutes to have you beggin' for mercy, will it? We
both know how scared you are right now—I kin smell
fear, you bastard, an' you're scared shitless, ain't you?
Ain't so brave without them guns, are you?"

The crowd stirred uneasily as the French soldiers came
to attention. In spite of himself, Steve had glanced upward
and to his right, where Colonel Devereaux stood in the
full regalia of his exalted rank. It was too far away for
him to be able to read expressions, but he needed to be
blind not to know that the woman who stood close beside
Devereaux was Ginny. Her shiny ball dress looked oddly
out of place here, and her hair, still worn loose, glittered
with a fire all its own under the sun.

The colonel had begun his speech, his best parade-
ground voice carrying clearly across the now-silent courtyard. Steve didn't hear him. So she really hated him that
much, did she? She had to watch, to gloat over his punishment. I'll be damned before I give the bitch that much
satisfaction, he thought suddenly, feeling the determination
he thought he'd lost come back to stiffen him. Deliberately
he looked away and met Concepción's eyes again. She
looked terrified, and he smiled at her encouragingly, seeing
her mouth open in a soundless gasp of concern. "Don't
worry, *chica*," he wanted to tell her, "it's not going to be
that bad. And don't do anything foolish. Try not to let
them see you're upset."

In this instance, Colonel Devereaux did not bother with
a long speech. Like Tom Beal, he was anxious to get
started.

Warned by the sudden stillness and Concepción's
widening eyes, Steve Morgan clamped his jaws together as
he heard the whistling sound of the whip, just before it
landed, with sickening force, across his bare shoulders.

The pain was worse, even, than he had expected. Liquid
fire, writhing snakelike over his cringing flesh. And before

Steve had been able to catch his breath the biting strip of leather had slashed downward again, tearing into his flesh so that drops of blood flew into the air. "God!" he muttered, his body shuddering involuntarily, and Beal, hearing, laughed wickedly.

"Whatsa matter, Morgan? Beggin' already?"

Every ounce of stubbornness and will power he possessed collected in Steve Morgan's brain, filling him with a dogged determination that almost wiped out everything else. He closed his eyes, teeth gritted, feeling the splinters from the wooden post embed themselves in the skin of his face and chest as he pressed against it. Concentrate, you have to concentrate . . . the thought pounded at him, blurring even the nauseating crack of the lash every time it cut into his flinching flesh. Beal, disappointed that he hadn't heard another sound out of his victim, went to work with determination.

The whip sang through the air, slashed through skin and muscle as Beal's arm worked tirelessly. The man was an expert, no mistaking it, the French sergeant thought with grudging admiration. The only question was, how long could the prisoner last under this merciless onslaught?

The prisoner, had he but known it, was almost beyond coherent thinking. His body now sagging against the post, held erect only by his bound wrists, Steve Morgan fought almost by instinct against the purely animal, primal urge to open his mouth and scream aloud with agony until his lungs burst, if screaming would bring him some relief. The muscles in his arms felt as if they were slowly being torn apart; his wrists were cut so deeply that he felt sure the rawhide strips had already penetrated to the bone. He held his breath, hoping that the lack of air would make him pass out, and then the whip would come down like a crimson explosion of pain, crushing him against the immovable post, driving the breath from his body with a gasp. He couldn't take this terrible punishment much longer—almost he prayed that Beal would strike harder, let his blows come faster, so as to make an end of it quickly, before he disgraced himself and still retained enough sense to face the bitter knowledge that he was a coward, after all, and just as weak as any other poor wretch who'd had to undergo this same ordeal.

Steve's mind sought desperately to escape—to detach itself somehow from the helpless agony of his tortured body. There was a dull pounding in his ears—each hammer-blow of his own pulse sending a separate vibration of pain through his entire frame.

Concentrate! For God's sake, for your own, concentrate on something, on anything other than this! The insistent screaming of his mind seemed almost to come from outside himself. He was on fire, if only he could find coolness somewhere, and peace! He fixed his dulling mind on water, deep and very cold. A spring in the high forest he came to once; so deep it seemed green and bottomless—dappled with pale sunshine filtering through the leaves high above. Rain forests, dripping with moisture; wet, dark—the only sound the steadily falling water. Miraculously, the pain of his racked and bleeding body seemed to be fading away, leaving only a creeping numbness in its place. He knew it, each time the whiplash connected with torn flesh and muscle, but only from the vibration and the helpless, involuntary writhing of his body's attempts to escape. He saw the icy breakers of the Pacific Ocean at Monterey, tumbling over each other as they foamed their way to oblivion among the wet black rocks. Unconsciousness came at last in great, smothering billows, like fog . . .

"Monsieur Beal! There's no use going on, he's unconscious, he can't feel anything now. The colonel says you are to stop!"

Tom Beal felt, what was almost a kind of madness, seize hold of him. His lips drew back from his teeth in a savage snarl of frustration. Damn it! Damn it to hell! This wasn't going at all the way he'd planned it. Why hadn't Morgan screamed out loud? Why hadn't he broken like all the others, begging for mercy, begging to be allowed to tell everything he knew? It wasn't possible that any man could resist the persuasion of the whip, especially when he, Tom Beal, the expert, was wielding it.

His arm ached—sweat poured down into his eyes, drenched his clothing. He was going to kill this bastard—he'd have them turn him around and tie him with his back to the post this time, so he could really go to work on him. When he got through, if Steve Morgan hadn't talked, he wouldn't even be a man.

"What does he think he is, a goddamn hero?" Beal swore aloud. He swung on the stony-faced sergeant. "What in hell are you waiting for? He's shamming—throw some water over him an' he'll be ready for more; and I can guarantee you that this time he'll start squealin' like a *Juarista* pig he is!"

Beal was so maddened with rage that he raised his arm again, wanting to strike, to maim, and he was momentarily disconcerted when Sergeant Malaval's steely fingers grasped his wrist, stopping his arm on its downward slash.

"I have said—it is the colonel's orders! It is his place to make the decisions here, and we will wait. You understand?" the sergeant added in a harder voice, watching the expression on Beal's face.

"Goddamit!" The American's voice was savage. "I had him—another minute would have done it. Your colonel better damn well make the right decision, or we ain't gonna be able to show our faces around here. Look at them—bunch of dirty peons starin' at that spy like he's some kind of God because he didn't yell yet. I'm tellin' you, Sarge—we better not back down, not now, or they'll all think they can get away with the same thing."

Chapter Thirty-seven

Colonel Devereaux, standing on the small balcony with his hands locked behind his back, felt almost as frustrated as Beal did. Why did this particular man, who had already given him so much trouble, have to prove so stubborn? Beal, as he well knew, was an expert—Esteban Alvarado, or Steve Morgan, whatever he chose to call himself—he should have broken a long time ago. And he, Raoul Devereaux would not have found himself in the quandary he did now.

Damnation! He should not, perhaps, have made this "interrogation" so public. But how was he to know? Crazy, arrogant, half-*gachupín* American! He'd meant to make an example of him, to show these peasants how easily these *Juaristas*, who raved of patriotism and freedom, could crack under a few swipes of the whip. Now, simply because the man had been too proud to cry out, they'd be thinking him heroic—a martyr of the revolution. He would not have it! Alvarado was a spy—a common criminal who had to be punished. He must show these people that the French dispensed stern justice to spies and traitors.

And yet—tempering his rightful anger, came the uncomfortable thought of possible repercussions. There was the woman to be thought of too. Now collapsed in a sobbing, crumpled heap at his side, with only the manacles he had ordered fastened to her wrists to keep her at the balcony rail, she was still a problem to be reckoned with. He had to remember that these were no ordinary peons he was dealing with. As his prisoner had already pointed out with supreme insolence, Don Francisco Alvarado was a man of far-reaching influence as well as being one of the richest *hacendados* in the whole of Mexico. He had hoped that with a full confession he would be able to forestall any angry reactions on Don Francisco's part. But now—Colonel Devereaux swore to himself again, his eyes lingering in spite of himself on Ginny's bright hair.

What a woman! He could feel himself flushing angrily when he remembered the insults and the threats she had shrieked at him when she found out what was happening to her husband. She would tell the whole world of the methods he used—how he had tricked her. She would have American armies here to avenge her—her uncle in Paris, who had the emperor's ear, would see to it personally that the colonel's career would be finished. Such threats—such fury! And then, typically female, she had begun to weep and wail and beg him to stop the torture. Even now, she sobbed uncontrollably, her shoulders heaving. He should not have brought her here perhaps, but *Dieu!* He could not help desiring her! He had thought to be subtle—to play with her, trick her and then cow her into submission. To possess her body and feel her trembling flesh under his as she opened herself to him. And she had dared threaten!

Did she really love her husband that much? How much? Maybe there was still a way he could achieve everything he wanted, without having to suffer any consequences ... yes, it was not for nothing his brother officers would sometimes laughingly refer to him as "the old fox" or "that wily devil, Devereaux."

An idea came to him, and he made an abrupt signal of the arm to Sergeant Malaval, who had been waiting, since they revived the prisoner, with an impassive face. Malaval wanted orders, did he? And those cowlike peasants down there, they waited to see what *el colonel* would do. No doubt Esteban Alvarado waited too—he hoped he was bemoaning his fate, that his flesh cringed with anticipation.

Yes, he could show them all that stubbornness didn't
pay—she, this trembling, weeping creature at his side,
she'd find that out too.

The sergeant had come up closer and stood at attention,
his face tilted upward, eyes squinting against the glare.

Devereaux barked out staccato orders in French, and
even before Malaval had saluted smartly and pivoted
around, the girl was staring up at him with wide, unbeliev-
ing eyes that were drenched with tears.

"No! Not that—for God's sake, I beg of you, have
pity!"

He forced his voice to be stern, although he triumphed
inwardly.

"And why, madame, should I have pity? He's a spy—
he's threatened me, and you have threatened me. A
colonel in the French army, madame, does not flinch away
from threats in the execution of his duty."

She flung her body towards his, the tears slipping down
her cheeks as she implored him again to be merciful.

"Please—oh, please! I swear to you, I'll say nothing—
I'll do anything you tell me to do—I'll do anything, anything, only—"

"A pity they have no Devil's Island for our criminals
here. Come, madame, what an exhibition! Perhaps your
husband will put up a better show, eh?"

She opened her mouth to scream wildly and he bent
down swiftly, clapping his hand over her lips.

"No! We'll have no more hysterics, if you please! I
thought you had more spirit." His voice softened as he
forced her eyes to meet his. "Perhaps, if you'll do as
you're told, we can strike a bargain, after all. I'm really a
soft-hearted man, I have no stomach for a woman's tears.
Will you be reasonable? Will you listen now?"

She nodded dully, and he removed his hand, fingers going up to stroke his jaw.

"I'll do anything," she murmured as if he had mesmerized her. "Yes, anything you say. Don't let them kill
him! For God's sake, spare his life at least!"

"Stand up!" His voice snapped the command. "You'll
stand up straight beside me here and watch your husband
branded with the mark of the fleur-de-lis—the way we
brand our incorrigible prisoners in France. One shriek, one
protest from you, and I'll have them repeat the performance, as many times as necessary, until you will hear him

screaming like a maniac as he prays for death to release
him. Do you understand me, madame?"

She nodded her comprehension like a puppet, a wooden,
lifeless doll, her face white, shining with small beads of
sweat under the pitiless glare of the sun. But in the end
the colonel had to assist her to rise; she seemed incapable
of movement, the only signs of her emotion now showed
in the stiffness of her carriage and the wide, staring green
eyes that still beseeched him.

Quelle femme! Devereaux thought again, admiringly. In
spite of her obvious distress she had enough pride left to
stand motionless, knuckles gleaming whitely as she
clutched onto the hot iron railing before her. He thought
he would take a great deal of pleasure in forcing her ul-
timate submission—even more in taunting her with the
fact that she was willing to turn whore in return for her
husband's life. Ah, she wouldn't be so proud then, there'd
be no more threats, no more insults! His desire swelled, so
that he had to tear his eyes away from the tempting
curves of her woman-flesh and look out again over the
parade ground.

They were heating the iron. He could not resist pointing
this out to her, and put a falsely solicitous arm around her
waist when she swayed slightly.

"Come!" he said in an overly sympathetic voice, "they
are almost ready, it will not take long. My men are ex-
perts—the sergeant will perform the task himself. We
brand horses and cattle every day, surely you've watched
it yourself?"

"Please!" she whispered in a choked, hoarse manner,
and he smiled. It would do her good to stay here with him
and watch her husband treated like a common criminal.
Perhaps it would make him less of a hero in her eyes, after
all. The application of a red-hot iron often had the effect
of making pleading, grovelling wretches out of the
strongest men.

He hoped that the prisoner would look up and see his
wife—believe that she was here in order to enjoy the spec-
tacle of his public humiliation. Yes, perhaps that thought
would help vanquish his damned stiff-backed *criolla* pride!

Frowning slightly, Devereaux admitted to himself that
after all, he hated the *gachupines*, who called themselves
criollos, and prided themselves on their pure European
descent. Damn *criollos*, thinking themselves better than

anyone else, even the Frenchmen who were here to help them and keep the emperor they had wanted perched on his precarious throne! Haughty, arrogant, proud-faced bastards, with all the airs of the first *conquistadores* about them still; cocooned by generations of wealth and power, and presuming to treat their own defenders with an overdone politeness that only barely veiled their patronizing attitude!

It felt good to be revenged on one of them at least, for all the slights, all the patient tolerance that he had fumed against for so long. Let's see how one of the *caballeros* feels, being treated like a *ladron*, worse than one of his grandfather's own peons! Yes, they would see how he despised them all, and especially the big *hacendados* who lived like kings and thought their power limitless. Men like Don Francisco Alvarado, who could have used the title of Marques had he not pretended a false, "democratic" humility; men like Don Juan Sandoval and his sneering pup of a son; yes, even his own parents-in-law, the Vegas, who were just as rich and just as overbearing. Did they really think that he was so stupid, so blind, that he hadn't known their lovely young daughter was no longer a virgin when he'd had her? Or that he hadn't known that was the only reason they had condescended to give her to him for a wife? Damaged goods, to be quickly foisted off on an ignorant Frenchman, who should feel himself lucky he was marrying a Vega! Bah! Whoever his little Alicia's lover had been, he'd taught her nothing at all about making love. She was a shrinking, frightened ninny of a girl, and not at all the passionate little siren he liked to imply that she was. Still, he'd desired her at first, because she was very young and pretty and had quiet, ladylike manners. And mostly because she brought with her an enormous dowry which he'd thought would compensate for her lack of a maidenhead. Yes, at the beginning, when the French rode triumphant on the tide of their victories, he had even thought of settling down here, becoming a *hacendado* himself, with peons slaving for him—accepted by the petit aristocracy of Mexico because he had married one of them. And then, everything had started to go sour.

The tide was turning. The followers of Juarez had proved stubborn, and with the help of smuggled American guns their generals were beginning to win victories of their own. Even Bazaine, that old ex-tiger, was beginning to realize it—he had decided to withdraw his troops towards the central provinces, to "concentrate" as he put it. What humiliation, what madness! But he had to follow orders, even though it went against the grain.

Devereaux frowned, thinking about the dust-covered messenger who had arrived only a short time ago, just before he'd given the orders to begin the afternoon's entertainment. They were to leave Zacatecas immediately, and march to Durango to reinforce the defenders there. "Leave tonight—the Emperor's Irregulars will take care of the mopping up afterward—" in essence, that was how his orders had read. That damned *criollo* down there, who had just been beaten like a dog for his crimes, he had known all this already. "You've lost the war. It's only a matter of time now," he had said in that mocking drawl of his. Didn't he place any value on his own life, that malcontent? How long could pride stand up to pain and torture, or a brace of rifle barrels staring you in the face? We'll see, Devereaux thought, we'll see!

He noticed that Sergeant Malaval was looking up towards him, waiting. Almost imperceptibly he moved his arm, giving the signal to begin. The girl stirred beside him and he tightened his arm around her waist as he heard her hissing, indrawn breath.

"Remember what I told you, madame. No shrieks, no hysterics. And then, when it's over, you can give me reason, perhaps, to spare your husband's life."

Ginny hardly heard what he said, in his softly commanding unctuous voice. In spite of herself, her eyes were glued to the courtyard below, her teeth caught in her lower lip.

If he can stand it, she thought frantically, then I can. I must not scream, I must not give way, or they'll do worse. Oh God, help me to bear this, help me to bear one more thing, help me to bear my own guilt! Her teeth caught, all unconsciously, in her lower lip, as she tried to persuade herself that this was all a nightmare, that she'd wake up soon to find Steve's arms around her, holding her close as they had done in the old days when their bodies had sought each other's warmth, even in sleep.

The sergeant was stirring the coals with the long-handled iron. She could hardly bear to look towards that still, bound figure that was soaked with blood—there was blood everywhere, his back had been torn to pieces by that monster! She remembered with a pang that seemed to pierce her heart the rippling play of muscles slippery with sweat under her fingers when she had clutched at him in the throes of love—yes, love! Why couldn't she have admitted it to herself before? She had loved him from the very first time he had kissed her so ruthlessly, laughing at her anger—a handsome, hard-faced stranger with the bluest eyes she had ever encountered. Oh God, why had she been so willfully stubborn? He had loved her, she realized that too now, with the force of a mortal blow. It was because of her that he was here now, tortured and perhaps dying. He would not have come back, having made good his escape if he hadn't cared. We were both too proud to admit it, she thought with a terrible, bitter anguish, and now it's too late. If they kill him now he'll die hating me, despising me.

Standing with his boots astride behind the prisoner, Sergeant Malaval was saying in his flat, expressionless voice,

"You still have an opportunity to confess, if you are sensible, *Juarista* dog! Can you hear me? If you do not talk fast, I'm going to be forced to take a hot iron to your sore back, do you understand? Your stubbornness will not last long then, you might as well spare yourself worse agony by being sensible for a change!"

Only half-conscious in spite of the buckets of water they had thrown over him, Steve Morgan heard the words come to him from far away and their full import did not penetrate his pain-fogged mind until he heard the concerted sigh of fear and compassion that went up from the crowd. Strangely enough he wanted to throw back his head and laugh with bitter, furious mirth. How very predictable, how pompous these French were! Such sticklers for old traditions! They were going to mark him with the fleur-de-lis—symbol of France, brand of French criminals. And for what? To leave a scar on his corpse? It was really surprising they hadn't brought their guillotine over here with them.

Tom Beal had failed, and the good sergeant was taking over. He had heard their muttered argument behind him before Beal had marched away in a rage. And now the sergeant was marching somewhere, tired of waiting for an answer. He could have told him ... Steve tried to blink the sweat from his eyes and focus them. He wondered vaguely why Concepcion was still here, why her face was so drawn and haggard and had taken on a pasty hue under the tawny-gold skin. Why? Oh, yes, they were going to make him a French criminal, they deserved a gesture in return, a final piece of useless, defiant bravado. He was expected to scream out loud, and he would. It might make them furious enough to kill him off and finish this ridiculous piece of play-acting . . .

Sergeant Malaval had grasped the handle of the branding iron in his gloved fist and now pivoted smartly on his heel, holding the metal rod before him.

No need to spit on it to make sure it was hot enough— the familiar shape of the emblem of France glowed almost white hot. Still holding the iron firmly before him, Sergeant Malaval took a step forward, aimed, and pressed downward, holding it down just long enough to hear the torn, bloody flesh sizzle and burn as the heat seared into it.

The prisoner's sagging, tortured body had gone rigid as the arms strained to break free and the exposed strips of muscle writhed and jumped with a life of their own.

His eyes closed, face contorted in an uncontrollable grimace of agony, Steve Morgan cried out hoarsely, but it was not the animal scream of pain and fear that Malaval had expected. With the charred flesh already turning black, outlining the fleur-de-lis clearly against the crimson, bloody mess that Beal had left, this stubborn dog had had the unmitigated audacity to shout, with the last of his strength, no doubt,

"Viva la revolución!"

In spite of the presence of a detachment of French soldiers, bayonets fixed to their rifles, a scattered, defiant cheer went up from the crowd. A pretty young woman, whom the sergeant had not been able to help noticing earlier, had the impudence to scream that they were butchers and torturers. An unidentifiable voice yelled, *"Mueran los Franceses!"*

Malaval looked up uncertainly at the colonel. Damn, he thought viciously, we're going to have a riot on our hands in a minute if he doesn't do something. This prisoner's made himself a hero with his insolent bravado! We ought to shoot him right now and make an end to it. But it was the colonel, after all, who made the decisions around here.

Devereaux leaned over the balcony rail, his voice loud with suppressed anger.

"Sergeant! Get those damned peasants off my parade grounds! Get them out, quickly, and close the gates behind them."

Malaval snapped to attention.

"*Oui, mon Colonel*! At once!" He hesitated, and dared to ask, "*Mon Colonel*—the prisoner—"

"Do as I say, Sergeant! Get rid of that crowd! The prisoner isn't going anywhere, let him bake in the sun for a while, until I decide what to do with him."

Saluting smartly, Malaval clicked his heels together and turned, shouting orders at his troop.

"Get rid of the crowd," the colonel had said. That was easy enough. Faced with threats and bayonets they dispersed like sheep, sullenly. Bunch of dirty, thieving peons! He, personally, would be glad to leave this stinking hellhole of a town. Get to someplace civilized, where a man could relax in a nice *cantina* occasionally, with a girl and a passable bottle of wine. They said Durango wasn't too bad. Well, they'd be on their way before nightfall, leaving the Irregulars behind to take care of things.

Malaval wondered, with a certain degree of curiosity, what the colonel was going to do about the prisoner. What a piece of effrontery that had been! The old man couldn't let him get away with it. But of course, there was the woman. She hadn't appeared to be a prisoner this morning, when they'd surprised her with the colonel over breakfast; perhaps she was his latest mistress after all.

The sergeant shrugged. It was none of his business. Thank God they'd be out of here before long. He chanced a quick look up at the balcony, and saw it was empty. 'So *monsieur le Colonel* is bound to be busy for a while' he pondered. Lucky Colonel!

Malaval posted two men in the smart green and white uniform of the Mexican Loyalist armies to stand guard over the prisoner and strode towards his own quarters. He might as well get packed.

Chapter Thirty-eight

The shadowed interior of the locked and shuttered room seemed intolerably hot and stuffy. A setting for a bad dream that went on and on endlessly, drawing Ginny into its vortex of horror.

Her fingers felt clammy and numb as she fumbled with the fastenings of her gown. Humiliation piled on humiliation—she had to undress for him, he had warned her that they had made a bargain and she must fulfill her end of it with the willing submission of her body. Willing! Dear God, how could this fat, obscenely smiling man who watched her every move so closely think she could ever be willing? He had made it clear what her position in this "arrangement" must be.

"You'll forgive me, my dear, if we dispense with the little niceties that take so much time? I suppose, like all clumsy soldiers I've learned to take my pleasures in a hurry, between wars, so to speak. This afternoon I shall enjoy your lovely body—this evening, it will be a long ride to Durango. I'm sure you'll give me some very pleasant memories to carry with me! Just remember, *ma petite*, I'm not the kind of fool you thought I was, am I? And I would never put up with a bad bargain."

The gown slipped from her body, and Ginny began to tremble. Her body felt like ice, it was all she could do to control the chattering of her teeth.

"Come now, madame! I really must request you to hurry! Remove your shift, I'm anxious to see what treasures lie beneath it."

Rigid with sick revulsion, her mind still dazed with shock, Ginny found herself complying with his demand. She stepped out of the shift. In spite of the stifling heat outside she felt so cold—so cold! She did not dare look up, she didn't have the courage at this point when her defeat was complete, to meet those yellow, greedy eyes that must now be devouring every inch of her cringing flesh.

When Devereaux came to her, his hairy, bloated body revoltingly white like a toad's belly, Ginny felt she must surely scream. Instead, forcing herself to remember the infamous bargain she had made with this monster, she stood quite still and allowed him to push her backwards onto the bed, only the tiny drop of blood that oozed from her lower lip where she had bitten into it revealing her inner agitation and torment.

"Let me look at you first. Ah, as I had guessed, you have a magnificent body, meant for love."

She had to fight back rising waves of nausea. How could he talk of love? This repulsive, hairy beast—what did he know of love? Love was the thundering pound of blood drumming in her ears, quickening her pulses when Steve touched her. His hands could be gentle, or harshly demanding, but always, sometimes even in spite of herself, he had been capable of making her feel. I loved him, even when I hated him most, she thought, and stared stonily at the ceiling while soft, pudgy fingers crawled over her body. How different from those long brown fingers whose touch her body craved so much and would never feel again! And I fought him, I told him over and over again how much I hate him, she thought with an anguish that was like a scream inside her mind. My love, my lover, my life—I almost killed him once, for doing this, when all the time I really wanted him in the same way—yes, he made me a woman, he made me need him, he taught me how to feel. And now—

The present was another man's hands, squeezing greedily at her breasts. Wet, horrible lips pressed against hers, unfamiliar tongue thrusting in her mouth. The present was unbelievable horror, and she wished she could die now, at this very moment.

Raoul Devereaux was like a pig—a fat, hairy, beastly creature pressing her body down under his repulsive weight, forcing his way into her.

Just as if she had really been a whore he'd bought for an hour or two, he was telling her what to do.

"Ah, you're a born coquette, aren't you little one? How cold you pretend to be on the surface, but your body is like a little furnace, isn't it? Hold me—yes, like that—and now your legs, yes, a little wider, throw them around my body, there's no need to be so shy, you've done this before, haven't you?"

I can't go through with this, I cannot bear another instant, no, I'll be sick, her mind screamed wildly, while her body submitted, even then. She moved under him, but only because he had slipped a hand under her, raising her up to meet his panting, grunting thrusts. She had to be free—and the thought made her squirm and thrash as she rolled her head from side to side, sobbing with pain, with despair, with hopelessness. His weight pressed down on her, she felt the slickness of his saliva on her face, her breasts, smelled the fetid odor of his breath.

"Little slut—little wanton—did he teach you all this? You need a real man for a change, don't you? I'll give you what you want, all right."

She moaned like a demented animal and he mistook her moans for sounds of pleasure. When she knew she couldn't stand this horror any longer, when she opened her mouth to scream her denial of the shame and degradation he was perpetrating on her body, he closed her mouth with his slobbering lips, with his own grunts of final ecstasy.

Afterwards, leaving her lying there so pale and exhausted she looked like death itself, he became all business, manner bluff and hearty as he began dressing himself again.

"I'm really sorry I have to leave you so soon, little pigeon. You were magnificent, just as I knew you would be once the shyness wore off, hmm? Quite the best woman I've ever had, and believe me I've had plenty, all over the world." He gave her his old twinkling look, actually winking at her. "I don't intend to let you get off too easily, now I've discovered how charming you are, don't you

worry about that! I'll tell you what, when I get to
wherever we're going in the end and get settled in, I'll find
a nice little apartment and send for you. How does that
sound, eh? Ah, we'll have some long nights of glorious
love, we won't have to be so hurried then—don't look so
forlorn, petite, it's not forever, you know—we soldiers are
always having to say goodbye!"

He thought, or pretended to think, that she was sorry
he was leaving! Oh God, didn't the man have any
sensitivity, any compunctions at all?

From somewhere in the depths of her shrinking,
degraded soul, Ginny summoned up the strength to remind
him about his promise. Licking her lips, she managed to
whisper the stumbling, hesitating words; almost afraid how
he might react.

"About my husband. You said—"

He gave her a sharp look that he quickly turned into a
debonair, slightly lop-sided smile.

"What! Still thinking of that no-good rascal? That's a
woman for you, I suppose! Never know when they're well
off. Yes, well—don't worry about it. I'll give orders before
I leave. They'll cut him loose tonight, after he's had plenty
of time to think about his misdeeds and be grateful he's
getting off so lightly. It has to be after dark, though—you
understand? I don't want the people around here to think
they can get away with the same kind of thing. I'll have
him sent on his way. Alive—quite alive! Feel better?"

He turned back to the mirror, adjusting the fit of his
starched, tightly fitting cutaway. "The Mexicans, the Irregulars, will take care of it. They're going to take over
here for a while, until we see how the land lies. But
listen," he continued, advancing towards the bed and staring down at her, "you're coming to me! No use going
back now—gossip travels. Who'd have you?" He gave an
abrupt chuckle. "Certainly not that strait-laced old
martinet, Don Francisco. The *criollos* are very strict about
family honor, especially when it comes to women! I hate
to sound so blunt, my dear, when you've been uncommonly sweet and obliging, but you have to face the facts
of life. You should be grateful to me, I've freed you from
the prisoner's life you'd have had to lead, like the rest of
these Mexican ladies. We'll have lots of fun together, you
and I. You'll find I can be more than generous! Now give

me a kiss like a good girl. I'll send Quita up here with something for you to eat, after a while."

Ignoring her instinctive shrinking and her pale, trancelike look, the colonel bent over, seizing her by the shoulders, and planted a wet, hearty kiss on her lips. No sooner had the door closed behind him than Ginny dragged herself from the bed, and staggering to the corner of the room was violently sick into the washbasin.

Going back to the bed with her knees weak and trembling with reaction, she buried her face in her hands, weeping helplessly. The colonel's words seemed burned into her mind, like the ineradicable scars of shame he had left on her body.

He's right—I'm done for now. Tarnished—dirty, dirty! They'd all turn away from me if they knew, and by now that brute of a man must have seen to it that everyone thinks I'm his willing mistress! I've saved Steve's life, but he'd never believe that—no, he'll go away hating me, despising me, thinking it was I who betrayed him. What's left for me now? I ought to kill myself—yes, that's it! She raised her head and her eyes stared wildly about the room, their green turned darker by the force of her emotions. I don't want to live any longer, she thought feverishly, I can't stand to feel myself torn apart by such shame, such agony! He's still out there—they've left him out there in the pitiless glare of the sun, to burn with thirst and suffer the agonies of hell—I'll throw myself from the balcony, and he'll understand what happened; that I didn't want to live without him.

She ran, stumbling, to the shutters, pulling at them violently, but the colonel had locked them securely and they refused to yield to her frenzied tugging and pounding. She sank to her knees, groaning out loud, and after a while some semblance of sanity returned and she threw herself across the bed once more, praying that the colonel and his Legionnaires would leave soon, giving her an opportunity, perhaps to bribe one of the Irregulars—she had heard that they were notoriously corrupt—perhaps they would let her talk to Steve . . . she would throw herself at his feet and beg his forgiveness, she would explain everything! She closed her eyes and murmured his name—"Steve—Steve darling." Stupid! As if by saying his name she could ever recall him to her side again! He'd never forgive her, how well she knew the extent of his anger, his arrogant, un-

bending nature! She thought, He'd prefer to die, rather
than to find out what I've done to save his life—he'd
despise me for my weakness, even if it was all for him!

Ginny lost all idea of the passage of time, or how long
it had been, after a while. Vaguely, she imagined that she
heard the sound of bugles, and shouts from the soldiers,
the clashing of harness as the Frenchmen rode away.
What did it matter now? It was too late for her.

She lay unmoving, as if she was dead already, and
prayed for oblivion. The Mexican woman had come, and
left some fresh fruit and water for her, but there was not
a trace of compassion in that brown, high-cheekboned
face. She brought some cotton garments with her too, and
tossed these on the bed. "You will find these clothes more
practical for riding, since you will be leaving soon. *El
señor Colonel* said so. He said you would let me have
your gown in exchange."

Without waiting for a reply, the woman was already
gathering up the dress that Ginny had kicked aside so
carelessly and still lay on the floor. She smoothed out the
wrinkles, folding it carefully, and Ginny could feel the
weak tears gather in her eyes once more. Her gown—her
beautiful, beautiful fire-opal ballgown! It was the last thing
that Steve had given her, that gown, and she had not even
thanked him for it. But she hated it now, she was glad
that this woman would take it away. The gown, her silk
shift, even her polished kid shoes—all gone, like her
virtue.

The coarsely-woven cotton felt rough and scratchy
against her skin, like the hair-shirt of a penitent. Ginny
pulled the simple garments on carelessly and lay back on
the bed again, her senses too dulled by what had happened
to wonder what would become of her now. She closed her
eyes and horrifying scenes danced behind her closed
eyelids. Oh God, oh God! Let me wake up now—let this
all be a nightmare, let me wake in his arms.

The rattling of a key in the lock suddenly sounded as
loud as an explosion, and she sat upright with a start, her
cheeks beginning to burn. What had happened? Who was
it? Had the colonel changed his mind after all and decided
that she must join him at once?

The door opened, creaking on its hinges, and Ginny
gave a gasp of terror when she recognized the man who
stood outlined against the fading light, stooping slightly as

he eased his long, thin frame through the doorway. He walked in without any preamble and stood looking at her, his pointed tongue running over thin lips that stretched in a wolfish grin when he saw her expression.

"Expectin' someone else, maybe?"

That was all he said then, but she was suddenly, frighteningly conscious of the fact that her skirt reached only to her ankles, that her feet were bare, and the blouse she wore was far too loose and cut too low. His eyes stripped her without any pretence, as if they had already penetrated her clothing; as if he knew she was naked under the thin cotton fabric.

Ginny cowered like a frightened animal under their pale, leering regard, her arms coming up to cross instinctively over her breasts.

"What do you want? What are you doing here?" Her throat was dry with terror and she had to force the words out.

He strolled closer, and stood looking down at her, pushing the door closed behind him with his foot. The little thud it gave made her jump.

"Nervous, ain't you? Colonel said I was to take care of you. Get you safely away before the whole town goes over to the *Juaristas*."

She jumped to her feet because sitting there on the edge of the bed had suddenly become intolerable under the knowing gaze of his pale, sneering eyes.

"But he said the Mexican army would remain here—what do you mean?"

"What do I mean? Shucks, I mean they're too damn scared to stick around, now that the Frenchies have pulled out. This whole dirty little treacherous town just loves *el presidente*, couldn't you tell?"

His voice sounded casual, normal, but he took another step towards her as she talked, and with a feeling of horror Ginny felt the heat of his body, like a physical, crawling thing.

If he touches me, she thought suddenly, it will be worse than anything that went before—it will be more than I can bear—it will be the end.

He started to laugh, softly, and reaching out, grasped the fullness of the cotton *camisa*, pulling her forward. There was no haste in his movements, no urgency. He kept laughing when her hands flailed impotently against

his chest, and then, with a quick movement that took her
by surprise, he had pulled the blouse free of the waistband
of her skirt and slipped his other hand under it.

"Easy now, easy!" he chuckled, and his fingers found a
nipple, squeezing viciously. She screamed, and the walls of
the room seemed to tilt and sway inwards as waves of
agony seemed to blacken and numb her mind. Suddenly,
he had swung her body around so that she leaned backward against him. His other hand came up and covered
her mouth, pressing down cruelly until her head fell
helplessly back against his shoulder. Looking down, still
grinning, Beal could see the white, strained arch of the
woman's throat, the muscles standing up along it like
cords. She tried to kick backwards, but the folds of her
skirt impeded her and she lost her balance, falling against
him.

Whimpers came from behind his hand. She sounded like
an animal, he thought.

"Stop struggling," he warned her. "I ain't got the time
to fuck you right now. Just wanted to show you
something." Deliberately, his hand moved over her
breasts, and when she tried to claw at him he caught her
nipple between his thumb and forefinger, squeezing until
the struggles stopped and she lay inertly against him,
moaning, her eyes closed.

"You had enough? You gonna come quietly?"

She made an inarticulate sound and he released her with
a contemptuous push that sent her sprawling to her knees,
bent over, her long, tangled hair shielding her face. She
kept sobbing with pain and shame. He unlocked the shutters and came back to her, hauling her to her feet, slapping her when she flinched away from him.

"You better learn fast that I mean business, miss high
and mighty! Give me any trouble an' you'll get more of
the same. Understand?" Grinning his thin-lipped, vicious
smile, he caught her wrist, twisting it up behind her back,
and pushed her ahead of him, out onto the balcony.

The Mexican *Cazadores* wore smart gold-trimmed uniforms that seemed to reflect streaks of red from the
torches that had been lit in the courtyard. There was still
light in the sky, although the sun had almost set, and was
lost behind the mountains now. Even their rifles looked
new and shining, their polished stocks gleaming.

In contrast, the ragged, uneven row of men who stood

lined up against the far wall looked like bedraggled scarecrows, hardly human any longer with their gaunt, bearded faces looking like grotesque masks in the play of light and shadow. None of them wore blindfolds, and some, barely able to stand, leaned up against the wall for support. They were manacled to each other, arms and legs chained.

"*Juaristas.* Orders from the general himself were to execute all prisoners. You'll make a might purty widow!"

Even now, dazed with pain, Ginny could scarcely comprehend what was happening. A sudden, muffled roll of drums almost drowned out Beal's words, and the shouted command of an officer. "Ready—aim—"

Rifles came up smartly, clapped against white-clad shoulders. "Fire!" The word was lost in the volleying explosion, like a crackle of thunder. Like wooden figures the broken bodies that had been men, had breathed, had feared, perhaps, jerked as shots tore into them; then pitched forward to lie still.

A thin, shrill scream tore itself from Ginny's throat as she flung herself forward. "No! He promised, he *promised!*" The pain from her twisted arm, which Beal still gripped so firmly, and the terrible, sickening shock of the sight which she had just witnessed made her crumple in the next instant, like a lifeless doll herself, as she slid into a dead faint.

Chapter Thirty-nine

"Consider yourself real lucky," Beal said. He laughed down at the anguished, half-demented squirming of the girl who lay under him on the bed of the baggage wagon, pinned down by his weight. "I could have had you shot too, after I was through with you," he continued in the same sneering voice. "Only carrying out orders, you see—you was a prisoner too, after all. But I always wanted to have me a *soldadera*, like them Mex soldiers—a white woman, not some greaser bitch. You might just do, baby-doll, once you've learned a few things."

The two other counter-guerillas, one riding his horse beside it and the other driving, laughed along with Beal. They found it amusing to watch Beal tame this woman who had fallen into their hands like a lucky windfall. He had already stripped her naked, and her frenzied struggles only served to present them with a better view of certain parts of her firm, long-limbed, sweat-gleaming body.

Matt Cooper, a big bearlike Arkansan, kept tilting a bottle of tequila to his mouth and looking over his shoulder, so that from time to time the wagon would lurch crazily and Beal would swear. Ordinarily, Matt was a bluffly kind man who would never have joined in Beal's kind of sadistic "fun," but when he was drunk Matt could become mean and dangerous, and right now, watching Beal with the girl, he could hardly wait to have his turn at her. God, but she was a beaut! And in spite of her seeming reluctance, she'd already sold her body to that fat colonel, hoping to save her lover's life. Beal had told them the story, laughing. "She ain't no better than a whore, any case," he had said. "Morgan—that damn turn-coat half-breed that just got an end put to his misery with them other *Juaristas*, he carried her all over the country with him—had her trained in some real fancy houses, I've heard. Like Lilas' down in El Paso. Now it's our turn, huh boys?"

Neither Matt, nor Pecos Brady, who kept looking over the side of the wagon and grinning, had contradicted him. Why shouldn't they take their turn? The colonel had instructed Beal to bring her to him in Durango, but hell, a lot of things could happen along the way! The colonel need never know, and there were other women he could get, with all his money.

The girl had bruises all over her body—there was a livid blue mark on her cheekbone, where Beal had hit her, and her lip bled. But she kept right on struggling, whimpering like a hurt animal.

Two Mexican officers, catching up with the troop that was already a few miles out of Zacatecas, rode up and started to laugh.

"Hey *amigo*—you got troubles? Caught yourself a wild one, eh?"

"You ought to do like we do to those *Juarista* women we catch, when they're not willing," the other officer said, his teeth a flash of white under his mustache.

"Won't take me long," Beal said between his teeth. He hit her again and she screamed. The imprint of his fingers flamed against the whiteness of her breast.

"But why waste any time at all? With four of us to hold her down a man could do as he pleased with her, eh? And perhaps she would not have the strength to struggle afterwards!" The Mexican who had spoken first was persistent, his small, bloodshot eyes were fixed on the pale, squirming body of the copper-haired woman. *Caramba*, but this one was worth having! Even if he had to pay the *Norteamericanos* for a share in their plunder.

"Ah, shit," Pecos grumbled, licking his lips, "why not,

Beal? Give her a taste of what's in store for her—she might's well get used to it!"

With a jerk, Matt Cooper pulled the mules to a halt. "I'm so goddam hard for her I can't stand to wait another minute, hear? I say let's get on with it."

His words were the last thing that Ginny remembered clearly of that night. For the rest of her life, she would try to push the memory far, far back into the recesses of her mind—so far that it wouldn't come back to haunt her nightmares. . . .

They tied the lantern to the side of the wagon and threw her onto the ground beside it. When she kept screaming someone stuffed a dirty, foul-tasting neckerchief into her mouth.

Strangely enough what seemed to hurt her most was the way they dragged her arms and legs apart and held them down. That and the thought of the obscenity of her position as they raped her, one by one. The degradation to her woman's soul was worse than what they did to her body, for it would heal, eventually. The stickiness of the blood between her thighs mixed with the drying semen. The animal grunts, eyes glaring down into hers, laughter that was not really laughter but a mixture of lust and excitement.

By the time the last man had his turn at her there was no longer any real need to hold her still. She was slipping into darkness, and did not even know it when Matt Cooper lifted her in his great, strong arms and put her down among the sacks on the wagon bed. Later, he came to lie beside her, while Beal took his turn driving the wagon. And it was in Matt's arms that Ginny woke up, moaning with pain, feeling her body one great, throbbing ache.

In his own rough way, Matt was kind to her during the weeks that followed—the weeks of gruelling, exhausting travel in the wake of the Imperialist Mexican armies commanded by General Mejia, who was far away himself, in Mexico City most of the time. Ginny found herself a camp follower, one of the wretched *soldaderas* who trailed their men, cooked for them, made and broke camp, and serviced their needs. *"La gringa soldadera"* they called her, and she gained a grudging acceptance from the other women when they saw that her lot was in some ways worse than theirs. For she, after all, had three men to take care of, after all, and one of them was that *Norteamericano* *"fiero"*—the man called Beal, who was liked by no one, not even his own compadres. A strange, coldly cruel man who loved to kill, but most of all to torture. It was he who questioned the prisoners they took. And when he took a woman there was always the pain he needed to mete out before his lust could be fully satisfied. Ginny was to learn this, just as she learned to tremble when he crooked his finger at her; to acquiesce quickly to whatever he wanted her to do, without question, because if she did not the agony of her "punishment" would stay with her for days. The man seemed to enjoy his absolute domination of her. Whereas Pecos was only interested in food and the fleeting pleasure he obtained by using her body as an outlet for his lust, Beal was more concerned with breaking her spirit completely. Time and time again, when she failed to satisfy him, or he found some fault he could accuse her of, he would beat her—using his razor strap with cold deliberation, laughing at her helpless struggles, until she was a collapsed, sobbing heap at his feet, pleading with him brokenly not to hurt her anymore. On one of these occasions Tom Beal did for the first time what he was to do again, when he thought she needed to be reminded who owned her. He knew that several of the Mexican officers wanted her—they would make excuses to ride back to the baggage wagons, and make bold, admiring comments, asking her to pull the ragged black *rebozo* off her head so they could see her hair . . . or to raise her skirts a trifle. She never answered them, and would look straight ahead until they got tired of their games and rode away. But Beal—Beal arranged to sell her to one of them, a *capitan* who fancied himself a great lover.

"He's promised me ten pesos," he told her, grinning wickedly. "See you bring it all back to me, you whore!"

She gave an uncontrollable cry of shame and fear and he caught her by the hair, tugging her cruelly back to her feet.

"Ain't so grand now, are you? I remember those fancy airs you useta have, just like you was a lady. But I knew you, bitch! I knew you for what you are, right from the beginning! An' remember this, you're mine—you'll whore for me when I tell you to, and you'll crawl to me if I say the word. Just you remember good!"

He flung her away from him and she lay still, only her shoulders moving as she sobbed, quietly and hopelessly.

But if Beal contributed to the hell that her life had become, Ginny found that Matt Cooper helped, in his way, to make it slightly more bearable. He seemed to take an almost childish pride in her, and if she had clothes to wear, such as they were, it was Matt who found them for her. It was Matt, too, who gave her a knife, and taught her how to use it.

"Some of these women are pretty wild, tough customers. They're always gettin' in fights—pullin' knives on each other. Wouldn't want to see your purty face marked up, baby. Matt's gonna teach you. Just be sure Tom Beal don't know nothin' about it, see?" Matt boasted he was the "best damn knife-fighter in the hills" and he taught her every trick he could think of. He enjoyed wrestling with her too, teaching her the names of various holds; shouting with laughter when her legs got tangled up in her skirt and she sprawled under him in the dirt. At times like this, all she had to do was haul the skirt up and "grab him a little bit" as he put it. The other women shrieked with laughter when this happened, but they forbore to start any fights with *la gringa*. "That one," they would say, half-admiring, half-disparaging, "she has learned to fight just like a man, no?"

Even the lazy Pecos began to think it looked like fun.

"Teachin' a woman to wrassle, ain't that somethin'? Like to see one of them other bitches try tanglin' with our little *soldadera*, huh, Matt?" He taught her some water-front tricks he'd picked up on the wharfs in San Francisco.

Mainly from a purely animal, primitive sense of self-preservation, Ginny learned fast. More, this same animal kind of furtiveness kept her from letting Tom Beal discover how much she was really learning. Beal, who took such pleasure in beating her, in slapping her around without provocation, reminding her she was a whore.

"Ah—leave her alone! She ain't done nothin'!" Matt would shout when he was around. And it was only the fact that Beal was the slightest bit afraid of big Matt and his temper that saved her from disfigurement or worse.

The Imperialist armies, a sprawling, disorganized collection of men and their camp followers, kept falling back. The gray-tunicked counter-guerillas ravaged the fringes of the retreating army, like a pack of snarling, ravenous coyotes—striking in the darkness at anything and anyone they could find. Most of them had ridden with Quantrill during the civil war in the States. Now, in name at least, they fought for the Emperor Maximilian.

Caught between opposing armies, the countryside lay bare and ravaged under an equally pitiless sun. This was the Meseta Central, the dry valley that sloped upward in a succession of plateaus until one came to the cool mountains of the Central Highlands. Mejia's army moved back and forth, trying to trap the army of *Juarista* General Mariano Escobedo. But Escobedo, who had learned guile, always managed to avoid an engagement unless it could not be helped. In the meantime *Juarista* guerillas harried the Imperialist soldiers in every way possible—striking; then fading back into the *barrancas*. Mejia sent a force to relieve Matamoras, the emperor's port on the Gulf, and found it already lost to the *Juaristas*. Rumor had it that Mejia himself had been captured, but released by order of General Escobedo. He went back to Mexico City, licking his wounds, leaving his army to keep fighting.

As the Juarists began at last to advance relentlessly, there came news that the French in their turn were pulling back even further. Chihuahua and Saltillo had been evacuated long before—Camargo had fallen. Durango was now their most northerly outpost to the west. And in San Luis Potosi the French bugles still blew over the parade grounds.

All this meant very little to the undisciplined Imperialist hordes, who felt that they were now being called upon to do most of the fighting. Refugees thronged the roads, overtaking the army in their headlong flight. These, of course were the supporters of Maximilian. Rich *hacendados* with their families and their most precious possessions, escorted by bands of armed *vaqueros*. Merchants, villagers who feared reprisals from the victorious *Juaristas* when their towns were taken.

The women would screech with laughter when smart, closed carriages rattled past them. They would spit in the road and jeer.

"They're all piss-scared of the *Juaristas*, look at them go! Afraid they'll steal their fat, ugly wives and daughters, pah, who'd want them?" They made obscene gestures at the ladies who watched through the canvas carriage blinds.

Only Ginny kept herself apart from such sport. Her

head and shoulders completely covered by a *reboza* that
hid her hair, she would ride the wagon with her bare legs
dangling—now as brown and thorn-scratched as the legs
of the others. Sometimes she walked, especially when Beal
was close. She never dared raise her head, on these occasions. Always the thought came to her that perhaps, in
one of those carriages, someone she had met might have
passed. What would they think, if they only knew? She
tried to stop herself from too much thinking of the past,
and did not much care what lay in the future. She had
forced herself into a kind of numbness, in which she could
accept everything that happened to her with a kind of
apathy. And the only time she seemed to throw off this
apathy, the air of sullen resignation that had become so
much a part of her, was when she danced. It was the only
occupation the women had to make them forget their
weariness and the hard work—the endless marching.

Someone would start to strum on a guitar, and demand
that the women dance. After a while, some of the men
would join in too. They danced the fiery peasant dances of
Mexico—the *jarabe*, the *corrido*—and sometimes the
fandango. Watching the Rositas, the Chiquitas and the
Lupes dance, Ginny could hardly fight the need to do so
herself. It was one thing she had always loved in Mexico—the music of the Spaniards. Wild, sobbing, primitive
music—dances that spoke of love and desire, passion and
hate and dishonor. Under the tutelage of some of the
other women, and to the accompaniment of delighted
"*olés*" Ginny actually found some pleasure in dancing—
even in learning the sometimes intricate steps—the *pal-
mas*, or hand-clapping, and the rhythmic finger-snapping.
She would think, bitterly, it's because I no longer have a
soul that I pick up things so easily. And then she'd think,
What do I care? I can lose myself in the music when I
dance, at least.

It was the only thing that made her forget that she had
become dirt—lower than the whores who walked the
streets of the cities. She despised herself for continuing to
live—for wanting to survive, with the fierce natural urge
of the starving and the destitute.

As they drew closer to San Luis Potosí, the rumors
continued to fly thick and fast, and no one knew what to
believe. The French were not "concentrating" as Marshal
Bazaine had pretended, but were retreating in earnest.

Their Emperor Louis Napoleon had denied the Treaty of Miramar—under the deluge of angry notes from Secretary Seward he was beginning to have second thoughts about the wisdom of continuing the French intervention in Mexico. Soon Maximilian would be on his own, supported only by the Loyalist armies of Marquez, Miramon and Mejia—and in the meantime the Juarist armies were being strengthened by volunteers from the provinces.

Ginny heard the gossip and its vehement denial with a kind of apathy. What difference did it make to her any longer? Now she had the *Juaristas* to fear as well, if she ever fell into their hands. They would rape and kill her without question and without mercy—was she not a camp follower of Mejia's army, and worse, the woman of the hated counter-guerillas? If only that terrible, bloody day and night had not happened! If only Steve was still alive. If only she had something to hope for!

They saw the flickering lights of San Luis Potosí late one evening, when the straggling "army" made camp on a mesa north of the town. Once a small mining town and a health resort of sorts it had suddenly become a city of bustling activity, surrounded by trenches and earthworks hastily thrown up by French sappers. Hotels were crowded, and *cantinas* did a thriving business. Performances were given every night at the small theater, which was always packed. Here in San Luis, pro-French sentiment ran high, and the *Juaristas* confined their activities to the nearby mountains, where they hid in small Indian villages and swooped down to harrass travellers on the mountain roads.

Beal surprised Ginny with a present of a garish red dress, picked up on one of his "raids" on a small *Juarista* village. He tossed it at her carelessly with his wolfish grin, and she could not help wondering, even as she took it, what had happened to the woman who had owned such a dress.

"Wear it tonight. We're goin' to town. An' don't get your hopes up either, he continued viciously. "There are Frenchies around here, but your colonel friend is still in Durango, fighting off *Juaristas.*"

She had learned to say nothing; to do nothing except what he told her to do. Under the pale scrutiny of his eyes, biting her lip to control her involuntary shudders, she began to pull off the ragged *camisa* and skirt. He watched her critically, noting the hollows at the base of her neck, and the way the thinness of her face exaggerated the high cheekbones.

"Shit!" he commented, "you're getting real skinny, ain't you? Don't forget to comb your hair out—an' get some color in your face, or I'll put some there like this . . ." and he slapped her, knocking her backwards. "An' you damn well better be on your best behavior tonight, too. We ain't been paid for quite a while, and I need me some *dinero*." He grinned at her, knowing that she knew what he meant.

"I'll be ready to leave in about fifteen minutes," was his parting shot. "Mind you're all spruced up and waitin' by then. Better take that new *reboza* Matt gave you—that one you bin wearin' recently looks too dirty and raggedy for company."

Ginny had hoped desperately for Matt's protection, but when Beal came to fetch her in a borrowed wagon, he was alone. He told her with a thin, evil smile that told her he knew very well what she was thinking that Matt and Pecos had already headed for a night of drinking and brawling on the town.

Ginny shivered from cold, in spite of the fact that her new white lace shawl was wrapped closely around her head and shoulders. San Luis in the fold of the mountains, and the night air seemed to pierce chilly through the thin material of her gown. It had been sewn for a woman much smaller than she was—cut low in front and at the back, and reaching just above her bare ankles. It clung too tightly to her slim figure, revealing all too clearly that she was naked underneath it. A whore's dress. But then, that's what I am, after all, she thought dully. What did it matter, after all? There was no escape from Beal, and he could make her do whatever he wanted, anyway.

French sentries hailed them, and she sat silently, her head hung under their bold scrutiny. Frenchmen. Even they seemed preferable to the kind of man Beal was—the kind of man he picked for her.

They rode through crowded streets, where well-dressed women strolled with their escorts, cocooned in their safe, pleasant world. French legionnaires, laughing and bright-eyed, strolled past, and the sound of their speech stirred a kind of nostalgia in her. A band played in the plaza; lights spilled out of the open doors of *cantinas*. But it was towards the other, shabbier part of town that Beal took her. Here the streets were narrower, the buildings closer together. Whores quarrelled in doorways—two drunken French soldiers, supporting each other as they reeled up the uneven sidewalk, sang a bawdy song off key.

He took her to a *cantina* that did not ever boast a sign over its open, cracked and warped shutters. Here was heat, at last, but it was the heat of unwashed bodies too closely packed together. The music, provided by two broken-down guitarists, was frenetic; the bar no more than a rough, wooden counter running the length of one wall. The laughter was loud, shrill and drunken. Men shouted at each other and called drunkenly for more tequila, for women. And the few women who frequented this place were, for the most part, sleazy slatterns, their dresses slit up the side to show skinny, bowed legs.

As usual, Beal chose a table where he could sit with his back to the wall—not too far from the door. When it came to self-preservation, he was a man of careful habit.

There were a few Frenchmen here—all soldiers. Some hard-bitten Americans, who seemed to keep to themselves. The rest of the crowd was composed mainly of *cazadores* of the Imperialist army, some of whom recognized Beal and shouted raucously at him, and a sprinkling of peons and *vaqueros* in their *charro* suits.

Ginny found a dirty-looking tin mug filled with tequila slapped down in front of her. "Better drink up, it'll make you look less sour," Beal ordered. She sipped obediently, watching his pale, shiny eyes survey the crowd; noticing how he had gulped his first drink down and was already ordering another. Some soldiers had made room for them at their table and they leaned over Ginny, trying to see more of her breasts, leering at her as they made sly, whispered comments. She pretended not to hear. A Legionnaire, wearing corporal's stripes, was leaning on the bar rather morosely. He began to stare at her and she found herself looking back at him almost pleadingly. Now I'm really becoming one, she thought sickly. But better a Frenchman than one of these pigs.

After a while the Frenchman nudged a companion and they both sauntered over. Beal, wearing the gray uniform of a counterguerilla looked up and grinned. "Seen any action here recently soldier-boys?" His voice sounded almost insulting, and one of the Frenchmen flushed and started to scowl. His companion, the corporal grinned back impudently.

"You are with Mejia's army, *oui*? Well, at least we haven't been running away from *Juarista* shadows. Some of us here are on our way to some real fighting, near Durango."

He stared through gray eyes at Ginny and she saw for the first time, with surprise, that he was quite young. But he had a tough and cynical look about him all the same. The look he gave her was bold, almost insulting, and she lowered her eyes, wondering why she was suddenly afraid.

Beal laughed thinly. "Me an' my buddies have been doin' some fightin' too—cleaning up stragglers, you might say. Those brave *Juaristas* scream a lot, like anyone else. Don't they?" He was looking at her—his hand reached out across the table and squeezed her wrist, so unexpectedly and cruelly that she gave a cry of pain. "Ask her—I took her from a *Juarista* spy she was supposed to be married to. After I'd gotten through with him. You remember that, don't you, dollbaby, huh?" He squeezed again, fingers twisting, until she let out a gasped "yes!" and he released her with a short chuckle. "See? She'd almost forgotten about him. Once I beat the fight outa her, she got to make a real fine little soldadera. She'll do anything I tell her."

Through a red mist of pain and humiliation, Ginny heard the inevitable, pretendedly careless bartering begin. The French soldiers sat down; the Mexicans, their obscene sense of humor touched, began making comments about her abilities.

"She's skinny, but she has good straight legs."

"I had her once—she was like a real wildcat, if you like 'em scratching and screeching!"

"Ah, but if she's for sale, in a place like this—why should my friend and I buy a pig in a poke, eh? I can't even see if her face is pockmarked or not, she's got that damn shawl wrapped so closely around her!"

"Yes, what is she hiding?"

The French soldiers were as cruel as the others, discussing her as if she was an animal to be sold, bargaining ... Beal had forced her to finish her tequila, and there was already another mug set before her. Ginny felt the hot color seeping into her face, her heart began to thud madly. This was much worse than anything he'd done with her before—to bring her here and put her up for public auction.

At least the other whores could choose their own customers, she was denied even that small privilege.

"Take the goddamned shawl off. Go on, take it off, you bitch."

Silently, in a daze of shame by now, she unwrapped the white lace and laid it carefully on the table, dragging out each movement as long as she dared. The tangled masses of her hair, now savagely pulled loose by Beal's rough hands, fell down over her shoulders, half-shielding her face. It shone like liquid copper in the dim light, and Ginny could clearly hear the gasp that went up. She felt as if the eyes of every man in the room rested on her, stripping her . . .

"Look up, damn you! Do I hafta tell you everything?"

Some hidden, forced-down instinct made her raise her head proudly, and her emerald green eyes flashed contemptuously from one man's leering face to another. "Animals!" she seemed to say, "dirty lecherous beasts! Look at me, then!"

"*Dieu*! She's lovely!" One of the Frenchmen said. The young corporal's eyes looked smoky in the gloom as he narrowed them, a smile curling his lips.

"She's a whore. She is for sale, is she not? But a face, even if enhanced by eyes like that, is not quite enough. I've seen whores as pretty in Marseilles, and even in Mexico City. And I've fought hard for my money."

"*Sí, amigo*, why don't you show them what they're getting? It seems they will not believe us."

Beal's face looked crooked with anger.

"You're damn right she's a whore. An' I tell you, she'll do anything I tell her to—anything you boys can think up. Just like a little performing animal, ain't you?" His hand shot out and Ginny screamed involuntarily as his fingers caught in the neckline of her dress, ripping it downward. Her breasts, even though she tried to cover them with her arms, gleamed milky white in the dim light.

"*Dios mío!*" a man breathed. "Such beauty should not be hidden. Show us more, *amigo*, and just for looking I'll give you a peso."

They were suddenly crowding around her like animals, so that she could hardly breathe.

"Please don't! Have pity," she looked straight at the young corporal, but his eyes were still narrow and he grinned his lust.

"Go ahead, why don't you do that? It'll make for some nice entertainment. And afterwards, if my friend and I like what we see, we'll have her for the night—it's been a long time since we've had a circus."

"Stand up." Beal's voice sounded vicious. When she couldn't move he caught her by the arms and pulled her erect. She felt his hand go behind her, heard the tearing of cloth, and the next moment she was bare to the waist, and he was holding her wrists, preventing her from covering herself.

"See that? Wanta see more an' you'll hafta pay—"

Her eyes glazed with fear, the blood pounding in her ears, Ginny heard the tinkling of coins as they were thrown to fall around her—on the table, on the floor. Some, flung straight at her, felt cold on her bare skin.

"No—oh God, no!" she sobbed frantically. "Not like this—don't!"

Beal released a wrist to slap her backhanded, send her staggering, only to be pulled forward again so that she fell against the table, feeling its sharp edge bruise her hip.

"You said she was tame—make her pull her skirt up. Or better still, have her pull it down . . ."

"You heard the Corporal. Come on, it ain't like you haven't stripped for a lot of men before. Do it, right now, or by God I'll beat you up so bad you won't be able to lie on your back for a week!"

Seeing that she had begun to sob hopelessly Beal released Ginny's wrists. Like a hunted forest creature she looked frantically around the room, and could see nothing but eager, desire-ridden faces; some staring, some smiling, all of them waiting—waiting.

Grinning at her, Beal raised his arm again, and something snapped in her mind, turning her, for a few minutes, into a wild, mindless madwoman.

Her face a white blaze in the center of her tangled mass of hair, she screamed, and he almost laughed at her sudden surrender, for her hand lifted her skirt, yanking it upward almost to the waist.

"You bitch . . ." he began and then he saw the knife flash in her other hand. The knife that she always wore strapped to her thigh since Matt had given it to her—the knife that flashed downward to bury itself in his throat and was the last thing that Tom Beal was ever to see.

He made horrible, gurgling noises in his throat, hands

clawing upward in the final throes of agony. She was to remember that, later. That, and the warm, sticky spurting of his blood that was suddenly everywhere, covering everything. The table—her face, and arms and even her breasts. It was like a frozen tableau, suddenly, with faces that grimaced, mouths that hung open, all motionless, suspended in time. Only Ginny moved, driven by the same unthinking desperation that had made her do what she had just done from instinct. Snatching up the white shawl she ran wildly for the door—was through it and out onto the street before anyone thought to begin shouting; before the French corporal, knocking over his chair, rushed after her, his friend close behind.

"Stop her! My God, what a wild animal! She killed him . . ."

"Yes, and she might have killed one of us, too."

She ran fleetly, desperately, the shawl streaming out behind her, dodging passersby who stopped to stare, wondering what had happened.

Out of the *cantina*, a whole crowd had begun to spill already. Some of them joining in the pursuit, some of them standing there to stare after her, talking among themselves.

"But why go after her? The French are in charge of the justice here, let them take care of it." "I certainly don't want to be involved. And besides they were both *gringos*." Some of the women even grumbled under their breath that the filthy *Norteamericano* had deserved it.

Even in her headlong flight Ginny could hear the pounding of their boots behind her, their shouts.

"You little murderess! You can't escape—better stop before someone shoots you down!"

"Didn't he say she was married to a *Juarista*?" the private panted. "*Merde*, she's probably one of them—it could have been planned."

She ran straight into the arms of a French patrol, four men, headed by a sergeant, who had been alerted by the shouts of her pursuers.

"What the hell is going on here? Hold her—she's trying to get away—"

"She's a damned *Juarista*, sergeant!" By this time the other two had come panting up.

"She killed a man—an American counterguerilla—back in that *cantina* there. She might have killed more of us."

"Ah, yes, she looks like a dangerous person all right!" the sergeant said with heavy sarcasm. By now the terrified girl was clinging to him, babbling to him in, of all things, his own language!

"Help me—don't let them take me—oh, please—he was trying to—"

"Don't believe a word she says!" The tough young corporal managed to hide his surprise at the fact that this little whore spoke French, but his friend had begun to gape. "Look at the blood on her—it's all over her, and she's messing up your uniform too!"

It was true—the woman, French-speaking or not, was covered with blood, and in addition to being quite hysterical she was half-naked into the bargain.

"Cover yourself!" the sergeant snapped. He himself wrapped the shawl around her shoulders. By now she was sobbing in a dazed, hopeless fashion and hardly resisted when he ordered his men to pinion her hands in front of her.

"*Allez, allez!* Be quick! Let's get her to the billets before this crowd gets any bigger, eh? We'll get to the bottom of this matter there. And you two," he added sternly, "you come along as well! I have some questions for you!"

In the center of a small crowd, the grim-faced, marching Frenchmen on either side of her, Ginny, feeling herself past all caring now, let herself be carried along. What does it matter? What does it matter? It might be better if they do kill me—I wonder if it'll be an execution, by a firing squad. Have they ever executed a woman before? Her thoughts were jumbled confusion, and she hardly heard the shouting of the crowd, the jabbering of the two French Legionnaires who had started it all at the *cantina*, and now marched alongside the sergeant.

The sergeant's office, a small room in the rest billets, seemed almost like a haven, with its sudden quietness, the warmth of a fire. Sergeant Pary, not an unkind man, gave the shaking, white-faced girl a chair. *Juarista* or not, she was a woman, after all, and she spoke French, which was unusual. What was she doing in a position like this?

He shouted for silence, drowning out the explanations of the two Legionnaires.

"But mon Sergeant ... she killed this man! With a knife."

"You'll answer my questions when I ask them! Be silent now!"

He turned to the woman. What to call her? *Mademoiselle*? They said she was a whore, a *Juarista* spy, but after all her French had been perfect, idiomatic. There was something strange here, something he sensed. And she was terrified, her whole body trembling from shock and reaction. She didn't look capable of killing, but then, with a woman, one could never tell.

Compromising, the sergeant addressed her sternly without prefacing his words.

"Now—perhaps you will be good enough to tell me what happened? And your name first, if you please."

She looked up at him, uncomprehending, and he had to repeat his question, while the Legionnaires grumbled to each other in low voices.

"My name?" He had spoken to her, automatically, in French and she answered him in the same language. But what name was she supposed to give him? Stammering, in a soft, strained voice, she said, "Virginie," and then, unable to help herself, sheer reaction from the nerve-wracking events that had taken place only moments ago made her start sobbing.

"Don't you have a last name?" the Sergeant began impatiently, and then he shrugged with annoyance. "Well, perhaps we'll get to that later. Tell me, did you really kill a man? Who was he?"

"I killed him! Because he was trying to—to make me—" Shock and humiliation at the memory made her lift her bound hands and cover her face with them.

"Ah, why bother to ask her, mon Sergeant? She's nothing but a lying whore, they're all alike! The man was an American counterguerilla, he said he'd taken her off a *Juarista*, and he offered her to us—yes, and to every other man in the room too! And then all of a sudden she went mad, she was carrying this little knife strapped to her thigh, a typical *poule's* trick."

"I've already told you to be silent!" the sergeant thundered. "I'll come to you two later." The woman was still weeping, but almost soundlessly now, her hands over her mouth. The sergeant caught a glimpse of white breasts, through the rents in the white shawl that was now covered with blood. A knife! What a dirty business! She seemed hardly capable of coherent thought or speech—

what was he supposed to do now? Hand her over to the
Mexican authorities? But if she was a Frenchwoman, then
. . . He was almost glad of the interruption that came just
then.

The sound of bootheels on the usual adobe floor, the
door flung open. The sergeant and his men came to attention, saluting the young captain who strode in, dusting off
his travel-stained uniform, his smart, dark-green cape.

"Sergeant! What the devil is going on here? I came to
find some horses, and I discover the whole place in mass
confusion! What's that crowd doing outside?"

"Your pardon, *mon Capitaine*! But there's been some
trouble. This woman here, they say she murdered one of
our counterguerillas. I've been trying to get some sense
out of her, but she—"

"Michel!" For a dazed moment the sergeant wondered
if she was really mad. She had sprung to her feet, her eyes
staring, her voice almost a shriek. "Oh, God—Michel, it's
you! Save me . . . help me, Michel!"

She was running towards the dumbfounded captain, and
when one of the soldiers tried to stop her headlong rush,
the shawl came off her shoulders, exposing her half-nude
body, covered only by the tattered remnants of the garish
red dress.

"Let her go!" the captain snapped. With a muffled oath
he had stepped forward to catch the sobbing, hysterical
girl as she fell against him.

"Ginnie? Ginette, am I dreaming? Is it really you?"
Even as he spoke he was tearing off his campaign cloak,
wrapping it around her body. Now he tilted her face up
with one hand, still keeping an arm around her.

She kept saying his name over and over, as if she could
think of nothing else. But yes, it was really her! His little
love, his Ginette, long-lost—turning up here, of all places!
And under arrest, half-naked, it was impossible!

The soldiers were all speaking at once until the captain
ordered them, in a voice taut with emotion, to be quiet.
Still holding the trembling girl in his arms, he looked over
her head at the confused sergeant, who by this time was
wondering if they all weren't going crazy.

"And now," he said, his voice steely, "let me hear your
explanations, if you please! What is this young lady doing
here, with you lot of ruffians? What have you done to
her?"

PART SIX

"La Cortesana"

Chapter Forty

The little townhouse that Michel had found for her in
the old Spanish section of Mexico City was on the Calle
Manzanares. To Ginny it became both a haven and a
refuge during the two weeks that followed his taking her
away from the horror at San Luis—a horror that still
haunted her sweat-soaked nightmares from which she
would wake up shaking, more often than not; sobbing
wildly. During the five days that Michel had managed to
stay with her, he would hold her closely, comforting her.

"It's all over, *petite amie*, don't think of it any longer!
It's finished, I'm here to look after you." He couldn't
forget how she had looked, that night; all but naked, her
big green eyes wide and terrified; the way she had
repeated his name over and over, begging him to help her,
to save her. The thought that if his horse hadn't happened
to go lame he might never have found her really horrified
him. *Dieu!* His Ginette, his little lost one, who had fought
so bravely to save his life—his little tarnished flower, what
terrible experiences she had been through!

Michel had been riding fiercely with a small body of
men—on his way from Durango to Mexico City, to ask
Bazaine for more reinforcements for the besieged garrison

there. Even after he had found Ginette he had not been
able to stay on at San Luis for more than a few hours.
Long enough to order the sergeant roughly to forget the
whole matter, that he would take full responsibility for the
lady. Carrying her in his arms, still wrapped in his cloak
and half fainting by now, he had taken her to a doctor,
had somehow managed to procure a gown for her, and
then they had to be off again. But this time, strictly
against regulations, Ginny had gone with him.

"I'm billeted in a house on the Torrez Adalid, but of
course it's out of the question for you to stay there. Don't
worry, I'll find a place for you," Michel had told her.
Felix, Prince du Salm, was a friend of his, and the prince's
American wife Agnes was a warm and friendly person, tactful enough not to ask too many questions. She offered her
hospitality to Michel's little friend at once, and Ginny had
stayed with them until Michel, by moving heaven and
earth almost, had finally found a small house. Hardly
more than an apartment, really, but the address was good,
and it was suitable. There was even a tiny, miniature patio
where she could take the sun away from prying eyes.

That first week, Ginny had clung to Michel as if she
were afraid to let him out of her sight, afraid to be alone.
It took several days before she was strong enough and
calm enough to tell him the whole story of what had
happened to her since the day she'd been abducted right
under his eyes. He could hardly believe that she, so soft
and feminine, so young, had actually been through so
much in the space of a few months.

She was so innocent, so pure, Michel thought painfully.
I was going to marry her, I wanted to be the first, and
then that American mercenary, that gun-hung bandit with
the blue eyes, the same man Sonya Brandon had told him,
weeping, had bothered Ginny before, he had taken her. By
force. He had dragged her everywhere with him as a
hostage, and had made her his mistress. He had actually
married her in the end, and probably out of gratitude, she
imagined herself in love with him. But when he thought
about this man, this Steve Morgan who had so casually
and belatedly given Ginny his name, Michel's fists would
clench and his fair brows draw together in anger. The
bastard! he'd think. *Merde*! He deserved his fate—he
deserved much worse! And as for the fat Colonel

Devereaux, the "wily fox" as his friends called him, he, Michel, would deal with him!

The young, popular Comte d'Arlingen, one of Marshal Bazaine's favorites, was not afraid of the consequences of challenging one of his superior officers to a duel. The circumstances were extenuating, and he had already told Bazaine, in strict confidence, part of the story. Michel was disappointed when he returned to Durango and found that the colonel had been killed a few days previously, by a *Juarista* sniper. Well, at least he could give Ginny the good news when he returned to Mexico City—he hoped that would not be too long, for to tell the truth he hated leaving her there alone. Agnes du Salm had promised to look after her, but Agnes was flighty and never lacked for escorts while her husband was away. She'd get Ginny involved in that fast crowd, and God knew what might happen.

Ginette—away from her, Michel wondered what would become of her. His little green-eyed, copper-haired siren! All the hardships and degradation she'd been through had not made her any less beautiful. She was thinner than he remembered, but it had only seemed to accentuate the fine bones of her face; give her eyes a new, vivid brilliance. He had remembered her as a girl, still shy and reticent. And he'd found her a woman. But what a woman, *quelle femme*! Unconsciously, Michel Remy echoed the late Colonel Devereaux' impression of her. The first few days, he had been carefully patient, overwhelmingly gentle with her. He had hardly been able to credit the fact that she'd endured so much, and still managed to survive. How she must hate and despise all men! He must be careful, he must not push her, he would try to make her feel that he was her friend, her protector, that he would never try to force himself upon her, no matter how much he desired her. And strangely, he desired her more than ever, in spite of all those other men who had used her—yes, in spite of everything!

The first few nights, he slept on a small couch in the big bedroom that occupied the whole of the top floor of their little house.

Then, the third night she'd awakened from a nightmare, moaning and sobbing wildly with terror, he had suddenly found it impossible to tear his arms away from around her shivering body, especially when her arms were clasping him so closely. The desire he felt for her overrode everything else, even though he tried to be gentle, to take the time to caress her and whisper words of love and encouragement in her ear. He couldn't help himself, he wanted her! He'd found her again, and this time he wouldn't lose her. In spite of the fact that she seemed unable to respond to him at first, Michel persisted. Very tenderly, very gently, finally breaking down her natural resistance.

On the last night that they had spent together, she seemed finally to abandon herself to him, forgetting her fear. He was amazed at her skill as a lover, once she had given in. Oh God, what passion! She drove him almost to the brink of madness with the wildness of her response. She was his now, exclusively his, or so he would like to think! She would be his mistress, his *petite amie*. She was different from those others he had taken to amuse himself with for an hour, perhaps a week, sometimes longer. He could take her out with him in public, yes even to the emperor's palace at Chapultepec, and not be ashamed of her manners or her appearance. And before he left Mexico City Michel made sure that Ginny would have carte blanche at the more exclusive dress boutiques. He wanted her to spare no expense, and when he came back, perhaps in less than a month, he would take her with him everywhere, he promised. She clung to him, half-crying, before he left.

"Oh, Michel! I'm going to miss you so much—I wish you'd take you with me. Please hurry back."

During the weeks that followed Michel's reluctant leave-taking, Ginny felt herself in a kind of limbo. At first, she could hardly believe that she was really free at last, that she was actually here, in Mexico City, with lovely gowns to wear again, and a maid and a cook to run the little house for her. It seemed strange to be a lady again, to have a friend like the bubbling, laughing-eyed Agnes du Salm, who insisted that Ginny must go with her everywhere, be introduced to everyone.

"It would be too silly of you to stay home, cooped up like a prisoner!" Agnes exclaimed. "Michel would be the last one to expect it, he's a man of the world, after all. And I did promise to watch out for you. Come along with me, do, I get frightfully lonely myself, and I don't really have a close woman friend."

Agnes coaxed prettily, and Agnes was used to getting her own way. They visited the theater together, attended masquerades and balls at the palace, and went to *tertulias* at the houses of the more liberal-minded Mexicans. At first Ginny lived in fear that she would run into someone she knew—into one of the Alvarado-Ortega clan. But Agnes, who knew something of her story made discreet inquiries and informed her laughing, that all of the richer *hacendado's* families always spent this time of the year in their summer *palacios*. "Mexico City is far too crowded with foreigners for that stuck-up crowd!" Agnes giggled. "You should have seen how some of them used to stare down their noses at me, because they all knew I'd been a circus rider! Really my pet, you're well rid of them—I've never known such stuffy, old-fashioned people. They act as if they're doing us a favor by letting us fight their battles, yes, really!"

Agnes's natural charm and her sense of humor were irresistible, and while she wondered guiltily if Michel would really approve, Ginny found herself swept along in Agnes's perfumed wake, realizing what magnificent foils they made for each other—Agnes with her dark hair and snapping dark eyes, and she with her pale-copper hair and green eyes. They became quite a familiar sight, these two, always surrounded by a crowd of admirers. Ginny would tell herself that it did not mean anything, she could hardly go about unescorted, and as long as she was faithful to Michel, that was all that mattered. She felt a tremendous sense of gratitude toward him. He had been so kind to her, he had saved her life and her sanity, she owed him everything! And as a lover he had been gentle and undemanding, trying so hard to give her pleasure. She too remembered their last night together, when at last, for a few moments, she had managed to close her mind to everything in the past and allow herself to be controlled by her body's innate sensuality. If it wasn't an experience filled with pain and a sense of degradation it was really quite easy to let physical sensation take over, to close her mind to memories.

On some nights however, or in the early hours of the morning, when she had just come home after a night of dancing, Ginny found herself haunted by the same memories she'd told herself she could shut out. It was not the state of degraded physical numbness that Tom Beal

had forced her into that she thought about at these times.
That time in her life, starting with her giving herself
willingly to Colonel Devereaux in return for Steve's life—
such a useless and wasted gesture, that!—she was now
learning to push away. But the memory of nights and days
spent in Steve Morgan's arms, even his occasional
cruelties, were less easy to cope with.

"A woman never forgets her first love, or the first man
who made her a woman, darling," Agnes had said when
Ginny tried to explain her occasional moodiness. "I can
understand how you felt about this man, your husband
who was a reckless adventurer, who taught you
everything. Yes, because my Felix is a man like that. But
what's the point spending your life regretting? There will
never be another first love, but there can be other loves.
Your Michel—didn't you say you once felt yourself in
love with him? And that he's a considerate lover? What
more can a woman ask for, after all? It's always so much
safer to love a little less than you are loved. You can't be
hurt that way. No, Ginette, you must learn to live for today, just like me!"

Of course Agnes was right, and she was always so practical. Having been deprived of luxury or even pleasure for
so long, Ginny felt that she appreciated life much more
now. She had no plans for the future—nowhere she
particularly wanted to go, no one she particularly wanted
to go to. So why not remain here, in this atmosphere of
almost frenzied gaiety? Why not take pleasure in living,
for a change? What did it matter?

She felt restless and adrift, without purpose. She felt
that yes, she loved Michel, when she thought about him,
but she wasn't in love with him. And, as Ginny was "discovered" by the cosmopolitan society of Mexico City, she
also found more and more admirers. Men who swore they
adored her and would die for a kiss. Men who offered her
anything, everything, if she would consent to accept them
as lovers. Now that she wasn't the one to be manipulated
by men, the feminist in her came to the fore and she
found how easy it was to manipulate men—to use them
and have them dancing like puppets to her tune. Even as a
girl, Ginny had always been a flirt, and now, as a woman,
she realized the power that flirtation could give her. She
would have traded it all to have Steve—but he was dead.
It had all happened so suddenly, so unexpectedly—she had

discovered what love really was, only to lose it almost at once.

'What does it matter?' It was the recurrent phrase in her thoughts. Like Agnes, she would learn to enjoy life, to snatch at its transitory pleasures while they were within her grasp. Tomorrow meant nothing, when there was nothing to live for.

At Michel's gentle urging, Ginny had dutifully written a long and rather ambiguous letter to her father. It told him only that she had been married to Steve Morgan. "I discovered after a while, that I loved him," she wrote, choosing words carefully. "I think that after all, he was in love with me too. He was not really as wicked as we all thought him at first, for he believed sincerely in Juarez and the revolution." She went on to say that she had been widowed. She explained that she had since met the Comte d'Arlingen again, and was now living in Mexico City, under the chaperonage of the Princess du Salm. "Please don't ask me to return yet," she added. "It's very gay here, there are diplomats from all over the world, and some of the richest men from Cuba and the West Indies come here on vacation—I find everything new and exciting, and I need to forget. You must not worry." Thoughtfully, biting the end of her pen, Ginny had added that she did not need money, for the property settlement made on her by her husband had left her quite well off. She'd frowned thoughtfully. It was true, after all. The papers had been drawn up and signed, the money somewhere safely in a bank. She remembered with a sudden, sharp pang that Steve had left a will leaving everything to her. But they hadn't talked to each other since, and all she knew was that he owned a ranch near Monterey. 'Perhaps, when all this is over, I shall go there to live. I'll become a recluse, I won't need anyone.' But in the meantime there was life, to be savored all over again.

Ginny sent the letter off, and hoped that her father and Sonya would understand. She supposed that she should write to Don Francisco too, after all, he had been so kind to her. But what would she tell him? How could she explain what had happened and expect him to understand? In the end, it was to Renaldo, who had been her friend, that she wrote. She could be frank with him, at least. She told him almost everything; almost, because there were still a few things she could not bear to talk about. But she was

blunt about the fact that she had been fortunately "rescued"
by a childhood friend from France, and was officially his
mistress now. "You will probably be shocked, my dearest
and kindest of friends, but I felt so depraved, and so
empty; almost past caring what happened to me. I was a
little in love with Michel as a girl, and he is kind and good
to me. I suppose I am as happy as it is possible for me to
be any longer. If there is some way you can explain to
Don Francisco without upsetting him too much, I'd be
grateful if you would do so. I suppose I am too much of a
coward to face him, after all this—I feel as if everyone
must think the worst of me. But I do want you to know
the truth, as painful as it is." Almost as an afterthought,
as if it had been forced out of her, she added at the very
bottom, in an almost indecipherable scrawl, "I loved him,
Renaldo. If only I could have told him so."

With the country in such a state of turmoil, com-
munications were at their very worst. Still, Agnes took the
letter and promised that she would have it delivered somehow. "Don't expect a reply too soon, my love," the
Princess warned her. "He might not even be there—
the province is almost completely in the hands of the
Juaristas, and most of the *hacendados* have fled to safety
unless they were Juarist supporters themselves." But at
least the letter was written, and Ginny felt slightly better.

When the Comte d'Arlingen returned he found his
mistress gay and sparkling, the toast of the town. She was
invited everywhere, and she insisted that he must take her.
She even swore that she'd been faithful.

"Michel darling, but I have missed you. Do you think I
could ever forget what you've done for me?"

"Oh, damn," he groaned, "it's not gratitude, I want
from you, Ginette! It's you—I've found myself thinking
constantly about you."

"And I've thought about you. Oh, Michel, hold me.
Please don't be jealous, when there's no need to be!"

He forgot everything in her arms. He felt hopelessly en-
tangled, all over again. Before—yes he had desired her
even then, but in the way that a man desires the woman
he might choose to make his wife. Now she was his
mistress; her lovely body, the same body that so many
men had used and abused, was all his. Or was it? It was
only in her arms that he could forget his jealousy. The

more he had her, the more he desired her—she was like no other woman he had ever known before.

The young *comte*, who had been one of the most sought-after bachelor officers, now dropped all of his other mistresses and let it be known, quite subtly, it was true, that he was Madame du Plessis' protector. He did not like the name that Ginny had chosen for herself, because it reminded him, as it did her, of a once-great courtesan of France. But as usual she had only laughed teasingly.

"But why not? I *am* a courtesan. At the theater the other night I heard an old woman whisper to her friend, 'look at *la cortesana!*' Don't look like that, I didn't mind! Aren't you happy that I'm yours?"

Yes, he was. He had to admit it. He was proud to be seen with her—pride mixed with jealousy, though, when he saw the admiring, envious glances that were cast their way. She did not seem at all to be the same Ginette that he had known and had been so passionately infatuated with so long ago. She was a different woman—but a *woman, Dieu,* yes. And what he felt now, like a constant ache in his crotch, was desire. I am completely obsessed by her, he thought gloomily, and then in her arms he forgot everything but the pleasure that she gave him, and would give him again and again, as long as he could keep her.

Ginny herself was not completely certain how she felt from one moment to the next. She loved Michel—yes, she did, as much as she was capable of loving any man again. But she had also begun to enjoy the open admiration of other men, the looks they gave her, the knowledge that she was capable of wielding a cruel power over them. When Michel had gone away she had missed him, for he had made her feel safe, he had been like a tower of strength that she could lean upon, as weak and frightened as she had been. And now, with her body filling out again, the fear gone as her mind began to heal itself, she was not quite certain what she wanted. Michel was jealous, although he tried not to show it. When flowers and little presents arrived for her, he was furious. And yet she had learned how to tease him out of his anger. It was really so easy.

Although the Comte d'Arlingen was now officially transferred to Mexico City, Bazaine kept him busy, as his trusted courier. He was constantly being sent here and

there, to French outposts—or on tours of inspection.
Wherever Bazaine went, Michel would have to go too.
And so there were evenings when Ginny, rather than stay
home alone, would accept other invitations; although she
always made it a point to go with Agnes, and was never
seen alone with any man but Michel. If he remonstrated
with her, she pouted.

"But you're always so busy! *Le marechal* has you at his
beck and call. What am I supposed to do? Must I give up
all my friends? Don't you trust me?" And he could never
bring himself to say that he did not.

On one of the occasions that Michel had to be away for
two days, Ginny attended a private masquerade at the
palace. The Empress Carlotta had just left for France on
a secret mission to the Emperor Louis Napoleon. Poor
Don Maximiliano needed cheering up! And besides, the
news was very bad, and getting worse—there were rumors
that all French troops were to leave Mexico soon. Why
not have fun while the golden bubble still lasted?

It was the height of summer—a summer which had
begun early this year of 1866. Here in Mexico City one
could feel isolated from the fighting going on everywhere
else, and all the unpleasant attendant rumors.

"Only a few people are to be invited on this occasion,"
Agnes whispered to Ginny as they planned their costumes.
"Just the cream of society, my love! Max's advisers—some
of the rich Mexicans who haven't fled from the heat yet.
And of course the handsomest of the officers and the
corps diplomatique. What fun it will be!"

Agnes was in her gayest, most devil-may-care mood, and
Ginny filled with a spirit of defiance herself, went along
willingly with her friend's mad idea.

"Let's shock them all! We'll go as ourselves—I mean,
of course, our real selves. Let me see—yes, I have it! You
know how they whisper about me behind my back, that
Felix married me out of a circus—well, it was true, and
I'm not ashamed of it! I'll go as a circus rider, and you—
you my love—" here Agnes narrowed her eyes and gazed
at Ginny consideringly. Suddenly her eyes began to
sparkle. "I have it! But do you have the courage? You
must go as a gypsy—a gypsy dancer—how many times
have you been told that you look like a *gitano*?"

Ginny began to laugh irrepressibly.

"Well, I must say I like the notion vastly better than

that of going as a *soldadera*! I should hate to have to wear such shabby clothes again! Oh Agnes, you do turn up with the wildest ideas!"

"But you agree? We'll do it?"

"Yes, of course—I only hope that poor Michel does not decide to turn up a day early, for he would never agree! You know how positively husbandlike he's been acting recently!"

"But he isn't your husband," Agnes said coyly. "He doesn't own you—high time he realized it!"

Chapter Forty-one

They talked about the masquerade ball for months afterwards. What a shocking scandal, whispered the older, more conservative members of society. The others merely laughed and said that it had been delightful. What a change from the usual, dull affairs of Carlotta's time! And of course, they would add, particularly the men, the other ladies were all jealous at having their dull and unimaginative costumes outdone by simplicity.

As they had deliberately planned, Agnes and Ginny made a late entrance, alone. Their escorts for the evening were to wait for them at the palace itself, and they had promised not to be too late.

Heavily cloaked, and riding in a borrowed carriage, Ginny had begun to giggle helplessly when the heavily-armed French sentries at the first checkpoint made some difficulty about letting them through.

"You're—entertainers?" the young sergeant questioned, frowning as he scrutinized their passes. "But no one told us—"

"Oh, you mean the musicians?" Agnes du Salm said sweetly, leaning forward so that the hood of her cloak fell slightly back from her face. "But they're with me, sergeant! I can vouch for them."

"We *always* take our own musicians everywhere with us," Ginny murmured, smiling innocently at the confused young man.

He colored, looking from one to the other of them. These ladies! He recognized the Princess du Salm at last, but not her companion. Obviously, they were up to some mischief, but he resigned himself to the fact that he could do nothing about it. Let the guards at the entrance to the palace itself worry about it! He stepped back with a stiff salute and waved them on, cursing his luck at having been appointed for guard duty tonight of all nights. It seemed as if he always missed the fun!

Monsieur Eloin, one-time court musician and now one of Maximilian's closest friends, was bustling about behind the raised marble dais, preparing for the entertainment of the evening. The little Belgian was not very happy with the fat Italian soprano who was to give a selection of operatic arias, but at such short notice, what could one expect? He only hoped that the guests would not show their boredom too openly, as some had done before, even in Carlotta's presence.

When the Princess du Salm made her sudden appearance through the servants' entrance, accompanied by her new friend and constant companion Madame du Plessis, M. Eloin gave a start of surprise. His astonishment turned almost to shock when the lady, her black eyes sparkling, whispered her scheme. He shook his head at first. "*Non*! No, it absolutely would not do! What would Prince du Salm have to say? And the *comte*, what about *him*?"

But poor Monsieur Eloin—he found himself helpless against the personalities of these two determined young ladies.

Agnes du Salm brushed aside his last objection with an impatient wave of her hand. "Nonsense, my dear Monsieur Eloin! You know how these people love to be surprised! Do you mean to say that they will prefer to hear the screeching of Signora Guzzi for the next hour?"

The guests, preparing for a siege of boredom, began to sit up and take notice when they saw the brightly-clad Mexican musicians walk on to the stand with their guitars. This did not appear to be quite M. Eloin's style of en-

tertainment after all! They all knew that his taste ran to
Bach and the opera—perhaps someone had persuaded him
to hire some dancers from the *Teatro Imperiale*!

The musicians struck up, the curtains parted, and there
was a concerted gasp of amazement, mixed with shock.
Agnes du Salm, dressed in her short, spangled circus rider's
costume actually rode her horse out onto the small stage!

In time to the music, the well-trained animal stepped
daintily round and around in a small, tight circle with
Agnes standing gracefully on its back.

"Hop la!" she said suddenly, and the magnificent Arabian mare leaped cleanly and nimbly from the stage. Alice
cantered it around the enormous ballroom, while the
crowd parted before her. She came to a stop directly before the Emperor's ornately-carved chair and dismounted,
curtsying to him demurely. Maximilian, whose face had
been a study a few moments before, now burst out into
hearty laughter, which was the signal for a storm of hand-
clapping and cries of "bravo!"

"My dear Princess," he said dryly as he handed the
smiling Agnes to a seat, "we can always count on you to
surprise and entertain us all! But tell me, where is your
lovely friend tonight? Surely she is not going to disappoint
us?"

"You know she wouldn't do that, sire," Agnes responded
demurely. "As a matter of fact—do please regard the
dais, the evening's entertainment has only just begun!" The
curtains, which had closed again when Agnes left the stage
were now flung open, and Agnes said softly, *"Voila!"*

The voluble chattering which had broken out after the
Princess du Salm's shocking performance was suddenly
hushed as the musicians broke into a wild gypsy dance.
That gypsy—that woman with her cloud of bright hair
flowing loose, clad in a tight, low-cut peasant blouse and a
bright red skirt reaching only to her ankles, surely that
could not be the sophisticated Madame du Plessis? But it
was. She gave them all a flashing glance out of familiar,
slanted green eyes before her bare feet began to move,
faster and faster; the skirt whirling up around her legs.

The musicians played as if they were beside themselves,
and Ginette danced like an angel—no, some women
whispered among themselves, more like a she-devil! She
seemed tireless. Her hair was like a shining, fiery cloud;
sometimes shielding her face, and sometimes tossed back-

ward as her body moved like a branch swaying in the wind. She seemed to change her mood as fast as the musicians changed their pace. Sometimes she was all languor, all supple, sensuous promise—a woman dreaming of her lover, waiting for his arms. And then she was a temptress, teasing, seductive, rejecting.

A man, a blue-eyed, fair-haired Mexican, dressed in a silver embroidered charro suit suddenly leaped on to the dais to join her as the music changed to a fandango.

There were whispers again. Colonel Miguel Lopez of the Imperial guard—one of the young Madame Bazaine's close relatives. They said he was one of the emperor's closest friends and confidants. What a striking pair they made, as they circled each other warily—now lovers, now antagonists. And the whispers began once more. Was the handsome colonel one of her lovers too? Or did he only plan to be? What would Captain Remy do when he found out?

Ginny, her breasts rising and falling with exertion, smiled teasingly at her partner. She began to seduce him, falling back when he came too close, promising him everything with the passionate movements of her hips as her skirt brushed against him.

"You little devil!" he whispered when they stood facing each other, her fingers snapping derisively over her head as she urged him on. "Is this what you really are under that passionless, ladylike exterior?"

"And is this your real self, colonel?" she teased him, tossing her head so that her hair whipped his face. "The lover, not the soldier?"

"Sometimes, doesn't a man have to be both, in order to conquer a particularly desirable woman?"

"Ah—now you are a *gallante*!"

She came close to him, her body all but touching his; offering herself for just a teasing instant before she whirled away, feet stamping.

He pursued her, a slight smile curling his lips under the thin mustache.

There was something in the insolent confidence of his manner that reminded her irritatingly and yet intriguingly of Steve. But he's *not* Steve, she reminded herself angrily. He's only a poor imitation. Only Steve had the power to make me completely willing, completely powerless to resist him, just by touching me.

Miguel Lopez whispered, "I know what kind of woman

you are—all passion, all fire. Why do you keep it all hidden? You could have any man here, and all his fortune, at your feet. Stop teasing me."

"You're flattering. And insulting too."

She made a small, almost indiscernible motion towards the musicians, and Lopez, his blue eyes gleaming with amusement, formed the word "coward!" with his lips. Traditionally, the dance ended with a declaration of passion. But after her formal surrender to his masculinity, when she would have drawn away, he put his arms around her and pulled her against him, kissing her.

Ginny's fingers were curled into claws when he released her. If not for their fascinated audience she would have clawed his face—she would have slapped that arrogant, self-assured smirk away! As it was, she merely gave him a daggerlike look and shrugged carelessly for the edification of the emperor and his guests who were now all on their feet, cheering, the shouts of "olé" and "bravo" intermingled.

"Come, I'll take you to Agnes, she looks impatient to talk to you," Lopez drawled, bowing to her. Again, she did not resist, but gave him her hand with a forced smile.

"You might have kissed me back," he murmured as they walked together through the crowd.

"I prefer to be asked, first," she responded icily.

"Then I'll certainly do so—the next time we meet."

There was no time for her to answer him, for he had led her before the emperor, and she was curtsying.

"You were magnificent, madame," Maximilian said, his rather watery eyes lingering on her breasts. "I hope you'll do me the honor of dancing for me again—perhaps somewhere more private . . ." his message was unmistakable, making Ginny recall, uncomfortably, certain reports she had heard of his strained relations with his wife. But she had no choice now except to smile and tell him she'd be delighted.

Then, at last, Agnes was clasping her hands, exclaiming that it had all gone off so successfully, and hadn't it all been such fun?

"We've really given the gossips something to whisper about this time, look at them chattering!"

Miguel Lopez had gone back to his partner, whoever she was, and Ginny subsided thankfully into a chair. She began to wonder, at last, what Michel was going to say.

He was furious, of course. Within hours after his return he had been told the whole story, with the usual embellishments. It seemed to make it worse, to him, that Ginny had stayed on, with the other guests, until the very end, dancing until dawn.

"Dear God! Couldn't you have thought of the consequences? You and Agnes—what an irresponsible pair you make! And I suppose you danced with Colonel Lopez again—haven't you heard what a reputation he has?"

"Haven't you heard what a reputation I have?" Ginny retorted angrily, stung by what she thought of as his uncalled-for jealousy. "After all, they do call me *la cortesana*! I'm your mistress, Michel darling—a cheap woman you literally picked up off the streets. You should not have such high expectations of me!"

"Ginny!" Thunderstruck, he stared at her.

A sudden pang of remorse seized her when she saw the white, tormented look on his face.

"Oh, Michel, Michel! I'm sorry! How horrible I am—I don't deserve any of your kindness. I should be grateful to you, and instead . . ."

She thought he was going to strike her, but he only seized her by the shoulders, fingers digging into her naked flesh.

"I don't want your gratitude!!" He shouted the words at her, wondering at the same time why she didn't wince, why she didn't shrink from his anger.

"Oh, Ginette, Ginette!" He said in a choked voice, "Don't you see that I've fallen quite wildly in love with you? I don't care what you say you are, or what you have been, it's nothing I can help, this feeling. But you're capable of driving me mad with jealousy, don't you see that?"

"I'm sorry, Michel," she repeated in a low voice. "It's not what I intended to do—I don't know what gets into me sometimes. I suppose I've just learned not to care about consequences. I haven't been unfaithful to you."

"No—not physically, perhaps! Not yet!"

Anger had begun to creep into his voice again, making it shake with emotion he could not control.

"Ginette—don't you understand? You've obsessed me, I can't eat or sleep for thinking of you, thinking of your body, the feel of your lips. You haunt me, I'm so infernally jealous that I—"

"No, Michel!"

"Yes, Ginette. You must listen to me, let me say it. I'm jealous! And not just of your pack of admirers—no, I'm sure they really mean no more to you than I do! Damn it, I'm jealous of your husband—the man whose name brings tears to your eyes—the same name you cry in your sleep sometimes ... it's like a knife in my heart! God knows he deserved to die, he deserved all that happened, but why does his memory have to stand in our way. Do you see how foolish I've become, how insane? I'm jealous of a dead man. I want to wipe his memory from your mind as well as your body! Oh God, if only I could be completely sure of you!"

It was a cry from the heart, and Ginny flung her arms around him.

"Darling Michel, please don't! I'm not good enough for you—I didn't intend to make you unhappy!"

"But you don't love me, do you? It's only gratitude that keeps you here. Gratitude! Don't you see that I would have done what I did in any case? I'm grateful to you. Yes, I'll never forget that day, how brave you were, how you saved my life by bandaging up my wound, and risking your own. It is I who owe you a debt, it is I who am privileged to be your lover."

She began to place soft kisses on his face, and as usual he was unable to resist the desire he felt for her.

"Oh, what a witch you are!" he groaned. "You bewitched me completely, I'm besotted!"

He carried her to the bed and could hardly wait until she had thrown aside the robe which was all she wore. But even after his desire had been sated, the torment still remained in his mind. She would never be his! How could he keep her?

All their friends, even Agnes du Salm, were astounded when their engagement was formally announced the following month. Colonel Miguel Lopez, who had continued to pursue Madame du Plessis with the persistance of a panther stalking its prey, was furious.

He made the Princess du Salm his confidant.

"But it's ridiculous!" he swore, pacing up and down her small sitting room. "Who ever heard of a man marrying his own mistress? He'll make himself a laughingstock!"

"I don't suppose he cares," Agnes said sweetly. "I think he's genuinely in love with her. And after all, why not? She's as well born as he is—I happen to know her whole story. Why shouldn't she marry him? Oh come, Miguel my pet," she added, seeing the feral glitter in his eyes, "you know as well as I do that all your influence with Max isn't going to stop their marriage. It's an open secret now that the French are on the verge of pulling out. It'll be brave soldiers such as you," she added maliciously, "and of course the mercenaries like my husband who fight wars because it's their only way of life, who will be left to save Mexico for the Emperor. Keep your mind on the war, I'm sure it'll prove much less frustrating!"

Putting on a smile and a casual air, he sat down by Agnes and held her hands.

"Come on, Agnes! You've been my friend for too long to deny me now. Why won't you arrange a private meeting for us? All right—so she's going to marry Captain Remy and make herself a *comtesse*. I suppose I can understand that ambition. But I want her, and I think she'd have me if I can only see her alone. Her fiancé need never know, nothing will be affected. I give you my word on that!"

In spite of her teasing and vehement headshakes, he continued to flatter and plead with her.

"We'll see—" was all Agnes would say, but since she combined the words with a half-smile he took heart. And the story she had told him, after swearing him to secrecy, intrigued him tremendously. Almost as much as the woman did. And, what an interesting life she had led—who would have thought it? He was determined to have her, though, at all costs.

The French withdrawal began, very gradually, in August. Feeling herself torn between two loyalties, Ginny made few comments as she listened to the talk that incessantly flowed round her. It was all the fault of the United States, and particularly Secretary Seward, who had always been vehemently opposed to the French intervention in Mexico. And now the man was actually forcing the Emperor of France to back down. Some of the French officers were talking of resigning their commissions to stay on and fight with the *cazadores* and the mercenaries from Austria and Belgium who also elected to remain loyal to Maximilian. The emperor himself, sick with the dysentery, seemed a lost, withdrawn man without Carlotta. And there were rumors about her too. She had met with Louis Napoleon and Eugenie, but they had rejected her pleas, weeping all the while. She was travelling to the Vatican to see the Pope himself, refusing to give up. And then— whispers of her "illness." The wild accusations she had made that the French Emperor had tried to poison her, that he had hired assassins to kill her. Poor Max! Ginny thought. What on earth will he do now? She really pitied him, of all people. He was such a good man, really—and he loved Mexico. What would happen to him in the end?

Because of Agnes du Salm's pleading, Ginny had begged Michel to stay in Mexico as long as she could. Strangely enough, she had almost begun to love the country herself. So much had happened to her here—and not all of it had been bad, after all. Mexico City itself was still a gay place to be, although its gaiety now seemed too loud and too spurious. There were still balls and *tertulias* and masquerades to be attended, and the theater was always crowded. Once or twice, Ginny had actually danced on the stage there, before an audience, when she was told that the proceeds were to go for hiring more mercenaries, buying more guns for the Imperialist armies. Even Michel had not dared to grumble too much, because after all, it was for the Cause! He seemed a little more sure of her these days, and talked of Paris, and the life they would lead there.

"You know that you're nothing but a little Parisienne at heart," he teased her. "Think how happy your uncle and aunt will be to have you there again! And I'd like to see the look on your cousin Pierre's face!"

Michel made an effort to keep her days filled with activity, and he escorted her everywhere when he was in the city, but his absences had begun to get on Ginny's nerves. She hated the thought of the risks he took, especially now that the *Juarista* guerillas were everywhere, and the armies of *el presidente* drawing closer, like a ring of steel. Juarez was in Chihuahua—he was moving up to Zacatecas, to make his headquarters there. Ginny heard the name again with a pang. What bitter memories that little town held for her! She could not help wondering too, how the advancing of the *Juarista* armies had affected the *hacienda* of Don Francisco. Somehow, she couldn't imagine that indomitable old man leaving his house to run away, or giving up any of his vast estates. And Renaldo. Had he ever received her letter? She had heard nothing from him—from any of them.

All the news they heard now seemed to be of Juarist triumphs. Porfirio Diaz, whom Steve had once called his friend, had escaped from prison in Puebla and returned to his province of Oaxaca, where he now headed an enormous army. Tampico fell—Guadalajara fell. Vera Cruz was now the only port that flew the Imperialist flag, and the diplomatic corps had begun to move slowly and unobtrusively out of Mexico City.

In October, Agnes du Salm came frantically to Ginny with bad news.

"Oh God! It's confirmed now, by transatlantic cable, of all things. Carlotta has been declared insane—they say she's lost her wits completely. Her brother is having her looked after at Miramar."

"But that's terrible!" Ginny was sleepy-eyed from a late night at a *tertulia*, but the news shocked her. "Oh, poor Max!" she burst out. "The poor, haunted man! Will he—do you imagine that he will really abdicate now?"

"I don't know! Nobody does!" Agnes shook her head distractedly. "They're trying to talk him into it, of course, but I don't think he understands what anyone is saying. He must feel as if he's been deserted by everyone." Then, with a flash of her old manner, Agnes added briskly, "That's why I'm here. The court is being removed to Orizaba—we've all been asked to stay at Max's little hacienda at Jalapilla, such a lovely, peaceful place! You must come with me, Ginny! The poor man needs time to think, I'm sure, and he'll need to feel he has friends around him. Come on! Everyone is going—you can't stay on here in Mexico City without any friends!"

"But—but Michel? He's gone again to Durango, they're really in a bad way there. And the general is right here—"

"Bah! Michel will understand! I've already talked to Marshal Bazaine, and he understands! He says he'll make it all right with Michel—and that in fact he'll send him to Orizaba as soon as he gets back. He was intending, in any case, to transfer Michel to Puebla—the French have their largest garrison there now, you know. And it's just a few miles from Orizaba. I won't let you refuse me this time, Ginny!"

In the face of Agnes du Salm's impatient pleading and her stubbornness, once she had made up her mind that Ginny must go with her, there seemed to be no alternative but to accede. Agnes was right, Michel would understand, especially when he talked to Marshal Bazaine. She couldn't let poor Max feel that she too had been merely one of the court sycophants, eager for invitations to the palace only when things were going well. And she had heard, many times how beautiful it was in Orizaba, the heart of the *tierra templada*.

"Oh, very well," Ginny said tiredly at last, "I'll go! But you must give me time to pack, and to write a letter to Michel."

"I'll be by with my carriage in two hours," Agnes warned her. "You must hurry, love, because we don't want to miss arriving there in the daylight, with all those guerillas haunting the *barrancas*. Although you needn't worry," she added cheerfully, already halfway down the stairs. "We'll have an escort, of course!"

In the end, in spite of Agnes's repeated urgings for Ginny to hurry, their journey seemed infuriatingly slow and leisurely. The Prince du Salm had already gone ahead with Maximilian and the rest of his entourage which included, Agnes whispered to Ginny with a flash of her eyes, that insufferable German Jesuit, Father Fischer. Ginny frowned, because she had never liked the thin, black-frocked man herself. But she was even more annoyed to find that Miguel Lopez was to be one of their escort.

Agnes, as usual, seemed in her element, surrounded by a bevy of adoring young officers. Her particular gallant of the moment was a dashing young Austrian Hussar in a spotless white uniform that looked as if it had never seen battle. In the end, because they had so much baggage between them, Agnes had brought two light, open carriages for herself and Ginny.

"This way, we can both be surrounded by our respective swains," she teased, pretending not to see the cold look that her friend shot at the handsome colonel.

It seemed as if they were merely going on some kind of a picnic, Ginny thought with annoyance. There was so much laughing and gay chatter—so many stops to admire the scenery! In the end, they had to spend the night at Puebla, and the only thing that Ginny could not complain about was the impeccability of Miguel Lopez manner towards her. She had to admit, grudgingly, that after all he was a gentleman. True, he had ridden by her all the way, and helped her in and out of her carriage each time it stopped, but his conversation dealt only with polite trivialities, and his compliments were merely polite, not bold, as they had been in the past. 'Perhaps he's changed, perhaps he's not too interested in me any longer,' she thought, and wondered why the thought gave her a slight pang of irritation. I'm really getting to be a horrible flirt, she scolded herself. I'm engaged to Michel, and I'm going to be happy with him. Why do I want every man I meet to adore me? And in any case, she reminded herself, Lopez had already made his advances and she had rejected them. It was a good thing he didn't plan to stay in Orizaba for long!

They left Puebla heavily cloaked and muffled against the morning chill—fortified by a magnificent breakfast provided by the French commandant. Before they left they had heard the French bugles, and seen the tricolor come up with the rising sun in the background. Little barefoot children came out to cheer the soldiers and gape at the fine ladies in their carriages. Puebla the impregnable fortress, Puebla, city of cathedrals. Ginny was almost sorry she had to leave it so soon—it would have been interesting to explore.

She turned back once, to see the twin volcanoes that towered above the twin forts of the city, their snow-capped peaks now pink from the newly risen sun. Popocatepetl and Ixtaccihuatl—harsh Indian names that were hard to remember, much less to pronounce. Then Lopez was at her side, leaning close to ask her if she was cold, if she needed anything. The moment of almost-sadness passed and she was the gay flirt again, her eyes flashing laughter at his sallies. She could not help thinking how charming he was when he wasn't trying to prove his own machismo. She was almost glad now that he was at her side, and not Agnes's. At least, he knew the country through which they were passing, and could describe what lay ahead, give her the names of every mountain, every river.

The highway seemed nothing more than a series of dry gullies or *barrancas*, running up and down like a switch-back. They had started out above the cloud level, and now began the slow and almost imperceptible descent into the *tierra templada*, with its warmer, more pleasant climate. The ladies discarded their cloaks and were daring enough to sip some tequila, in small silver-chased goblets that

Colonel Lopez had produced. Every now and then they halted, while the small company of soldiers who had also accompanied them scouted ahead for any sign of *Juarista* guerillas. And it was for this same reason, too, that they avoided many of the small villages they must otherwise have passed through.

"Too much chance of an ambush there," one of the Austrians said tersely. "They're all *Juarista* sympathizers, anyway!"

The roads seemed incredibly narrow, but at least here everything was green, and flowers grew in profusion on the mountainsides.

"But wait until you're near Orizaba!" Agnes called back to Ginny. "It's really beautiful there—you'll think you've never seen such a profusion of tropical beauty!" She smiled when she saw that Ginny had just accepted a small bouquet of flowers from Miguel and had tucked them into her shawl.

They encountered a heavily escorted wagon train, hauled by mules, and had to pull off to the side of the road until it had passed.

"It's silver, from the mines nearby," Colonel Lopez explained. "They'll take it back to Puebla first, and then the soldiers will take it back to Vera Cruz."

"Mines, in this part of the country? It doesn't seem possible," she murmured, looking up into his handsome face. He smiled down at her.

"Oh yes, why do you think my ancestors came to Mexico? Gold, silver, precious stones, they are everywhere! But it's hard work for those poor devils in the mines. The Indians don't like to work down there any more, so they use convicts, most of the time. That's where we put some of our Juarist prisoners."

He was giving her a piercing look, as if he expected her to make some kind of reply, but she only shrugged and turned away. Why speak of such unpleasant things on a beautiful day like this? The war, for once, seemed like a bad dream and she didn't want to think about it.

It's really beautiful, far lovelier than I could have dreamed, Ginny thought. I had no idea Mexico had this profusion of beauty, of contrast! How far away she was now from the dry harshness of the vast Meseta Central, across which she'd trudged or ridden so many times in the worst of circumstances. How different it was today, to be travelling in such comfort with such wonderful companions!

When they neared Orizaba, Agnes insisted that she and Ginny must ride too, for she was tired of being cramped in a carriage.

Agnes wore a deep burgundy velvet riding habit, trimmed with sable, and on horseback, she looked really magnificent, riding like a young Diana.

"You shall take the black mare today," she told Ginny, "and I'll take the white stallion!" Her eyes laughed. "Let's show these men that women can ride as well as they!"

To tell the truth, Ginny was relieved to be on horseback again herself. At Agnes's insistence, she had even worn the new, frighteningly expensive riding habit that Michel had ordered especially for her. When she threw aside her shawl and allowed Miguel to help her mount the restive black mare, Ginny thought she had seen again the barely controlled flare of desire in his eyes. She was aware that she looked exceptionally well.

The habit was of white watered silk and clung closely to her figure, showing every detail of its perfection. The only touch of color, added at her own insistence, was the green velvet ribbon that trimmed it, and set off the small white hat, perched becomingly forward on her shining hair.

"You look like an angel—a vision!" Miguel Lopez whispered. His hand squeezed hers for a moment, although he released it quickly soon afterwards.

As always, riding exhilarated Ginny. She wanted to laugh, to urge her mount to go faster, so that she could feel the wind on her face. Yes, she told herself, I've been too long in the city—this is what I've been missing!

The path they followed broadened, as they rode downward towards the town of Orizaba, nestled under a whitecapped mountain of its own. They passed more people, obviously refugees, some of them foreigners like herself. All of them, their belongings piled in carts dragged by oxen, seemed to be hurrying.

"They're like rats, scurrying away from rumors!" one of the Belgians snarled. "Why don't they wait until the railroad is built?"

"What railroad? I thought the railhead from Vera Cruz ended at Paso del Macho!" someone else interjected.

"Ah, but our good French allies have sent their engineers, and they're hurrying to put the rails down as fast as they can—perhaps, with luck, they'll reach Puebla before long."

"God and the *Juaristas* willing!" one of the other Mexican officers snickered, and Lopez frowned.

"Of course it will be built! It's money from the silver mines that's paying for it, after all! The mine owners want a faster, safer method of transportation for their ore."

"Who's building it, though? I thought it was hard to find labor in these parts, for the peasants refuse to be parted from their lands, and the *hacendados* won't release any of their peons."

"Ah!" Colonel Lopez shrugged, kneeing his horse closer to Ginny's. "More convict labor, I'm afraid. But we have plenty of that, and now we've stopped executing our *Juarista* prisoners—we send them to the mines or the road gangs instead. It's more practical, you'll admit, and the hard work kills most of them off in any case!"

He caught a slight shudder from Ginny and smiled at her.

"What an angel you are—do you even feel pity for *Juaristas*? I wish you were as soft-hearted towards your ardent admirers, cold one!"

"Why Colonel, are you really one of my gallants? You flatter me exceedingly!"

"You're playing with me," he said in a low voice. "I wish I could find the key to unlock that heart of yours— even if only for a moment!"

"Perhaps I don't have a heart," Ginny retorted, her eyes meeting the challenge of his without flinching.

"In spite of your cruelty, you have a spirit that I cannot help admiring," Lopez said. "Never mind—perhaps there'll be a moment when you'll feel some slight degree of warmth for me. I'm a patient man."

"You play the gallant admirably!" she said coolly. And then, "can't we ride a little faster? Aren't we in sight of Orizaba yet?"

"Patience, *petite*, we're getting there." A Frenchman, a friend of Michel's rode up, grinning. "Phew! It's really getting hot, isn't it?"

Miguel's manner had reverted to that of formal gallantry, no more.

"But there's no point in exhausting the horses yet. Remember that the Emperor's hacienda at Jalapilla lies a little beyond Orizaba. In the meantime, why not enjoy the scenery?" They were passing what appeared to be the outskirts of a small village, beyond which stretched a tremendous orchard.

"How pretty it is! What's this village called?" Ginny dropped back slightly to hear his reply.

"That, *belle madame*, is no village, I'm afraid. It's part of the *hacienda* of the Conde de Valmes. In a short while, we'll pass the high stone walls which surround the *palacio* of the *conde* himself. You've met him surely?"

"You mean that stooped over little man with the very white hair and great big mustaches? That *conde*? The one we are always saying is Max's shadow?"

Ginny opened her eyes wide in surprise, and Miguel gave a rather sarcastic laugh.

"Precisely! That one. But he's too busy playing courtier to bother with the running of his *hacienda*. He leaves that to his wife, who is quite young and er—active, one hears."

"But that's incredible, that he should have a young wife. Is she pretty, the *condesa*? Does he always leave her locked up here alone, or does she ever come to the city?"

"Ah, now at last I've managed to pique your woman's curiosity!" Miguel laughed. "I don't think you've ever met her—Soledad doesn't visit Mexico City very often, she says she finds it too boring. However, she's hardly a prisoner here! She finds plenty to keep her busy, and this part of the world does have its amusements, you know!"

"Stop teasing, Miguel!" Agnes had reined up beside them, her face flushed and smiling. She turned to Ginny. "No, really! He won't tell you too much because she's a distant relative of his, isn't that so, Miguelito? But you know me, I've no qualms about gossiping! Our *condesa* is quite young, compared to her husband, if you can call fortyish young, that is! And she's considered attractive, too, in a full-blown way! As for her amusements—"Agnes turned her laughing eyes on the Colonel, who had the grace to flush, "what Miguel means is that she doesn't lack for gallants. Most of them young, and quite handsome! She has quite a discerning eye for strongly built young men—perhaps it's her mothering instinct, for they never had a child. Don't look so curious, my pet, you'll probably meet her at Jalapilla! She'll be invited to one of our *tertulias*, I'm sure, even though her old bore of a husband is sick and lying in bed in Mexico City, surrounded by doctors! *La Condesa* won't miss him."

They all burst out laughing at Agnes's irrepressible air of mischief, even the colonel.

"You're quite impossible, dear Agnes!" he murmured to her and she replied with a saucy look, "Am I though? You must admit I'm a born intriguer, isn't that so?"

He inclined his head at this, with a certain light in his eyes, that had narrowed slightly in appreciation of her innuendo.

It was a gay company that rode so light-heartedly into the outskirts of Orizaba. Even Ginny hardly looked up, except to give one short glance of pity when a ragged, filthy line of men, their legs chained to each other, wrists manacled by long lengths of chain, were ordered to get into the ditch and stay there until the small cavalcade had passed.

"Are those miserable vermin your railroad builders?" one of the Austrians asked. "Well, here's part of the railroad, and I suppose those anxious-looking men are your French engineers!" another officer replied.

"I'm surprised that any of them has the strength to lift a pick, much less one of those heavy sledge-hammers!" Agnes said with a shudder. "Poor devils!"

Ginny continued to smile at something the colonel had said. Really, she didn't want to be bothered all day by thoughts of men chained like animals, having to work their miserable lives away in this heat! She heard Alice say petulantly, "I do feel sorry for them, but I wish their guards wouldn't let them stare so! Fancy, they probably haven't seen a woman in months—and in spite of the rags and those heavy chains I'm sure they're quite dangerous!"

At the moment, Miguel Lopez had picked up Ginny's hand and was kissing it. "You're the dangerous one," he murmured. "Who can blame any man for wanting to stare at you?"

"And you're far too bold!" she said, but her voice didn't sound angry, and she was smiling when she said it.

Well content for now, Lopez dropped her hand, but continued to ride by her side all the way into Orizaba.

Chapter Forty-two

The Emperor Maximilian's little *hacienda* near Orizaba was every bit as beautiful as Ginny had been led to believe, with its meandering streams, great old trees and profusion of tropical vines and flowers. And yet, as the first week dreamed by, she found herself filled with a strange discontent, almost a feeling of malaise.

After all, except for the really beautiful scenery around here, was it any different from the city? Here were the same faces, the same ceaseless round of forced gaiety. Only the emperor himself seemed withdrawn and serious—always closeted with Father Fischer, or one of his generals. He had not yet made up his mind what he would do. He spent his time in a dreamy-eyed fashion, arranging picnics for a few chosen guests, or writing endlessly in his study, leaving his guests free to amuse themselves. And Ginny found herself growing tired of this endless round of amusements.

Michel still had not come, and she hadn't heard anything from him—not a line! As for Miguel Lopez, he was constantly in attendance, she could not turn without finding him at her side, alternately bold, sly, sarcastic and charming. Their friends began to take it for granted that the handsome colonel would be Madame du Plessis' escort wherever they went; whether it was to Cordoba to visit the colony of settlers from the southern United States, or to Orizaba itself—now full of foreigners and diplomats, all waiting to see what Maximilian would decide to do. Would he abdicate? Or would he decide to do what his poor Carlotta had wanted and remain as Emperor of the Mexicans without the support of the French? It would be foolish, Ginny thought, if he did anything but leave, in the face of the recent *Juarista* victories. But one could never tell, with poor Max. She had begun to call him that too, picking it up from Agnes. Yes, poor Max—poor vacillating man!

Agnes was constantly nagging at her friend to do more with herself, to act more cheerful, smile more often.

"Are you pining for your Michel? It doesn't seem possible. You're not in love with him are you?"

"Oh, Agnes, of course I love Michel! Why else would I marry him?"

"For security and a title perhaps?" Agnes threw back at her saucily. Then, catching sight of Ginny's perturbed expression she went on more gently, "Oh, come on my love! Pray don't look so gloomy! We're here to amuse poor Max, aren't we? Why won't you let yourself be amused as well? Take a lover—perhaps that's what you need. There's always Miguel."

There was, indeed, always Miguel. She grew almost too weary of fending off his advances. He was always snatching at her hand, stealing kisses, swearing his devotion one minute and the next, chastizing her for her coldness and her cruelty.

"Are you really marrying for love, beautiful one?" he asked her one day, when they had gone out riding together. "Or is Captain Remy merely substituting for a ghost? Is that the secret of your coldness?"

"What do you mean? You're always talking in riddles, Colonel!"

She looked at him almost wildly, her small teeth worrying her lower lip. His laughter was a trifle cruel."

"Who do you think Agnes entrusted with that letter you sent to Renaldo Ortega? I'm the only person who has what you might call 'connections' in both camps, my dear! Don't glare at me that way, of course I read it! All the young *hidalgos* in those parts are well-known Juarist sympathizers—how did I know that you were not a spy? Of course, I didn't really know you then, did I? Since then, I've gone to a great deal of trouble to learn as much as I can about you."

"You—you're really vile! What did you hope to gain by all this—this spying into my private life?"

Furiously, Ginny glared at him as if she hoped her looks would strike him dead. Instead they only moved him to amusement and he smiled at her, revealing perfect white teeth under his slim mustache.

"Rage becomes you! And in answer to your question, I wanted to—shall we say—understand you better? Yes— who would have thought that the fashionable, sophisticated young Madame du Plessis once careered around the countryside as the hostage of a villainous outlaw? Or that her charms melted even this dangerous character in the end, so that he married her? Much more interesting, I thought, was the fact that you didn't even spend your wedding night together."

"Stop it!" she gasped. "What do you expect to gain by all these—these revelations? I know very well what happened to me, and I choose to try and forget it!"

"*All* of it, *querida*? Even the undying love you declared for your husband?"

"Leave him out of it! What are you driving at with all this?"

"I was merely trying to explain why you fascinate me. I know you're a lady, it shows all over you. And yet, underneath—yes, what *is* underneath? It intrigues me to know that once you were a *soldadera*, a—if you'll pardon my bluntness—little girl who had many, many unpleasant experiences forced upon her. I ask myself, is she as passionate as she seems to be when she abandons herself to wild gypsy music? Is she capable of giving herself completely and without reserve? You see how you've been tormenting me, Ginette!"

She had begun to stare at him with wide, uncomprehending eyes, as if she was seeing him for the first time.

"What kind of man are you? Don't you have any scruples at all?"

"When it comes to what I want—none at all, I'm afraid."

She suddenly kicked her heels into her horse's side, sending it leaping forward with a bound.

"I won't listen to any more," she called over her shoulder. "Please don't bother to pursue me any longer!"

But he followed her, still laughing.

"We'll see, little enigma, we'll see!"

So Colonel Lopez was closing in for the kill—and there was still no sign of Michel.

As she dressed rather half-heartedly for a *tertulia* to be held outdoors that evening Ginny found herself wondering for how long she could continue to resist the man's concentrated stalking of her. He must be crazy, she thought. Fancy going to such lengths to find out all about me—it's only because he isn't used to rejection that he continues to hound me.

Agnes was escorted by her husband, the Prince du Salm this evening, and as Ginny descended the low stone steps that led out into the gaily-lit ornamental gardens, she saw that Miguel waited with them, his usual rather sarcastic smile flashing as he caught her eyes.

"Isn't it lucky that you have such a devoted admirer, darling!" Agnes said in her high voice. "You'd have had no fun at all if you moped around waiting for Michel!"

"Ah, don't be so cruel as to remind this vision of loveliness that she has a fiancé," Miguel Lopez exclaimed in an exaggerated fashion. "I'm sure no one could adore her as much as I do." He took her hand and bent over it, his lips lingering far too long, seeming to burn into her flesh. "You did promise me all the waltzes, did you not, madame?"

With Agnes and her husband leading, they strolled out to join the emperor's party.

As she always did when she was a trifle nervous, Ginny drank too much champagne. When they danced, Miguel held her too tightly, whispering his innuendos in her ear until she felt breathless.

"I'm beginning to think you're afraid of me," he whispered. "Or is it of yourself? You're more of a challenge than any woman I've met before, *mi alma*. Won't you let me find out if I can melt that icy little heart?"

The light-headed feeling she always got from champagne made her laugh.

"Oh come, Colonel Lopez! Just think how disappointed you'd really be if I gave in too easily—the hunt would lose all its savor then, wouldn't it?"

"Does that mean that you do intend to give in at some time? Or only that you're playing cruel games with my devoted heart?"

Something like a premonition seized her for just an instant and she said in a quiet voice, "I think you are the one who enjoys playing games. You frighten me just a little bit, you know!"

He laughed delightedly, squeezing her waist.

"That's a good sign, little cold one. It proves, at least, that you're not quite indifferent towards me."

She wasn't quite certain how she felt about the devoted, attentive, and yes, handsome, Colonel Lopez. He never left her side once that whole evening, and later when at the emperor's especial request Ginny kicked off her shoes and danced by the pool, she was still conscious of his eyes on her body. They seemed to watch—and to wait. But what did he want, apart from another conquest to add to his already formidable list of conquests?

He was perfectly frank with her later, when he had seized her boldly in his arms after her dance was over; carrying her wrapped in his cloak like the prize of some medieval knight in spite of her struggles and cries of angry protest.

"Colonel Lopez—Miguel—have you gone completely mad? Put me down—where are you taking me?"

His voice, for once, sounded quite serious.

"Tonight, whether you knew it or not, you danced for me, *querida*. You were aware of my eyes, and your body offered itself to me—teased me, challenged me. Tonight, at last I take up that challenge!"

"Don't—stop it!" She struggled furiously, but he only laughed. "Do you realize what this will do to my reputation? You know that all the guests—all our friends saw you carry me off in this ridiculous fashion like a . . ."

The words choked in her throat when she saw where he was taking her. The tiny, deserted summerhouse they had discovered one day on one of their rides. He had said then, very casually, "What an ideal place this would be to make love! Look, the roof has fallen in, and the moon could watch . . ."

He carried her inside and laid her on the improvised divan he had created there, with cushions and soft silk and velvet coverings.

"A couch of love for a lovely courtesan—you're a fit prize for any Eastern sultan's harem, little Ginette!"

She was frightened of the determination she read in his face as he slowly began to undress—and of her own weakness at this moment. Oh, if only his eyes had been a darker blue, like a stormy sky—his hair jet black like an Indian's! Yes, then—then she would have thrown herself at him, as wild with desire as he appeared to be. Why did she always have to think of Steve when she was with another man?

"You're so silent—don't be afraid. Little flower—little green-eyed gypsy!" He came to her, his voice low and ardent, and she felt his fingers against her skin, numbing her first shamed reaction of withdrawal. He mustn't haunt me any longer, she thought wildly. I must, I have to forget him—I'll never have him again.

And so, with something close to a sob, Ginny gave herself to Colonel Miguel Lopez, that puzzling, persistent man. His reaction, after his breathing had slowed and he lay quietly by her side, was even more puzzling to Ginny.

"So—it's true after all. You're one of those—a born courtesan. I had hoped for something different from a woman of your unusual background, Ginette!"

"What?" She raised herself on an elbow and stared uncomprehendingly down at his set face. What do you mean? What is wrong with you now?"

"With me! Why nothing! Except I'm not the sort of man who likes to be fobbed off with a sugar tit—a mechanical, rather resigned bodily reaction with the mind completely uninvolved. "Yes," he added fiercely, throwing a leg over her to keep her still, "yes, little one, I, Miguel Lopez have known enough women to understand that for a woman the involvement of the mind, even a little bit, as well as of the heart, is everything. It is what adds warmth and passion to this kind of embrace. But there was no true warmth in you tonight—your dancing was a lie, just like your feigned passion!"

"Oh!" she gasped angrily, "But you expected far too much then, Colonel Lopez! You carried me off here tonight just as if I was a prize of war! And I gave in—surely you didn't expect more of a woman you yourself called a born *cortesana*! Really—your arrogance and your conceit are insufferable!"

"And I also find it insufferable that there is so much

wasted passion, such wasted potential hidden inside you somewhere, *chica*! No, don't try to get free yet—at least let's have some honesty between us now, for a change, eh? Are you capable of that much?"

His face, with a fixed, sneering smile, seemed to loom over hers and she turned her own away.

"Oh, Miguel, please! What more do you want of me? That I should force some emotion I can't feel any longer? Is that what you want me to admit?"

"Admit the truth, *querida!* Yes, admit it to yourself, if not to me! You are not in love with Captain Remy—if you had been you would not have left Mexico City, and you would not have played your teasing games with me. But have you ever really loved? Are you capable of it? Or is it your husband who's spoiled you for any other man?"

"Yes!" she cried wildly. "Yes, then, if you *must* know, if you *will* torment me! I loved him, and I still do. Is that what you had to know? Is it?"

"So that's the secret to your puzzle. Perhaps I should have guessed it before—there were enough clues, were there not? Half the men in the city at your feet, and you're in love with a ghost. Or is he a ghost? Are you sure of it?"

She stared at him fixedly, her face becoming pale. She was suddenly deathly afraid—suddenly quite positive he was going to tell her something really terrible—something she wouldn't have the strength to face.

"What's the matter? You've gone quite white. Don't you want to hear the good news I'm about to give you?" Miguel Lopez' voice softened, almost to a purr of cruelty. "You ought to be grateful I'm such a soft-hearted fellow that I can't bear to see a beautiful woman suffer. Prepare yourself for a pleasant shock, madame. Your husband is alive."

For a long time, as she continued to stare up at him, Ginny could hear the repetition of his words in her numbed brain.

"Your husband is alive . . . alive. . . ."

She gave a sudden shriek of pure agony and began to struggle wildly under his pinioning body.

"Oh God! Don't lie to me! No—not about *that*! Why must you torment me so? I tell you I *saw* him die! The execution squad—I saw it, I saw it! Do you think I don't wish I hadn't? I prayed that I could have died too. Oh, my God, if I weren't so weak I'd have killed myself."

"But that would have been such a pity, little one! Think of all the experience you've gained—think how joyous it will be to be reunited with this paragon of a man again! Only"—his voice grew slower and more thoughtful and she waited for the further shock she somehow knew he would deal her—"only I'm afraid that by this time there might not be much manhood left in him. I'm afraid we do not treat *Juarista* prisoners very well in our prisons here. Perhaps by now he wishes that they *had* executed him!"

Chapter Forty-three

Steve Morgan was alive only because his body insisted upon survival. It was as simple as that.

He had very few recollections of the nightmarish, jolting ride; lying manacled hand and foot in the bottom of a wagon; when he had wondered distantly, in his few moments of lucidity, why he was still alive. After a while, he had relapsed into a black delirium of pain and feverish darkness, overshot by occasional flashes of more agony. Sunlight had almost blinded his eyes once; another time, someone bent over him—hands touched his back, intensifying pain, and he heard, with shame, his own scream of agony resounding in his ears as the blackness swallowed him up again.

Later, as his body began to heal and some power of understanding returned to his mind, he found that he had awakened to blackness; worse than that of unconsciousness. He was in a cell, alone, and his arms and legs were still manacled with lengths of chain; his arms behind his back. The floor of his cell might have been stone—it was cold. The only movement possible to him was crawling, and even for that there was no space, for the cell was hardly wide enough to take the length of his body.

His mind tried to remember what had happened, why he was here, but he felt too weak to make too much effort, and kept drifting off to sleep or unconsciousness. Once, during that first day of lucidity, a tin plate with some kind of slop on it that he couldn't even see was thrust through a small opening at the bottom of the door. He heard a voice call, "If you are alive, *gringo* pig, you'd better eat."

He was suddenly very hungry. He felt the uncontrollable knotting of his belly that told of emptiness, the saliva in his dry mouth as he crawled to the plate and ate from it like a dog, uncaring about anything but the assuagement of his terrible, gnawing hunger.

He ate, and slept again, and after a while the guards came for him and half-carried, half-shoved him down a dimly lit corridor to the prison doctor.

"So! You've decided to live, eh, blue eyes? It's a good thing you have a strong body—it's healing well."

The doctor was a slim young creole in the uniform of the Imperial army. He smiled rather contemptuously under a pencil thin mustache.

"You should be really grateful to me for saving your worthless life, you know," the man continued, long fingers probing the half-healed cuts on Steve's back. "Whoever did this job on you was pretty thorough. You should have died—but you'll live to work hard in our silver mine; our armies need money!" In the face of Steve's silence the young doctor gave a rather high-pitched laugh. "You must have made that French colonel who had you sent here very angry, for some reason! A *Juarista* with the mark of the French fleur-de-lis—really ironical, don't you think? And you—for a *gringo*, you're rather a puzzle. You talked French and Spanish when you were delirious. Some day you must tell me all about it—why such a linguist should end up *here!*"

It was a question that Steve too, in the weeks that followed, was to ask himself bitterly. And then, with the eventual dulling of his mind and spirit he could only wish that he had been allowed to die.

The mines were passages cut deeply into the bowels of some mountain, with cells opening off these same passages to accommodate the miserable wretches condemned to work here. Many of them died. There was no sun—they had no conception of night or day or even time itself.

Their leg and wrist irons were welded on, and when they were taken out of their cells to work, they toiled in a long, ragged file; chained to one another. Three men, also manacled to each other, shared each tiny, filthy little cell that was hardly larger than the one Steve had found himself in at first.

To Steve Morgan, who had always had more than his share of pride and arrogance, this living death, where men were reduced to a bestial level, was the hardest thing to endure. With a cowardice he hated to discover in himself, he longed for death, but his body forced life upon him. He tried to resist, at first, some of the unendurable conditions forced upon them, but the prison guards were used to dealing with recalcitrant convicts, and like the others he broke at last under the constant beatings, the starving, and solitary confinement in a pit where a man could neither stand, lie down or sit but was forced to kneel with his arms manacled to the wall behind him.

When he stopped being stubborn they put him back to work and his body performed all the required motions quite mechanically, while his mind closed upon itself and he almost ceased to think.

Reality was a darkness only slightly less than the inky blackness of the prison cell where they were put when the day's quota of work was done. The flickering orange glow of lanterns or creosote torches lit straining bodies, streaming with sweat, nostrils and mouths continually gasping for air. The whips of the guards, curling around their bodies to leave scars on backs, bellies and thighs, reminded them that they were alive. Reality was constant agony, growling, half-starved bellies, eyes that cowered and closed at occasional glimpses of the sunlight "out there." If a man didn't groan or cry out under the lash the guards kept whipping him until he did—or was dead. They had no names, these animals who had been men. It was "you!" or "dog" or "filth" and this too they accepted dully. The only release they could look forward to was death, and quite often a prisoner would contrive to strangle himself with his chains.

The young doctor sent for the prisoner he insisted on calling "*ojas azules*"—"blue eyes" one evening. Wondering only what offence he had committed this time, Steve was brought into his presence soon after the *teniente* had eaten his dinner.

The sight of all the half-empty dishes on the table, the smell of tobacco, was almost like a physical blow. Steve felt suddenly sick and faint with hunger, so that he swayed. The guard hit him.

"Up against the wall, filth. The *señor* doctor does not like to have pigs staring at him while he's enjoying a meal!"

They shoved him against the wall and he stood there obediently like the animal he had become, hearing the doctor's sneering, sarcastic comments with only part of his mind.

"A pity you've come to this—and you used to be quite a handsome specimen of a man, too. Now you're as bad as the others, a dirty, cringing beast. But still"—the voice became slower, as if considering. Leaning his forehead against the coolness of the wall, Steve heard the doctor say, "You can leave him here for a while—I'll be quite safe, don't worry. I doubt if he's capable of violence any longer." And then he heard the soft snickering of the two guards and remembered the things he had heard them say about the doctor.

Later, as they prodded him, half-shuffling, half-stumbling back to his cell, the laughter and the gibes of the guards added to the demented, frustrated rage that had begun to pound in his brain.

"Why were you so stubborn, blue eyes? It's seldom the *señor* doctor takes such a liking to one of you pigs! Just think, you could have had a bath, clean clothes, a good meal—how long before the doctor makes you his *puto*, eh?"

The dregs that remained of his pride and self-respect fought against the gnawing pains in his belly and his body's scream for survival, at all costs. How long had he been here? A month—two months—three, perhaps? And how long before he'd give in, spirit completely annihilated; or before the doctor lost his patience and forcibly made his degradation complete?

He shuddered in the darkness, wanting to retch weakly, remembering; those soft, crawling hands on his body, assessing what the doctor had chosen to call his "potential." If his hands had not been manacled behind his back he would have leapt at the man and smashed his smiling, taunting face against the wall. The young lieutenant must have sensed this in some way, for he had moved back slightly, his smile growing rather weak.

"I hate to see such waste," he'd murmured. "You'll find out that life, even in a hell-hole like this, can be quite pleasant if you decide to make it so. Yes, even for me it's rather lonely. I'm a man of some refinement, I used to enjoy the theater when I lived in the city; books, music. Perhaps we can find much in common, eh? You're an educated man, even if you are rather a mystery."

When Steve said nothing, the doctor had shrugged.

"Ah, well! I'm quite a patient man—I really hate to take by force what I'll have in the end anyway. There's nothing more exciting than a willing—uh—victim!" And he had given that high-pitched giggle again, grating on Steve's nerves.

The whips of the guards seemed to come down more often, during the days that followed; the slop that passed for food grew smaller in quantity, so that he was constantly hungry, weak with craving for water that was doled out less often.

And then one evening when they were locking him back in the cell the guard said in parting, "hey, blue eyes— you've got something to look forward to for tomorrow— the *señor* doctor wants you in his quarters, first thing in the morning!"

He tried to strangle himself that night, with the length of chain that joined his wrists. The frightened shouts of his cellmates, afraid of the guards' reprisals if they didn't betray him, brought the guards running, and he spent the rest of the night in solitary, his arms doubled up and shackled to the wall behind him.

They came early to haul him out of the cell, barely able to stand by now, his brain too numb to care about their taunts, or whatever fate awaited him next.

"What's the matter, *gringo* pig? You want to leave us so soon? Has death become so tempting to you that you go to seek it, eh?"

They dragged him out into the sunlight, with a black cloth hood over his head, like a condemned felon and he began to hope, with whatever capability of thought was left to him, that they were going to kill him at last.

But then they staked him out, spread-eagled, in the harsh, hot sun of the prison courtyard and he began to

realize what kind of death they had in mind. The wet
rawhide they had used to tie his wrist and ankle irons to
the stakes dried out quickly and he felt his body stretched
to almost beyond the point of endurance against a burning, blazing rack of pain. Too far gone in despair to do
more than groan at first, he screamed with agony only
when the ants, attracted by the smell of fresh blood, came
to sink their millions of tiny pincers into his lacerated
flesh.

The doctor came out into the sunlight only after the
screams had died away into choked animal groans from a
throat too dry and sore to do more.

He stood looking down at the tortured rise and fall of
the prisoner's chest, now the only sign that the man was
still alive, and nudged him in the ribs with his polished
boot.

"You—move your head if you can hear me—I have
some good news for you." He noticed the barely percepti-
ble movement and his voice sharpened with anger. "You
might easily have saved yourself all this pain, *caballero!* I
had expected a little more sense from you, considering—
yes, especially considering! You see—I know who you are,
Don Esteban. Why didn't you tell me you were a *criolla*,
like myself? I have such an especial hate for *gringos*!" The
boot nudged Steve's ribs again, more painfully this time.
"You deserve punishment—for stupidity, more than anything else. But I'm really here to tell you that you obviously have friends in high places. Your life's been saved
again. Learn a lesson from this, if you can, and you'll do
better on the road gang, building a railroad for the
French, than you did in the mines!"

Two days later Steve Morgan, together with fifteen
other men, began the long march down to Cordoba.

He found that building a railroad, under the direction
of a couple of French engineers, was infinitely preferable
to the eternal darkness of the mines and the scheming attentions of the young prison doctor. There were still the
guards who wielded their whips freely, but even they
seemed in a better humor under the sky, and preferred to
spend most of their time in the shade of the supply wagon
while the convicts labored in the sun.

The sun! Once his eyes had again grown accustomed to
its brightness Steve felt as if he couldn't get enough of it.
They worked out in the open and they slept outdoors,

even when it poured with rain; but a man could still smell the fresh air, the scent of newly cut hay, the odor of cooking.... Even the food was much better here, for the Frenchmen insisted that well-fed men were capable of more and better work than starved animals.

They labored unceasingly from sunup to sundown in a fight against time; still manacled, chained to each other by the leg. But still they were outdoors, and slowly becoming aware of the world around them—a world that they had all felt cut away from before.

Part of Steve Morgan's mind that had kept him numb and closed away from reality began to open again as he began to feel himself as being human, capable of thought once more. He was even capable of thinking about escape.

The thought began to obsess him, but along with humility he'd learned patience. He watched the steadily growing stream of refugees on their way to Vera Cruz when he could see for the sweat that streamed down into his eyes, and was sometimes lucky enough to overhear the French engineers talk about the war, and how badly it was going. Quite by chance he learned what month it was. October.

The railroad, snaking its way past Orizaba, was protected now by French and Mexican troops, since there had been rumors of guerilla activity in the vicinity. The filthy, ragged convicts were herded together under the rifles of the guards one day when the emperor himself came to inspect progress. Having just arrived in Orizaba after hearing the tragic news of his wife's mental collapse Maximilian seemed a sad and withdrawn man, his golden beard blowing in the wind. How much longer could his bubble empire stand against the steadily advancing *Juarista* armies? Even the guards gossiped about it, and Steve heard names of battles that had been fought and won—names of Juarista generals suddenly sprung into prominence. Thirstily his starved mind absorbed it all, even while on the surface his manner showed no change and there were no more explosions of anger or defiance from him. He couldn't take a chance on being sent back to the mines! So he accepted the whip, the taunts and the insults and the worse feeling of being chained up at night like an animal. Because now he knew he wasn't an animal—he was past that stage of black, blank despair

and numbness, he was beginning to think. And he
wondered who had had him sent here, and why. Was
Devereaux the "friend in high places" that the prison doctor had referred to? Had his grandfather discovered where
he was? And if so, why was he still here?

The work they did, as back-breaking as it was, had
developed a power and strength in his muscles that was
almost unbelievable. The convicts worked, and baked, in
the sun—bare from the waist up, their straining muscles
standing out like cords along bare, scarred backs. There
was no time to think or to ponder their fate, no time for
pausing while the sun was up and there was work to be
done. They obeyed orders blindly, knowing that to slow
down or stumble meant the whip. Building a railroad, for
the goddamned French invaders. To carry their supplies
and ammunition to them quicker, to bring down the silver
from the mines so that it could be shipped from Vera
Cruz and bring more money with which to pay Imperialist
mercenaries.

If I only had some way of laying my hands on some
dynamite, Steve thought tiredly when he should have been
sleeping. If only, among all those refugees I'd see someone
I recognized. If, if, if! Again, he felt sheer physical strain
and tiredness begin to push his mind into a kind of
hopeless resignation. What chance was there of escape
when they were chained together every night, more often
than not, tethered to trees like cattle? And when, in the
daytime, the railroad was so carefully guarded by armed
soldiers? They were building now on the land of the
Conde de Valmes, who had given his gracious consent,
and the strip of land ran beside the roadway that led into
Orizaba. And what chance was there of being recognized
when he was as sun-blackened, as dirty and ragged,
bearded and shaggy haired as the rest of his companions?
In any case, when they worked alongside the road, they
were always herded into ditches when a big convoy of carriages clattered past, throwing up clouds of dust. The fine,
respectable people must not have their eyes or noses of-
fended by prison scum!

Bitterness cut as deeply into Steve Morgan's soul as the
irons he wore on his ankles and wrists. With the power to
think came memory, and with memory hate, as he cursed
the fate and the circumstances that had put him here.

On the third day after the railroad ribboned out of the

outskirts of Orizaba they had begun to lay trestles when they were ordered into the ditch, half full of dirty, stagnant water.

The French engineers climbed onto the side of the road to get a better view of the leisurely cavalcade that passed, with an escort of mounted soldiers in their spotless, gleaming uniforms.

"More guests for the emperior's *hacienda* at Jalapila," the man called Ledoux muttered to his companion. Only lately arrived from Mexico City, he was the source of all the latest gossip and scandals. "This time there are some beautiful women to cheer poor Don Maximiliano up! Perhaps they will persuade him to stay."

"Isn't that the Princess du Salm? I've seen her before, but who is that lovely vision riding the black horse? The one in white, with Colonel Miguel Lopez of the Cazadores. *Bon Dieu*, what hair! And what a figure," the man continued in a lower voice.

Standing waist deep in filthy, odorous water, feeling the blood beginning to pound in his head, Steve Morgan looked up, staring like the others, and saw his wife. It had been a long time since he had even thought about a woman—that need having been replaced by the other, more urgent instinct of survival—but now he felt the ironic frustration of his predicament like a blow, and the need to live was replaced for just a crazy instant with the desire to kill. Ginny! Ginny laughing, her hand being kissed by the handsome Lopez—Ginny of the flashing green eyes, dressed all in white, like a virgin, like a bride. Ginny who had arranged for his living, slow death, because the firing squad would have been too quick and too merciful—he was sure of that now. Without conscious thought he made a sound in his throat and would have flung himself forward if not for the shackles that held him and the quick movement of the man on his right.

He barely heard the hoarse, urgent whisper. "For God's sake! Do you want to get us all killed under the whip? What's got into you?" He stood still, breathing heavily, like a man in the throes of a bad dream, and he hated her.

Alice du Salm glanced towards the prisoners and said something in a pitying, rather high voice. Ginny continued to smile at Colonel Lopez.

"That's Madame du Plessis. No one knows from where she turned up, but they say she's a French courtesan.

Would you guess that she is actually engaged to the Comte d'Arlingen?"

"Perhaps she's the kind of woman who believes in having more than one string to her bow!" The Frenchman who had spoken gave a short, ribald laugh.

Their conversation penetrated dimly through the red mist that had collected in Steve Morgan's brain. He saw the riders disappear in a cloud of dust, and they were ordered back to work. He stumbled along with the others, his movements slow and mechanical, barely remembering to respond to the whip with a groan.

"What is the matter with you, *Americaine*? Has the sun gotten to you at last?" The only reason that the Frenchman bothered to show any pity was because this man had blue eyes, and was, after all, of European descent.

Steve shook his head, not daring to speak in case he screamed his hate and his bitter frustration out loud.

Ginny! That she should have gone this far to be revenged on him—and he had actually begun to love her, once. 'Fool! *Idiota*!' The far-away echo of Concepción's voice came back like a goad. Madame du Plessis—French courtesan—how far she'd come since the time he'd married her in such a hurry. Married her! It was really laughable. She was his wife, of all things, and now she had found her French count again and planned to marry him. She had had him sent here, and now she was going to have him killed, so that she could marry again. How long did he have left? She had sworn to make him suffer—how well he remembered that! No doubt she wanted him to go on suffering for as long as possible. Right up until her wedding day, perhaps, and then she would quietly get rid of one husband in order to marry another. How steadfast she was in her determination to be revenged. At least in that . . .

The rain, long overdue, slashed down in buckets one night, some ten days later, soaking the shackled, shivering men to the skin, washing off dust only to replace it with mud. What did it matter? They should be used to these sudden storms by now, and if it rained during the night the morning would surely be sunny; the air washed clean, the smell of freshly wet earth in their nostrils as they worked.

Steve was almost glad of the excuse not to sleep, afraid of the choking nightmares that might return. While the others huddled together, knees drawn up to their chins, he lay on his back and let the rain beat down on his face. Perhaps it would drown him! Ginny. Ever since he had seen her again he had not been able to think of anything else. All his instincts had told him to stay away from her in the first place, and yet he had found himself wanting her. Even in the face of her screaming hate he had continued to want her. And even now, torturing him, was the knowledge that even while he hated her, he craved her. Just once. To take her just once more, to wipe from her mind and her body the memory of all the other men she must have had, and then, when she began to moan her defeat under him, to squeeze the life from her lying, treacherous, beautiful throat.

"It's too damned wet to get very much accomplished around here this morning," one of the engineers was saying dolefully to the mud-spattered young soldier who sat astride his horse beside the cook wagon. He turned around when the prisoners shambled up; all of them looking bloodshot-eyed and unutterably weary. "They're a sorry lot, aren't they? They send their prison dregs here to us— all lifers. Dangerous characters too, though they don't look it. Still, they're strong enough—look at all those muscles." Used to being talked about as if they were animals that couldn't even comprehend speech, the convicts showed no reaction as they waited, bodies sagging with tiredness.

"The Condesa de Valmes needs the wall around her *hacienda* repaired, and her peons are all off trying to save the coffee crop. We're sending you along to build that wall—and you'd better have it done by nightfall!"

Just before midday, the Condesa de Valmes, who was a soft-hearted woman, sent her servants out with food and water for the toiling wretches who worked so hard at repairing her wall. A little later, she emerged from the house herself, trailed by two *vaqueros*; twirling a dainty parasol over the high-piled hair on her head. She wanted, she explained in a dear sweet voice to the overawed guards, to see for herself what progress was being made. Her husband was returning next week, and she wanted it to be a surprise to him.

"It was really very kind of my nephew, the Colonel Lopez, to arrange for your men to come out here this morning," she said to one of the guards, a heavy-bodied,

taciturn man they called Rodriguez. "I'm afraid I would
not have been able to spare any of my men to repair it
otherwise." While she spoke, her eyes travelled idly over
the men who labored so silently, muscles ridging in their
backs, the sweat shining on their bodies. She could not
help but notice the deep crimson, almost purplish scar in
the shape of the fleur-de-lis that marred what would otherwise have been the almost perfect symmetry of muscle
and flesh on one particular back. A young man, obviously,
and taller than the rest. With the eye of a connoisseur, the
condesa continued to study this particular man with interest. Aloud, she said to the guard, "Please don't let me
disturb you! If you don't mind, I think I'll just stay out
here and watch for a little while."

Touching his forehead to show his respect, the guard
turned away to supervise, his growling voice raised now
and again as he shouted threats or instructions.

Soledad de Valmes watched, with a little, thoughtful
frown puckering her white brow. The one with the brand
of a French criminal. Was he the one Miguel had meant?

"They have an American, a *gringo*, on that road gang
I'm sending over to fix your wall. One with blue eyes. I
know your tastes, dear *Tia*, and you might find him—interesting."

She thought, What a beautiful body he has! Like a
Greek athlete. She watched him heft a large boulder that
no man should have been able to lift, gasping with the effort, muscles straining as he lifted it into place. She had
seen how the muscles in his slim flanks, covered only by a
ragged pair of *bombaches* had hardened and tightened as
he levered the rock upward; noticed the broadness of his
shoulders, and with pity, the raised lash weals that criss-
crossed them.

He stood panting, after the effort he had made, head
hanging with exertion, and suddenly one of the guards had
raised his arms to bring the whip slashing down.

"Back to work, you *gringo* filth! Do you think we have
all day?"

The man had raised his head, and for just an instant his
pain-glazed, startlingly blue eyes gazed directly into hers.
A strange shiver, almost like premonition, ran through her
body. What eyes! she thought. He's like a young god—under that filthy beard and hair he must be very handsome.

The guard brought the whip down brutally again. "Did you hear what I said, pig?"

With a wince of pain that was too close to a shrug, Steve Morgan turned away to take up the pickaxe he'd been using, and the guard, rattled by the presence of a lady, reading defiance into that shrug that had not even been preceded by a groan, lost his temper.

"You're overdue for some real discipline, blue eyes! Now get down on your knees and put your hands behind your head. I'm going to make you scream for mercy like you did that day in the courtyard, when the ants reached you!"

With a horrified gasp, Soledad de Valmes pressed the back of her gloved hand against her mouth. Steve Morgan, his back rigid with a wave of hate and anger he could no longer suppress, stood without moving. If I'm going to die in any case, at least I'll die like a man, not a crawling dog! he thought.

The guard's flat-featured brown face had gone almost purple with fury. He forgot about the grand lady who was watching, he forgot everything but his rage and the need to punish this stubborn, mulish prisoner.

"You dare to disobey? Have you forgotten what happened to you in the prison? Move! Down on your knees, you doctor's *puto—joto*!" His arm rose and fell in a passion of hate as the whip bit deeply into the prisoner's brown back. But only once— His arm had risen again when Steve Morgan whirled around with an almost animal growl of fury. He swung the pickaxe in his manacled hands as he turned, and its point caught the guard full in the chest, piercing his heart.

"Get Fuentes!" Steve yelled, but the other convicts, desperate with rage and a crazy excitement, had needed no signal.

There were only three guards today, and the other two had been distracted by what had been happening. Before they could recover from their shock, they had been beaten down. The men used shovels, pickaxes, anything they had their hands on. One of them, half-sobbing with blind hate, brought a rock smashing down on the head of the man that Steve had just killed.

The *condesa* screamed shrilly, and it was like the breaking of a spell. Her *vaqueros*, both fully armed, brought their rifles up to point menacingly at these dangerous

wretches who had suddenly gone berserk; and the convicts, suddenly aware of their peril, seemed frozen.

Only Steve Morgan had the presence of mind to move.
He threw himself on his knees and gazed pleadingly into
the horrified brown eyes of the lady.

"*Condesa!* In the name of heaven, tell them not to
shoot. We wouldn't hurt you."

His flawless Castilian Spanish at least had the effect of
startling her and making her *vaqueros* hesitate.

In a trembling voice she said, "Wait!" Keep them
covered, but—wait."

She found she could not turn away from those very
blue eyes that continued to look so piercingly into hers.
He spoke to her again, his voice hoarse, shaking slightly
with reaction.

"I beg you, Condesa de Valmes, only to listen. We're
not all such evildoers that they had to whip us and chain
us like dogs and treat us even worse! You see what happens when men are treated like animals—they react
like animals. We've killed those men who were our guards,
it's true, but they deserved it. It's you who are our judge
now, sweet *señora* with the face of a merciful angel—
what will you decide to do with us? If you send us back to
the others, we're going to pray for a quick and merciful
death. Could you condemn any man to such a fate? You
can give us either life or death—but I beseech you, if you
decide on death, then let it be quick, under the rifle bullets
of your *vaqueros*."

"He talks like an advocate, *Condesa*," one of the vaqueros growled in a rather familiar voice. A grizzled,
straight-backed old man, he held his gun with its muzzle
pointing unwaveringly at Steve's chest. "The question is,
what are you going to do with them? You can't release
prison trash like these men to menace the whole countryside . . ."

"Oh God!" Soledad de Valmes said distractedly, "I don't
know—I don't know! Do be quiet a moment, Hernan—I
must think!" Her eyes kept clinging to those other eyes—
how blue they were! Even when he knelt to her, as he had
refused to do for that brutal guard, he was still beautiful,
like—like Lucifer, she thought, like a fallen angel—surely
he couldn't really have deserved a fate like this!

"*Condesa*," Steve said quietly, and then in an even
softer voice, "Soledad." He saw the muzzle of the rifle

come up a fraction and caught the old man's frown, but he continued to speak quietly, desperation tinging his tone. "I know I'm not fit to touch you, nor even to come too near you now, but once—once you let me put my arms around your neck while you kissed me on the forehead. I don't expect you to remember—but I've never forgotten it. You were so far above me, even then; so unreachable! But you were the first woman I loved, and I'm asking you to spare us all—not for my sake, because I don't deserve such bounty, but for my mother's."

The flowing Spanish language lent itself to the phrases he used, and Soledad found herself spellbound, her eyes widening as she continued to stare at him.

"Your—your *mother?*"

"For God's sake, *Condesa*," Hernan said roughly, "what kind of madness is this? How can such vermin presume to speak so familiarly to you? I tell you, we had better shoot the lot and make an end of it—they're all murderers now!"

"No!" The *condesa* suddenly screamed the word, and her face had gone very white. "No—I remember! It's your eyes—Luisa's eyes! You must be her son. How can it be? What happened to bring you here?"

Still on his knees, Steve said in a voice that was steadier and less emotional, "It's too long a story to tell, *Condesa*. But I can tell you this much, we're none of us murderers, except for this. I'm here because I admitted to being a supporter of Benito Juarez—so are they all." His head indicated the silent, gaping men who stared so imploringly at her. "They thought it would be a nicely ironic touch, to have a bunch of revolutionaries working on a railroad to bring supplies to the French. But if you will let us go we will manage to find our way to General Díaz and fight like men—" he shot a rather mocking look at Hernan, who looked nonplussed. "We certainly won't ravage the countryside here—believe me, we'd like to see the last of it!"

"But—but Esteban—yes, that is your name, I remember you now, you were such a handsome little boy!" She clasped her hands together, almost wringing them in her distress. "But how will you ever contrive to escape? And in those chains . . . what can I tell them?"

"You can tell them we threatened you—that you were a helpless hostage, and we forced your blacksmith to file off our fetters. If we had horses—no, not even one apiece, I wouldn't ask that much, and we could ride double—we could get away. . . ."

"You should have been a general yourself!" She was half-crying, half-smiling. "For heaven's sake, get off your knees! You don't have to kneel to me, have you forgotten that I'm your godmother? But come quickly into the house, before the peons get back from the fields—I can trust my *vaqueros*—Hernan!" She turned to the dumbfounded old man, "You heard what the *señor* has suggested . . . get the blacksmith!"

It took less than two hours, and Steve Morgan used part of that time, once his shackles were cut away, to bathe and shave, while Soledad cropped his hair. She insisted that she must talk to him and sat rather nervously on the edge of her bed while he took a bath, stepping out of it quite unself-consciously to towel himself dry and get dressed in the clothes that Hernan, scowling, had found.

"You're going to Porfirio? He's a relative of mine, you know. I've always had a sneaking fondness for him, even though that silly husband of mine is so loyal to the emperor!"

He looked so different from the dirty, ragged convict he had appeared as only a few moments ago. He was positively handsome—yes, a young god—she found herself wishing that he could have stayed.

He was smiling at her, just as if he had read her thoughts. "So—you're a *Juarista* at heart too, are you? I'm glad of that—I'd like to be on the same side you are."

She said nervously, "You had better hurry, I suppose! Hernan will tell you the best routes to take, so you'll be in the mountains before they look for you. I'll see that you have weapons, all of you—no, don't say anything! You could never hope to survive without something to defend yourselves with!"

"In a way—I wish I didn't have to hurry away." He took both her hands in his and kissed them. "Soledad—beautiful first love—can I come back and see you?"

"It would be madness for you to think of it!"

"I'd be crazy if I didn't. Don't worry, I'll be careful. But I'll come back . . . and I'll bring you Don Porfirio's regards, as well as my heart."

He truly loved her at that moment, as she stood looking at him with tear-filled eyes. Yes, she had been his first love—his godmother, his mother's lovely young friend.

"Esteban—you must go!"

But before he left the room he kissed her, deeply and passionately, with all the stored up desire in his starved body.

She remembered that kiss, and its promise, even after he had ridden away with the others. He'd come back— yes, somehow she was sure of it now.

'After all,' she told herself, 'it's not as if we were *blood* relatives! And if he was only a boy when I saw him last—he is a *man* now!'

Chapter Forty-four

The Condesa de Valmes sent a messenger, who conveniently managed to lose his way first, to the Frenchmen and the rest of the guards at the railhead. Such a terrible, terrible thing had happened! She was quite prostrated with shock—fancy these miserable convicts turning on their guards to murder them, and then daring to take her hostage!

"I can't see anyone—I'm still far too upset!" she told the servant who came to announce a visitor the following day.

"Of course she'll see me—I'm a member of the family, am I not?"

Colonel Miguel Lopez, looking extremely smart in his uniform, strode into the room and bent to kiss the *condesa's* cheek.

"*Tia*—you always contrive to look beautiful—even when you are prostrated with shock!"

The servant had left, tactfully closing the door behind him, and Soledad looked weakly at her smiling nephew.

"Really Miguel, you're so unsympathetic! You can't think ..."

"Come, Tia Soledad! Let's not have any pretence between ourselves, eh? They escaped—how very convenient! I'm only surprised you did not keep the blue-eyed *gringo* behind here when the others rode away on their—um, *stolen* horses! Are you sure you haven't got him hidden away in the cellar?"

"Miguel! How dare you talk like that? And in any case," she added a trifle sulkily, turning her face away from his mocking look, "there was no *gringo* among them."

To her growing dismay, Miguel had seated himself on the arm of her chair and had taken her hand.

"Indeed? Well in that case dear *tia*, you must tell me all about it—every little detail, yes?"

For Ginny, the nightmare that had begun when Miguel Lopez had first informed her so off-handedly that her husband was still alive grew even more nightmarish following Miguel's return from the home of his relative, the Condesa de Valmes.

Ever since he had told her that Steve, her Steve, had actually been one of the men on the chain gang they had passed on their way here, she had been in an agony. To have passed so close to him, without even seeing him! All she had seen from a distance was a collection of ragged, dirty men, chained together like animals, and she had turned her head away to look into Miguel's eyes instead. No wonder he had given her such a peculiarly intent gaze—no wonder he had dropped so many hints, asked so many questions. He had known—all the time, while she was so sure that Steve had died, that her capacity for love had died, Miguel had somehow known the truth!

"I hate you, I despise you!" she had screamed at him that night. "How could you have been so cruel? Why did you let him suffer and continue to suffer?"

"But my dear," he had responded, quite unperturbed by her hysterical rage and grief, "I really thought you wanted him to suffer! How was I to know you didn't have him sent to prison for some devious reason of your own?"

She raised tragic, streaming eyes to his face, everything leaving her but grief.

"Do you really think me such a good actress? Oh God, Miguel, why did this have to happen? Why didn't I *know?*" Suddenly she was clutching his shoulders, clinging to him in a frenzy. "Miguel! Miguel, please! You can do something—you must save him! I'll do anything you want, I swear it, anything at all! But I beg you, I *beg* you!"

Gently, he disengaged her frantic clasp, his eyes looking down at her with rather a strange expression.

"So you really do love him!" he said in a thoughtful, wondering kind of voice. "You'd do anything you said—and yes, I believe you at last! I believe you would do anything. Poor little Ginette! Poor little *cortesana*—so warm to touch, so frozen with grief inside! I'm really developing quite a softness towards you, you know! It's seldom I've encountered a woman who has done everything you have and still continues to love one man. You're really to be admired for that!"

"Miguel—Miguel, please help me!"

It was a wail of grief, of pleading, of despair.

"I'll see what I can do," he said shortly. And for the moment, she had to be content with that.

She was in an agony of impatience when he returned from his visit to the *condesa*. And the news he brought threw her into a frenzy of despair.

"He's *gone*? He escaped? But where is he then? Oh God, where has he gone? How will I ever find him now?"

"But, *querida*, I thought you would be glad of the news." Miguel smiled down at her with his twisted, sarcastic smile. "After all, he's a free man now, he's no longer in chains—although, of course," he added thoughtfully, "he won't dare show his face around here again—he's a murderer, along with those other wretches. They all have a price on their heads now."

She looked at him wildly, and he put his arms around her, drawing her rigid, unresisting body against his.

"You mustn't worry, *chica*. If he had enough presence of mind to kill a guard and seize his chance to escape, I'm sure he'll know where to go. My guess is that he's gone to find Díaz. Yes, I'm almost sure of it, now I recall that my *Tia* the *condesa* is a distant family connection of Don Porfirio. Perhaps that's where she sent him."

She felt so numb. The effects of the shock she had received, and the even worse shock of knowing that having been so close to her, Steve had disappeared again, made Ginny move through the days that followed like a somnambulist. She felt so empty inside—so drained of everything, even the pride and stubbornness that had enabled her to survive all that she had gone through up to this point. She had finally learned to accept the fact that Steve was dead, that she would never see him again, and then suddenly she was informed that he hadn't died, that he was alive; only to have him snatched away once more.

There was also the frightening realization that he might not want to see her again. He must hate her of course, after the rotten trick that Colonel Devereaux had played on them both. He probably blamed her for everything—perhaps he had even forgotten about her, if he hadn't seen her that day ... and if he had, then he must think the worst.

It was agony to know all this, and to have to go on existing, pretending to everyone but Miguel that nothing had changed, that she was still the same light-hearted, flirtatious young woman they all thought her to be.

Strangely enough, she was more than ever in Miguel Lopez' company these days. She felt that in his own peculiar way he was the only person who knew her real self, and understood her pain. He was the only person she could talk to honestly—there were no more pretences between them, and so therefore, an almost grudging friendship, if one could call it that, grew up between them. She had almost forgotten about Michel, except when Agnes, or some other catty woman would ask about him.

Ginny knew very well that they all whispered that she was Miguel's mistress—he her latest lover. Not a few of the other women hoped secretly to be the one to comfort the poor young Captain Remy when he found out how his fiancée had been behaving. But by now Ginny didn't even care.

Colonel Lopez seemed to take a peculiar pleasure in parading the lovely Madame du Plessis as his latest mistress. She was one of the most beautiful and sought-after women in Orizaba, as she had been in Mexico City, and he had conquered her citadel. He had made her his, even though it was widely known that the Comte d'Arlingen had actually asked her to marry him! Women whispered to each other that Miguel Lopez must be an exceptionally charming and virile man to make a lovely woman jeopardize the prospect of an extremely good marriage and in fact her very reputation, just to be seen with him everywhere.

They did in fact go everywhere together, with Miguel playing the assiduous gallant. They went riding alone and

did not return for hours—it was a well-known scandal
that Colonel Lopez was more often in the bedroom of
Madame du Plessis than he was in his own—and in the
emperor's own *hacienda*, under his very nose in fact, the
gossips whispered. Miguel took all kinds of public liberties
with her—he kissed her boldly on the lips when they
danced, or let his fingers brush across her breasts when he
leaned close to whisper something in her ear. And Ginny
still did not care, even when Agnes warned her that she
was being foolish to allow her reputation to be ruined.

"But Agnes, what is my reputation after all?" Ginny said
wearily when Agnes taxed her with it. "You know what
they all said when Michel first produced me as his
mistress—why should I care now?"

"Michel, at least, was a gentleman about it! You know
how unexceptionally he behaved towards you in public,
never showing anything but the greatest respect. But
Miguel—he's a show-off! He wants to make sure everyone
knows when a woman has given herself to him. He may
be—what is the word they use?—yes, 'macho,' but
basically he's not a gentleman, at least where women are
concerned."

"But you were all for my taking him as a lover! You
encouraged it, don't you remember?

"Of course I did!" Agnes said impatiently, "but I didn't
expect you to lose your head! Every woman needs a lover,
especially when she has a fiancé who's not around. But
for God's sake, you should be more discreet about it!
What will happen when Michel finds out?"

Ginny had been wondering, in a passive kind of way,
why she had heard nothing from Michel. She had imagined that perhaps he had heard all the stories that were
circulating about her, and had decided he did not want to
see her again. And she began to think that perhaps that
was best—she could not possibly marry Michel now,
knowing that Steve still lived; but still, she could not bear
the thought of hurting Michel, who had been so good to
her. Yes, it was best this way—and there was always
Miguel, and their strange, almost unnatural alliance.

Then she received word, by a special messenger sent by
Marshal Bazaine himself, that Michel had been wounded
during the siege of Durango, when the French had been
forced to retreat, leaving the fortress to the victorious

Juaristas. His wound was not serious, but it was bad enough to put him in the hospital in Mexico City.

When Ginny left Orizaba, early in November, Miguel Lopez went with her. The emperor had decided to stay in Mexico and fight for his crumbling empire. He was talking of coming back to the city himself, and Colonel Lopez was to see that the old palace was prepared for his arrival.

"He says he can't bear to live at Chapultepec again. It has too many memories of Carlotta." Miguel, riding beside her open carriage, bent his handsome blond head to Ginny's pale, upturned face. "But you, *querida*—what will you do now? So you've decided to run back to your handsome, wounded hero to nurse him back to health. No doubt he'll carry his arm in a sling and have an interesting pallor in his cheeks for a while. But what are you going to do about him? Will you throw yourself at him and confess everything? Will you sacrifice your one great love to his need?"

Miguel's drawling, sarcastic words grated on her nerves, and she started chewing her lip angrily.

"Must you always sound so callous? Of course I'm going to see Michel. And the very least I owe him is honesty! I feel so guilty as it is."

Miguel groaned dramatically.

"Dear God—the sentimentality of women! First you're half-dead with frustrated passion for your long-lost husband, and then you feel guilty because you can't have your *comte* as well! Make up your mind, *chica*—or better still, play your cards right and you might have both in the end!"

"Oh you! You're really insufferable, do you know that? You're the one man I've met who is absolutely devoid of principle!"

"How very cruel and unfair you are, *querida*!" Miguel picked up her hand and held it to his lips. "Here I travel all the way to the city with you, and all I hear is reproaches. What would you have me do to prove my devotion to principle? Shall I make a clean breast of everything to Captain Remy and fight a duel with him? But of course—I'd forgotten his wound. That's too bad. Think what a buzz of gossip we could create!"

Because she had learned that the best way to combat Miguel's constant barbs was to ignore them, Ginny forced herself to shrug lightly.

"Please Miguel! At least let me see poor Michel before we decide what to do with him!"

He gave a delighted laugh. "You're learning, *chica*, you're learning! We'll make a good pair, you and I."

She was to think of that later, when she moved into Miguel's little apartment—the one where he always kept his current mistresses.

Yes, she thought bitterly, we really do make a fine pair! Both opportunists—using whatever weapons we have to gain our ends. Miguel is right, I'm almost as heartless and as calculating as he is!

The thought of her last, painful meeting with Michel still twisted like a knife-blade in her heart. He had been so hurt! So angry! Try as she would, she could not forget the bitter, hurtful words he had flung at her.

"To think that I loved you and respected you enough to offer you marriage! And then the minute my back is turned you embark on a flagrant affair with Miguel Lopez—that rake! That roué! You knew his reputation, and yet you had to make a public show of your affair with him, and drag my honor in the dust along with your own! Don't come running back to me when he throws you over—I've done with you forever!"

I deserve it—I deserve everything he says about me, she kept thinking while he continued to flay her with his caustic words.

"I really loved you, Ginette! And God knows how much I tried to make you love me back. I thought of you as the beautiful and unworldly girl that I had known—even though you had been dragged through the dust, I continued to think of you as a heroine, a degraded angel who was capable of rising above anything! But now I'm beginning to believe that you are past redemption, that you actually enjoy degradation and the kind of life that can only lead you from one vice to another."

"Oh stop, Michel!" she had entreated him at last, "please stop—please don't upset yourself so! I know I deserve your scorn and your anger as well, but you have to admit that I never pretended, with you, to be what I was not! Didn't you enjoy the art of lovemaking that I had been forced to learn? Wasn't that what obsessed you in the first place? You never would have dared to make the old Ginette your mistress, but you enjoyed the new

me, didn't you? You asked me to marry you because that
was the only way you could be sure of me—because deep
inside you felt you could not trust me, isn't that true?"

"What a glib tongue you've developed!" he sneered at
her. "How easily you've learned to twist everything, so
that you can avoid believing the truth about yourself! You
never loved me—all you could offer me was gratitude!
Good God—*gratitude*, when I worshipped you, I adored
you, and wanted only your true affection in return! What
does Lopez give you? What kind of satisfaction do you get
from being his public plaything, his little *poule* of the moment?"

"He can help me to find my husband!" At last, goaded
beyond endurance, she had almost shrieked the words at
him. "Would you have preferred me to enter into a
bigamous marriage with you, Michel? Heavens, what a
juicy scandal that would have created! But I couldn't do
that to you, nor to myself either, and as for Miguel Lopez,
he is about the only man who understands—who is willing
to accept me as I am. You see, he knows that I still love
my husband—in a way, he saved him for me!"

She saw Michel's pale, suddenly tortured look, but even
that could not stop her now. "Michel, Michel—you knew
that I still loved Steve! How many times have you accused
me of yearning for a ghost? Well, he's not a ghost, he's
alive, somewhere, and I'm going to find him. No matter
what it takes, no matter what I have to do, to what depths
I might have to sink, I'll do it!"

"So when Lopez has had enough of your rather publicly
advertised charms he will find your husband and push you
off into his arms—is that how it's supposed to be? In a
way, I almost pity this husband of yours—I wonder how
he will feel to get his rather used wife back!"

She paled as if he had struck her. "Yes, I've thought of
that too," she said in a whisper. "But that is a chance I
must take." She had turned and fled from him then, unable to face any more. And had gone to Miguel, just as he
had expected.

Chapter Forty-five

Being Miguel Lopez' official paramour was not really too bad after all, Ginny discovered as society began to return to Mexico City in throngs, in the wake of the emperor. The city returned to its old frantic gaiety, and she attended just as many balls and *tertulias* as she always had, with the difference that Miguel, and not the Comte d'Arlingen, was now her 'protector', and Miguel was not in the least jealous.

He took her to all the more important functions, and seemed as devoted and attentive as ever in public. In private, he made few serious demands on her, except to oblige him when he decided he wanted her—and as a lover he could be quite exciting, if a trifle perverted in his tastes. Ginny refused to let this upset her. After all, why should it? She had done almost everything, she had learned all the tricks of a whore—what difference did it make? At least, Miguel did not use force on her, and he was always impeccably clean. He made her feel, at such times, as if they were playing some kind of game; competing with each other as if they had been children. And they could be perfectly honest with each other, with no need for play-acting.

Miguel Lopez enjoyed showing her off in public as his latest acquisition. It gave his rather jaded reputation a kind of cachet to have it known that he had stolen her from right under the nose of a French nobleman, and almost on the eve of their wedding, at that. If she had decided to take another lover, or more than one, he would merely have laughed and asked her for details. He had grown quite fond of her, he admitted, but he was hardly in love with her. After all he was married—and kept his wife safely tucked away in his small *hacienda* in the country, protected from the corruption of the city. And he had other women—he made no bones about it.

He made Ginny his confidante and related endless stories of his various conquests, his amours. Sometimes he even went so far as to ask her advice or help in some affair of the heart.

"Fancy, *chica*," he laughed, "you're the first woman I've really been able to talk to quite frankly. You've made our little arrangement a pleasure."

"But what about your side of the bargain?" she said quickly. "Haven't you been able to find out anything yet?"

"Patience, *querida*, patience!" he cautioned her. "You know I've been working on it, but these are such uncertain times, and he appears to be an extremely difficult man to pin down." He smiled lazily at her, playing with a lock of her hair. "Did you know that some Porfirista guerrilleros blew up that painfully constructed railroad they were building to Puebla? Yes—in spite of all the precautions we had taken, they sneaked through our armed soldiers like puffs of smoke—destroyed all those months of hard labor! And then disappeared quite safely, to make matters worse. On top of everything else, it's really a bad business!"

She sat bolt upright. "What are you trying to say? Do you think that he was one of them?"

"Oh, I've no doubt he engineered the whole thing! Such multi-faceted talent—such a resourceful man, isn't he? I suppose I'll have to send down to ask my dear aunt the *condesa* all about it—I'm sure he must have paid her a visit at the same time. Did I tell you how struck she was by him? I was quite bored, listening to her rattle on about his good looks, his magnificent physique, his—er—other qualifications."

"Oh, damn you, Miguel, damn you! I do hate you when you're in a cruel mood like this!" She beat at him furiously until he caught her wrists, still laughing, and held them over her head while he brought his face down.

"I think I have a way of making you forget how much you hate me," he whispered, and after a while her furious struggling stopped. It was the kind of defeat he enjoyed inflicting on her, and she thought with a pang, how much Steve had enjoyed doing the same thing. Steve—Steve— she closed her eyes. *That* would be her revenge on Miguel!

In spite of the almost endless round of amusements that Mexico City provided, Ginny found the time dragging. Christmas came and went—the rain showered down and then the sun came back and baked them. She kept reminding Miguel about his promise until he pointed out that she was becoming a nag, and he was doing his best. All she had to sustain her was the thought that Steve was still alive—Miguel was able to tell her that much at least. And she had learned this much about Miguel, that he had his own peculiar sense of honor in spite of his deviousness and cynicism. If he took the trouble to give his word, he would keep it.

But Miguel too was preoccupied these days. The war was going very badly—that was all everyone could talk about, and Ginny sometimes thought she would go mad, listening to the endless discussions, the battles refought. What was the point? It was now one victory after another for the Juarists, and Maximilian still vacillated dreamily while his generals talked of nothing but "*mañana*," when they would push the hated revolutionaries back to the sea, with or without the damned turncoat French.

It was now an established fact that the French were packing up to leave. The Emperor Louis Napoleon, preoccupied by the war with Prussia, had finally given in to the adamant demands by Secretary Seward of the United States. He promised to withdraw his troops, and made repeated requests, echoed by the Emperor of Austria, that Maximilian should give up this mad venture and return to Europe himself.

Maximilian, his pride pricked, listened instead to the urgings of his generals. He had adopted Mexico as his own country, he announced. He would never leave it. He could never desert his loyal Imperialist troops, nor abandon all those who had supported him to the not-too-tender mercies of the *Juaristas*. Stories of brutalities, of torture and mutilation of prisoners, of mass executions of defeated Imperialist troops by the *Juaristas* began to float around the city.

"They say it's only in revenge for the Black Decrees, and for what the French did to them, but do two wrongs make a right?" Agnes du Salm sounded vehement. "That Juarez is a monster—did you know he is pure-blooded Indian? If he had been Spanish he might have been more honorable."

"Were the French all honorable?" Ginny retorted, stung. "You forget, Agnes, I've been at the receiving end of some of their brutality."

Her friend shot her a strange look. "I do keep forgetting that your husband is on the other side. And here you are, with Miguel of all people. Are you sure you two are not in contact with each other?"

Ginny stared at the other woman disbelievingly. "Are you accusing me of being a spy? Oh, really, Agnes, this is too much, even from you! If I knew where Steve was I'd be with him—I don't care on what side!"

"Ginny, I'm sorry! I truly am—of course I didn't mean anything—it's just that this damned war has got on all our nerves! You'll forgive me?"

Agnes threw her arms round Ginny and pressed her face against hers for a moment. "Darling," she went on, "I understand how you must feel. And believe me, I do wish you luck—you deserve some good fortune."

Ginny thought bitterly that fortune seemed to have deserted her entirely. Miguel was too busy with the war to pay her more than token attention—she attended theater parties and went to balls with escorts who couldn't seem to wait to put their hands on her and whisper propositions in her ear.

Quite often, these escorts were American. Mexico City seemed to be thronged with them now. Businessmen, newspaper reporters, hard-faced mercenaries. The diplomats had all moved to Vera Cruz, for even Orizaba, as close as it was to Puebla, was now menaced by the steadily-growing, slowly advancing army of Porfirio Diaz.

The *Juarista* Generals Escobedo and Corona, winning victory after victory as whole provinces fell into their hands, continued to advance from the north and west. Acapulco fell—Taxco—even Cuernevaca, where the Emperor had his summer palace. More and more rich *hacendados* who had supported the Imperialist cause left

Vera Cruz, the only port now belonging to the empire. Refugees choked all the roads leading to Vera Cruz, travelling in convoys and in fear of their lives, because now the *guerrilleros* were everywhere—their daring raids coming closer to the border of the City itself.

Where is Steve? The question plagued Ginny constantly. Is he with Díaz? Is he one of those *guerrilleros* everyone is so frightened of? What is going to happen?

Michel Remy, still bitter and unforgiving, had already left Mexico City and was on his way to France when, late in January the French made their last preparations to quit the city for good. They began to make their final march through Mexican territory, to the port of Vera Cruz, where their troopships already awaited them. And the emperor announced, smiling, that he was at last free. With his loyal generals, he would defend Mexico himself.

"The poor, deluded man!" Ginny exclaimed when she heard. "Loyal generals indeed—they're all cutthroats, it's only because they know what kind of reprisals they're in for if the Juarists win that they remain so loyal!"

"So now you're a little politician as well, eh?" Miguel teased.

He seemed in an exceptionally good mood that evening, in spite of all the bad news they had been receiving of late.

They were dressing for a *tertulia* at the house of some American friends, and he came up behind her to help fasten her dress. Ginny frowned slightly as she watched his face in the mirror.

"You're up to something, Miguel! I can always tell, when you have that particularly innocent smile on your face. Are you going to let me into the secret now, or will I have to wait?"

"Ah, but you know me too well, I can't keep anything from you!" He gave her a pat on the bottom as he finished fastening her gown, and continued a trifle obliquely, "so—the vultures continue to gather for the kill. Have you noticed how many new faces we see recently as the old ones fade away? Mexico City is no longer such a gay place to be, I'm afraid. Yes, in fact it's a place we're all better out of. I've even heard rumors that Max plans to go to Queretaro soon, to organize its defense." His sarcastic smile flashed. "No doubt we'll all go trailing after him there—his loyal friends—his last loyal friends! Except those of us who have more sense and leave for Vera Cruz instead, even if it does mean braving those overcrowded roads and the *guerrilleros*!"

Something in the tone of his voice made her swing around to face him, her silk skirts swishing. Her eyes had gone very wide, almost pleading.

"Miguel! For God's sake—tell me! You've heard something."

"But how would I manage to glean any real information about one of our enemies? Don't you think they'd be afraid I might betray their whereabouts? We still have an army of sorts, you know." His voice suddenly became abrupt. "Don't stand there staring at me as if I've destroyed all your hopes, *chica*. Cheer up. Tonight I intend introducing you to an American gentleman who most certainly knows where your husband can be found. A Mr. Bishop, who carries a newspaperman's credentials from the Washington *Star*. Of course, I happen to be one of the few persons who knows that Mr. Bishop is in reality an agent of the United States—another one of the vultures, I'm afraid. But your Esteban used to work for him, and I've reason to believe they still keep in touch. I'll perform the introduction, but you must do the rest, *querida*. For obvious reasons, I can't afford to be mixed up in such a matter. Be bold—blackmail him if you have to—use your charm!"

He took her arm, while she still stood rigid, staring at him.

"Don't you think it's time we left? We'll miss a magnificent supper if we're late, and there's a pretty young American actress who will be waiting for my arrival with a beating heart. Come along, Ginette."

If Jim Bishop was surprised when he recognized the beautiful "Madame du Plessis" as Steve Morgan's wife, he hid it well under his stiffly formal manner. Ginny, on the other hand, could not prevent her little gasp of shock when she recognized the same man who had given her away at her long-ago wedding.

Since Miguel had left them together after he'd made the introductions, Mr. Bishop had no choice but to offer Madame du Plessis his arm, and escort her in to supper. When she insisted, in a low voice, that she must speak to him in private, on a very urgent matter, he did no more than nod his head politely as he acceded. However he did look slightly shocked later, when she invited him to visit her apartment.

She gave a slightly hysterical laugh. "Mr. Bishop! I swear I don't mean to seduce you. But really, it's the most private place I can think of. The servants have the night off, and as you can see, Miguel has found—a friend to occupy his time with. I don't expect him to visit me tonight. Won't you trust me?"

He gave her a bluntly direct answer that surprised her. "I really don't know, madame. But"—he gave a small shrug and a thin smile touched his lips for a moment— "you hardly leave me with an alternative, do you? Very well. And as a matter of fact, I should warn you that I have a few words for you, as well."

She was so excited, so deathly sick with anticipation, that she could not eat, and she hardly knew what she said to anyone else for the rest of the evening. Miguel had gallantly left her his carriage, and when at last she thankfully emerged into the cold night air, Mr. Bishop himself took the reins while she gave him directions.

Ginny came directly to the point when they were comfortably settled in the small *sala* of her apartment. She offered the gentleman some champagne which he refused with a slight lift of his eyebrow, and then she leaned forward, fixing her eyes on his.

"Mr. Bishop, I want you to send me to join my husband. No," she hurried on, noticing the slight contraction of his brows, "please don't say anything yet—until I have explained. You see, I didn't know, all these months, that he was alive—that he had been sent to prison. I thought he had been executed! And I didn't betray him, you must believe that. It was a trick that Colonel Devereaux played on us both—making Steve believe that I had been the one to plan it all—making me believe that he would spare his life if I'"—she bit her lip and looked away for a moment. "I suppose he did keep his word to me, in a way! But, oh God, if I'd only known!"

Bishop cleared his throat in an embarrassed fashion. "Really madam, I see no point in your—er—upsetting yourself in this manner! But as for sending you to your husband—that's quite another matter! You must realize it is out of the question! In fact, I had intended to ask that you leave Mexico City immediately, for Vera Cruz. Although it's very difficult, I think I can arrange a passage for you. Your father, the senator, is extremely concerned for your safety, as you can imagine. In fact, he has even talked to President Johnson about it. I have been instructed to see that you leave here as soon as possible, and I must remind you, madam, that it is now only a matter of months—perhaps even weeks, before President Juarez will be back in Mexico City to take up the reins of government. Your remaining here, with the risk of fighting imminent, is out of the question!"

"Mr. Bishop!" Ginny's eyes flashed like green flame as she clenched her teeth together. "I will not be ordered to do thus or so, by anyone! Not my father, not even the President of the United States himself! I've become quite used to taking care of myself, and I'm capable of continuing to do so. I want to see my husband. I love him, can't you understand that? I will not and cannot leave Mexico until I have at least spoken to him face to face, and settled matters between us. I can't have him go on thinking that I was responsible for what they did to him! I must see him! And if you won't help him then I'll go looking for him myself—do you think I care so much what happens to me? It can't be worse than what I've already had to endure."

"Madam, I must insist." Mr. Bishop's voice, usually so colorless had sharpened with impatience, but Ginny, who didn't really know him, ignored this symptom of his perturbation.

"It is I who must insist, Mr. Bishop! Steve Morgan is my husband, and I have a right to know where he is!"

"Very well, madam." Pale gray eyes looked into hers as the quiet voice continued. "Mr. Morgan is a captain in General Porfirio Díaz' army. But he also plays another role, with the full knowledge and cooperation of General Díaz himself. He has been on temporary assignment, at various times, with certain guerilla bands." Bishop permitted himself a thin smile. "I'm sure Colonel Lopez was able to tell you that much, at least. In addition, since he is still, technically at least, an undercover agent of the United States, he also manages to keep in contact with me—or certain of our other representatives here. He is usually somewhere in the vicinity of Oaxaca province—sometimes even closer to the east—but I'm afraid that it is, well, almost impossible to keep track of his exact movements."

"But you said he keeps in contact with you—how could you know where to reach him, then?"

"I said, madam, that *he* keeps in contact with me." Bishop's voice was dry. "It is he who makes all contacts. I merely arrange to have messages waiting, if I happen to have something important to communicate to him. And I should not even be telling you as much as I have. You are really a very disrupting influence, young woman!"

He watched, with disapproval, as she tilted her glass of champagne, draining it to give her courage.

"Mr. Bishop," she said at last, "I do not intend to give up! Do I make myself clear? I will not go anywhere unless I go to my husband. And you can send me to him. I warn you—I can be thoroughly unscrupulous when I have to be. And I will see Steve again!"

"Am I to understand that you are threatening me, madam?"

Bishop's impeccable poise slipped for an instant, and the shocked surprise was obvious in his tone.

"If you want to call it that—yes!" Ginny gave a careless shrug and looked directly into his eyes. "You see, Mr. Bishop—you will not be rid of me unless I can meet my husband, and talk to him. Just once is all I ask. And after that—if he does not want me—I'll go to Vera Cruz or anywhere else you say, without making a fuss."

Chapter Forty-six

They were jogging down the great highway that led out of Mexico City and all the way east to the ocean, and already, though the sun had just risen, the beaten-down, rutted roadway was crowded with other refugees.

Ginny sat hunched on the uncomfortable wooden seat of the little creaking oxcart, her *rebozo* wrapped tightly around her head and shoulders to keep her warm in the chilliness of dawn. Beside her, her companion, the man who was supposed to pass as her husband, sat in sullen silence except for the occasional grunting noises he made to the two emaciated oxen. It was clear, in spite of the wide sombrero that partially covered his face, that Paco Davis was not at all happy.

"What a coincidence!" he had said ironically when he first saw her, dressed in the shabby garments of a Mexican peasant woman, her face smudged with dirt. "One is always meeting old friends, in my job—and especially *here*. Tell me, how did you manage it?"

Ginny had frowned at him crossly. "What do you mean? I'm sure your Mr. Bishop told you the whole story."

"He told me some of it," Paco had continued in the

same ironical tone. "But then, I was rather drunk at the time—I'm not used to the fleshpots of Mexico City, you know! I did gather, though, that I'm supposed to take you to the place where I usually go to drop off messages. And that you were my responsibility." He had given her a wry look, and noticed her frown deepen.

"I'm sorry if I've put you out. But, as I managed to convince Mr. Bishop in the end, I'm perfectly able to take care of myself. Surely you can't throw any more objections in my way than he did!"

"I won't even try! You're here, aren't you? But I ought to warn you that this whole idea is crazy! It's the damnd-est thing I ever heard of—taking you to meet your hus-band in the middle of a war—just as if this was some kind of pleasure jaunt! I think Bishop's crazy too, for letting you talk him into it!"

"I'm afraid poor Mr. Bishop didn't have much choice," she'd said sweetly.

"Well, anyhow—remember to keep your hair covered, for God's sake—and lower your eyes—in spite of those clothes and the mud on your face I'm afraid you don't look at all like the wife of a poor peasant like me!"

"You can always say I'm some *puta* you picked up in one of those—those fleshpots you were talking of!" she retorted, beginning to get angry. "Shall I convince you that I can pass as one of those quite easily?" In the same sweet voice she released a string of expletives that made even Paco flush—both with surprise and embarrassment.

My God, he thought, what's happened to her? He remembered her as a headstrong, willful girl, with the potential of great beauty some day. He had seen her dirty, dusty and dishevelled; and dressed like a debutante. But she had still been just a girl, all the same, and now here she was, dropped on him from out of the blue—very obvi-ously a woman now, in spite of her ridiculous attire; and a woman with quite a past, to judge from her language!

As they rode on in silence Paco found himself thinking, I wish Bishop had told me more about her—why does he have to be so close-mouthed? She disappeared, we all knew that, and then she suddenly turns up in Mexico City—a high-priced *cortesana*, if what they say is true. But what is she doing here? Why is she suddenly so insis-tent on seeing Steve? He almost shuddered at the thought of that meeting. Steve had always been close-mouthed, and since he had escaped from that hell-hole they'd put him in, he'd appeared even more reserved; and bitter, into the bargain. Not that he blamed him—he'd seen the scars on Steve's back, and could imagine what it must have been like. But Steve seemed to have withdrawn himself into a hard, coldly implacable shell of late. He had always been cool-headed and almost nerveless when it came to fighting—now he was quite ferocious, and merciless. A killer. Paco had seen some of the damage the *guerrilleros* had done—and some of the victims they left behind. Steve never talked about his wife, but he hated to think what he might do to her, especially if she turned up like this— quite suddenly, without any warning. If he still thought that she had been the cause of his betrayal . . . in spite of his annoyance at having Ginny foisted upon him, Paco had to admire her courage. Yes, she had changed all right. She had grown tougher, more resilient. And used to getting her own way.

A baby started to squall in the back of the wagon, and Ginny leaned back to pick up the blanket wrapped bundle.

"It's really heartless of you to bring this poor little mite along, just as a cover! A baby! How could you do such a thing? How do you expect to feed it?"

Paco jerked his head backward with a grin, at the sad-looking goat that trailed behind the cart. "You'd better know how to milk her! That's a woman's work. And besides," he added in an exaggeratedly patient voice, "I already told you that this poor infant was abandoned. What did you expect me to do, leave it screaming its head off in the middle of the street until someone ran over it? No—I used my head instead. Now we look like a real family, unless someone gets close enough to see your eyes."

"Well, I'm sorry I can't cover *them* up too!" she snapped at him. She started to rock the baby, crooning to it in the Mestizo dialect they had agreed to use when they spoke to each other. A short while later she handed the infant to him without a word and jumped off the cart, carrying a little tin cup. He shook his head in grudging admiration when she came back with milk.

By the time she had cooked a meal when they stopped for the night, most of his anger had evaporated. Having her along hadn't been at all bad after all. Unlike most women, she was silent most of the time, and she did what had to be done without any complaints; without even having to be told. She fed and cared for that little brat as if she'd had one of her own—when they started to get up into the mountains she had helped to push the wagon—she had walked beside it, barefoot, for several miles; and all without a grumble. And she could cook!

They had stopped in a little clearing with a lot of other wagons and carts—all huddled together for safety from *bandidos*. Just as a Mexican wife would have done, Ginny had cooked their meal, served him his portion first, and then retired to spread her blankets under the cart, hugging the baby to her breast. He had grumbled to Bishop, imagining that she'd be a millstone around his neck, with all the dainty airs and graces of a society woman. Now he understood that thin, secret smile that Bishop had given him. "I think you'll be surprised," was all Bishop had said at the time. Well, he certainly was—and pleasantly too. He found himself thinking, as he sat around a small fire chatting desultorily with some of the other men, that she might after all be able to hold her own with Steve. He even hoped so.

The fire had gone out when Paco came back to crawl under the small cart, which was the only shelter they had.

"I'm sorry," he whispered. "But they'll think it strange if I don't."

"That's all right," she whispered back coolly. "I can manage to control myself—if you can!" But he noticed that she laid the baby between them, and grinned to himself.

When they started out the next day, very early in the morning, they were able to converse in quite a friendly fashion.

She asked him about Steve, of course. She couldn't resist it.

"Paco—tell me, has he changed a lot? Does he hate me? Does he ever talk about me?"

He glanced sideways at her, and decided to tell her the truth. After all she deserved some sort of warning—and he was really beginning to admire her quiet stamina.

"He's changed. I think those months in the prison did it—although he won't talk about it much. But you know his damned stubborn pride—I think what he can't stand is that they broke it—for a while, anyhow."

"Oh God! Does he blame me for it?"

"I don't know, *niña*. He's rather more silent than usual these days. But I must warn you—he's still got that temper. Look"—Paco went on quickly before she could interrupt—"why don't you change your mind about all this? I can take you straight on to Vera Cruz—you can see him after all this is settled, when he's had time to get over whatever's eating at him right now, turning him into a devil. I don't trust you with him—damn it, he's my friend, I know him, as much as anyone does! He's been riding with one of the roughest, toughest bunch of dirty fighters you can imagine—those *guerrilleros* don't give anyone any quarter—they're out for revenge now. Steve's one of the worst of them, I could tell you things"—he cut his speech off abruptly when he saw her stubborn, closed face, and gave a fatalistic shrug. "I can see that you're not even listening to me! But I tell you, you're making a mistake. Give him time, Ginny! He'll come to his senses in the end."

"I've wasted too much time as it is! Oh, Paco—you can't imagine how—how horrible it's been. Like a nightmare—all those months of thinking him dead, of not caring what happened to me, or what I did! I existed, that's all. And I didn't even know why! Then, when I heard—it was like coming alive again—like discovering something I was meant to live for. Can't you understand? I must go to him, I must find out for myself, once and for all, if things are still the same between us."

"Thank God I'm not a woman!" he said gruffly. "All I can say is, I never did understand feminine logic. I still wish you would come to Vera Cruz with me!"

"I promised Mr. Bishop that if Steve didn't want me to stay I would go directly to Vera Cruz. In any case, he said he couldn't promise to get me a passage on an American ship until at least the sixteenth of March—it seems everyone is running away! But don't you see, Paco? That gives me time."

"I see that you're a stubborn, pig-headed female! Think, Ginny. Even if Steve is happy to see you, what the devil do you expect him to do with you right in the middle of a war? You know he's an officer in Díaz' army—pretty soon he's going to be recalled to his official duty, and I've no doubt the regular discipline will do him good. But for God's sake—what about you?"

"I'll meet that problem when the time comes," was all

she would say, and in the end he gave up trying to reason with her.

Their journey seemed painfully, unbearably slow, and the crowded state of the roads did nothing to help. On several occasions they had to pull off to the side, while heavy baggage convoys lumbered past.

"So at last it's really goodbye, *los Franceses*," Paco muttered. "Their ships have started to take them away already. They'll be all gone by the end of the month, and the war will end more quickly."

"The emperor's going to Queretaro, with his generals—they say he insists on being in the forefront of the battle himself, now. And Queretaro has always been loyal. So has Puebla. Do you really think it can be finished off that quickly? There are still thousands of loyal Imperialist troops."

"Yes, and there are some of them now! I think they pay more attention to the cut of their uniforms than they do to fighting!"

Ginny saw a troop of Cazadores ride past, and with them, some bearded men in a familiar gray uniform that made her heart pound with terror, even though all that was so far behind her now.

"Counterguerillas!" she said in a low, choked voice that caused Paco to shoot her a questioning glance.

"Yes, that's right. American mercenaries—still fighting on the wrong side, it seems! They seem to be going in the same direction we are—perhaps they're going to try and stop Díaz!"

Paco seemed to think this very funny, but she did not. She was thinking of Steve, who was probably somewhere in the vast province of Oaxaca. Or perhaps he was even closer now—every day brought new rumors of the steadily advancing army of the south.

The route they were taking was almost painfully familiar to Ginny now, although the conditions under which she travelled were vastly different. There was no smart carriage with its escort of handsome officers—no picnics along the way. They skirted Puebla, its church spires etched against the background of twin volcanoes, still capped with snow. The tricolor still flew over the heavily barricaded twin forts, but for how long? There were still French soldiers everywhere here, and all along the road that led to Orizaba, but they all looked jubilant instead of menacing. They were going home!

Swinging around Orizaba, they followed a low-lying, humid valley that led southward, and Paco at last confided to Ginny that they were going to a small *hacienda* near Tehuacan, the town that bordered the province of Oaxaca.

By now there were fewer travellers on the road, and Paco hid a rifle under the seat. "There are still bandits in these parts," he confided, "although it's unlikely they'll attack such poor and unimportant people as we appear to be. If we do come across anyone, don't forget that you're very shy. Pull a corner of your *rebozo* across your face, look down and giggle. And if there are questions asked, remember that we are from near Orizaba—I have been working for the Condesa de Valmes"—here he shot her a sly look. "And we're on our way to visit my mother's younger sister, Sancia Rodriguez. Her husband is the manager, if you can call him that, of the *Hacienda de la Nostalgia*. They have only three children," he added, "and will be glad to take that one"—jerking his head at the baby in Ginny's arms.

But she had seized on the name. "*The Hacienda de la Nostalgia*! What a quaint and unusual name! Is it as beautiful as it sounds?"

" 'The place of longing.' Perhaps its former owner felt it was a place one would always be homesick for. Who knows?"

"You said its former owner. Who owns it now? Won't they mind our going there?"

"I really don't think so." Paco gave her a strange look. "You mean that Bishop didn't tell you? I must say, this is rather awkward!" He clicked his tongue at the oxen and she put her hand on his arm impatiently.

"Paco! Why are you suddenly being so mysterious? What did Mr. Bishop omit telling me?"

"I suppose you might as well know. As a matter of fact it belongs to you, *niña*! You probably won't remember, but before you married Steve his grandfather drew up a property settlement for you. Do you recall it now? There was not only a considerable amount of money involved but land as well. He deeded this little *hacienda* to you. I believe it was part of the dowry he intended for the Dona Luisa. Well, in any case—it's yours now. And very convenient, I must say, for our purposes!"

She was staring at him, lips parted. "I don't believe it! It's too much of a strange coincidence! Mine you say?"

"Yes, *niña*, all yours! But of course, since Steve is your husband, he's been using it. Don't look so hopeful—he doesn't live here, you know! As I said before, it's been convenient. Few people come here, there's only an old man who's worked for the Alvarados for years to take care of the house. And the peons are fanatically devoted to Steve since he freed them. They elected to stay on and work the land—everything has been neglected for years, I'm afraid, but they make quite enough to live on comfortably."

"And he comes here?"

"Yes. Quite regularly, just as I do. If we miss each other, old Salvador takes care of the messages. We use a code, of course, to be perfectly safe, but I rather doubt that this place will ever be bothered!"

Ginny could hardly contain her excitement now, until they reached the *hacienda*. Her land. Her property. Already, she had fallen in love with its name. Yes, it would be beautiful—and it was in some way fitting that she should first meet Steve here of all places, after they had been parted for so many months.

As they travelled closer, and Paco began pointing out landmarks, Ginny's sense of anticipation grew so that she could hardly bear the slow pace at which they were travelling. A few times she jumped off the seat of the slow-moving *carreta* and walked beside it, to stretch her legs, she told Paco.

Finally, about an hour before noon, Paco told her they had just reached the border of her land. The path they travelled now was little more than a grassy, rutted track, winding amid thickly-leafed old trees, hung with vines. Here and there a cane brake, the tall, thin stalks growing close together, testified to the neglect that showed everywhere.

Small, cleared patches of land showed occasionally through gaps in the trees, but there was not a sign of anyone—only the distant barking of a dog the plaintive mooing of a cow gave evidence that people lived here.

"It's too close to the time of siesta to find anyone working," Paco explained. "In any case the peons here don't need to turn in a daily quota to the manager. I believe they work just hard enough to feed themselves and their families." He lifted his arm suddenly to point through the trees. "Look—there's the old warehouse. I doubt if they keep anything in there now. Only all those vines keep the bricks together, looks like. But you'll find that the distillery is still in pretty good shape—they make some really good *aguardiente* here. Down that way," he pointed again, "is the small store—the *tienda*. There's still an old sawmill down by the river—the usual collection of buildings you'll find on any *hacienda*." They had turned rather a sharp bend and were now passing by a small cottage, set some way back, with a tiny flower garden bordering a neatly kept path leading to a painted door. At Ginny's inquiring look Paco said, "That's the Rodriguez house. He's the estate manager—technically that is. The place seems to manage itself these days, that's the trouble with absentee landlords like you!"

But Ginny was, by this time, far too filled with excitement to respond to his teasing.

"Oh, Paco! Everything is so beautiful, so old—I feel as if time has stopped here, as if one could feel detached from everything unpleasant and dream one's life away."

"Wait until you see the old mansion. It's badly in need of repair, like everything else around here; in fact only one wing is at all liveable. Still, you'll probably like it. At first sight it is really quite pretty—the flowers grow almost as thickly as a jungle in front, and the trees that surround it are very old."

They moved along what had obviously once been a wide, tree-shaded avenue. Now grass had overgrown the carriage drive, and the trees were draped with moss and brightly-flowered parasites.

"There it is," Paco said suddenly, as they emerged from beneath the gloom of the trees and out into a small clearing. "Your own *estancia*, madam. What do you think of it?"

She was speechless, at first. The house itself was quite large, built in a style that was typically Spanish. It nestled like a jewel in its own grove of trees that seemed to enclose it on three sides. In front, as Paco had warned her, everything had gone to seed, except for a cleared-off section directly in front of the wide stone steps that led down from a covered verandah that extended across the whole front of the house.

On the left, and a little to the side, a small herd of

goats milled uncertainly about in an improvised corral—chickens ran squawking everywhere, scattering wildly as they approached and Paco called out loudly through his cupped hands, *"Hola*! Where are you, *el viejo*? Is everyone dead around here?"

"I love it already," Ginny was murmuring as her wide eyes took everything in. "I can hardly imagine it's really mine! And look, Paco—look at the goats, there'll be plenty of milk for the baby! I hadn't expected . . ."

She broke off abruptly as a girl came flying down the steps, her bright red skirts whirling around slim, bare ankles.

"Esteban! *Querido*—is it really you at last? I have been so lonely!"

She stopped suddenly, hand shading her eyes, to stare at the small cart.

"Oh Lord!" Paco groaned softly, "believe me, Ginny, I hadn't expected this either! Now—don't you fly off the handle, just let me handle this."

"Oh, it's only you!" The girl was saying in a sulky voice. "I thought . . ."

Paco heard Ginny's smothered exclamation of rage beside him and winced.

"Now listen to me, Ginny—," he began, but he might as well have been talking to air.

She pushed the baby at him unceremoniously, forcing him to take it, and the next minute she had jumped down off the wagon to confront the girl who stood there with her mouth open—surprise written all over her face.

"What are you doing here?" Ginny flung at her in a cold, hard voice that shook with rage.

The girl gave her an amazed look that slowly turned to one of contempt. She looked beautiful as she stood there, so sure of herself—her vivid gypsy coloring seeming to glow like a rose in the sunlight.

Deciding to ignore Ginny she looked over her head at Paco.

"Paco, who is this woman you have brought with you? I think she is insolent."

"This is too much! It's you who are insolent, and if you know what's good for you you'll leave my house immediately—before I lose my temper!"

All but stamping her foot Ginny snatched the *rebozo* from her head and flung it aside. She stood there reminding Paco of an angry Fury, with her coppery hair gleaming in the sun. Her eyes, although Paco could not see them from where he sat as if spellbound, were narrowed like those of an angry cat. Concepción! Ginny was thinking. To find her here, cosily ensconced in Ginny's own house—waiting for her husband—

The stunned expression on Concepción's face had slowly begun to change to anger as she regarded Ginny.

"You! How dare you come here? Traitress—French whore! It's you who had better get out of here in a hurry, for if Esteban ever sees you he'll kill you—if I don't do so first!"

"*Ramera*—if you don't take your offensive self from my sight it is I who will do the killing!"

All the vilest words and phrases that Ginny had learned during the time she'd been a *soldadera* came back as she planted her feet astride and glared warningly at Concepción.

It was plain that the other girl had again been startled by Ginny's command of the vernacular and her attitude of fearlessness. Concepción wasn't used to being taken lightly—not by anyone.

By this time an old man, slightly stooped over, his hair snowy white, had appeared at the top of the steps where he stood as if rooted to the spot, staring stupidly at the two women.

"*Madre de Dios*—a *gringa!*" He muttered and crossed himself. Concepción and Ginny seemed embarked on a screaming match of bitter vituperation as they circled each other warily. Paco, suddenly recovering his senses, jumped off the cart and ran up the steps to hand the baby to Salvador.

"Here old man—take it, for God's sake! There'll be murder done here in a minute if I don't do something."

"How dare you come here looking for my man?" Concepción was yelling. "In whose arms did he sleep on your wedding night, *gringa puta*? Into whose eyes did he look for comfort when the French soldiers tortured him and you stood laughing on the balcony with your fat lover?"

"*Hija de putana!*" Ginny hissed. "My husband may have used you—particularly if you offered yourself to him and there was nothing better available; but don't forget that he married me!"

"A marriage that was never consummated? Don't

worry, *puta*—I'll see he gets an annulment quickly; that way he'll be safe from French knives in his back!"

"And a knife in your black witch's heart is exactly what you'll be getting if you don't get your carcass off my land!"

Paco leaped between the two women just as they advanced on each other, their fingers like claws reaching for each other's eyes.

"For God's sake!" he yelled, "have you both gone *loco*? There's no reason why we can't all discuss this matter in a civilized manner in the house. Do you realize your screeching has brought you quite an audience?"

This much was true, for several men had suddenly appeared and now surrounded them, muttering to each other in amazement, their eyes staring curiously at the sight.

Ginny and Concepción both burst into speech almost at the same time.

"I won't have this filth in my house!" Ginny flashed as Concepción screamed, "she shan't dirty the home of my man, after all she's done to him! *Gringa* traitress!

It's just like Steve to leave such a mess for me to have to settle, Paco was thinking wildly. What on earth am I going to do with the two of them? They seemed oblivious of his presence between them—like a pair of angry cats they kept circling him, trying to get at each others throats. To Paco's dismay, Concepción had pulled a knife, and its long blade was glittering in the sun. Before he could say a word he saw Ginny pull up one side of her skirt, tucking it into her waistband as she snatched a knife from the sheath that was snuggled against her thigh. So along with the other bad habits she'd picked up she'd taken to carrying a knife as well!

There was no help offered by the peons who had collected around them—they were murmuringly loudly that this was better than a cockfight, and they ought to make a few small wagers on the outcome.

"I don't know who the *gringa* is but she certainly looks like a fighter," one man said. "Look at the way she holds the knife—it's plain she knows how to use one!"

Another man said in a low voice, "*La gringa*—is she really the wife of *el señor*? I do not think he is going to like this too much . . ."

There was a brief moment's uneasy silence as the

women glared at each other, and then Concepción decided to try for blood. Red lips drawn back from her white teeth, she spat an insult as she lunged forward, the knife-blade glittering wickedly. And for just the fraction of an instant its glitter, reflecting into Ginny's eyes, almost blinded her. It was only instinct, and the warning that the other woman's hissed invective had given her that enabled her to move fast enough.

"*Olé!*" one of the men said softly. The women ignored him, intent on each other.

As the knife flashed down Ginny whirled and threw her body backward against Concepción's even as her knife parried. Concepción's free hand clutched air as Ginny's left hand chopped viciously downward. The knife flew out of Concepción's numb fingers—she started to fall and found her wrist caught firmly as Ginny bent over, allowing the momentum of Concepción's forward movement to help her throw the young woman so that she landed a few feet away with a thud that knocked the breath from her.

When she knew what was happening next, Ginny was kneeling over her with a knife blade at her throat—knee digging painfully into Concepción's belly.

"Make one move and I'll gladly slit your evil, lying throat," Ginny said through her teeth. Through the blood pounding sickly in her head Concepción was painfully, shamefully aware that the men had crowded close—laughing and making admiring comments.

"I'll never give him up!" Concepción sobbed defiantly, her breath coming in loud gasps. "Even if I have to leave here—he will come looking for me—he'll leave you—if he doesn't kill you first for what you've done to me—"

"In that case, bitch, maybe I should kill you first and feed your body to the vultures!"

Concepción could read absolutely no mercy in those cold green eyes that glared down into hers, and she began to scream wildly.

"This woman is crazy! She'd kill me—"

"Maybe I should just carve up your face a little, eh? Maybe that'll keep other women's husbands from taking too much notice of trash like you in future!"

"No—no! Paco, help me!"

Paco himself could hardly believe that this woman was Ginny—this raging virago who could speak so coldly about scarring another woman for life!

"Ginny—damn it, you're going too far! Now let her up!"

"Not until I've heard her promise to leave here and leave Steve forever!"

Before Paco could move a muscle Ginny had used her knife to scratch a thin, oozing line across Concepción's heaving belly. The girl closed her eyes and shrieked like a madwoman.

"You shut up and swear you'll leave my husband alone or I'll really mark you good!" Ginny threatened.

"I swear—yes, I swear! Take her off me! Help me!"

"Ginny!" Paco bellowed, moving forward.

But Ginny was already springing back to her feet.

"Since you're so concerned about snivelling little Concepción there you'd better get her out of here fast."

She turned on the other men, who all stepped backward with something between awe and admiration on their faces.

"So! You all thought it was a real sport, didn't you? I hope you had the sense to put your bets on the right one, that's all! And now—what are you still staring at? You never saw a *gringa* before? Maybe I should go find your wives and tell them how you've been gaping."

"*Señora*—no—we beg the *señora's* pardon."

One man, bolder than the rest grinned and said, "Well at least *I* had the sense to put my money on *la patrona* here—no offence meant, *patrona*!"

She began to laugh, hearing herself called *patrona* for the first time under circumstances like these—also the man had a bold and somewhat engaging grin for all that he spoke quite respectfully.

"Well—I suppose we'll all make each other's formal acquaintance later," Ginny said pointedly to the men after a minute. But her laughter had taken away some of the sting of her words and she found them all grinning back at her with friendly respect.

"You'll need some help up at the house, *patrona*—we'll send some of our women up after a while," one of the men offered. "Yes. But please don't tell them too much about the—the fight, *patrona*!" Another one chimed in.

"Better help him take care of her first!" Ginny pointed to where Paco was trying to comfort a sobbing Concepción.

Then she turned and walked, with all the dignity she

could muster in torn clothes and bare feet, up the steps that led to her *estancia*, taking the now-howling baby from the shaky arms of the old man who still stared at her as if he could not believe his eyes.

Chapter Forty-seven

"I must say that I no longer feel quite as uneasy as I did about leaving you here alone to face that husband of yours," Paco Davis commented later that day. Already dressed for travelling again, he sat across from Ginny at the small table she'd ordered brought into the patio so that they could eat outdoors and enjoy the coolness of approaching evening.

"I told you that I was quite capable of taking care of myself!" Ginny retorted tartly. "But I do have my doubts about you—travelling all the way to Vera Cruz with that gypsy bitch on your hands. Better watch that she doesn't stick a knife in you while you're asleep!"

Paco paused to stare at Ginny reproachfully, his tortilla halfway to his mouth. "Do you have to hurt my feelings, *niña*? I would have preferred your company, quite frankly, but alas, since you're married to a friend of mine I think I got quite a good bargain—all in all! Besides, don't worry, I think I can manage to make Concepción forget about Steve in not too long a time—what do you think I am, a goat in the matter of lovemaking? Yes, I've managed to leave my share of happy women behind, you know!"

Ginny began to laugh rather wildly. "Oh, Paco—I have

a feeling I'm going to miss you—you've been a good companion. I only hope . . ." she broke off, biting her lip, and he changed the subject quickly and tactfully.

"Hey, you know what? I can hardly recognize this old place since you've been cleaning up all afternoon! It takes a woman with real energy to accomplish so much in such a short time! What do you think of your new home now, eh?"

Her face softened. "It's like a dream! I kept pinching myself, telling myself it's really mine! I do love it all, Paco—the rooms are so big and so cool inside—did you know the walls are more than a foot thick everywhere? And this patio—with those vines growing down over the old walls and the smell of all the flowers—wait until after you see it again!"

"So you are going to enjoy being a little housewife, eh? This I can hardly imagine, I must confess! I will drop back for sure as soon as I can—you'll save a guest room for me?"

"*Mi casa es su casa*," she said seriously, her eyes shining into his. In spite of her simple clothes he thought she seemed like a great lady, aglow with beauty and an inner excitement.

If Steve does anything; if he hurts her, I'll see to him myself! Paco thought suddenly—surprising himself with the thought.

"Well," he forced himself to say lightly as he took a last deep swallow of wine, "guess I had better get on that trail before it gets too dark. I have to be in Vera Cruz within three days. You won't forget everything I've been telling you? Or your promise to Bishop?"

"I remember everything," she said quietly. And then, surprising him with the admission, "I'm afraid, Paco! But I won't let him see it. And don't worry, I'm certainly not going to try and cling if I'm sure he doesn't want me. It's just that I have to be sure, one way or another, about him. Because I know about myself."

He got up and came to bend over her, kissing her lightly on the cheek.

"I know, *niña*. But you take care of yourself all the same. Don't let him—oh hell, it's none of my business, *si?* But you remember—I'm your friend. Any time."

She called softly after him, *"Vaya con Dios,* Paco." After he had left, striding almost angrily away without a

backward look, she went back into the house to help
Salvador light the lamps.

It became cold enough, late at night, to warrant a small
fire in the bedroom Ginny had chosen for her own. By
about eleven o'clock, she was so tired that she turned
down the last lamp that still remained lighted in the
house—the one in her bedroom.

Only the light from the small fire she had made brightened the room, throwing strange leaping shadows on the
walls and ceiling. I shall never be able to fall asleep
tonight! Ginny thought, moving restlessly in the big bed.
Too big to comfortably fall asleep in alone—but in her
rage this afternoon she had been determined to use
nothing that Concepción had used—to keep nothing
around that would remind her of the gypsy woman and
her casual assumption of belonging here.

The first thing that she had done was to clear
everything out of the room that Concepción had obviously
shared with Steve.

"It'll do as a storeroom for the moment, I suppose," she
had remarked carelessly to Salvador; and they had proceeded to pile all the old and broken bits of furniture in
the center of the room.

Ginny's arms and legs ached with the effort she had
made to make at least part of the old house more presentable. But after all, it's *mine*, she kept telling herself to
ward off the unpleasant feelings she had experienced when
she saw that bedroom—Concepción's bright, pretty clothes
scattered all over it; and the rather narrow bed which
would force two people sharing it to lie very close
together. It felt so strange, suddenly, to be competing for
the favors of her own husband—to wonder how he would
greet her unexpected appearance here. Would he give her
a chance to explain?

The thoughts went round and round in Ginny's head
while she lay in bed and stared at the fire. Yes, what will
he do when he finds me here instead of Concepción? She
felt suddenly quite chilly, and pulled the blanket over
herself. The sheer, silk and lace shift she had smuggled
here in the small bundle of possessions Paco had permitted
her to bring along was scarcely any protection against the
cold. With the last thought, Will I succeed in making him
forget the past? she fell asleep quite suddenly—worn out
from her exertions that day.

The crashing noise the door made as it was kicked open to smash against the wall on its hinges woke Ginny with a start so that she sat bolt upright in bed, almost forgetting where she was.

"What in hell is going on here? There's not a light in the house and I almost broke my neck bumping against that pile of furniture you left in the bedroom. What kind of fancy notions have you developed now?"

She'd know that voice anywhere—harsh, full of anger—and suddenly, now that he was here and in the same room with her, obviously mistaking her for Concepción, she found that her throat was too dry to utter a single word. She simply sat there, staring as he walked over to the fire and dropped more wood on it, kicking it so that the flames flared up suddenly. She noticed that he seemed taller than ever—the glint of the bottle he carried in his hand and was now tipping up to his mouth as he swallowed—that he wore a loosely fitting pair of peasant's trousers and a white *camisa*, open at the chest—and then at last he turned to snarl something else at her and froze.

Her eyes hung on his, watching the thunderstruck expression on his face begin to turn slowly to black, dangerous fury as he recognized her. She drank in every detail of his appearance while they continued to stare at each other in silence. His black hair was slightly longer than she remembered seeing it last, and the dark thick sideburns had been allowed to grow almost to the jawline to meet the downward, somehow villainous curve of a closely-cut Mexican style mustache. It only emphasized the lean, reckless face with those hard blue eyes that were just as startling against his sun-browned skin.

His eyes, narrowing, seemed to pierce her like daggers. Without a word, he tilted his head back and drank again from the bottle he carried—wiping the back of his hand across his lips when he had finished. And because he still had not spoken Ginny began to think, desperately, I must say something—anything—I can't bear to have him look at me like this.

But in the end, when she opened her mouth, all that emerged was his name, in an imploring whisper—all the cool, rational words she had been preparing all these days had fled from her mind.

"Steve—" she whispered, "I . . ."

"*You!*" His one word, full of contemptuous rage,

slashed across her faltering speech like a knife thrust. He
continued in the same hateful tone, "*Por Dios*! I had a
feeling my evil genius was at work today! First I have a
run-in with two separate troops of counterguerillas, and
then find *you*—here, of all places!"

His anger seemed to reach across the room at her, making her shrink back quite involuntarily when he took one
forward step—then stopped himself abruptly.

"Am I supposed to be honored by this surprising visit?
Madame du Plessis—the highest-priced *cortesana* in all of
Mexico City—the woman who threw over a French count
for a Mexican colonel. The barefoot, sensual dancer at
Maximilian's private parties—my wife, the whore!" He
began to laugh cruelly at the flush that came up in her
face. "Can you still blush? You never cease to amaze me,
madam. So here you are—" his harsh laughter jarred on
her already exacerbated nerves, so that her hands flew up
to cover her ears as she shrank from it. "I must say that I
almost admire your cool effrontery! What kind of dirty
trick do you have hidden up your sleeve this time? Do you
have soldiers hidden in every room here to take me? Or
perhaps you planned to do it all yourself—do you happen
to have a gun concealed under that pillow? What's the
matter, madam, what's happened to that sharp tongue of
yours? I've never known you to be so silent!"

Sheer desperation made Ginny find words to defend
herself with—any words, just so she could make him stop
his scathing, blistering attack on her.

"Must you attack me so cruelly without even giving me
a chance to defend myself? Must you always believe the
worst of me? Oh God, Steve—if you'll only listen to me,
give me a chance . . ."

"Chance, madam? Chance for what? To betray me
again? To gloat over your own cleverness as you were doing the last time I saw you? Damn you for the lying little
bitch you are! No. I've had my bellyfull of your lies and
deceit—as you ought to know, by now! Why *did* you
come here? What made you tear yourself away from the
many delights of Mexico City? What in hell did you want
this time?"

He had emptied the bottle in his hand before she could
reply, and now with a vicious, sweeping gesture he sent it
smashing against the wall, breaking into a thousand tiny
shards that lay glittering like drops of blood on the floor.

As if his action had broken a spell Ginny came to her feet, facing him, her eyes shining with unshed tears.

"Are you actually going to give me a chance to explain? Your Mr. Bishop sent me with a message for you. *Paco* brought me here . . ."

"Paco! By God, does your outrageousness know no bounds? Did you manage to seduce him too? And Bishop—he must be crazy! To trust you, of all people."

"You—you're as pig-headed and as insufferable as you always were, Steve Morgan! Don't you realize that I believed you were dead? Don't you realize that Devereaux played a little game with us both that day—that he tricked you into believing I'd conspired with him to—to—oh God! If I became a whore, then the first time was for you, Steve. He promised to save your life if I—"

"To save my life! Is that what you call that prison you had me sent to? You dare call that living hell *life?*"

"Steve! Only listen to me . . ."

"No!" He flung the word in her face like a slap. "There is nothing you can tell me that I want to hear—Madame du Plessis. If you value your own rotten life I advise you to take yourself out of my sight—you can damn well spend the rest of the night writing out any message you have for me because I swear that if I have to spend one more second looking into your lying whore's face I'll break your neck!"

Instead of running from the look in his eyes, she went straight to him on her bare feet, and put her arms around his neck; clinging with a strength that he found amazing, even in the midst of his own blind rage.

"I came here because I love you, Steve. Kill me if you want to—do anything you please—it doesn't matter."

His hands went round her throat with an almost animal growl of rage, choking the words from her, as he planned to choke all the breath from her body. She saw sparks of light begin to dance before her eyes as his fingers began to tighten very slowly, his voice coming from a distance.

"This is what I dreamed of doing with you, you whore! From that moment when I saw you in Orizaba, dressed all in white like an angel—so pure outside, so corrupt inside—did you know I was watching you with the rest of those wretched, chained felons who stood shivering in that ditch filled with dirty, stinking water while you passed by, laughing so gaily when your newest lover kissed your little

hand? You should not have come here, Madame du
Plessis!"

She realized, dimly, that he intended to kill her—that he
was slowly and inexorably choking the life from her. But
instead of struggling to be free some deep-seated instinct
made her lean her body limply and heavily against his
while with the last remaining strength that remained in
her she desperately pulled his head down to hers.

She seemed to be offering her white throat to his
strangling hands like a sacrifice as her head tilted back.
Unable to utter a sound, her parted, gasping lips seemed
to fasten themselves to his.

Is there absolutely no limit to the tenacity of this
woman? he thought, why isn't she fighting for her life?
What does she hope to gain by this?

Did he really *want* to kill her? Could he bear to have
her dead? Steve was suddenly, intensely aware of her
small, firm breasts against his chest—the particular fra-
grance of her body that belonged only to her—the taste of
her tears, the silky-soft texture of her hair. Without knowing how it happened he found his fingers tangled in her
hair, instead of around her throat, and he was kissing her
like a starving man; too much aware of the sudden, strong
wave of desire that almost made him groan out loud with
its intensity.

Damn her, damn her! He had almost killed her, and still
she continued to cling to him, her little tongue darting into
his mouth as she began to kiss him back with a fervor that
surprised him even while it disgusted him.

It was intolerable to have his own treacherous weakness
discovered and used by her to trap him—to wonder, even
while he couldn't stop kissing her, how many other men
had been trapped by her beauty and their own desire—
had kissed her and felt her kiss them back just as
warmly—had taken her and buried themselves in her corrupt softness just as he longed to do.

He'd cursed her name and her memory a thousand
times at least—over and over, until he felt the hate and
disgust he'd begun to feel for her seared indelibly into his
brain. And then she had to turn up out of the blue and
throw herself at him shamelessly—tempting him almost
beyond endurance . . .

With a sudden, brutal motion born of hate and desperation and self-disgust Steve brought both his hands down on

her shoulders; fingers biting into soft flesh for just an instant before he flung her away from him—sending her staggering against the door. She stood there leaning there with her palms flat against it for support, her breathing sounding like sobbing, her eyes wide with shock.

"Oh—why? Why, Steve? Please—"

He ignored her panting, breathless cry of pleading; too busy with finding his own self-control again to care for her pain.

"Don't push your luck any further, Ginny." His voice was flat, harsh. "If you won't get out of my life gracefully, then I'll take myself out of yours—I don't think I care for the thought that you still carry my name—even if you had the decency not to use it. If you won't get an annulment, then I will."

"Annulment!" Her sudden, passionate cry of rage made him lift one eyebrow in amazement. A moment ago she had been crying—pleading brokenly—and now she stood with her back straight and stiff against the door, her bare feet planted apart, chin tilted defiantly. "Do you dare remind me again of that night when you should have been with me and you chose Concepción instead? Is that why you want an annulment now? So you can marry that slut you had the bad taste to keep here, in *my* house?"

His voice sharpened with anger. "Concepción—what has she to do with this—this farce between us? And what did you and Paco do with her, anyway? Christ—did you think that by substituting yourself for her you could fob me off with your cheaply bought favors?" He took a step towards her, his mouth twisted dangerously. "You bitch! Where's Concepción?"

"I got rid of her! Yes—did you think I'd tolerate your mistress here a minute after I'd arrived? She's lucky I didn't carve her up and destroy those overblown charms forever! You see, at least I have the courage to fight for what I want—which is something you seem to have lost."

"What in hell are you talking about, you little *puta*? And how dared you send Concepción away?"

"I'll tell you how I dared—by scaring the death out of her! And believe me, I'm beginning to feel you weren't worth it—you coward! Yes—you can scowl all you want—do you think you scare me any longer with your loud threats and your blustering? You want me—you want me as much as I've wanted you all these months—and yet you're no longer man enough to admit it! There was a time when you were sure enough of yourself to have taken me without another word, but no—you were afraid, weren't you? Is that your problem now, Steve? That you feel you're no longer man enough to please me?"

His face had gone white with anger under her wild, scornful words.

"Christ—," he said softly, the words coming from between his gritted teeth, "is there no trick you're incapable of using? Is there anything too low for you? My problem, if you can call it that, is that I've stood here far too long—wasting my time on you. You can think what you please, Ginny, and do as you please. I've no more stomach for this pointless argument, or for you!"

He made as if to brush past her, actually laying his hand on the doorknob when the peculiarly taut, barely-controlled note he heard in her voice forced her back to his unwilling attention. "Steve!"

He swung around angrily to face her and thought bitterly that the tone of her voice should have warned him. Suddenly, amazingly, she had a knife at his throat; and as fast as his reactions usually were, this time the very unexpectedness of her smooth, pantherish movement took him completely by surprise. Moving very quickly on her bare feet she had suddenly pressed her body against his in almost the same motion; her left arm going around his waist while the knife point pressed threateningly against his neck, just below the ear.

Unbelievingly he began to laugh. "My God! This is too much—even from you!" He felt the pressure increase very slightly, just enough to break the skin, and stopped laughing, his eyes looking down into hers wonderingly.

He heard her say in the same coldly uninflected voice, "In case you're wondering how far I will go, Steve, I should tell you that I've killed a man before, with a knife in his throat. So when you raise your arms, please don't try anything foolish—this blade could slip very easily, as I'm sure you realize. Now if you'll clasp your hands behind your head—and please move very slowly. . . ."

"This is not happening—the crazy bitch—what in hell is she up to this time with this ridiculous game she's playing?"

And yet at the same time he was thinking he'd begun to grit his teeth with rage and frustration, knowing he would play her stupid game to the finish—until he could get his hands on her.

Hardly daring to breathe, Ginny saw the anger flare in his eyes, making them glitter in the firelight as he narrowed them at her. Still, he obeyed her quietly enough although the rigidity of his muscles under her hand made her move the knife very slightly so that the slightest move on his part would indeed cause it to slip very easily, just as she had warned him.

"Are you going to tell me what you hope to gain by this stupid trick? Did you go to all this trouble merely to make sure I was dead this time?"

Surprisingly her mouth had begun to curve into a taunting, teasing smile.

"I don't want you dead, Steve. I came here to find a husband. And since I've been reminded far too often that our marriage has never been consummated, I think you ought to remedy that. After all, you do owe me certain rights. I'm still your wife, whatever else you may choose to call me."

"*Dios!*" Forgetting himself he swore in Spanish, hardly able to believe his ears. "You *are* crazy! Tell me, madam, do you seriously expect me to play the part of your—your damned stud—and at knife-point into the bargain?"

"Since you will be enjoying the favors of the highest-priced *cortesana* in all of Mexico City for nothing, don't you think it's a pretty good bargain, all things considered?" she said sweetly and then as his face darkened with anger her voice rose slightly. "Why do you look so stunned? How many times did you take me by force? Remember how you ripped the clothes off my body when I resisted you? Remember when I—"

"I remember a time when you used a knife on me before—" he said in a strange voice and she said abruptly, biting her lip to hide her emotion, "Lower one arm—your left—very slowly; and unbuckle that belt. How does it feel now it's your turn to undress for *me,* lover?"

"I really can't believe that you mean to go through with this ridiculous performance! Damn it, Ginny—" he broke off suddenly when the knife drew blood and stared down at her disbelievingly.

"Unbuckle your belt, Steve," she said flatly and this time he lowered his left hand without another word and began to fumble with his belt buckle, still staring at her, with a new, strange expression creeping into his eyes.

"And now?" he said suddenly in a voice that sounded oddly choked with some kind of emotion she couldn't read.

"Step out of them."

He shrugged. "I've really got to hand it to you—I never thought I'd shuck my pants for a woman who held a knife at my throat! Do you make a habit of this?"

"Only when a man is extraordinarily stubborn," she whispered, her hand beginning to caress his back.

His voice sounded sarcastic, but for an instant she thought she heard a note of repressed laughter in it. "Tell me, ma'am, do I have to wait for step by step instructions from you, or am I allowed to improvise occasionally?"

She became aware quite suddenly of the warmth of his hand against her belly, moving deliberately lower.

"How's that, ma'am—does that please you? Anything to oblige the lady with the sharp knife."

She gasped sharply, and found his eyes holding hers, with the dancing light of the fire reflected in their blueness.

"Don't!"

"Why not? You know I'd forgotten—how soft your hair is—even here—"

"No, Steve!" All her anger and her defiance left her quite suddenly and she began to tremble.

"Be careful with that knife, Ginny—don't you think it's in the way now?"

His right hand was suddenly caught in her hair and she let the knife fall with a clatter between them. He kicked it away, along with his pants. With a sudden, savage movement he took a hold of her shift at the back and ripped it apart.

"Now we're even," he said softly. And then, as he lifted her into his arms to carry her over to the bed, "What a persistent little vixen you are! I'm afraid I'm not strong enough to resist either your body or your threats—you see how easy I am to rape?"

He almost flung her down onto the bed and took his shirt off without removing his eyes from the seductive curves of her body. She was actually here—the little green-eyed, passionately sensuous woman he'd dreamed about and lusted for and hated. And she was his—he still could hardly believe the lengths she'd gone to just now, just to force him to admit that he wanted her. And God knew that in spite of every instinct that screamed warning at him he wanted her . . .

She held her arms out to him and clasped him passionately to her softly yielding body when he came to her. The passion that had always existed between them took over and she was ready for him without wanting or needing any further preliminaries. Her body arched fiercely up against his, just as achingly impatient for that first joining as his was.

She alone has the power to defeat me, Steve thought suddenly. She means trouble—she alone, of all the women I've known has been my downfall, my fatal weakness—but I'm incapable of resisting her any longer! She's a bitch—she's been a whore—but at this moment she's only mine.

Never before, when they had made love, had she called out to him aloud, sobbing her love and her need as she did now. He felt a raging pang of jealousy for a moment, until her caressing hands, the spontaneous movements of her supple body blotted out everything but the fact of his own insatiable, unsatisfied need for her—for this particular woman above all others; this wild, bold, sensual creature who gave herself to him with such complete abandonment that it was hard to believe that anything had ever existed between them but desire.

Chapter Forty-eight

"What a lot you've learned!" Steve said reflectively. He leaned over Ginny's prone body, propped up on one elbow; his free hand caressing her smooth flesh almost absentmindedly. "I'd always told myself what an apt pupil you were, but now I confess that your talents amaze even me."

He bent his head to kiss the hollow at the base of her throat, feeling her pulsebeat under his lips. His exploring hand went lower and he heard her soft sigh. Her teeth caught in her lower lip as she stirred under his caresses.

He lifted his head suddenly and looked mockingly down into her half-closed eyes. "Yes—you certainly have changed, my sweet. You've lost that delightfully intriguing modesty and shyness you once possessed! Now, when I tell you to open your legs you do so with no fuss. If I tell you, 'turn over, we're going to do it that way'—you oblige. Tell me, is there anything you haven't tried yet?"

With her eyes closed, Ginny averted her face, turning her head sideways on the pillow.

"Steve—for God's sake! I've told you everything—must you go on punishing me?"

"Perhaps I'm punishing myself as well—" he dropped

his nude body over hers and caught a handful of her hair; rubbing his face in its softness. "You know—" he continued softly, "I've asked myself at least a thousand times why I didn't kill you when you threw yourself at me so boldly. And why I continue to want you! Perhaps it's because for a woman, you're almost as depraved as I— and you make me curious." His voice roughened. "Who taught you all your little whore's tricks?

Without any warning she felt his teeth sink savagely into the soft flesh of her shoulder and she shrieked; digging her nails into his back, only to find that just as suddenly he had begun to kiss, very tenderly and gently, the aching wound that he had just inflicted on her.

Why did he still have the power to do this to her? It's because I love him, she thought hopelessly. It's because I can't stop loving him—in spite of the fact that he has never once told me that he loves me.

He had cupped her face between his palms as if he thought to mold and memorize its contours as he studied it through slitted blue eyes.

"You've grown more beautiful—your cheeks have developed the slightest hollow, and it serves to emphasize that wicked slant to your eyes. You look like a Hungarian gypsy! And your mouth—" he kissed it gently, "you have the most sensuous, promising mouth in all the world. I suppose I ought to consider myself lucky that I got you back—even if you are a trifle shopworn!"

He kissed her savagely, before she could do more than let out an angry gasp at the sudden brutality of his attack.

They spent three days together—alternately quarrelling or making love. Their quarrels had become duels of wits as well as words as they regarded each other cautiously, like adversaries.

In spite of the weakness in her that she admitted to herself, the hard lessons that Ginny had been forced to learn during the past months now stood her in good stead. She had learned how to erect a shell around herself and to withdraw sullenly behind it; allowing no trace of emotion to show on the surface. Sometimes, in sheer self-defense, she would throw up this same barrier between herself and Steve, particularly when he pushed her too far.

And it was this, above all things, that infuriated Steve Morgan most about his wife. She had changed, there was no doubt about it. And he had had no part in this

change he resented so bitterly. He found himself wondering what kind of experiences had contributed to the
strong, self-willed, independent woman she had become.
She could use a knife with almost careless skill and swear
like a man—and on the other hand she could cook better
than most peasant women. She had changed in other ways
too, as he was quick to point out to her. She had certainly
learned all the techniques of a whore, along with a
passionate abandon that was all her own. More
particularly, she had learned how to resist—to withstand
his cruellest taunts, his most calculated thrusts; retreating
behind a shrug or a blank silence. She had become
resilient almost unreachable.

Ginny, his wife—during the short time they spent
together he had learned that she was no longer the green
girl he had first possessed. The very stength that she had
gained from all the degrading experiences she had been
subjected to, and the fact that she had somehow managed
not only to rise above them but to win her own brand of
independence against tremendous odds, annoyed him more
than he could ever admit to her. She should have broken,
and she had not. It was he who still bore the scars of his
experiences and still held the canker of bitterness locked
inside him. She appeared to have managed quite easily to
forget everything unpleasant; he could sense that she had
glossed or skipped over some of the worst parts of her
story when she had told it to him. How could she remain
so unaffected? What kind of a woman had she really
become? He couldn't forgive her for the things she had
done of her own accord and even some of the things she
had let herself be forced to do—and what made it worse
was that she had never asked him to forgive her either!

Three days. Steve had told her grudgingly that it was all
he could manage at the moment, and he had no idea when
he might be back next. Alternately happy and miserable,
Ginny had to be content with that.

At least she had found him again! She found herself
wondering about the changes she noticed in him; studying
this stranger who was her lover and her husband in almost
the same covert way that she sensed he was studying her.

He wanted her. She could be sure of that much at
least. She exulted in the blaze of desire she could always
discern in his eyes when he looked at her, and yet—he
never spoke of loving her, only of wanting her. Just once

she had dared to ask him boldly if he loved her, and his derisive laugh pierced her more deeply than she let him see on the surface.

"Love! That's a funny word to hear on your lips, baby. Is that what you called it when you gave yourself to a legion of lovers?"

"Oh God, Steve! You're the only man I have ever loved. Why else do you think you have the power to hurt me?"

"I don't think any man can really hurt you, sweetheart. You're too strong, too resilient—you'll always manage, somehow, to survive—won't you?"

He was cruel, and yet he could be tender with her too. He wanted to know everything about her past—every sordid detail he could force her to admit to; and yet he would tell her very little of what had happened to him. Jealously, Ginny pressed for more details of his relationship with the Condesa de Valmes, and he raised an amused eyebrow.

"Soledad? She's my godmother, you know. And still a very beautiful woman. You've met her, haven't you?"

"Oh—I suppose so! I'd hardly remember."

"I'm not surprised, as busy as you were while you were visiting Orizaba. But Soledad remembers you very well!"

"Oh, she does?" Ginny turned on him furiously, stung by his sarcastic tone of voice. "I've no doubt she was the one who gave you all the worst gossip she could pick up about me. I suppose she was jealous!"

"I hardly think so, sweetheart!" He said cuttingly, the meaning behind his pointed words so obvious that angry color stained her cheeks.

Whatever remarks she might have made to contradict his insinuations were blotted out, as usual, by the sudden pressure of his lips over hers. He could make her forget all his infidelities and all his cruelties with his kisses, or an occasional moment of tenderness.

To counteract her own treacherous vulnerability Ginny showed him a pride that matched his own—a temper that flamed up to meet his when he got angry. He began to show her almost a grudging respect at such times, although it annoyed him inwardly that she had learned to take such good care of herself. Only in his arms, with his lips on her lips or travelling all over her body, did she submit and become weak.

Steve Morgan saw her cry for the first time since they had found each other again on the morning he got ready to leave the *hacienda*. He covered his surprise at her unexpected tears by speaking to her roughly.

"For God's sake! What's the matter with you now? This sniveling doesn't suit you—and it's not going to move me into taking you along; I've already told you it's out of the question. You must just do as you think best, sweet. Stay here if you want to, after all the *hacienda* is yours, as you've reminded me often enough. And if you get too bored, there's always Vera Cruz—I'm sure you'll run into lots of your friends there. Salvador can escort you, and I've left you with enough money to manage on until that ship Bishop booked your passage on is ready to leave."

As usual, he seemed to pick on exactly the right words and phrases that would hurt most.

"Don't you care? Doesn't it make any difference to you at all whether I'm here when you return or not?"

When she glanced up at him through eyes that were blurred with tears she thought she noticed an almost imperceptible softening of the harsh tension lines at the corners of his eyes and mouth.

"I don't know, Ginny," he said slowly. "Damn it— I'm not used to being owned, and neither are you, it seems. We've both become used to doing without each other—sometimes it's as if we were strangers; coming together only in bed. Are we really ready for ties, either of us?" He shrugged fatalistically and repeated, "*quien sabe?*"

For two long, dragging weeks those words were all she had to go on.

Here, in the isolated world of the little *Hacienda de la Nostalgia*, even the war seemed too far away to be real, or to affect Ginny in any way. Where before she had been caught up in a whirl of pointless activities, always with some new item of gossip or news of the most recent battle to be discussed; here it always seemed as if time had been suspended.

Almost thankful that there was so much to be done both around the *estancia* and within it, Ginny tried to keep herself both busy and tired, so that she would fall into bed before nine o'clock each night—too exhausted to stay awake and think.

The house began to shine inside as Ginny had the old

furniture repaired and polished, the windows washed; found bright scatter rugs for the floors. She had lots of help, for the peons sent their wives and daughters up to the house to assist *la patrona*, and even came themselves to help with bigger jobs like repairing roofs and walls.

They were all proud of their *gringa patrona* with the bright hair and eyes like the sea—a woman who was not too proud to set her hand to any task, no matter how menial. "Truly," they would say, wagging heads knowingly, *"el patron* chose well when he chose this woman. She is of the people." It was the greatest compliment they could give her, these simple Indian peasants, and they developed a fierce loyalty for her.

She visited their houses, carried and changed their babies, and could even sit down with the other women and pitch in unself-consciously when they were grinding the meal for tortillas. She could cook over a little open-hearth cook fire, and get clothes clean on a flat rock by the river. And she could ride a horse bareback and astride, like a man.

Even old Salvador, who could remember Steve's mother, gave Ginny his grudging stamp of approval. When she came into the kitchen to help him he no longer muttered his objections, but would sit down to gossip with her and give her the news he picked up on his infrequent visits to the nearest village.

It was from Salvador that Ginny learned that the armies of *Juarista* Generals Escobedo and Corona were closing, like an iron ring, around Queretaro.

"Soon, they will have the foreigner emperor trapped like a rat there—with no way to escape," the old man said with a ring of triumph in his voice.

She learned of the daring raid that General Miramon had led on Zacatecas, where his cavalry had cut the garrison there to pieces and only narrowly missed capturing Don Benito Juarez himself. She had met General Miramon, she remembered. A tall and grizzled old creole officer, with a face like granite. A veteran of other wars. Ginny wondered if his exploit meant a turn in the waning fortunes of the Imperialists, until a week later Salvador brought her the news that General Escobedo had routed Miramon's sadly out-numbered little army.

"To teach a lesson to these dogs El General Escobedo had a hundred Imperialist officers executed," Salvador went on; "and one of them was the brother of Miramon himself!"

Ginny could not help feeling a pang of pity. She recalled Agnes du Salm's bitter words to her one day that two wrongs did not make a right. Was it really necessary to be so brutal in order to teach the Imperialists a lesson? They were all fighting, after all, for whatever they believed in—although Ginny could not help remembering Miguel Lopez' cynicism about the loyalty of Maximilian's three top Generals.

At least Salvador had good news for her about Díaz. The army of Don Porfirio was still moving steadily towards the borders of the province of Puebla. They should be in the province itself within the week.

It meant, Ginny knew, that there was a good chance Steve might make the short detour to see her. If he had rejoined the army permanently, he would be so close! But had he rejoined the army, or was he still skulking in the mountains with the *guerrilleros*? She had to tell herself sternly that she must be patient—she mustn't let herslf hope too much.

Two weeks after Steve had left, Salvador came padding into the small room Ginny had appointed as her "study," his face set in disapproving lines . . .

"There is a man who says he has come to see you, *patrona.*" The corners of the old man's lips dropped sourly. "He does not look like a good man, *patrona.* He looks like a *bandido* to me! Who else would come softly out of the shadows after dark? But he says the *señor* sent him . . ."

Ginny jumped to her feet, her green eyes shining like lamps.

"Oh, Salvador! Why did you not say so before? Where is he? Have you offered him anything to eat?"

Without waiting for a reply, she had run past him to the kitchen, where the man who straightened up from his lounging stance against the wall as she entered was certainly one of the most villainous-looking characters she had ever seen. He had been eying the little maid that Ginny was training with a calculatedly evil leer that had her cowering up against the stove, but now he betrayed what was almost a startled surprise when he saw Ginny.

Indoors, she discarded the *rebozo* she normally wore to cover her head and shoulders from the sun, and her hair glowed as brightly as the richly polished copper pans on the wall. She was barefoot, for comfort, and wore a low-cut white blouse and brightly patterned skirt such as the local Indian women wore. Her lips, when she smiled rather questioningly, revealed small, pearly-white teeth. The man, whose name was Manolo, found himself regarding her almost with awe.

He dragged off his wide-brimmed sombrero to reveal a shock of long, badly-trimmed black hair as he shuffled his booted feet rather awkwardly, unable to take his eyes off Ginny.

"You have a message for me? From my husband?" Her voice was just as he had imagined it would be—low, and rather husky. He thought, Wait until I tell the others! Esteban will never lack for volunteers to take his wife messages in the future!

Grinning to cover the trend of his thoughts, Manolo produced a crumpled piece of paper from a pocket in his silver-embroidered vest. The vest had been taken off the body of a dandyish young lieutenant in the Cazadores, who had had a weakness for a certain *cantina* when he was off duty, and Manolo was proud of it, although the crossed bandoliers he wore detracted from its beauty.

He kept grinning while the red-haired woman held the note in her hands almost as if she was afraid to open it. She was looking at him inquiringly.

"Have you eaten? You must be tired—Salvador here will be glad to give you a meal, and some tequila to wash it down with if you have time to rest for a while."

The old man had followed her into the kitchen and now stood by the stove frowning darkly, but when Manolo admitted that he was indeed very hungry he turned to the stove and began clattering pans loudly, muttering under his breath.

Salvador looked even more disapproving when *la patrona* offered the "*bandido*" a chair and sat down across from him at the little kitchen table herself. The *señor* keeps bad company, he was thinking as he dished out a meal. It's too bad he could not have found someone better to send here! The *patrona* should not sit at the same table with such a bad one—nor talk to him in such a friendly fashion either! He sent Maria scurrying off to her home, having noticed the way the man had been eying

her. At least he would not dare to act so disrespectfully to
the *patrona*.

Ginny sipped at a glass of wine under Manolo's admiring glances and tried to question him about Steve, but he
either knew nothing or wasn't prepared to say. He
shrugged often as he said that he did not know when Esteban would be back here; and as he admitted rather
proudly that they never stayed in the same place for too
long.

"But when is he going back to join the army?" Ginny
persisted and got another shrug from her taciturn visitor.

"*Quien sabe*? Perhaps it will be soon. Soon we will all
be joining the army on its march to Mexico City itself!"

He disappeared almost as quickly and as silently as he
had appeared after he had eaten, and Ginny took her letter along with her to her bedroom to read in privacy.

The first letter that Steve had ever thought to send her.
What an unpredictable man he was!

She unfolded the creased and crumpled piece of paper
and found only a few scrawled words on it, with no
salutation nor formal ending.

"We've been very busy—moving a lot—but at least
things are looking up. I'll see you soon, perhaps—if you're
still there."

That was all. Even from a distance, she thought bitterly, he could still hurt her. The note could have been
written to anyone at all—there was nothing personal in it,
just for her, except that mocking half-promise—"perhaps
I'll see you soon." What made him so afraid of commit-
ting himself?

Oh Steve—Steve, she thought despondently, why do I
continue to love you? Why can't I take you as lightly as
you seem to take me?

There were no answers to be found in herself. She
would just have to be patient—to wait.

Chapter Forty-nine

Steve Morgan, never a very patient man under any circumstances, was also doing his share of waiting—in this case for Díaz' huge army to move into a position where it could menace the twin fortresses of Puebla. But Díaz, sure of his objective and its eventual surrender, was taking his own time—preferring to play a cat and mouse game with the Imperialist garrisons who had the task of defending not only Puebla itself but Orizaba, Cordoba and Vera Cruz; to name a few of the more important cities along the thin strip of territory that was now Maximilian's only pipeline to the ocean.

Steve continued to enjoy the danger and excitement of being a *guerrillero*, but he was getting rather tired of the constant moving around they had to do—the long hard riding that never allowed a man enough sleep or rest.

Since he could just as easily pass for American as he could for a Mexican, he was almost always the one who scouted for them—riding boldly along the highway or into towns and villages bristling with Imperialist troops or mercenaries who still fought for Maximilian. There were Americans everywhere, and they hardly excited curiosity any longer. Hard-bitten men who had fought in the Civil

War and enjoyed fighting for its own sake—men who came to observe the end of a war and to write about it— men who were curious—men who hoped to make some profit for themselves when the empire toppled and there would be lands and estates belonging to Imperialist sup- porters put up for sale.

Usually, Steve did what he had to do with a coldly cal- culated concentration that could explode into ferocity when he had a gun or a knife in his hands and was about to use it. Women were instruments of pleasure—put in the same category as a good meal and a comfortable bed in which a man could get a safe night's sleep—to be thought of only when he had the time. A few of them, like Con- cepción and the *condesa*, he could even think of with an absent-minded affection.

But before Ginny had hurled herself so unexpectedly back into his life he had not let a woman affect either his judgement or his reactions.

Concepción had been dancing in a small *cantina* in Orizaba, when he had run into her again. Disdaining the risks he took, he had taken to visiting the *Hacienda de Valmes* as often as he could—especially since he had found out that Soledad's husband was still trailing around behind his emperor. By the time he saw Concepción again, the wildly passionate affair that had started up between him and his godmother had tapered away into a loving friendship; particularly since Soledad was deeply religious in her own way and her confessor had spoken to her sternly about what he called an almost incestuous relation- ship with her godson.

Whether it was partly gratitude and partly because he had not had a woman for so long, Steve had found him- self getting almost too involved with her. She was still beautiful, with the figure of a young girl still, because her husband had not been capable of giving her a child. She was experienced—and she was just as insanely attracted to Steve as he had been to her at the beginning. But after a few times, the flame began to burn out and they began to talk more than they made love; their relationship actually became more comfortable, and Steve had to admit to a feeling of relief. He hated ties!

Concepción with her wild gypsy ways was the direct op- posite of Soledad. She had been almost out of her mind with joy and relief when she saw Steve, and it was she, catching him in a weak moment, who had persuaded him to take her along with him as his mistress. He thought at the time, Why not? The *guerrilleros* had no *soldaderas* to follow them around and hardly any time to stay in any place long enough to find a steady woman. He told himself that it would be nice to have a warm woman waiting in bed for him when he had a few free days. And at least, Concepción knew and understood him well enough not to expect any commitments on his part.

It had been a mutually pleasant, uncomplicated relationship, and he had almost managed to get his green-eyed tramp of a wife off his mind when she had turned up.

Now, in spite of himself, Steve caught himself thinking far too often about Ginny—when he should have been thinking of something else. The vision of her face and her peach-tanned, softly sensuous body interfered when he should have been snatching what sleep he could.

He wondered bitterly how she had contrived to bewitch him, and why it had to be her, of all the women in the world, that he craved incessantly. He should have kept on hating her—even now he would not admit to himself that he felt anything more than desire for her; and that was bad enough! After all, how many other men had desired her? Every time her arms reached up to clasp him closer to her he had jealous visions of the number of other times she must have made exactly the same motions, offered her lips to other lovers in exactly the same way. He remembered how hard she used to fight him in the days when he had been her tutor in the arts of sensuality—but obviously, somewhere along the line she had forgotten how to resist and had learned to yield instead. And how passionately she yielded! Not only that—but she had even learned how to take the initiative in lovemaking . . .

In spite of his irrational anger at Ginny's newly acquired accomplishments, Steve could not help grinning when he thought of the way she had reacted to his first rejection of her. The little bitch! She had all but raped him! It didn't seem possible that she could have changed so much in so short a time, but he had the uneasy feeling that the changes in her went even deeper than she would admit—that there were still secrets she continued to hide from him. What was she hiding? And why?

"Damn her—right from the beginning she's managed to

be an irritant in my life. She's been the only woman who's been able to confuse my thinking!"

Steve Morgan stared rather morosely into his beer, one elbow propped on the splintery wooden bar of the *cantina* he preferred to frequent during his visits to Orizaba. Ever since he'd been back at the *hacienda* he'd find thoughts of Ginny popping into his mind at the most unexpected moments—and usually at the wrong time. Why couldn't he forget about her, just as he'd forgotten all the other women he'd taken and used and left when he was ready to move on? Why had he married her? But even as he damned her savagely, he found himself wanting her—wondering if she were still at the *hacienda* waiting for him, or had decided, after all to go back to pick up the threads of her old life. That was the trouble with her—she was completely unpredictable! But perhaps it was that very quality that intrigued him, and made him wish, even now, that he had not volunteered for this mission tonight. It was his own fault—if he hadn't been so determined to prove to himself that he could still do without her, he would be halfway to Tehuacan by now, and in a much better frame of mind!

A man at the other end of the bar muttered in the local Indian dialect,

"Too many *Norteamericanos* in here—why can't these *gringos* stay on their own side of the river?"

Some of the other Mexicans laughed; but softly, for there were just a few of them in this particular *cantina*, and besides the particular group of *Norteamericanos* their *compadre* had been referring to were hardly the kind of men one wanted to get on the wrong side of.

The group of counterguerillas had ridden in only about an hour ago, and now occupied several of the tables at one side of the room. They complained of enormous thirst, and the room was filled with the noise of their laughter and loud boasting in their own language.

These were the same men who had been organized into groups by Colonel Dupin and paid well by Bazaine. Now that all but the last shipload of Frenchmen had left Mexico, their wages consisted of occasional payments in gold or silver from the severely-depleted treasury in Mexico City, and whatever else they could pick up in the way of booty from the *haciendas* or villages of suspected *Juarista* supporters. Hard looking, gun-hung men, their beards making them look even more dangerous, they stayed on in Mexico because the risks they took here were considerably less than the risk of going back to the United States, and the excuse of fighting a war gave them license to rob and plunder almost as they pleased. Most of the soldiers of fortune who had come to Mexico in droves after the war, attracted by the high pay and the prospect of being on the winning side for a change had already returned when the tide of war had changed in Juarez' favor. Those that remained were the dregs—outlaws, men who had ridden with Quantrill's raiders and enjoyed killing, deserters from the Union army who had nowhere else to go.

The gray-tunicked counterguerillas were good men to stay clear of, but they had also been giving the small band of *guerilleros* that Steve rode with a lot of trouble recently. Having nothing to lose, these bearded killers took more risks than any troop of Imperialist soldiers would have dared—and did more damage. They were an annoyance—and more than that, a hindrance to the great, sprawling army that advanced towards Puebla. Therefore, they had, somehow, to be eliminated.

Steve drained the bitter-tasting beer in his glass and slid it across the bar. "Better make it two more," he told the pock-faced bartender. "Tonight I have a great thirst." He pretended not to catch the rather surprised look the man exchanged with the small group of Mexicans at the end of the bar. So this *gringo* spoke their language, did he? And quite well too, so they had better be careful what they said. He did not look like the kind of man who would take to insults kindly, this hard-faced, blue-eyed *Norteamericano*.

The bartender brought the two bottles of beer in rather a hurry, and Steve counted out his change carefully, giving the impression that he was short of money.

"Hey—you're an American too, ain't you? How come you speak their damn lingo so well?"

The American who had just come up to lounge against the bar next to Steve had short-cropped red hair and enormous handlebar mustaches.

"Just curious," he said hastily when he met the hard blue eyes that seemed to narrow slightly as they bored into his. "I bin here about a year myself and still don't know more than a few words, mostly for the things I want most!" He gave a course, meaningful laugh, but his eyes were still inquisitive.

Steve shrugged shortly, sipping his beer. "I had plenty of time to learn it," he growled. "Didn't have a choice." He let his glance at the other man become openly suspicious. "Why'd you want to know?"

"Hell, no particular reason, I guess! Just tryin' to start up a conversation with a fellow American. A man can get real homesick for the sound of his own language, sometimes."

"I guess. Ain't had the chance to speak it too much recently."

Steve kept his answers short, slightly sullen, as if he was determined to remain suspicious. He finished both bottles of beer and grudgingly allowed the man to buy him a drink.

His name was Cole, and he was from Texas. He said that after the war he had "just drifted over here" and had ended up joining the counterguerillas for the money. Steve, acting as if the liquor was just beginning to get to him, admitted that he was a Californian.

"My folks came down the Oregon trail from Missouri, though. One of the earliest wagon trains, my old man use to boast. They were dirt farmers in Missouri and they stayed dirt farmers in Oregon. But me—I got the hankerin' to see California—an' after that, the rest of the world. Shit!" he grimaced. "Shoulda known better!"

"I did all of my travellin' in the States, with Quantrill—things seemed awful dull after that—that's why I decided to join up with a couple of my friends and get mixed up in this shootin' war."

Expansively, he bought Steve another drink and took him back to one of the tables to meet some of his friends.

Predictably, their conversation seemed to center around wars and women. The presence of a stranger in their midst who was also an American seemed to make a few of them curious, although with their own strange code they didn't press him too much. It just seemed natural, after a few more drinks, for him to admit that he hadn't seen much of the Civil War since he had deserted the Union army in '62.

"Got in a fight, one time—how was I to know he was an officer? He wasn't in no uniform, an' he was carryin' a gun. Anyhow, after that I didn't have no choice but to drift."

"Hey listen, you shoulda joined our side! We were doin' some real fightin' then, weren't we boys?" The laughter was boisterous, but not derisive.

Steve let his words slur very slightly. "I didn't have too much sense, back then. Got back to San Francisco to celebrate missin' the war and ended up on a damn ship . . ."

"You mean you were shanghaied? Happened to a friend of mine once, an' he never did come back home. How'd you end up here?"

Steve let his eyes travel around the circle of bearded faces as if he was making up his mind whether he could trust them or not, and then he shrugged.

"Seems like I was just born to do the wrong thing! I jumped ship at Vera Cruz an' managed to hide out until she sailed. An' then I find that the pretty little Pepita I was shacked up with had a jealous husband, an' he didn't like *gringos* particularly. So"—he gave a wry, half-angry grin. "So I got myself thrown in jail, an' they left me there to rot. Any of you fellers been in a Mex jail? I didn't believe they still had dungeons until they put me in one. Some of those cells fill halfway up with water when the tide comes up—an' they make you work like a dog for the slops they feed you. But I sure learned the language!"

"You bust out?"

Steve gave them all a wary look. "Hey—you fellers kinda work for the government, don't you? I tell you, only way anyone's gonna get me back in that jail is feet first, an' I ain't so slow with a gun that I won't take some company with me!"

"Simmer down, buddy—ain't nobody here going to turn you in. I'll bet most of us here have seen the inside of a few jails ourselves, huh?"

The speaker, a big man with enormously strong shoulders winked reassuringly at Steve, and pushed a bottle across the table. "Here, have another snort. You oughta think about joining up with us, if you're at loose ends."

"Thanks, but I'm beginning to feel like I'm bad luck, even to myself. Guess I'm gonna try and make my way back to California."

"Better watch out for them *Juaristas* along the way then! Them bastards even got an army pointed this way."

Still pretending to be half-drunk, Steve listened as the liquor loosened the tongues of his companions and they began to discuss the war; their comments about the Imperial troops not only contemptuous but verging on being insulting.

"At least the French were fighters, an' they knew what they was doing. It was them kept that Juarez in his place."

"Only good thing I can remember about bein' attached to Mejia's army was the women—the little *soldaderas*." The big man who had spoken began to chuckle, his eyes crinkled with nostalgia.

"I recall when me an' a couple of my buddies had our own little gal—an' she weren't no ordinary Mex whore either. Purtiest thing you ever did see—half French an' half American, with hair like polished copper. Tom Beal took her off some French colonel—you remember Tom?"

"Heard he got killed in San Luis."

"She killed him. Put a knife in his gullet, slick as a whistle. I taught her to use that knife, too." Matt Cooper gave a reminiscent chuckle and Steve, every muscle in his body rigid, the rage almost blinding him to all reason, used every ounce of will-power he possessed to remain seated, his body slouched back in the chair. If he moved, he would kill Matt Cooper.

Unaware of the effect his words had caused, Cooper was going on with his story, bottle clutched in his hairy fist.

"Not that Tom didn't deserve to get hisself killed. Funny guy, Tom. Mean and cold, and a deadly fighter. Hated women, in a way. Useta get a real kick out of hurtin' them. Pecos and I, we kept him from hurtin' our gal too bad, when we was around, but that day we had just got in town and while we was getting ourselves drunk, Beal took her down to some *cantina*—he useta make her whore for him when he needed money, see? Only this time he went too far, way I heard it later. Started to strip the clothes off her, right in front of that whole roomful of grinning apes—feller I knew said it was like a slave auction—he was goin' to sell her to the highest bidder. Only she went crazy all of a sudden and let him have it with the knife . . ."

"You ever hear what happened to her?"

Cooper shrugged, his huge shoulders moving bearlike under his tight jacket.

"That was when the French were runnin' everything back there. We went down to the guardhouse after we'd sobered up, Pecos and I, and all that sergeant would do was shrug his shoulders. Told us some French officer came in while they was questioning her, and took her off with him to Mexico City. But I bet she fell right on her feet there, just like a little cat. She sure was something!"

Steve kept looking at the buttons on Matt Cooper's open tunic, planning just where he'd put his knife in. His mind had begun to function again, but the cold rage he'd felt when the big man started on his rambling discourse still remained, making his resolve implacable. Now that he knew where the counterguerillas were going he ought to get out himself and plan a little surprise for them. But first he was going to kill Cooper.

It was a good thing they thought he was drunk, and were going on with their own conversation. He could feel the fury in himself, coiled like a rattler ready to strike, in the pit of his stomach. So that was part of her story she hadn't told him. He remembered her saying, that first night, "I've killed a man, Steve," but she hadn't told him who the man was, or why. How much more had she kept hidden from him behind those slanted green eyes of hers? Ginny—his sun-haired darling, with her softly parting thighs, her seductive, temptress mouth opening under his kisses—how many men had experienced the same delights that he had? She had killed one of them, driven to God knows what depths of desperation and degradation; and another sat across the same table from him, swilling his liquor like the swine he looked to be. Had they vanquished her stubborn spirit, dragged her spit-fire pride in the dust, broken her just as he had been broken in that wretched prison? He had never felt such a fierce, frantic desire to kill as he did at this moment, even though the rational, thinking part of his mind told him coldly to wait—the time would come.

It was easy to pretend drunkenness when he finally stumbled away from the table, chair scraping noisily as he did. They were all more than a little drunk by now and hardly noticed his weaving departure. Only Cole called after him, his voice a raucous bellow.

"Hey, Steve! You decide to join us, remember we ride out in the morning!"

He muttered something unintelligible and found himself in the coolness of the night air outside; sucking in great gulps of it, as if he'd been holding his breath a long time.

PART SEVEN

"La Guerra"

Chapter Fifty

On March 12, 1867, the last shipload of French soldiers left Vera Cruz harbor, and on the same day Steve Morgan came back to the *Hacienda de la Nostalgia*.

He was wearing a uniform—it was the first thing Ginny noticed when she came running down the steps. She was still damp from the bath she had just taken—wet curls pinned carelessly on top of her head, her skin still glowing with moisture.

He was just dismounting from his horse when she stopped abruptly, not two feet away from him, teeth worrying her lower lip, green eyes starting to shine with anger as she remembered how enraged with him she was.

"Well?" He cocked an eyebrow at her.

"Well! Is that all you have to say? It's been almost a month, and all the word you've bothered to send me was that—that note that said *nothing*, which you might as well have written to Salvador!"

"Since it made you so angry, I'm sorry I didn't tell Manolo to hand it to Salvador instead." He stood looking down at her, a strange, hard smile on his mouth, his blue eyes blazing with some kind of emotion she couldn't fathom.

"Well, at least Salvador has been bringing me news of the war," she said sulkily, adding almost unwillingly, "I see you've joined the real army at last! When did that happen?"

"A couple of weeks ago, after we wiped out a troop of counterguerillas who had been bothering us."

He turned away from her rather abruptly and began to take his saddlebags from the horse, and she noticed that he moved one arm rather stiffly, as if it hurt him.

Her anger evaporated immediately and she ran to him, eyes wide with concern.

"Steve! You've been wounded, haven't you? Oh, for God's sake, why didn't you tell me? Why didn't you let me know?"

Her arms seemed to fly up around his neck, and the sarcastic comment he had been about to make died under the sweet, familiar pressure of her lips. He dropped the saddlebags and began to kiss her roughly, savagely, as if he had to seal his possession of her. There was only one thing to do, he found himself thinking crazily, and that was to take her to bed. He had had too much time alone with his thoughts, there was too much bitterness, like poison, collected inside him.

They did no talking in the bedroom afterwards, except for the occasional, half-breathless words of love and passion that came quite naturally as they rediscovered each other's bodies and their capabilities.

He wanted her! In spite of the note of harshness in his voice and the sarcastic twist of his lips when he had first spoken to her; once she was in his arms he had held her as if he couldn't bear to let her go. And in spite of the grinning, watching faces of old Salvador and the peons who had come up to greet him he had carried her in his arms and straight into the bedroom, kicking the door shut behind him with a bang that they must have heard outside.

Drowsily content, Ginny lay with the weight of his body still pressing hers down as he lay half-asleep, his breathing slowly becoming more regular. He had come back to her after all, just when she was beginning to despair that he ever would. Her fingers gently stroked the ridges of scar tissue on his back, moved to touch the bandage that he still wore, wound tightly around his chest and shoulder to keep the thick wad of dressing in place. He had been wounded—he must have been in some battle he hadn't yet had the time to tell her about. She had started to ask him about it when he had crushed her words into silence with his lips.

That's why he didn't come before, she thought, and in spite of the terrifying knowledge that he might have been killed without her even knowing it, she was somehow glad that it was his injury, and not his indifference, that had kept him away so long.

The patterns made by the late afternoon sun as it slanted through the window she had left half open for coolness were beginning to look faded, like the old-gold roses on a damask curtain she had seen once. In the kitchen, Salvador would be preparing dinner, his old, seamed face probably sour as he wondered if they would eat it or not.

Ginny hadn't been eating very well lately, but now, suddenly she felt as if she had been starving for weeks. And Steve must probably feel the same way too. He looked thinner, and his face had tired, tense lines in it she hadn't noticed before. And he had had a haircut too—she touched the back of his neck with her fingers, discovering where his hair was just beginning to grow long enough to curl slightly.

His face had been buried in the curve of her shoulder and neck, in the masses of her hair, but now he suddenly turned it so that his lips grazed her cheek.

"You're restless, *chica*. What's the matter?"

"Oh, I was only wondering if you were hungry," she confessed shamelessly. "I haven't been able to work up an appetite all week, and now suddenly I feel as if I could eat anything! A mountain of tortillas—two bowlsfull of chili, oranges and papayas—and oceans of wine to wash it all down with!"

He began to laugh softly.

"That's a hell of a thing to be thinking of in the position you're in! What a set-down you've given me, especially since my hunger at present is all for you—you tempting little baggage!"

Holding her pinned down he began to nibble at her breasts, his lips and tongue teasing her nipples until she began to writhe under him, moaning helplessly.

"Oh, Steve! Oh, Steve—yes!"

"What does that mean? Have I really managed to arouse some other hunger in your wanton body?"

He rolled over onto his back, grinning at her, while she almost cried with frustration, her fingers clawing at his chest.

"Oh damn you, Steve! You can't do that to me! I won't let you!"

"As a matter of fact, I'm rather tired—and now you've mentioned it, the thought of food does sound mighty tempting."

"You—you brute! You horrible wretch! You're saying that on purpose to tease me!"

She squirmed over on top of him and began to pummel at him with her fists until he caught them.

"Hellcat! What are you trying to do—open up that wound of mine again? I can think of better ways for you to work up an appetite once more."

Suddenly catching his meaning she began to frown with anger and then dissolved into helpless giggles until he pulled her face down to his and began to kiss her, his hands moving to caress her body until desire made her almost mindless and she did exactly as he wanted.

They ate their dinner very late, after all, because Steve had insisted on taking a bath and she went to find some fresh clothes for him in his saddlebags, which were still outside in the living room where Salvador had put them.

Ginny had resisted the urge to peek—to go through them to learn what he was carrying and where he had been, but the only thing she could find was lying right under the clothes he had asked her to bring him, and she stared at it, frowning, for a few minutes. An Arkansas "toothpick"—a knife she was only too familiar with, but which it was strange to find Steve carrying about with him. He preferred a Bowie knife, and had often told her it was the only knife worth carrying. "You can find all kinds of uses for a Bowie," she remembered him telling her once on their travels. He had used his for cutting branches to make shelters for them; for skinning the animals that he had shot. And she had once stabbed him with that same knife.

She longed to pick the new knife up and examine it carefully, for it looked strangely and almost ominously familiar, but something stopped her, and with a shudder she left it where it was. No—let Steve tell her if he wanted to—she was not going to let him think she had been prying.

Ginny chattered almost nervously right through their
dinner, longing to ask him questions but afraid to do so in
case she brought that sarcastic, almost hateful look back
to his face. She told him about small things—unimportant
things—the repairs she'd made to the *estancia*, the herb
garden she had begun. And all the time she sensed that he
was watching her—even when he gave her a lazy smile
occasionally and told her politely to go on, he was interested in her doings.

At last, when she had lapsed into an uneasy silence and
began to drink her wine too fast, he leaned back in his
chair and began to scrutinize her openly, as if he'd only
met her a few hours ago.

"Domesticity certainly seems to agree with you, love.
And I like that tan you've acquired. It gives your skin a
certain bloom. You remind me of a peach—all over."

Memory of the afternoon they had just spent in bed,
thoroughly exploring each other, suddenly made her blush
and lower her eyes. Why did he look at her so strangely,
almost as if he hated her, even while he was paying her
compliments.

"What a shy, innocent look you can put on sometimes!"
he went on. "Who, looking at you now, would think that
you were once a whore?"

The suddenness of his attack made her flinch visibly,
even while she raised her eyes challengingly to his.

"Oh God! What kind of cruel game have you decided to
play this time?"

He shrugged coolly, his eyes capturing hers with their
hard, inquiring look.

"Why should I want to play a game with you? It's just
that I ran into a friend of yours a few weeks ago, and his
conversation about certain incidents in your past was most
enlightening." She gave a gasp, and his voice hardened
into what was almost a snarl. "Tell me—what did Tom
Beal usually charge when he rented you out to his friends?
How many others did he share you with for free?"

Her voice was an agonized whisper. "Oh no—no!"

"You didn't tell me everything, did you? You didn't
tell me he sold you to any man who could afford a few
pesos to sample your charms."

"Stop it!" She jumped to her feet, hands pressed over
her ears. "Stop it—I don't want to listen to any more!"

Like a panther he came at her with one long stride;

catching her wrists, pulling them downward until he held
them imprisoned before her.

"Goddammit, you *will* listen—at least until I'm through!
How do you think I felt—to hear your sordid career discussed so casually in front of a roomful of gaping men?
Your friend Matt Cooper—the same one who taught you
to use a knife so well—he hadn't forgotten you—nor how
good you were. In fact, he and a friend went back to look
for you, after they'd heard how you killed Beal. Oh
Christ!" He flung the oath in her face savagely, his fingers
tightening around her wrists until she screamed with pain
and fear. "Why didn't you tell me? What kept you from
the truth? And how many other incidents like that are you
still hiding?"

Suddenly she threw her head back, her eyes streaming
with tears, but still able to glare defiantly at him.

"Isn't there something that *you're* hiding from me?
Some—some incident so horrible, so impossibly vile that
you can't even bear to think about it? You have no right
to sit in judgement over me—you're not a woman, so you
can't possibly understand what terrible degradation a
woman can be forced into—you can't understand how it
felt to be—to be exhibited like an animal to all those
men—their eyes staring, their mouths open with lust—
staring—yes, and screaming obscenities while he—while
he told me I had to undress so that they could see what
they were getting! And then when I wouldn't—I
couldn't—he started to—to hit me and rip that rotten,
sleazy gown he made me wear off my body—and all the
while they were throwing money—it came at me from
everywhere—money, to see the clothes torn off me as if
I—I went crazy then! I remembered I had the knife—I
didn't even know what I was doing when I plunged it into
his throat and heard the awful noises he made, with the
blood spurting everywhere—everywhere!"

Her voice rose into a tormented scream, and she hardly
realized that Steve had released her abruptly and was staring at her, his face whitening under the brown of his tan.

"Ginny."

She thought he was going to sieze her again and backed
away from him, her eyes staring.

"No—I don't want you to touch me—not now—I'm
dirty, remember? I'm a whore—dozens of men have used
me—and you'll never forgive me for that, will you? Not

even if it wasn't my fault—because I survived, even though I wanted to die—because *you* want to be the one to destroy me, where *they* couldn't—and you know why you can, Steve? Do you know?"

"Shut up! Damn you—is that what you're trying to do now? Make *me* feel guilty for the things you did?"

"Stop it!" She shrieked the words at him, panting with the force of her emotions. "Haven't *you* been human enough to suffer from beatings and starving and—and torture until—until you'd do anything, *anything*, just to go on being alive? Have you never known what it was to be forced to do things your mind shrank from, because you had gone past the point of *caring?* I was a body, that's all—a *thing*, to be used, to be sold—I was dead inside, and I stopped caring what happened to me, because *you* were dead—because I had loved you, and they had killed you, and nothing mattered . . ." she began to laugh wildly with the tears still slipping down her cheeks. "I used to tell myself that, all the time—like a litany of hopelessness—'it doesn't matter—it doesn't matter—nothing matters any more.'"

"You're hysterical. Can't you see there's no reason for you to cry?" She was suddenly in his arms, feeling their hardness like steel bands around her, pulling her against his body. She kept sobbing helplessly, her tears soaking his shirt.

"Listen to me," he was saying in a strange, expressionless voice, "he's dead. Do you think I could let him live after what he said?"

"Steve," she tried to pull away from his encircling arms, but he only held her more tightly, pressing her face against his shoulder.

"I was in Orizaba looking for those damned counterguerillas who had been giving us such a bad time. I ran into them—and *him*—your Matt Cooper. I waited for him outside in an alley. I knew where they were staying—they told me, the damned careless fools! There were three of them—two more than I expected, but at that point, I didn't care—the thought of you has always managed to chase away all the caution I've ever possessed! There was quite a battle, I can tell you—but I'd taken their guns first—they thought I wanted their money, the bastards!"

"Don't—don't!" she began to whisper. "I don't want to hear it."

His voice became harsh. "Why not? Don't you want to know that you were revenged? That I was man enough to kill at least one of your lovers? The other two were easy—they were too drunk to put up much of a fight, but Matt Cooper—I'll say this much for him, he's a fighter. He went for his knife—and he knew how to use it. That's where I got the new wound you were so curious about! But I'll take a Bowie any day. I had to kill the others very quickly, so they wouldn't make too much noise and bring everyone running, but I took my time with Cooper—I told him why I was going to kill him, and he fought like a lion—silently, too, as if he knew he'd had it coming a long time."

"And you killed him. It was his knife I saw in your saddlebag."

"I thought maybe you'd like a souvenir, baby."

She said very quietly, "Oh—dear God!" And he laughed, a short, bitter sound in his throat.

"I admit it was a stupidly reckless thing to do. I was only supposed to find where the counterguerillas were, and in which direction they were going next. But as things turned out, we fixed up a nice little ambush for them—that's when I took a stray bullet in the shoulder. It was worth it, though, because we wiped them out."

As if she hadn't heard him, Ginny whispered, almost to herself, "You killed him—because of me! Poor Matt—he was the only one who was *kind*—he protected me from Beal, when he was sober." She felt his arms tighten with the anger she could sense in him again, and said in the same husky whisper, "But *why?* Why did you bother, Steve? You'll never forgive me—you'll never forget what I became—you don't even care about me any longer, if you ever did! So—why?"

"Why do you think I'm here? You're right, I can't forget any of it—it's been like a festering, cancerous sore ever since you came back—your past! But all the same, I want you—you've become like a drug, like a sickness I can't shake off—I want to punish you for what you've become, and still, at the same time, I want you!" His voice became hoarse, she felt his hands move slowly up her back, caressingly, until his fingers caught in her hair, grasping handfuls of it. "I crave your flesh, and your softness, and your firmness and the feel of your hair like silk under my hands—I want to hear you scream softly under me—to bury myself in you—I've never encountered another woman who's satisfied and tormented me as much as you have. For God's sake, woman, isn't that enough for you? What else do you want of me, except the same thing I want from you?"

She began to sob again, and to beat at him wildly with her fisted hands.

"It's not! It's not that way! You talk as if I'm your whore, not your wife!"

In spite of her fury he lifted her easily in his arms, slinging her roughly over his shoulder when she continued to fight him.

"What's the difference? Why not *my* whore for a change? And if you really want to feel like a wife, then you'd better start acting like one—there's one wifely duty at least that you perform extremely well!"

"Oooh!" she screamed aloud with rage and frustration as he started to carry her off into the bedroom. He began to laugh.

"You want Salvador to think I have to rape my own wife? Be sensible, Ginny! After all the only way we really seem to hit it off together is in bed—why can't we make the best of it?"

He laid her none too gently on the bed and lay over her, his eyes blazing down at her with passion and hate and desire—everything at once—until, as he knew they would, her struggles stopped. Still sobbing, she put her arms around his neck.

Chapter Fifty-one

When Ginny awoke the next day she realized that some instinct had made her reach gropingly out beside her, only to encounter emptiness. She levered herself to a half-sitting position, squeezing her eyelids together against the bright sunlight that streamed into the room.

"Where is he? It's late—perhaps he's only gone outside—in a minute he'll come back in and wake me," but even as she tried to console herself with cheerful thoughts some deep-seated instinct made Ginny go cold with fear.

When Maria knocked gently at the door and then opened it, her eyes very large, her face solemn, Ginny knew, even before she saw the piece of paper that the girl held in her hand that her worst fears were about to be confirmed.

"I'm sorry, Ginny, but I never did get around to telling you I have to leave first thing this morning—*c'est la guerre!* It will probably be quite some time before I pass this way again."

Why does he bother to write? Ginny thought savagely. Why doesn't he at least leave me to draw my own conclusions?

All the bitter memories of the previous night came back

and she covered her face with her hands; not sure whether she hated him or herself more. How cruel he had been! How unfair—how unreasonable! And he had admitted, bluntly, that he could neither forget nor forgive her past—he actually blamed *her* for everything, when it had all been his fault in the beginning! Oh God, what could she do? She felt as if she couldn't possibly stand any more hurt, and she knew that he would continue to hurt her and continue to use her body, for as long as she'd let him. That was all she meant to him—a woman's body for his use. And after all, she thought bitterly, why not? After all it was she who had followed him here and thrown herself at him, forcing him to accept her.

He's never once told me he loves me—he's been honest in that respect at least! And he's even admitted he had no intention of consummating our marriage—not even in the beginning! So all the time it was *I* who cared, *I* who gave my heart to him—he only married me because of a promise he made his grandfather! Is it fair to him, to saddle him with a wife he obviously doesn't need?

When Maria came back in the room with the *señora's* chocolate she found the *señora* in tears. The girl's eyes became sympathetic as she tiptoed out of the room. It was natural, she supposed—how sad to have just one night of love and then have one's lover torn away by a war! Maria herself was too young, her mother said, to think about young men yet, but she had her thoughts all the same! She hoped that the *señor* would return very quickly so that the *señora* would begin to smile again.

Steve Morgan, however, at that very moment, was riding as hard as he could away from Tehuacan and towards the mountains that sheltered Puebla. He felt unutterably tired, and his mood was none too good, although it improved slightly when he caught up with his troop at the place they had decided upon earlier.

Sergeant Manolo Ordaz came to meet him, a wide grin on his face. "I thought maybe you'd changed your mind!" He winked. "If I had a wife like yours I'd find it almost impossible to tear myself away from her arms!"

The familiarity that had been born between them when they were both *guerrilleros*, constantly on the run sometimes sharing the same canteen, made Steve force a tired grin.

"Well, I'm here, as you see! Let's get moving—we have less than a week to get this job done."

The men were already mounting up. A picked troop of twenty-five men, mostly ex-*guerrilleros*, men who knew these mountains and every narrow trail and bit of cover they afforded. At their head, Captain Esteban Alvarado, especially chosen for this mission because he had once been an inmate of the very prison they were going to visit.

This was an official sortie, so they were all in uniform. A matter of obtaining silver ore, badly needed in order to be exchanged for money to pay the *Juarista* armies—to pay for the guns that were still pouring in from across the border.

General Díaz had been very specific as to the procedure to be followed. It was to be an official, straightforward confiscation. The owner of the silver mine had already fled the country, leaving the small military garrison and the prison guards to protect his interests. The silver mine now belonged to the State—and in effect, the State was now El Presidente Benito Juarez.

There were other mines that had been similarly taken over, of course, but they were far away. This one, nestled in the hills overlooking Puebla, would provide silver for the army of Porfirio Díaz and at the same time would not be allowed to make more shipments to Vera Cruz, to line the pockets of the Imperialist armies.

What this all really meant was hard days and nights of riding, especially since they had to avoid the highways and more frequently used paths and snaked their way through the mountains, using goat trails when they had to. It was like being with the guerillas again, the men often muttered to themselves. They were all travelling extra light, because of the silver they were supposed to carry back with them. Two men shared a canteen sometimes—they foraged for food wherever they could, sometimes reduced to eating cactus-pulp and piñon nuts.

As they penetrated further and further into the mountain fastnesses the air became colder and thinner. Sometimes a damp, chilly mist hung over everything, so that their uniforms seemed to stay perpetually soggy. Thank God the Imperialist armies were too busy trying to guard the four major cities which were all that remained of Maximilian's empire, to spare the men to patrol such remote areas. Thank God, even, for the mists which hid their furtive passage! The men gave more attention to their horses than they did to themselves—the loss of a horse would probably mean disaster and death for the man who had been riding it. They snatched at their precious hours of sleep, spending most of the time in the saddle. The sooner they arrived at their destination, the sooner they would be able to turn back.

Steve Morgan found himself unusually absent-minded during the long days and nights that followed his hasty, almost surreptitious departure from the *hacienda*. He told himself angrily that his preoccupation nearly amounted to an obsession. Damn it, why did Ginny keep obtruding herself into his thoughts even now? Why did he actually feel guilty that he had left her as he had?

He remembered the way she had looked asleep that morning—her eyelids still red and swollen from the tears he had made her shed, her hair lying in tangled strands across her face. He hadn't had time to write her a longer note—he hadn't felt in the mood for lengthy explanations—the probable tears and recriminations he would have had to face if she was awake. So he had left her, still sleeping—and now he couldn't get her out of his mind.

The past was catching up with a vengeance, Steve thought grimly. First hers and now his. He thought of that prison, and felt a pang of pure hatred flash through his mind as he wondered if the effeminate young doctor was still there. What had been his name? Cabrillo—yes, that was it. Doctor Cabrillo. He rolled the name on his tongue like a foul, bitter taste, and felt all his old scars begin to ache again. The leg and wrist irons, digging deeply into flesh, almost to the bone—solitary, and the slow corrosion of the mind while the body continued its blind functioning. That morning when they had taken him out into the sun, the indescribably horrifying feeling when the ants had begun to crawl curiously over his shrinking flesh—the doctor's shiny boot, digging into his ribs—and yet, he had survived. He was here, riding back of his own free will. What an unpredictable irony!

They were suddenly caught in a blinding rain shower as they worked their way farther into the remoteness of the mountain called Malinche. The trails they followed—little more than animal tracks—became slippery and they were thankful for the shelter of the closely growing piñon trees.

Still, they were too close to their destination to pause.
They kept going, slowly and cautiously, their horses picking the way.

The cold was biting, through their soaking wet uniforms. Steve, like the others, had turned the collar of his
uniform up and pulled down the visor of his forage cap to
protect his eyes from the cold needles of rain.

Adelante! Keep moving! The rain dripped from the pine
needles and made a soft soughing noise as it filtered
through the trees. Somewhere to the right of them came
the sound of rushing water down a steep *barranca.* Water
going down to join the river, ending in the sea. What
would happen when they reached the prison? Would their
carefully planned bluff work?

Steve shot a quick upward glance through drooping
branches to see if there was any chance that the rain
would stop, but the sky looked steel gray, menacing. What
a hell of a way to fight a war! But then, was there anything else he was good for? He realized with what was
almost shock that he had spent over a third of his life doing just this. Travelling—moving—sometimes the hunter
and sometimes the hunted. Nights spent sleeping on the
ground or in tawdry hotels and barrooms. Faceless, innumerable women—chance encounters with predictable,
inevitable endings. Always brief, always meaningless in
retrospect. Except for one. He remembered, far too
vividly, riding with her in the rain, her body held before
him in the saddle, curve of her back pressed closely
against him. Heat of her body under one, thin blanket.
Taste of the rain and salt tears in his mouth.

How he had made her suffer! And had delivered her,
without his realizing it, into even worse suffering and
degradation. Yet, she had been strong enough to live
through it all—stronger, in her way, than he had been.
Her scars were deeper than his, even if they didn't show;
and she wouldn't let them show—she was too proud! She
had too much pride, she was too strong. He had tried to
make her crawl to him, begging his forgiveness, and she
had refused to do so.

The only thing she would admit to was her love for
him, and he had thrown it back in her face, too much of a
coward to admit the truth—that he was making her pay
for the very crimes that had been committed against her.
He had acted like an adolescent in the throes of his first

romantic love; not being able to countenance the fact that his idol had suddenly developed dirty feet and a tarnished halo! After all, what did it really matter? She had been with other men, had used her body as an instrument for survival. Would he really have preferred to hear that she had killed herself instead? Could he have borne the thought?

She had begged him for understanding, and he had given her rejection. *Perdición!* he swore to himself, suddenly remembering the heartbroken look on her face. I call myself a civilized man, and I've acted worse than any illiterate savage! How many women have I slept with, merely to satisfy a passing appetite? Didn't I first take her for the same reason? He thought about Concepción—installed as his mistress when Ginny turned up. And she had fought for him, his little termagant! He had a sudden wild, crazy longing to feel her arms go around his neck, to hold her against him and kiss her endlessly. "Ginny—Ginny—*sangre di me corazon, amada mia....*" Why had it always seemed so difficult to say the words to *her?*

The rain had lost some of its force and came down like a fine cobweb, a mist of moisture. He turned back to look at the miserable-looking men who followed him.

"Come on—we have to keep moving—it's only a little way now . . ." They rode out of a narrow *barranca*, and started down the mountainside, the trees soon giving way to shale and rocks. Another rise, another descent, and they would see the reddish stone walls of the prison.

Steve left five of his men spread out as much as possible under cover and took the remaining twenty with him, riding boldly over the stretch of open ground that led to the massive gates.

"I think this is the most uncomfortable experience of my life," Manolo said out of the corner of his mouth as they came abreast of the gates.

They were challenged from one of the watchtowers when they had come close enough for their uniforms to be seen.

"Alto! Quien es?"

Steve found he had to swallow hard before he could answer. He made his voice as hard and commanding as possible.

"Capitan Alvarado—Ninth Cavalry Regiment, serving under General Díaz. I have business to discuss with your commander—better open up quickly, my men and I are very wet."

There was a short pause, in which they could almost sense the surprise and consternation of the men who had just hailed them.

Finally, another voice called down, a note of doubt in it.

"General *Díaz*, you say? You're *Juaristas*?"

"General Díaz serves our *presidente*, Don Benito Juarez. We represent the government of Mexico, *señores!* What's the meaning of this delay?"

"Just a minute—you will have to wait just a minute until we tell our *capitan*. . . ."

They waited, the seconds seeming interminable. Easy targets—Steve prayed that the men hidden behind them would be able to cover them with their fire in case they had to beat a quick retreat. But at this range, how many of them would live to gain cover?

The gates suddenly swung open, creaking on their heavy hinges. A man in the uniform of a captain in the Imperialist army was revealed in the opening, and then as the gates opened wider, the men who formed a tight semicircle behind him, rifles at the ready.

"You may enter, *señores,* but you will have to explain . . ."

Steve allowed a tight smile to touch his lips as he gave his counterpart the formality of a salute.

"Do we have to explain the obvious, *señor capitan*? The war is all but over. We have just taken Puebla, and the whole of this province is under the command of our Supreme Commander—General Porfirio Díaz."

He kept the faintly sarcastic smile, hoping fervently that the men in this isolated garrison had not had any news recently. He could feel the tension in the men who sat their horses so rigidly straight behind him, and his own muscles ached with the strain.

"But what are you doing here, Capitan?" The commander of the small garrison kept pulling at his mustache nervously, as if he was uncertain what to do next.

"It is my duty to inform you, sir, that this place is now the property of the state—you understand the policy of the government with regard to the holdings of certain people who conspired against the state?" As if to take some of the sternness from his words, Steve gave a small shrug.

"As for you and your men, Capitan, you are soldiers, are you not? I've been given orders that there are to be no reprisals against loyal soldiers who fought for the last government, and that you are to be given the chance to transfer your allegiance to the present and rightful government of Mexico." He added with a wry smile, "to tell the truth, Capitan, neither my men nor I have the stomach for this kind of duty—it's too isolated out here, and we're in a hurry to join the march on Mexico City."

"On Mexico City you say? The war's progressed so far?"

"You can hardly call it a war any longer, I'm glad to say. It's merely a rout, now! Our presidente is in San Luis Potosí—as soon as Queretaro is taken he'll travel to Mexico City for his formal inauguration. Do you still have any doubts as to where your loyalties lie, *señor Capitan*?"

For the length, possibly, of a couple of heartbeats the nervously scowling captain seemed to hesitate, and then suddenly he drew himself up, clicking his heels together as he bowed formally.

"I am Capitan Juan Figueroa, at your service, Capitan. You must understand my hesitation—as you pointed out, we *are* rather isolated up here, my men and I. But believe me, as soldiers, we live to serve the government of Mexico!"

Steve saluted shortly.

"Capitan Esteban Alvarado. And just to make sure we understand each other and there are no more doubts, would you like to see my credentials, sir?"

He thought he saw a gleam of relief in the other man's eyes as he took the stiffly crackling paper that Steve handed to him, drawing it carefully out of its oilskin covering.

"You will observe, Capitan Figueroa, that it bears not only the signature of General Díaz but of our presidente himself. I hope it makes my instructions and my mission here quite clear?"

Still scrutinizing the amazing document carefully, Captain Figueroa answered almost absentmindedly, still tugging at his mustache.

"Oh, yes—certainly, Capitan!"

There was no mistaking its genuineness, of course. General Díaz' bold, flourishing scrawl—the smaller, neater penmanship of Don Benito Juarez himself. Yes, it was all too real—what they had all feared had happened, and in a way it was a relief to have it done with! The prison—the silver—he had begun to feel it was far too great a responsibility. Now he could hand it all over without the loss of either his honor or his life!

Watching the changing play of expressions on Captain Figueroa's face, Steve let some of the tenseness leave him as he began to relax imperceptibly.

"We've made it! He's going to hand it all over without a fuss!" He felt a surge of triumph, of relief, go through him as the captain looked up, folding the document carefully as he handed it back to Steve.

"You must excuse my lack of manners, Capitan Alvarado! Please to dismount, you and your men—perhaps you would care for a drink in my quarters before we get on with our—er—business transaction?"

Figueroa cleared his throat rather awkwardly as he continued, with a dry smile, "After all, Capitan, you are now technically in charge here—my men and I will be happy to cooperate in carrying out whatever orders you may have."

"Thank you Capitan. I must admit, it's been rather a long and tiring ride up here. I will make sure that General Díaz hears of your—excellent cooperation!"

Chapter Fifty-two

By the time they had shared a few bottles of wine and partaken of a hastily prepared hot meal—the first Steve and his men had tasted for almost a week—the atmosphere had lightened and the tensions relaxed.

The soldiers, Juarist and ex-imperialist fraternized in a friendly fashion, and there had even been some laughter when the five men Steve had left on the hillside to cover their possible return had joined them.

"So! Your *capitan* takes no chances, does he?"

"Not our *capitan*!" Manolo boasted. "That's why General Díaz sent him on this mission. He's a good leader—we've fought together for a long time."

The atmosphere in Captain Figueroa's quarters was just as expansive. A *mestizo* himself, the dark-featured *capitan* still held a kind of grudging respect for the *criollos*, who had been the ruling class in Mexico for so many centuries. He found that this young Capitan Alvarado, however, in spite of his lisping Castilian Spanish, was no chocolate-box soldier like so many other creole officers. Alvarado had seen a lot of fighting—he had the look of a fighting man, with his rather hard, reckless brown face and blazing blue eyes. He even listened sympathetically to the story of all

615

the problems Captain Figueroa had had to face since he had been here—his feeling of humiliation at being appointed to a prison, of all places!

"Perhaps we can arrange for a transfer—I'll speak to General Díaz myself," Steve promised.

"You know the general, then? Personally?"

"His brother, Colonel Felix Díaz, was quite a good friend of mine many years ago," Steve said casually, lighting a cigar. "And as for General Díaz, yes, I've met him, several times. He's the kind of man you'd be proud to serve—the finest general in all the world!"

Captain Figueroa mentioned diffidently that he felt sure he himself would be proud to serve such a man.

If he wondered why Capitan Alvarado did not remove his wet tunic, and had removed only his forage cap, he was too polite to mention the fact. Perhaps General Díaz insisted on strict formality on the part of his officers.

Asking searching questions as if he really knew nothing about the prison or the operation of the silver mines, Steve discovered that there hadn't been many changes made since he'd been here. The silver was still kept in a tightly secured strong room underground, with soldiers guarding the door in shifts. Work in the mines had slowed down somewhat since the war had come so close—the perilous state of the roads leading down to Vera Cruz had made sending any shipments down there too risky.

As for the prison itself—Captain Figueroa gave an expressive shrug. He did not interfere too much in the running of it—he had only been here a few months himself. There was a mine manager who ran everything "down there" and saw to it that the guards were paid. The soldiers were here mainly to keep off *bandidos* and other marauders who might be tempted by so much silver lying in a strong room.

And the conditions in the prison? Again the captain shrugged. They were the same in most prisons, he expected. He did not know for what offenses the men were here, but he had been informed that they were some of the worst felons in the country, most of them sentenced to life imprisonment or having their sentences of death commuted to life so that they could make up to society for their crimes.

"You mean they're all thieves and murderers?" Steve persisted, wondering why he did.

"I am forced to believe so, Capitan. They're certainly a wretched lot. But you don't have to worry about going down there—they're all locked up in their cells by this time. And in any case the guards always have the situation well in hand—they have their ways of taking care of recalcitrant troublemakers."

Steve raised an eyebrow. "You don't mean to say you allow any really bad treatment here? Surely the guards don't resort to torture?"

"Capitan Alvarado—you know how it is! Those guards—some of them are very hard, brutal men. I was given orders when I was transferred here not to interfere with the way they keep discipline. It's the only way, I suppose—some of those men are worse than animals."

"I suppose the orders came because of the influence of Don Hilarion Delgado in high places," Steve said sarcastically. "He was the former owner of the mine, you know."

He saw the curious look that Captain Figueroa gave him and decided that he should curb his tongue. Unfortunately, he was not here to release any prisoners but to get as much silver as he and his men could carry and get out. The general's instructions had been strict.

"There will be time later, Capitan Alvarado. But Mexico must be taken first. Those men, if they've survived this long, will manage to survive for a few more weeks."

Seeing the practicality of the General's viewpoint, Steve had not pressed the issue. Now, he was almost sorry.

It felt strange to be descending the steep, winding steps that led down into the mines again. A surly, taciturn guard opened the heavy wooden trap-door for them. The manager, who had objected strenuously to what he termed "theft and invasion of private property" had been locked in his quarters under armed guard. Steve, who remembered occasional glimpses of the red-whiskered man, was glad he hadn't had to face him again. As it was, he kept the visor of his cap pulled low and hoped his clean-shaven face and pure Castilian Spanish would keep any of the guards from recognizing him.

The trap-door thudded shut, enclosing them in the familiar darkness. The lanterns carried by the guards who led the way, and by Captain Figueroa himself, gave the impression of hell.

Steve heard Manolo, who followed close behind him,

whisper *"Dios mio!* Am I glad I don't have to live down here!" An involuntary shudder that he passed off as a shrug ran through his body as his nostrils were suddenly assailed by the same close atmosphere, the ineradicable prison stench that he remembered only too well. It was all he could do to continue taking the steps steadily, one by one, reminding himself to be careful, controlling the impulse to retch.

It was the irrepressible Manolo who commented, "Faugh! Does it always stink like this down here?"

Captain Figueroa grimaced apologetically. "I'm afraid so. If you have a handkerchief to cover your nostrils it might help."

He produced one himself and continued, as Steve followed suit, "One gets used to it, after a while. It's these torches, you see—and of course the dirty bodies, crowded too closely together . . ."

They were walking down a familiar, narrow passageway with the creosote torches flickering in brackets on the walls. One of the guards who preceded them held his lantern up high so that they could get a better view of the tiny, barred cubicles they called cells. They could hear the rattle and clank of chains as the men inside stirred uneasily. A steady, animal moaning came from somewhere up ahead. The punishment cell? The pitch-dark pit they called "solitary" where a man could feel his body and mind slowly rot in that impenetrable blackness?

Steve felt as though he could hardly breathe. Only Captain Figueroa's voice brought him sharply back to reality.

"Capitan Alvarado—are you all right? Forgive me for asking, but this place has a way of affecting newcomers. I felt the same way, the first time they brought me down here to inspect the mines."

Forget it! Steve told himself. Walk past the cells—ignore the chained beasts in there—pretend it doesn't affect you in the least. They'll all be new faces anyhow—if one could recognize a face under the matted beards. Who could last more than six months down here?

One of the guards, a man Steve recognized with hatred, was pointing out some of the diggings with the handle of his coiled up whip. Enrique had been quick to use it too—he was one of those who really enjoyed his work. Pablo—the dark, squat man there, with the beady eyes— had preferred using his fists on the manacled men.

Captain Figueroa was doing most of the explaining and Steve forced himself to ask intelligent, interested questions.

This shaft produced so many ounces of silver per day. The quota was never less—the guards saw to that. Now this other shaft over here—it was comparatively new. They had struck a really rich vein of ore—over a pound of the stuff in three days, wasn't that amazing?

How many lashes on how many bleeding backs to produce that much ore? How many deaths for each ounce of pure silver after it had been purified? Dios—curse his weakness, but he actually felt sick in here. How long had this lot lived away from the sun? How long did it take to turn a man into a creature like a mole, eyes cowering from the light? Remembering the lice that used to crawl all over them, Steve felt his armpits begin to itch. He broke out into a sudden bath of sweat, in spite of the bitter cold down here.

Captain Figueroa was asking him a question, he had to bring his mind back to reality with an effort.

"What are we to do about all this now? Do you still want the same quota produced each day, or should we slow up until we can be sure of getting the shipments through safely?"

He kept his voice steady. "I think you should have them slow down. I'll be giving you a receipt for the silver we take with us, of course, but as for later shipments—well, we'll have to see what El Presidente decides to do. In the meantime—" his voice hardened, "It's only a suggestion, you understand, Captain Figueroa, you're still in charge here, but I hope there are enough cells up there in which to put these men. The conditions down here are hardly human, even for such hardened criminals as these must be."

"But Capitan!" One of the guards began furiously, and Captain Figueroa snapped, "You heard! I'll have my soldiers help clean the cells overlooking the courtyard."

They kept walking—and he thought how good it felt to walk—to take long strides instead of having to shuffle.

The moaning they had heard earlier seemed to have intensified. One of the guards banged threateningly on the black, closed trap-door set into the ground at the blank end of the passage they had followed.

"Shut up, you filth, or I'll really fix you good this time!"

"That's the punishment cell," Captain Figueroa

whispered. "Only the worst trouble-makers, the really stubborn ones, get put in there."

I know, Steve thought. God, yes! I remember! Did I sound like that? An animal in pain, screaming his guts out—sounds of your own screams bouncing back off the walls, raking cruelly over eardrums.

Unable to control the impulse, Steve said suddenly, "How can you stand that racket? The man sounds as if he's in real agony. In the army we'd get him to a hospital or shoot him to put him out of his misery if we couldn't. Don't you have a doctor around here?"

Behind him, he heard Manolo and another of his own men mutter angrily. The guard who had banged on the trap-door turned around with what was almost a sneer in his voice.

"The capitan is too soft-hearted. Animals like this understand only the kind of treatment we give them."

Steve dropped his hand casually to the butt of his revolver and the man shuffled his feet.

"I asked you a question." He rapped out the words coldly, and saw the man's eyes drop from his.

Captain Figueroa spoke quickly to avert an incident, a trace of embarrassment in his voice. "We did have one, as a matter of fact. He was my predecessor—a lieutenant. Unfortunately, he had an unfortunate accident."

"Lieutenant Cabriollo allowed himself to be too kind to certain prisoners," one of the guards said, a grin overspreading his face. "What happened was that he got himself killed by one of them—a man he took a fondness for and made his *puto*." The man made an obscenely descriptive gesture with his hand, still grinning. "He did it with a broken bottle, after he'd smashed off the top—you understand, Capitan? Up *there* . . ."

There was a burst of laughter from the guards, and Captain Figueroa burst out furiously, "By God! You brutes forget yourselves! The señor doctor was an officer."

"But he was also a *joto, señor Capitan!*"

Steve felt such a cold, murderous rage take hold of him that he was glad when Manolo nudged him sharply.

He'd stayed down here too long—he had too many bad memories; and as long as he stayed here he was playing with fire. Captain Figueroa was right—the guards were all brutes, toughened and twisted in sick patterns by their own warped brutality.

"By God, I think I've had enough of this pesthole to last me forever!" he said abruptly. He had to think only of the twenty-five men he'd brought along with him, and the silver they had come to get. That was all. But some day—some day he'd volunteer to bring some of his guerillero friends down here and clean this prison up!

They began, at last, the slow, careful ascent back into the blessedly clean, blessedly cool night air. And thank God the rain had stopped. It would make their return journey a lot easier and faster.

Riding back the way they had come with their saddlebags weighted down with silver, Steve felt as if he could never breathe in enough of the air up here in the mountains. His wet uniform had dried out and he hardly felt the chill of the night.

It was clear, with millions of stars that seemed very high above them, very far away. They stopped to drink their fill of water at a tiny spring, bubbling out of the ground. In the daytime, with the sunshine filtering through the ferns that surrounded it, it would probably look like Ginny's eyes. Beautiful, fathomless green eyes—and how warm her skin would feel now, against his! He had to see her again, as soon as he turned the silver over. He had to explain—he remembered her crying out at him, "And isn't there something that you're hiding from *me*? Some incident so horrible, so impossibly vile, that you can't even bear to think about it?"

He could tell her everything now—about the prison— even about Doctor Cabrillo—yes, even that sick feeling had left him now. He felt free; with most of the bitterness starting to ooze away—leaving more room for her. He could face the fact now that she had captured his mind, as well as his loins. He loved her after all—why had he been trying to escape from that inescapable, unavoidable truth?

Chapter Fifty-three

The port of Vera Cruz had never been so crowded, in spite of its limited accommodations. The harbor itself could not contain all the ships that arrived daily, and sleek vessels lay at anchor even beyond its limits, waiting for a berth.

Here, in the humid, tropical climate of the *Tierra Caliente*, Europeans usually found the heat unbearable. Even the Mexicans themselves preferred to take longer siestas than usual, and until the glaring sun began to slip down behind the distant mountain ranges of the *Tierra Templada* and *Tierra Fria*, there were usually very few people to be seen on the narrow, dirty streets.

In spite of the overpowering heat and unpredictable tropical rainstorms that beset Vera Cruz, several Europeans remained. A few diplomats had decided to "wait it out" now that the outcome of the war was beyond question. And there were still the refugees—American, Belgian, even Austrian, who had clung hopefully and tenaciously to their newly acquired lands and possessions until the very last moment. There were even a few newspaper reporters, too nervous to approach the encroaching battle fronts, but deciding that since they were here, after all, they would stay and get a story. Everyone, it seemed, was waiting for something! Sometimes it was for a ship to take them home—sometimes for news of friends or relatives who still fought in the war.

Ginny, who had arrived in Vera Cruz almost a week ago, was still waiting for the *Yankee Belle* to be cleared by Customs and Quarantine and obtain a berth in the harbor. By now, her anxiety to leave and be done with it, bordered almost on desperation.

She hated this town! A collection of squat adobe buildings, its architecture patterned on the Spanish style, with red roofs and peeling wrought iron grill-work. Narrow, impossibly dirty streets, with squalid, odorous alleys where the displaced actually slept at night. And the ocean-front itself consisted of desolate, humped sand dunes, their shapes constantly changing under the furious onslaught of the fierce Atlantic winds—scrubby palm trees that seemed grotesquely bent and twisted by the force of those same winds. Even the nights were impossibly hot, and she understood why this was referred to as the "fever belt." How could people possibly choose to live here?

'I hate it. I can't wait to leave this place!' she told herself each day as she woke up very early for her regular visit to the shipping agent. And each day the news was the same.

"There are other ships that have priority, ma'am, the *Yankee Belle* has to wait its turn. Don't worry," the blunt-featured American had added once, taking pity on her pale, pensive looking face, "they're not going to leave without you! They have a shipment of silver to pick up from my warehouse."

She had even asked if she couldn't possibly go aboard the ship right away, and wait—but he had shaken his head regretfully.

"I'm afraid not, ma'am. There are all kinds of rules, you see. And in any case, it really gets rough out there in the ocean, you won't find any of these little rowboats willing to go outside the harbor!"

And so she waited, spending most of her time in the tiny room she had managed to obtain for herself in one of the smaller, shabbier *posadas*—not daring to open her windows because of the smells from the alley below and the chance of picking up some infection.

The *posada* fortunately boasted its own tiny walled in

patio-garden, with a rickety collection of tables and chairs that did not match. But it was pleasant out there when the sun wasn't directly overhead and the stunted palm trees provided a little shade. She ordered *naranjada,* orangeade, constantly, always remembering to caution the waiter to be sure that the water was boiled first.

Sometimes, on an exceptionally clear day, one could catch a glimpse of the peak of Orizaba, white snow glistening in the sun. Beautiful, vine-hung Orizaba—the little town nestling at the foot of the peak—the gay days—dancing for the Emperor beside his gardenia-strewn pool—the days when she had been a butterfly, never thinking too much, skimming the surface enjoyment of life. Alice, with her shrill gaiety, and handsome Miguel, her charming lover who had brought everything crashing about her ears ...

Ginny wondered about Miguel, sometimes, using his memory as a talisman to stop herself from thinking about Steve. Miguel in Queretaro with poor Max—the ring of *Juarista* soldiers closing tightly around them—"trapped like rats in there" Salvador had told her triumphantly on that day that seemed so long ago now. What would become of them all?

Already, Ginny had run into several people she knew, or remembered seeing at the balls and parties she had attended almost nightly in Mexico City. Listlessly, she began to allow herself to be drawn into their company, their almost pathetic attempts at amusing themselves of an evening. Anything to stave off depression, the tension that came from waiting—waiting. The month of March continued to drag on—she heard from a new arrival that General Marquez, with a hand-picked cavalry detachment, had managed to cut his way through the besiegers of Queretaro and had gone to Mexico City to drum up reinforcements. But her informant had commented dryly, "Who will he find? Those scared politicians who are left there are going to tell him to get out quickly, to go off and try to keep the *Juaristas* out of the city."

Everytime she heard them talk of the *Juaristas* she would wince. But after all, who would imagine that she, the intimate friend of the Princess du Salm, once engaged to a French captain; sometime mistress of Colonel Miguel Lopez—that she might actually be married to one of these same *Juaristas* they feared so much?

How could she stop herself from thinking of Steve? She wondered where he had gone that morning, leaving her so suddenly, so heartlessly, without even a farewell kiss. And where was he now? Sitting outside Puebla with the rest of Porfirio Díaz' army? Had he bothered to go back to the *hacienda*? Had he read the long letter she had left for him?

When the ocean reflected the bold, dark blue of the sky she would remember his eyes. Blazing with passion sometimes—cold as sapphires at other moments, when he was angry. When she tried to read, the memory of his face came between her eyes and the page to haunt her. How she had loved the crisp feel of his dark hair under her fingers! She remembered wistfully that the harshly handsome hardness of his face could soften when he smiled—when he *really* smiled—the deep grooves in his cheeks and the dancing lights in his eyes making him suddenly appear younger and less remote. Did he ever think about her? Would he miss her?

All he wanted me for was as an occasional bed-partner, she thought, someone who could slake his desire quickly so that he could leave again. No, I could not have borne to suffer and go on suffering any longer! It's best this way—if he wants me, he will have to come after me this time. She would berate herself for her pointless longings, her impossible hopes. He didn't love her, and he never had. It was she who had been stupid enough to read something more than plain unvarnished desire into his words and actions. I will not continue to beat my head against a stone wall any longer, she told herself sternly. And yet, all her friends had been quick to notice and to point out that the charming Madame du Plessis was not her usual gay self—that she was pale and tired-looking as if she did not sleep very well—that in repose her face bore a withdrawn and pensive look.

It was because she had grown tired of having people ask her if she felt ill, and remarking on her lack of vivacity, that Ginny allowed herself to respond to the eager, curious overtures of a Mrs. Baxter, a middle-aged American widow from Boston who was travelling with her companion.

Unable to speak a word of Spanish, Mrs. Baxter had overheard Ginny talking quite companionably to the little maid who was supposed to clean their rooms at the *posada*, and she had immediately bustled up with a beaming smile on her face, her slightly protruberant eyes gleaming with curiosity.

"Oh, my dear—pardon me for approaching you without a formal introduction, but you must be European! You do speak English?"

Hiding a smile, Ginny admitted that indeed she did. From that day on Mrs. Baxter seemed to monopolize her company, to the decided annoyance of several gentlemen who had had the same idea.

She plied Ginny with questions without the slightest trace of embarrassment at her own probing curiosity. A young American woman who dressed and spoke like a lady, all alone here? Mrs. Baxter appointed herself Ginny's unofficial chaperone immediately, especially when she contrived to discover that Madame du Plessis was none other than dear Senator William Brandon's daughter. She had actually met the Senator once, during her dear husband's lifetime—it had been at a grand reception in Washington. Now, how was that for coincidence? It seemed to be an ever greater coincidence to find that Mrs. Baxter had actually been a passenger on the *Yankee Belle*, and planned to go all the way to California to visit her son and daughter-in-law in San Francisco. She admitted that she had had to pay an *enormous* sum of money to have herself rowed into the harbor.

"But after all my dear—you can't imagine how choppy it is out there! I had a terrible case of *mal de mer*, and so did dear Sophy here—she was absolutely no use to me at all! And I asked myself, why should I be so uncomfortable on board ship when I have the perfect opportunity to see something of Mexico? Particularly in these exciting times!"

In spite of Mrs. Baxter's grumbles about her accommodations on board ship, she complained even more about the room she was forced to occupy at what she termed a "third-rate hotel." It was too small—too shabby—badly furnished—and the heat, of course, was intolerable. Still, the lady managed to survive and take a lively interest in Ginny's many friends and admirers.

She preferred the dark Southern gentleman, that Mr. Frank Julius with the charming manners to a plump and slightly balding Belgian banker who was decidedly too old for Ginny. She wanted to know everything about the grand days when Maximilian and Carlotta had their court in Chapultepec—about the gay life in Mexico City—about the beautiful but rather fast Princess du Salm.

Ginny had taken to coming out into the tiny walled garden of the *posada* a trifle later than she usually did, because Mrs. Baxter liked to rise early, and usually retired to her room when the sun began to get too hot.

She sometimes ordered her dinner outdoors in the evening too, when they lit the flickering torches that hung on the bouganvillia-covered walls. On these occasions, in spite of the fact that Mrs. Baxter was always in attendance, there were usually three or four gentlemen who also begged to be allowed to join the ladies. Frank Julius, who had been one of the southern colonists in Cordoba, and Bernard Bechaud, a merry-faced Belgian—one of "Carlotta's crowd," who had tried his hand at planting coffee and tobacco in Oaxaca until Díaz armies drove him out—these two were Ginny's most constant swains. Monsieur Bechaud was content just to be in Ginny's company and to bask in her occasional flashing smiles, but Mr. Julius, a darkly handsome ex-colonel of the Confederate army, wanted a little more than smiles. When she had first met him, she had been with Miguel—and later he had been one of the emperor's guests when she had danced by the pool at Jalapilla that night. He knew she had been Miguel's mistress, and before that, the *petite amie* of the Comte d'Arlingen. When she rebuffed his rather bold advances he told her smilingly that he could wait—she was too beautiful, far too charming to remain alone.

"Are you asking me to become your mistress, Mr. Julius?" Ginny asked him pointedly, her chin up, her green eyes shining dangerously.

"And if I were, would you agree? I'm not a rich man at this moment," he went on, ignoring the angry tapping of her foot, "but then—I'm not a poor one either. I mean to make my fortune before too long."

"For heaven's sake! Of what interest is that to me? I assure you, Mr. Julius, I am not looking for a protector!"

She thought that her anger might drive him away, but it did not. His attentions, his smiling gallantry, were as assiduous as ever.

They played cards on some evenings, piquet and bezique, and once, even a game of poker, after Mrs. Baxter

had retired early. The men were delighted to find that
their charming companion could play as well as a man.

On some evenings, the men hired a ragged group of
Mexican musicians to provide some music for them. The
waltz, of course was beyond them, but they kept begging
Ginny to dance, and she kept refusing, shaking her head
angrily.

One Friday evening however, having just received the
good news that the *Yankee Belle* would have a berth in
the harbor early next week, Ginny finally gave in to their
incessant pleadings. The night was unusually clear, with
even a full moon that defied the tawdry orange glow of
the torches. The musicians played "*La Paloma*" and some
other melancholy pieces, and the wine, for a change, was
actually slightly chilled. Ginny drank too much of it, trying to keep up her air of spurious gaiety. She kept thinking— Next week! I will be really leaving here next
week—and suddenly Mexico seemed more like home to
her than the distant California she hadn't yet seen. I
wonder if Salvador is looking after the little hacienda—my
own, my very own home, she couldn't help asking herself.
I wonder how Marisa is—if she's grown any fatter—
her thoughts were suddenly insupportable.

"Ginette, won't you please dance for us? We have only
a few days left of our pleasant little gatherings here."
Bernard Bechaud's humorous smile was unusually
appealing.

"Please—it would be such an honor," Frank Julius
added, his hand surreptitiously touching hers.

Even Mrs. Baxter suddenly added her pleas.

"Indeed, you must oblige us all, my dear Ginny! You
must dance divinely, if you've danced for an emperor!
Please do!"

"There's no reason to feel embarrassed, madame," the
brown-haired, open faced Mr. Rutherford put in rather
shyly. "See—we are almost the only people left out here."

"It's getting rather late," Ginny said distractedly, but
they began toasting her with their glasses of wine.

"If you won't dance for us, why don't you pretend you
are dancing for a lover?" Frank Julius whispered in her
ear, and she flushed with annoyance. His whisper had carried, and Mrs. Baxter was staring at him in a slightly disapproving fashion.

"Oh, very well!" she cried at last with exasperation in her voice. "At least, have them play something a little more lively!" Perhaps if she danced for them they would leave her in peace, and she wouldn't have to listen to any more of Mr. Julius' sugar-coated innuendos. She tossed off the whole of her glass of wine, ignoring their surprised and pleased looks, and kicked off her shoes. In a way, this would be her farewell to Mexico, with all its life and rich laughter, and all the memories it held for her!

The musicians, encouraged by the coins thrown at them began to play furiously—a fiddle and two guitars; not the Spanish *fandango* but the *jarabe* of the peasants and the gypsies.

Walking defiantly over to the small, tiled part of the patio where the musicians stood, and ignoring their looks of surprise, Ginny began to snap her fingers, and then as the rhythm began to flow into her body, loosening her muscles and sending the blood beating faster in her temples, she began to dance.

Even the waiters and the two maids came out to watch, but she ignored them just as she ignored the others at her table. She was dancing for herself, for Mexico, for her lost love. Attracted by the clapping and the olés, a few more people had begun to edge their way outdoors from the small *sala* of the *posada*. A *gringa* who danced like a Mexican gypsy? Incredible!

Her hair started to come loose and she let it—shaking its rippling waves free around her shoulders. She lifted her skirt, showing her ankles, and then let it drop, teasingly. Her eyes half-closed she danced first slowly and then faster, until her cheeks were flushed, her body beaded with perspiration. She danced as a woman dances for a man, her lips parting slightly as she panted to show a glimpse of small white teeth, her arms stretched imploringly, first above her head and then before her, entreatingly. And then she became a tease—a woman who half-promised, but would give nothing in the end.

"Who are you dancing for, green-eyes?"

The words had been spoken softly, but she heard them over the music, in spite of the thudding pulse in her temples. The bold words of an impudent stranger, but she knew that slightly mocking, slightly impatient voice; she would always hear it, no matter how softly he spoke.

Her half-closed eyes flew open, everything seemed to stop as she looked into his eyes.

"For *you*, only for you, Steve!" It was all she had time to whisper before she flew into his arms.

Epilog

Chapter Fifty-four

"Do you know, you impossible woman, that you dragged me away in the middle of the most important battle we have yet fought? I had the devil's own time getting here! As it is—no more leave for me until the war's ended."

In spite of the pretended harshness of his voice, she was in his arms, Ginny thought, and that was all that mattered. He loved her, he had come back for her—she could stand anything now, even the separation he threatened her with again.

They were in her room—she could almost start giggling all over again when she remembered the startled, shocked, and then disbelieving looks on all their faces down there, to see her suddenly swept into the arms of a strange, travel-dusty, stubble-bearded American who kissed her as if he would never stop. What a shriek of dismay Mrs. Baxter had given when she saw him lift Ginny in his arms and start to carry her off! Only pity for that poor lady's sensibilities had made her call back over Steve's shoulder,

"Please don't worry, he's my husband!"

He had only paused to ask her grimly where her room was.

"And don't tell me it's on the top floor; I've been travelling all day, and I'm damned tired!"

Then he had set her down on her bed, not taking his arms from around her, and started kissing her again.

In between kisses she tried to ask him questions.

"But—what are you doing here? How did you find me? The town is so crowded! Did you get my letter?" and then finally, in a choked voice, "Oh, Steve! I thought you wouldn't come! I thought you didn't want me."

"What does a man have to do to convince you, you ir-ritating, stubborn little bitch? Do you want me to go on my knees to you and beg you not to leave me?" He added in a changed voice, "My God, I believe I'd even do that! Do you see what you've brought me to? I ought to beat you for a runaway wife! That's what you really deserve for going off and leaving only that ridiculous letter! I came straight to the *hacienda* after leaving that silver we went after at Díaz' headquarters, and instead of you I found only Salvador. And then, madam, I had to turn around and go all the way back to our headquarters because they only gave me twenty-four hours leave! If I'd met you along the way I'd have broken your pretty neck!"

He was really angry with her, in spite of the fact that he couldn't seem to keep his hands off her. He had ridden back to her as fast as he could, hardly stopping to change horses—only to find her gone. And it was then, when he stood there staring down at her letter, all smudged with tearstains, that he admitted his own final defeat. He loved her—he realized that if he lost her now he'd never have her again—and the thought was beyond bearing.

All the way down here he had kept praying—he, who never prayed, that the ship she planned to take had not left yet. He had damned her, damned Bishop, damned his own pig-headedness and his temper. And then when he had finally found her, after visiting half the *posadas* in this pigpen of a town, she had been dancing! It was the first time, since their wedding night, that he had seen her dance—and if she had been only learning then, now she was magnificent! How could he bear to let a woman like that out of his sight?

She was yielding to him as she always did, her cheeks

still flushed and wet with tears. She was soaked to the skin with perspiration, even her hair felt damp.

"Goddamit Ginny! Why is it that the minute I see you I begin to desire you? Change your clothes"—he began to pull them off her himself, growling angrily that he had to be back near Puebla within the next twelve hours.

But when Ginny started to get up off the bed, he pushed her down again, leaning over her.

"Steve! You told me to change."

"I didn't mean this very minute, and you damn well know it!" He began to undress, throwing off his clothes and grinning at her. "I know I'm dirty and sweaty and haven't bothered to shave, but you had better get used to that. We don't always have time for the pleasant niceties in the army. And once we've taken Puebla it'll be march, march, march again—this time to Mexico City. I hope your legs are still as strong as they used to be."

She could hardly believe her ears—her eyes widened, shining in the semi-darkness like twin green flames.

"Do you really mean—oh, Steve! You'll take me with you?"

"What do you think I've been talking about? Do you think I can trust you out of my sight?" He came to her and lay propped up on his elbows over her, staring down into her face. "I'm afraid I can't offer you very much right now, sweetheart! Not until we've taken Mexico and Juarez comes driving into the city in his little black carriage. You'll just have to be prepared to be my *soldadera*—you'll have to cook and drive the baggage wagon, and wash clothes, and see to all my other needs as well!" He put his mouth close to her ear, biting it gently. "And let me warn you right now, if I ever catch you looking at another man I'll beat the hell out of you! You'd better start remembering that you're my wife, and you belong only to me!"

She clasped him closer, feeling their bodies join and become one. And now, at last, as he began to kiss her tenderly, he murmured all the words she had waited so long to hear.

"Ginny—my beautiful green-eyed vixen—you've driven me half-mad ever since I set eyes on you! Didn't you

sense, with your woman's intuition that I loved you? That
I always loved you?" He whispered to her in Spanish, wiping out all the other love words she had ever heard,
"Ginny—*mi alma, mi vida—amada mia . . .*" and she
knew that all her memories in the future would begin with
this moment.

FLAME AND THE FLOWER

Kathleen Woodiwiss

The Tempestuous epic of America's deep south at the end of the eighteenth century.

Heather Simmons escaped from the drudgery of her aunt's farm to what she imagined would be the magnificence of London high society. Instead she fell into a far more degrading captivity which took her from a squalid London dockside to the splendour of a Carolina plantation, as the unwilling companion of arrogant and devil-may-care Captain Brandon Birmingham. A man who had abducted her, robbed her of her virtue, and sworn never to let her go.

POLMARRAN TOWER

Charlotte Massey

Polmarran Tower stood high above the Cornish cliffs, a landmark for wreckers and smugglers, frowning over the sea.

Katherine Ainsley came to Polmarran as a governess to Adelaide Northwood, but found herself drawn into a vortex of terror. For over the house brooded the spirit of a woman who had once lived there, a woman whose very name drew a chilling silence from the Northwoods of Polmarran, and over Katherine's charge hung the shadow of a mystery that threatened the lives of both pupil and governess.

FALLS THE SHADOW

Regina Ross

Beautiful Nicola Beaufort is spirited, stubborn, and determined. Top British Intelligence agent Charles Forsyth is tough, resourceful, sardonic and experienced. Their initial encounter at Heathrow Airport is violent and explosive, setting a pattern that is to be repeated in the days ahead in distant Rumania, where both are seeking, for different reasons, Tony Rothman, fellow operative of Forsyth, and former lover of Nicola.

Plunged into a whirlpool of intrigue and violence, Nicola and Forsyth are drawn together against their will in a desperate race to reach the missing agent, as they realize that the key to their search lies in the discovery of the 1,000-year-old Crown of St Stephen, symbol of the Hungarian monarchy, buried somewhere in the heart of the mountains.